# The Practice

# The Practice

## Alan E. Nourse

**HARPER & ROW, PUBLISHERS**

NEW YORK, HAGERSTOWN

SAN FRANCISCO

1817    LONDON

For ANN, who persevered

FIRST EDITION

*Designed by Sidney Feinberg*

Library of Congress Cataloging in Publication Data

Nourse, Alan Edward.
  The practice
  I. Title.
PZ4. N92Pr    PS3564.08    813'.5'4    75-25094
ISBN 0–06–013194–2

78 79 80 81 82 10 9 8 7 6 5 4 3 2 1

## Author's Note

This book is a novel—a work of fiction, plain and simple. In it I have tried to set forth certain ideas about the nature of rural medical practice in America today, in both its good aspects and its bad, and about some of the people who do the work of rural medicine and the things that can happen to them. Although in any work of fiction the author inevitably draws inspiration from multitudes of diverse personal experiences, this novel is not, nor is it intended to be, biographical in any degree whatever. The settings, events and characters—except for obvious existing place names—are totally imaginary, and any resemblance to actual settings, events or persons living or dead is purely coincidental.

*North Bend, Washington*
*May 1977*

# Part I

# 1

The rain had begun at noon in Pocatello and followed them north for the next nine hours, a steady, relentless, pounding deluge. Hunching behind the wheel of the old Chevy wagon, Rob Tanner peered through sheets of rain at the winding highway ahead, following the center line doggedly as twilight turned to darkness and obliterated all view of the road's shoulder. The driving had been torturous all the way, through mountain and canyon and wilderness, dragging the heavy U-Haul trailer behind them and the little blue Vega on a tow bar behind that, like a gypsy caravan, never exceeding forty miles an hour since the Chevy's clutch had started slipping in midmorning. All day they had crept northward, up through the Idaho lava beds, north through the Big Lost River Valley, crossing the Salmon near Challis and winding still northward up the Gorge. Now at last, moving ever more slowly through dark and downpour, they were climbing the long grade north toward Lost Trail Pass and the Montana border, somewhere up ahead.

Glaring lights exploded behind Rob and a huge double-trailer rig roared past on his left, hell-bound, unnervingly close, throwing up a blinding wave of roadwash in its wake. Rob cursed and slowed as his wipers struggled to clear the windshield. The woman beside him stirred, sat up to peer through it. "Trouble, hon?"

"Can't see the goddam road," Rob muttered.

3

Ellie rubbed sleep from her eyes. "I thought Montana was sup-posed to be dry."

"We're still in Idaho. Seems like we've been in Idaho for fourteen years. And anyway, it's eastern Montana that's dry. In the western part you get mountains, and with mountains you get rain. Or snow."

"In June?"

"Could be. You get high enough up, anything can happen, and we've been climbing for hours."

Ellie shivered, then poured lukewarm coffee from a thermos on the floor and handed the cup to Rob. She was a small-boned woman in her mid twenties, with dark auburn hair pulled back in a ponytail from her pale forehead. Her face was plain except for the wide-set serious eyes. Now she looked weary and drained as she took the cup back for a sip. "How much water are we taking in back there?"

"Not much. I tightened the ropes when we got gas in Salmon. A chair leg's gone through the tarp, but it's only leaking on the kitchen stuff in the rear." Rob ran a hand through his dark hair, a solid but spare man with appraising blue eyes and a stubborn set to his jaw. His long fingers gripped the wheel as another truck passed. "Sure wish this rain would quit, though."

As they rounded a curve, a signboard floated by in their dim lights:

CAUTION—MOUNTAIN PASS
CONSTRUCTION AHEAD
DELAYS POSSIBLE

Rob sighed and geared down to a crawl, dodging construction signs and creeping through muddy detours. A few miles farther along, with the car's temperature just below boiling, they finally reached the crest of the pass, marked by a large WELCOME TO MONTANA sign. Then, as the grade eased, Ellie sat up sharply. "Rob, watch it. There's something wrong down there."

Peering ahead, Rob saw a line of cars and trucks slowly descending the grade, bumper to bumper, with the blue lights of a patrol car flashing down beyond a curve. "Looks like an accident," he muttered, braking behind a huge semi. He squinted through the streaming wind-shield. "Isaacs said cars are getting smashed up here all the time. Curves are too sharp, especially in winter or bad weather."

The line of traffic stopped altogether as red and yellow flashers appeared down the road, and a tow truck came blundering up the hill

4

and swerved through the mud onto the right shoulder below the patrol car. Then as they inched forward again, Rob saw a red sedan nose-down in the right-hand ditch, hood buried in the mud, windows splintered, the rear end thrust up in the air. "Jesus. That's the job that passed us going ninety about an hour ago."

"Rob, you'd better stop and take a look."

"Yeah." He pulled the caravan off the road above the patrol car. Grabbing his bag from behind the seat, he climbed out, waved on a truck that was hesitating behind him, and plodded through the rain toward the ditched car. Two patrolmen in rain gear were standing above it, holding lights on the wreck, while a third one down below was trying to pry open the driver's door with a crowbar. One officer turned as Rob came up. "I'm a doctor," Rob said. "Need any help?"

"Sure do," the patrolman said. "There's blood all over the place down there."

Rob slithered through the mud down to the wreck just as the driver's door finally burst open with a wrench of twisted metal. The sole occupant of the car was a young woman, strapped in at the waist and leaning forward over the wheel, shaking her head and moaning. Rob took the officer's flashlight and peered in at her. Blood was dripping from her nose, forming a gelatinous mass in her lap. Rob took his handkerchief and wiped her face, then gently pressed at the bridge of her nose, her forehead, her cheekbones.

"What happened?" the woman said. "Why'm I bleeding?"

"You slammed your face down on the wheel," Rob said. "Take it easy—there's probably nothing broken there. Just a hell of a nosebleed. You hurt anywhere else?"

"God, yes—my chest. Hurts when I breathe. And my foot."

Rob shone the light down. The right side of the woman's chest was rammed against the steering wheel, her right foot twisted and wedged against the floor where the motor, steering post and all, had been shoved back into the front seat. Carefully Rob leaned across to press her ribs and heard her cry out as he touched her. "Easy, now. You may have some cracked ribs. Don't try to move; just let us work you loose. It'll hurt, but it won't take long."

He stood up beside the patrolman. On the road above, a white emergency van had arrived, red lights blinking, and a pair of men were skidding down toward the car with a stretcher. Rob looked at the patrolman. "Maybe you can get in the other side and help me work her free. She's probably got broken ribs, and that foot may be broken too."

5

He ducked into the car again, searching with the flashlight for the seat-adjustment lever. He pulled it, felt the seat move back an inch as the woman cried out. The second time he gave the seat a backward shove and it moved another inch. "Good," he said to the patrolman leaning across from the other side. "Try to get her foot and ease it onto the seat."

They worked for five minutes, Rob gently edging the woman's body toward the door, the patrolman controlling the injured leg. The emergency men brought the stretcher close to the car door, and one took the woman under her arms, freeing Rob to control her hips. Slowly they inched her out full length onto the stretcher. "Fine," Rob said. "You guys have a pillow and some roller bandage? Okay, let's splint that foot with the pillow and hold it with the gauze. Easy, now—not too tight. What about a chest binder?"

As one attendant finished splinting the foot, Rob quickly checked the woman's abdomen, heart, lungs. The other man produced a canvas chest binder and Rob worked it under her back, outside the windbreaker she was wearing, and then cinched the lacing snugly up the front, splinting her chest. "That feel better?"

She nodded grayly. "Still hurts, though."

"We'll give you something to help for the moment." By flashlight he filled a syringe from his bag and pressed the needle into the woman's arm. "That's just a little Demerol," he said. "It'll help with the pain. You just lie flat and relax." He pulled a pad from his pocket, scribbled out the drug dosage and the time, then tore off the sheet and secured it to the top button of the woman's blouse. As the men started hoisting the stretcher up to the emergency van, Rob turned to the patrolman. "Where are they going to take her?"

"Twin Forks Hospital, twenty-five miles down the hill. No need for you to follow her down, though. There's a doctor already standing by down there."

"Oh, good. Dr. Isaacs?"

"No; Florey's got accident call this month." The officer glanced up. "You know Doc Isaacs?"

"I'm going to work with him."

"Oh, yeah? No kidding. Good man. Well, I guess you're getting broken in early. We got this kind of thing going on all the time."

Back in the Chevy, Rob reported to Ellie, then with extra caution pulled the caravan onto the highway again and started through the wet and darkness. The descent was steep, with the road twisting dangerously. Halfway down, red flares marked a mud slide partly covering the highway, and a road crew with a front-end loader worked to clear the debris and flag the traffic past in a one-way pattern. Finally, some sixteen miles from the summit, the road began to flatten out. Rob eased his grip on the wheel and sat back in the seat, stretching kinks from his arms.

"Rob?"

"Mm?"

"Is this really going to be what you want?"

He glanced sharply at his wife. "What do you mean?"

"This place up ahead. This town we're going to. Way out in the middle of nowhere." She looked at him in the darkness.

He hunched his shoulders. "Hell, honey, *I* don't know. I was only here for a day, and Isaacs was putting on the best front he knew how. It's a town, and it needs another doctor. It looks a lot better than some places we've thought about. There's a hospital of sorts, and a modern office with a good staff. Plenty of hunting and fishing, maybe hiking in the summer. Step out your back door and shoot a bear, Isaacs said."

"I know. It just seems so remote."

"It's not that bad. There are good hospitals in Missoula, just seventy miles up the pike, when we need them. Not places like Graystone, but big enough. Plane connections to Spokane or Great Falls, so we can get out for meetings." He hesitated. "And anyway, we've both had enough of big cities, haven't we? Five years in Philly—Lord, I thought we'd *never* get out of there—and then these last three in Seattle. Just too many people; you said so yourself. In a small town like this, maybe we could put down some roots, if we wanted to. And after all, a small town is what family practice is all about, isn't it? Sick people, and no big Graystone Clinic full of hotshots to take care of them. You see everything."

"Including a lot you can't really handle."

"But you handle it, all the same. There's no choice—you're all there is. And there won't be any sitting around waiting for patients to turn up, either. Isaacs wouldn't be hollering for help if he didn't have more work than he could handle right now." He paused, glancing at Ellie. "I know the money's not the greatest—a lot of groups are offering three thousand a month to new guys right out of training—but fifteen hundred is better than a kick in the head. We'll have plenty to live on compared to the peanuts we were getting at Graystone. And I won't have to spend a nickel for office equipment, either. It's all here."

"It's not the money," Ellie said. "I'm just worried about you. And me. It's time we had a real home for once, started thinking about a family. And I've never lived in a small town."

"So we give it a year, okay? We can take anything for a year. If we don't like it then, we move on. That was the deal. No strings. That's what Isaacs said."

"It just seems that so much depends on him."

"On Isaacs? Well, you met him. What did *you* think?"

She laughed. "What could I think? I met him for three hours one evening, and I was so worried about burning the roast I hardly even remember him."

"Well, I liked him. He seemed honest enough and he didn't duck questions. And from what he said, the other men in the group know what they're doing too." He chewed his lip. "Look, Ellie, it can't rain all the time."

"I know. It just seems like it." She sat silent for a minute. "Looks like town coming up."

Roadside buildings had begun appearing for a mile or more; now town lights appeared ahead, around a curve. Rob heaved a sigh of relief. "Guess we've made it."

Ellie sat forward, peering through the windshield. "Doesn't look very big."

"It isn't very big; just a little lumber town." Rob slowed to a crawl as they passed the town limit sign. "What time is it?"

"Almost ten-thirty," Ellie said.

"Isaacs said to give him a call if we got in before midnight. The clinic's down this first street—we might just swing by."

"Oh, Rob, do we *have* to? *Tonight?* We've been driving for ten hours straight. And I know you: once you get your toes wet here, you're going to be in right up to the neck—"

Rob laughed. "All I want is to say hello. We've got two whole days before I have to start."

"Yes, and we're going to need every minute of it—finding a house, moving this junk in, getting unpacked. This is no big city full of places to rent. We may be lucky to find *anything.*" She spread her hands helplessly. "I'm just afraid once you start, you're going to be buried, just like you were at Graystone. And this hospital-widow stuff is getting pretty tiresome."

"Look, there's only two thousand people in the whole town. They can't all get sick at once. I'm going to have lots of time."

8

He took the first turn to the right and drove past the low, squat cinder-block clinic building, a block off the highway. It was dark and deserted; a dim night light over the front door made the place look shabbier than Rob had remembered. Back on the main street, he pulled up to a gas station phone booth. He dialed Dr. Isaacs' home number, but got an answering tape instead of Isaacs. *Sorry, Dr. Isaacs is not in. Dr. DeForrest is taking calls. If you wish to leave a message, wait for the beep—* Rob rang off, irritated. He dialed another number Isaacs had given him in case he got the tape, and let it ring a dozen times before he hung up.

"Glad we're not bleeding to death," he said, climbing back into the car.

"Maybe the doctor on call would know where he is."

"Oh, the hell with it. Let's get a room somewhere." Rob pulled out onto the rain-swept road again. One motel looked plausible, but there was a NO VACANCY sign. An old square hotel building in the center of town had a light on, but the last room had just been rented to a pair of youngsters who looked too young to be renting a hotel room. The desk clerk shrugged. "You can wait, if you want," he said.

"Any other place around?"

"There's Hadley's Motel, a mile up the road. Just keep on drivin'; you'll see it."

They spotted it, finally, through the rain: a dismal little place with a dozen shacks around a flooded parking court. In the office a tight-mouthed matron peered at Rob suspiciously over a pair of half-glasses, gave him a smudged registry card to sign, then studied it closely, and finally, grudgingly, accepted his ten dollars and handed him the key to Cabin 8. "No pets, though," she said as he started for the door.

"Is my wife all right?"

"If you've got some luggage."

"Lady, I've got five tons of luggage in a two-ton trailer out there. You want to check it out?"

The woman's mouth tightened. "Just don't go tracking in any mud," she said. "And you'll have trouble with the hot water. The heater's on the fritz."

Pulling his caravan into the parking court, Rob found Cabin 8 near the back. The court was ankle deep in water and they both soaked their feet hauling their suitcases out of the back seat. The cabin was dry enough, but the water heater was indeed on the fritz and the shower head was so clogged there was no alternative to a cold tub bath. Ellie

9

undressed and climbed in, shivering, as Rob fiddled with the rickety space heater and finally got it to light. When his turn came for the tub, he made it quick. She was already deep under the covers when he emerged from the bathroom, naked. As she peeked out, he made an elaborate ritual of pulling down the shade on the single window, then pounced on her, stripping the blankets off.

"Oh, Rob, for God's sake—"

"Got to get warm somehow." He pinned her, still struggling, kissed her ear, then her lips, and felt her yield, her arms tightening around his chest. He kissed her again, more deeply, then suddenly pulled back. "Hey, we forgot something."

"Rob—"

"We were going to celebrate." He leaped from the bed, burrowed in the bottom of his suitcase and emerged with a bottle of California champagne and two squashed Dixie cups. "We can just stick it in that tub to chill—"

"Robbie, *honestly.*"

"First night in our new hometown, honey."

She sat up against the headboard, giggling, pulling the blankets up around her. He popped the cork, caught the overflow in a cup and handed it to her solemnly. "To a practice in wonderful western Montana," he said. "Welcome to Twin Forks."

# 2

By morning the storm had gone and a hot summer sun beat through the tattered window shade. Rob Tanner was still snoring when Ellie had risen, dressed and slipped out half an hour earlier; now she was back with coffee, banging the door open and throwing up the shade exuberantly. "Up, you bum," she said, snatching away his pillow. "You've slept long enough."

He groaned and sat up. "What's going on out there?"

"Oh, Rob, it's *beautiful*. I had no idea." She held out the coffee. "Come on, you've got to see it. The trees, the mountains—they're all around us!"

Rob climbed out of bed, stood in the doorway in his pajamas, sipping coffee. Across the highway, rising abruptly, were green-clad hills with rocky outcroppings emerging at the top. Though it was not yet seven o'clock, the sun was high in a cloudless sky, and a warm, humid breeze held a promise of gathering heat. The air smelled of flowers and pine. Ellie joined him at the door and he hugged her close. "Look, we've got till noon before we have to check out of this place. Let's drive around, get some breakfast and see what we can see."

"Do you suppose Dr. Isaacs would know of a place for rent?"

"Could be. He might even have a place himself. He sounded like he owned half the town." Ten minutes later Rob was dressed and had the little blue Vega unhitched from the trailer. They turned left onto the highway and headed back toward town, following the winding course of a turbulent clear-water stream. Rob felt a sudden urge to have a fly rod in his hand. "That's the Icicle River," he said. "It comes down from the mountains there to the west, and feeds into the Bitterroot River farther north. There's another fork that joins it right in the middle of town. Full of trout, Isaacs said, and hardly fished at all if you get back upstream a ways."

"That's assuming you have any time for fishing."

"Don't worry; there'll be time. I'm supposed to be free from call every other weekend, and I'll get one day off during the week as well. Plenty of time."

Scattered buildings began to appear near the highway now as they approached the town. The flashing river and the surrounding mountain ridges were undeniably beautiful, and in an oddly sprawling way, the town fit the setting. Twin Forks lay in the center of a broad, flat valley, flanked by mountains rising abruptly on three sides, and by rolling foothills stretching northward toward Missoula. Through town the highway widened to four lanes, lined with squat and weather-beaten buildings. Nothing looked really new, but the antiquated false fronts gave the buildings a sleepy, ageless appearance. There was a small bank building of aging red brick, with a rustic wooden sign over the door; a clothing store; two drugstores; a restaurant; a cramped-looking super-market; three gas stations. Toward the north end they crossed a bridge at the confluence of the river, then turned right along the River Road. Storefronts gave way to snug frame houses with rockwork pillars sup-porting the porticoes. They passed a frame church rich with new red paint, with a high steeple and fresh cedar shakes on half the roof. Presently the road forked; Rob turned the Vega left up the hill past more substantial homes standing back from the road in groves of long needle pine and fir. A huge black dog charged out from one, barking at their tires, and they slowed to avoid a couple of ducks waddling and quacking across the road. "I think Dr. DeForrest lives up here some-where," Rob said. "He's the internist in the office. The surgeon lives in Missoula, only comes out once or twice a week, except for emergencies. Isaacs lives down in town near the clinic. Here, I'll show you."

They had reached an overlook high above the village, and Rob pulled over beneath a cluster of trees. The edge dropped off sharply, and the whole valley was spread out below them.

"Oh, Rob, it's like a postcard," Ellie sighed.

"You can see most everything from here," Rob affirmed. "There are the two forks of the river, and that's the clinic building, off there to the right. That big, wooded place behind it is Isaacs' house. I guess a lot of the town fathers live in those big old houses down beyond there —Riverbend, they call it." He pointed across the valley. "That rise over there is called the East Ridge. You can see the hospital up near the top. Pretty slippery climb up there in the winter, I guess, but Isaacs says they always plow and sand it first whenever it snows. There are still more homes back behind it. Then right down below us here is the railroad spur that brings logs in to the mill and hauls finished lumber out."

"I don't see any mill."

"It's back behind this hill, out on the River Road. Big place; lumber and plywood. One of the last of the big independent mills. It used to be a lot bigger; there was a whole company town back there, and a lot of the millworkers still live in the old tin-roof shacks along the river in Tintown. Isaacs says Boise Cascade wants to buy the mill and put in a whole new plywood plant here. He says it would be good for the town, but the environmentalists are fighting it. And of course, the town gets a lot of its money from tourists now too—skiers in the winter, hikers and fishermen in the summer and hunters in the fall."

"It's beautiful," Ellie said, staring down at the sleepy village, "but it sure doesn't look like any two thousand people."

"They're there, all right. Plus another couple thousand or so scattered all up and down the valley. Isaacs said he sometimes drives twenty miles to make a house call."

Climbing into the car again, they drove back down to the River Road. "You know," Ellie said thoughtfully, "I haven't seen a single house for rent anywhere."

"Neither have I. But there's bound to be something. We can try the real estate offices after breakfast—I saw at least two of them."

Turning back onto the main street, they recrossed the river bridge and pulled into a parking lot beside a ramshackle two-story white frame building marked COLONIAL INN/BAR-NONE CAFE. Inside was a large U-shaped lunch counter, with booths around the outside. They picked a booth with a view of the bridge and the river, and a girl brought them menus. Moments later they were sipping coffee from heavy white mugs and ordering sausage and eggs.

The place was humming with early-morning business. Men in work clothes were eating at the counter, laughing and flirting with the waitresses, and several other booths were filled. Just as the Tanners' orders arrived, a door at the rear, marked with a Kiwanis emblem, burst open

13

and a group of men in business suits and open-necked shirts filed out, apparently at the end of a breakfast meeting. As they moved past Rob and Ellie, one man stopped short and turned back. "Well!" he said in a booming voice. "Got here a little bit early, I see."

Rob looked up, startled, at the big white-haired man. Then he smiled and struggled to his feet. "Looks like you're up pretty early yourself," he said. "Ellie, you remember Dr. Isaacs?"

"Of course she does." The big man nodded to Ellie and reached over to shake Rob's hand. "Sit down and move over, Rob. I'll have some coffee with you while I'm here."

Rob slid over to make room as Isaacs flagged the waitress. Once again he was struck by the sheer size of the older man. Martin Isaacs was big in all dimensions, a large-boned meaty man, towering six inches over Rob's six feet. With his thick snow-white hair sweeping back in luxuriant waves from his ears, Martin Isaacs looked like an old-time senator from Texas, but there was no sense of softness about him. His shoulders were heavily muscled, his neck powerful and bowed slightly forward. Only his hands, lean and long-fingered, seemed delicate, and his eyes, behind old-fashioned wire-rimmed glasses, were by moments watchful and sly. "Hey, Mabel," he called out, "bring some coffee over here, will you? And put these breakfasts on my tab."

"Are you a Kiwanis regular?" Rob asked.

"Not really. I just come around to meetings when I can. Good for business." Isaacs threw Rob a sidelong glance. "When did you get here?"

"Last night, in the middle of a rainstorm."

"Yeah, that was a beauty," Isaacs said. "You should have called me when you got in, like I told you to."

"I tried both numbers," Rob said, "but I didn't get too far."

Isaacs shook his head. "You should have tried the hospital. I was up there all night, delivering a pair of twins. Knocks the statistics all to hell, but this was my third set this year and I've still got two more coming up. Must be uranium in the mountains around here; we get more twins than you know what to do with."

Rob laughed. "How'd it go?"

"No problem; just a damned nuisance. This makes nine kids for this woman. She could have delivered a Mack truck with room to spare."

Rob whistled. "What's she going to do with nine kids?"

"Beats me," Isaacs said. He looked at Ellie. "What would *you* do with nine kids?"

14

"I'd do something to keep from having any more," Ellie said.

"Well, maybe your husband here can talk this gal into it. I sure can't. If the damned fool woman could just manage to keep her legs crossed once in a while, she'd be okay."

Ellie frowned. "Are you sure it's all her fault?"

Isaacs gave her a flat look. "What else?"

"She doesn't have a husband around?"

"Sure she's got a husband around," Isaacs said sharply. "But *she's* the one that keeps getting pregnant. What she needs is to have her tubes tied, once and for all. Now's the time to do it, too—they're right up front there, all ready to go—but she won't have anything to do with it." He sipped his coffee in disgust and turned back to Rob. "It's good you got here early, though. These OBs are really driving me nuts. Every time I sit down to dinner, there's one of them going into labor. Sometimes I feel like pulling the phone right out of the wall."

"How many OBs do you have?"

"I had a hundred and twenty last year, and this year looks even worse. And that's on top of everything else too. Of course, you'll have to get on to the way I handle them here. This is no big city hospital. We have to make do with what we've got."

"You mean like no caudal anesthesias?"

"Not unless you want to sit up with them all night yourself. But I manage. Agnes—that's my OB nurse—she helps a lot. She's real good with the girls in the office, and she helps me with all the deliveries. Soon as you get the routine down, maybe I can relax a little and let you take over. Fact is, you might as well start today, since you're here."

Rob cut off Ellie's protest. "Fact is, I already started last night," he said. "There was an accident up in the pass as we came over."

Isaacs looked up sharply. "About ten o'clock? Did you treat that woman up there on the road?"

"I helped them pry her out of the car and get her onto a stretcher. Gave her a little Demerol to carry her down the hill."

Isaacs hit his forehead with the heel of his hand. "Oh, good Lord. And that bastard Florey waiting down here to grab her right out of the ambulance! Jesus! Why didn't you come on down with her?"

"The cop said I didn't need to."

"So you handed her over to Florey instead."

"Well—maybe so. Who's Florey?"

"The man in the other office, down in Tintown. He's a real prince, he is. He'll steal 'em right out from under your nose if you give him a chance. You just watch: he'll give you the glad hand, tell you how great it is having another doctor in the valley, and then he'll screw you purple the minute you turn your back. Just wait, you'll see."

"Well," Rob said, "this couldn't have been any great coup for him. All she had was some cracked ribs and a twisted foot."

Isaacs just looked at him. "Listen, buddy, nobody in *my* practice is going to give away four hundred dollars in fees without hearing from me."

"Four hundred dollars! You can't be serious."

"I can't, huh? Listen: he's going to bill her seventy-five just for standing by for a highway emergency last night, okay? And another forty or fifty for sewing up and dressing all the cuts and bruises. Then another hundred or so for fixing the foot under anesthesia—it was dislocated—and taping her ribs, and a hundred more for follow-up care in the hospital, because he's not going to let her out of there for the next three weeks if he can manage to keep her in. And even then he's going to make a mess of things. He already should have had a plastic surgeon down from the city to look at her face, pretty girl like that, but he hasn't, and he's not going to, either. He'll just muddle along and hope for the best, and then collect four or five hundred in fees before he gets through. You just watch." Isaacs finished his coffee and pushed the cup aisde. "Well, there's nothing to do about it now—but next time, for God's sake, don't mess around. You just climb into that ambulance and ride it right on down the hill. Give the patient a break, as well as yourself." Isaacs shook his head. "Look, come on up to the hospital now and check out those twin babies for me."

"Rob, we've really got things to do," Ellie protested.

Isaacs looked at her. "Like what?"

"Like finding someplace to live," Ellie said. "Unless you've already rented a house for us."

"Well, no," Isaacs said lamely. "Can't say I have. Not much for rent around here. Might be a couple of places for sale; I don't know. I'd ask you to come stay with us, but Jennie's down with the flu or something right now." The big man rubbed his chin. "Tell you what, though: old Judge Barret has his law office just across the street, and he's got a little cabin on the river he might sell. Just a summer place, but you could fix it up. It's worth asking about." Isaacs stood up. "Look—really, nobody's going to be around this early. Come on up to the hospital and check those babies for me. We'll be back in an hour, and then you two can go house-hunting."

16

Rob looked at Ellie. "That okay with you?"

"I suppose so," she said. "Maybe I can go check with the real estate people in the meantime. I know you're itching to get started."

"Well, he won't have to itch too long," Isaacs said. "He's already got patients scheduled in the office on Thursday morning. Nobody sits around with his feet up very long in my practice."

The big man paid the breakfast checks and Rob followed him out, leaving Ellie to finish her meal alone. In the parking lot Isaacs eased himself into the driver's seat of a big new pearl-gray Buick sedan. "Say, I didn't mean to just drag you away," he said. "Hate to have your wife sore at me before you even get started."

"She won't mind snooping around town a bit," Rob said. "She's never really looked at a small town before."

"City girl, eh?"

"Philadelphia. Studied nursing at Penn, and then we've lived in cities ever since we were married."

"Well, Twin Forks is sure no city. Not too bad, as small towns go. It's got good things and bad things." Isaacs eased the car out onto the highway, honking and waving at a man hurrying across the street. After crossing the bridge they turned left, swung past the clinic building, and then headed up the hill toward the hospital. "I've got about ten people up there now," Isaacs said. "Three OBs, a coronary, a couple of accident cases. The usual mix. You didn't meet DeForrest when you were here, did you?"

"No, he was at a meeting in Spokane."

"He should be up here by now. And then there's Harry Sonders. He's our surgeon, comes down from Missoula on Tuesdays and Thursdays. You remember him. He's doing a couple of T&As and a hernia repair this morning."

Rob nodded. He vaguely remembered the small, dapper surgeon he had met six months before on the flying trip he had made to Twin Forks when he finally decided to accept Isaacs' offer. It had been a hasty, hit-and-run visit, and now there was little that Rob really *did* remember other than Isaacs himself: a brief and fuzzy picture of the clinic building in a snowstorm, a swift, almost meaningless tour of the little hillside hospital, a hazy recollection of the little red-haired surgeon ducking in for a cocktail after an emergency appendectomy that had brought him out on a Saturday night, and over all, the odd impression that everyone he met was trying fiercely to be as charming as possible —flattering to him, in a way, but also a little disquieting. . . .

17

In the end, Rob realized, what had finally sold him on the practice proposition had been Isaacs himself—a strangely impressive man, charismatic in some curious way, physically powerful and blunt in his manner, yet surprisingly quiet and unhurried. It was Isaacs who had patiently sketched the situation in Twin Forks and answered Rob's questions to his increasing satisfaction. The need for a new doctor there had not arisen suddenly, but it was very real. First there had been Isaacs alone, fifteen years before, coming to the little mountain town as a solo practitioner with two years of obstetrical residency and a few years of city practice behind him, and locked from the first in bitter conflict with an older, better-established doctor practicing down the valley. Seven years later Isaacs had coaxed Jerry DeForrest into the practice, a man who was qualified to take specialty board examinations in internal medicine but always seemed too busy to bother, once his office hours were established. Three years after that Harry Sonders had joined the partnership, an ambitious young surgeon based in Missoula but willing and eager to expand his practice and income by spending two days a week in the OR of Twin Forks Hospital, handling the surgery that the other men found for him to do.

Yet even with this help, Isaacs and DeForrest were hopelessly mired in an ever-increasing influx of work. They found themselves still in the office seeing patients at ten o'clock at night, dogged by emergency calls at all hours, the once orderly pace of their practice gradually transformed into an endless nightmare. They had held up stubbornly for a while, yet both of them realized finally that they had to have help.

It was Isaacs who took the bull by the horns. First he placed ads in the medical journals, announcing the practice opening. Then he took a whirlwind tour of Western hospitals, talking to residents completing their training, supplicating them to consider the situation: a practice ready made and overflowing; an office building with x-ray and lab facilities already installed; an "adequate" local hospital, as Isaacs rather circumspectly described it; consultation in obstetrics, surgery and internal medicine provided by himself or others in the group; a reasonable starting salary, with the prospect of full partnership in the group after a year's trial period; and to top it all, the physical beauty of the town, with its mountains and rivers and hiking trails.

Isaacs had met Rob Tanner at Graystone Memorial Hospital in Seattle during that trip, introduced by a friend on the Graystone Clinic staff. They had talked during lunch in the hospital cafeteria and Rob, drawn to the man and the prospect, asked him home to dinner that evening. Ellie had come through with a juicy beef roast on last-minute notice; Isaacs had been gallant to her in his blunt way ("Hard to believe a gal could get off ward duty at County at three o'clock in the afternoon and have a dinner like this ready at seven!") and then completely ignored her for the rest of the evening as he talked long and earnestly to Rob about the practice opportunity he had to offer. Ellie had quietly darned socks while Rob listened, intrigued despite the seeming remoteness of Twin Forks, Montana, and the change it would present from the city hospital life he and Ellie had known since the day they were married.

Nothing was decided at the time, but Rob was strongly attracted. Since his first years of medical school he had dreamed of a family practice, and his internship and general practice residency at Graystone had been planned accordingly. The problem was money. Rob had none left, after eleven long years of college and medical training, nor did his family. With his meager resident's stipend from Graystone and Ellie's even smaller salary as a pediatric nurse at County, they had managed to limp along—but nothing was ever left over. True, he was emerging from training free of debt—but the cost of starting a new practice would be staggering. Office equipment alone could easily cost fifty thousand dollars, and staying alive through the first lean months or years could run to thousands more. He knew he could find a place in the Graystone Clinic if he stayed on to train as a city specialist—but that was far from his dream of a general family practice.

That dream had seemed more unattainable with every passing month—until the day Martin Isaacs had appeared out of the wilderness of western Montana and offered him a small country group practice just waiting for the right man to move in. "Don't decide now, if you need time to think," Isaacs had said finally. "Talk it over with Ellie. Even better, grab a weekend and come see the place. The timing would be just perfect—Jerry and I can sweat things out till you finish here at Graystone in June. But we'd need to know that you're coming for sure within a couple of weeks."

After Isaacs had gone, Rob and Ellie had talked about it for long hours into the night—longer, perhaps, than they had ever talked about anything before in the whole seven years of their marriage. Close as they had been at times, there had never been much chance for talking. He had met her in Philadelphia during his first year of medical school —the only daughter of a busy Main Line doctor, just out of Bryn Mawr

19

and enrolled in the School of Nursing at Penn—and they had shared being new and green and uncertain in their fields. Soon he was spending more time in her tiny efficiency apartment than in his own barren rooming-house quarters near the med school. In those days a young man didn't live with a girl very long before the question of marriage arose, and it did, and they were married, quietly and simply, that first Christmas holiday, with neither family happy about it, sudden as it had been, but with not much they could do about it.

The marriage was companionable, the sex great, but from the beginning there wasn't much talk. Long days in the wards and clinics for Rob, long silent evenings hitting the books night after night, with Ellie also in hospital training and bent to her own studies. Money was sparse till she took her R.N. and went to work as a floor nurse at Philadelphia Children's; Rob doggedly refused to accept a dime from her father, and his own family, simple tradespeople from Paramus, New Jersey, had precious few dimes to offer. Once Ellie was working, they saw each other even less, with her odd hours and broken shifts, like ships passing in the night sometimes, so that when they *did* catch an evening off together it was like some kind of special date. Once or twice they even managed an outing—Ellie especially loved camping and hiking, and spent her graduation money for an overpriced pup tent and sleeping bags—but such excursions were rare indeed. She didn't like the constant separation any more than Rob did, but medical training was medical training, and what could they do? And then when he was tapped for residency training at Graystone in Seattle, one of the few really good Family Practice programs in the country in those days and the one place he really wanted to go to, he ran into a work load more intense and demanding than anything he'd ever dreamed of before, and time and talk with Ellie became scarcer than ever. . . .

Now, with Isaacs' proposal squarely before them, Rob had wanted Ellie to share in the decision, but she was curiously reticent. "Rob, *you're* the one who has to decide," she told him. "You're the doctor around here, not me. You've got to go where you want to go to practice, and wherever you choose, I'll go along. It's got to be that way; it always has been."

"But dammit, Ellie, it matters what *you* want too."

"Not when it comes to choosing a practice, it doesn't. Sure, I'd like to go where I wouldn't have to work double shifts so often. I'd like to spend some time just being a wife, for once, maybe even get to *see* you once in a while. But that's not the issue right now. Once we're settled

20

somewhere and you're doing what you want to do, then we can worry about making a home and starting a family and all those things. That'll be *my* end of it, and I'll tell you what I want then, don't worry. But where we go and when has got to be your choice, all the way."

It was infuriating, but she could be stubborn as a Kansas mule when she didn't want to be pushed, and Rob knew better than to try. *Might never know how she really feels,* he reflected. *Maybe she doesn't know herself.* And in the end, as he thought it out, Rob kept coming back to Isaacs the man—solid, quiet, blunt-spoken. "In a solo practice, you're on your own," Isaacs had told him, "but in a group, you have to work with others, and those others matter. You've got to count on them and trust them. Everybody has to pull his own weight; if somebody doesn't, it all falls apart at the seams." Isaacs had said that in parting, and more and more it seemed to Rob that Martin Isaacs might be the sort of man who would pull his own weight and more. . . .

Ultimately, as Ellie insisted, Rob had made the decision himself. There were real concerns, of course. "I'll bet that hospital doesn't have an Intensive Care Unit," he said at one point, weary from dogging an acute coronary patient at Graystone all day. "I'm not even sure they've got an ambulance. And as for entertainment, forget it! There won't be any plays or concerts. Maybe not even a movie house." He shook his head. "There'd be a lot of things we'd have to get used to in a little place like Twin Forks. Family feuds, snoopy neighbors—"

"But we could always get away to the city when things got too thick," Ellie said. "You said so yourself."

"I suppose. Except I'll bet we don't very much. Even Missoula will be a seventy-mile drive, and once we get dug in, there'll be so much work—"

"You've decided we're going, then?"

"Yes, I think we will."

With that bridge crossed, Rob's hurried trip to Twin Forks had been more ritual than necessity, merely reaffirming a decision he had already made, fixing his name to a formal letter of agreement, and shaking Martin Isaacs' hand. "I'll need a week or so of vacation in late June before I start," he had said, "and a few days here to get settled. Let's make July first the starting day," and Isaacs had nodded his agreement. And then, back at Graystone, his plans finally clear, his future determined, Rob dug in for his last six months of hospital routine, too busy to think about the forthcoming move to Twin Forks. When the final days of June came at last, they had shopped for a small car for Rob to use in the practice, packed their goods in a U-Haul trailer, tuned up the old Chevy wagon to pull the caravan, and then headed south and east for a few days of camping in Oregon before reporting for the new job, and the time for second thoughts had come and gone.

# 3

The Twin Forks Hospital sat in a pleasant grove of firs on the East Ridge, overlooking the town, isolated from the residential areas and the hustle of cars. A low, white-walled, shake-roofed building, it sprawled like a badly planned ranch house, its footings set in the bedrock of the hillside. In a sense it was poorly located, at the summit of a steep, winding drive. In summer, though, the high, open location proved its worth. There was always a mountain breeze sweeping down from the hills, and families visiting patients would bring picnic hampers and eat under the trees. Now Isaacs turned his Buick into the hospital drive, swinging past the general parking lot and the emergency entrance to park in the doctors' lot behind the building. Climbing out, he led Rob through the wide doors of the emergency room and up a ramp into the central lobby.

The building seemed to have no definite form, for it had been built like a nautilus, a chamber at a time, as need and use had demanded. The original building, almost forty years old, was a long rectangle divided by a central corridor lined on either side with two- and three-bed rooms and leading to the "men's ward"—a large eight-bed solarium lying across the end. The nurses' station, entrance lobby and business offices had been built later in an adjoining wing set at right angles to the old building and providing a small but comfortable room for patients to check into the hospital, for expectant fathers to wait and pace, or for families to sweat out the results of midnight consultations.

Yet another angling corridor led to the two "business rooms" of the hospital—the operating room on the right, the delivery room on the left, separated by a scrub room with sinks against the wall and high cabinets full of sterilized surgical packs. Next to the delivery room, a door opened on a tiny doctors' dressing room, with lockers for street clothes, an ancient sofa, a small desk and dictating equipment. Finally, to the rear of the hospital was the diet kitchen, with a small adjacent dining room where the hospital staff took their meals and where the doctors would congregate for consultations, coffee and doughnuts. The emergency room, on a lower level, had been the last part of the hospital to be completed, with an x-ray cubicle and a tiny laboratory housed to the rear. The only elevator in the building, barely large enough to admit a wheeled cart and an attendant, creaked and groaned up and down between the ward corridor above and the x-ray room below. On the other side of the ramp was a tiny lower-level patient room with an ISOLATION sign hanging on the closed door.

Isaacs led Rob up the ramp, past the nurses' station, now empty, and past the OR corridor to the doctors' dining room. At the table, with coffee and cigarette, sat a small, thin man with a cadaverous, almost lupine face and oddly yellow eyes under a shock of yellow-brown hair. He looked up at Isaacs as they came in. "About time you got here," he said. "Your girl Millie is looking for you."

"Good God," Isaacs said. "I was just up with her all night already."

"Well, you stitched her up too tight or something. She's ready to expose herself to anybody she thinks might help."

"Okay, I'll check her. But right now we've got company. Rob, this is Jerry DeForrest."

DeForrest reached up to shake hands. "So you're the long-awaited Dr. Tanner, eh? Very good. You came early. That wasn't wise." He gave Rob a wolfish grin.

"I just couldn't wait," Rob said.

"Oh, I'm not objecting," DeForrest said. "It's not a day too soon for me." He looked sharply at Rob. "Where does the 'Rob' come from? Robert?"

"No; Robinson. Don't ask me why—my mother never would say."

"Maybe she was frightened by a desert island," DeForrest said. "Well, stick around. Harry Sonders is just finishing up a T&A in there; you'll want to meet him."

"Who's in the delivery room?" Isaacs asked.

24

"Some woman of Florey's. He's got the block in, but there's not much going on, as far as I can tell."

"If he'd just put on a pair of forceps once in a while he'd save everybody a lot of grief," Isaacs said. "Say, what do you think of my man with the arrhythmia?"

"Hard to say. I ordered another tracing—the one you sent up from the office looked like it had been through the shredder." DeForrest frowned. "How much digitalis have you been giving that guy?"

"Not enough to stir his heart up like this," Isaacs said.

"I just wonder if he's had enough to do anything at all. It sure doesn't show up on the EKG."

"Hell, Jerry, you know I get nervous giving these old goats digitalis. Why don't you just take over the case? Give him anything you want to."

"Well, I might just beef up the digitalis and see what happens," DeForrest said. "Hate to start quinidine if the digitalis will do it. Might toss in a little phenobarb too; he sure seems jumpy. Anyway, I'll check him."

"Good," Isaacs said. "I'm going to show Rob around."

Out at the nurses' station, a small, middle-aged woman was making up a medications tray. She had faded red hair pulled back in a bun behind her nurse's cap, and pale blue eyes peering through rimless glasses. "Nellie, meet Dr. Rob Tanner," Isaacs said. "He's my new doctor, coming to work on Thursday. Rob, this is Nellie Webster, head nurse on the seven-to-three shift."

The little nurse gave Rob an appraising look and then smiled. "Welcome to the zoo," she said. "It's about time we had another doctor around here. These men have been working too hard. They need a rest."

"Sounds like I'll have plenty to do," Rob said.

"You just wait," she said soberly. "You'll find out what hard work is." The nurse looked up at Dr. Isaacs. "Do you want me to make rounds with you, Doctor?"

"No; you're busy and I'm late," Isaacs said. "Where's Happy this morning?"

"She's helping Dr. Sonders in the OR. Esther wasn't feeling good this morning, so she's just coming in for the hernia case. Happy's good with the T&As."

"Well, we'll just snoop around by ourselves. Oh oh, here comes trouble. Say a prayer for us, Nellie."

A tall, prim-looking man with thinning gray hair was bearing down on them from the direction of the business office, an expression of vast disapproval on his pale face. "Dr. Isaacs, I've simply got to talk to you—"

"Later, Roger. Meet Rob Tanner here, the new man I told you was coming. Rob, Roger Painter manages the hospital."

Painter gave Rob a cold look and extended a limp hand. "Delighted," he said. "I trust you'll find things satisfactory here. But, Martin, you simply must talk to Harry Sonders about these little fits of pique of his."

"Oh, God, not again! Like what this time?"

"Like dumping a whole tray of instruments on the OR floor because he couldn't find the clamp he wanted."

"Oh, hell, Roger. So he's a little temperamental sometimes."

"Temperamental or not, it costs this hospital ten dollars and forty-five cents to wrap and autoclave a tray of instruments—"

"So that's why we have you around—to worry about the cost."

"That may well be, but it's very hard for me to explain to the board of directors."

"Okay, I'll take care of it," Isaacs said in disgust. "Just don't bother me anymore." He turned on his heel and started pulling charts from the rack as Roger Painter retired, still twittering angrily. "That goddamned Sonders," Isaacs muttered, shoving charts into Rob's hands. "Picks a fight every time he walks into this place. Drives Roger right up the wall."

"Surgeons can be pretty fussy," Rob said.

"Yeah; well, this one is getting a little bit too fussy to live with," Isaacs said heavily. "Come on, let's make rounds."

He started down the ward corridor, with Rob behind him. The place was buzzing with morning activity. A nurse's aide was retrieving the last of the breakfast trays, while two others were making beds and helping patients with wash basins. An elderly man in white pushed a woman on a wheeled stretcher up the corridor toward the x-ray elevator, and a girl in a long white lab coat came trundling by, lugging a small portable EKG machine, and disappeared into the solarium. To Rob it seemed like a morning on a ward at Graystone but on a miniature scale, with everything compact and crowded. "How many beds do you have here?" he asked.

"Twenty-four, counting the one in the delivery room—it doubles for a labor room too—and that one in the isolation room down below."

"Ah. I was wondering about isolation."

26

"Well, it's not much, but it's away from the rest of the patients. We try to keep infectious cases at home, if we can, and hold the isolation room for somebody that needs to be away from noise and activity. Florey's got an old lunger down there now, emphysematous old goat with flu and pneumonia. Most times it's empty, though, so the doctors can sack out there while they're sweating out an OB or something." He paused by the first door. "Now, these two rooms are usually kept for post-partums, or for OBs in early labor. Let's see how this gal of mine is doing."

The room was bright and pleasant. In the bed by the window the recent mother of twins was resting, cheerful enough, but complaining of a sore bottom. "We'll get the heat lamp going on it this afternoon," Isaacs said, "and I've ordered something for pain too. You just tell Nellie when you need it." He introduced Rob. "I'm going to have Dr. Tanner here check those babies out. He's real good with babies."

"I hope they're all right," the woman said. "The nurse said they had to go in the Rockette."

"I always put twins in the Rockette whether they need it or not. Helps 'em get used to breathing. Then day after tomorrow I'll circumcise 'em both. You do want them circumcised?" It was more of a challenge than a question.

The woman frowned. "Well—I don't know. I'd better talk to Joe."

"Always have them circumcised," Isaacs said flatly. "Easier to keep 'em clean, and it helps prevent cancer later on. You tell Joe I said that." He gave the girl a nod and crossed the room to the woman in the second bed. "Rosie, you about ready to go home?"

"Oh, I'd like to, if I could."

"No reason why not. You can go along as soon as Dr. Tanner here checks the baby. Just keep taking those same pills I've got you on now until I see you in the office on Friday. They'll keep your milk dried up just fine."

Out in the hall again, Rob looked at Isaacs. "How long do you keep the mothers after delivery?"

"Three days, unless there's some problem. Old Florey keeps 'em in five, calls it 'extra precautions,' but that's a bunch of old-fashioned crap. I get a lot of his women coming to me after they get slapped with that big hospital bill."

They went on down to the men's ward. There was a boy who had run a fishing spear into his leg, convalescing alongside the old man with the arrhythmia. The new EKG had just been taken; the big doctor ran

27

the tracing through his fingers, shaking his head. "I can't read these things for beans. If I can just get DeForrest to take over here, that'll suit me fine."

"Eh?" the old man said.

"I said Dr. DeForrest's going to take over your case," Isaacs shouted. "He's the heart man around here."

"He ain't gonna make me swallow no goddam string again, is he?"

"Well, I don't see why," Isaacs said. "Never can tell, though, Jake. You'd better watch him."

"Ain't gonna swallow no goddam string again," the old man grumbled. He quieted down as Isaacs listened to his chest.

"You're still thumping along all right, Jake. Dr. DeForrest'll have you straightened out in no time. He'll see you again this afternoon."

"What was that about the string?" Rob asked as they moved on.

Isaacs chuckled. "The old guy had an ulcer a couple of years ago, and Jerry ran a string test on him. Jerry's a great one for the string test."

"I'm afraid I never heard of it."

"It's straight out of the Middle Ages," Isaacs said. "He thinks there might be an ulcer or something down there bleeding, so he gives them this long piece of grocery string to swallow overnight, and then pulls it back up next morning and checks it with benzidine for blood. He says it's more accurate than x-rays, but I don't know. Of course, you're supposed to leave one end out, taped to your cheek, so you can haul it back up, but that old guy swallowed the whole damned thing. Had to sit watching his rectum for three days to retrieve it, and he was fit to be tied. Wouldn't even speak to Jerry on the street for six months."

Moving on up the corridor again, Isaacs pointed with his thumb to a room where a woman was cranked half upright in bed, dozing, her face swollen and purple, her right foot in a cast propped up on a pillow. "There's your accident case from last night," Isaacs said. "You might want to take a look at her x-rays, just for kicks."

"No harm in saying hello to her, is there?" Rob said.

"Well, you'd better just check with Florey first or you'll have him right up your ass. Say, here comes our surgeon. Let's see what's bugging him today."

A small, dapper man with close-cropped curly red hair and an almost invisible hairline mustache was coming down the corridor, dressed in a green scrub suit. Isaacs flagged him down. "Harry, what the hell's been going on in that OR this morning?"

"A tonsil case," the little man said. "Bloody damned mess, too. Is

28

there some reason you can't clean up their infection a little bit before you schedule them?"

Isaacs looked startled. "I've had 'em both on Ampicillin for two weeks," he said.

"Well, that last one bled every place I touched him," Sonders said disgustedly.

"That's still no reason for dumping instruments on the floor," Isaacs said. "Roger is having a fit."

The surgeon's face darkened. "You just tell Roger to go fuck himself," he said. "Those idiot girls can't put a tray together to save their lives. I ask for a clamp and they hand me a pipe wrench."

"Well, I warn you, Harry, I'm getting damned sick of your little temper tantrums," Isaacs said, "and so is everybody else around here. Every time you walk in here we've got a big fat hassle on our hands."

"Hell, Martin, you're lucky to get anybody at all. I've got to be out of my mind to come operate in this bug house." The little surgeon glanced at Rob. "New man here already, huh?"

"Yeah," Isaacs said. "You remember Rob Tanner."

"Sure." Sonders shook Rob's hand. "Say, you don't want to help me with a hernia, do you?"

"Not right now. I've got to go hunt houses. Maybe next week, though."

"Sooner the better," Sonders said. "Old Jerry is nothing but thumbs in the OR, and Martin here is only interested in female troubles. He's just not happy unless he's squeezing ovaries."

"I thought Esther was coming in to help with the hernia," Isaacs said.

"Oh, she's here, all right, but it's that time of month again. All she's going to do today is bitch. Every month it's the same damned thing, just like clockwork."

"Maybe she just needs her ovaries squeezed," Isaacs said.

"She needs something, I can tell you that," the surgeon said. "Ever since that husband of hers ran out on her she's been hell on wheels. If you ask me, what she needs is some good, steady—"

"Yeah, we know what she needs," Isaacs said, "and you'd better just lay off, too."

Sonders looked up slowly. "Is that some kind of an order?"

"Just a friendly suggestion, Harry. This is a very small town. You do your surgery and keep your fly zipped up and everything will be just fine." Isaacs started to turn away, then paused. "You didn't really have

29

trouble with those tonsils, did you?"

"Nah, not really. That second one was pretty dirty, had a big pocket of pus back of the left tonsil, but the other one went okay. I'll check them out later this afternoon and probably let them go home."

"Well, get down to the office as soon as you're through with the hernia. You're booked solid all afternoon. And I meant what I said, Harry. Watch your temper up here. Roger is going to have a stroke one of these days."

"That'd be great," Sonders said. "Then maybe we could get something moving around this dump."

As the surgeon disappeared down the hall, Isaacs led Rob across to the newborn nursery. "You don't mind checking out those babies, do you?" he asked.

"No, that's fine."

"There's nothing wrong with them, but the mothers will feel better. And if you can take over the baby care around here, that would suit me fine. Nothing I hate worse than squalling babies."

They slipped on gowns and masks in the nursery anteroom, scrubbed and gloved themselves and then went in. The new twins, out of the Rockette by now, were sleeping in a double bassinet, a sturdy-looking pair of five-pound boys. Rob checked each of them carefully as Isaacs stood by, then checked over the baby girl who was waiting to go home. "Do you record Apgar ratings on your newborns?" he asked.

"Oh, sure, that's routine. But when it comes to fine-tuning these little ones, I'm completely at sea. Fact is, they scare me stiff."

"Well, these look fine to me," Rob said, "and I'll be glad to follow them up in the office if that's what you want."

They were slipping off their gowns when Nellie Webster stuck her head in the nursery door. "Dr. Isaacs, we've got a patient for you down in the emergency room."

"Oh, damn." Isaacs looked at his watch. "I've got to get down to the office or Terry is going to be sending up flares for me. What's the trouble?"

"Ed Butler cut his arm splitting wood."

"Well, I guess we'd better see him." Isaacs dropped the charts off at the nurses' station and Rob followed him down the ramp to the emergency room. An elderly man with thick, bushy eyebrows was sitting there with his forearm wrapped up in a bloodstained white towel, his wife hovering nervously beside him. "Ed, what the hell have you done to yourself?" Isaacs said.

"Not much, Doc," the man said. "I was just splitting some alder and a piece of the wedge broke off and nicked me."

Isaacs unwrapped the man's arm to reveal a long, ragged laceration. He spread it a bit, peering inside. "Looks like quite a nick to me," he said. "Let's see you move your fingers."

"They move all right," Ed Butler said, "but I can feel a kind of an electric shock down this forefinger."

"Well, we'd better get an x-ray. You've probably got a piece of steel in there." Isaacs looked at his watch again. "I've just got to get down to that office. Rob, could you take care of this?"

"Well, sure; I guess so."

"I'd ask Harry to do it, but that would keep Ed here waiting half the morning."

"No problem," Rob said. He introduced himself to the man. "I'm going to be working with Dr. Isaacs."

"He'll do a good job," Isaacs assured the man. "I'll send Raymond down to get a film, and Happy Cumley will help with the suturing."

"Look," Rob said, "my wife is going to be waiting down there—"

"I'll explain everything," Isaacs said. "I'll send her on up here. This won't take you long. And if you run into any trouble, just get Harry Sonders to take a look at it." The big man gave Ed Butler a pat on the shoulder and then headed back up the ramp again.

Inevitably, the job took longer than expected. The x-ray revealed a small fragment of steel embedded deep in the tissue of the forearm. "It's probably touching the nerve," Rob told the man. "That's why you feel that shock when you move your finger." A few moments later a nurse appeared and set up a minor-surgery tray. She was a handsome woman in her late thirties with wide-set eyes and freckles across her nose. "I'm Gladys Cumley, Doctor," she said. "Everybody around here calls me Happy."

"Well, we're going to have to dig for some steel here. Maybe Mrs. Butler would like to wait up in the lobby."

With the man's wife dispatched, Rob bent to his task, injecting a local anesthetic and gently probing the wound with a hemostat in search of the fragment, with Happy working efficiently at his side. It was a tedious affair as Rob searched the wound to its depths, anticipating the touch of metal on metal yet failing to find it. Happy patiently sponged and irrigated the field, retracting the tissues gently, while the patient looked on with nervous interest. Rob sighed and stretched a kink out of his back. "We know it's in there," he said. "Let's look a little deeper."

"You'll find it," Happy said. "You work just like Dr. Isaacs."

"Is that good?"

"Oh, yes. He has such a gentle touch."

"Better watch her, Doc," Ed Butler said. "Happy here has had a case on Dr. Isaacs for the last ten years."

"That so?" Rob looked up, saw the nurse flush crimson. "What kind of a case?"

"I just happen to think he's the finest doctor we've ever had here," Happy said, "that's all."

"Well, if that gentle touch would just work for me now— Hold it!" He felt something grate against the hemostat and saw Ed Butler flinch. "Okay, that's where it is. Happy, can you straighten that light a little?"

The nurse adjusted the light, hovered beside him with a gauze sponge handy. He dabbed away blood, spread the tissues with a larger pair of forceps, and then saw the black fragment momentarily. "There, now. Just hold tight." An instant later he caught the fragment with the hemostat and withdrew it. "Good. Now we just have to close it up."

"Make it neat, Doc. That's my fly-casting arm," Ed Butler said.

"You're a fisherman?"

"You bet your life, Doc. That's what I retired for." He looked up at Rob. "You do any fishing?"

"Every chance I get."

"Worms or flies?"

"Dry flies," Rob said. "I used to tie my own when I was a kid, but I think I've lost the knack."

Ed Butler beamed. "You never lose it, Doc, you just get rusty. One of these days I'll show you a gray hackle I use that really murders the trout around here. Ouch!"

"Sorry. I'm about done here." Rob tied the painful suture, then placed a small rubber drain in the wound before completing the closure. It had been over a year since his emergency room duty at Graystone, and his fingers felt like thumbs, but he finally finished and dressed the wound with an elastic pressure bandage. "There," he said. "You let that dressing be—don't disturb it and don't get it wet. I put a drain in there because there'll probably be some infection. I'll prescribe an antibiotic for you to take, and then let me see you down at Dr. Isaacs' clinic day after tomorrow. I'll take the drain out then and see how it's coming. Okay?"

32

"Fine."

"And bring that gray hackle with you. I'd like to see it."

Ed Butler went up to join his wife and check out at the hospital office, while Rob stopped at the nurses' station to file an emergency room form on the case. As he sat writing he heard the unmistakable wail of a newborn child. Presently the delivery room door burst open and a nurse scurried by with a blanket-wrapped bundle in her arms, heading for the nursery. Out in the lobby a worried-looking young man, hardly more than a boy, leaped to his feet, pale as a ghost. Nellie Webster saw him. "That's all right, Mr. Roberts. Dr. Florey will be out in a moment."

The young man waited at the door as Rob went on with his charting. Five minutes later the delivery room door swung open again and a small, portly man came out, his bald head gleaming as he pulled off his surgical cap. A mask hung from his neck, and he was completely swathed in a white surgical gown that was splattered with blood from top to bottom. Beaming, the florid little man walked over to the young father, who had turned a sickly gray at the sight of all the blood. "Well, Donnie," the doctor said, seizing the boy's hand and pumping it. "By golly, we saved her! I thought she was in trouble for sure there for a while, but we pulled the fat out of the fire."

The youth, goggle-eyed, was practically blubbering. "Oh, God, Doc, I hope she's going to be all right."

"Well, it was touch and go for a while there, but I think we've made it. She's not out of the woods just yet, but maybe the worst is behind us now."

Rob sat frozen in his seat, his jaw sagging in disbelief as the fat man chattered on, with the youth pumping his hand for dear life. "Baby's okay, a fine boy, never had any doubt about the baby, but it was rough on that little lady. I'm not sure right now if she should be having another little one or not. We'll just have to wait and see how she comes out of this, wait until I give you the go-ahead. But you just quit worrying now, everything's under control, and we'll get her down to her bed in a bit. If she's all right then, we'll let you go down and see her." He led the youth back to a seat, still chattering.

Rob stared up at Nellie Webster. "My God," he whispered. "What *happened* in there?"

The nurse laughed cheerfully. "Just a routine delivery," she said. "Sometimes Dr. Florey lays it on a little thick, that's all."

Rob pursed his lips and went back to finish his note. A moment later the doctor came back to the nurses' station, pulling off the blood-spattered gown. He took a pair of half-glasses out of his pocket, put them on, and then peered at Rob over them. "Well, now! You must be the new man."

Rob stood up. "Right. I'm Rob Tanner."

"That's right, Tanner was the name. John Florey here!" He seized Rob's hand, beaming, and pumped it vigorously. "Glad to meet you, son, glad to have you in the valley. Going to work for Martin Isaacs, eh? Well, let me tell you, Martin's a fine man, a mighty fine man. People around here have got nothing but respect for Martin Isaacs. He'll break you in right, let me tell you! And if there's anything I can do, you just let me know, eh? Anything at all."

"Matter of fact," Rob said, "I might like to look in on your new accident case, if you don't mind."

The fat man's smile congealed like cornstarch pudding. "Now, what accident case would that be, son?"

"The woman I saw up at the pass last night. Broken ribs, bloody nose . . ."

Florey frowned. "You saw her up at the pass? Funny the aid car men didn't say anything."

"I left a note buttoned to her blouse," Rob said.

"Did you, now? I didn't notice any note." The man regained his composure. "Well, you understand she's under control now. Ribs were just cracked, and the foot is all taken care of. She's resting now and everything's fine. Of course, you can stop by later to say hello if you really want to. Always glad to oblige."

Before Rob could respond, the little man turned on his heel and vanished into the doctors' dressing room. Rob finished his emergency note and handed it to Nellie Webster. Out in the lobby the young father was still pacing, puffing fiercely on a cigarette, and now Rob saw that Ellie was waiting there too. He joined her, and together they went out to the car. "How long have you been sitting out there?" Rob asked.

"Long enough to get an earful," Ellie said grimly. "Who *was* that horrid little man?"

"That is the sinister Dr. Florey," Rob said. "He and his partner have an office down near the mill. I gather he's the competition around here."

"Some competition! Why, he had that poor boy scared half to death, and him preening as if he'd saved the world or something."

"Maybe he just knows his patients," Rob said. "Sometimes you have to ham things up a little or they don't think you've done anything."

"Well, I think it's disgraceful. If I ever heard *you* talking to a patient like that, I'd leave you in a minute. And I can see why Dr. Isaacs doesn't like him too, stealing accident cases and all."

"Oh, but Florey thinks Isaacs is the salt of the earth. He just said so himself."

"He did, did he? Well, I hope you kept your hand on your wallet while he was telling you all this." Ellie sniffed disdainfully. "And as for your Dr. Isaacs, I could break his neck. Does he always mean three hours when he says one?"

Rob sighed. "Things just got a little involved. Man with a cut arm I had to sew up. I'm sorry you had to wait."

"Well, the time wasn't all wasted. I went in to see that Judge Barret that Dr. Isaacs mentioned—he's really only a justice of the peace—and we might just be in luck."

"You mean a house?"

Ellie smiled. "Wait and see what you think," she said.

# 4

Without another word Ellie turned the car down the hill, then swung north onto the highway through town and crossed the River Road bridge. The heat was shimmering on the broad streets now, the sky cloudless. Rob watched his wife in silence for a while. Then, finally, he said, "Okay, what have you been up to?"

"Lots of things," Ellie said. "First, I got us checked into the Sundown Motel. They want a small fortune for their rooms, but at least there's hot water, and they even sent a boy out to Hadley's to haul our trailer back for us. Then I tried the real estate offices, but that was a total loss. There isn't a single house for rent in the entire valley." She slowed for a dog crossing the road, then headed on north out of town. "You know, I just don't understand your Dr. Isaacs. He's known we were coming for six months now. You'd think he might at least have told the real estate people to keep their eyes open for something, wouldn't you? But no. He hadn't even talked to them."

Rob shook his head. "He's a funny guy. I'm not sure it even entered his mind that we might need someplace to live when we got here."

"Well, thank God he mentioned Judge Barret. The Judge doesn't have a place to rent, but he does have a place to sell. It's in awful shape, but—oh, Rob, you've just got to *see* it."

"Way out here?" They were a mile past Hadley's now, and the valley had widened out, town dwellings having given way to small

36

farmhouses with black cattle grazing in the fields. Presently Ellie turned left onto a blacktopped crossroad that passed through pastures and pine groves, heading toward a shoulder of fir-covered hills. They crossed the river on an old steel bridge, its ancient trusswork painted a hideous faded chartreuse. Beyond the bridge an unpaved road cut left, passing between the shoulder of the hill on the right and the river on the left. Taking another turn, Ellie swung into a driveway behind a small house, painted the same hideous chartreuse as the bridge and facing directly on the river.

At first Rob thought it was just a fishing shack like others he had seen, but at closer range it appeared more substantial, a low, one-story building with an attached garage, stacked full of debris. With Ellie leading, they entered the back door, which opened into a kitchen and dinette, divided from a long living room by a louvered railing. On the river side the kitchen and living room walls were entirely of glass, with French doors leading out to a tiny triangular patio overlooking the river. Behind the living room and kitchen were two small bedrooms, each with windows facing a pine grove, and separated by a bathroom. At the end of the living room was a red brick fireplace with a tiled hearth, supplemented by a small oil space heater in the corner.

Rob sniffed the musty air of the place, and stepped out onto the patio. The house stood on a rise some fifty feet above the river, with wooden steps leading halfway down the bank to a small pump house. The river below was wider than in town, with huge boulders breaking the quiet flow of water into foamy riffles and deep green pools. A much smaller shack with boarded-up windows sat fifty yards or so upstream, but the house was turned so that the neighboring building was invisible from the patio.

Back inside, Rob looked around more closely. The place was in a dismal state of repair. A hole in the roof had allowed water to soak the fiber ceiling board until it sagged wetly; two pieces draped down like soggy curtains. A huge water puddle filled half the living room floor, with cheap asphalt tiles peeling loose in the middle of it. Other floor tiles were ripped up, broken or scuffed aside. Two of the glass window panels facing the patio were smashed, leaving the room open to the air, and a third was cracked. The construction was crude, as if the place had been built by a walleyed carpenter, with cracks and gaps appearing in unlikely places. Outside, Rob found a ladder in the garage, set it up against the roof and climbed up for a look as Ellie steadied it. "Oh, good Lord," Rob said. "That hole's big enough to throw a cat through. We'd have to replank a third of the roof, and tar-paper the whole thing." He examined the flashing around the chimney and the bathroom vents. Then he scrambled down and poked and prodded at the foundations. "Not very high, but the concrete looks sound enough, I guess. Is it insulated?"

"No, but there's some insulation stored in the garage. They just never got it put in. Oh, Rob, can you *see* it?"

"I can see a hell of a lot of work," he said.

"But the *possibilities,*" Ellie cried. "We could get those windows fixed in no time, and a couple of boards would stop the major roof leak. Then we could at least sleep and eat in here while we fixed it, and by fall it could be snug as can be."

Rob looked around disconsolately. "That green paint would have to go."

"Yes, but think of it with red barn paint and white trim. And that garage—we could put in a window and a door onto the patio and you could have a wonderful study, or maybe a guest room. We could put down some good vinyl tile in the living room—that wouldn't take long. . . ."

He could see it, yes. A lot of work—but the place was big enough, close enough to town, with power and phone lines installed, and the quiet river with its trout pools right below the patio. . . . "I suppose he wants an arm and a leg for it."

"That's just it, Rob, he doesn't. He admitted we'd have to spend a couple of thousand for repairs even if we did the work ourselves. But he's only asking sixty-five hundred. A thousand down and forty dollars a month."

Rob whistled. "There's got to be a hitch."

"I don't think so. He said we could have the stuff in the garage and all. There's a lawn mower in there, and all kinds of tools. The lot's not very big, just a little wedge of land, but there's the river, and the land on the other side is just used for grazing. We'd have enough privacy."

Rob looked at her. "You really like it, don't you?"

"Oh, Rob, I *do.*"

"You'd have to do most of the work, you know. I'm not going to have much time, once I walk into that clinic."

"I wouldn't mind the work, for heaven's sake; it'd be a challenge. And you'd at least have weekends and days off to help with the really heavy stuff, wouldn't you?"

"I suppose." Rob scratched his chin. "It would clean out our savings

38

—we've only got about fifteen hundred left—but maybe Isaacs would advance us a little for materials. Let's measure those smashed windows; they'd have to come first. Then let's go talk to the Judge."

As he started for the door Ellie turned and faced him. "Rob, are you sure you don't want to look at other places first?"

"Do you?"

"Not really."

"Then what's the point?" he said. "Honey, I don't know any other places to look at. If this looks good to you, let's grab it."

She threw her arms around him, hugging him, and there were tears in her eyes. "Oh, Rob, I'm going to like it here, I know I am!"

It was a whirlwind decision for him, Rob realized, as they drove on back toward town. Instinct cautioned him to wait, consider, think about the costs, the possible irritations—yet the almost idyllic location and the very simplicity of the place appealed strongly. And there was no mistaking Ellie's enthusiasm. Clearly the place on the river had struck a deep chord in her mind, promised fulfillment of some deeply felt desire, and Rob could not have denied her even if he had sensed far more crushing disaster than anything that entered his mind now. It would be work—but for once they might be building something of some permanence in their lives. The cash demands would be great, but not all that great. And where else would they find a place to live for forty dollars a month?

The interview with Judge Barret in his tiny law office across from the Colonial Inn was brief. A tall, lean, stooping man with wispy gray hair and a thin hawk nose, the Judge was ready to seal the bargain with a handshake. No need for earnest money; Martin Isaacs wouldn't be hiring a man if you had to be scared of his word. The tools and materials in the garage went with the deal, and the power and telephone were already connected. The Judge would bring papers over to the clinic in a day or so, but they could start fixing it up anytime. "If it helps Martin get you settled and happy here, that's good enough for me," the Judge told them. "I owe that man a lot more than I could ever pay him, the way he took care of my wife's cancer. You know, some docs just lose interest when a cancer case goes bad on them. Not Martin Isaacs. He helped Harry Sonders do the surgery, up in Missoula, but when the cancer came back he was right here. He stood by her to the end, and I'm not liable to forget it." The Judge took a deep breath and stood up. "Some people around here don't like Martin Isaacs. You'll hear all kinds of strange stories. But if you practice medicine here the way he does, son, you'll be all right."

At the door, the old man pointed out Al Davidson's lumberyard down in the next block. While Rob loaded the car up with supplies there, Ellie went across the street to a small grocery and bought bread, cold cuts and beer for a picnic lunch. Ten minutes later they were driving back toward the river.

"Talk about gossip," Rob said.

"What do you mean?" Happily, Ellie threw her head back on the seat.

"Secrets sure don't last long around this place. That guy in the lumber store knew all about us."

Ellie giggled. "Same thing in the grocery. And old Ernie at the Chevron station had me spotted the minute he saw your credit card."

"Well, we'd better watch our p's and q's," Rob said. "Make sure the blinds are pulled or they'll be making check marks on the wall."

"Oh, Rob! You're the new doctor in town, that's all. So everybody's interested. You should be flattered."

He turned off the highway, Ellie sitting close to him on the seat. The afternoon sun glinted on the river as they crossed the bridge, angled left and turned in behind the cabin. Out on the patio a warm breeze swept up from the river, sultry and cooling at the same time. Ellie's hair glinted a rich red-brown as she spread the lunch things out. "Rob, look in the garage. I'm sure I saw an old chaise longue in there."

He found it, a dilapidated plastic-webbing affair, dusted it and hauled it around to a corner of the patio secluded from view of road and bridge. A moment later he was leaning back on the chaise sleepily, sipping cold beer from a can, opening one for Ellie as she fixed sandwiches. A gray camp robber flew from across the stream and settled in a small fir beside the house, watching them. There was a steady, pleasant gurgle from the river below.

They ate in silence, Rob on the chaise, Ellie on the footrest. She finished her sandwich and tossed a crust to the jay, which swept down instantly to retrieve it, then fluttered nervously back to its perch to gulp it down. "Move over, you bum," she said, poking Rob in the ribs. "You can't have it all."

He shifted over to make room and she lay down beside him, one leg thrown over his. He kissed her lips, kissed a pulse throbbing in her neck as she closed her eyes. "You look warm," he said.

"Pretty warm."

He slipped her blouse open, kissed her shoulder and her throat. "Damned jay bird's going to make a check mark on the wall."

"Let him. He's *my* jay bird now; he won't tell. . . ."

He made it a sleepy ritual, loosening bra and shirt, tossing trousers aside in rising urgency. Her skin was pink and gold in the sunlight, her hair thick about her shoulders, breasts firm, mouth hungry. His hand was gentle on her thigh and back, became ungentle on her breast, and she moaned as she pressed to join him. He guided her, oblivious to the awkward curve of the chaise, oblivious to the hard aluminum arm in his back as she rocked with him, meeting him fiercely, unremittingly.

Later they dozed awhile, still joined, Rob perspiring gently, her own skin smooth and cool. The jay came down and pecked at the grocery bag, unnoticed. "Rob?"

"Mmm?"

"It could be just perfect here."

"Well—nothing's ever perfect, honey."

"I suppose not. But things *are* going to work out in the practice, aren't they?"

He sat up, staring at her. "Honey, of course they are. Why shouldn't they?"

"I don't know. Dr. Isaacs, I guess."

"Dr. Isaacs!"

She nodded, looked away. "I don't think he likes me very much."

"Oh, come on. What gives you that idea?"

"I don't know, just—things. Like not even asking about a house for us. Or the way he acted at breakfast this morning, putting me down every time I opened my mouth. Hauling you off to the hospital regardless of what *you* wanted to do."

Rob laughed. "Honey, you're dreaming. He's just an overworked country doctor, and probably a pretty good one at that. But he's worn out, and now he's got a new doctor to help him, and he can't wait to get him working. So what's wrong with that?"

"I don't know. He just acts like you're his personal property, and it worries me, that's all."

"Well, you've got him all wrong. You'll see. And meanwhile we've got *real* things to worry about—like fixing those windows." He kissed her lightly. "Let's get moving."

They dressed then and got to work, Rob tackling the windows, Ellie prying up loose floor tiles. They labored silently for a couple of hours until Rob finally finished the third window. Next he went down with a coffee can full of water to prime the pump. It squeaked and wheezed and delivered a reluctant trickle up to the kitchen sink.

41

"That's not so good," Ellie said.

"Just needs new leathers." Rob looked at her. "You know, if I could get those tomorrow, so we have water and a toilet, we could bunk in here with our sleeping bags, and to hell with the Sundown Motel."

"I was thinking the same thing."

"But I'd better get another look at that roof from the inside." He brought in the ladder, crawled up between the ceiling joists where the ceiling tile had fallen, and poked and probed with a flashlight and a pole. "Couple of spots of dry rot," he announced. "But the rafters look okay."

The phone began ringing as he clambered back down. Isaacs was on the line. "So you made a deal with the Judge, eh?"

"The Judge was very obliging," Rob said. "Almost too obliging."

"Oh, don't worry about the Judge," Isaacs said. "He's the one honest man in town. Crafty lawyer when he wants to be, but he's honest."

"Well, he said we could start work," Rob said, "so I took him at his word."

"Fine. You could have a real nice place out there, once you get it fixed up." Isaacs paused. "I just called to be sure you had a phone in. And you'd better do all the heavy repairs tomorrow. We'll be looking for you at the office Thursday morning at nine—get you oriented and all."

As Rob rang off Ellie was at the sink filling the coffeepot. "Ready for a break?"

"Yeah, but we'd better not trust that tap water yet. I'll go down and get some fresh." Down at the river's edge Rob dipped a coffee can and paused to take a drink. The water was icy cold, and so clear he could see every rock in the bottom of the stream. A trout jumped in a pool not two yards from his feet. He stood there for a long moment, staring out at the river with the water can in his hand. Then he pursed his lips, shook his head and started up the bank again.

The trout would still be there tomorrow, and he'd find a minute somehow to try a cast or two. He went back up to Ellie with visions of fly lines dancing in his head.

# 5

At eight forty-five on Thursday morning Rob faced the Sundown Motel mirror for a final check, adjusted his tie and brushed lint from the shoulders of his only business suit, a threadbare and lumpy blue gabardine he had owned since his senior year in medical school. Then he found his black bag in the corner, snapped off the light, and let himself out into the raw morning air. The day had dawned overcast, with a chill breeze gusting down from the mountains as he drove to the clinic. Just as well, he reflected, that they had not yet moved into the river place after all.

It was not that they hadn't tried. By the time they had quit on Tuesday evening, they were both determined that a full day's work on Wednesday would at least allow them to camp on the floor of their new home by that night. Ellie had turned in early to get rested for the hard day coming up, but Rob had decided to go see the accident patient at the hospital before calling it a day.

"Just to spite Dr. Florey?" Ellie teased.

"I suppose. But she's been on my mind anyway."

At the hospital he learned that Dr. Florey had already been in, but the woman was still awake. First Rob checked the x-rays—the chest film with a suggestion of some fluid collected at the base of the thorax on the right; the rib films revealing crack fractures of the ninth and tenth right ribs; films of the dislocated foot, showing a successful reduction; and perfectly normal skull films. In her room, the woman was propped up in bed, leafing through an old *Time* magazine. When he came in, she looked surprised, her honey-blond hair still in disarray, her nose, cheek and forehead puffy with bruises, her right eye swollen half closed. "Hi," Rob said. "You're Christine Erickson, right?"

"Just Chris is fine."

"Age twenty-six?"

"Maybe. Why? Who are you?"

"Rob Tanner. We've already met."

The girl stared at him for a moment, then slowly raised a finger and pointed at him. "You're the doctor that stopped to help me up at the pass," she said.

"Right. You were quite a mess just then."

"Still am," she said wryly. "What I need is a long hot soak, but they won't even let me in the shower."

"Plenty of time for that later."

"I suppose. But I'm glad you stopped up there. I really thought I'd had it when that car went off."

"It was a bad night," Rob said. "Still hurting anyplace?"

"A little. Not much. Do you think this face of mine will ever get back to normal?"

"In a week's time you'll be gorgeous again," Rob said.

"If you're right, I'll owe you a kiss," she said. "Hell, I owe you a kiss anyway. Thanks for helping. We can use a Doctor Galahad around this valley."

"You live here?"

She nodded. "For the summer, at least. I work in the forestry lab, down at the mill."

"Well, you'd better get some rest now. I'll drop by again when you're a little more gorgeous." He touched her shoulder, felt her hand touch his. Back at the nurses' station he considered writing a progress note in her chart, then decided not to. *Why irritate the old fart? She's going to be all right in spite of him.* Suddenly weary, he drove down the hill and rolled into bed without waking Ellie.

They had started early on Wednesday, labored from sunrise to dark, and still could not get the place ready even for camping. Too many basic things to be done: new leathers for the water pump, dismantling a jammed and corroded shower head, replacing a fuse and a thermostat on the hot water heater, and two grim hours spent snaking out the toilet plumbing until they finally got it to flush. They had paused

44

briefly at two o'clock for cold cuts and soda, then worked doggedly on. By 9 P.M. they had finally quit, grimy and exhausted, with the roofing job really only started. Back at the motel, they had sipped a drink in silence, then walked over to the Bar-None for steaks. While they ate, Rob scribbled a shopping list on a paper napkin and handed it to Ellie. "Sorry, but it's going to be all yours tomorrow," he told her.

"I know," she said, fiddling with her steak. "It's going to take weeks, I can see that now—the roofing, the insulation, replacing all those tiles and those rotten rafters. God. Any idea what your call schedule is going to be?"

"Not for sure," Rob said, "but it's going to be tight, at least for a while." He explained the situation: that it was Isaacs who needed the relief, as DeForrest was purely an internist, no help at all with OBs or surgery. So Isaacs had been getting nailed all the time. "I think I'm supposed to take over DeForrest's call opposite Isaacs, but really *cover* —OBs and surgery and everything—and only call in DeForrest when there's a real medical emergency."

"You mean like a bad coronary?"

"Or a diabetic coma or something like that. In addition, I guess DeForrest wants to spend more of his office time on the really sticky diagnostic problems and leave a lot of the routine stuff to me. And Isaacs wants me to take on the pediatrics too, so I'm going to have my hands full."

They had finished dinner then and walked back to the motel. Ellie had been noticeably glum, but she was up before him this morning, taking the old Chevy wagon and heading for Davidson's with her shopping list as he dressed for his first morning in the office. Now, approaching the clinic building, he saw a change from two days before. The white TWIN FORKS MEDICAL CLINIC sign hanging from the double posts on the lawn near the front door bore a new name below the other three:

ROBINSON TANNER, M.D.—FAMILY PRACTICE

Cars were already arriving in the parking lot, although it was still an hour before office hours began. Rob drove around to the rear entrance the doctors used, just as Martin Isaacs pulled up in his gray Buick and parked beside DeForrest's shiny green Volkswagen.

Inside they found a middle-aged woman in a nurse's uniform drawing a cup of coffee from an urn in the rear nurses' station, a tiny room crowded with canisters, supply cartons, laundry bins and a small steam

45

autoclave. The woman had a stocky, solid look about her, with graying hair, strong hands and pleasant crinkles around her eyes. "Agnes, this is Dr. Tanner," Isaacs said. "Have you got Room 5 set up for him?"

"Just about," Agnes said. "We've still got to get an x-ray viewing box up from the basement, and wheel that old pediatric table into his examining room, but then he'll be all set."

"Sounds fine," Isaacs said. "Ask Jerry to come down to my office, will you? We need to meet for a few minutes."

The older man drew coffee for both of them, then led Rob down the hallway. "Agnes is my OB nurse; works with me in the office here and stands by for deliveries too. You'll have Dora for your regular office nurse, but Agnes will help with your OBs as well as mine. This'll be your office, here on the left, with your examining room connecting with it."

It was the first time Rob had seen the clinic by daylight; it seemed much smaller and more cramped than he remembered from his brief evening glimpses of it some months before. The building, though not new, was freshly painted in off white on the inside and the brown floor tile gleamed. The corridor ran the length of the building, with three office examining room suites near the front, together with a fourth suite used as a business office and insurance-billing room. At the rear of the building was an x-ray room and darkroom, a small cubbyhole of a laboratory, and the nurses' station on one side of the hall. On the other side, between Rob's office and a small minor surgery, was a large treatment room with a couple of wheeled stretchers, a diathermy machine, an EKG machine and sundry other equipment stored about in jumbled fashion.

"The place was perfect for two men," Isaacs said as he ushered Rob into his consulting room, the largest and brightest of the three. "Then when we brought Harry Sonders in two afternoons a week we began to get crowded. With you here, I'm not sure what we're going to do for space."

"It seems pretty well organized," Rob said.

"I planned it all myself when I had the place built," Isaacs said. "Things may be a little tight, but we'll get by."

The older man sat down behind his desk as Jerry DeForrest came in with a huge file of chest x-rays under his arm. "I'm finally getting caught up on those damned things," he said. "Got them read clear up through April."

"You call that caught up?" Isaacs said. "This is July already. What about the EKGs?"

DeForrest shook his head sadly. "I don't know. Maybe we should ship them all up to Missoula for Blomberg to look at; give us a fresh start."

"What, and pay him half our fee just for reading them? Forget it. You're just going to have to start taking them home at night, Jerry, that's all."

"I suppose so," Jerry said. "We're taking too damned many of them, that's the problem. They just pile up."

"Got to have EKGs," Isaacs said. "Maybe Rob here can help you."

Rob shook his head. "I'm not too sharp on EKGs."

"You'll learn," Isaacs said. "You'll *have* to learn, the rate Jerry here gets them read." He locked his hands behind his head and leaned back as Rob found a chair and Jerry perched on the corner of the desk. "Okay, let's get Rob organized. Most things are pretty simple. Office hours start at ten in the morning and run till six at night. It's clumsy, but we have to stay open that late because lots of the millworkers don't get off until four-thirty or five, and if we were closed by then, Florey would grab every one of 'em. We try to take an hour for lunch between one and two, but that's every man for himself, depending on how far behind schedule he's gotten by lunchtime. Hospital rounds are before office hours in the morning and again in the evening. The man on call makes the evening rounds for everybody. As for call—Rob, it's going to be you and me. I'll take Monday, Wednesday and Friday nights. You'll take Tuesdays and Thursdays, beginning with tonight. Then we'll alternate weekend call, with you taking the weekend coming up—that okay with you?"

"Fine," Rob said. "But I may need a little backup at first."

"Oh, sure. You're going to find that office practice is a whole new ball game, after Graystone Hospital. You holler for help whenever you need it. Call Jerry on medical problems, even if you just want a second opinion on something. Call Harry Sonders for surgery. He can get down here from Missoula in an hour and a half when he has to. But you'd better check with me first, to begin with, so we aren't hauling him down here for things we can handle ourselves."

"That sounds fair enough," Rob said.

Isaacs took off his glasses and began polishing them with his handkerchief. It was the first time Rob had seen the older man without glasses, and the change in his appearance was almost shocking. His eyes seemed suddenly large and protuberant, with an odd owlish expression, his face puffy and naked, almost childlike. For a moment, as he held the

47

glasses up to the light and peered at them, his face seemed to take on a sly, slightly sinister expression. Then the glasses went back on again and the old Martin Isaacs looked up at Rob, bland and fatherly. "Okay," he said. "The next thing is your day off. Jerry's taking Tuesdays off and I'm going to start taking Thursdays now that you're here—no appointments, no calls, no nothing, it's the one day I can really disappear if I want to. So what day do you want?"

Rob scratched his chin. "Mondays would be great, especially after a weekend of call."

"Well, Monday's a real bad day," Isaacs said. "Everybody's picking up the pieces after the weekend, a lot of things postponed until then. Another day would be better."

"Okay, then Fridays," Rob said.

Isaacs looked uncomfortable and tugged his ear. "Yeah. But then you'd be coming into the weekend cold, wouldn't know for sure what was going on up at the hospital when you started weekend call. And we get a lot of millworkers on Fridays, too. They sort of save things up for the end of the week."

"Then that kind of boxes me into Wednesdays," Rob said, exasperated. "Like it or not."

"Well, I don't mean it like that." Isaacs rubbed his nose. "I suppose you could try Fridays and see how it works. What do you think, Jerry?"

"One day's as bad as another," DeForrest said, shrugging.

"Okay, make it Fridays for now. At least you'll have a long weekend when you don't have the call, and you'll need it." Isaacs looked up. "So. Anything else?"

"What's the story on accident call at the hospital?" Rob asked. "Like the woman that ditched her car."

"Oh, that. It's one of Florey's cute little deals. Used to be when the hospital had a drop-in without a doctor, or an accident case from the pass, they'd just call whoever was around. Then Florey and Ted Peterson—that's his partner—started screaming that Jerry and I were getting all the juicy cases and they were getting all the kids with earaches, so they made a big fuss and we ended up splitting it down the middle. They get the calls one month, we get them the next. That's why Florey got your accident case—it was still June. We've got it now for July—but if there's any problem about the hospital not calling you, just let me know. You've got to fight that bastard every inch of the way. If he isn't pulling one trick, he's pulling another."

There was a rap on the door and Agnes stuck her head in. "Dr.

48

Isaacs, you'd better get moving. You've got ten patients waiting, and Rochelle Gallagher just called in and thinks maybe she's starting in labor."

"Oh, Christ. Tell her to come on over."

"I already did."

"Okay. If she'll just hold off till tonight maybe we can bump her and get it over with." He looked at Rob. "Damned woman pisses along for two solid weeks before she gets down to business; a guy can't get any sleep at all. But maybe we can get her off it now. Rob, you go find Bev Bessler in the business office. She handles accounts and billings, and she can show you around a bit."

In the business office he found a tall, dark-haired girl dressed in a trim blue-green pants suit that seemed to be the uniform for all the office staff except the nurses. "I try to keep the business end of the office going as smoothly as possible," Bev explained, "and we have a girl who works afternoons on insurance forms—we're always behind. Terry is on the appointment desk. . . ." She led Rob forward to the front desk facing the waiting room, where a blond girl was laboring over a huge appointment book. "We stick to appointments as much as possible, but we have lots of drop-ins too, and so we take care of them the best we can. This is your column here in the book. You've got Ed Butler coming in at ten —he's the man you sewed up at the hospital on Tuesday—and then there are two new babies Dr. Isaacs delivered a couple of weeks ago and a little girl with a sore arm. They're all scheduled before lunch. You also have a patient coming in for a checkup—headaches, I think—and a couple of pre-T&A checks on children for Dr. Sonders. Then this afternoon we'll try to shift some of Dr. Isaacs' patients over to you if possible. He's double-booked all day, as usual."

Briskly the woman went over details on chart forms, the lab, x-ray and EKG forms, the charge slips, the fee schedule and billing procedures. "Any question about fees, just buzz me. Most of our patients are very good about their bills, and I get after the ones that aren't. A few families are really hardship cases, and we take care of them the best we can—we usually ask them to pay at least something on their bills and then write off the rest. But then we have some deadbeats too. You'll spot *them* soon enough."

Rob nodded. "I suppose I will. Do the partners all own the clinic together?"

"Oh, no. Dr. Isaacs owns the building and all the equipment. There's a long-term lease agreement, and the rent comes off the top of the practice income each month, just like the rest of the overhead, and goes to him before the rest is divided up." Bev smiled. "Of course, that won't affect you while you're still on salary."

By then it was almost ten, and Bev led him back to Room 5, a narrow office with a desk, a swivel chair, a portable x-ray reading box set on top of a low bookcase, and a chair across the desk for the patient. The room was connected to a small examining room by means of a sliding door. "Your nurse will bring the patients back to the examining room, and pop their charts into the box on your door after she records their temperatures and blood pressures," Bev explained. "When you want her for help with a patient, just push that buzzer by the sliding door. You'd better use one long buzz—Dr. Isaacs uses two short ones and Dr. DeForrest one short one. You'll share Dora Hoffman with Dr. DeForrest. Dr. Isaacs keeps Agnes running all by himself."

He met Dora back in the nurses' station: a pleasant-looking woman of sixty, buxom and motherly, with purple-tinted white hair and a pair of alert brown eyes. She went on loading the autoclave with instrument packs as Rob sipped a cup of coffee. "We're certainly glad to have you," she said. "Dr. Isaacs has just been run ragged these last few months."

"Well, you'll have to show me some of the routines," Rob said. "If I do things wrong, speak up."

"Don't worry, I will," Dora said cheerily. "And anything you need to know, just ask. *I've* been the baby doctor, almost, up until now."

"Dr. Isaacs really doesn't like babies?"

"Hates 'em. Says he's always scared he's going to drop them on the floor. Of course, he's really very good with them, but he hates 'em all the same."

"Well, I can cover the babies, all right," Rob said. "I'm not so sure about the OBs."

"Oh, Agnes will help you with them; don't worry." A buzzer sounded, and Dora glanced out into the hall. "I think that's your man with the arm. I'll bring him back into the minor surgery, if you have stitches to take out."

"Just the drain comes out today, but I'll need scissors and forceps."

Dora ducked down the hall and returned presently with Ed Butler in tow, bushy eyebrows and all. The dressing on his arm was tattered and dirty. Dora led the man back into the minor surgery and stuck a thermometer in his mouth. "Dr. Tanner," she said, "Dr. Isaacs wants another x-ray to be sure you got all the foreign body out of that arm. Shall I take that before you see him or after?"

50

It hadn't occurred to Rob, but he nodded. "Better get it first," he said. He finished his coffee and returned to his office just as Agnes came by and dropped two charts into his box. "Couple of babies for you to see," she said cheerfully. "They're in the rooms I've marked on the slips."

Rob donned the white coat hanging on the back of his office door, and found his way to Room 4. A young mother was waiting there with a very small baby in her arms, feeding it from a bottle. "So you're the new doctor," she said as he walked into the room. "Dr. Isaacs said you were good with babies."

Rob smiled. "Babies are fun," he said, "especially the new ones. Of course, I don't have to change the diapers and all." He took the child up, placed it gently on the examining table. "When was this one born?"

"Just two weeks ago. He's my first."

"Well, it sounds like there's nothing wrong with his lungs." The infant had started wailing the moment the bottle was taken away. Gently Rob undid the clothing, then checked the baby over from top to toe as Dora Hoffman joined them in the room. He was a strong, husky child, flailing his arms and legs in rage as Rob checked eyes and ears, mouth, heart and lungs, abdomen. Both the navel and the circumcision were healing well. "I don't see how you can hear a thing with all that noise," the mother said as Rob put his stethoscope to the baby's chest.

"Oh, that's just background music," Rob said. "You'd be surprised what you can hear right through it." He straightened up. "The baby has a little tongue-tie; nothing serious. We'll just nip it here and now. Dora, do we have one of those little slotted tongue-lifters around?"

The nurse already had it in her hand, together with a sterile gauze sponge and a small pair of surgical scissors. "Won't it hurt?" the mother asked fearfully.

"He's so mad right now he won't even notice it." Skillfully, Rob lifted the baby's tongue with the metal paddle and clipped the thin strip of membrane restricting it. "There may be a drop or so of blood later," he told the mother, "but don't worry about it. The only way a tongue-tie like that can cause trouble is if you leave it there. It's all taken care of now." He surveyed the baby again. "This rash is prickly heat; you may be keeping him a little too warm. On hot days let him go without any clothes at all except a cotton diaper."

"How about disposable diapers?"

"Only for short stretches, like when you go shopping. Otherwise use cotton; they're a lot better for his bottom. And no plastic pants at

51

all. They'll give him a diaper rash every time."

Dora started re-dressing the baby, and Rob sat easily on the corner of the examining table, checking with the mother for problems and ordering a richer formula for the baby. "Dora, what does Dr. Isaacs do about the PKU test?"

"We should run that today."

"Okay; maybe you can help collect a specimen." He looked at the mother. "Just a screening test for a rare illness newborn babies sometimes have," he explained. "If you don't hear from us by tomorrow, you'll know it's okay. Then let me check the child again in two weeks, and we'll start his baby shots."

It had been the simplest of basic well-baby checkups, yet Rob found himself perspiring by the time mother and child were gone and he was back in his office. His hand was actually trembling as he wrote out his brief examination note. The reaction was startling, even embarrassing. After all, he'd been seeing patients for years now, ranging from newborn babies to aged grandmothers. Yet here he was shaking like a freshman med student. Of course, he realized why this seemed so different. For the first time in his life these were *his* patients he was seeing—people who would either come back to him again for years to come, or else be put off by some idiot misstep, some irritant or silly omission, and go find another doctor. *Back at Graystone it didn't really matter,* he thought. *There were always far too many patients to think about anyway. But here it matters a very great deal.*

Dora came in, smiling. "It's always a little scary at first, I guess," she said.

"It sure is." Rob grinned. "It's ridiculous, but there you are."

"Well, you'll get over it. Dr. DeForrest was all thumbs when he first came here. He'd sit down to do a pelvic and drop the speculum on the floor. It took him a week to settle down. You'll be all right soon enough. At least you've got a good way with babies." She peered at him over her glasses. "That x-ray is ready now."

He walked back to look at Ed Butler's film. It was perfectly normal. In the minor-surgery room Dora had already cut off the ragged bandage and had a sterile drape ready. "He has a little fever, Doctor—99.4 degrees."

"That's not surprising," Rob said. "How does it feel, Ed?"

"Not too bad; just a little sore."

"Let's see you move your fingers." The man complied. "Still get that tingly feeling?"

"No; that stopped as soon as you took the chip out of there."

"Fine." Rob peered closely at the uncovered wound. Then he slipped on rubber gloves, clipped the stitch holding the rubber drain in place, and withdrew it. A drop of clear amber fluid appeared where the drain had been. "No pus down there; that's a good sign. You're still taking the antibiotics? Okay; keep on using them till they're all gone." He paused, looking at the wound. "Dora, didn't I see a diathermy machine in the other room?"

"Yes, you did, Doctor."

"Okay, let's use it. We need some heat on this, but I don't want him soaking it just yet." As Dora dressed the wound, Rob leafed through the man's chart and frowned. Ed Butler, almost seventy-two, had been seen by Dr. Isaacs repeatedly over the years for colds, stomachaches or minor injuries, yet his chart was almost blank except for a handful of one- or two-line notes. "Ed, when did you last have a really thorough physical checkup in here?"

The man looked startled. "Hell, Doc, *I* don't know. Doc Isaacs gave me a chest x-ray a couple years ago when I had a little bronchitis, I think."

"It says here that was seven years ago. And you're past seventy—time a man should at least have his heart checked out; some other things too."

Butler looked at Rob, puzzled, his bushy eyebrows twitching. "I suppose. But hell, Doc, I ain't sick. I feel great."

"Good. We'd like to keep it that way too." Rob sat down across from him. "Think about it," he said. "These stitches have to come out next Tuesday. Why not tell the girl at the desk to block off an hour for a good, thorough physical exam? It'll cost you some money, but it could be worth it to stay ahead of trouble if you want to keep on fly fishing for a while."

Butler blinked. "Well, I'll think about it," he said. "And say, I brought you that gray hackle." He pulled a plastic tube from his shirt pocket with a tiny gray fishing fly in the bottom. "Give it a try on a one-pound test leader, right there in the river below Judge Barret's place, along about dusk. If you don't get yourself a mess of trout with it, I'll *buy* you a mess of trout."

"It's a deal," Rob said. "Now you go with Dora."

Back on his office door the patients' charts were piling up. There was a week-old baby to be seen, a man with a wax plug in his ear, another with a head cold—the sort of commonplace minor problems he

53

had not thought about for years, if he had ever thought about them at all. Gradually he felt his tension ease. *Not terribly interesting things,* he thought, *but not terribly difficult to solve, either.* He worked slowly, carefully, trying to miss nothing. Most of these people had come in to see Dr. Isaacs, but agreed to see "the new doctor" when they learned that Isaacs' schedule was already crammed. And indeed, Martin Isaacs seemed to be moving people in and out of his office on a veritable treadmill, patient after patient after patient, a long succession of pregnant women trundling up the corridor under Agnes's cheery eye to be weighed in and leave their morning urine specimens before seeing the doctor. Occasionally Isaacs appeared in the hallway for a moment, or ducked back for a gulp of coffee, but for the most part he was in his office or examining room, and the corridor rang with his peremptory double-buzz signal for Agnes every few moments or so.

"He seems to keep busy," Rob said to Dora during a momentary break.

"Oh, Lordy, yes. On his OB day he's always got a crowd in here. He's plenty busy other days too, but he works very fast." She hesitated. "Sometimes a little too fast. Some of the patients complain that they're in and out of his office so fast they hardly see him."

Rob moved on with his own schedule; a succession of minor ailments or consultations. Presently he ducked back to the nurses' station to join Isaacs for a cup of coffee. "Say, how come you ordered another x-ray on Ed Butler's arm? There was only one chunk of metal in there on the first film, and I took it out on Tuesday morning."

Isaacs looked at him. "You mean you'd swear in court that you were one hundred percent sure there wasn't another little piece hiding behind the big one?"

"Well—ninety-nine percent sure."

"I see. But if this just happened to be that other one percent, you could have that guy suing you for your back teeth if you didn't have a clean post-op film to back you up. Don't even think twice about it— *always* take a post-op x-ray in a case like that. You just never know when somebody's going to come back and kick you right in the balls."

"I suppose you're right," Rob said reflectively. "But are people really as suit-happy as all that?"

"Not everybody. Hell, I've been in practice here for fifteen years and I've hardly even had a case up before the Grievance Committee. But you never know when a bad one's going to come along, and one

54

malpractice suit can put you right out of business. Why put *your* neck on the block just to save somebody a ten-dollar x-ray fee?"

Dora appeared to tell Rob he was getting behind, and he dug in again. The woman with headaches took him almost an hour, sixty long minutes of frustration. She'd seen everybody over the years—Isaacs, DeForrest, three specialists in Missoula—and she still had the same old headaches. *What do you do when everybody else has given up, and there she sits in your office?* he wondered. *Spend her money on more fruitless lab tests? Tell her it's all in her mind and invite her to get lost? Go back to the books and review every detail you can find about possible causes of obscure and recurrent headaches? Maybe so. What else can you honestly do?* Finally, unhappily, he postponed decision until the lab work was back—*a cop-out, or just being realistic?*—and made a reappointment to see her the following week, sensing that the woman was as disconsolate when she left as when she came in, that somehow something, however indefinite, had been expected of him that he had failed to produce. . . .

It was almost one o'clock when the last morning chart went *plop* into his box. *Sharon Lendy, age 6—arm hurts,* Dora had written in the chart. In his examining room he found a harried-looking mother with two children, a six-year-old girl and an even smaller boy. The children were fighting vigorously over a comic book, the boy trying to tug it out of the girl's arms, the girl holding on for dear life, while the mother clucked at them ineffectually like an old hen. The struggle stopped abruptly when Rob came in. "Mrs. Lendy? This must be Sharon. What's the problem with her arm?"

Mrs. Lendy didn't know. A month or so before, the child had fallen off a swing onto her right arm. It hadn't seemed to bother her much, she went right on using the arm, but now a month later she still complained that it hurt.

Rob looked across at the child. A more subdued struggle for the comic book had resumed, Sharon maintaining possession with full vigor. Finally she let loose a roundhouse blow at her brother with her right fist. "Well," Rob said, "she can't be hurting too badly. Let's have a look, Sharon."

He examined the arm, extending and flexing the elbow, moving the whole arm through its full range of motion, wondering what on God's earth the child was doing in a doctor's office. At only one point, when he squeezed her upper arm, did the child wince. "Hurts there?" The girl nodded. "Really?" She nodded again.

"I sure don't see much," Rob told the mother, "but I guess we'd better have an x-ray anyway."

He went back for more coffee as Dora shepherded the girl down the hall to the x-ray room. A few moments later Dora stuck her head in. "That film's ready, Doctor."

Rob lifted the wet x-ray out of the water bath—and gaped at what he saw. The big bone of the upper arm was broken cleanly and completely through in midshaft. It was a recent fracture, but not fresh; a large lump of calcium had already formed a neat join around the broken ends. The alignment was perfect, and there was no sign of shortening of the bone.

Dora brought the mother into the darkroom to look. "You mean she *broke* it?" the mother said.

"She broke it right straight through. And she's also practically healed it already. That lump there is a new bone joining the broken ends. They're stuck tight. She's done a better job than any doctor could do."

"Then why does it still hurt?"

"There's still a little swelling and reaction there at the break, that's all. It'll go away." He went into the minor surgery and made a loose gauze sling for the girl's arm. "Just have her go easy on the arm for the next week or two, keep it in that sling, and give her a little aspirin if it keeps hurting."

The mother looked at him suspiciously. "That's all there is to it? She doesn't need a cast?"

"Nope, nothing like that."

Rob charted the Lendys' visit, then waved at Dora and headed over to the Bar-None for a sandwich. It was almost one-thirty by then and he was ravenous. Walking back a few minutes later, he wondered with a pang of guilt how Ellie was coming with the roof. Back at his desk, he dialed the river house. The phone rang ten times before Ellie answered. "I nearly broke my leg coming down that ladder," she said, panting.

"I'm sorry. I just wanted to see how you were doing."

"Oh, I'm doing all right," she said gloomily. "The nasty stuff is all dried up and stuck down to the boards, but it's coming."

"Well, I should be out of here by six for dinner. I've got call tonight, and all weekend, but I'll be off tomorrow to help you some."

"Great," Ellie said without conviction.

56

"Well, Jesus, kid, I did accept a paying job here."

"Oh, I know." Ellie sounded contrite. "I should be asking you how the office is going."

"It's busy as Billy-Be-Damned. I see now why Isaacs was hungry for help. I've been running my ass off, and he's been seeing ten people to my one. Look—can we camp at the house tonight?"

"We're going to," Ellie said grimly, "ready or not. I've got the sleeping bags airing right now."

He rang off just as Isaacs and Harry Sonders came in through the rear door. The little surgeon's face was flushed and his voice cut sharply down the hallway. "I'm just telling you, Martin, that drunken Sara Davis bitch has got to go. I can't do surgery out here if I have to spend half my time up at the head of the table giving anesthesia too."

"Oh, Christ, Harry, it's not that bad."

"The hell it's not. She almost went to sleep on me three times this morning, and when she was awake she could barely lurch across the room without falling down. Well, I can sneak by with that on a hernia case, maybe, but what am I going to do when I've got a tough one on the table?"

"Well, I'll talk to Roger, but it won't do any good. Last week he said the woman has been very good lately. Florey's been giving her Valium or something and she's been coming along fine."

"She must be eating the damned things like popcorn," Sonders said. "Since when do you put a lush on tranks, anyway?"

"Sometimes it calms them down so they don't drink so much."

"Well, tranks or booze, I've just about had it with this babe. One of these days she's going to kill somebody."

"So what am I supposed to do?" Isaacs growled. "Wave a magic wand? She's all we've got for anesthesia, and you're just going to have to live with her. Why don't you just use more spinals so it won't matter what Sara does? Do without her."

Sonders swore. "I can't use spinals out here, and you know it. Florey has got people scared shitless that they're going to be paralyzed if they have one."

"Well, then get some help down from Missoula, at least for the tough cases," Isaacs said angrily. "I can't just pull anesthesia out of my hat, and neither can Roger. And frankly, I'm getting damned tired of these fights all the time. You might think about that too."

The voices fell off as Isaacs headed down the corridor toward his office. Rob looked up at Dora. "Are they always scrapping like that?"

Dora sighed. "It's getting worse and worse, these last few weeks. They never used to fight, but Dr. Isaacs wants things done *his* way, and Dr. Sonders balks, and they start fighting. I don't know where it's going to end—"

She broke off as Sonders appeared at the door. "Getting dug in?" he asked Rob.

"Bit by bit," Rob said.

"Well, when you make rounds tonight, check out those two T&As I did this morning. If they aren't bleeding or anything, let 'em go home. And check the hernia case I did too. Make sure he's urinated before you turn in for the night."

"What if he hasn't?"

"If he hasn't, you'd better go catheterize him, or the nurse that comes on at eleven will haul you out of bed at three in the morning to come do it."

"Can't she do it?" Rob asked, startled.

"Well, she's an old maid," Sonders said, "and she's got a thing about grabbing some husky young logger's dong and shoving a tube up it. She'll get you out of bed every time."

"I see," Rob said. "I guess this *is* a pretty small town."

"You'd better believe it, boy." Sonders slipped into a white coat and started down the hall. Rob took his first chart and dug into the afternoon's work. He was already five patients behind, and it seemed that the faster he worked, the faster Dora plopped more charts down in his box. About four o'clock he saw a middle-aged housewife, in for an annual checkup, and found a nodule in her thyroid. Sonders came in to check it and affirmed his finding. "Have you gotten thyroid assays on her?" he asked.

"They were ordered with the rest of her lab work."

"Okay, have Bev call Missoula and set up an iodine uptake test and scan."

"Is it serious?" the woman asked.

"You mean like cancer?" The surgeon smiled. "It's possible, but not very likely. I wouldn't fret."

"Will I have to have surgery?"

"Too early to say. Let's get the tests first and then we'll go over the whole picture."

Back in the nurses' station Rob found Isaacs pouring some coffee. "Say, that Lendy kid you saw this morning," Isaacs said. "You know, the broken arm?"

58

"Right," Rob said. "Weirdest thing I ever saw. She's been going around with it broken for a month."

"Well, the mother just called me, all upset. Said you didn't do anything but put it in a sling."

"What else?" Rob said. "The bone's stuck tight as it's ever going to get."

"I know, I saw the film, but you still should have put on a cast."

"What for?"

"Look, use your head. The kid's arm has been hurting for a month, right? So you take a picture and tell the mother the arm's been broken all that time. Makes her feel like a damned fool. So then you laugh and tell her it's already taken care of itself, and that makes her feel like even more of a damned fool. Makes her think she's been a lousy mother."

Rob scratched his head. "Maybe so—but what does she want?"

"What she *really* wants is peace of mind," Isaacs said. "What she *thinks* she wants is something to help heal the kid's arm. The old laying-on-of-hands bit, and you didn't provide it. She can't believe that arm has healed all by itself after being broken clean through. *You* know there's nothing to be done, but *she* knows different, and that's all that matters as far as she's concerned."

"So what should I do? Have her bring the kid back in this afternoon?"

"Nah, then *you'd* look like an ass," Isaacs said. He looked at Rob. "I lied a little: told her I'd seen the x-ray and that it looked okay to me, but that *you* said that if the kid was having any more pain by Saturday morning—any pain at all—she should bring her back and you'd put a hanging cast on it. Okay? Don't worry, she'll be back. Just make sure the cast doesn't interfere with the kid's arm motion, and then just leave it on for a few days. The mother'll be happy, and the kid will have something to show off, and you'll look like a hero."

"Okay," Rob said dubiously. "It just seems pretty silly."

"Of course it's silly. But when people go to a doctor, they want something done. They may not know *what*, exactly, but there's a deep-seated need, and if you don't fulfill that need, they'll go right down the street to somebody who will. You'll learn."

Dora Hoffman dropped two more charts into Rob's box, so he gulped down the last of his coffee and waded back in. Dora, he noticed, was constantly on the move, ushering in an apparently endless succession of postoperative patients for Dr. Sonders to see, moving up and down the corridor like white lightning, yet always on hand when Rob

59

buzzed for her. About five o'clock the little surgeon headed out the back door with a wave of his hand. "Don't forget to check those T&As," he said. "See you Tuesday morning." Rob saw more and more of his own charts piling up, and tried frantically to increase his pace. By five-thirty or so his energy was beginning to flag. It was not that he had seen all that many patients—Isaacs and Sonders between them must have seen ten to his one—but the pace was unrelenting, with no opportunity for rest or rumination. A dozen things had come up that he would have liked to check out with Isaacs, but the opportunity just hadn't arisen, and then Isaacs too was gone. As the clock pushed six-thirty he was examining his last patient, a child with an earache, when Dora stuck her head in the door.

"Doctor, can you come a minute? We've got some trouble in the treatment room."

He followed her down the corridor. "What's going on?"

"It's John Polnick, an old ulcer patient of Dr. DeForrest's. I think he's bleeding."

He was bleeding, all right. He was sitting on a chair at the side of the room, supporting his head over the wash basin, a muscular man in his middle thirties. The sink was full of black gelatinous stuff that looked like coffee grounds. As Rob came in the room, the man retched and vomited again, spitting more black stuff into the sink. His skin was the color of putty, and he was soaked with perspiration, his blue work shirt rancid and splotched with it. He looked up weakly at Rob for a moment, then returned to retching. Rob leaned over him, grabbing a wrist to feel for a pulse. The heart rate was fast and thready. "Mr. Polnick. *Hey!* Can you hear me?"

The man nodded weakly.

"We've got to get you onto a stretcher before you pass out," Rob said.

The man nodded again and lurched to his feet, throwing an arm around Rob's shoulder. Polnick's knees began to sag, but Rob half walked, half dragged him across to the wheeled stretcher. With Dora's help he laid him out flat with his head turned to one side.

"Do we have any shock blocks?" Rob asked.

"Right over in the corner."

"Okay; let's get them under the foot of the stretcher." A moment later the stretcher was tilted up, with the man's feet a foot higher than his head. Polnick's blanched face took on a tinge of color, and he stirred, trying to sit up.

"Just lie still, Mr. Polnick. You passed out for a minute."

"Gotta throw up," the man groaned.

"Okay, here's a basin." Rob held it to the man's cheek and Polnick retched a couple of times but nothing more came up. When he had relaxed again, Rob checked out his story. The man had had a stomach-ache all day, then started vomiting black stuff about five in the after-noon. Three times before in ten years DeForrest had treated him for peptic ulcer, but there had never been any bleeding. "Well, you've got some bleeding now," Rob said. He checked the man's sagging blood pressure and shook his head. "We've got to get you up to the hospital and get this under control."

"Can you call Dr. DeForrest? I couldn't get him on the phone."

"He's off today, but we'll reach him. Meanwhile I'm going to take a blood sample and start some fluid going into you." Dora already had an IV setup ready; Rob sent her to call the aid car while he drew blood and started the IV. "What do we do for transfusion blood around here?" he asked when the nurse came back.

"The hospital sends Raymond Potter into town to get some."

"To *Missoula?* Good Christ. Well, we need two units crossmatched and out here as fast as we can get it. Meanwhile, a dose of the poppy may help quiet him down. Get him a sixth of morphine."

Rob was taping the IV needle down more firmly to the man's arm when two burly men from the aid car came lumbering down the corri-dor with a stretcher. Moments later John Polnick was loaded into the back of the ambulance, while Rob climbed into his Vega to follow them. "Oh, Dora," he said, "my wife was expecting me home for dinner. Will you call her and tell her to hold it? I'll let her know when I'm free. And tell the hospital we're on our way."

# 6

By the time they reached the hospital, the ulcer patient was drowsy from the morphine, and his retching and vomiting had stopped. Rob helped the driver and his assistant lift the stretcher down, patient and all, and wheel it through Emergency and up the ramp into the hospital. A nurse Rob had not seen before was waiting for them, a small, blond girl with large, round glasses. "I'm Janice Pryor, the three-to-eleven nurse," she said. "Mr. Polnick having more ulcer trouble?"

"He's bleeding, and it's probably an ulcer," Rob said. "We've got to get him crossmatched for whole blood as soon as possible. Is it true the nearest blood bank's in Missoula?"

The girl nodded.

"Not even a storage unit for stand-by blood out here?"

"I'm afraid not," the nurse said. "Raymond will take the crossmatch sample in right away. It'll take four hours—seventy miles each way, and an hour for the crossmatch." She looked up at Rob. "If you really need it fast, you can specify a ten-minute crossmatch, and Raymond can start back with the blood that much sooner. They'll finish the full crossmatch after he's left and call us if there's any trouble." She held up a clipboard with a blood bank requisition for him to sign.

"And then if it doesn't crossmatch, we're stuck, eh?"

Miss Pryor nodded. "Except for some freeze-dried plasma we have around."

62

"And if Raymond's car breaks down halfway to Missoula—oh, Christ!" Rob scribbled a requisition for two units and handed the slip to the thin, balding man who had just come up. "Better wait for a full crossmatch," he said.

"Okay," Raymond said. "You going to want any x-rays before I leave?"

"You'd better just get the blood here as fast as you can." As Raymond headed down the ramp, Rob turned back to the nurse. "The first thing we'll need on that man is a Levin tube into his stomach and some suction to keep the acid away from the ulcer. Make it continuous drainage. And we'll also need a blood pressure check every half hour until we're sure he's stopped bleeding. That IV is five percent glucose in water, and I'll want another one to go in when this one runs out."

A few moments later the groggy patient was in bed at the end of the men's ward with a thin plastic Levin tube inserted into his right nostril. Rob checked his blood pressure again, found it low but stable. As Miss Pryor set up the second bottle of glucose water, Rob continued to probe the man's history: recurrent ulcer symptoms over ten years; three separate programs of treatment, each discontinued when x-rays had shown that the ulcer had healed; then occasional recurring symptoms over the past six months, without treatment. No previous bleeding, but at least one episode of bowel obstruction two years earlier on account of the ulcer. "Doc DeForrest said I was plugged up completely," the man said. "Had to have the tube down that time too."

Finally satisfied, Rob went back to the nurses' desk and dialed Jerry DeForrest's home number. After eight or nine rings DeForrest came on the line.

"Jerry, I've got a problem. I just admitted your old ulcer patient, John Polnick."

"Haven't seen John in a coon's age," Jerry said. "What's the trouble?"

"Bleeding like a stuck hog. I've got him in bed with a tube down him and some blood ordered as soon as it gets here."

"I see. How much has he lost?"

"Maybe a couple of pints, maybe more. His hematocrit was down to thirty-five in the office; he could have been oozing for a week." Rob waited, but DeForrest remained silent. "I think you'd better come up and check him," Rob said finally.

"Well—you say he looks stable now? Probably not much I could do but order up some Banthine or something like that to cut down on his

63

secretions. We can check his electrolytes in the morning."

"Well, sure," Rob said, "but you might want to look at him tonight, at least set up his fluid balance. We know he's going to be short on chlorides with this continuous suction going."

"True," DeForrest said. "Why don't you order a liter of glucose in half-normal saline to follow the IV you've got running. Otherwise it sounds as if you've got him under control." There was a long pause. Then: "I suppose I can come up and see him later on, if you think I need to. I'm right in the middle of dinner just now."

Rob rang off, exasperated, and sat chewing his thumb for a moment. Then he began writing admission orders for the patient. The blond-haired nurse with the round glasses came up and peered over his shoulder. "How long do you want the every-thirty-minute blood pressures?" she asked.

"All night," Rob said. "He's bled a lot and he may bleed more. It was a hundred and ten over seventy a few minutes ago, and that's fine, but if it drops below one hundred systolic, you'd better get me up here in a hurry."

"Okay, we'll keep checking. Do you want all the blood given when it gets here?"

"Just one unit, as long as he's stable. Then we'll have one left if his pressure drops, or if he starts to bleed again."

He was tired and hungry by now, but he decided to make rounds of the other hospital patients before starting home. He checked Dr. Sonders' two T&A patients, a boy and a girl, and wrote discharge orders, telling the mother to call him if there was any sign of bleeding. On the men's ward he found the patient who had had the hernia repair that morning, confirmed that he had been up on his feet and emptied his bladder since recovering from anesthesia. He was just going up to check on Florey's accident case when he saw a very pregnant woman and a harried-looking man with a suitcase trundle in from the lobby and stop by the nurses' desk. At the same moment the nurse called down the corridor. "Dr. Tanner? Dr. Isaacs is on the phone."

Rob took the instrument from her hand. "Oh, Rob," Isaacs said. "I just sent Rochelle Gallagher up there."

"You mean the OB? She just walked in."

"Good. I bumped her with a little Pit this afternoon and I think she's in labor now. Check her and give me a call as soon as she's in bed, okay? Agnes will be up in a few minutes."

The blond evening nurse had already escorted the woman back to the labor room. A moment later Agnes Miller came in, wearing a light summer print dress to replace her office uniform. "Got one coming along, have we?" she said.

"Looks like it," Rob said. "I'm supposed to tell Dr. Isaacs how she's doing when you get her in bed."

While Agnes went to gown up, Rob wrote orders on the other patients he had checked, then walked back for some coffee in the little dining room to the rear. Try as he would, he could not shake off the sense of disquiet, the growing uneasiness he felt as he thought about the ulcer patient down the hall. Lord knows he had nursed enough ulcer patients through acute attacks, bleeding episodes, obstructions, perforations, everything imaginable. But things had been different at a big city hospital. At Graystone John Polnick would already have received whole blood to replace his loss, with additional units crossmatched and on stand-by in case of an emergency. At Graystone an expert intensive care nursing unit would already have swung into action to monitor the patient, and a surgeon would have been alerted in the event that the bleeding did not stop and surgery became necessary to stop a hemorrhage. The lab would already have assessed the patient's electrolyte balance, his clotting power, a dozen other things. Indeed, the more Rob stewed about it, the more things he could think of that needed to be done, that ought to have been done already. . . .

But this was not Graystone Memorial Hospital, in the heart of a big city. This was Twin Forks Community Hospital, a tiny institution in a remote corner of the wilderness. Blood had to be brought from a blood bank seventy miles away. Some lab work was available, but other things would have to be sent to the city, and God alone might know when the reports would get back. The nearest surgeon, seventy miles away, didn't even know the patient was in the hospital; and the nearest internist wasn't about to be stirred away from his dinner.

Rob shook his head as his concern mounted. *What are you going to do if this man really opens up and bleeds?* he asked himself. *You can't go in and tie off a bleeding artery. You don't have the training. You'd just kill him all the quicker. You don't even have blood on hand to cover a fall in blood pressure. He could bleed to death right before your eyes.*

Agnes Miller stuck her head in the door. "She's in labor, all right, Doctor. I think she's dilated about four centimeters, but maybe you'd better check."

"Okay." Rob pushed aside his uneasiness and followed the nurse into the delivery room. Rochelle Gallagher was in the "labor bed" in the corner of the large, brightly lit room. Rob introduced himself, told her Dr. Isaacs had asked him to check her. He was just finishing when Isaacs himself walked in.

"Well, how's she doing?" he demanded.

"She's coming right along," Rob said. "Agnes just gave her some Demerol."

"Good. Hang around and you can help me wrap it up." Isaacs disappeared into the doctors' dressing room. Rob went down to Mr. Polnick again, found him sleeping, with Miss Pryor just checking his blood pressure.

"It's a hundred and twenty over ninety, Doctor."

"Great." Rob checked the drainage bottle. There was no sign of blood now, only a half inch of clear yellowish fluid. "Good. We may just luck out on this one. But watch him like a hawk."

He found Isaacs back in the coffee room. The big man studied him narrowly. "You look worried," he said.

"I *am* worried." Rob told him about the ulcer patient. "What do we do if this guy goes sour on us in the middle of the night?"

"He still bleeding?"

"Not at the moment, and I've got some blood coming, if it ever gets here. But what do we do if he really starts dumping it out along about midnight? He could float right on down the river, and *I* sure don't want to have to go in there and tie off a bleeder at two in the morning."

Isaacs frowned. "What does Jerry think?"

"Who knows? It's almost nine o'clock now and Jerry still hasn't even seen the guy."

"How about Harry? He know the man's been bleeding?"

"Not that I know of. He was already gone when this guy came in."

Isaacs pulled off his glasses and polished them. "Well, Jerry probably just hangs on to these people too long, that's the trouble. Harry should have had this guy's stomach out years ago—but Jerry doesn't believe in surgical treatment for ulcer disease. And he usually sneaks by." Isaacs put his glasses back on. "You're probably fretting about nothing. When a bleeder like this settles down, he usually stays settled down. But if you're really worried, call Harry yourself. Pack the guy into the ambulance and ship him on into town."

Rob grimaced. "I hate to make a big fuss. Maybe I should wait until Jerry sees him, at least."

"That's probably safe enough. But Jerry should get on the horn to

66

Harry about it in the morning, just the same."

Agnes looked in again. "If you guys are going to deliver this baby, you'd better get cracking," she said. "She's going to be ready for the block pretty soon."

Rob changed into a scrub suit and joined Isaacs at the scrub sink between the surgery and the delivery room. "No trouble with this woman," Isaacs said. "She's already had two big babies, nice wide pelvis with plenty of room, so we'll do fine with a saddle block. She'll be pretty uncomfortable by now, but once we get the block in she'll work like a trouper. You just pay attention and help out where you can. It's all pretty much routine."

In the delivery room Agnes gowned and gloved them. Rochelle had already been shifted over from the bed to the delivery table, clearly uncomfortable with her contractions but doing well with them just the same. Isaacs checked her and nodded. "Let's get her up for the block," he said.

Rob watched as Agnes helped the woman sit up, with her legs dangling off the table. Isaacs pulled up a kick stool with his foot, painted a patch on the woman's back with Merthiolate and began probing for the familiar lower spine landmarks. An instant later Isaacs had slipped the needle into place, so swiftly and deftly Rob could hardly believe his eyes. When clear drops of spinal fluid appeared, he injected the anesthetic solution, withdrawing the needle just as the woman tensed for another contraction. Then, as the anesthetic took effect, he helped Agnes ease the patient back on the table, and turned to change his gown and gloves.

From that point on things went so smoothly, so unhurriedly, that it seemed more like a staged performance than the delivery of a newborn baby. Free of discomfort, and encouraged by Agnes's cheerful banter, the mother worked vigorously with her contractions; in between there were pleasantries, some idle conversation, and some instruction as Isaacs outlined his delivery procedure to Rob. "It sounds like routine," he said, "but it never really is. Every woman is different, and every delivery is different. I follow a pattern as far as possible, but you've got to be ready to shift gears fast if something unexpected turns up. Fortunately, most times things go pretty smoothly."

Rob looked at the open delivery pack on the tray stand at Dr. Isaacs' right. "What about forceps?"

"I almost always use them, and I always tell my patients why in advance. Better control, fewer lacerations, less trauma to the support-

67

ing muscles—better deliveries all the way around, for my money. Florey makes a big issue about 'natural deliveries' without forceps, and tries to make it look as if I'm forced to use them because I don't handle things right. Of course, that's just a lot of crap, and it used to make me mad as hell. But then after a while I quit worrying about it, just did things my way and ignored him. He gets more of his women back for perineal repairs later on than I do, but that's not my idea of good medicine."

The moment of truth had come, and Isaacs placed the forceps and delivered the baby with almost offhand speed and gentleness. He held the child carefully as Rob clamped the cord. "Well, Rochelle, it looks like the Gallaghers have another gorgeous daughter."

Tearful mother greeted wailing child as Agnes held it cradled in the receiving blanket. Rob inspected the infant briefly and nodded to Isaacs. "Looks like Apgar ten to me; no problems."

"Of course there are no problems," Agnes said good-naturedly. "We'll just take her down to the nursery and get her cleaned up a little and then let the father have a look." As she went out with the howling child, Rob turned to help Isaacs repair the episiotomy incision made to ease the delivery, but Isaacs was already almost finished.

A moment later the placenta was delivered and the big doctor was massaging the patient's abdomen. "Rob, give her the Ergotrate in that syringe over there. I'm going to have Agnes hook up half a liter of glucose with some Pitocin in it to that IV, just in case this gal has more flow than usual. Might as well let you get a little sleep tonight."

Rob struggled out of his gown and gloves and walked back to the nurses' desk. Isaacs was talking quietly to the anxious father. "No problems . . . good, strapping eight-pound girl. You should have joined the party, Jack. Maybe next time, eh? Agnes will let you know when you can have a look, and your wife will be back down in her room in a few minutes. You'd better just give her a kiss and go on home, though; she's pretty tired."

The clock over the nurses' desk said 9:45. Back in the coffee room Rob found Jerry DeForrest scribbling a note on John Polnick's chart. "So you finally got here," he said.

"Little hang-up at home," Jerry said. "But then, you've cured him without me. He's snoring away back there. Stomach drainage is clear, and his blood pressure is stable. We'll just keep him emptied out tonight and start him on fluids and antacids tomorrow morning."

"How about the blood?" Rob asked.

68

"It's here, but I think we'll wait until we can check his hematocrit in the morning before we give him any. No point complicating things tonight with a transfusion reaction."

"That sounds reasonable." Rob regarded DeForrest's lean face, yellowish in the poor overhead light. "Even so, I really think we ought to let a surgeon know what's going on."

"Well, it's pretty late." DeForrest fiddled with his pen. "Maybe it can wait till morning. I've got to call Harry then anyway."

Rob shrugged. "Okay. I guess I'll check that new baby out and then go home." Leaving DeForrest to his writing, he walked down to the nursery and did a quick exam on Rochelle Gallagher's new baby. On the way back he passed Chris Erickson's door, paused, then walked in. The girl was sitting up in bed, peering intently into the mirror of a small vanity case. Rob watched her for a moment. "Is this the face that launched a thousand ships?" he said finally.

Chris gave a start. "Two rowboats and a garbage scow," she said in disgust. "God, what a mess."

"You're just impatient," Rob said. Despite the purple bruises, most of the swelling was down, revealing an oddly attractive face, delicate and fine-featured, with slightly slanted green eyes and a small, tilted nose. Her honey-colored hair, freshly shampooed, lay close to her head in natural curls. Rob regarded her with increasing approval. "Things are definitely improving," he said.

"I hope so. Dr. Florey tapped some fluid from my chest this morning." She pointed to a spot near the base of the ribs in the back. "He also put a walking heel on this damned cast, but he won't let me walk on it." She held up her casted foot for Rob's inspection.

"He probably will tomorrow," Rob said.

"I hope so." She glanced up at him. "Isn't there some way you could take over on this? Dr. Florey doesn't exactly send me, with his damp little hands poking around. . . ."

Rob shook his head. "Not while you're still in here, I can't. Ethics, and all that. Very bad scene. Of course, once he lets you out, you could sure call me if you're having any trouble."

"I'll do that," she said, smiling. "Seems to me a person might have all kinds of trouble."

Walking back up the corridor, Rob glanced momentarily at the girl's chart. *At least the fat bastard saw the fluid in her chest too,* he thought. *Can't be quite as sloppy as Isaacs claims.* He rechecked his orders on the new baby, made sure that Miss Pryor had his home phone

69

number on her call list, and then slipped on his jacket and headed the Vega down the hill toward home.

It was past ten when he walked in, and Ellie was dozing over a magazine. Out on the patio she let Rob poke the charcoal fire back to life while she prepared steaks to grill. "I thought you must have died up there," she said. "What happened?"

"A little bit of everything," Rob said. "A couple of sick people to get settled, and then Martin had a delivery he wanted me to help with."

"Everything's going all right, though?"

"I guess so."

She looked at him. "You don't sound too sure."

"Well, it was a little weird. I had this guy bleeding from an ulcer, kind of an urgent problem, you'd think, with no transfusion blood anywhere in sight, but it took four hours to get DeForrest out to see the man, and the surgeon still doesn't know he's in the house. Even Isaacs doesn't seem to think it's anything worth worrying about."

"And the man's still bleeding?"

"Well, not right now, knock wood. But I think I'll say a little prayer before I turn in for the night."

They ate their steaks and salad on the patio, with a pleasant breeze coming up from the river to cool them. Ellie described her progress tearing off the old roofing. She had sleeping bags and air mattresses out for sleeping on the floor of the bedroom under an undamaged part of the roof. "If you can help tomorrow, maybe we can get the whole thing watertight," she said.

"That'd be fine, if calls don't keep me up all night," Rob said. He was bone weary by now, aching in every joint, and was sprawled out sleeping soundly by the time Ellie finished the dishes and followed him in to bed.

He didn't sleep long, however; the hospital emergency room calls began about midnight, in an unrelenting stream. A baby with an earache, a woman with a painfully infected finger, a truckdriver with a cinder in his eye—minor things, irritating things, and in each case Rob was just crawling back into bed when the phone rang again. Then about three-thirty a more worrisome problem turned up: a four-year-old boy found on the floor beside his bed, "acting funny" (according to the father) and bleeding from a cut lip. Rob told the parents to bring the child up to the hospital, and started back up the highway once again. In the emergency room he found the child sitting in a half stupor under the bright lights, his fingers and arms twitching uncontrollably. A single

70

glance told Rob the whole story as the tall, gaunt night nurse took the boy's temperature.

"You must be Jessie Hodges," Rob said to the nurse.

"Right," she said. "Eleven P.M. to seven in the morning. Nobody else'll take the shift."

"Well, we've got a hot little boy here. His temp is 105 degrees or I'll eat my shirt."

"You're close enough," Jessie Hodges said grimly. "I get 104.6."

"Okay; let's sponge him down quick before he fires off another one." He talked to the parents as he undressed the boy. The child had been well all day, just a little cranky at bedtime. Then at 3 A.M. the mother had been awakened by a crash in his bedroom.

"He was just lying there, out of bed, banging his head on the floor," she said. "He didn't even seem to know me."

"He was having a fever convulsion," Rob said. He opened the boy's mouth, saw the bitten lip and tongue as the night nurse sloshed him down with alcohol and water. "Has he ever done this before?"

"Nothing like this; no. Sometimes he gets a little twitchy when he has a fever."

"Well, that's your clue. The high temp irritates the nervous system and all of a sudden he's convulsing. Then afterwards he's rum-dum for a while, almost like he's drunk."

The father looked up at Rob. "Does this mean he's an epileptic?"

"No, no; nothing of the sort. It's just a response to high fever. Some kids are more sensitive than others, that's all. They usually outgrow it." Rob turned back to the child, examined him carefully. He saw the irritation of the eyes, the red throat and angry red lining of the child's mouth. He checked heart, lungs, abdomen and joints, then looked up at the night nurse. "Are you thinking what I'm thinking?"

The nurse pursed her lips and nodded once, solemnly.

"Red measles?"

She nodded again. "Red measles."

"Then we'd better get him out of the emergency room, right?"

"Right," she said, with the faintest flicker of a smile.

"Okay; get him a little phenobarb and a couple of aspirin, and we'll move him on home." Rob turned to the parents. "He's never had a measles shot?"

"Doc, we've been moving around so much all the kids' shots are fouled up."

"Well, now's the time to straighten them out. This boy will have a

71

lovely rash in another few hours. Give him aspirin and sponge him down to control the fever. I'll order something to block the convulsions and let him get some rest. Then on Saturday you bring the other kids to my office and we'll start getting their shots up to date."

While the nurse helped dress the child, Rob walked quietly down to the men's ward and examined Mr. Polnick's drainage bottle. Back at the nurses' station he checked the man's chart. No sign of fresh bleeding, and the blood pressure was stable. In the chart Rob wrote: "Recommend surgical consultation; Dr. DeForrest please assume care." He hesitated a moment, looking at what he had written, then closed the chart with a snap and walked back out to his car. It was almost broad daylight as he drove across the bridge and turned into the drive behind the house, and he was numb with fatigue. Ellie stirred sleepily as he came in, a smudge of tar still visible on her cheek. With a sigh Rob collapsed on his sleeping bag. The next thing he knew it was almost noon and he woke to thumping on the roof and the smell of fresh coffee perking.

# 7

His first impulse was to rush up to the hospital to see how his ulcer patient was doing, but he blocked it firmly. *Jerry's got him now, and if Jerry screws him up, that's Jerry's headache. This is your day off, before a long duty weekend. Better make the most of it.* He dressed, poured some coffee and climbed up the ladder to track down the roof-thumping. Ellie had accomplished wonders; the old, torn-off roofing was piled in dirty heaps all over everything. Ellie herself, clad only in blue jeans and a bra, was struggling fiercely with a stubborn piece that wouldn't tear loose. Rob climbed up to relieve her. "You stay up here dressed like that, you're going to sunburn like hell," he said.

She dropped the pile of debris with a thud. "I guess I woke you up," she said. "Did you get any sleep at all last night?"

"Not much."

"Is there any coffee left?"

"A cup or two. I'll bring some up."

A moment later he returned with two fresh cups of coffee and a cotton blouse for Ellie. Together they sat cross-legged on the roof, sipping. Almost all the old roofing was off now, exposing the dried planking. "I've been trying to hurry," Ellie said, "before we get rain. I've put new boards over the hole, but we've got to go buy a pot of sealer before we can put the roll roofing down."

"So let's go get it," Rob said. The trip into town in the Chevy wagon

73

was brief. Al Davidson at the lumber store seemed to know what they needed, piling tar pots and brushes into the rear of the wagon. Driving back out the highway, Rob vaguely noticed an aged woman walking along the roadside in the noonday sun.

Ellie turned and looked back. "Rob, stop. That little old lady lives just down the road from us. She must walk all the way into town and back every day."

He pulled over and backed up along the shoulder toward the approaching figure. She was wrapped in a huge woolen overcoat, despite the heat, and held a bulging shopping bag in each hand. A faded print dress showed under the coat, with long black stockings and weather-worn black shoes beneath. On her head was a blue beret, wisps of white hair emerging on all sides. As she came up to the car, Rob saw a deeply wrinkled face and a pair of sharp blue eyes peering out at him curiously. "I suppose you're thinking I'll never make it," she said in a crackly voice. "I've never failed yet, though. I could outwalk you young things any day of the week."

"Maybe so, but it's pretty hot out there. Hop in; we're going your way."

"I know." The woman glanced at Ellie. "Saw her up on the roof this morning, pounding away. Like to wake the dead." She climbed into the back seat and settled back with a sigh.

"You must be the Mrs. Foreman who goes with the green mailbox down the road from us," Ellie said.

"Florabelle Foreman," the woman affirmed. "Folks call me Belle. Think I'm crazy, just because I keep cats."

"There's nothing wrong with cats," Ellie said.

"You haven't seen my cats," Belle said, and laughed in a high-pitched cackle. "Drove three husbands off, they did. Ah, well, everybody to his own poison." She looked around at Rob with a sly grin. "You, now, you've got your own kind of poison to deal with, going to work for Martin Isaacs."

Rob looked around at her. "You know him?"

"Sonny, I've known Martin Isaacs for more years than I care to think about," Belle said. "Know him better than he knows himself. Hard man to deal with, if you don't agree with him. He's been trying to put me away in a nursing home for the last ten years, but he hasn't made it yet, and what's more, he's not goin' to."

As Rob crossed the bridge and swung left, Belle sat forward, clutching her bags. "I can walk from here," she said. "You've got things to do

74

besides drive me around." Rob stopped to let her out, watched her juggle the bags for balance. "You come down and see my cats," she said to Ellie. "And as for you, sonny, just don't let Martin Isaacs wear you down. He'll try."

She hobbled along the road, and Rob turned in to their house. "Sounds like maybe she's got his number," Ellie said.

"Or else she's a little crazy," Rob said. "Wonder what's wrong with her cats?"

"Maybe I'll go see tomorrow. Right now we've got work to do."

They plunged in, then, to a grueling afternoon of tar paper, roll roofing and foul-smelling, sticky black sealer. Then at four o'clock, with the job half done and Rob at his gooiest, the telephone rang. They exchanged a long look, and Rob scrambled down the ladder to get it. "Rob, I've got to do a Caesarean on a woman in labor," Isaacs said. "You'd better come up and help."

"Martin, I'm covered with tar."

"That's okay; just use a little paint thinner. It'll come off."

Rob swore under his breath. "How soon do you need me?"

"Thirty minutes. You'd better hustle. She's a repeat section, and I don't want her to stretch that old scar too much."

Rob scraped off tar, showered, changed and started down the road, leaving Ellie working grimly on the last half of the roof. "I shouldn't be more than an hour," he told her, but even then he knew better.

At the hospital Esther hadn't yet arrived to set up the OR. "I'm going to give the woman a spinal myself," Isaacs told her when she finally did arrive. "I don't want to have to wait for Sara Davis to get off her ass and get up here." But even so, it was an hour and a half before they even got started. When things were finally under way, Isaacs went about the surgery calmly and cheerfully while Rob silently stewed. "She had a lot of bleeding with her first baby, so I had to section her then," Isaacs explained. "And you know the old rule: once a Caesarean, always a Caesarean."

"I thought the experts threw that one out the window years ago," Rob grumbled.

"Oh, yeah? Well, maybe *they* have, but *I* haven't," Isaacs said. "One good hard contraction and she could split that old uterine scar wide open. And believe me, boy, when you've got a ruptured uterus on your hands in a place like this, you've got trouble. The experts can play around all they want to, but me, I'll do a repeat Caesarean every time."

It was a smooth, uncomplicated procedure with a pink, squalling baby delivered within five minutes of the first incision, and a long, tedious closure that Rob thought would never end. It was almost eight o'clock when he got back home and found Ellie sitting like Tar Baby in the middle of the living room floor, sipping a drink.

"Sorry, kid," Rob said. "I can help now."

"You don't need to. It's done."

He blinked. "All finished?"

"All finished. And if it leaks with the first rainstorm, you can go up and plug the holes with your fingers."

"Honey, I'm sorry, but he had to have help. . . ."

"Sure. I know." Ellie stood up wearily. "If you want to help me wrestle that stove in from the trailer, I'll cook you some dinner. Otherwise you can go down to the hamburger stand."

Rob found the range near the back of the U-Haul and together they lugged it in through the kitchen door and plugged it into the 220-volt outlet. Ellie started cooking dinner while Rob watched her in strained silence. Finally he said, "Ellie, it wasn't *his* fault the woman went into labor on my day off. He had to do a section fast and he needed some extra hands."

"I know; it's nobody's fault. There's just so much to do here."

"Well, one way or the other, the roof is on."

She nodded. "So that just leaves the insulation and the ceiling board and the floor tile and the house painting, among other things."

"I can work on it after dinner."

She turned from the stove and hugged him for a moment. "Forget it; I'm just feeling sorry for myself. You must be bushed, and you've got weekend call coming up. You'd better go to bed after dinner."

He felt guilty, but he didn't argue with her. As soon as dishes were done he collapsed on an air mattress in front of the fireplace fire. "Nuts," he said sleepily. "I forgot to check that ulcer guy while I was up there."

"Won't Martin be making rounds?"

"I suppose."

"So let it be," Ellie said. "Martin can certainly cover. You just get some sleep." But Rob was already snoring.

# 8

Nellie Webster was just coming on duty at seven o'clock Saturday morning when Rob walked into the hospital. He found Jerry DeForrest back in the doctors' room scribbling a progress note on John Polnick's chart and sipping a cup of coffee. The internist looked up as Rob walked in. "Ah, there you are. I think our friend is out of the woods."

"No more bleeding?" Rob said.

"Not a bit. I started him on fluids by mouth yesterday and pulled the tube this morning. He can go on a soft ulcer diet today, and home tomorrow if he's still okay."

"Fine," Rob said, relieved. "How about his blood picture?"

"Down to nine grams of hemoglobin yesterday, so I gave him a unit of blood last night. We'll see how he checks out in the office on Monday before we send the other unit back."

"He's going to see you, then?"

"Or you; either way."

"Well, I really think you'd better follow him up," Rob said, irritated. "What did Harry Sonders say?"

DeForrest scratched his jaw. "Matter of fact, I never did call him. Nothing for him to do now anyway. We can get ulcer films on the guy in a week or so, and then talk it over with Harry."

Rob just looked at him, bemused. "Okay, whatever you want," he said finally. "Are you going to be around this weekend?"

"Part of the time. Amy and I may go up to Missoula for a while, but we should be back tomorrow. I think Martin's going to be around."

"Any special problems I need to know about?"

"Not really." The internist stood up to go. "I did put a kid in the house last night with croup. You may want to let him go on home if he's settling down."

As DeForrest left, Rob walked down to the men's ward and found John Polnick eating puréed oatmeal and custard for breakfast. He was washing it down with a large cup of very black coffee. "Good God," Rob said. "What are you doing with *that?*"

The man gave him a sheepish grin. "I talked old Jessie out of it before she went off duty," he said. "Gotta drink it fast, though. Nellie Webster'll snatch it away for sure if she sees it."

"So will I," Rob said, picking the cup off the tray. "Look, my friend, do you really *like* sitting around this place with a tube down your nose?"

"Aw, Doc, one cup of coffee isn't going to hurt my ulcer."

"And how many do you drink in a day?"

"Maybe two or three."

"Or maybe nine or ten," Rob said.

"Well—maybe."

"Okay; look. You want to get home tomorrow—why not get smart and just not drink any? Putting that stuff down there is like pouring acid over a cut. You fool around now and you're going to be bleeding again, sure as night follows day."

Rob moved on to check the other patients. Florey, he found, had discharged Chris Erickson the night before. "She said to tell you thanks a million," Nellie Webster said, and Rob nodded, regretting that he hadn't looked in on her when he had been up there the previous afternoon. Rochelle Gallagher was busy nursing her new baby with a bottle; mother and child both looked radiant. The child with croup was sleeping, and Rob didn't wake him, just checked to make sure he was breathing freely. No rush about sending him home, he decided. He had had hair-raising experiences with croupy children during his pediatric training—children with swollen, infected larynxes that simply choked off their breathing a little after the onset of the telltale croupy cough, so that breathing tubes had to be inserted to keep them from suffocating. He'd even inserted such tubes himself on occasion, but he hated it: there was something about the thought of driving a scalpel blade into the front of a baby's throat that brought sweat out on his forehead.

Several new patients of Isaacs' were in the house, and Isaacs himself came in to check them as Rob was reading their charts. "Nothing to worry about here," he said, "but you're going to have an officeful of patients this morning, and highway call as well. Give me a ring if you get snowed under. I'll be around home most of the time."

It was a quarter past nine when Rob headed the Vega down toward the office, trying to shake off the odd sense of coiled-spring tension he was feeling about the weekend ahead. Not that weekend call was anything new—he had spent many a harrowing weekend at Graystone, weekends of frantic, steady work from Saturday morning to Monday morning with hardly time for a cat nap. But even at its worst, he had never stood alone at Graystone. There was always help within easy reach when serious problems arose. There were all the facilities of a modern city hospital to draw upon—round-the-clock lab work, excellent x-ray coverage, surgical help and skilled anesthesia all ready at a moment's notice, intensive care facilities for the critically ill—everything one might need immediately at hand. But here, by contrast, Rob felt unnervingly alone facing the weekend. Lab and x-ray facilities, at best, would be limited. Jerry DeForrest might not be much help in a pinch—was the man *always* so blasé when confronted with trouble? Of course, Isaacs might respond more swiftly in a crisis, but the main reason Rob was there was to relieve Martin Isaacs of the burden of incessant call. *It would have to be quite some crisis,* he thought, *before you call him out.* And as for the surgeon, it remained to be seen what *he* might do when the fat was in the fire.

Turning into the clinic parking lot, Rob pushed aside his gloomy thoughts. He was a novice here, just as he had been a novice at Graystone. He had muddled through then, and he would muddle through now too. He'd only just begun to explore the pattern of work here, the strengths and weaknesses of his new colleagues and his own capacities and limitations. Naturally there would be tensions and uncertainties, probably even foolish mistakes—but he would learn. And he would also learn to live with the limitations that existed here, or else find ways to change them. Martin Isaacs had lived with them and still managed to practice a respectable quality of medicine. And maybe Jerry DeForrest was right too. Maybe it didn't help to be too tense, to look too hard for potential catastrophe. Maybe too much tension would really be more hindrance than help.

Maybe.

Dora Hoffman was busy setting up the office when he walked in. "Glad you came early," she said. "You've got five people waiting already, and it's just you and me today, so we're both going to be hopping."

He started in at a run—and ran all morning. Sure enough, the little girl with the broken arm was back, just as Isaacs had predicted. The mother was adamant: the child's arm was hurting worse than before, and aspirin was no help. "After all, Doctor, it isn't like a headache; she has a broken arm. . . ."

Rob listened, then winked at the child and worked with Dora to put a light cast on the arm, leaving the elbow free to move. "There," he said finally. "That should do it."

"How long will it have to stay on?" the mother asked.

"About ten days. Let's see her next Wednesday and then we'll decide." He gave the child a pat on the bottom and packed her off with suckers and balloons from a box in the hall closet.

Other patients were piling up, and Rob moved from examining room to examining room, with Dora just a step ahead of him. In one room four boys of assorted ages, all from one family, were waiting for pre-camp physicals. "Dr. Isaacs just checks their heart and lungs and sees that they don't have hernias," Dora said. "He doesn't usually even make a charge." Two men waiting to have insurance policy physicals took more time. The first, a young logger, presented no problem, but the other, a pudgy thirty-year-old furniture salesman named Peter Brennan, had a blood pressure reading of 160/120. Rob frowned, rechecked it, then took the reading on the other arm.

"Let's have you lie down for a while and then I'll check it again."

Rob ducked out to see another patient, returned a few minutes later. The reading was 160/110. Rob shook his head. "Peter, this blood pressure is way too high. The insurance company is either going to turn you down or rate your premium up into fairyland somewhere. You'd better come back another time, first thing in the morning, and see if we can't get a reading closer to normal."

"Gee, Doc, can't you just fudge it a little?"

"No way; they could put us both in jail for fraud." Rob looked up at him. "That's not really the point, though. This blood pressure is dangerous to *you*. How long has it been high?"

"I never knew it was."

"Well, now you know. And you're going to be in real trouble if you don't get it under control."

"So what should I do?"

"Come in here next week when we can both take some time and

find out what's going on with you. Check with Dora for an appointment time. If we can't cure it, at least we can control it before it beats your kidneys to a pulp."

He moved on, forcing himself to rush as more and more charts piled up on his door. Noon came and went without even a pause for coffee. By one-thirty he had the crowd in the waiting room thinned down to half a dozen people, when Dora put her head in his office door. "I think we've got a sick one in the treatment room, Doctor. Dan Harrison from down in Tintown. Can you take a look?"

The man was in his early twenties, tall and gangling, with a shock of black hair falling into his eyes. He was sitting on the edge of the examining table, looking gray. "Sorry to bother you, Doc, but I didn't want to go back to Dr. Florey again, and something's sure wrong."

"What's the trouble?"

"Gut ache. It really hurts."

Quickly Rob got the story. The man had awakened at four in the morning with cramping pain in his abdomen—a pain that came and went. Finally, about 5 A.M., Dr. Florey had seen him up at the hospital. "He just said it was stomach flu and gave me some pills," the man said. "Seemed kind of pissed off that I got him out of bed."

"So what happened then?"

"Well, I went fishing like I'd planned, but my belly kept aching, really hurting steady. I finally threw up, but it just hurt all the more, so I figured I'd better get some help. Didn't want to bother Dr. Florey again, and Doc Isaacs said to come in and see you."

Rob nodded and glanced at Dora's note in the chart. Dan Harrison's temperature was recorded as 99.6 degrees. Rob checked out details, a danger flag waving in his mind. No urinary trouble, no diarrhea, no previous illnesses. Finally he had the man undress, examined his eyes, ears, throat and chest. For a fleeting second he thought he caught a faint rotten odor on the man's breath, but he couldn't be sure. Then he laid the man down on his back, gently felt his abdomen. Dan Harrison winced and pulled his legs up. "Take it easy, Doc, that's mighty sore."

"Okay, relax." Rob pressed again, even more gently. The man's belly muscles tightened involuntarily. Rob pressed in over the lower right quadrant, then lifted his hand suddenly. The man groaned and nearly jumped off the table. Rob turned to Dora. "I need a blood count and urine on this man."

"I can call Ginny in to do them."

"Fine. I'd also like a flat plate of his abdomen."

"What's going on, Doc?" the man asked as Dora left.

"I think you've got a hot appendix, and if I'm right, it's going to have to come out. I want you up in the hospital, and I want Dr. Sonders to see you. He's a surgeon."

"Gee, Doc Florey didn't think it was anything like that," Dan Harrison protested.

"True, but that was nine hours ago. He'd think differently now." Rob paused. "If you'd rather I gave Dr. Florey a ring, I'll be glad to."

"No; Sonders is okay. He took care of my ma when she had a cyst last year. And I reckon you know your business."

"Then you get on up there while you can still drive. I'll get hold of Dr. Sonders."

As the man got dressed Rob went on to see the remainder of his waiting patients. By then the lab work on Dan Harrison was done. The urine was clear, the white blood count elevated. Rob took one look and dialed Harry Sonders in Missoula. It took most of an hour to reach the man through his answering service, but he finally returned Rob's call. "White count's eighteen thousand, you say? And he's definitely got rebound tenderness?"

"No question," Rob said.

"Ah, shit. There goes my golf game. When did he eat last?"

"Just a little breakfast about six this morning."

"Okay, tell the hospital to call Esther and get the OR set up. We'll do him at five o'clock."

Rob called orders to the hospital, left Dora to close the office and drove home for lunch. Ellie was up on a ladder tacking insulating batts to the ceiling joists in the living room. "Late dinner tonight," he said. "We've got an appendectomy at five o'clock."

Ellie sighed and came down the ladder. "Okay. Did you get a call from a Chris Erickson? Something about chest pain. Or a Mrs. Haskell with a sick baby? The numbers are by the phone."

Rob dialed the first number and heard Chris's voice on the line. "I know this is silly," she said, "but my chest has been hurting again, right down where he tapped it, and I've been short of breath all morning. Do you suppose you could see me?"

"Sure. Meet me at the office."

"I would, but I've got no way to get there. That car of mine was totaled."

"True. Then tell me where you are." Rob wrote down the address, a small apartment court down near Tintown, with directions for reaching it. "I'll be over in a few minutes to take a look," he said. Hanging up, he returned the second call—an infant with diarrhea, now becoming very lethargic. He told Mrs. Haskell to bring the baby to the hospital for him to see in half an hour or so. Then he gulped down a sandwich and headed out the door again.

Chris Erickson was hurting, but not because something had gone wrong. Rob listened carefully to the bases of her lungs on both sides, heard air moving freely, with no sign of more fluid gathering. "Let's face it, Chris, you've got a couple of cracked ribs, and they're going to keep on hurting for a while, no matter what anybody does. You're worrying too much."

"It just makes me so *mad*," the girl said. "I just *despise* being sick, and it seems like I'm aching in every bone, and I don't see why I can't just snap out of it." She gave a hassock a kick with her walking cast, and then winced. "This miserable foot along with everything else."

"When your car hit that ditch, your whole body got jarred from top to toe," Rob said. "It's no wonder you ache. But nothing *bad* is going on. You're just going to have to be patient."

"I suppose. And patience is not my long suit, either." She grinned. "Well, thanks for checking, anyway."

"Anytime." He left her with some Darvon to help with the aching and drove on up to the hospital. It was past three when he arrived, and the Haskell baby was already there. The child was dehydrated, but not yet dangerously so; Rob prescribed some medicine to combat the diarrhea and urged the mother to encourage fluids every hour for the rest of the day. "If the diarrhea keeps on, or the baby throws up at all, let me know and we'll see about intravenous fluids. But chances are this is only a summer diarrhea and will settle down with just what we're doing." He felt uneasy about it; his mind was on other things, and it seemed awfully vague, inconclusive advice to be giving, but the mother was relieved and promised to call back later if the trouble continued, and Rob reflected again on the old bromide he had heard so often in pediatrics: Treating the baby is 99 percent treating the mother.

Up at the nurses' station Janice Pryor was busy on the telephone. "I'm sorry, Sara, but Dr. Sonders said five o'clock, and that's what he meant. You'd better be here." She hung up the receiver, shaking her head. "I swear, it's like pulling teeth to get that woman out on a weekend."

"Who's that?" Rob said.

"Sara Davis, the anesthetist. She knows perfectly well she's on call, but you practically have to beg to get her to come, and even then she's likely as not to be—" She stopped abruptly, biting her lip. "Well, keep your fingers crossed. Will you tell Esther that I finally reached her? I've got to be sure the patient gets his enema."

Esther Briggs, the scrub nurse, was in the anteroom to the surgery, laying out surgical packs in preparation for the case. She was a tall, homely girl, all bones and angles, with her hair trussed up in a scrub cap and a pair of glasses so thick that her brown eyes looked huge behind them. "I know—I heard," she said sourly as Rob started to pass on Miss Pryor's message. "I don't know why Roger keeps that woman around; she's such a pain, and she just makes Dr. Sonders see red."

"Is she a doctor?"

"Heavens, no. She's a Registered Nurse Anesthetist, and she does fine when she happens to be sober. She just doesn't happen to be sober very often." Esther dropped a surgical pack on the counter with a plop as if to emphasize her disgust. "Just hope for the best, or you're liable to end up passing the gas yourself."

Rob took Dan Harrison's chart into the coffee room and started writing up an admission note. He was halfway finished when the door burst open and John Florey marched in. "Dr. Tanner," he said, "will you please tell me just precisely what's going on with this Harrison boy?"

"He's got a hot belly, I think," Rob said, still concentrating on the note he was writing.

"Is that right! Well, I came up to see that boy right here in the Emergency Room at five this morning. What are *you* doing treating him?"

Rob looked up then and saw that the fat little doctor was absolutely furious. "I'm treating him because he came to my office this afternoon," Rob said. "It looks like appendicitis, and we're probably going to open him up when Harry Sonders gets here."

Florey was so angry he spluttered. "He's my patient, and you know it damned well."

"Well, I didn't see your name on him," Rob snapped. "Matter of fact, I offered to call you and the man said no, not to bother you again. Now, if you're offended, I'm sorry, but that's the way it is."

Florey stared at him for a moment, fairly quivering. "Well, I see you learn fast," he said finally. "I'd have expected it from Martin Isaacs, but not from you—until now." He turned abruptly, almost colliding with Harry Sonders in the doorway. With a snort, he elbowed Sonders aside and stalked out to the nurses' station.

Sonders looked after Florey, bewildered. "What's eating him?" he said.

"He claims I stole his appendectomy," Rob said. He told the surgeon what had happened.

Sonders grinned, then threw his head back and laughed. "You just have to realize how it is with Florey and Isaacs," he said. "They hate each other like poison, and if this case were the other way around, old Martin would be up here screaming like a panther. That's the way it usually is, too. John Florey's the one that's always pulling the slick tricks."

"Well, I don't want any part of their fight," Rob said heatedly, "but I don't want that fat fraud crawling down my throat, either."

"Well, let's just go see the boy," Sonders said. They found Dan Harrison in one of the three-bed rooms, looking even sicker than when Rob had last seen him. Sonders made an offhand examination, sniffed the man's breath and nodded. "Appendicitis, all right," he said as they walked back out into the corridor. "You can smell it."

"I thought that was an old wives' tale," Rob said.

"Oh, yeah?" Sonders laughed. "Could be, but I'll bet you ten to one that he's got a gangrenous appendix in there. Let's get changed and get him some premedication. Esther says we're ready to go as soon as anesthesia gets here."

Rob was just getting on his scrub suit when Miss Pryor banged on the dressing room door. "Dr. Tanner? We've got an OB in labor for you to see."

"One of Dr. Isaacs'?" Rob asked, coming out to the nurses' station.

"No, somebody from out of town. They just walked in the door."

The girl was certainly pregnant, seven months along by her dates, and she was also certainly in labor. The couple lived in Kalispell, well north of Missoula, and were driving home from a vacation in Colorado when the girl's membranes ruptured on the way up Lost Trail Pass, with labor pains starting immediately thereafter. With Miss Pryor helping, Rob checked the woman. The contractions were about three minutes apart, but the baby's head was still high, and once the girl had quieted down a bit she wasn't too uncomfortable. Even so, Rob hated just to send her on her way. Anything could happen before she reached Kalispell. After hesitating a moment, Rob called Isaacs to see what he thought.

"You sure don't dare let her go," Isaacs said, "but if she's that early, you'd better try to stop the labor. Give her some Demerol and Seconal, really lay her out on her ass and see if she doesn't quiet down. But get Agnes up there to watch her, and have the incubator ready. If she delivers, it's liable to be a small baby."

Rob called Agnes, then checked his plan with the girl and her husband. When Agnes arrived, he ordered the medications. Agnes nodded.

"That may do it, if she's really that early. She looks awful big for seven months, though. Are you going to be home?"

"No; we've got an appendectomy coming up, so I'll be around. Just holler if something starts to happen."

It was past five by then, and no anesthetist. Both Sonders and Esther were chafing, with Esther banging instrument trays around in the anteroom and Sonders pacing angrily, looking at his watch every two minutes. "I swear I spend my whole fucking life waiting for that bloody woman," he muttered. "If she ever once turned up on time, I think I'd drop dead from shock." Then around five-thirty Sara Davis finally appeared—a huge, heavy woman of fifty with faded red hair and watery blue eyes. She fairly reeked of licorice, and kept wrinkling her nose and sniffing as if she needed a handkerchief. "Sorry, but I just couldn't get away any sooner," she said in a defensive whine. "I've got a family to think about, you know."

Esther Briggs sniffed pointedly and turned away. "Everything's ready as soon as you're set up in there," she said. She wheeled a patient cart down the corridor and returned a few moments later with Dan Harrison draped in a crisp sheet. Rob went in to join Sonders at the scrub sink. The surgeon seemed suddenly relaxed and cheerful now, whistling tunelessly as he scrubbed. "Say, do you want to do this one?" he asked.

Rob looked up, startled. "I'd love to, but I'd better not. I've got a pregnant girl liable to pop right in the middle of things. Unless you'd feel like breaking scrub to deliver her."

"Uh—no, thanks. I'll stick with surgery."

"Well, ask me another time, eh?"

"Sure, why not? You and Martin don't need me out here for a case like this. You guys should be doing all the simple stuff—appendectomies and hernias and T&As, that sort of thing. Martin's funny, though. He'll do his own Caesareans without even blinking an eye, blood from here to Guinea and back, and he just sews 'em up, calm as you please. But when it comes to something simple like a T&A or an appendix, he backs off like it's poison or something."

"Well, he's had some OB training," Rob said.

"Oh, yes, a couple of years. He should have finished while he was at it, but he ran out of money or something. Well, let's get going here."

After all the delay, the surgery itself went swiftly. Since the beginning of his training Rob had come to realize that surgeons approached their work with varying degrees of intensity. Some were like coiled springs—tense, demanding, explosive—while others worked so quietly and smoothly they made any procedure, however difficult, look like child's play. Sonders was one of the latter: unhurried, confident, almost casual as he made his incision, tying off the skin bleeders as Rob clamped them, then proceeding with his dissection until the peritoneum was incised and retractors were placed. As he worked Sonders teased Esther unmercifully about her love life and Rob about his clumsiness. At the head of the table Sara Davis slouched, a sullen mountain of flesh, occasionally adjusting the flow of gases from the anesthesia machine, with her maddening *sniff—sniff—sniff* going on like a slightly irregular metronome. At one point Sonders said something sharp to her—Rob didn't quite catch what—and the sniffing increased abruptly in frequency as she sat up and checked the patient's blood pressure. Finally the appendix was exposed, angry red and swollen, slightly blackened near the tip, and Sonders grunted in satisfaction. "How about that? Right on the nose."

"None too soon, either," Rob said.

"Nope; another couple hours and he'd have been in the soup. Watch how you clamp that, now; I don't want it near anything—there, that's fine. Just hold it there." A moment later the infected organ was excised, the specimen wrapped in gauze and dropped in a pan. "Good. Pathologist can't bitch about that one." Quickly, then, the surgeon closed the incision, leaving the last few skin sutures for Rob to complete.

"Very nice," Rob said as he joined the surgeon back in the dressing room. "What post-op routine do you want?"

"Just the usual. But make damned sure he's recovered from the anesthesia and responding before you leave. You can't count on Sara. If she's in a rush, she just pulls the tube out, says a little prayer and takes off."

"Okay, I'll watch it." As Sonders wrote post-op orders, Rob went back to check the pregnant girl. He met Agnes coming out of the room, finger to her lips. "She's quieting down nicely, almost asleep. I wouldn't stir her up right now."

"Fine," Rob said. "If you can stand by, I'd like to duck home for dinner as soon as Dan Harrison's awake. Call me if there's any problem." Walking down to Harrison's room, he found that Sonders was right: Sara Davis had stayed just long enough for the patient to stir, and then she had vanished without a word to anyone. Rob waited until the man was awake enough to respond to questions and then checked out to Happy Cumley.

It was seven-thirty when he got home, and Ellie had a stew warming on the stove. Rob found a Diet Pepsi in the refrigerator and tried to relax for a moment. He had been running full speed for almost twelve hours without a break, and his whole body seemed to be vibrating with a sense of frantic tension. He looked around at Ellie's handiwork. The ceiling joists were festooned with insulating batts, and all the water-stained ceiling board had been torn out. Even in the bedroom, where the ceiling board was still mostly sound, insulation had been installed clear out to the eaves. "How'd you get that stuff out there?" he asked.

"I just lay down on the ceiling joists and wiggled," Ellie said.

"Jesus. You've practically got it finished."

"Oh, that's not all. I've decided we need battens for the ceiling—narrow strips of board to cover up the seams between the ceiling boards. Mr. Davidson showed me how they'd look, so I bought some." She led him into the other bedroom, where she had the narrow batten boards spread out on newspapers on the floor, all freshly stained and varnished.

"So that's why it smells like paint in here. I thought it was the stew."

"Oh, the hell with you." She looked at him. "How'd the case go?"

"Okay, I guess. But from the looks of that anesthetist, we're walking on thin ice out here every time we take a patient to surgery. There's got to be some better system than this—there's just *got* to be."

They ate, and took their coffee out on the patio. Ellie was still smeared with smudge and varnish, and her hair, back in a ponytail, was coming loose at the edges. "I went down and paid a call on Belle Foreman this afternoon," she said. "She lives in a little log cabin back in the woods down the road a ways."

"Did you see her cats?"

"Oh, yes, I certainly did." Ellie paused. "She's got forty-five of them, by last count."

88

"Forty-five *cats?* I told you she was crazy."

"Oh, but she's *not,*" Ellie said. "That's just the thing. She's sharp as a needle, that old woman. But honestly, Rob, it would have been funny if it weren't so pathetic. She lives all alone back there; her husband walked out twenty years ago and she's been living like a recluse ever since. Never goes anywhere except to walk into town for groceries. And those cats—they're all inbred, some of them blind, stub tails, deformed paws and ears, wild as bobcats, and she just tends them like babies." Ellie sipped her coffee. "About ten of them are her Indoor cats, and another twenty are her Outdoor cats, and she keeps another fifteen way out in the barn. And then there's Princess, her favorite. A big, ugly Manx tabby that follows her all around."

"I wonder what it smells like in there," Rob said.

"Pretty awful, I'm afraid. She wouldn't let me in the house, just stood there on the porch and talked. I'll bet she hasn't had a visitor there in twenty years, the poor thing."

"Well, don't get too involved," Rob cautioned. "She really *could* be crazy—"

The telephone cut him off, with Agnes Miller on the line. "You'd better come up right away, Dr. Tanner. This girl has started up again and I think we're going to have a baby."

Rob slipped on his jacket, told Ellie not to wait up, and headed back to the hospital. He found Agnes taking sterile packs down from the delivery room anteroom. "What happened?" he said.

"She woke up half an hour ago with contractions, and this time I think she means it," Agnes said. Rob found the girl just recovering from an intense contraction. There was perspiration on her forehead, and little beads of sweat on her upper lip. When he checked her he found the baby's head very low, well lodged in the birth canal, the cervix dilated a good four fingers' breadth. "Okay, you're going to have a baby," he said.

"How soon?" she asked.

"Hard to say. Maybe an hour, maybe less. But you're doing fine." He ordered a small dose of Demerol and then stepped out to brief the girl's husband. Half an hour later, as he was finishing evening rounds, Agnes flagged him. He scrubbed and gowned as she shifted the girl from the bed to the delivery table.

"Do you want a saddle block?"

"Not this time," Rob said. "Pudendal block will be better. Got a long needle?"

It was only a local anesthesia, but it was effective, and above all, safe. He could tell from the girl's face that the block was good; within a few moments the tension had eased and she smiled and nodded. "Yes. Yes. That's much better."

"Good girl. Now work with the contractions." She worked, and five minutes later the baby was delivered, howling with gusto. It had none of the waxy, unfinished look of the premature baby, nor did it seem unusually small.

Agnes shrugged. "Guess her dates were wrong."

"Just as well. But check the weight anyway."

Later, after the mother was back in bed, Rob went in to see her. "Feeling better?"

"Oh, I'm glad it's over. Was the baby very small?"

"Five pounds three ounces. Only a couple of weeks early at the most. And he's healthy as healthy can be."

"Then he won't have to stay in the incubator?"

"I doubt it. We'll see how he does in the next day or so. But for now, you get some sleep. I'll see you in the morning."

It was well past ten now, and most of the patients were asleep, but Rob made a quick check for last-minute problems. Dan Harrison was doing fine, and the baby with croup was afebrile and sleeping soundly. Rob thanked Agnes as she was leaving, then changed back to his street clothes. He dawdled over a cup of coffee as he wrote up his delivery note, suddenly realizing he was totally exhausted. He greeted Jessie Hodges as she came on for the night shift, gaunt and owly, and then checked out for home. The place was dark when he arrived. Ellie was asleep and the house still reeked of paint. On the bathroom mirror she had taped a note. *I love you,* it said. Rob sighed, tucked it in his wallet, undressed and collapsed into his sleeping bag. For over an hour he lay there, sleepless and tense, waiting for another call; then finally he drifted into restless sleep.

# 9

The calls began an hour later, and didn't stop for the rest of the night. The first, at 1 A.M., was from Vern Bradley, the town's chief of police. "Got a guy here you'd better see, Doc. I'll meet you at the clinic."

Rob shook his head, groggy from sleep. "Hospital might be better," he said.

"Uh—let's make it the clinic, okay?"

The police car was waiting by the back door when Rob got there. The constable was a thin, wiry man, trim in his blue uniform, with a huge holstered pistol at his belt. He half dragged a sullen youth in handcuffs out of the car. "Goddam transient," Bradley said. "Found him snooping around the back of the drugstore."

In the bright light of the minor surgery Rob stared at the youth, suddenly wide awake. The boy's face and scalp were covered with ugly purple welts and swellings. Blood was still oozing from two or three of them. "Good Christ. What happened?"

The constable shifted uneasily. "He started to lip off, and I kinda lost my temper."

Rob looked at his pistol. "I see." Grimly he examined the youth, checked his pupillary reflexes. His upper lip had swollen his mouth almost shut, and two upper incisors were snapped off at the gum line. Ignoring Bradley, Rob led the boy down to the x-ray room, got his name and took skull films. As he examined them on the darkroom view box the constable stood nervously in the door.

"He ain't really hurt, is he?"

"He's still alive, if that's what you mean." Rob dressed the oozing welts as best he could. "He could be bleeding inside too."

"I'll watch him real close," Bradley said.

"You've watched him close enough already. He needs to be in the hospital."

"Doc, I can't take him up there. Hell, I just lost control for a minute —you don't want to get a man in trouble for that, do you? Doc Isaacs wouldn't—I mean, we keep a real close eye on his place here at night, all the drug addicts coming through. . . ."

Rob turned away, disgusted. "This man needs hospital observation for your protection as much as his. If you insist on keeping him, he's your headache. If he goes into coma or starts convulsing, that's also your headache—I won't be responsible. But what I write up on his chart here is a legal document, and I'll swear to it in court if I have to."

The constable was adamant, so Rob let them out, then returned to his desk so furious he could hardly hold his hand still to write up his examination note. *This is our police force? Good Christ.* The phone jangled and he grabbed it before the tape could cut in, heard Jessie Hodges' stentorian voice on the line. "Better come up here, Doctor. A couple of loggers have been having it out down at the Wagon Wheel."

They had indeed; they looked somewhat worse than Vern Bradley's prisoner, and reeked of whiskey till it made Rob's eyes water. Raymond was already there taking x-rays and Jessie Hodges came down, with an air of massive disapproval, to help Rob sew up a lacerated lip and a torn ear and set and cast a broken hand. Just as he was finishing, a mother came into the emergency room with a howling child in her arms. "Better put these two lunks into bed till they sleep it off," Rob told Hodges. "They could both have concussions and we'd never know it."

The nurse reluctantly agreed and corralled Raymond to help her bed them down while Rob checked the baby. It had a spiking fever and a fiery red throat streaked with pus; he started antibiotics and gave instructions for fever control and sent mother and child back home. By then two other patients were waiting—a night cook from the Bar-None with a nasty grease burn on her arm and an aged gentleman in congestive heart failure. The burn was easy enough to dress, but the old man was a real problem: off his digitalis, off his diuretics, wheezing and foaming and gasping for breath, his heart fluttering along at 240 beats

92

per minute. It was a classic medical crisis and Rob heaved a sigh and dug in—a chest film to rule out free fluid in the chest cavity; intravenous digitalis and aminophylline; tourniquets on his legs to reduce the circulating blood volume temporarily and help the heart rally; oxygen by mask until Hodges could get a bed ready upstairs ("Positive pressure? We've got one, but the valve jammed the last time Dr. Peterson used it, and it hasn't been fixed yet. You'll have to settle for catheter oxygen"); and a sixth grain of morphine to help quiet the old fellow down. By the time they finally got him into bed his breathing was easier, his heart rate a little slower, and Rob breathed a silent prayer and walked to the nurses' station to write up his chart.

Jessie Hodges met him with a phone call from Jim Blair, a retired millworker who lived on Camp 13 Road south of town. "Can you come out and see my mother, Doc? I think she's having one of her little strokes. Just lies there and groans; I can't get her awake real good."

"Any way to get her up here for me to see her?" Rob said.

"Not without a derrick, Doc. She's half paralyzed anyway, and we can't afford the ambulance. Doc DeForrest usually comes out."

"Okay, how do you get there?" Wearily Rob scribbled notes on a pad, only half listening, his mind still busy with the heart failure patient. "South to Camp 13 Road, left at the first fork, two miles beyond Rainey's pig farm, big brown house on the right. Fine, I'll get there as soon as I can."

He drove down the hill and south on the highway, but something was clearly wrong with his directions; he found what he thought was Camp 13 Road, but it didn't seem to fork, and there wasn't any pig farm that he could see. In five miles the road deteriorated from gravel to mud to jeep trail. He got stuck trying to turn around, and had to jack up the rear wheels and throw rocks under them to get free again. As dawn lighted the sky he found yet another road, equally unproductive, and finally headed back to town, thoroughly disgusted, and called the man from Ernie's gas station. When he found the place at last it was almost seven, and the crisis was over; Granny Blair, aged ninety-seven, was sitting up in bed scolding her son like a shrew and drinking camomile tea. Rob made sure she had no cardiorespiratory distress, nor any further neurological loss, and promised to report her trouble to Dr. DeForrest. The Sunday sun was high in the sky, and he met Nellie Webster coming on duty as he arrived back at the hospital.

Sleepily, he made morning rounds. Dan Harrison had a sore belly and winced whenever he had to cough, but he had been up on his feet

93

to the john already, clutching a pillow around his middle, and complaining of being hungry. The new mother from Kalispell was sleeping soundly, so he didn't wake her. The baby was doing fine. He checked the child with croup and went to write a discharge order. As he sat at the charting desk John Florey came up the ramp, dressed in a florid sport shirt.

"Well, you're up early," he said cheerily. "Beautiful day."

"Yeah, beautiful," Rob said.

Florey looked at him. "You know, I didn't mean to jump on you yesterday," he said. "Sorry if I seemed snappy."

"Don't worry about it."

"Just wouldn't want you to think we sit around this place fighting each other all the time, that's all. Plenty of patients here, God knows; no need to scrap about 'em, eh? Better to cooperate, give each other a leg up when we can."

Rob nodded, and Florey beamed and headed for the dressing room. Nellie Webster watched him go. "That Dr. Florey," she murmured, "he's *such* a nice man," and Rob thought: *Yeah, excepting when he's not,* and went back to his charting.

By eight o'clock he was home, feeling punchy. Ellie was wrestling with four-by-eight slabs of ceiling board, looking defeated. "Oh, for Christ sake," Rob snapped. "You can't get those up by yourself. Why try it?"

She looked at him. "We've got to get the ceiling up somehow."

"Fine. Sometime in the next week or so we'll get the ceiling up, but there's no sense killing yourself. Right now I need some breakfast and then some sleep. If there isn't another damned call first."

She got breakfast, and Rob ate in silence, too groggy even to think by now. He got three hours of sleep, finally interrupted by a call from a mother with a sick child. He dragged himself into the car and headed over to meet them at the clinic. The child was not seriously ill—a modest upper respiratory infection—but the mother was a wreck: tense, fearful, verging on hysteria. Patiently Rob focused on her problem, instructing her in the care of a sick child at home—fever control, fluids, danger signs to watch for, confidence that things would get better. On the third repetition the mother seemed to understand, and Rob encouraged her, but inwardly he was appalled. *God, what's wrong with the people around here?* he thought. *A mother with three kids all under four, and she doesn't know how to take a temperature, control a fever, recognize an earache! Why not? She's seen the doctors here a thousand times. Why haven't they taught her anything?*

He was dog tired, and he knew that was part of it. But there was something else involved, far more basic and alarming. He'd seen mothers of ghetto children in Philadelphia with this same gaping lack of comprehension—but this was no ghetto here. *The doctors are at fault, that's what's really wrong. The men here are just fucking off. They aren't teaching the mothers, and I'm getting these silly, needless panic calls because these poor women don't know what else to do with a sick child.*

He sent mother and child along, quieted, with instructions to see him again in two days. When they were gone, he sat there, still sluggish, feeling slightly stunned by his insight. The whole valley full of people here, and not one mother knew anything. It suddenly struck him that the need for simple, basic health education in this area was going to be enormous, perfectly staggering, and if he was going to be the baby doctor around here, he was the one who was going to have to take the bull by the horns.

The phone rang, with Nellie Webster on the line. "Dr. Tanner, there's a patient of Dr. Isaacs' up here, an eight-year-old boy with a fractured arm. Can you come see him, or should I call Dr. Isaacs?"

Rob was instantly awake. "Fractured arm? No, I'll come. Call Raymond in to get x-rays, will you?"

At the hospital the boy was sitting on the x-ray table, his carrot-red hair sticking out in all directions. He was clearly in pain, but determined not to cry. *Tommy Hart, age 8,* the x-ray slip said. "Well, Tommy, what happened?"

"Fell out of a tree," the boy said. A tear oozed from his eye and trickled down his cheek.

"Okay, let's take a look." He nodded to Nellie to support the pillow splint on the boy's arm while he gently undid the wrapping. Mother and father stood nervously by. The forearm was clearly broken, both bones, with a definite angulation at the fracture site. The skin was not broken, however, and the arm was well supported by the bulky pillow. "Whoever splinted this did a good job," Rob said. "Wish they'd all do it like this. Let's see the films."

It was a double fracture, with both bones badly displaced and the bone ends overriding. "I'm afraid it's a bad fracture," Rob told the parents, "and we'll have to put him to sleep to get it set. I'd be glad to call Dr. Isaacs if you want."

"No; he knows about it," Mr. Hart said. "He said you'd take care of it."

"Okay, then we'll get things going. You'd better wait in the lobby."

This time it seemed he was in luck; Sara Davis responded on the first call and said she'd be right up. "Right up," however, proved to mean "in an hour or so"; it was well past one o'clock when she finally arrived. Esther Briggs came in immediately, and looked at the x-rays with Rob. She pursed her lips. "You really going to try a closed reduction on that?"

"Sure; why not? If Sara can get him good and relaxed, we'll just pull those bones out straight and get the broken ends together and then slap on a cast."

"Just like that, eh?" Esther stared at the films a moment longer. "Last one of these we had, Dr. Florey just shipped the kid right in to a bone man in Missoula. Wouldn't even touch him. They can really be nasty."

"It looks pretty straightforward to me," Rob said.

"Well, suit yourself. I'll get the OR set up if you say so."

"Sure; set it up."

Her caution seemed puzzling to Rob. True, he'd never actually set such a fracture before, but he had assisted with several single-bone fractures of the forearm, and this one seemed much the same to him. Even so, while waiting for Sara, he went into the doctors' dressing room and took down a handbook on fractures he had seen there. The book had little to say about this kind of fracture, merely stressed the need for relaxation of the arm muscles and warned about nicking the artery or vein with the fractured bone ends. Finally he pushed it aside and slipped into a scrub suit.

Then Sara finally arrived, and Rob embarked upon an afternoon he would not soon forget. He asked Sara for complete relaxation of the patient, and he got it. For all her incessant sniffing, Sara was clearly trying hard to please him; the boy was laid out like a poleaxed mule. Even the odor of licorice was missing today. *Maybe she doesn't drink on Sundays,* Rob thought, *or maybe not until dinnertime,* recalling an old alcoholic at Graystone who had insisted with the utmost gravity that no civilized person drank martinis before eleven in the morning. The problem with Tommy Hart was not the anesthesia; the problem was that the front and back half of his forearm, no longer joined by solid bone, refused to get together. By tugging fiercely and angulating the arm, Rob could get the broken ends of the radius overlapped—but when he tried to pull the ulna fragments into alignment, the radius slipped off. Raymond had a portable x-ray machine ready in the OR; four times in succession Rob asked him to take films, certain that he had a good reduction; but each time, after holding the wretched arm rigidly in position for the seemingly endless interval it took to wet-develop the x-rays, he saw little or no improvement in the bone position. "Jesus," he said to Esther after two solid hours of futile work, "what am I doing wrong?"

"You're not exactly doing anything *wrong,*" Esther said. "You just aren't doing it right. That's why the bone men open these up and pin them. It's almost impossible to get both bones right at the same time, and then hold them long enough to get a picture, much less apply a cast. . . ."

This was fast becoming obvious as Rob grimly bent to the task of yet another attempt. He knew he shouldn't keep the boy under such deep anesthesia much longer; even Sara Davis was growing restive, peering nervously at Rob over the anesthesia drapes and sniffing fiercely. He drew out the fractured arm once again, angled it to get one of the bones overlapped, pulled less and less gently to get the second fracture hooked, then felt the first one give again with a grate of raw bone ends that sent a chill up his back. He was sweating now as he pulled once more. *This isn't going to work,* he was thinking, *and what are you going to do? You can't open this arm up and try to put pins in. You're no orthopedic surgeon; you don't know beans about pinning fractures.* As the bones grated and slipped again, he felt a wave of panic. *You started this, you boob, and you're going to have to finish it if it takes you all week.* Desperately he considered getting just one bone overlapped and letting the other be—but he knew that wouldn't do; there would be angulation, a shortening of the other bone, maybe a nonunion—surely a botched-up mess.

Esther interrupted him. "Dr. Tanner, there's something wrong with his hand."

He relaxed his grip and saw that she was right: the boy's hand was suddenly a pasty yellow color, noticeably cool to the touch. What was more, the middle of the forearm was beginning to bulge like an over-stuffed sausage, thick and doughy-feeling. Even as he watched it seemed to be swelling more and more.

At that point Martin Isaacs walked in the door, wet x-rays in his

97

hand. "Rob, what in *hell* do you think you're doing, fooling around with a fracture like this?"

"I—I thought I could set it," Rob said.

"A double forearm fracture? You're out of your fucking mind." The big doctor pushed Rob out of the way and peered at the tense, swollen forearm. He pressed the swollen area with a forefinger, felt the cold yellow hand. "Holy Jesus," he said in a half whisper.

"What is it?" Rob said.

"Hematoma—what do you suppose? You've sliced a major blood vessel in there with those ragged bone ends, and if it's the radial artery you got, this boy could lose his arm." Isaacs looked up at Esther. "Get me one of those rubber wrappers the bone men like to use, huh?"

Esther unwrapped a six-inch roll of rubber sheeting. Deftly Isaacs wrapped the fractured forearm, pulling the rubber tight, from above the elbow down to the wrist. "Sara, bring him up," Isaacs said. "Raymond, get a sugar-tong splint on this forearm and then wrap it tight to his chest. He's going to have to go into town fast."

Stalking out to the nurses' desk, Isaacs started dialing, got his party after three tries. "Charlie? Martin Isaacs in Twin Forks. I'm afraid I've got a mean one for you out here. Eight-year-old boy with a double fracture of the right forearm. I—ah—tried a closed reduction, and I shouldn't have. May have nicked the radial; we've got a big hematoma in there all of a sudden. . . . Yes, I've got it wrapped. . . . No, no, I'll ship him on in; you're obviously going to have to open it up. Right. He'll be on his way in a few minutes. Maybe you could give me a call when you finish, huh? Oh, and Charlie, this is a little bit embarrassing to me, what with the parents and all, if you take my meaning. . . . Right, right. A little leg up would help a lot; I'd take that very kindly."

He pushed the telephone aside with a sigh and glowered up at Rob. "What the hell school did you go to, anyway? That's the most God-awful fracture there is; even the bone men won't try a closed reduction very often. Whatever were you thinking of?"

Rob spread his hands. "The wrong thing, apparently."

"You can sure say that again." Isaacs shook his head in disgust. "Well, Charlie Feldman is a good orthopedist. He'll pull this one out of the fire if anybody can. And he'll be discreet. . . ."

"You didn't really have to cover for me," Rob said.

"What do you want—I should tell every doctor in Missoula that I've got an idiot working for me out here? I've been around a while, I can stand a little static, but you aren't even in the medical society yet. All we need is to have them hang up your malpractice insurance on account of some asshole blunder. You just keep your mouth shut and let me talk, okay? And that goes for talking to the kid's parents out here, which we'd better go and do right fast."

Rob followed him out to the lobby. Isaacs did the talking, with Rob feeling so appalled at his blunder that he barely heard what the older man was saying. ". . . had an awful time getting those bones to stay in the right position," Isaacs told the parents. "Neither one of us could get them to stick right, and then one of those broken bone ends nicked a blood vessel—that often happens; they're sharp as razors in there—so we had a lot of swelling as well, and we finally both just decided the best thing for Tommy was to back off and send him in for a bone doctor to look at. Dr. Feldman's top rate; he'll probably just open the arm up and put pins in to hold those bones. It's always better if you can do it the easy way, but that just didn't work this time." He went on to tell them he'd given the boy something for pain and splinted the arm so they could safely whisk him in to Sacred Heart in Missoula, where Dr. Feldman would be waiting to meet them. All told, it was a triumph of diplomacy, Rob reflected miserably. The parents were thanking Isaacs for all he'd done as they drove off with the boy, and the big man was perspiring through his shirt as he came back to the coffee room to rejoin Rob. "Well, keep your fingers crossed," he said heavily. "If you haven't sliced up a nerve or two in there too, we may pull out of this smelling like a rose."

"I'm sorry," Rob said glumly. "I just didn't think it out."

"Well, don't fret about it. Everybody pulls a dumb one once in a while."

"I should have listened to Esther. She told me I was crazy to try it."

Isaacs nodded. "It pays to listen to Esther. She's one of the few around here that knows where straight up is."

"I don't know, Pryor seems to be sharp. And that surgical aide isn't so bad, either."

"You mean Happy? She's okay; just hasn't got much training or experience. Esther's an R.N. and scrubbed for five years in Missoula before she moved to Twin Forks. Aside from her, we're still in the Stone Age out here. Which means you've got to be doubly careful." Isaacs pushed his coffee aside. "Well, I'll be down home. Holler if you need help. And I mean *holler*. No more hero acts."

Rob sat there staring at the wall for a long time and feeling dismally depressed. The fracture case had been a drain, physically and emotionally; Isaacs was right—he should never have gone near the damned thing—and he felt a perfect ass about it. *And if that kid should really lose an arm—oh, Christ!* He shoved the thought away fiercely and got up to make evening rounds. It was past five o'clock, the afternoon completely gone, and he hadn't even seen it pass. He realized he was actually feeling punchy; more than anything he wanted to get away from the phone for a little bit, go down and have a quiet dinner with Ellie and then crawl into some nice hidey-hole and be left alone for a while, just have a chance to catch his breath and get his feet back under him again. . . .

A lovely thought, but he was out of luck. Janice Pryor had come on duty while he had been in the OR. Now she looked up from the phone as he came back up the hall. "You're not planning to leave, I hope. . . ."

"I was. What's wrong?"

"There's a two-car accident in the pass. The patrol wants somebody standing by down here, and you've got the highway call. The ambulance is already on its way up there. Three people hurt, I think."

"Oh, Christ." Rob picked up the phone and rang Ellie. "Sorry, kid, but I won't be down for dinner. I'm stuck. No telling when I'll be through. . . . No, I'd better eat up here; I could be all night. . . . I know, but that's the way it is. I'll see you"— he groped for a word—"someday, I guess."

# 10

Ellie had just dragged a stepladder in from the garage when Rob's call came. After he had rung off she stood looking at the phone for a long moment, then gently put it back on the hook.

*Damn.*

She opened the oven door and looked in at the four-pound pot roast that was cooking, then snapped off the oven. She had purposely chosen something that would keep for two or three hours, if necessary. *But all night? What am I going to do with this now? Grind it up into hash? He could heat that up for himself, anytime he got around to it.*

She walked over to the patio windows, stared out at the river as it sparkled in the afternoon sun. The weekend had seemed interminable, with a long day in the office for Rob tomorrow whether he got any sleep tonight or not. Even at Graystone he'd been able to check out to somebody else and get home for dinner once in a while. But here there wasn't anybody to check out to. . . . She shook her head, forcing back the anger and frustration. *It can't always be like this; it's his first call weekend, and he's just getting started, that's all. People are bound to test him out, maybe just call him to get a look at him. And you can't be forever nagging him, either; that would really wear thin in a hurry. If you're patient, it'll settle down after a while. It's bound to settle down.*

With a sigh she turned around, surveyed the half-finished living room grimly. Right now there was the ceiling board, stacked on edge against the wall in four-by-eight-foot sheets. Not really heavy—it was just fiberboard—but clumsy, God! Still, she had finally found a way to get it up—she hoped. She placed the stepladder, stacked a foot or so of scrap lumber on the platform at the top, then wrestled onto that one end of a sheet of ceiling board so that it was supported a few inches below ceiling level. Holding the other end of the sheet, she stuck a couple of nails into her mouth, grabbed a hammer and climbed on a chair, raising her end of the sheet over her head and into a place against the ceiling joists. Holding it up, she finally got a nail in place and started hammering upside down. Halfway in, the nail bent. Her effort to knock it straight again bent it the other way. Suddenly a week's frustration became focused in that one stupid nail; she flailed away more and more wildly, then aimed a mighty whack, missed the nail and buried the hammer head in the fiberboard two inches off target. "Oh, *shit!*"

"My, how ladylike," a woman's voice said from the kitchen.

Ellie gave a start, lost control of the ceiling board and saw it crash to the floor, breaking a foot off one corner. Furious, Ellie hurled the hammer into the fireplace. "Ladylike, *balls,*" she snapped at the intruder. "Who in the hell are *you?*"

The stranger was a tall, ungainly woman in her thirties, with pipe-stem legs and faded red hair and a touch of Southern drawl in her voice. "Why, honey, I'm Amy DeForrest," she said.

"Oh, dear," Ellie said, coming down off the chair.

"Don't sweat it, honey," Amy said with a smile. She had the same thin face as her husband, and the same wolfish gleam in her eye. "Work like a slave, swear like a slave, I always say. But you really should call the man to do all this."

"We don't know any man to call," Ellie said. "And we couldn't pay him if we did know. But I'm sorry; come in. I look a mess."

"That's fine; you should see me after a day cleaning out the garage." Amy DeForrest looked around the room, looked out the patio windows and nodded approval. "You're going to have a lovely little place here when you get it finished."

"If we get it finished. I'm beginning to wonder."

"Oh, you'll get it finished, all right." Amy spied the coffeepot, helped herself to a cup. "I suppose I should have called first, but then I decided I'd just swing by to say hello. At least get acquainted before the party."

Ellie blinked. "Party?"

"You haven't heard about the party?" Amy DeForrest threw back her head and roared with laughter. "That's Martin Isaacs for you. Plans a welcome-to-town party, and then forgets to invite the guests of honor! Well, brace yourself, honey. Dr. Isaacs is throwing a welcoming party for you and Rob. He wants to let all the town burghers know that Rob's here, and he can't advertise in the newspapers, so this is the next best thing."

"Well, that's nice," Ellie said dubiously. "When's it going to be?"

"Tomorrow night. Cocktails and buffet."

*"Monday?* That's a weird time to have a party."

"Honey, that's not the only weird thing you're going to run into around here." Amy gave a horsy laugh. "It makes perfect sense to Martin Isaacs to have a party on a Monday night, if that's when he decides he wants to have a party. Just count your blessings. *We* didn't get any welcoming party. Oh, by the way, it's at our house."

"*Your* house? I thought you said—"

"I did. It's his party. He just never entertains at home, that's all."

"I see . . . I guess." Ellie scratched her head. "Well, it was certainly nice of you to offer—"

"Honey, we didn't offer, we were *told.*" Amy laughed cheerfully. "Don't get me wrong. We don't *mind;* this is just the way things work around here. Martin walks in one morning and says, 'Jerry, we're going to throw a party for Rob and Ellie Tanner, at your house,' and Jerry says, 'Yassuh, boss, when is dis heah now pahty gon' be held?' and Martin says, 'Monday night, so have everything ready,' and Jerry says, 'Yassuh, boss, we gon' have one mighty fine pahty Monday night at my house.' So we have a party."

"I see." Ellie looked at the woman, groping for something to say, uncertain whether Amy was angry or merely sardonic. "Well, at least we'll have a chance to meet Mrs. Isaacs."

"Well, now, I wouldn't count on that too much. Maybe you will and maybe you won't. It all depends."

"On what?"

"Well, never mind. Let's just say if you think *Martin's* a little weird, you ain't seen nothin' yet." The woman gave another horsy laugh. "Anyway, we'll look for you around seven."

"Tell me," Ellie said, "is Dr. Isaacs always so—*imperative* about everything?"

"Oh, you'll get used to it," Amy said. "I'll say one thing for Martin: he's consistent. He just likes to get things done, that's all. Preferably

103

*his* way. In fact, you might say, his way or no way." Amy smiled. "Just remember that, honey, and you can always get along with Martin Isaacs. You can do it the easy way, or you can do it the hard way; it's all up to you. If you want to make it easy for yourself, you'll do things his way and not worry about it. If you want to make it hard—I mean, if you really *like* to bang yourself in the head with a hammer—then you fight him. You'll end up the same place, either way, but how you get there is purely your choice. Same thing goes for your husband." Amy sighed and put down her coffee cup. "Me, I used to be an old head-banger from way back when we first came here—until I finally decided it wasn't worth it. It's been much easier since then."

"I see," Ellie said. "Well, thanks for the tip. Unfortunately, I'm afraid Rob is a head-banger."

"Ah, well, he'll get over it soon enough." Amy smiled. "I'd better get along now, go haul Jerry out of that garden. Don't fret, honey, things will work out. And we'll see you tomorrow night. . . ."

She went as quietly as she had come, leaving Ellie staring across the room in silence. She blinked at the ruined sheet of ceiling board, the stepladder with the boards piled on top. Presently she went and retrieved the hammer from the fireplace, but she did not go back to work. Instead she stood staring out the window at the river for a long while, gently tapping the hammer head against her temple.

# 11

An hour after the accident call had come down from the pass, Rob was still waiting at the hospital with no accident to treat. He drank coffee, ate a plate of lukewarm spaghetti from the diet kitchen, drank some more coffee, and waited. Finally he walked out to find Janice Pryor. "No sign of them yet?"

"Not a sign, Doctor."

"They wouldn't have taken them somewhere else, would they?"

"Oh, I doubt it. Sometimes they take them right on into Missoula, but they'd have let us know if they were doing that."

Rob stalked back into the coffee room, sat down at the table and waited another half hour, dozing. Then at last he heard a distant siren and saw the ambulance coming up the hill, red lights flashing, followed closely by two patrol cars. A moment later the whole hospital seemed full of strange people wandering around at random. Two men on stretchers were unloaded and wheeled into the emergency room on carts; two patrolmen helped a third man down, half supporting him between them. Janice Pryor shooed a crowd of other people up to the hospital lobby, then returned with Raymond at her heels.

Rob never did find out what had taken so long; he was too busy to ask. The men on the stretchers were officers of a Missoula bank, driving back together from a conference in Boise. The third man's car, going the other way, had swung suddenly across the center line and crashed

105

into them head-on, going sixty miles an hour. The driver, reeking of gin, was now snoring loudly on the stretcher in the upstairs corridor; he had been walking around, apparently uninjured, at the scene of the accident, but had passed out coming down in the ambulance.

The bank men were not so lucky. Both had gone through the windshield. One had been thrown completely clear of the car and had slid on his face through the roadside gravel; he had a deep laceration of the chin and several smaller cuts on his face and neck, but was conscious and able to respond. His friend had a long laceration straight across his forehead, still leaking blood all over his face. He had been unconscious, but was showing signs of coming to, groaning and reaching a hand up to his face.

With Miss Pryor and Raymond there, Rob swiftly set up priorities. "First, get needles in their veins. Five percent glucose IV is fine for now; just keep the veins open. Then we've got to monitor pulses and blood pressures—can Happy do that? Then I can see what injuries we're dealing with and order x-rays."

The examinations were clumsy, cutting off blood-encrusted clothes amid showers of broken glass and gravel, then checking for head or neck injuries, ruling out spine injuries, checking the long bones for fractures, finally examining heart, lungs and abdomen for internal injuries. It was just preliminary, searching first for immediate threats to life. Satisfied that there was no gross hemorrhage and no breathing impairment, Rob helped move the half-conscious man onto the x-ray table first. "We'll need skull films and cervical spine," he told Raymond, "and then a chest film and some views of the right ribs. Oh, yes, that left forearm too, where he has that big bruise. I don't think it's broken, but I don't want to take any chances. Janice, you draw blood for a blood count and a typing and crossmatch when you start that IV, okay?"

The other man was more responsive, sitting on the cart holding a gauze pad to his chin by the time Rob got to him. His name was Fred Mallory, and he was willing and able to talk. When Rob asked him where he hurt, he said, "Everywhere, man. *Everywhere.*"

"I believe you, but let's narrow it down." Rob had him move his fingers, hands, feet and legs. With the bloody shirt off, it could be seen that abrasions from the roadburn involved his left shoulder; the whole left side of the man's face was encrusted with ground-in gravel. "Okay, now take a deep breath and then blow it all out. Good. Does that hurt anywhere?"

"No; it's my face that's killing me." He paused. "How's Jim doing?"

"He's just coming to, and we're checking him out. What's his name?"

"Jim Tice. Doc, what happened? Last thing I remember was when we stopped over in Idaho for coffee. Then next thing we were in the ambulance coming down the hill. Everything in between is blank."

Rob nodded. "That's called retrograde amnesia. It's a natural mental defense. Some of it may come back later, some may never come back. Doesn't matter, though. There were people that witnessed the whole thing. Right now we're going to take some films and get you patched up. I'm going to take your buddy first, though, make sure he's out of the woods."

While Raymond was getting the x-rays, Rob took a look at the man from the other car. It wasn't much of a look, because every time Rob touched him he started fighting, flailing his arms and muttering, "Don' want no goddam doctor."

Finally satisfied that he had no major injuries, Rob turned him over to Miss Pryor. "Might as well leave him right there on the cart till he sleeps this off and decides to cooperate. Just shove him off in a corner somewhere. Better take off his pants and shoes, though, so he doesn't just wander away. The cops have a hold order on him."

The skull and neck films on the two bank men looked normal. Jim Tice had two broken ribs on his right side, but his lungs were expanding fully. The bruised arm was not broken. The ribs would need splinting, but the laceration of his forehead was more urgent. Esther was already there, getting the OR set up. "Are you going to want Sara?" she asked.

"Not on this one. I don't want to risk a general anesthetic, and I think we can do just as well with local procaine. I'll need 4–0 chromic catgut for the deep sutures, and the smallest silk you've got for the skin. Lots of it."

She was ready by the time Rob had scrubbed and gowned. The man was conscious now, and his blood pressure was stable, so Rob dug into the repair work. The laceration crossed the forehead from above one eyebrow to the other, with the skin lifted up like a flap, but it followed a natural crease in the man's forehead almost perfectly. Despite the swelling of the contused tissues, a good repair could be done. It merely took time. Rob sat huddled over the man for two hours, then three, then almost four, fighting the delicate suture material, fine as spider web, trying to use as little of the injectable anesthetic as possible, yet watching the total used mount closer and closer to the maximum he dared administer in a six-hour period. At long last he pushed back his kick stool, stretched his cramped back muscles and surveyed the job. "Still with us, Jim?"

"Yeah, but I sure wish you'd finish."

"We have. All we need is a pressure dressing on this and you can get to bed." Two minutes later the dressing was in place, with a binder on the chest. He helped Esther wheel the man down to Room 6. As they passed the nurses' station he saw Pryor checking out to Jessie Hodges, and realized it was 11 P.M.

Fred Mallory came next. While Esther set up the OR again, Rob looked over a sick child who had been waiting an hour to see him, then saw another just arriving—sore throats and fever. Done with that, and nearly famished, he rummaged in the diet kitchen for a sandwich. As he ate, Hodges looked in. "Dr. Isaacs on the phone," she said.

*The Hart boy.* Rob took the phone, suddenly tense. "Any news?"

"Yeah. Charlie Feldman just called. You're in luck; you just nicked a little feeder vein, not a main vessel. The arm's all pinned and the kid's doing fine."

Rob thanked him and rang off, feeling almost buoyant as he scrubbed and gowned to dig in to the Mallory case. Mallory's lacerations were easier to repair, but the work was unmercifully tedious; the man's cheek, neck and shoulder had been scraped along the highway, with multitudes of ground-in chunks of gravel and dirt to pick out, piece by piece. Again Rob used a local anesthetic, cleaning as much as possible by gentle scrubbing with gauze and surgical soap, then sitting there picking, picking, picking. Presently he handed Esther one of the needles he was using to dislodge the tiny rock fragments and told her to join the party. She did so, working deftly with the needle in one hand and a pair of tiny tweezers in the other. Bit by bit they completed the picking, leaving the abraded areas remarkably free of detritus except where the skin was so badly macerated it would surely slough off anyway, taking its burden of dirt and gravel with it. By 3 A.M. they finally finished, packed Fred Mallory down to bed and retired, exhausted, to the coffee room. Esther collapsed into a chair. Rob drew coffee for both of them and sat down. "Lousy mess, that gravel," he said.

She nodded. "One of these could do me for the rest of my life." She looked up at him through her thick glasses. "Whole weekend's been a bitch. You must be pooped."

"I'm pooped, all right. Is it always like this?"

"Oh, no; sometimes it's much worse." She laughed. "Just wait for winter—that's when we get the real beauties down off that highway.

I've seen times when every doctor in this valley has been in here working at the same time, all weekend long."

"Encourage me some more," Rob said.

"Then other times nothing happens—*nothing*—and you wonder if your phone has gone out, or if everybody's dropped dead at once." She yawned and stretched. "As for me, right now I'm just glad I don't have any morning cases. Peterson's got a couple of T&As, but Happy scrubs on them."

"Well, I've got eight hours in the office," Rob said, "so I guess I'll go sleep while I can." He dumped out the rest of his coffee, checked out with Jessie Hodges and headed for home. As he crossed the bridge he could see the eastern sky already beginning to brighten. He dropped his clothes on a chair and collapsed into his sleeping bag, but weary as he was, he couldn't sleep. There had been too much happening too fast, decision after decision, tension piled on tension. Gradually pale daylight crept through the house. Ellie slept curled up in her bag, snoring daintily, her hair tangled and dark in the dim light. *At least,* Rob thought, *this next evening I'll be completely off, just walk away from the office at six and forget everything.* . . .

He was finally dozing when the phone rang. He cursed and grabbed the receiver, heard Jessie Hodges' hoarse voice on the wire. "Dr. Tanner, there's been a bad accident down by the Bar-None. Three boys in a car hit the bridge. We're going to need you."

He dragged himself out, dressed and splashed water into his face, rubbed the stubble on his chin. A moment later he was on the highway, heading back through town. As he approached the bridge he saw blinking blue lights from a patrol car parked athwart the northbound lanes. Two patrolmen stood in the road as the ambulance pulled out and started up toward the hospital. One of them flagged him to stop, but he held his black bag up to the windshield; the cop saw it and waved him by. As he passed the bridge he noticed a heap of wreckage, almost unrecognizable; the car had struck the concrete abutment head-on, and a severed steering wheel lay out in the road like a severed hand.

He pulled in behind the ambulance, and met Hodges at the emergency room door. "You'd better see the one on the x-ray table," she said. "I don't think you're going to help the others much."

The ambulance men were lifting a stretcher down, and Rob saw the heap lying on it under the blanket. The skull was crushed like an egg, the face totally destroyed. He pushed the blanket back to cover the mess, shaking his head. The other stretcherload was even worse. "He

109

was in the middle," the ambulance man said. "Bridge just split him in half."

"Well, they're both dead, if you need a pronouncement," Rob said. "Where's the other one?"

"The driver? He's in there." He pointed in the direction Jessie had taken.

The driver was on the x-ray table, moaning but alive, a boy of sixteen or seventeen. Raymond was already there, getting films. The boy's right hip was held at a grotesque angle, either broken or dislocated, and there was a huge welt on his chest where the steering wheel had struck. Rob asked Raymond for rib films too, and walked out of the x-ray room to wait. The patrol sergeant was standing there. "What's with that one?" he asked.

"Some broken bones. Maybe not too bad."

"The son of a bitch," the sergeant said.

"What happened?"

"Came down off that hill like he was shot from a gun. Truckdriver stopped down here, said the car passed him just this side of the pass. He was doing sixty-five himself, and they went past him like he was parked." The sergeant shook his head and pointed to the two heaps on the stretchers. "And I get to call the families," he said.

A moment later Raymond came out. "Those films are ready. Talk about luck. Just a dislocation."

He was right. The ribs were fine; the hip was dislocated to the rear of the socket, but with no sign of fracture. "Must have just rammed his knee into the dashboard," Raymond said.

Rob nodded and went back to look at the boy. It was ten minutes to seven, and Sara Davis had just come in for the morning surgery schedule, so there was anesthesia—but Rob was at a loss. He'd read about hip reductions years ago, but he'd never even seen one done, much less done one. He was just deciding, reluctantly, to call Isaacs when the man himself came walking in, looking bright and fresh and rested. "Hear tell you've been busy," he said.

"You might say." Rob rubbed his eyes and yawned. "I need some help here too. How do you set a dislocated hip?"

"Nothing to it but hard work. Tell Sara to bring the gas machine down. We'll put him to sleep right where he is."

It sounded simple, the way Isaacs described it, but it was no mean feat, even with the boy deeply anesthetized and relaxed. Rob pulled laterally on the thigh with all the strength he could muster while Isaacs

110

flexed the hip repeatedly, trying to lever the bone back into its socket. They worked until they were both red-faced and panting. Then Isaacs said, "Let's give it one more try, and this time when I say pull, *pull*. Okay—now *pull!*" Rob hauled at the thigh with all the strength he had, then felt something shift with a deadening *thunk* and the leg extended straight for the first time, the dislocation reduced. Isaacs pulled out a handkerchief and mopped his forehead, and went up to make rounds. Rob wrote an admission and operative note on the boy, then just sat at the charting desk, suddenly feeling so groggy and stupid he hardly knew what to do next. When Isaacs came by, Rob told him briefly who was in the house and why.

"We need a blood count and hematocrit on Jim Tice, then we can decide whether to order blood or not. And we've got to keep a close check on his chest. The others are all right for now, I guess. Better have Jerry check the old guy with heart failure. His patient anyway, I think. I've got to get home now and get some sleep before the office opens."

He headed down the hill in the bright morning sun. *Sleep would be nice, but an hour or so will just leave you worse than ever. A dip in the river would be smarter.* At least he'd have time for a shower and a shave and a quiet breakfast with Ellie and a little planning before he walked into the office at ten, with a duty weekend behind him at last and his first full week of practice in Twin Forks, Montana, coming up. In an odd way, it felt as if he'd been there a month already, a desperately hard-earned month, and as he drove across the bridge the thought came, almost objectively, that if practice in Twin Forks was all going to be like this, it was going to either make him or break him. *Well, it hasn't broken Martin Isaacs,* he thought, *so it's not going to break me* —but then he laughed, because he knew, despite the brave sound of it all, that he wasn't really ready, right then, to take any bets.

# 12

"Well, I think it's idiotic, throwing a party tonight," Rob said, struggling into a fresh shirt and tie. "He knows I've been running my ass off all weekend. When am I supposed to sleep?"

"Relax; you'll make it," Ellie said.

"All he wants is to show me off. He practically said so himself. He even dragooned Jerry DeForrest into taking call so we could both be off at the same time."

"Well, if you're going to be shown, you'd better be there. Now quit complaining. I've got to get dressed."

Rob went into the kitchen and poured a stiff bourbon over ice for himself, a lighter one for Ellie. She had broken the news of the party during breakfast, and he had been no more enthusiastic than she was. Now, after dragging his way through eight hours in the office, he wanted nothing more than a quiet dinner and a full night's sleep. "What are you planning to wear?"

"Nobody said, so I decided to go elegant." Ellie stepped back so Rob could review the new wine-colored cocktail dress she had bought at the Twin Forks Bo-Teek that afternoon. "How about this?"

"Say, that's great, if you don't lean over and fall out of it. You'll put the rest to shame."

"Better finish zipping me, then."

He zipped her up, then kissed her lightly on the neck. "Just too

112

damned bad we have to go out. . . ."

Ellie wriggled away. "Well, we do, and we'd better get ready." Rob sipped his drink and watched her admiringly as she went to the bathroom mirror and started applying eye makeup. "What do you suppose Jennie Isaacs is like?"

"Beats me. I've never even seen her."

"Amy DeForrest implies she's a little odd," Ellie said. "But then, Amy DeForrest struck me a little odd herself."

"Fact is, I doubt if it's even occurred to Martin to bring us around to meet his wife. Never entered his head. Seems like half the time his mind's off in the next county somewhere."

"So is yours sometimes," Ellie said. "Or did you plan to wear brown shoes with that blue suit?"

Rob shifted to black shoes and finished his drink. A few minutes later they were in the little Vega, crossing the bridge and driving into town. The day had been hot and cloudless; only now, as the late-afternoon sun angled down the river from the west, a gentle breeze had arisen, cooling and freshening the air. As they turned up onto the ridge from the River Road the pine scent was strong. A few moments later they turned into the long drive leading up to the DeForrests' house, with Isaacs' gray Buick close behind them, and Harry Sonders' little red Porsche following second.

The place was beautiful, an expansive ranch-style house set among pines high on the ridge. A beautiful garden of rock and foliage surrounded the place—apparently Jerry's major hobby—and on the far side of the house a large patio faced on a lovely view of the valley and town below. As they pulled up into the parking area, Jerry and Amy came out to greet them, Jerry dressed in his usual slacks and jacket, his wife in a flouncy summer print that seemed somehow too small for her gangling figure. The gray Buick pulled in next to them and Martin Isaacs climbed out, white hair flying in the breeze. He opened the passenger door for a small, dark-haired woman to emerge, and took a huge gift-wrapped package from her arms. "We decided to make this a housewarming too," he said, "since you're moved into the Judge's place." He looked over his shoulder. "Jerry, haul in this booze, will you? Then we'll come help get the food in."

He pushed the huge package into Rob's arms, then put his arm around the small woman at his side and brought her forward. "Ellie, you've never met my Jennie—we've been very remiss. Jen, this is Ellie Tanner and Rob."

"Oh, yes." Jennie Isaacs smiled tentatively and took Ellie's hand in hers. She was a small, once handsome woman, now appearing slightly frayed and dowdy, almost wraithlike, with hesitant, fluttery movements and an odd look of caution in her eyes. "We've so much wanted to have you over, but everyone's been so busy. . . ." Her voice trailed off. "You know how it is."

"Yes, I certainly do," Ellie said. "I just hope things will ease up a little when Rob gets broken in."

"Oh, I'm sure they will. . . ."

Amy came up and pecked Jennie on the cheek. "Nice to see you, honey," she said. "You all just come in and make yourselves at home. Oh, there's Harry and Karen! Jerry, dear, why don't you get drinks going before everyone else gets here? Then we can put Harry to work tending bar and give you a chance to ogle his wife. Better meet Karen while you can, honey," she added to Ellie in a lower tone. "Harry only takes her out for housewarmings and funerals."

Sonders had parked behind Rob's Vega and now came up, dapper in a checkered sports jacket and pale green open-necked shirt, with a strikingly pretty blond woman by his side. She was wearing a gauzy summer dress that exposed legs and bosom almost to excess. "Darling, how *daring,*" Amy cried, "and all for us country folk, too." She took the blond in tow and brought her over to Ellie. "Karen Sonders, Ellie Tanner. Oh, dear, I see that Harry's following the booze in. Hope there's no surgery tonight."

"Don't worry, dear—Ted Loftis is covering," the blond girl said sweetly. "And in a pinch we've always got Jerry." She turned to Ellie. "Harry says you've started remodeling your house all by yourselves. I mean, with your own little hands!"

"It's true," Ellie said. "There was this big hole in the roof, and soggy ceiling board all over, and all the floor tile peeling. You'll have to stop by and see it."

The women followed the men into the house as other cars began turning up the driveway. Inside, Isaacs had set up a bar in the huge open kitchen and Jerry DeForrest was emptying a bag of party ice into three ice buckets. Rob had followed Harry Sonders in; the moment they stepped into the living room, the surgeon stopped and looked around admiringly. "I must say Jerry did all right with this place. They were just building it when I was last here. Quite a spread." He looked up at Rob. "How's *your* remodeling going?"

"Ellie's doing most of it," Rob said. "The way you guys have been

114

running my ass off, I've had no time."

"Well, it'll be snug when you finish. You know, I looked at that place a year or so ago, figured I could use it to hole up in when I was out late on cases, but Jesus, it looked like such a wreck it'd take ten grand just to get it closed in."

"Well, it isn't going to take any ten grand," Rob said, "just a lot of hard work— Hey, I think the drinks are on."

DeForrest was taking drink orders. Isaacs shoved a bourbon on the rocks into Rob's hand and herded him toward the living room. "Come on, get your wife and stand by to meet people; lots of folks coming. Jennie, where the hell did you put the crackers and cheese? They were in the bag next to the turkey. . . ."

Others were arriving now; Rob joined Ellie and Amy near the door for greetings, while Isaacs stood by introducing them like a couple of pet poodles at a dog show. Joe Pollard, the banker, came in, a small, weasel-faced man with his overweight and effusive wife. "Joe, Carmen, glad to see you," Isaacs boomed. "Meet Rob Tanner here—he's my new doctor. Ever need a personal loan, Rob, just see Joe here, he'll take care of you. . . ." Judge Barret was right behind them. He shook Rob's hand and leaned over to kiss Ellie's cheek.

He thrust a tall, narrow package into Rob's hands. "Just a little cheap champagne to warm the house up," he said. "But don't share it; stick it in the refrigerator and take it home when this is over. Then you can see if you can pop the cork into the river from the patio. We used to make it every time, when my wife and I were living out there summers."

Still more people were arriving thick and fast; for a while it seemed that half the town had been invited. Esther Briggs drove up in her dusty old Ford, followed by Roger Painter in his pale-blue Mercedes, greeting Ellie with a frosty nod and offering Rob a damp hand before repairing to the bar. ("Just Seven-Up, Jerry. I really can't stay.") Next came Al Davidson, the little hunchbacked lumberyard man, and his wife; Agnes Miller with her long, thin scarecrow of a husband, badly crippled with arthritis and leaning heavily on a cane; Nellie Webster and her husband, a rough-hewn, muscular man with a face weathered by years of work in the woods and hair as red or redder than Nellie's; and Dora Hoffman, her white hair freshly and handsomely set, arriving with Bev Bessler. Rob went to get drinks for Dora and Bev; as he returned, he was startled to see Chris Erickson coming in, accompanied by a tall, gray-haired elderly couple. "Rob, this is John and Mary Stanley," Isaacs said, "and

115

Chris Erickson. John is the manager of the mill down in Tintown and Chris—"

"Oh, we're old friends," Chris said, smiling. She gave Ellie a long, appraising glance. "I'm the one your husband put in the ambulance the night you arrived at Twin Forks. You could say I was his first patient." She took Rob's arm and squeezed it.

"Lucky for you we happened by," Ellie said coolly. "You seem to have recovered all right."

"Oh, I bounce right back," Chris said. "I always have."

"You sure look better than the last time I saw you," Rob said. The bruising and swelling were almost gone now, and her face, he reflected, was startlingly attractive, with a sleepy smile and eyes so vividly green they caught him quite by surprise when he found himself looking directly into them. "No more chest trouble?"

"Well, a little, but nothing that's holding me down."

"That's right," John Stanley said. "She stumped into our forestry lab this morning, cast and all, to get back to work. If we're lucky, we'll have her here until Christmas—right, Chris?"

"If the moths cooperate," Chris said. "Frankly, I could stay here forever. To an Iowa girl these mountains look like heaven."

Jerry DeForrest came up to take drink orders and Rob and Ellie turned to greet more newcomers. Already the party was spilling out onto the patio, still warm from the sinking sun. Jerry and Isaacs were setting up tables for the buffet, while their wives busied themselves warming food in the oven. Housewarming gifts for Rob and Ellie were displayed on a side table: a set of wrought-iron fireplace tools from the Isaacses; a striking watercolor of a wintry South Ridge in a snowstorm, done by Amy DeForrest and splendidly framed; a bartending set from the Sonderses; a half-dozen other small gifts. With the last guests arrived and the buzz of talk at a self-sustaining level, Rob gave Ellie a wink and a squeeze and began moving from cluster to cluster of people, catching fragments of conversation here and there. He refilled his glass at the bar and stepped out on the patio, where Martin Isaacs and Al Davidson were huddled in deep conversation, the little lumberman arguing vehemently while Isaacs shook his head and Roger Painter stood by tight-lipped, his face a picture of pained distaste. "I don't care what you say, Al," Isaacs was saying. "There's no way that hospital's going to charge any less, if you kick and squeal till you're a hundred."

"Why, Martin, when I saw my wife's bill for her pneumonia I almost dropped my plates on the floor. I thought the hospital room rate was

116

supposed to pay for *something*, but hell, it didn't pay for *anything at all.*"

"Nah, you just didn't look at the bill, that's all. It takes money to run a place like that, and you're just damned lucky to have it here at all. If you had to go to a Missoula hospital, your bill would be twice that big."

"Well, all I can say is that we need a few young Turks around here to shake things up in that place," Davidson said, winking at Rob. "A little new blood is what we need—right, Doc?"

"Could be," Rob said. "In fact, blood is one thing that hospital needs in the worst sort of way. I don't know about the bed rates, but I know it doesn't make sense for a bleeding patient to have to wait four hours for transfusion blood."

"There's no money for a blood bank," Roger Painter said. "The directors would never buy it."

"But that doesn't make sense, if you're trying to run a decent hospital," Rob said. "You don't need a whole big blood bank operation —but you need some way to have blood on hand in that place for emergency use without riding a bicycle to Missoula after it."

"Like what do you suggest?" Isaacs said.

"Well, I don't know. You could at least have a modern, refrigerated storage unit to keep blood here."

"All right, that's five thousand dollars right there. Where you going to get five thousand dollars?"

"Organize a citizens' committee," Rob said. "Get people stirred up, get a fund-raising campaign going. Then get hold of the Red Cross or whoever provides blood in Missoula or Great Falls. They could ship blood here by bus twice a week, if we had someplace to store it. We could keep it ten days and ship back what we haven't used. Let them send a bloodmobile down here twice a year for donations. And in case of a real pinch, we could organize a walking blood bank right here in Twin Forks. Get every able-bodied man and woman in the valley here to come in and be typed, and then keep a list for emergencies."

"You can't just up and do that sort of thing," Roger said primly. "You'd have to have licensing, costly personnel to administer the program—"

"So let the hospital get a license, formally sponsor the whole thing," Rob said. "Make the hospital really look good around here."

"Well, it won't work," Isaacs said flatly, "so you might as well forget it. The hospital won't buy it in a million years."

"Then maybe the hospital needs some new directors," Rob said. "If we got enough people in this town stirred up to have a good blood service here, the directors would *have* to listen."

Al Davidson grinned broadly at Isaacs. "Better watch him, Martin. This boy's liable to get out of hand."

"Oh, yeah?" Isaacs laughed. "He's just got a lot to learn, that's all."

Moving on, Rob found Jerry DeForrest and Judge Barret with their heads together, sampling trays of hot goodies Karen Sonders had just brought out from the oven. "I still say you lawyers are to blame for this malpractice mess," Jerry said, spearing a prawn expertly with a toothpick and swallowing it whole. "And then people wonder why our fees go up. Well, when a man's got to fork over six thousand dollars a year for the same malpractice insurance he paid three hundred dollars for ten years ago, he's going to raise his fees to cover it. And that's only part of it. He's also going to order every test known to man on every patient he sees, just to protect himself, and the patient pays for all that too. You legal boys have got it fixed so a doctor's judgment doesn't mean a thing. All that counts in court is what he *does*, whether it's necessary or not. So he does *everything*, whether it's necessary or not."

The Judge coughed apologetically. "Of course, theoretically the doctor could be held negligent for doing unnecessary things, just as well as for neglecting to do things that *were* necessary."

"Well, maybe, but it's not very likely," DeForrest said. "The rule today is 'When in doubt, do it,' and the doctors damned well know it."

"Maybe that goes for blood counts or chest x-rays," the Judge said mildly, "but if you're talking about taking out a woman's uterus, for example . . ."

Jerry grinned. "Okay, you'd hesitate a little about that. But when an accident comes in off the highway, believe me, you leave no stone unturned, no matter what you think is really necessary. Or take headache problems. Some patient comes in complaining about headaches. Nothing else, just headaches—"

"Jerry, you're going to give the Judge more than a headache if you don't lay off him," Isaacs said, walking over to join them. "You just don't know when to shut up. Why not go in and make drinks for a while? Couple of people here are ready for seconds. Oh, and, Jerry"—he turned aside slightly and lowered his voice—"see that Jennie just gets ginger ale, okay? And keep her away from the bar, if you can."

Over by the barbecue John Stanley was talking to Agnes and Jim Miller as Isaacs herded Rob over. "Important man to get to know," Martin said in Rob's ear. "He can throw us a lot of business or cut us off

118

at the pass; depends on how he feels. Hey, John, you're looking good this summer. Got a little weight off, I see."

"Right." The mill manager looked at Rob. "So how do you like the practice, now that you've got your feet wet?"

"Gets pretty wild sometimes," Rob said. "Of course I like it—at least most parts. Some things are going to take getting used to, though."

"Oh?" Stanley looked at him sharply. "Like what?"

"It's just a whole lot different from hospital training, that's all. Back at Graystone, just about every patient I saw was really *sick.* You'd work like hell to pull them out of the fire, and get them stable, and send them home, and they'd hardly be out the door before the bed was filled with another one even sicker. A sort of never-ending cycle. Out here you work, all right, but it's different."

"You mean the people you see out here aren't sick?" Stanley said.

"Well, some are, but not that many. Cut fingers, sore throats, rashes —a lot of people who think they might be sick but really aren't and just want to be reassured, maybe have some pills prescribed. So you pat them on the head and tell them everything's going to be all right, and charge them ten dollars for it."

"You're damned right you do," Isaacs said. "What's more, they're happy about it, because you're giving them just what they want."

"Maybe so," Rob said, "but you end up cheating them. Pretty soon you're merely running a first-aid station instead of a doctor's office."

The mill manager scratched his head. "I don't quite follow you."

"If you're running forty people through your office each day, you can't begin to practice good medicine. All you're doing is taking a quick look, patching them up and sending them home. If they're in trouble you bail them out, and then they're back next week and you bail them out again without getting close to what the trouble might be. If they've got a headache, you give them some pills and out they go. If they've got a sore throat, you give them penicillin, and out they go. You see a leak in the dike, you shove in a cork and send them home and never stop to wonder why the dike's leaking. You just crank 'em through the office, get 'em out of there, and listen to the cash register jingle."

Rob paused, feeling his drinks a little, realizing his voice was getting strident. The mill manager was watching him, half amused. "So what do you recommend?" he asked.

"Maybe slowing down a little, taking time to really be thorough. A patient may think you're great for curing his sore throat so fast, but the truth is he's been ripped off. Any boob could throw pills at his sore

119

throat. What he *really* needs a doctor for is to spot his pernicious anemia, or find the cancer in his lung, or knock his blood pressure down before it blows a hole in his brain." Rob turned to Isaacs, who was listening to all this with an expression of pained indulgence. "Why, hell, Martin, there are people who have been through that office twenty times in the last ten years and have never once had a chest x-ray, not even a blood count or a urine check. There are women coming in for ten years for vitamin shots or diet pills who haven't once had a Pap smear. Sure, a good workup might cost them a couple of hundred bucks, but hell, people spend that much on a set of new tires just to stay alive on the highway, and never give it a thought. Why can't they spend it to hang on to their health? It's the doctor's job to *sell* them on it, that's the truth."

"Out of the mouths of babes," Isaacs said. "John, do you have trouble with your newest millhand coming in and telling you how to sell plywood after one week on the job?"

Stanley chuckled. "No, can't say I do."

"Yeah. Well, these smart young punks just out of training give me a pain in the crotch," Isaacs said. "They think they know everything there is to know about medicine, and they don't mind telling you about it, loud and clear. I mean, they've got the *answers*. Of course, it's still kind of nice to have an old Stone Age muddler like me hanging around to bail 'em out when they get in trouble treating bad fractures—right, Rob?"

Rob flushed. "I sure can't argue with that."

"Well, you stick around awhile and keep your eyes open and you'll find out some of the old boys have a few tricks up their sleeves." Isaacs laughed. "Go get yourself a drink before you break John's ear off here."

Rob moved away, feeling thoroughly ridiculous and angry at himself as well. *They aren't here to listen to your Expert Theory of Medical Practice, you stupid ass. And Martin doesn't need a lot of instruction. He was working here in Twin Forks when you were still in high school, for God's sake. And these other people don't need your wisdom, either. They're just here to have a pleasant drink and take a look at you and wish you well, and you talk to them like they're a bunch of clods.* He skirted two or three other groups, searching for Ellie in the crowd. He spotted her in the kitchen with Amy DeForrest and Nellie Webster, pulling turkey and ham from the oven and popping rolls in to heat. She leaned over and kissed him on the cheek. "How are *you* doing?" she said.

120

"I'm busy making a jackass of myself," Rob said. "Next time you see me start preaching to somebody, kindly come stick a towel in my mouth, okay?"

"Oh, you've just had two drinks, that's all." Ellie handed him a tablecloth and pointed to the living room. "We're about to serve up a buffet on those tables there and let people help themselves. Why don't you spread this out for us?"

Rob started for the living room with the tablecloth, but Jennie Isaacs intercepted him and took it from his hand. "You go back and visit with people," she said. "I'll take care of this."

"Fine," Rob said, "but let me help."

"Nope, you kids're not supposed to be working today. Martin'll be very angry if he sees you working. And we can't have that, can we?" She was speaking very deliberately, placing each word with extreme care, as if tiptoing across a stream on rocks. She held the cloth in one hand and looked at her empty glass. "Make you a deal. You go get me a drink and I'll set the table. Just a little one, bourbon with ginger ale."

She handed him the glass and turned toward the table, lurching slightly and catching the table edge for support. She fluffed the cloth out, then snatched at it to keep it from sliding off onto the floor. "None of that now," he heard her mutter to herself. "Tablecloth, *behave,* dammit!"

Rob glanced at her sharply. Her eyes were clear enough, but her cheeks were flushed, and she moved with a sort of studied precaution, reacting a split second too slowly for the tablecloth she was trying to drape, and once again almost tottering for balance. *God, she's tense,* he thought, *or else stone drunk.* He took the bourbon bottle from the kitchen bar, hesitated, then poured a scant ounce over ice cubes and filled the glass quickly to the brim with ginger ale. He shot a glance across the room at Isaacs, feeling almost guilty, but the big man was busy talking to Dora Hoffman and Joe Pollard, with his back to the kitchen. Rob brought the drink to the table, saw that Ellie had come to the rescue with the cloth. Jennie brushed off a fleck of lint and then looked up at him. "Oh, you're a dear," she said. With a pat to his arm and an odd little smile, she took the drink and turned toward the roomful of people.

By now some of the other women were moving food and dishes out to the table, and Amy flagged Jerry down to carve the turkey. Rob continued making the round of guests. Two men by the window were discussing the merits of a new rotary mower one had just bought.

121

Raymond Potter from the hospital and Judge Barret were debating fly-fishing techniques and assured Rob that both streams and nearby highland lakes were superb for trout from the middle of July on. At the far side of the room Rob spied Chris Erickson, standing by herself, nursing a half-gone drink and staring pensively out the window. He crossed over to join her. "Bored? Or just dreaming?" he said.

For an instant the girl looked startled. Then she smiled. "Me? Neither. I was just listening to the sound."

"Of the birds?"

"No, the party."

"Just sounds like a cocktail party to me," Rob said.

She smiled again. "Then you're not listening. You'd be amazed how different parties can sound. This is not as bad as some. Not quite the tension you feel at the business parties John Stanley has to give sometimes. Nobody here laughing too loud."

"Which means?"

"Not much. Just that nobody has to. Most of the people here are enjoying themselves. Well, maybe not the big white-haired man, Dr. Isaacs. He isn't happy in this kind of situation, somehow. He doesn't resonate right, everything he says is a little awkward, like an off-size shoe. And that poor little woman . . ."

Rob looked sharply at the girl. "Is it that obvious?"

"Not yet. She covers up pretty well. But it will be. He's taken that drink away from her three times now in the last quarter hour, and something's going to pop if he doesn't stop it."

"And you get all this from clear across the room?"

"I just pick up signals, I guess. I don't know exactly how. I get feelings, vibrations, whatever you want, and they usually turn out true." She looked at him soberly. "Is that so strange? You doctors must do the same thing every time a patient walks into your office. You must pick up signals like mad whenever you see a patient."

"Never thought of it that way," Rob said, "but I guess you're right. You see something odd, hear something that doesn't click, and you're right on top of it, bang. You can be half asleep and it whacks you right between the eyes, and you *know* something's wrong. Chances are you know *what*, too."

She nodded. "Like ESP."

"Well, not really. The clue is right there in front of you, whatever it is, and your mind grabs it and runs a chain of associations, and then,

122

whammo, there's the answer. No magic about it. None of your fancy vibrations."

"Oh, but I *like* my vibrations," Chris protested.

"Well, for a doctor it's just plain practice and hard work and training. You spend years getting all your senses keyed up, like a safecracker sandpapering his fingertips and tuning his ears so he can hear and feel the faintest click of a tumbler."

"Ah," she said. *"All* the senses?"

"That's right; even smell: You'd be amazed how it helps. Back before antiseptics, a doctor could diagnose a case of childbed fever just by walking in the patient's room and sniffing. Even today you can tell a person with severe liver damage just from the odor on his breath. It's called hepatic fetor and there's no other smell quite like it."

"Sounds absolutely nauseating to me," the girl said, "and if you keep on talking you may yet drive me down to Dr. Florey for my physical exam."

Rob grinned. "You mean I've made a convert?"

"Well, you didn't sell John Stanley, but it makes sense to me. And for all his roaming fingers, Dr. Florey didn't once check anything that wasn't actively hurting all the time I was in the hospital. Not that I'm sick. Except for the accident, I've never felt better in my life, and I haven't darkened a doctor's door since I was a college freshman and wanted a prescription for the pill. But maybe the time to look for trouble is when you feel just fine."

"It's great preventive maintenance," Rob said.

"Like an oil change every two thousand miles," she said dryly.

He started to answer and then realized she was laughing at him. "Well, if you decide you need an oil change, just call for an appointment," he said. "If you're going to be around."

"Oh, I'll be around, all right. The grant money came through and Mr. Stanley has given me lab space at the mill."

"To do what, exactly?"

"To study moths."

Rob blinked. "Moths? You mean . . ." He fluttered his fingers.

"Right. Those nasty little guys that have been killing off all the Douglas fir trees up in Washington and Oregon, and you have to use DDT to kill them, and then everybody has a French fit about using DDT."

"So you're a chemist?"

123

"Geneticist. At least, I'm working for my doctorate in genetics at the university in Missoula, School of Forestry, but at the moment I'm sort of on loan to the timber company, trying to stir up trouble for these moths. Right now I'm trying to interfere with their love lives so they can't reproduce properly."

"It's a little impractical to spay them, isn't it?" Rob said suspiciously.

She laughed. "We're much more subtle than that. Nobody really knows how they reproduce, but it involves some chemicals called pheromones that the female secretes when she's in the mood, in order to stimulate the male to mate. Maybe it just makes it easier for him to find her; nobody really knows. But I'm trying to tamper with the genes that control pheromone production so the female moths can't attract mates and the moth population drops below the point that can maintain the population. . . ." Her voice trailed off. "I'm afraid it's not very interesting," she said apologetically.

Rob roared with laughter. "I think it's wild," he said. "You're getting paid good money over there to try to raise a bunch of funny moths."

"You could say that. There's a lot of field work too, climbing up and down mountains catching specimens."

"Sounds like it keeps you busy."

She looked at him. "Not too busy to get into mischief."

"I see. What do you do in your spare time?"

"If there's nothing better to do, I hunt mushrooms."

"Oh, come on, now."

"No, really. That's one of the great things about working out here; there are more wild mushrooms than you can shake a stick at. There are mushrooms around here nobody's ever *seen* before."

Rob shook his head wonderingly. "That sounds as wild as your funny moths. Or your vibrations."

Chris smiled. "You get a free hour sometime and I'll teach you all about mushrooms. But right now I'm getting vibrations that your wife is getting sore and you'd better grab a plate and start the serving line or there's going to be thunder and lightning. See you later."

She was right; Ellie was coming across the room—but she was not angry at him. "Rob, we've got some trouble. Can you help?"

He followed her toward the kitchen. There seemed to be a cluster of people there—Jerry DeForrest, Amy, Karen Sonders, Agnes Miller. As he came up, Rob saw Isaacs in the middle, tall and angry, facing his wife. Jennie stood spread-legged, glaring at him, a full glass in her hand.

124

"—truth is you're nothing but a big, nasty bully," Jennie was saying in a high-pitched, hysterical voice. "You think you can run everybody's life any way you want, but sometimes the mice give a squeak or two when you slap 'em down. Squeak, squeak!"

"Jennie, put that damned drink down. We're going home," Isaacs said.

"Don' want to go home. I'm havin' a good time. Don't often get a chance to squeak at the big, nasty bully." She broke into hoarse laughter.

"Jennie, I'm telling you we're going home. Now put the drink down."

"Not goin' anywhere." She leaned toward him, holding the drink at arm's length off behind her. "Jus' because *you* say so doesn't mean I have to leave."

"God damn it—" Isaacs lunged for the drink, but she evaded him, stepped back suddenly. "You wan' my drink? Okay, you've got it." Quite suddenly she dashed it into his chest, drenching his shirt and trousers and throwing the glass crashing to the floor. "Satisfied?"

He faced her, jaw clenching, arm raised. Then, shaking his white head, he drew back. "Jerry? Give me a hand." Isaacs seized Jennie under one arm while Jerry took the other.

"Don' want to go home!" Jennie screamed, first struggling and then slumping. Together they lifted her like a sack of oats and started out the door, as her voice rose to a wail. *"Don' want to go home. . . ."*

For an instant the people in the house stood frozen. Then they turned away, embarrassed, and those nearest the buffet started serving themselves, grateful for something to do. A moment later Jerry came back in, shaking his head. "It's all right," he said. "Let's everybody help themselves."

Gradually conversation came to life again. The buffet was beautiful and bounteous: a roast turkey, a huge ham, a seafood casserole, three kinds of salad, buttered vegetables, two kinds of cake and three pies, with more apparently waiting in the kitchen. Harry Sonders, growing more expansive by the minute, was snapping flash pictures as Ellie and Rob joined the serving line. Tables had appeared on the patio; it was almost dark now, but tiki torches had been lit at the patio's edge, providing a romantic, flickering light. Rob and Ellie joined Agnes and Jim Miller and the Stanleys at a table, groping for small talk at first; the conversation limped along from the problems of living in a small, secluded lumber mill town like Twin Forks to the difficulties of maintain-

ing a small hospital in a community with such a limited pool of professional nursing help to draw from. "It's easy to blame Roger Painter,"
Agnes said, "but the truth is you just can't get registered nurses from
the city to come out and work in a place like this. In fact, you can't get
nurses at all unless they already live here. You can't match the salaries
the big city hospitals pay, and there are too many other problems, living
in a little place like this."

"Oh, I don't know," Ellie said. "It can't be all that bad. We had our
fill of city living. A small town is kind of refreshing."

"You were just ripe for a change," Agnes said. "Wait awhile. It's all
you can do to find groceries out here at prices you're willing to pay, and
if there's anything else you want, you've practically *got* to go to the
city."

"Like nuts and bolts," John Stanley said. "Two hardware stores in
Twin Forks just filled with junk you wouldn't think of buying in a
million years. But try to find a nut to fit a bolt, and they won't have it.
Doesn't matter what size. It'll be on order, but don't hold your breath.
It'll never actually get here."

The talk drifted to other things, insignificant things. Rob helped
himself and Ellie to seconds, wondering how soon they could leave, and
later coffee was ready as the big house and patio were filled with quiet
murmuring. The summer breeze was sultry, setting the torches to
flaring and flickering, and Rob felt a lazy drowsiness overcoming the
shock of the scene between Isaacs and Jennie. Suddenly he experienced
a wave of irrational good will toward the people gathered here. *They're
good people, friendly, able to overlook an unpleasant scene, welcoming
strangers without restraint.* He looked around, saw Harry Sonders on
the other side of the patio, his face florid now, eyes very bright, smiling
and laughing, teasing Esther Briggs across the table, leaning forward to
whisper in her ear, while Karen Sonders sat stiffly across from them,
smiling only with her lips. At another table Al Davidson and Raymond
Potter were in animated discussion of a boat-building project as their
wives waited patiently for the subject to change. Rob looked from table
to table, involuntarily searching, until his eyes found Chris Erickson
deep in conversation with Nellie Webster and her husband. She met his
gaze, momentarily, with an almost startled look, as though he had
caught her in some surreptitious act, and he saw her suddenly in odd
perspective: with the group but apart from it, an elfin creature with a
trim yet voluptuous figure, a vibrant, animated face, and such very
green eyes. . . . He frowned and forced his eyes away, almost embar-

126

rassed that she had caught him staring.

"She's certainly attractive," Ellie said close to his ear. "In a cheap sort of way."

"Mm?"

"The girl."

"Yes. She works with moths." He felt himself flushing. "Good party?"

"It's a party," Ellie said. "But I wish we could go home."

"Then let's go."

Others rose with them and prepared to depart. They smiled and shook hands as Agnes and Jim Miller drifted along, then Harry Sonders and his wife, then the Davidsons. The Stanleys were leaving just ahead of them, with Chris, and Rob felt a pang of regret that he had not talked more with this odd girl with her odd interests, yet sensed in some disquieting way that more had been said, somehow, than had been said. Finally they were in the car, driving down the hill in silence, through the darkened, sleepy town, out the highway to home. In their own living room Rob tossed aside his jacket and tie, then uncapped a beer and went out on the patio. Ellie joined him a moment later and they stood together listening to the quiet sound of the river.

"Nightcap?" Rob said at last.

"No, not now."

"Nice party. Nice people. They really seemed to be wishing us well. If it hadn't been for . . ."

"I know," Ellie said.

"Poor guy, with a wife like that."

Ellie turned on him. "Poor *guy!* My God, Rob, what about *her?* She was so pathetic, such a sad little wraith. Every time I spoke to her she seemed to be off in neverland somewhere, as if she couldn't understand what I was saying."

"She was very drunk," Rob said.

"I suppose. But she didn't seem to be drinking so much. . . ."

"Then she was loaded before she got there. But most of them behaved themselves." He forced a laugh. "Nobody fell through the windows, nobody broke any furniture. Everybody was pleasant. Some were even interesting."

"Especially the one with the green eyes."

"Oh, her. She studies moths and hunts mushrooms."

"Well, she'd better keep her green eyes where they belong," Ellie said. "And as for your brown eyes, buddy, you'd better get them closed before you pass out. You haven't slept for three days."

"I know. I could sleep for a week. But I won't."

She kissed him lightly, caught his arm. "Oh, Rob, I hope so much it's going to work out here."

"Don't worry," he said grimly. "One way or another, it's going to work out."

# Part II

# 13

One thing was certain: as July gave way to August, the summer weeks in Twin Forks passed with incredible swiftness, a succession of hot, dry, sun-baked days that turned only slightly cooler in the late evening hours. As week followed week, the only break in the weather was an occasional rousing thunderstorm in midafternoon, with ominous clouds rolling in from the mountains and then spending themselves as quickly as they came in a few moments of drenching rain. The river dropped steadily from the full watercourse of late June to a crystal-clear streamlet in late August, filling only the deepest channels and gurgling through dark, tranquil pools. People in town called it the driest summer in years and worried lest their lawns and gardens scorch in the sun; on any night on the ridges above town one could hear the swishing of water sprinklers blending with the buzz of cicadas. The cars and campers of tourists abounded, and fishermen plied the stream from dawn until dark, with the happy weight of full creels on their shoulders.

The trout were there, beyond doubt, but neither Rob nor Ellie threatened them. For Ellie it was a long summer of sawing and pounding and tacking and painting as she drove home the remodeling job with the determination of a badger. For weeks they were buried in sawdust, tile scraps, bent nails and wood shavings, the place reeking of paint remover and turpentine. Ellie would quit each day with her eyes red and swollen from the fumes, only to dig in the next morning with

131

miraculously renewed determination. On rare occasions Rob had a day free to help—but for the most part, with equally dogged determination, he spent his nights and days in the superheated crucible of a growing medical practice in Twin Forks, Montana.

Nothing was said next day about Jennie Isaacs' outburst at the housewarming party. Isaacs offered no apology, nor any other comment, when he appeared in the office next morning. Indeed, he huddled with Rob only once, briefly, to point out that the office load traditionally turned heavy in the summer months, and that Rob had better be prepared to "move his ass" now that he was broken in.

Not that Rob needed the reminder, as the days and weeks whipped by. If he had ever imagined that those first few frantic days had been a fluke, some kind of ghastly initiation rite, he soon was disabused; the practice pressure was intense, constant and unremitting. In the office, his hours were packed from the start with a continuing stream of patients, and the patients' demands on call nights and weekends were, if anything, even more extreme than during that first exacting week.

At first he blamed himself: his slowness to adapt to the demands of a private practice, so frustratingly different from his hospital training. *There's got to be some way to move faster,* he told himself, *some way to get more done in less time.* And speed up he did, budgeting every minute possible, moving ever faster from patient to patient, making one hospital trip do for two or three calls as he saw Martin Isaacs do— and still the load did not ease. Isaacs continued to see five times as many patients as Rob did, even as Rob's facility increased. On Isaacs' OB day in particular the clinic was like Grand Central Station, with an unbelievable parade of women passing through in all stages of pregnancy. Yet slowly Rob began to realize that Isaacs, for all his incredible instinctive know-how and experience, was not doing the thorough, painstaking job that Rob had been taught to do in his hospital training. The time Isaacs spent with a given patient had no relation whatever to the patient's complaints. It seemed more related to the number of patients still waiting to be seen; the more charts Agnes Miller plopped down on Isaacs' door any given hour, the faster he moved. Miraculously, his stream of patients would always dry up by six o'clock in the evening and suddenly, without a word, Isaacs would be out the back door while Rob worked doggedly on for another two hours to finish up his schedule. Yet by that six o'clock witching hour Isaacs would already have seen twenty more patients than Rob had seen and sent them packing off.

"I don't know how you get away with it," Rob said one day when

132

they were pausing for coffee in the back room. "You never quit moving, you never stop to talk to them, you just move them through like cars on a conveyor belt. Like that Bradley woman you just saw: she was still talking to you, telling you her troubles with her husband, and you just walked off down the hall in the middle of it—"

"Hell, she'd talk all day if I let her," Isaacs said. "I can't listen to them talk all the time. My God, I'd *never* get out of here if I did."

"But what do they get out of seeing you?"

"Hell, *I* don't know—but they seem to be happy. They come in with complaints, so I listen a minute to the complaints and then I do something about them. Mostly I look for trouble and if I don't see or hear any, I do something that won't do any harm and pack them along. If I sat and listened to them forever, I'd be dead by now."

"Maybe so," Rob said. "But it seems like you're just sticking on Band-Aids, by guess or by God."

"I take care of an awful lot of complaints that way," Isaacs said.

"I just wonder how much you miss."

"Not much," Isaacs said.

"I don't see how you can help it."

Isaacs gave him a long look. "You'd just be surprised," he said. "Look, people are going to *tell* you when they're sick. You don't have to go hunt up trouble. You've got to spot what's significant, sure, and you've got to keep your eyes open, but you don't miss much. And if you *do* miss something one time, they stay sick and come back and you don't miss it the next time. If you sit and talk to them, and get all involved in their troubles, you're not going to think about what they need right now; you're going to try to make their lives over for them, and that's not what they came for."

"I still think you must miss things you shouldn't miss," Rob said.

Isaacs laughed. "Okay, have it your way. You do what you want and I'll do what I want, and anytime you catch me out, you just tell me and I'll buy you a drink." And with that he was down the hall toward his office again and the endless stream of patients.

The odd thing was that Rob seldom did catch him out. Indeed, he only rarely saw Isaacs' patients at all. A great many people, he found, had a curious affection for the big white-haired doctor, a fierce sort of loyalty that Rob found difficult to account for. Many, at first, refused to see "the new doctor," preferring the longer wait to see Dr. Isaacs, so that Rob was assigned only the patients coming to the clinic for the first time. Only slowly, as his name became more familiar, did he really begin to receive the overflow of patients from the other two doctors, and to recognize the curious differences in the kinds of patients they examined. If Isaacs primarily saw the OB patients and the women with "female problems," Jerry DeForrest took on the elderly, the emotionally crippled and the chronically ill. Far from displaying the speed and abruptness of Martin Isaacs as he went about his work, Jerry DeForrest often took inordinate lengths of time with his patients, to no discernible purpose whatever.

DeForrest was constantly and chronically behind. He would arrive for morning hospital rounds just as Rob and Isaacs were finishing up and departing for the office; he would breeze into the office ten minutes late, take fifteen minutes to get settled down, and remain increasingly behind schedule for the rest of the day. As lunch hour approached, Terry at the front desk would frantically begin rescheduling his leftover morning patients for afternoon; the already overcrowded afternoon schedule would become packed, and Jerry would still be laboring to finish even after Rob himself had departed the office for evening rounds.

It did not follow, however, that DeForrest was any more thorough or painstaking than Isaacs—nor was he particularly helpful to Rob. His lengthiest attentions were reserved for a certain small coterie of patients of whom DeForrest seemed particularly fond. But when Rob referred a patient to Jerry for help with a difficult diagnosis, nothing much seemed to happen. Jerry would order a lab test or two, perhaps make a vague therapeutic suggestion or mention an offhand list of things "one might consider," and nothing more. Rarely did he come up with a new idea, even more rarely a firm recommendation for treatment. When Rob mentioned this to Isaacs one day, the big man just rolled his eyes back and waved his hand. "Don't ask me what's going through his mind," he said. "I quit sending patients to Jerry for consultation long ago. I don't send them to him at all unless I'm really up a tree, and then I just hand 'em over. He muddles through somehow, or the patient gets disgusted and goes somewhere else, or else the problem just goes away. Sometimes I think Jerry talks it to death."

"Doesn't he ever take a fresh look at a problem and come up with a good clean answer?"

"Well—sometimes."

"I guess I just haven't been here long enough to see it," Rob said sourly. "Most times he merely hits the same ground I've already covered and comes up with a big fat zero."

134

"I know."

"But Jesus, Martin, I can't have all *that* many answers. Jerry's had three times the training I've had in internal medicine. Yet it seems like I'm way ahead of him nine times out of ten."

"Maybe you're expecting too much," Isaacs said. "Jerry's just naturally lazy. He doesn't always dig as deep as he should, but he wears pretty well in the long run. I don't know what he does with all that time —he'll spend two solid hours in there with some old goat like Mike Rainey, the guy with the pig farm down the valley, and won't end up doing anything but adjusting his digitalis by a grain a week—but somehow his patients keep stewing along okay."

"That's great," Rob said, "but I still don't know what to do when I get a tough one on my hands."

"Well, if it's somebody you're really worried about, and Jerry doesn't help, send them in to see one of the boys in town. You may just have to work *around* Jerry sometimes."

It wasn't much of an answer, Rob thought, but what else could he do? For the most part, he settled down to being his own internist. But even that didn't help with the ever-increasing stack of unread x-rays and electrocardiogram tracings piling up in Jerry's office. Jerry was formally responsible for the official cardiogram readings, but the piles merely increased. Once a week Isaacs would kick and scream and tear his hair, and Jerry would reluctantly, dutifully, take a few home for an evening of work—but a week later the piles would be higher than before.

As a result, Rob began to read his own. Never skillful at analyzing cardiograms, he pulled his textbooks out of their cartons in the garage and spent long evenings reviewing them in order to read the tracings he needed to read for his patients. Alternatively, he would trap Jerry in his office or in the coffee room for a spur-of-the-moment consultation on a cardiogram he needed urgently before it got lost in the limbo of the "in" pile on Jerry's shelf. It didn't help reduce the backlog, but it gave Rob the readings he needed when he needed them—and at the same time he learned.

Chest x-rays were a different matter. With part of his training spent in a tuberculosis sanitarium in California, Jerry DeForrest was truly expert in interpreting the shadows and markings on chest films, and Rob hated to by-pass his readings. After some weeks of limping along with hasty curbstone consultations, Rob thought of a way to speed things up. One morning a week, he proposed, he and Jerry would make hospital rounds an hour early and come down to the office for an hour-long chest film conference before office hours began. DeForrest finally and reluctantly agreed, and the sessions began. They meant an extra hour of work every Tuesday morning, but they proved doubly fruitful: not only were the chest films read within a reasonable period after they were taken, but the sessions allowed Rob to polish his skill at reading and interpreting the films. Occasionally Isaacs would look in on the sessions, and then move on with a sly grin at Rob. "You must be some kind of a wizard," he told Rob on one occasion, "just getting him to sit down and *do* them. I've been trying for years and got nowhere."

Rob found himself seeing all kinds of patients during those hot summer weeks, but the vast majority fell into a single group: the children of the practice. Jerry DeForrest, it seemed, disliked pediatric cases only slightly less than Isaacs himself, and both referred children's cases to Rob with almost pathetic eagerness. It was only gradually, however, that Rob began to realize how truly neglected these small patients had been, and to what degree they had been shucked off by the other doctors with a minimum of stopgap, first-aid treatment.

To Rob, it was profoundly disturbing. Nowhere in the clinic could he find a well-ordered, comprehensive plan for new-baby care—or for the care of older children, either. True, a pile of mimeographed instruction sheets gathered dust in the back of the samples cabinet, but the information they offered could have been taken *in toto* from a baby food ad. Even worse, in reviewing children's charts, he found no consistent office policy for immunization shots, no growth and development records, no pattern for well-child care—virtually none of the things that were vital for the proper health care of children.

When he queried the nurses, they spread their hands helplessly. "We've done as well as we could," Agnes said defensively. "Of course, the doctors have always seen them for colds or sore throats or earaches, but as far as changing formulas or starting babies on solid food or scheduling baby shots is concerned, it's all just been dumped in our laps."

"Well, I think that's got to change," Rob said. "Not that you've done anything wrong—I think the two of you have done wonders, under the circumstances—but Jesus! We've got to have some kind of a program so you at least know what to tell the mothers when—and so these kids don't miss half their polio vaccine. We've got to make out a list, a complete care program for these kids from the time of delivery on. And you're going to have to help me set it up."

136

They went to work on it, with Agnes and Dora both eager to contribute. The three of them met in the office for two or three evenings of concentrated work, slowly hammering out a baby care program. Rob turned thumbs down on mimeographed instruction sheets. "It's got to be a booklet, something they'll keep and read and refer to," he said. "We'll get Twin Forks Printing to set type and print it, with stiff paper covers. We can call it 'Your Healthy Baby' or something like that, and give the mothers a booklet for each child. Maybe we can use the inside of the back cover for a permanent record of baby shots, and list the actual dates we want to see these babies for well-baby checks after the mothers take them home."

The nurses were delighted, each taking a crack at the manuscript as Rob worked it out, suggesting additional topics that needed to be covered. Martin Isaacs was not so delighted. "You think we're made of money?" he said as he looked over the manuscript. "Why not just run photocopies? Hell of a lot cheaper."

"Martin, you know what happens when you hand a mother a bunch of photocopy sheets. They go into the wastebasket the very next day. I want a neat little booklet, maybe with pink or blue cover stock, depending on the baby's sex. I'll bet we could get five hundred copies printed, half pink cover and half blue, for maybe a dollar and a half a copy."

"Good God! Well, I suppose we could charge them for their copies."

"*Charge* them! What for? Why not absorb the cost in their OB fee, for God's sake? It just isn't that much. What worries me is not the cost but the *care* they're missing. We shouldn't have five-year-old kids in this valley who have never completed a polio series, Martin. My *God!*"

"Well, you're right about that," Isaacs conceded. "So go ahead, if you can get them printed for a buck and a half a copy. Just be damned sure you *charge* for all this well-baby care you're promoting. You try to do it for free and we'll all go broke."

DeForrest dragged his feet, but finally went along. "If Martin thinks it's okay, it's okay with me, I guess," he said.

Rob moved fast then, before either of them changed his mind. His cost estimate was way off—the total job cost twelve hundred dollars for five hundred copies—but within ten days the job was done and a stack of "Your Healthy Baby" booklets took its place on the shelf in his examining room. Meanwhile Rob unearthed an old baby scale and pediatric examining table from the clinic basement and hauled them

137

back upstairs to a "baby corner" in the treatment room—and the new "baby doctor" was in business.

It went slowly at first. Mothers were suspicious of Rob's fancy new ideas about child health care, which were going to cost them money they'd never had to spend before. Presently, however, word got around that Dr. Tanner might have something to listen to. Mothers stopped to query Agnes or Dora on their way out of Isaacs' or DeForrest's office. The booklet proved surprisingly popular. One evening Rob was asked to address the local chapter of the Ladies of Sacred Heart, a group supporting the big Missoula hospital with the proceeds of rummage sales and bake-ins; he spoke for an hour on well-baby care and was kept talking past eleven o'clock with questions. "You don't *want* to wait till the baby's sick to do something," he told them. "That's the worst possible time to have to call the doctor." Expensive? Maybe, but not really. Think of the cost of a case of polio, with a child maybe crippled for life, or whooping cough, with the permanent lung damage it could cause. He talked, he exhorted, he pleaded, and some of them, a few of them, listened.

Determined, he sold his well-baby program to every mother who came into his office. Whenever he examined a child, he asked if there were other children in the family, and then and there pulled out their charts. A few, he found, were up to date on their immunizations, and had been seen by a doctor at least on reasonable occasions—but more often the charts would show only the sketchiest of notes, or no notes at all, infrequent physical checks, no lab work, spotty immunization records, failed follow-ups of illness. In such cases he would virtually beg the mothers to bring in *all* children for updating of immunizations, and for well-child exams, blood counts and urine checks at the same time. Some dragged their feet, but for many his enthusiasm was contagious and the appropriate appointments were made then and there.

And bit by bit the labor paid off. Fees were set that the mothers could live with. Isaacs grumbled that they were far too low, but Rob made them stick. Within weeks Rob was seeing mothers and children by the droves—not just those with newborn babies, but many who had not darkened the clinic door in years. Some became old, familiar faces around the office. Tommy Hart, whom Rob saw at weekly intervals at Dr. Feldman's request to check his pinned and casted forearm, proved long overdue for both polio and triple-vaccine immunizations—and Tommy had four younger brothers. It took effort to persuade Mrs. Hart to bring the others in for examinations and immunizations, but once she

138

agreed, she went whole hog, keeping careful records of the shots as they were given and setting up examination times for each of the children in turn.

The Harts were pleasant, rewarding patients: cheerful, uncomplicated people with bright eyes and mischievous schemes, possessed of an irrepressible vigor and zestiness despite their decidedly skimpy financial means. Tommy threatened continually to refracture his arm, and always needed repair work on the cast; Mollie Hart would listen good-humoredly while Rob scolded and cajoled the boy, threatening dire consequences if he damaged the healing arm inside. "You don't *need* to hit Billy on the head with your cast," he would plead. "You could just use a stick or something, couldn't you?" Tommy would swear that he didn't hit his younger brother very hard with it, and the mother would laugh and say, "If you've got some magic way to keep a thumb on that kid, Doctor, you'd better speak up. I never did know how." And Rob, in the end, would put plaster patch on top of plaster patch, convinced from the most recent x-rays that somehow, miraculously, the pins were holding and the bones healing in spite of everything.

The other Hart children presented few surprises as they came in for physical exams and vaccinations. They were not always immaculate; neither they nor their mother saw any virtue in combing their hair when it would just be mussed up again five minutes later, and if a brief immersion in a lukewarm tub didn't always get all the dirt off, there was just that much more for the next bath to work on. The children were forever promoting an extra sucker or balloon from the goodies box, offering to carry out the trash for a nickel a day or trying to sell Agnes futures on a dead mountain beaver for forty cents; there always clung to them the oddly pungent aroma of furnace oil from the smoky space heater in their ramshackle house in Tintown; but their bodies, if somewhat less than clean, were healthy and strong. There were few luxuries possible on George Hart's meager logger's salary, but there was always food on the table and there were outlets for the children's high spirits, and a mother who worried about them only when worry was necessary and largely simply enjoyed them as they were, slightly disheveled but perky.

Not all the children he saw were as happy and irrepressible as Mollie Hart's. One early patient was a distressing case in point. Jerri Harlow, mother of a newborn baby girl, was a thin, gray-looking woman with high cheekbones and a once-attractive face, now marred by lines of apathy and resignation. Matt Harlow worked with the logging crew up in the woods, in daily peril of his life scaling logs down the hills from wherever they were felled, murderous labor for little pay. It was well known in town that Matt found his way to the Wagon Wheel Tavern in Twin Forks with his weekly pay check every Friday night before he went home, and other nights too: a man of ugly temper in his cups, with a defeated wife who tried to make what money was left stretch as far as she could. The new baby girl was slightly premature, a small, dainty fairy creature clinging to life by the slenderest of threads; Rob took extra pains to explain his well-baby program to Jerri, urging her to bring in her other child, a five-year-old boy, to catch up on the immunizations that had lapsed two or three years before. He chalked up the woman's washed-out appearance to the fact that she had just delivered a baby, but when she returned a week later with five-year-old Bobby in tow, Rob saw a clearly discernible bruise on her cheek below her left eye.

Cautious, he said nothing, turning his full attention to the boy: a small, scraggly youngster in a ragged T-shirt and worn-out sneakers, with disorderly brown hair recently subjected to a heavy home trimming. At first he saw nothing, yet he sensed something odd—the child's apathy and resignation, the lackluster, downcast eyes with no gleam of vitality whatever. The boy responded to questions only with nods or shakes of his head. He didn't look to his mother for support, as a shy child might. He didn't look anywhere except down, as if waiting, numbly, for a blow to fall.

Rob frowned as he examined the boy. "Any problems here?" he asked the mother. "All the chart shows is a couple of colds."

"No, he ain't been sick."

"Good appetite?" He looked at the bony shoulders, the jutting shoulder blades.

"Good enough, I guess. He eats what I give him."

Rob nodded, certain that something was wrong, something obscure he was seeing but missing. He thought, suddenly, of a picture he had seen of a starving boy in the African famine belt, apathetic, dull, sickly. He examined ears and throat, listened to the boy's lungs and heart, thumping regularly but almost inaudibly. Rob frowned. "Now take a *deep* breath," he said.

Bobby Harlow did so, thrusting his bony rib cage out. Rob probed the chest wall with his fingers, feeling the little lumps of cartilage that joined each rib to the breastbone. "Now stand up and let me see your legs."

140

"Seems like he's getting awful bowlegged these days," Jerri Harlow said.

"So I see. For how long?"

"I don't know. Maybe a couple of months."

Rob sat the boy back on the table, examined his teeth and gums with the aid of a flashlight, probed his abdomen gently, squeezed his knobby knees and ankles. The room was hot, and somewhere a fly was buzzing loudly. There was a line of perspiration on the mother's forehead and dark splotches under the arms of her dress. Rob chewed his lip. "How much milk does this boy drink?"

"He don't drink milk. Always made him throw up."

"Then what *does* he drink?"

"Lot of Cokes. And he likes Kool-Aid."

"How much milk do *you* drink?"

She met his eyes for an instant, then looked away. "Not much. I have to get it for the baby, but milk's more than a dollar a gallon, Doc."

"Yes, I know." Rob sighed. "Look, we need some x-rays of this boy —one of his chest and one of his legs."

Jerri Harlow looked up, alarmed. "Is somethin' wrong?"

"I'm not sure. The x-rays may tell us." Rob buzzed for Dora, ordered the films he wanted, and left the mother waiting as he went back into his consulting room and closed the door. There were other patients to be seen, but Rob pulled a book from his shelf, pored over it for a few moments, then sat back in his chair, rubbing his eyelids with his fingers. A few moments later he was in the x-ray darkroom, holding the dripping films up to the view box. Jerry DeForrest came by and Rob called him in. "Tell me what you think of these," he said.

Jerry peered at the chest film. "Looks pretty clear to me," he said. "What's this other one? Lots of leg bones— Hey, hold it." He frowned, squinting at the knee and ankle joints, then at the chest film again. "I'll be damned," he said. "Where'd you find this kid?"

"Right in my office. What's wrong with him?"

"It's right there on the films," Jerry said. "Those joints are absolutely typical; so is the rib cartilage. But where'd you dig him up? I haven't seen a case like this in the valley for years."

"I've never seen one before anywhere," Rob said. "But I've sure got one here, big as life."

Back in the examining room Rob had Jerri Harlow feel the child's ribs with her fingers. "Feels like little bumps," she said.

141

"That's right. That's where the cartilage joins the ribs to the breast-bone, and it's swollen."

"That mean there's somethin' wrong with him?"

"I'm afraid so. This boy isn't getting enough vitamin D, either from his diet or from the sunlight. Doesn't he ever play outdoors?"

"Not much. The other kids torment him, he's so small. He watches TV a lot."

"Well, that's part of it. He's also not getting calcium and phosphorus, without any milk in his diet. Those lumps on the ribs are part of it, and those sore, swollen knees and ankles, and the bowlegs too. It's a vitamin-deficiency disease called rickets. If we don't treat him, he's going to get sicker and sicker and fall farther and farther behind until he's permanently crippled. Fortunately, there's a treatment that will cure it and keep it from coming back. It won't go away overnight, it's been developing for years now, but if we really go after it—"

He stopped, nonplused. As he talked the woman's eyes had filmed with tears; now they poured down her pale cheeks and she lowered her forehead to her hand, sobbing silently. "I done the best I could by him," she wept. "I don't know how I could have done better. I've tried to feed him right and dress him right, but what can I do when there's no money? And now he'll need medicine, and I don't know how I'm gonna pay for it. I keep tryin' but there's never enough, it's never any good. . . ."

"Look," Rob said, "I didn't mean it's your fault—"

"I *know* it ain't my fault," she flared. "It's that goddamned bastard of a husband of mine, that's who. He wants to get laid every night, you can bet on that, but he don't give a damn about nobody or nothin' the rest of the time."

"Okay; maybe we can't change that right now, but we *can* do something for the boy, and it won't have to cost you a lot. He's got to have vitamin D every day until his body starts building good bone again. We've got vitamin samples back in the box that you can have for free; they'll get you started. Look—here, wipe your face." He held out a box of tissues. "But he also needs milk. Forget what happened when he was a baby; get him to drink it now. Make cocoa, malted milk, Ovaltine, *anything.* Powdered milk is just as good as fresh and a whole lot cheaper. Maybe cheap enough for you to have some too."

As they talked about ways to reverse Bobby's vitamin deficiency within reach of a scanty budget, Jerri Harlow dried her tears and settled down. Rob spent additional time explaining why milk and vitamins

142

were vital for the new baby too; by the time the woman was ready to leave, she was in command of herself and convinced that she could somehow manage the problem with help and support from the doctor along the way.

When she was gone, Dora shook her head sadly. "Poor woman, stuck with that dreadful man," she said.

"Drinks up his pay check, huh?"

"It isn't just the booze," Dora said. "Matt Harlow is *nuts*. Came in here with a pistol one day, threatening to shoot Dr. Isaacs. Claimed he'd been playing around with Jerri. Dr. Isaacs, yet—can you imagine? Vern Bradley finally got over here and got the gun away from him, but we were all sweating blood before *that* was over."

Fortunately, the case of Bobby Harlow was unusual. Most of the children Rob saw were essentially healthy. A couple were asthma victims, which meant extra time spent learning their particular medical histories; three children he saw had had rheumatic fever and were taking prophylactic penicillin to prevent recurrences. One already had unmistakable evidence of damage to his heart valves from the illness, and required still more time for Rob to develop a long-range planning program. But more and more mothers were drawn just by the rumor that the new doctor liked to work with children, and most of these small patients were fun for Rob to see—until one day a real shocker came along.

It was a hot August afternoon when Dora interrupted in the midst of a physical exam. "Dr. Tanner, can you come for a minute?" Out in the corridor he found her standing, white-faced and trembling, with a chart clutched in her hand. "I think you'd better see this baby right away. She looks just awful."

Rob frowned, taking the chart. "Do I know her?"

"I don't think so. It's Janice Blanchard's baby. Dr. Isaacs delivered her about six months ago; it was a Caesarean, I think. She had the baby in for him to check about a month ago and it looked just fine, but now . . ." Dora took a deep breath and shook her head, almost tearful. Rob glanced at the chart, then followed the nurse down the corridor to the pediatric examining room. He walked through the door, about to speak, and then stopped short at the sight of the baby.

He had never in his life seen an infant so ghastly, so shockingly white. Its skin was whiter than the sheet on the table beneath it, relieved only by a grayish-blue cast around its eyes. Even from the door he could see the swollen abdomen, the eyes bulging as the baby fought

143

for air with little gasping, grunting movements.

Rob nodded to the mother as he undressed the baby. The child's skin was hot to his touch. "When did she get sick?" he asked the mother.

Janice Blanchard shook her head. "I don't know. The—the breathing trouble just started this morning. It's been getting worse just this last hour."

"And the pallor?"

"I can't be sure. Maybe a week or two, maybe only three or four days."

"You mean she was perfectly pink and good-looking when Dr. Isaacs saw her last month?"

"Perfectly fine; there wasn't a thing wrong."

He looked up at Dora. "Temperature?"

"It's 104 degrees, Doctor."

"Okay, we'd better sponge her off." Rob pulled down the baby's eyelid, saw a pale gray mucous membrane with only the faintest tinge of pink. He listened to the child's chest, heard the wet, sticky sounds over the lung fields, the galloping rhythm of the frantic heartbeat. Then he felt the abdomen, the enormously swollen liver and spleen. He looked at Dora and shook his head. "Let me sponge while you get Ginny to do a stat blood count and differential. Then get the oxygen bottle and that little mask I've seen around."

The mother was watching him with growing alarm. "Doctor, what's wrong?"

He shook his head. "I can tell you better when I see the blood count. The lungs are full of fluid, either from pneumonia or heart failure or both. The question is why. Here, help me sponge this fever down."

He gave the mother the sponge, kept her busy wiping the baby's skin while he fanned the air around the tiny body. The mother started another question, but he just shook his head and motioned her to continue with the sponging. Presently he said, "We're going to have to move this baby to a hospital in Missoula, and get a pediatrician's help. Do you know one?"

The mother shook her head.

"Okay; Dr. Isaacs often consults with a Dr. Bauermann there."

"Is she very sick?"

"I'm afraid so." Rob stepped aside as Dora brought the oxygen tank and mask up on a cart. Out in the corridor he met Ginny coming out of the lab with a report slip in her hand. "You're not going to like this, Doctor."

144

"Leukemia," he said. It wasn't even a question. "Lymphatic?"

She nodded. "There's nothing but lymphocytes, billions of them. And hardly any red cells at all. The blood looked like pink water."

"That's why they call it leukemia," Rob said. "White blood." He looked at the report slip, shook his head, and went in to the telephone on his desk. A moment later he had Dr. Bauermann on the phone. "No question about the diagnosis," Rob said after describing the baby's problem. "The total white count is 550,000 and the differential is 99 percent lymphocytes. Liver and spleen are both down below the navel. With this anemia, the breathing problem is almost certainly congestive heart failure, but there's a high fever too."

"Well, send the child in," Dr. Bauermann said. "Better make it by ambulance and have them continue the oxygen." He paused. "You can beg the question of what's going on, if you want to."

"I'd probably better tell the mother straight," Rob said. "But you can spell out the prognosis. I'll just tell her that it's bad."

"Okay, but don't say too much. Sometimes we can tease one of these along for four or five years if we start fast enough. The problem now is to get the child here alive. I'll keep you posted."

With Dora calling the ambulance, Rob told Janice Blanchard. "It's leukemia, and the sudden lack of red cells has put a terrific strain on the baby's heart. We'll use the ambulance so she can have oxygen on the way to town, and Dr. Bauermann will meet you at the Community Hospital emergency room."

The woman shook her head, stunned. "I don't see how it could move so fast."

"Sometimes it does, especially in these little ones. But sometimes things can be done. You go along behind the ambulance, now, and drive with care."

He went back to his earlier patient, heavy-hearted, and later wrote a lengthy note in the Blanchard baby's chart. Acute lymphatic leukemia, congestive heart failure, possible pneumonia . . . He stared at the words. Six months old, a healthy, happy baby; and then, in a single month, this. And despite what Bauermann said, Rob knew there would be little help for this child. A murderous disease had moved too far too fast for *anything* to stop it.

He wanted to alert Isaacs, but the older man was gone for the day and no one answered at home. Rob went through the motions of work for the rest of the afternoon, preoccupied, wishing the day would end. A little after six he finished his last patient, and headed for the hospital.

145

He was in the middle of rounds when Janice Pryor paged him for a phone call, and a moment later he heard Dr. Bauermann's voice on a bad connection, sounding hundreds of miles away. " . . . just too far ahead of us, unfortunately. We didn't even have time to crossmatch blood before the baby went out. Maybe a blessing in disguise; it's sometimes easier to see them go when they're tiny like this than when they're five or six years old. . . ." Rob listened, and thanked him, and then rang off. Later, as he drove down the hill for dinner, the man's words came back, and he shook his head. A blessing? Maybe; maybe not. As with so many other things recently, he suddenly realized that he simply didn't know. . . .

# 14

With the sun high in the sky, and Rob long since packed off to the hospital for morning rounds, and the breakfast dishes done and the bed made and the house straightened up, Ellie rechecked her shopping list —Al Davidson's lumberyard, the supermarket, the bank—and headed out to the old Chevy wagon a little before ten, more depressed than she'd felt at any time since she'd arrived in Twin Forks. Not just blue-moody today, not just feeling grumpy. Downright depressed, much as she hated to admit it.

Part of it, she knew, was the seemingly endless task of the house repair, day after dismal day of it, paradoxically wearing thinner and thinner the closer it came to completion. Part of it was Rob, so exceedingly gray the night before—a baby suddenly dead of leukemia before they could even get started treating it, sickening to death in just a few days as they sometimes did, those little ones; enough to make anyone feel gray. But part of it was something else altogether—something in the town itself that she'd found herself facing day after day as she made her shopping rounds, and knew she was going to face again this morning, just as always.

Al Davidson's lumberyard first. The little hunchbacked owner hobbled out from behind the counter to greet her. "Mornin', Mrs. Tanner. What's it going to be today?"

"Al, I need some one-by-four stripping of some sort, something I

147

can paint and use for valances over the drapes above the windows. You know what I mean?"

"Sure thing, Mrs. Tanner. I've got some nice, clear spruce back here ought to be just the ticket."

"Fine; I'll take some. And, Al—why not just make it 'Ellie,' huh?" She laughed. "After all, I'm spending about half my life in here."

Al Davidson laughed too. "By golly, Mrs. Tanner, that sure is just about right, isn't it? Not that I'm complainin', you understand. Never complain about too much business. Now, then, how much of this stripping do you think you're going to need?"

A bit later, then, on to the little supermarket. Always crowded at ten in the morning, housewives by the dozen getting their shopping done early so they could get back to the soap operas, gathering in little groups of twos and threes over their shopping carts, talking cheerily, checking out all the little things that had happened since they'd seen each other the day before. Millworkers' wives, shopkeepers' wives, schoolteachers' wives, bankers' and lawyers' wives. Most of them recognized her by now, and they'd smile at her, guardedly, and nod to her, and stop dead in their conversations until she had gone past them, searching the shelves for the things she needed

Back by the meat counter she found Mary Stanley, the mill manager's wife, chattering heatedly with Carmen Pollard, the overweight spouse of the bank manager, whom Ellie had met at the party. "Well, I just told *him,*" Mary was saying, "if *that* was the way he was going to finish a job, dripping hot solder all over my kitchen tile and then walking off and leaving it for me to clean up, we could just manage to find ourselves another plumber if we had to call one from Missoula—" At this point she saw Ellie and stopped abruptly, her mouth still open. There was the barest instant of hesitation; then both women smiled at her at once. "Why, Ellie Tanner," Carmen Pollard said. "It's *nice* to see you again."

"You too," Ellie said. "Isn't it a gorgeous day?"

"It certainly is," Mary Stanley said. "Of course, that's what we have this time of year. Sunny and hot."

"And dry," Carmen added. "Just bone dry. I only hope they don't have to shut down the woods. . . ." Her voice trailed off as Mary Stanley shot her a sharp glance.

"Yes. Well—I guess that wouldn't be so good," Ellie said into the awkward pause. When the women didn't respond, she glanced at the meat counter. "Anything good on special today?"

148

"Fryers for fifty-nine cents, if you can eat those scrawny little things we get from Arkansas," Mary said. "It's getting so you can't find a decent chicken anymore." She sniffed and glanced again at Carmen Pollard.

"Yes, it sometimes seems that way." Ellie worked up a smile. "Well, nice to see you both," she said, moving on with her cart. "Have a good day."

On then to the bank for an unimportant little chore she just hadn't got around to doing yet. The skinny girl in the teller's cage gave her a bored smile. "Morning, Mrs. Tanner."

"Hi," Ellie said. "I need to draw a little cash. And I'd like to open a small personal checking account. Just a hundred dollars or so. One of those little ten-cents-a-check economy accounts—you know?"

The girl blinked at her, puzzled. "But you've already got an account," she said.

"Yes, I know," Ellie said. "But that's our regular joint account, for paying bills and things. I'd like this one just in my name." She looked at the girl, who stood gazing at her. "Is there some problem?"

"Well, no, I don't suppose so. Just a minute." The girl disappeared from the cage and went back to poke through a small card file. A moment later she was around at the bank manager's desk, whispering in Joe Pollard's ear. The little weasel-faced man came up to the cage and showed Ellie his false teeth. "Can I help you, Mrs. Tanner?"

"Well, yes. I'd just like to open a small personal checking account, separate from our joint account, just for myself," Ellie said.

"I see." Pollard hesitated, looked down at his nails, then back up at her. "No problem with the joint account?"

"No, of course not. I just like to have a small convenience account in my own name. I've always had one. Like, if I wanted to buy Rob a small present sometime without him knowing what it cost . . ." She looked at the man, beginning to feel a little desperate. "Is there something strange about this?"

"Oh, heavens, no. Nothing *strange*." The man flashed his teeth again. "Just not too common a request around here, is all. But if that's what you want, we can sure set it right up. Now, we've even got a nice selection of decorative checks here you can choose from, some real nice Montana mountain scenes. . . ."

At dinner that night Ellie watched Rob plow into the pizza casserole. "Honey, what's wrong with me?" she said suddenly.

"What do you mean? You're not feeling good?"

149

"I don't mean my health. I mean *me.*" She thumped her chest with a finger.

He regarded her a moment, deadpan. "Well—a little heavy in the breast, maybe, if *that's* a problem," he said finally. "Hips a little too wide . . ."

"I don't mean that, either, you bum! I mean the way I seem to strike the people in this town. Every time I come near them, they back off. You'd think they were scared I was going to bite them. I try to reach out a little, and there's no response whatever. Just *nothing.*" She told him about her encounters with Mary Stanley and Joe Pollard. "Is there something wrong with the way I'm dressing? Or acting? Or talking? Or what?"

He shook his head and took a bite of pizza. "Ellie, these are plain, ordinary closed-up country people, and you're still an outsider. That's all that's wrong; nothing else. You're just impatient. Give 'em a couple of months."

"They've already *had* a couple of months, and it's still just as if I were a brand-new tourist coming through."

"Then give 'em another couple of months, I guess."

"But what can I *do?*"

"Just be yourself, and ignore it. Grin and bear it. *I* don't know." He scratched his head. "Maybe this is one you could check out with that old hen down the road. *She* must know how these people think by now."

It was no satisfaction, Ellie reflected, clearing the table and cleaning up the kitchen later. No satisfaction at all—but maybe he was right. Maybe she was crowding it, expecting too much too soon. Maybe she *should* ask Belle Foreman about it—but somehow she wasn't too sure that Belle was going to have any answers, either.

For Rob, despite the gradual acceptance of his well-baby program, all did not go smoothly in the practice those first summer months. If he had the capacity to win the hearts of the clinic nurses and many of the mothers, he also possessed an inordinate capacity to irritate people. If he was gentle and supportive with most of his patients, he was sometimes blunt, outspoken and imperative with others. John Florey was infuriated from the first, complaining far and wide that Rob acted as if no doctor in the valley had ever treated a child properly before. Some mothers in Florey's practice were also indignant, and didn't mind saying so. These things Rob passed off with a shrug; he didn't expect Florey

150

to be happy with him anyway, and frankly didn't care. But Roger Painter was a different matter.

As early as the second week Rob, still upset about the bleeding ulcer patient, confronted Roger in his hospital office one morning. "The more I think about it, the more I'm convinced that we have to do something about this blood situation," he said.

Roger leaned back in his chair, slender fingers tip to tip, and looked up at Rob through his rimless glasses. "There's nothing to be done," he said coldly. "We've already checked out everything."

"But there's got to be some way we can have blood here on standby," Rob said. "The Red Cross at Great Falls has a big bank, supplies dozens of small communities like this with stand-by blood."

"We can't have stand-by blood without a proper storage unit," Roger said, "and a proper storage unit would cost us five or six thousand dollars. To say nothing of the cost of a lab tech to do the crossmatches, an incubating oven, and the place to put them all. Nobody's got that kind of money here, and the directors aren't about to borrow it."

"So what do you do when somebody's bleeding to death on the operating table?"

"You put a clamp on and send them to Missoula. Or else you use freeze-dried plasma."

"Yeah, five units you've got here," Rob said bitterly, "and two of them outdated. I've looked. Oh, yes, there's a case of dextran around somewhere."

"None of the other doctors have been complaining," Roger said primly. "Now, can I help you with anything else?"

"Well, while we're at it, what about this anesthetist?"

"Sara Davis is all we've got, so she's all we've got."

"But she's a walking disaster," Rob said, feeling his temper slip. "Hell, this whole place is a disaster waiting for the right time to happen."

"If you're just going to insult me, Doctor, I have other things to do."

"Oh, hell, I don't mean to insult you," Rob said. "I'm just trying to *tell* you something. What about other emergency facilities? Maybe I'd better know what's here and what isn't."

"Like what facilities?"

"Well, power, for instance. With this little co-op electric company we have out here, the power must go out with every storm. What do we do in the middle of surgery when the lights go out?"

"We've got a full emergency system, battery-powered, cuts in the

151

instant the power goes out," Roger said.

"Sounds great. Can you show me?"

"*Show* you?"

"Well, yes. Just in case I'm the one who has to go throw a switch someday. Okay?"

"If you insist." Quivering with indignation, Roger led him down the ramp to a small cinder-block room in the basement. "The batteries are there on constant trickle charge, the automatic switches there, the manual controls there. We test the whole system every month."

"Fine, let's test it now. Cut the power."

"Damn it, man, there are suction machines going up there, a delivery in progress. Oh, hell, if you've *got* to see . . ." Roger threw the main power switch. The room blacked out for an instant before the lights flickered and went back on with the emergency power. A moment later an overload switch popped and the room fell dark and stayed dark.

Roger cursed. It was silent for a long moment. Then Rob said, "Uh —maybe you'd better turn the power back on."

"I don't understand it," Roger snarled. "It was tested just last week. Something must have shorted out." He threw the main switch, restoring the power, then flipped an intercom switch. "Raymond! *Get down here.* God damn it, where's Raymond?"

"Raymond's probably out to lunch," Rob said.

"Oh, be quiet. I'm telling you, it's always worked before."

"I see," Rob said. "So what about other things? Have you got a shock box in the place?"

"Of course we've got a shock box. It's in the Emergency Room cabinet."

"What about a resuscitator?"

"We've got a Byrd valve up in the OR."

"Positive pressure?"

"Of course it's positive pressure."

"But the last I heard, it was jammed or something."

"Well, it's fixed now, so you can quit worrying. Now if you don't mind, I've got work to do."

Rob watched as Roger flounced angrily up the ramp in search of Raymond. An hour later, down in the clinic, Isaacs collared him. "Rob, you've got to lay off Roger."

"Why? He's the one who's supposed to make things happen, isn't he?"

"Yes, but harassing him isn't going to help."

"Well, *somebody's* got to harass him," Rob said, "and if nobody else will, I guess it's up to me. I think we need stand-by blood storage up there, one way or another, and I'm going out to get it."

Isaacs laughed. "If you insist on pounding your head on the wall, go right ahead. But humiliating Roger isn't going to win you any friends, I'm afraid."

He was right, Rob realized in a calmer moment. "I guess it really wasn't very smart," he conceded to Ellie that night. "Make a man feel like a damned fool and he's going to hate you forever."

"Maybe so," she said, "but for something as reasonable as this, you'd think he'd listen."

"I'm not so sure he's a reasonable man," Rob said, "and Isaacs is sure offering no help. But maybe I'd better cool it." He even half apologized to the hospital manager next day, although it came out sounding more like justification than apology, and—for the moment— he laid off Roger Painter. For one thing, he wasn't really quite sure which way to move at that point. For another, he found he had his hands full irritating his own office colleagues in quite a different area.

Despite his preoccupation with child care in those early weeks, Rob found himself seeing a wide selection of other patients too, some old and familiar to the practice, many more brand new, with problems ranging from the profound to the ridiculous. And the more such people he saw, the more he found himself doggedly insisting, one way or another, on doing a thorough and painstaking diagnostic workup on every new patient that came through his door.

Isaacs and DeForrest didn't exactly *object* to the policy, at least in principle. They admitted it was probably good, sound medical practice. They simply didn't think it would work. "People just aren't going to stand still for it," Isaacs protested. "Somebody comes in here about an earache, and you want to run a liver profile on him!"

"He may need the liver profile a whole lot more than he needs ear drops," Rob said.

"He also may not," Isaacs said. "As far as he's concerned, you're just trying to sell him the clinic."

"Then I have to make him understand why he needs it," Rob said.

"People don't want to hear that sort of thing," Isaacs said. "When you spend a whole hour doing a physical exam, you've got to charge them at least forty bucks for your time alone. A chest film and a cardiogram is another forty. Blood and urine work pile another ten or twenty on top of that. And where are you going to quit? You going to take IVPs?

153

Gall bladder series? Spine x-rays? GI series? First thing you know, you've run this guy's bill up to three hundred dollars, and all he came in for was an earache."

"Well, that's one side of it," Rob said. "But Jesus, Martin, you've got patients coming in here three or four times a year who haven't had a good thorough physical exam in fifteen years—and then they drop dead because nobody's ever taken a cardiogram on them."

Isaacs raised his hands in defeat. "Look, *I* don't care; do it any way you want. Just one thing: you make damned sure you charge for all this extra work, and make sure Bev can collect the money. That's all I ask. I don't think people are going to buy it for sour apples, but go ahead. Try it and see."

Rob tried it. Day after day he talked physical exam to his patients. Many seemed far less entranced with the idea than Rob was—but those who consented seemed oddly pleased by this new young doctor and the intense approach he took to caring for his patients. And as more and more patients began passing under Rob's intensive scrutiny, he began turning up health problems no one had suspected were there—and Martin Isaacs sat up and took notice.

The two bank men Rob had treated from the auto accident in early July were cases in point. After they recovered enough to return home to Missoula, both Fred Mallory and Jim Tice elected to return to Rob in Twin Forks for their weekly follow-up visits. What was more, both elected to have exhaustive physical checkups as part of their treatment. The results were interesting. Mallory came up with a clean bill of health except for a high cholesterol level, a condition he faithfully undertook to treat under Rob's guidance. Tice, however, was found to have early but unmistakable glaucoma in both eyes, and Rob insisted on referring him to an eye specialist in Missoula. This was precisely the sort of health threat that a thorough examination was intended to turn up—a problem that could easily have cost the man his eyesight if someone had not caught it early. Tice saw the specialist, but still came back to Rob for follow-up, and Isaacs was increasingly nonplused to see these two men spurning the excellent medical facilities in the city to place their health care in the hands of an obscure young general practitioner in an obscure country town seventy miles away. "Damned if I ever saw anything like it," Isaacs muttered one day, shaking his head. "What's more, they even pay their bills. . . ."

The case of Peter Brennan proved even more arresting. The pudgy young furniture salesman, upset about his insurance examination, came

154

in for a thorough, painstaking check-out just as Rob had urged him to. After taking a detailed and totally unilluminating medical history, Rob invited the man into his examining room and checked his blood pressure first of all. He looked at the reading, checked it again, then checked it a third time with a different pressure cuff. "Now, that's damned strange," he said finally.

"You mean it's still way up there?" Brennan asked.

"It's not up at all," Rob said. "That's what's strange about it: a hundred and ten over seventy. Mine should be so low." He looked at Brennan. "You haven't been taking some kind of medicine, have you?"

"Just a little aspirin for my headaches, Doc."

Step by step Rob went on with the exam—completely normal from head to toe. Then he checked his blood pressure again, scowling at the pudgy little man. It was still 110/70.

Something stank.

"Just a little aspirin for your headaches," Rob said at last. "So you do have headaches."

"I sure do," Brennan said. "Real bastards, too. They come on just like *that.*" He snapped his fingers. "They even wake me up at night. Like my head's exploding."

"How often do these happen?"

"Maybe three or four times a day."

"A *day!*" A bell rang somewhere in Rob's mind. "Peter—stand over there on the floor and touch your toes."

"I'm pretty fat for that, Doc."

"That's all right; try it anyway."

The little man waddled over, bare naked, and started to bend, missed the floor by a foot. Rob urged him on to a second and third attempt. "Doc, this is giving me a headache."

"Okay, up on the table, quick," Rob said. "Lie flat." Before he was even down, Rob had a pressure cuff on his arm, squeezing the rubber bulb. The pressure was 170/120. Rob, perspiring more than the patient, sat back on a kick stool, his heart thumping. "Peter, I want you to go into town to see our surgeon, Dr. Sonders. He's going to put you in the hospital, run some tests on you. You've got something funny going on, and I think I know what it is. If I'm right, Dr. Sonders can maybe cure this blood pressure, once and for all."

He had Bev make an appointment for next day through Sonders' office nurse in Missoula. Later, on the phone, he told Sonders his findings. "You'll need to get IVPs there," Rob said, "and he needs some careful, controlled observation, a Regitine test, probably renal arteriograms—can you handle it?"

"Well, sure," Sonders said. "But Jesus, Rob. You've really got nothing to go on but a funny story—"

"And a very funny blood pressure," Rob said.

"Well—maybe. Sure, send him in. But meanwhile you'd better check those pressure cuffs for leaks."

Two days later Sonders was on the phone again. "Say, boy, you really nailed it," he said. "Pheochromocytoma on the left, big as a goddamned grapefruit, according to these arteriograms. I'm doing him tomorrow morning at Sacred Heart. You want to call his wife and tell her?"

Rob got Mrs. Brennan on the phone, told her about Peter's problem, reassured her. "It's a tumor of the adrenal gland, a big one, and it has to come out. . . . A cancer? No, it's not malignant. It just makes a whole lot of extra adrenaline and squirts it out into his bloodstream from time to time, and that pushes his blood pressure up and gives him these headaches. Dr. Sonders will take it out tomorrow, and that will be that. No more trouble, no more high blood pressure. It's one of the few kinds of high blood pressure we can really *cure.*"

Ed Butler's exam was less dramatic but—at least to Rob—even more rewarding. Ed, his bushy eyebrows quivering, was skeptical about the whole thing. "Never felt better in my life," he grumbled as Dora drew blood samples. "Just because I got a piece of steel in my arm, for God sake . . ."

It was his wife, Emma—small, gray-haired, motherly—who was Rob's champion. "Don't you listen to him, Doctor," she said. "When it comes to taking care of himself, that man hasn't got a brain in his head. All he ever thinks about is fishing. You check him over good."

Rob did, and found nothing alarming. Ed Butler, who had spent twenty-five years working in the mill, seemed as healthy and hearty as a young steer. And late one Thursday afternoon, going over his exam results, Rob told him so.

"Hell, I could have told *you* that, Doc," Ed said. "I've always lived clean, never drank too much, never smoked too much, never went whoring around. Not that I mind bein' checked, you understand. Emma, she's always peckin' away at me to go get looked at, and I figure you done a good job of lookin'."

Rob shrugged his shoulders. "The only worrisome thing I can find is a little weakness down in your right inguinal ring."

156

"Now, what in hell is *that*, Doc?"

"Down in the groin, where men tend to get ruptures. No, you haven't got one; we just ought to check it once every six months to be sure that you don't, is all."

"I gave up heavy lifting a long time ago, Doc."

"That's probably why you haven't ruptured. Just keep it that way. Otherwise your exam is clean as can be, and that's the best news I could give you."

"Well, I appreciate that." The old logger looked up at him. "Say, Doc, you off tomorrow?"

"That's right."

"Let me take you fishin'."

"Oh, boy. I'd love to. But my wife. . . . fixing that place of ours up . . ."

"Tell her to go to hell, Doc. You need to relax a little. I'll swing by for you at five."

Ellie wasn't happy about it, but she didn't really object. "I suppose you need to unwind. Does this Ed Butler—well—fish all day?"

"Probably. But I don't have to stay out all day. He can bring me home."

At five next morning Ed was there, in an old Ford pickup with four-wheel drive. They drove south on the highway, starting back up the pass. Presently Ed turned off on an unmarked country road heading into the mountains. In a mile or so the road became a narrow jeep trail, heading steeply up toward a gap. On the other side a fantastically beautiful blue-green lake appeared with a single shack on its shore. "Lake Marian," Ed said, pulling up to the shack. "Had this place for years, Doc. Emma don't hardly come out here anymore, her arthritis gets her, so I've got it all to myself."

It was a lovely place: snug, rustic, clean, with elk horns over the door and a huge granite fireplace inside. In a shed to the side was a huge pile of firewood, neatly split and stacked. Ed dragged a boat out of the shed, together with a pair of oars and an antiquated two-horsepower air-cooled outboard motor. "Can't use it for water-skiing," he said, "but you can muddle around the lake with it." Rob shoved them off, and they drifted along the shore. "That gray hackle I gave you will work fine here," Ed said, "but I make a little coachman that works even better, if you're going to fish dry. Wings are a little duller, the body a little brighter red—here, try this one."

They fished, with Ed sculling them down along the shoreline. On

157

the third cast Rob had a lovely rainbow on for a while, lost him, then snagged another. Ed fished a wet fly, retrieving it just beneath the surface, and after he brought in three rainbows and a Dolly Varden trout in rapid succession, Rob could even see the fish swirl under the surface as they struck. Then a sixteen-inch golden trout rolled belly-up through the water to take his dry fly and Rob paid attention to his own line, working ten minutes getting the fish quiet enough to boat. As the sun rose higher, Ed fired up the motor and they crossed the lake to a shaded ledge near the far side. He dug a six-pack of beer out of his old knapsack and tossed one to Rob. For an hour they fished in silence. Then Rob dug out another beer. "Tell me something," he said.

"Will if I know the answer."

"You've been around here a long time, Ed. What do you have to do to get something done in this town?"

Ed gave him a long look from under his bushy eyebrows. "Depends on what you want to get done," he said. "Now, if you want to get a piece of land rezoned, something like that, first thing you do is buy the mayor and each of the town councilmen a bottle of good whiskey, except for Al Davidson—he prefers gin. Then you get your head together with Selma Sharf, the town clerk, and—"

"That's not quite what I had in mind," Rob interrupted. "I'm talking about something that would benefit the health care of the whole town—like a blood bank storage unit up at the hospital."

"Ah. Something that would cost a lot of money, I suppose."

"Maybe five thousand dollars," Rob said.

"Well, if it's going to cost money, you don't want to take it up with Roger Painter."

"I've already got that message, right from the horse's mouth."

Ed looked at him. "I see. What you're after is somebody who can get people stirred up, eh?"

"Now you're right on target."

"Well, *hell.*" Ed looked thoughtful. "You need somebody like Dottie Hazard. You know her?"

"No."

"You've seen her around. Cute little black-haired Irish gal, blue eyes—she's Tim O'Hagen's daughter. Married to Joe Hazard, couple of kids, pregnant as hell right now. Doc Isaacs is taking care of her, I think. Thing is, she's into everything—town planning commission, head of the library board, president of the League of Women Voters. When she decides she wants something, she'll stand this town on its ass until she gets it."

"That's my gal," Rob said. "Hey! That was a nice one I missed."

"Better pay attention to what's important, Doc. These fish ain't gonna wait for you all day."

An hour later they had both limited, and Ed set the little motor putt-putting them back toward the cabin. When they beached he was out of the boat, hauling it up toward the shed, before Rob could help. "Now, that's what you've got to quit doing," Rob told him. "For God sake, Ed, get yourself a winch to do the work."

"Yeah, you're right, I should get a winch." The older man looked around. "You like it here?"

"It's great," Rob said.

"Thought you'd like it. Well, I always keep an extra key up on the right side of the woodshed wall here. You feel like coming out here once in a while, you just come along, don't bother to ask. Be my guest. I'm not up here much anymore, and there's nobody else ever uses the place. You ever want to get away from people, get yourself together, just come along. Or when things get too hot for you down in town. Anytime."

"Thanks, Ed," Rob said. "I appreciate that—and I'll do it too."

It was a thoughtful offer, even though it seemed unlikely to Rob that he would ever take it up. There were certainly times, as the weeks passed, that he wished he could just bag things for a few hours and get away from problems, from calls, even from Ellie—but the opportunities were diminishingly few. The more he pressed complete exams on his patients, the more the pressure on his time increased, both during office hours and beyond. Even the time he was supposed to be off was interrupted incessantly with calls, follow-ups or special appointments; if Rob's "Friday off" was the only day he could get a patient to come in for a physical exam, he would schedule the patient for Friday morning and come into the office to do the job, ignoring Ellie's increasingly restive protests.

It was not that the others didn't help with the load, to a point. Cases like that of Peter Brennan quite clearly shook Isaacs up. He was even more shaken when Rob discovered a case of dangerously active diabetes in George Crenshaw, the local high school principal, who had come in to have Rob suture a finger he had nicked in a buzz saw. Isaacs grumbled a lot, claimed he just wasn't cut out to sit down and do a two- or three-hour medical school workup on people anymore, muttered

159

that some of the people would drive him right up the wall if he had to sit and listen to them all afternoon, claimed he had to keep moving, had to see them and get them out of there—yet when he put the idea to some of his older patients, he found they accepted the concept, some almost eagerly, and was thoroughly disconcerted at the unexpected findings he turned up. In the course of one particularly productive week he found a suspicious thyroid nodule in one patient, a long-neglected hernia in another and positive Pap smears in two ex-OB patients who had not had thorough examinations in years, and he went down the corridors of the clinic shaking his white head and muttering to himself.

Even Jerry DeForrest began, rather reluctantly, to tighten up his procedures with the patients he was seeing. But inevitably much of the additional work fell to Rob. More and more often he found himself making hospital rounds an hour early in the morning in order to catch up on the previous day's left-over charting at the office before the new rush of patients began; more and more often his lunch hour was engulfed by patients, and more and more he was the last one to leave the clinic in the evening, later even than the ever-lagging Jerry DeForrest.

"I just can't work as fast as the others," he said to Ellie one evening over the third warmed-over dinner in a week. "I don't dare start cutting corners—I'll start missing things—and of course I'm getting the extra load because I've been asking for it. I'm the one that wants to do things the others haven't been doing, so they're giving me my chance."

"I suppose so," Ellie said. "But good Lord, Rob! There's got to be a limit somewhere. You're on that phone or up at that hospital constantly, whether you're on call or not, and the little I do see of you, you're so worn out you can hardly keep your eyes open."

Rob speared another pork chop. "Come on, now. You're beginning to sound like your mother."

Ellie banged her fork down. "Now you listen, buddy. My mother spent twenty-five years of her life married to a man who wouldn't give her the time of day because of his medical practice and she was sucker enough to buy it. The practice always came first, no matter what, and she limped along for years playing the sweet little helpmeet and martyr. She complained enough to *me* about it, but she never once complained to *him,* and the only time in twenty-five years that she got a real good long look at him was when he was in his coffin. Well, that was *her* bed of nails, she let it happen, but that's not the bargain *I* made for the long term, and I'm not going to let it happen to me. I married a man

160

to be my husband, sooner or later, and it's getting later now, and I am jolly well going to start seeing him once in a while now or I'm going to find out why not."

Rob spread his hands. "Honey, it's not going to *stay* this way forever. I know you're hurting for help on the house—"

"That's not really the problem."

"Okay, then that's not the problem. The problem is that I'm taking a different approach to the practice here than the others have taken, a better approach, and we've just got to hang on until I can get the bugs out of it."

"Were things really all that bad before?"

"I don't know. Maybe not. No worse than a lot of other small-town general practices around the country, I guess. But they've been getting sloppy. They've been working themselves to death just to keep up with the people walking in the door, and they've been *missing* things. And when you're the only medicine there is in a place like this, you just *can't* be missing things, and *know* you're missing things, and still live with yourself."

"But, Rob, you're not going to get men like Isaacs and DeForrest and Sonders to change their ways at this stage of the game."

"I can sure as hell try."

Ellie sighed and poured coffee. "Then to top it off, there's all these meetings all of a sudden."

"You mean the Blood Bank Committee?"

"Yes. Who's this Dottie Hazard that keeps calling you all the time?"

"She's the town activist. Knows everybody in town, talks constantly, belongs to every organization there is. She's picked up this blood bank ball and she's running with it. She's set up a steering committee, started negotiations with the Red Cross people in Great Falls, started dickering with Greyhound about bus delivery of blood, and she's lining up groups for me to go speak to. She's a real bulldog, with deep roots in this town; her old man was one of Twin Forks' first mayors. If anybody can get a groundswell going, she can."

"And what does Martin think about all this?"

"He's sore because she's due to go into labor in the next few weeks and he's afraid she's going to precipitate on a downtown street corner. Doesn't seem to hold *her* down any, though."

"Well, she sure has *you* running," Ellie said wearily. "Two evening meetings last week, two more this week . . ."

"I know."

161

"But *why?*"

"Because I'm going to get a blood bank going in this damned town if it kills me," Rob said.

"But why does it have to be your private fight?"

"Because nobody else will do it. Roger Painter won't even talk about it. Martin just laughs. Jerry doesn't have an opinion, and if he did he'd never back it up, and Sonders couldn't care less. So that leaves me."

"But how are you going to shove something through if you can't get support?"

"I'll get support, don't worry. You just watch."

"I'll watch," Ellie said quietly, "but you'd better watch too. Because I meant what I said."

One final problem had begun to surface during those weeks as late summer merged into early fall—in some respects the most disturbing problem of all. After his first three weeks or so in the practice, Rob found it increasingly difficult to reach Harry Sonders during night and weekend call.

At first he thought it was just poor communication. Sonders' office hours in Missoula ended at five, and like many city surgeons, he had both his home and office phones connected to an after-hours answering service. Of course, he had a second, unlisted home phone for personal use, and Rob was given the number, but he soon found that Karen Sonders or the housekeeper always answered, and Harry was practically never there. But going through the answering service was equally aggravating. Sonders carried an electronic beeper to notify him of incoming calls, but more often than not he either ignored the signal completely, or merely picked up the caller's number from the service and then neglected to call back until hours later.

It was not that there were so many crash emergencies that demanded Sonders' immediate, personal attention in Twin Forks. Often Rob merely wanted a brief telephone consultation when some problem on his hands happened to have surgical overtones. In other cases he had specific diagnostic questions he wanted to ask, or felt Sonders ought to have early warning of a potential surgical problem. But half the time Rob found he couldn't get hold of Sonders at all, and the rest of the time he had to spend hours nailed down beside a telephone waiting for a return call that might be half the night coming.

At first Sonders blamed his answering service. "Those girls are a bunch of idiots," he would say. "Never *can* get a message straight. If you

162

have trouble, just hang up and call back in a half hour. They'll get me sooner or later." But soon it became clear that the answering service operators were not idiots, and that they really were trying their best to transmit his calls to Sonders. The surgeon was simply not responding.

On most occasions it was merely irritating to Rob. One hot Monday evening in August he was called to see an eight-year-old girl who had broken her finger in a softball game, a nasty multiple fracture. Checking the x-rays, he was undecided whether to go ahead and set the bone and cast it, or merely immobilize it until Sonders could handle it next day, so he put in a call for the surgeon about eight-fifteen. At 9 P.M. he called the service again. Yes, they'd reached Dr. Sonders. Yes, he'd said he would return the call—but they would try to reach him again. A third call thirty minutes later brought the same answer.

At that point Rob gave up in disgust, went ahead and set the broken finger with a local finger block for anesthesia, and held the reduction in place with a curved finger splint embedded in a cast. He had sent the child home long since and was buried in other hospital work when Miss Pryor interrupted him at eleven to take a call from Dr. Sonders.

"Yeah, what's the problem?" Sonders asked.

"Well, the main problem right now is that it's eleven o'clock and I've been trying to get you since eight," Rob said angrily.

"Oh, for Christ's sake, Rob. I've been busy."

"Yeah, well, so have I," Rob snapped. He told Sonders the problem and what he had finally done.

"So it sounds fine," Sonders said. "What's the big deal? If I don't like the looks of the films tomorrow, I'll just take the cast off and pin the damned thing."

"I know—but a simple phone call could have saved me a lot of sweating," Rob said.

"Ah, you let things bug you too much. You're calling me about some damned thing or another every other night you're on call. Relax. You're doing fine."

A week later the same sort of thing happened, except that the patient was an accident case with a question of internal abdominal bleeding, and Sonders didn't return his call for over six hours. Rob sweated it out, watching the man desperately for some conclusive evidence that he really was bleeding internally, or—preferably, of course—that he wasn't. Rob became so tense he finally phoned Isaacs to come take a look—only to find that Isaacs had gone to an obstetrical meeting in Missoula and wouldn't be back until after midnight. Then, when things had just about reached the breaking point and Rob was ready to pack the man into the ambulance and send him to town to see a surgeon, any surgeon at all, the patient had an enormous bowel movement, and all traces of his abdominal pain vanished. Chagrined at his own near-panic state, Rob exploded when a call from Sonders came through an hour later, with the patient happily snoring in the back corner of the men's ward. "I just don't get this, Harry. When I call you for help I need help *now*, not sometime in the dim, distant future. This old foot-dragging crap is getting to be a habit—"

"Yeah, but now you tell me the guy dropped a fecolith on the floor and cured himself," Sonders said.

"In this particular case, yes."

"Well, if it isn't one thing, it's another," Sonders said. "Jesus, Rob, I can't sit around and hold your hand every time somebody around there gets a gut ache."

"I'm not talking about every time; I'm talking about the few select times when I want contact with a surgeon. I don't care if I'm way out in left field about the diagnosis. If I need contact with a surgeon, I need contact with a surgeon."

"Oh, crap," Sonders said, and hung up.

Since Rob by then was as disgusted with himself as he was with Sonders, he let the matter drop and didn't even mention the incident the next time he saw the man. But then a week later a mean one came along. A young millhand, fiddling with a power lawn mower blade, got his hand caught and mangled. It was a nasty mess and a challenge for any surgeon; one finger dangled by a strip of skin and muscle, several tendons were cut and the multiple wounds were filled with ground-in leaves, grass and gravel. Sonders had left the clinic only an hour before the victim was brought in to the hospital, and as soon as Rob got the bleeding under control and an IV going, he was on the phone, leaving urgent messages for Sonders to call as soon as he made contact.

As he waited for the return call, he and Happy Cumley set about debriding the dirty wound as best they could with a minimum of local anesthesia, and Rob grew more tense by the minute. He was no expert on hand injuries, but he knew that time was of the essence in the successful restoration of a half-severed finger. He also knew that infection was the deadly enemy of tendon repair, and that every passing minute reduced the chances of a good final result. After waiting an hour he went back to the phone, tried Sonders' answering service again. Yes, Dr. Sonders had checked in forty-five minutes ago. Yes, he got the

164

message and said he'd call right back. Slowly Rob set the receiver down, stared at the wall clock in cold fury, watched the sweep-second hand move around and around. He sat there for twenty long minutes, tapping his fingers on the desk, watching the clock. Then he pulled out the Missoula phone book, found the number for Jack Evers, a plastic surgeon Isaacs had once spoken of, and placed a call. Three minutes later he had Dr. Evers on the line and Rob was describing the problem. "The man is stabilized here, but I can put him in the ambulance and shoot him in there fast, if that's what you want."

"Yes, you'd better do that," Evers said. "Sounds like an all-night job, and the anesthesia could be tricky. Tell them to take him to the Municipal Hospital Emergency Room. I'll be waiting there to catch him."

Ten minutes later Rob watched the ambulance drive down the hill with the patient. It had just disappeared from view when Sonders' return call came through. "What's the trouble now?"

"No trouble," Rob said tightly. "I just had a man here with a mangled hand, was all. Power mower."

"Oh, good Christ. That's all I need now, farting around all night sewing up tendons," Sonders complained.

"Well, you won't have to. I just shipped him in to Jack Evers."

"You *what?*"

"I sent him to another surgeon, that's what."

"Oh, good Christ." There was a long pause. "Why couldn't you just sit on him for a while?"

"Because he had a dirty wound and he needed attention, that's why. Now if you don't mind, I'm busy. Enjoy your evening."

Rob was still stewing an hour later, sitting in the hospital coffee room writing up his note on the patient, when Isaacs came in. "Say, what the hell is going on up here? Sonders just called me and damned near burned my ears off. Says you just handed Jack Evers a thousand-dollar fee."

"Well, if I did, there wasn't any other choice," Rob said. "I've just about had it trying to get hold of Harry Sonders when I need him. You can't get him direct, and he won't return calls till Christ knows when."

Rob told him about the girl with the broken finger and a couple of other incidents still fresh on his mind. "He's just ducking me, that's the truth of the matter."

Isaacs' face had darkened as he listened. "Well, I wish I could say it was a fluke," he said finally, "but it's not. He's been pulling the same

165

thing on me, and I don't like it any more than you do. He's getting paid a full partner's share of the income from this practice for half-time work, and lately he's not even giving us an honest half-time job."

"Well, maybe you can get through to him somehow," Rob said wearily. "I can't even seem to make a dent."

Isaacs stood up, then paused at the door and looked down at Rob. "I'll get through to him, all right," he said heavily. "One way or another." He left then, and Rob finished his note. It was not until hours later that the ominous undercurrent in Isaacs' voice really struck him.

# 15

For Ellie Tanner the summer days were long and increasingly lonely as she saw her husband vanishing into the vortex of a frantically busy practice. At first, of course, the remodeling work sustained her, solitary as it was, with long hours of physical work to leave her exhausted at night, and the satisfaction of seeing a tacky little broken-down river cabin gradually transformed at her hands into a snug and attractive home. But presently the hard work was completed, with only the lighter tasks of painting, varnishing and finishing left to be done, and time began to weigh on her hands.

Rob was aware of her problem, and made sympathetic noises, but he was really no help at all—up and out by seven every morning, rarely back before eight in the evening, interrupted incessantly by phone calls when he did get home, constantly and increasingly absorbed with his patients and the practice problems. After the first week or so he never got home for lunch, with little more than five minutes between patients to gulp a sandwich and run; evening hospital calls that promised to be "brief" kept him buried for hours; even the Fridays he was supposedly off became peppered with calls, which he unfailingly answered himself, and during his off weekends, even when the phone let him be, he was too exhausted for anything but sleeping, or sitting torpidly leafing through the week's collection of journals.

At first Ellie had told herself it had to be that way—he *had* to get into the practice, *had* to make himself available, *had* to run at Isaacs' bidding. But as days and weeks wore by and Ellie saw his little free time steadily diminishing, she found her patience flagging as a solid, almost frightening backlog of resentment began to build. *If only he'd try to set some limits,* she told herself again and again; *if only he'd pass one call on to Isaacs just once when he was supposed to be off*—but no such pattern appeared.

Perhaps hardest of all, she found she couldn't force herself to complain too much. She knew the rules for doctors' wives all too well: shut up, adapt, concede that the practice comes first. She knew all the trite clichés—*He's got enough on his mind without having to worry about you too . . . The patient always has priority . . . A doctor's time is never his own . . . Your job is to have things ready when he can get home*—and she hated every one of them; but the few times she did explode, like the evening he compared her to her mother, she spent the rest of the night feeling guilty, blaming herself rightly or wrongly for bitching to him about something he was helpless to change, determining to just shut up and sweat it out, whatever it might mean, even when she hated *that* decision as much as she hated the role of martyr her own mother had so untiringly played.

She sought to get out and *do* things, but found that there were limits. She was welcome enough at the Ladies of Sacred Heart Hospital guild meetings, but the welcome was more coolly correct than generous; she came away with the sense that her presence had tied knots in tongues and dampened what might otherwise have been a delightfully juicy gossip session. She heard that there was going to be a local Boy Scout jamboree at a camp up on Lake Vivian, and with her nursing background she sought out the local scoutmaster and offered her services as a volunteer camp nurse—but was told, politely but firmly, that arrangements had been made for that two years before. People were civil enough to her on the street or in the supermarket, but none came eagerly forward to greet her; she continued to feel more like some sort of exotic specimen, being regarded with a certain cautious bemusement, than a new housewife to be taken into the community.

Nor could she turn to the other doctors' wives for company and acceptance. Two overtures to Jennie Isaacs to join her for coffee came to nothing. The first time her call met with no answer at all; the second time Jennie did answer, but greeted Ellie's invitation with such a long silence that Ellie thought the line had been disconnected, and then said, "Oh, my . . . I—I'd love to, but there's *so* much to do . . ." and then, vaguely, "Maybe—maybe sometime next week I'll call you . . ." but of course she never did. As for Amy DeForrest, she proved all too willing to drop by for coffee—and the rest of the day as well—but Ellie soon found that the combination of her laid-on Southern "sweetness" and her brittle sarcasm toward her husband, the practice, the hospital and just about everything else was more than she could take after the first dose or two, and Ellie herself began drawing away. On two occasions they took a day shopping together in Missoula, but the second of these day-long immersions in Amy's bitterness left Ellie feeling so angry and depressed and totally frustrated that she never agreed to make a third trip.

The one light that glimmered for Ellie during those summer months was her growing companionship with Belle Foreman. After her first visit to Belle's back porch and her introduction to Belle's many hierarchies of cats, she made a practice of walking over every two or three days to chat. At first it was from a sense of compassion: the aged woman seemed so very lonely, so forlorn, so pathetically forsaken and so timidly eager to welcome Ellie's company. She would not yield her privacy—they always talked on the back porch step, or while walking through Belle's fantastic and jungle-like garden—but Ellie came to look forward to these small human contacts far more than she had ever expected. And as the weeks passed, the relationship gradually turned in some subtle way; it seemed almost that Belle was taking Ellie in like another stray kitten, hearing out her frustrations and grievances, comforting her, supporting her.

Bit by bit Belle came forth from her seclusion. Every other day, rain or shine, she would hobble down the road, wrapped up to her neck in her old woolen overcoat despite the summer's heat, shopping bags in either hand, blue beret askew and wisps of white hair pointing wildly in all directions, her wrinkled face browned like old leather in the summer sun, en route to her shopping mission in town. She began stopping by, briefly, to greet Ellie and check on progress of the remodeling. At first she would merely come and peer in the back door, chirruping something to catch Ellie's attention and offering to "pick up something in town" if Ellie wanted it. Steadfastly she refused a ride, even when Ellie was planning to drive to town anyway—"These old legs have done me fine for seventy years and they'll do me a few years more. Got to keep the blood flowing—" but occasionally, on very hot days, she would accept a ride partway back if Ellie timed her trip just right. Sometimes, then, she would stop longer at the cabin, setting the bulging shopping bags down outside the door and coming in to sit at the kitchen table for a glass of lemonade or iced tea before trudging on home.

These were times when Ellie could relax a bit and open up without feeling guilty of sounding querulous. Belle Foreman, she discovered, knew more things about more people in Twin Forks, Montana, than anyone suspected—yet, oddly enough, Belle was not a gossip. "I just keep my ears open and my mouth shut," she would say with a sly grin. "Been doin' it for years. You learn a whole lot that way, if you just pay attention." She was full of tales of the old days in Twin Forks, but about current times and people she was decidedly reticent. Once in a while she would express a sharp opinion, dismissing such as Jerry DeForrest with a contemptuous gesture ("Lazy man; you could die choking before he'd come see you on a rainy night"), but more often she would turn a query aside, gently but firmly, even humorously. "You can't trust an old woman's judgment; all we see is cobwebs. Better you judge for yourself."

One hot August morning they sat longer than usual, as Ellie unloaded her apprehensions about Rob and the practice pressures. "He just seems more and more preoccupied with the hospital and the office and the patients," she said. "I barely see him from one week to the next, it seems. And I don't expect it to get any better, either."

"Nor I," Belle said. "It may well get a whole lot worse before it gets any better."

"You really think so?"

"Yes, I'm afraid I do. Most men have their hands full with one taskmaster. But he's got two. The practice, and Martin Isaacs. That's enough to keep any man preoccupied."

"Martin surely does seem to push him," Ellie conceded.

"My dear, Martin pushes everybody. And pushes, and pushes. It's his nature."

"But somewhere there's got to be a limit."

Belle gave her a sharp glance. "If you think that, you just don't know Martin Isaacs. He'll push your husband just as far as he can, and he'll keep on pushing till he's forced to stop. And that may take some doing."

"You could be right." Ellie sighed. "What scares me is that Rob doesn't respond to pushing too well. He pushes back."

"Then he may be in for some interesting times." Belle smiled ruefully. "And you as well."

"It isn't just Martin, though," Ellie said. "Rob's upset about this blood bank business—he can't get either Martin or Roger Painter to help—and he's upset about the anesthetist, says nobody can count on her, and I guess they're *all* upset about the surgeon, trying to get him to respond when he's needed." Ellie shook her head helplessly. "I don't know what to tell him, even if he'd listen. Mostly, I'd like to get better acquainted with people in town, get involved in things, but everyone seems to back away somehow."

"It's a small town," Belle said, "and you're new and strange. But the *real* trouble is you're a doctor's wife, and that makes it even harder. They all figure that everything the doctor knows his wife also knows, and nobody wants to snuggle too close."

"But that's just not true!" Ellie protested.

"Of course it's not true," Belle said, "but *they* think it is, and that's what counts. They can't *believe* that you don't know everything that's going on in the practice." The old woman shrugged. "They'll get over it, if you live long enough. They may always think you're in on all the secrets, but at least they'll learn you don't spread them around, and things will soften up sooner or later."

"And meanwhile?"

Belle's blue eyes twinkled. "Meanwhile we'll just transplant flowers, and to hell with 'em."

Ellie smiled and went to the refrigerator for more lemonade. "You know what I wonder? I wonder what Jennie Isaacs is really like."

Belle looked up sharply. "Haven't you met her?"

"Just once. At a party. It wasn't a very good introduction."

"No, she might not be at her best at a party." The old woman pulled at her lip. "Can't say I really know *what* Jennie is like today. I remember when she first came to Twin Forks, years ago. Handsome woman. Gracious, thoughtful, had a good word for everybody. Even spoke to *me,* now and then." Belle smiled gently. "Yes, she was a fine-looking woman in those days. But then things changed." She sighed. "A lot of water's passed under the bridge since then. As for what she's like now, you don't want an old woman's cobweb view. You'll have to judge for yourself."

After she left, Ellie went back to her painting. At lunchtime, however, she stopped and took a sandwich out on the patio, sat quietly for

171

an hour or more, watching the jaybird watching her sandwich, watching small white clouds move gently in the sky, but mostly watching the river swirl and eddy down among the rocks and pass swiftly under the bridge. . . .

# 16

As the hot days of August gave way to the first chill mornings of September, Rob found his patient schedule at the office ever and increasingly more jammed. He also observed an odd permutation of Parkinson's law at work: the faster he moved and the longer the hours he put in, the more patients appeared for him to see.

Many, of course, were patients new to the practice—people just moved to the community, younger women seeking him out for the care of their first pregnancies, or older folk who had never cared for Isaacs or DeForrest but were not entirely enchanted with Florey or Peterson either. Many others were the oddballs and outcasts of the practice—the chronic problem patients, the ones with apparently endless lists of complaints and few or no answers to match. Among these were a number of the "town squirrels," as DeForrest called them—eccentrics who had long since exhausted the patience of every other doctor in the valley and were drawn to the office in search of new blood.

Rob saw them all, assuming (not unreasonably) that his efforts to fill this chink in the practice wall would meet with nothing but approval from Martin Isaacs. Yet soon he discovered that this was by no means always the case. He found that Isaacs' pleasure did not always conform to reasonable standards. The practice, it seemed, was curiously booby-trapped with a succession of unwritten rules regarding who was to see what patient when. Indeed, it appeared that there were certain select patients whom he was not supposed to see at all—although no one told him in advance precisely which ones these patients were.

One such case involved Sara Sandalman, a short, stocky, sandy-haired woman who wandered into Rob's office late one afternoon of Isaacs' day off. She carried one infant under her arm like a sack of flour while two others, only slightly older, toddled after her, saucer-eyed, tugging on the back of her skirt. Sara Sandalman suspected, through some arcane divination of her own, that she was pregnant again (*"If it's September, I must be pregnant,"* Rob mused) and she had come in to "make arrangements." From the woman's chart Rob learned that she was a refugee from Florey; Isaacs had delivered her last two children, the sort of coup Isaacs seemed to relish beyond any others. Perhaps that alone should have alerted Rob, but the thought of conflict never entered his mind. Quite the contrary: he assumed that Isaacs, still complaining almost daily of the burden of his OB schedule, had directed the woman to him to lighten his own load. *And about time too,* Rob reflected, *if he really wants relief.*

In any event, he reviewed Sara Sandalman's recent menstrual history, confirmed her pregnancy, took blood and urine samples, and set a time for her to return early the next week for him to do a complete obstetrical physical examination. When the time arrived, however, he did not see Sara Sandalman. Instead he received a peremptory summons to Dr. Isaacs' office, where the older man sat at his desk, leafing through her chart. "This woman," Isaacs said. "What are you doing with her?"

"It seems she's pregnant again," Rob said. "I scheduled an OB physical."

"With *you?* How come?"

Rob blinked. "She came into my office on your day off last Thursday," he said. "I assumed you'd sent her over."

"I sure as hell did not," Isaacs said. "And she's all upset about it. Called me up this morning practically crying. Wanted to know why she had to go see you."

"Well, Jesus, Martin, I didn't go out and *trap* her," Rob said. "She wandered in under her own power. And I thought you wanted to get rid of some of your excess OB load."

"Sara Sandalman's not excess," Isaacs said indignantly. "She's an old patient of mine, I've delivered her last two babies, and some of these women are very sensitive. She shouldn't have to go to anybody else."

"Look, I don't care *where* she goes," Rob said. "If she wants you,

174

that's great. But do I have to ask your personal permission for every new OB I take on?"

"Of course not. Don't be ridiculous. You don't have to ask me about anything, ordinarily. You can do whatever you want, see anybody you want, do all the fancy workups you want, just as long as you don't get in my way. But when my OB patients walk in this place, I want them in *my* office—understand? You just keep that in mind from now on."

It was baffling to Rob, as well as irritating, but Agnes Miller didn't seem surprised when he queried her about it. "It doesn't make any *sense,*" she said cheerfully, "but he's an awful Nervous Nellie about some of those OB patients of his. Especially the ones he's 'rescued' from John Florey. Maybe if you have any question, you could check with me. He's just liable to get all stirred up. He's a real bug about patient loyalty." It didn't seem a good answer to Rob, but for lack of any better he agreed, and even asked Terry at the desk to make doubly sure that any OBs posted to his office were checked with Agnes before the appointment was made.

About a week later, however, an even more peculiar conflict arose, and this time the problem had nothing to do with obstetrics. It happened on an unseasonably hot day in mid-September. Rob, as usual, had been running all day, and by late afternoon he was bushed, ready for quick rounds at the hospital and an evening free of call. He was at his desk charting, with half a dozen patients still waiting to be seen, when he saw Martin Isaacs whisk up the hall and out the back door without so much as a nod, start up his Buick's engine and buzz off down the street.

Five minutes later an uneasy Agnes came by with a chart in her hands. "Dr. Tanner, Dr. Isaacs had to go up to the hospital or something, and he's got a patient here. Do you think you could see him?"

Rob sighed. "Sure, just put him over in Room 3."

Agnes hesitated. "It's Herman Barney," she said, as if that somehow explained something.

"Never heard of him," Rob said.

"Oh, dear. Well, he's pretty sick. Maybe you could see him out in his car."

"In his *car!* Oh, come on, now. Get a wheelchair if you have to, and I'll help you get him in here."

With that Rob ducked in to see another patient for a few moments. When he emerged, he found Agnes standing disconsolately in the corridor with a wheelchair. "I don't think this is going to work," she said.

Rob took the chart from her, saw that she had written *Heart Failure* with a big question mark at the top of a fresh progress sheet. "What do you mean?" he said. "You think the two of us can't get a patient into a wheelchair? Come on now."

He followed her out the front door of the clinic, pushing the wheelchair himself. In the parking lot he saw an old and battered two-door Ford with a very thin elderly woman in the driver's seat. As they came closer, Rob frowned at the apparition in the passenger seat beside her. At first he thought it was a child, because only the head appeared at the window. Then he got close enough to look in, and saw that the entire passenger seat was filled to overflowing with a perfectly huge human body.

Rob gaped for a moment, stared at Agnes and waved the wheelchair away. They didn't need a wheelchair; they needed a fork-lift. The man in the passenger seat was incredibly, grotesquely obese. He was wedged tight into the car, his abdomen and chest crammed against the dashboard, his immense weight squashing the seat down to the floorboards, his legs completely filling the space beneath the dash. His eyes were buried in deep, fatty pouches, and his head, cheeks and chin, all bulging, seemed to merge into the immense torso without any discernible neck at all. It struck Rob that the man must have weighed seven hundred pounds; that he had managed to squeeze himself into the car at all seemed a miracle.

In any event, the man was in trouble. The skin of his face was a grayish-blue color and he breathed in rapid gulps, his mouth popping open with each gasp, like a fish out of water. As he looked up at Rob a series of curious rhythmic wheezing sounds emerged from his mouth, and his massive body began to jounce in the same rhythm; it took a moment for Rob to realize that the man was merely coughing, trying to bring sputum up from his chest. For a few seconds the man's face turned a deep purple, and then the sputum came up in a bubbling, pink-tinged fountain; he leaned his head out the window and spat, and spat, and spat again, barely missing Rob's foot. After that he sat back to catch his breath for a moment, then looked malevolently up at Rob. "Where's Isaacs?" he said in a wheezy rasp.

Agnes stepped forward. "Mr. Barney, Dr. Isaacs had to go up to the hospital."

"Hospital, my ass. I saw the goddam bastard drive out of here when we drove in." He pointed a thumb at Rob. "Who's this?"

"This is Dr. Tanner, our new doctor. Maybe he can help you."

176

Barney began wheezing and jouncing again in another strangulated coughing spell. Recovering, he took a deep breath and said, "Goddam bastard said he'd be in this afternoon. I don't want to see no new doctor."

"Well, he's gone, and he won't be back," Agnes said. "I think he's delivering a baby."

"Baby, my ass!" the fat man snorted. "Goddam bastard's hiding, that's what he's doing. I could sit here and choke to death for all he cares"—and off he went again into a paroxysm of wheezing and coughing.

Agnes started to say something, but Rob shushed her. "Look, Mr. Barney, maybe I can help. What's the trouble?"

"What the hell does it look like?" the fat man roared. "I can't breathe, that's what's the trouble."

"I can see that, but when did it start?"

"I already told Isaacs, God damn it! All week long I can't breathe, and all he tells me to do is take some more of them heart pills—"

"He's supposed to be on digitalis," Agnes said, "but he always quits taking them."

"So when I finally get down here to see him, he takes off like a big-assed bird," Barney said. "Goddam bastard wants me to die, that's what he wants."

"Look," Rob said sharply, "if you really want to sit here until Dr. Isaacs comes back, that's fine with me, but you may have quite a long wait. If you want me to help, you might try shutting up for a minute so I can listen to your chest."

Barney glowered up at Rob, and then across at his wife, and then back at Rob. "So listen," he said finally.

Rob reached through the car window and loosened the man's shirt, drew his undershirt up to his neck. For a long while he searched the vast expanse of chest with his stethoscope for heart tones, finally caught a faint, rapid galloping sound typical of congestive heart failure. Three times he was interrupted by Mr. Barney's spells of wheezing and coughing, and both lung fields sounded full of water. And indeed, the man's face was turning noticeably bluer even as Rob examined him. "Okay; when did you quit taking your heart pills?" Rob asked finally.

"Week or two ago," the man gasped.

"You haven't taken any at all in the last week?"

"No. Hate the goddam things."

"Well, you may hate them, but you're going to die for sure without

177

them." Rob turned to Agnes. "This is ridiculous," he said. "I can't treat heart failure in the front seat of a car. But if I open that door he's going to roll right out onto the ground. Can't we get him to the hospital?"

"No way. You just mention the word 'hospital' and he'll have a stroke right here in the parking lot."

"Okay, then I guess we treat him in the front seat of the car. Get me a sixth of morphine in one hypo, and seven and a half grains of aminophylline in another, and an ampule of Cedilanid in a third. And you'd better bring a long needle. I don't know how I'm going to find a vein through all that blubber."

While Agnes was getting the medicines, Rob took Barney's arm out the car window, searching for a vein. The fat man watched for a moment, then pointed with his other hand to the inside of the bend of the elbow. "Isaacs always gets it right *there,"* he said.

"Okay, we'll try it. You just hold still." He took the aminophylline syringe from Agnes and inserted the needle almost to the hilt where Barney had pointed. To his amazement, he hit the vein on the first try, and slowly began administering the medicine.

"Pretty good," Barney wheezed. "Isaacs has to try six times."

"Beginner's luck," Rob said. "You just hold still so we don't jar it loose." With the first medication given, he switched syringes to administer the digitalis preparation, and then, after a moment of misgiving, the morphine. Barney had another violent wheezing and coughing spell as Rob removed the needle, but this time after he had coughed and spat, he looked a little pinker.

"Breathing better?" Rob asked.

"Yeah. Matter of fact, I am." Barney took a deeper breath. "Say, that's more like it."

"Well, let's give it a little more time. Agnes, you stay here with him. I need to check his chart."

In at the front desk, Rob sat down and leafed through the chart, a long, dismal record of multiple automobile consultations just like this one. It had been five years since Herman Barney had actually been inside the clinic, with his weight recorded then at 573 pounds. Each subsequent visit had been during an episode of congestive heart failure precipitated by the patient's dogged refusal to continue taking the digitalis prescribed for him.

Rob sighed and went back out to the car. Herman Barney's heart was still fluttering away at 220 beats per minute, but his color was far better, his wheezing much less marked and his breathing obviously

178

improved. "You got a good touch, boy," he said. "Whatever you give me done the trick—my breath's comin' back just fine now. So you can tell that goddam Isaacs to go screw himself. Mabel's going to take me home now."

"Well, hold it a minute." Rob leaned in the window and looked the fat man in the eye. "How many of those heart pills have you got left?"

"Whole goddam bottle full."

"That's great. When you get home you start taking those pills again."

"I ain't takin' none of them pills. I'm breathing just fine right now."

"Listen, my friend, you do what I'm telling you or you may not be breathing *at all* by midnight. Without those heart pills you're going to be drowning in your own juice again before twenty-four hours are out, and the next time it may be too late to bail you out."

The fat man looked up at him. "How long do I have to take them?"

"Until I tell you to stop. You take those pills and you *keep* taking them—and come back here in three days for me to check you again. Got that?"

"Three days?"

"Three days. That means Thursday afternoon."

"You gonna be here?"

"I'll be here—but I want you to take those pills."

Barney looked at him disconsolately. "How many?" he said.

"Two of them tonight and two more tomorrow. Then one a day until I check you again on Thursday." Rob looked over at the woman behind the wheel. "You hear that, Mrs. Barney?"

"I hear it," the woman said wearily, "but I can't make him take those pills, Doctor."

"I don't want you to," Rob said. "It's his heart, and it's up to him whether he wants more trouble or not. I just want you to know the dose in case he all of a sudden can't remember."

"I can remember, God damn it," Mr. Barney said indignantly.

"Then remember, at least until Thursday. Now, there's one other thing. How did you get from your house to the car, with all that weight?"

"I've got crutches," Barney said, pointing into the back seat. "I get around when I'm not short of breath."

"Okay, then on Thursday I want to see you *inside the clinic.* No more of this out in the car business. If I'm going to take care of you, I need to see an electrocardiogram and a chest x-ray on Thursday and I

179

can't get either one of them out here. So you walk inside. Got that?"

The fat man scowled as he met Rob's eye, then looked away. "I suppose."

"Fine. Now you go home and find that pill bottle."

Rob turned and walked back into the clinic with Agnes as the heavy-laden car groaned and squeaked its way out of the parking lot. Agnes was shaking her head. "You'll never see him again till he's right back in the soup," she said grimly.

"Oh, really? Why not?"

"Because he's a pigheaded old fool, that's why not. He's not going to do what a doctor tells him. He never has."

"I believe you," Rob said. "What's more, I bet he gives the doctors hell every time they do see him, while they plead with him to behave himself, right?"

"More or less. Dr. Isaacs reads him the riot act, but he never pays any attention."

"Why should he? He's a great big overgrown baby, and he's got everybody treating him like a baby and trying to protect him like a baby too. How do you think he got so fat? That poor woman must just feed him continuously. Well, I'm not about to scold him. If he wants help from me, he's going to do things my way and take some responsibility for himself. If he doesn't like that, I'm going to tell him to go chase himself." Rob tossed the chart down on his desk. "What's more, I think he knows it."

"Well," Agnes said, "I guess we'll find out on Thursday."

It seemed a simple enough situation to Rob. He had filled in where Isaacs had defaulted, seen a man Isaacs wouldn't see anymore, and followed some sixth sense in dealing with him. Either Herman Barney would follow orders or he wouldn't, and that, Rob thought, would be that. But if everyone else at the clinic seemed to think that he had dealt splendidly with the irascible fat man, it appeared that Martin Isaacs disagreed. To Isaacs, Herman Barney's response to Rob's ministrations was nothing less than a defection of loyalty—and Martin Isaacs did not like it.

Nothing was said at first. Rob had indeed found Isaacs at the hospital after the Barneys had departed for home, but there was no woman in labor there. Isaacs clearly had fled the clinic to avoid seeing the fat man, and he must have known that Rob knew it; indeed, he made a rather shamefaced point that he had been busy making evening rounds so that Rob wouldn't need to—doing penance, Rob thought wryly, for

180

cutting and running when the whites of Herman Barney's eyes had appeared. Nor was anything said in the next day or two, although Rob noticed that Barney's chart, with his notes of the Monday evening visit, had found its way to Isaacs' desk before it went back into the chart file. *Probably just curious,* Rob thought, *to see what he missed out on.* The trouble exploded on Thursday afternoon, when Herman Barney reappeared at the clinic on his crutches, with his wife on one side and a scarecrow of a son on the other to keep him from falling on his face. Slowly and painfully, wheezing with every breath, the fat man inched through the door and up to the reception desk, demanding to see "that new young whippersnapper that told me to come back on Thursday."

It was a victory, of sorts, that set the clinic staff abuzz. Mr. Barney had not crossed the threshold of the building in years, always demanding to be seen in the front seat of his car, or calling the doctor out for a house call at two in the morning when his troubles became acute. He didn't like it; he complained profanely with every step that his breath was giving out, the crutches hurt his arms, he was going to sue them all if he tripped and fell—but in he came. Dora was ready for him, guiding him back to the treatment room with as much dispatch as possible, even luring him onto the two step-on scales they pushed together in the corridor along the way, one foot on each, to record his first weight measurement in five years—a hefty 627 pounds. Rob came in to help Dora ease the man down on the treatment room table so that Ginny could run an electrocardiogram. "Glad you made it," Rob told him. "As soon as we get this and a chest film done, I'm going to check you over from top to bottom."

He walked back for some coffee, feeling immensely pleased with himself. Then, without warning, Martin Isaacs came storming down the hall. "What the hell are you doing with that fat son of a bitch in the treatment room?" he demanded.

"Trying to get a cardiogram," Rob said, "if we can get any signals through all that blubber."

"Well, *get him out of here,*" Isaacs said.

Rob stared at him. "What do you mean?"

"I mean just what I said. Get him *out* of here. I don't want him anywhere near this place. I've had enough of that fat bastard, and so has Jerry. He never does anything you tell him, and he torments you night and day on the telephone, and I don't think he's had a bath in ten years. How'd you get him in here in the first place?"

"I told him to walk in or go to hell," Rob said. "So he walked in."

"Good; then he can walk right out again too. I'll be damned if I want him in my clinic again, and I'll be damned if you're going to waste time and money on him, either."

It suddenly dawned on Rob that Isaacs was dead serious. "For God's sake, Martin," he said. *"You're* the one that dropped him in my lap. So now I've got him. You don't have to be bothered. What's eating you?"

"He's going to make a monkey out of you—that's what's eating me."

"But suppose he doesn't? Suppose he does just what I tell him? Then what?"

"Well, he won't, that's what," Isaacs spluttered. "God, all that fat! It makes me sick just to think about him. Never pays his bills, either, you ask Bev; she's got to fight for every nickel. Well, he can go to hell, as far as I'm concerned."

"But he's not *dead* yet," Rob said. "He was damned near it the other night, but you took off like a rocket when you saw him drive in, so I got the fun of bailing him out. Now he's back because I told him to come back, and he walked in because I told him to walk in, and if I can get a decent look at his heart and lungs and kidneys, maybe I can straighten him out a little. And if you want him to take a bath, I'll see about that too, when I get a chance."

"Look, God damn it," Isaacs cut in furiously, "this is my clinic, and I'm telling you I don't want Herman Barney in here wasting your time and my money."

Rob just stared at him. "Martin, this is ridiculous. The cardiogram is already done and they're taking the chest film right now. What am I supposed to do, tear them up?"

"I don't care what you do with them. Just get that bastard out of here."

"Well, I'm sorry, but it can't be done. There's no ethical way I can dump that man at this point, and I'm not about to try. What's more, I'm going to get him out of heart failure before I quit on him, and if you don't like it, you can go piss up a rope."

Shaking with anger, Rob picked up Barney's chart and stalked past Isaacs into the corridor. He found the fat man in the treatment room, still panting with exertion from his trip back to x-ray. "Okay, Herman," Rob said, "how are you doing?"

"Lousy," Barney snarled.

"Really? Your breathing still bad?"

"Oh, not like the other day. Just when I move around too much."

"Well, let's have a listen." Rob undid the fat man's gown, listened first to his chest, then to his heart. He could still hear squeaks and wheezes, but the lung fields were far clearer than three days before, and the heart rate had slowed to ninety beats per minute. Barney watched with childlike curiosity as Rob went on to complete his examination. "Why are you squeezing my ankles?" he asked at one point.

"To see how much excess water you're carrying around. You've got a good twenty pounds of it right there."

"In my *ankles?*"

"And legs, and other places. When your heart doesn't work right, a lot of water seeps out into your tissues."

"How's my heart doin'?"

"Better, but not good enough. You're going to have to keep taking those heart pills. What's more, I'm going to order another medicine to dump off some of this excess water. That alone will make you feel one hundred percent better. Then I want to see you again next week to check how things are going. That's next Thursday, without fail. Make an appointment when you go past the front desk. Got all that now?"

Barney nodded. "Seems like an awful lot of pills," he grumbled.

"I know, but you need them. And you'll have to take them if you want to get well. All I can do is point you in the right direction."

Barney nodded again. "I suppose."

"What's more, the pills are just openers. We haven't even *talked* about the real problem yet. You know that, don't you?"

"I know," the fat man said, almost inaudibly.

Rob looked at the man for a long moment, studied the gray face, the pudgy hands, the bulging rolls of fat, the little beads of perspiration on his upper lip just from the effort of breathing. "Tell me something, Herman. How long has it been since you really felt good? I don't mean just breathing a little easier or moving around a little more. I mean when did you last feel *good,* really top-rate in every way?"

"Oh, God, Doc." Barney stared off across the treatment room. "Fifteen years? Twenty? I don't know." Suddenly, unexpectedly, the fat man's eyes filmed with tears. "Would you believe there was a time when I worked up in these woods, falling and bucking trees? Would you believe that, Doc? They used to pay us piecework, so much per thousand board-feet of lumber we dropped. My partner and I, we worked like demons twelve hours a day, running up the slope to the next tree before the last one hit the ground. We pulled down ten, twelve, fourteen grand apiece in a season, and that was *money* in those days." He looked at Rob, shaking his head. "Would you believe I used to hike up to the high lakes up behind Iron Mountain just for a day's fishing? Ten miles of steep trail, hardly more than a goat path, and I'd go up it in three hours with a pack on my back. There were trout up there as long as your arm, you'd fight for an hour just to beach one, and I'd cart home four or five for Mabel to smoke up or can. Well, *those* were the days when I felt good. But then I broke a hip, and laid in a hospital bed for six months, and still couldn't go back to the woods, and then the mill cut back and I was laid off there, and there was nothing to do but eat. . . ."

Rob nodded. "Okay, so you had some bad breaks. But something else happened too. Somewhere back there you tossed in the towel. Well, you can't get your youth back, but you can feel good again—really good—if you want to work for it. You just have to go back and pick up that towel."

"How you going to make me lose this weight, Doc?"

"I'm not. There's no way I can make you. It's got to be *you*. But if you want help, I'll give you help. As long as you work for it."

The fat man sat silent, staring at his hands for a long moment. "So what do I do?" he said.

"First, get your heart bailed out and get rid of some of this fluid. By next week we'll see how many pounds of water you've dumped off. After that, if you really want to dig in, we'll talk about a plan."

He left a strangely subdued Herman Barney to dress himself and took the man's chart back to his office. Still baffled and angry at Isaacs' outburst, he began drafting a skeleton program. It would take time, and work, and patience, and after all that it still might fail. *Isaacs could be right: you could end up squandering endless time and effort, all for nothing. But treating the heart failure is pointless if you ignore the rest. Unless you tackle the weight loss and win, he's a walking dead man.*

Dora came back with other patients, so he pushed the Barney chart aside and moved on. Later he confirmed that Barney had indeed made a reappointment for the following week, and nodded in satisfaction. *A minor victory, maybe, but a victory.* He worked on through the day, passing Dr. Isaacs in angry silence once or twice in the hall. Then, as he was wrapping up the afternoon's charting, the white-haired man suddenly appeared at his office door. "Oh, Rob, have you got a minute?"

Rob looked up. "If it's about treating Herman Barney—"

"Oh, hell, Rob, I didn't really mean what I said. It just made me burn to see that fat bastard taking up a lot of your time and attention,

184

and I guess I lost my temper. *I* sure don't want to see him, but you do whatever you want."

"Well, I'm not going to nursemaid him," Rob said. "But if he wants to work, I think we can offer him something."

"*You* can offer him something," Isaacs said.

"Okay, *I* can offer him something."

"Fine; I just wish you luck. But look, don't get upset if I blow my top once in a while, okay? On some things I've got kind of a short fuse."

It seemed fair enough to Rob. Certainly it restored tranquillity to a suddenly tense office. Yet the abruptness of Isaacs' explosion, and certain of the undertones, continued to bother Rob. He told Ellie of the incident, and she listened with a little frown. "It's hard to figure," she said finally. "Of course, he had the whole practice to himself for so long, before Jerry came, and then you, he's bound to figure it's still his show. And if he gets mad at a patient, I suppose he figures you should be mad at him too."

"Maybe so," Rob conceded. "It just kind of shook me, was all. He's usually at least *reasonable* about things, and then all of a sudden, blooey, he blows up in my face over nothing, really. Makes you wonder what's going to be next."

Jerry DeForrest passed it off far more casually. "Don't let it throw you," he said. "Martin has a sort of proprietary attitude toward just about everything in this valley, one way or another. He'll blow up about some damned thing or another and make a perfect ass of himself, and then spend the rest of the week trying to get his foot out of his mouth."

"But what do you *do* when he does that? Tell him to drop dead?"

"Doesn't matter too much. It sure doesn't do any good to *argue* with him; when he gets irrational, he does it in spades. Best thing is just to walk away until he quiets down. Once in a while he even apologizes, but you'd better not hold your breath waiting. Mostly he just forgets about it in a day or so and assumes that you have too."

It still seemed odd to Rob, but as the days passed it did indeed appear that Isaacs had forgotten the contretemps over Herman Barney. And the fat man's condition began to improve sharply. Clearly he had been on the edge of heart failure for months, perhaps even years, before Rob first saw him, largely because he had ignored Isaacs' treatment instructions for so long. Now, accepting the same instructions from Rob, Barney found himself breathing more freely, sleeping more soundly and moving about more readily than at any time in recent memory, and although he complained incessantly to his wife at home,

185

to Terry at the front desk, to Ginny in the lab and to Dora on the floor, he seemed never to complain very loudly to Rob. He was flatly astounded to see from the clinic scales that he did indeed lose some fifteen pounds of excess fluid in the course of the first week, just as Rob said he would, and another five pounds the second week. Finally, warily, he expressed a willingness to make a try at true weight loss, and Rob set out the program he had planned, bringing Mrs. Barney into the discussion as a logistical consultant. The initial goal they set was quite modest, but at least realistically attainable in a matter of two weeks or so—and it *was* attained. The next goal, set by Barney himself, was not so modest; the fact that he failed to reach it was not so remarkable as the fact that he missed it by only three pounds, and Herman Barney became positively beatific when he found Rob encouraging rather than scolding him for his failure. The goal was simply reset and reinforced, and as day followed week the weight that Herman Barney registered on the clinic scales began slowly but steadily to drop.

In the meantime, Martin Isaacs had nothing more to say in the matter, his objections apparently forgotten. And if some half-sensed concern about Isaacs' sudden explosion still smoldered in Rob Tanner's mind, he shrugged it off impatiently. There was not, he decided, any point in borrowing trouble.

# 17

"Dr. Tanner, you had a couple of cancellations, so I let Terry book an extra physical exam this afternoon," Dora said. "I hope you don't mind."

Rob sighed. It was two o'clock on a hot September afternoon, and he had been hoping to get away an hour early for once. "I suppose," he said. "What's the problem?"

"No problem. It's Chris Erickson, the girl from the forestry lab. She's canceled out twice already, and then she called Monday and said she could come over on short notice, so I thought we'd better grab her while we can."

"Okay, set her up. Routine lab work and cardiogram, and I'll want a chest film to check those ribs and an ankle film as well." As he went on to examine another already waiting patient, he found his spirits suddenly and surprisingly buoyant. He had seen Chris from time to time since the housewarming party, but seldom with an opportunity to talk. She had been in once to have her walking cast replaced by an elastic ankle support, but Rob had been rushed that day and looked in only briefly, leaving the dirty work to Dora. Later he had occasionally seen her come barreling down Main Street in the weather-beaten green timber company jeep she drove these days, complete with open sides, back-country tires and a pair of roll bars over the driver's seat. Once or twice she had hailed him with a jaunty wave and squealed to a halt in a cloud of dust to chat for a moment before roaring off again—but that was all. She had also become active with the Blood Bank Committee meetings at Dottie Hazard's house, where she tended to raise uncomfortably practical questions about what the committee should plan to do if the hospital directors turned a cold eye on the action program they were evolving. But Rob's participation at those meetings had been piecemeal at best, since he was invariably called away right in the middle of things, and he had never found a chance to exchange more than casual greetings with the girl. He had wondered, vaguely, if she ever did really intend to come in for the exam they had discussed at the party, and he had finally concluded that she didn't—until now, quite suddenly, she was there sitting in his office.

"So why now?" he asked, facing her across his desk. "I'd just about given up on you. Or is something suddenly falling apart?"

She laughed. "Heavens, no. I've been feeling absolutely splendid since I got that cast off. You might say I'm just taking my doctor's advice, like a good girl."

"I see," Rob said dryly.

"Or you could chalk it up to sheer boredom," Chris said. "The night life in Twin Forks just isn't that stimulating."

"You should try making the scene down at the Wagon Wheel on a Friday night," Rob said. "All those lusty young loggers down from a week in the woods . . ."

"Yes, I know. All of them randy as goats and smelling like sweat and sawdust and bad whiskey." She wrinkled her nose. "No, thanks. I'd like something more than a quick scramble in the back seat of a car. Something with a little challenge to it."

He turned their talk to health problems then, but there was really little to go on. Chris had no symptoms or complaints other than an occasional twinge in her chest when she coughed and some swelling of her injured ankle when she was on her feet too long at a time. Her past health problems seemed few and minor as Rob took a more sketchy than usual medical history; she talked briefly about her dull childhood in Iowa, some traveling she had done, her work at the university, and Rob found himself far more preoccupied with her slightly tilted green eyes and her easy laugh and her trim figure than with anything she was saying. Finally there seemed no further excuse for prolonging the visit; he sent her into the adjoining examining room to gown, and then proceeded with his examination. She was a small woman, slender and light-boned, with the smooth musculature of good physical condition-

188

ing, a flat stomach and small breasts and a barely visible furze of golden-blond hair running down her spine, broadening to a trapezoid at the base. With Dora's assistance he finished with a pelvic and rectal exam, then helped Chris sit up on the end of the examining table. "Nothing bothering you at all, then?" he said at last.

"Really no, nothing to speak of." She laughed. "Unless you count silly things like my right hand going to sleep whenever I lie down."

"Just your right hand?"

She nodded. "It's always all numb and tingly when I wake up in the morning. Goes away as soon as I'm up for a few minutes. It's been doing that as long as I can remember."

"How do you sleep? On your side?"

"On my back, mostly."

"With your right arm up over your head?"

"Mostly, yes."

"Well, it's probably nothing. Some vagary of circulation on account of your position." He took her right arm, found the pulse at the wrist, strong and bounding, then raised the arm above her head, still feeling the pulse. There seemed a slight difference in that position, but he couldn't be sure. "Well, you'll probably live," he said, lowering her arm again. "In fact, I don't see any problems at all at this point, but I'll want to check your lab work and your x-rays and get the report on the Pap smear just to be sure. This is Monday. If you can come back for a few minutes on Thursday, I can give you a final report then."

She agreed and went on her way while Rob started through the rest of his afternoon schedule. At four-thirty he was called up to the hospital on various errands and was hurried for the rest of the day. It was not until the next morning that he got back to check Chris Erickson's x-rays. The ankle was completely healed. So were the ribs, visible on the chest film, and the lung fields were clear. He was about to drop the film back on the pile when he did a double take and stared at the plate, hardly believing his eyes.

He blinked at it for a long moment, then let out a whoop and headed down for DeForrest's office, film in hand. "How about a pinpoint diagnosis?" Rob said, popping the film up on Jerry's view box.

"Looks like a chest film," Jerry said dryly.

"Right," Rob said.

"In fact, aside from some healed rib fractures, it looks like a *normal* chest film."

"Ah, but it's not. Take another look."

189

Jerry sat back and stared at the film for almost a minute, then said, "Beats me."

"Suppose I told you that her right hand goes to sleep when she lies down."

Jerry looked again, then suddenly sat forward. "I'll be damned," he said, pointing. "She's got a cervical rib."

It seemed impossible to miss, once it had been spotted: a small, two-inch curve of bone located just *above* the highest normal rib on the right. "It must press the subclavian artery just a little every time she raises her arm," Rob said, "and she doesn't notice anything at all unless she has her arm up a long time, while she's sleeping. And everybody missed it completely on the chest films at the hospital."

"Well, *I* sure missed it," Jerry said. "Maybe you should have that girl stuffed and stand her in the corner of your office."

"Maybe so," Rob said. "There's sure not much to *do* about it, without any symptoms to speak of."

"Except to impress a pretty girl with your cleverness and acuity," Jerry said.

"Well, yes, there's that . . ."

As trifling as it was, and as medically insignificant, the discovery of this anatomical curiosity pleased Rob enormously and left him feeling ridiculously buoyant for the rest of the day. More than once he was tempted to ring Chris at work to tell her why her hand went to sleep, but he pushed the impulse aside. Even so, he felt a sense of excitement and anticipation about her forthcoming Thursday visit all out of proportion to the medical findings he had to report. He knew he would not have felt the same if the patient were a seventy-year-old grandfather; he was suddenly looking forward to seeing Chris Erickson, not as a patient coming in for lab reports, but very much as Chris Erickson of the green eyes and lithe body and too much unoccupied time on her hands—

He pushed the image away sharply and turned his attention to the work at hand, blocking his thoughts of Chris with an almost ruthless clinical precision. It was nothing new to Rob, such blocking. It was a doctor's major defense, a part of the professional insulation he constantly used to muffle the variety of stimuli, erotic and otherwise, that he faced day by day. There was an ancient and bedraggled myth that doctors, of all men, were somehow impervious, immune to intensely personal thoughts and feelings in dealing with their patients. He had heard it piously proclaimed again and again, but he knew, of course, that it was a fraud, that myth—a false and soothing lie to hide behind. The human organism was not so readily thwarted and the doctor was not made who did not respond, however silently and privately, to the stimuli of sex and other emotions in his office. But by throwing a mental switch almost automatically, he defended the professional façade. And the stronger the stimulus, the more overtly compelling, the higher and thicker the defensive wall was erected.

So he blocked Chris Erickson, firmly and dutifully if not too completely. A corner of his mind escaped, and he saw her in surreal fantasy, dressed in blouse and dungarees, confronting an immense enclosure of moths, tending them, releasing them, mysteriously recapturing them— followed by a sudden, unbidden image, almost overwhelmingly vivid: the exquisitely erotic curve of her back, the honey-colored skin, the narrow waist and the flare of the hips, the fine peach-fuzz growth at the base of the spine, the small, perfect breasts, the certain knowledge that she was not virgin, somehow erotically surprising, with the instant, scornful reaction: *So? As if for some reason she should be, you ass. Twenty-six years old—she's a big girl now.* And yet again, the curiously exciting image of that small, sun-drenched body, so coolly controlled at the party, moved to passion, inflamed, taken and joined by another— Once again he blocked fiercely as he moved on from patient to patient, with Dora glancing at him oddly, then shrugging and moving on.

The image recurred through the rest of the day as he went about his work with half a mind, only vaguely aware of routine things: the hum of cars going by on the street outside, the quiet pad-pad of Dora's rubber-shod feet hustling down the corridor, the peremptory buzz of Isaacs' signal for Agnes. . . . Home for a quick bowl of soup and a sandwich for lunch and a preoccupied word or two with Ellie as she dressed for the Ladies of Sacred Heart Hospital guild meeting that afternoon, then back for a full afternoon schedule. Late away from the office, and still buoyant, he made his evening hospital rounds and returned home for a late dinner, then sprawled on the couch with a handful of new journals that had just come. Presently he realized that Ellie was talking to him. "Huh? How's that?"

"This weekend," Ellie said. "Martin has call, doesn't he?"

"Yep."

"Then let's go somewhere."

He looked up at her. "Like where?"

"I don't care where. Anywhere. Let's just pack up Friday morning and take off."

191

Rob shook his head. "There's a Blood Bank Committee meeting Friday night. We're nailing down a sponsorship proposal to hand to the hospital directors next week."

"Okay, fine," Ellie persisted. "Then let's pack up Saturday morning and take off."

"Kind of hard. Martin's got three OBs ready to pop, and I've got one of my own about due too."

"I see."

Something in her voice caught his attention. "Look, maybe the next weekend I have off would be better. Maybe we can plan something."

"Maybe."

"I'll just tell Martin we're going to be gone, and that'll be that."

She was silent for a moment. Then she said, "I thought the idea was that you two were going to trade off covering these women on nights and weekends."

"It was. I've just been waiting for Martin to give it the nod, that's all."

"I don't think he's going to," Ellie said. "It must be kind of nice for him to have you around to help all the time. That way he can keep you under his thumb better."

"Oh, come on, now."

"Honey, Belle Foreman says he's going to push you just as far as you let him."

"What does she know about it?"

"I don't know," Ellie said, "but she seems to have *his* number pretty well."

"Well, she's nuts," Rob said. "But maybe I should say something. I'll nail him down about it the first chance I get."

The opportunity came sooner than he expected. He was about to make a final telephone check with the hospital before turning in when the phone rang, with Isaacs on the line. "Rob, Janet Marks is on her way up to the hospital in labor. Why don't you come up and give me a hand?"

"Why don't I just take it?" Rob said. "I've got the call."

There was a startled silence. Then: "Well—I don't know. I've been following her along in the office all afternoon. It'd look kind of funny."

"Okay, I'll come help." He hung up and slipped on his shoes, suddenly more irritated with Ellie for forcing the issue than he was with Isaacs. He knew she was right, of course. It had indeed been the idea

192

that he and Martin would start trading off OB coverage sooner or later —but in the course of almost three months no such thing had begun to happen. He also knew that Isaacs had to be certain of Rob's delivery room expertise before letting go of the reins. Isaacs was a careful obstetrician, and the fastidiousness of his care was reflected in the unhurried, unruffled smoothness with which he conducted his patients' labors and deliveries. Even in unusual circumstances—the woman the previous week with a marginal placenta and considerable bleeding during labor, or the patient three days before who had entered labor with a breech baby—Isaacs' attendance was undisturbed and placid. He wanted no heroics, no midnight disasters, no hysterics and no dead babies, and by and large he got what he wanted. He was also an excellent delivery room teacher—but there had been no single case yet in which he had stepped back and let Rob take over.

Now Rob found the older man already in a scrub suit, sitting back in the hospital coffee room playing solitaire with a dog-eared pack of cards. Rob sat down across from him. "So. What's going on?"

"She's just piddling along," Isaacs said. "She'll start moving pretty soon."

"Then why call out the troops so early? We could be here all night."

"Not with this one. Once Janet takes off, she goes like a rocket. Last time I gave them half an hour to get her prepped and I damned near didn't make it. The one before that she had in the car." Isaacs flipped down another card, pursed his lips, and played it to open up a column.

"I thought you were getting tired of sweating out these OBs on your off-duty nights," Rob said.

"Boy, am I ever! Jesus! I've got ninety-five undelivered OBs on my schedule right now—would you believe it? That's almost three a week for the next nine months, and it sure is getting old."

"Well, I've got a few coming up myself," Rob said, "and more turning up every week. So when are we going to start covering for each other, like we planned, so only one of us has to work at a time?"

Isaacs sighed. "That sure would be the day, all right."

"So what's the hang-up? I'm ready to start anytime."

The older man shuffled the cards in silence and then began dealing them out methodically into columns again. "It's not quite that easy," he said finally. "With OBs there's no substitute for experience."

Rob frowned. "Hell, Martin, I know enough to holler if I get in trouble, and I can certainly handle the uncomplicated ones on the nights and weekends I'm on call."

"I suppose," Isaacs said dubiously. "But there are other problems too—"

A rap on the door cut him off and Agnes looked in. "You'd better check this girl, Doctor. She's going like a three-alarm fire."

Isaacs headed into the delivery room while Rob hurried down to change into a scrub suit. He was almost too late; Isaacs was already delivering the baby by the time he got back. "Did you get the block in?" he asked.

"No time," Isaacs said. "I got a little procaine into the perineum for the episiotomy, and then the baby was right there. When this girl finally gets going, she doesn't mess around—right, Janet?"

The woman nodded, looking remarkably chipper. "Beats the back seat of the car," she said. "I just sort of relax, and there it is. Like natural childbirth."

Agnes took the baby down to the nursery and Rob stood by, feeling foolish, while Isaacs sutured up the small episiotomy incision. Later, as they changed back into street clothes, Isaacs said, "Now, there's a perfect example. No other woman in the valley would have a baby like that, and if you'd tried to get a saddle block in, she'd have had the baby on the floor before you knew what happened. Even if I'd warned you in advance, you wouldn't believe it unless you'd actually been through it with her once before."

"So maybe this was a special case," Rob conceded. "But you must have plenty that aren't so tricky."

"Mm. The problem is getting the patients to go along," Isaacs said.

Rob stared at him. "You can't mean that these women seriously expect you to stand by on uninterrupted call seven days a week, three hundred sixty-five days a year," he protested.

"Well, maybe not for little problems along the way. But for delivery, that's something else. They don't want some stranger walking in and delivering them just because their doctor happens to be off call that night. If I started pulling that, these women would head down to John Florey's office so fast it would make your head swim."

"Oh, John Florey be damned! That man can't come near you on OB care, and you know it as well as I do. And those women wouldn't go *anywhere* if you prepared them a little bit in advance."

"What do you mean?" Isaacs said suspiciously.

"I mean telling them, right from the start. They know I'm here. They know I'm covering for you on other things. Just tell them that we work together and if they happen to go into labor when you can't be reached, I'll always be there to cover. Get them in to see me once or twice when they're getting near term, so I'm not just a stranger."

"I don't think they'll buy it," Isaacs said.

"You've got to *make* them buy it, if you really want to get out from under this load. There's no other way. Sure, if somebody really violently objects, maybe you'd be stuck with that case—but most of them won't object."

Isaacs sat for a long moment looking at Rob. "I don't know," he said finally. "Maybe it'd work. I'll just have to think about it."

"Okay, think about it," Rob said. "But then let's either do it or quit pretending we're going to—okay?"

He was both puzzled and irritated at the older man's reluctance, and his irritation carried through the rest of the week. To Rob it didn't make sense; hardly a day had passed since his arrival that Isaacs had not muttered and complained about the merciless pressure of his OB load —yet now he was acting as if covering for each other was a totally new and suspect idea. *Well, maybe he's just too set in his ways,* Rob reflected. *Maybe the time has come to start pushing it.*

Thursday dawned gray and drizzly, matching Rob's mood. At the office his irritation was compounded when he learned that Chris Erickson had postponed her morning appointment until late afternoon. "Maybe she needs the day with her moths," Dora offered, and Rob conceded grumpily that maybe she did. It was a long morning, rushed but uninteresting, filled with a multitude of mundane problems. At lunchtime he caught a sandwich at the Bar-None and plunged back into an afternoon of sniffles and early-season flu. Then at five-thirty Dora handed him a chart as she passed him in the corridor. "Chris is here now," she said. "I put her in your office."

The moment he saw her he felt himself tighten up, blocking, feeling tense and uneasy and not a little wary. "So," he said. "Are the moths all in good health?"

"The moths? Oh, yes." She smiled. "They're always in fine shape."

"Well, it looks like you are too," Rob said. "Your lab work is all normal, the Pap report is good, the x-rays check out fine." He paused. "I can even tell you why your hand goes to sleep."

"Oh, good. Tell me."

"You have scalenus anticus syndrome."

She burst into laughter. "Oh, I'm very impressed! Now tell me in English."

"You've got an extra rib on one side."

"I've got a *what?*"

He stuck the chest film up on the view box, pointed to the small curving bone. "Whenever you raise your arm, that presses on a muscle, which presses on an artery, which cuts down the circulation a little bit. It doesn't mean a thing, and there's nothing to do about it—it's just a curiosity, is all."

Chris giggled. "I think you waved your magic wand and put it there," she said. "I'm going to call you Merlin from now on."

"Well, magic wand or not, you're a rare specimen. Perfectly healthy; just . . . peculiar."

"My husband always told me I was put together wrong," Chris said.

Rob looked up, startled. "Husband?"

"Yes. Didn't I tell you I'd been married?"

"No, you didn't."

"That was ten years ago, when I was just out of high school." She shrugged. "I got pregnant, and where I came from, in those days, that meant you got married. And then when all the fuss was over I lost the baby on the honeymoon."

"Miscarriage?"

She nodded. "It happened twice again, later on. I could get pregnant like you wouldn't believe, but I couldn't hold on to one. The doctor gave it some nasty name—habitual abortion, I think." She sighed. "It was just as well, in the long run. He was a sweet enough guy in his way, but God! We were both just kids, we had no business being married. He went to work in his daddy's dime store—there wasn't much else he could do—and I wanted to go back to school, and we had many fights about that. And then one morning I woke up and saw him getting fat and me getting dull, and I said, Chris, baby, if you're ever going to go, you'd better do it now. So I went."

"And you never checked out the miscarriages? Tried to find out why?"

"Not really. The doctor was pretty old-fashioned; he just sort of shrugged and told me to forget about having babies."

"And your husband never saw a doctor?"

"Ted? Heavens, no. He said he would, but he never got around to it." She sat silent for a long moment. "How'd we get into this, anyway? We were talking about my weird bone structure."

"Yeah, your bone structure," Rob said. "Trouble is, that doesn't mean anything. Recurrent spontaneous abortions could. But then, you may not want to dig into that."

196

"Maybe not right now. It's a little depressing." She looked at him narrowly. "Matter of fact, you don't seem too cheerful yourself right now."

"I guess I'm not. It's been a bad day."

"Doctors aren't supposed to have bad days. They're always supposed to be bright and chipper and positive about everything."

"I know. But sometimes things pile up."

"Like what things?"

Rob sighed. "Nothing important, really. It's just that coming into a practice like this can be frustrating as hell. Nothing ever goes the way it ought to, and when you try to get things to move, they refuse to budge."

Chris looked at him. "With that crowd I see out there in your waiting room, you can't tell me you're having trouble breaking the ice."

"Oh, I'm *busy* enough, God knows. There are more patients than I can keep track of, and some hellish long hours to boot."

"And no social life at all," Chris added.

"Not much. You see a lot of people, but a medical practice isn't a social life, and they don't really mix too well, either. I don't mind so much for myself. I love the work and there's plenty to do. But Ellie finds things pretty slow and dull."

"What does she expect in a town like this? Fireworks every night?"

"Well, not really. But I'm not free very much, and when I am we don't find a whole lot to talk about."

"Ah. But you can't blame the practice for that. That's purely up to you and Ellie, isn't it?" She looked at him quizzically. "You know, there's a lot going on in this world besides medical practice, Merlin— or have you just forgotten? Maybe you should open your eyes and look around a bit. And as for Ellie, if she's finding things dull in that little nest of hers out by the river, that's for *her* to think about. Why should she bother *you* about it? She must have known what a doctor's life would be like. If she didn't want it she shouldn't have bought it." Chris tossed her head scornfully. "There are plenty of things she could do around here if she wanted to! If she really wants to isolate herself, she's going at it the right way—but that's her problem, not yours. Why should she come whining to you about it?"

There was a rap on the door and Dora looked in. "Dr. Tanner, I'm sorry to interrupt, but Mrs. Lendy needs her baby checked, and she has to drive her husband to work. Can you take just a minute?"

"Oh, sure." Rob pushed back from his desk and stood up abruptly.

197

"We were just wrapping it up, anyway. I'll be there in a minute."

As the door closed again, Chris looked up at him. "Sorry, Merlin," she said.

"Why?"

"You're angry."

"Maybe a little. But it doesn't matter."

Her eyes, intensely green, met his. "I didn't mean to sound so nasty," she said. "I should learn to keep my mouth shut. But sometimes I get carried away and say what I really think."

"So I see." He took her hand as she rose to her feet. "Maybe you're just cutting a little too close to the bone; I don't know. Don't fret about it. I'll see you tomorrow at the Blood Bank meeting."

He watched her a moment as she walked down the corridor toward the front desk, then went in to check the Lendy baby and finish out the afternoon's schedule. She wasn't entirely right, he reflected, or even fair in what she'd said. Ellie *wasn't* deliberately isolating herself; in fact, she was trying her damnedest not to, and just getting nowhere. But Chris had struck a nerve about one thing: for whatever the reason, practice or otherwise, his relationship with Ellie was indeed going downhill, maybe a lot more so than he wanted to think about. And he *was* angry; for a moment it had seemed that he and Ellie had been glimpsed, however briefly, by the cold scientific eye of an outsider, pinned to the wall like an interesting specimen. Yet somehow he could not think of this green-eyed girl entirely as an outsider. There was a sense of comfortable easiness in her presence, an odd sense that they had somehow known each other for many years and talked long and intimately many times before, without any need for dissembling. And what bothered him most was that possibly what Chris had said was precisely the truth as she saw it—and perhaps a lot closer to home, in some ways, than he had any idea.

# 18

The Friday evening meeting at Dottie Hazard's was suffused with a sense of excitement and accomplishment. It seemed to Rob that half the town was crowded into the tiny living room—Al Davidson, with his fluttery wife; Gordon Jenks, the pharmacist; Chris Erickson; Judge Barret, settled back contentedly in a threadbare old easy chair; Janice Blanchard, mother of the leukemic baby, and her heavy-set, red-faced husband; a half-dozen others. Dottie Hazard—small, dark-haired and immensely pregnant—was running the meeting, with her husband, Joe, leaning back on a kitchen chair puffing sleepily on a pipe. The only one conspicuously absent was Roger Painter.

"Okay; I think we've finally got this proposal in shape to hand it to Roger," Dottie was saying. "He said he'd present it at the next hospital directors' meeting, and we're going to hold him to it. I've followed Dr. Tanner's advice and cut out anything that sounded like criticism or finger-pointing—just presented the case the way we see it: if the hospital will sponsor the project, get the necessary licenses and cover the cost of lab work from ongoing hospital charges, we'll raise funds for the storage unit." She handed out photocopies of the proposal to everybody. "If any of you see any problems, speak up now."

There was a shuffling of paper as people read the draft. Al Davidson coughed. "I think you've put it pretty well," he said. "What do you think, Judge? You're on the board of directors."

199

Judge Barret shrugged. "Looks pretty straightforward to me," he said. "They'll either say yes or no, and it shouldn't take them a lot of time to decide." He adjusted his glasses. "Where it says here: 'the Committee is determined . . .,' that sounds a little bit militant and threatening. Maybe you could just say: 'the Committee is eager . . .'"

Several others murmured assent. "Okay, I'll change that," Dottie conceded. "Now, where do we stand with the money?"

"We've got five hundred and fifty dollars in the bank," Janice Blanchard said. "That's plenty to cover newspaper appeals, make up fliers and pay postage. Members of the committee have got another five hundred dollars pledged. Chris says John Stanley has practically promised that the mill will give two thousand dollars if the hospital sponsors it, and we certainly ought to be able to get a thousand dollars from each of the clinics." She gave Rob a long look over her glasses. "With a lot of smaller donations, we should have the storage unit paid for in a couple of months. Put a big fund-raising graph down in front of the post office where everybody can see how it's going."

"Fine." Dottie looked around at the crowd. "The only remaining question is who should take this to Roger Painter. Seems to me it should be one of the doctors."

"Not me," Rob said. "Roger doesn't like this to begin with, and I'd just make things worse. I think a delegation of just plain citizens would be better. Judge, you're one director who's on our side already. Dottie, you're obviously going to be a customer of the place any day now, and Gordon gives Roger a fat discount on all the drugs he orders. Why don't you three go?"

"Sounds good to me," the pharmacist said. "When's the next board meeting, Judge?"

"Next Friday night."

"Then let's go see Roger on Monday, beard the bastard in his den."

As the meeting began to break up, Chris Erickson came over to Rob. "Still angry, Merlin?"

Rob grinned. "How could I be angry, when we've finally got this blood bank thing rolling?" he said. "I actually think we've got half a chance to win. And we owe nine tenths of it to Dottie here and her superior organizing ability."

Dottie Hazard flushed. "Don't thank me," she said. "Without you we'd never even have gotten started. I just hope the directors buy it, that's all. Maybe I'm just overnervous in this delicate condition of mine,

200

but I keep thinking what might happen if I were to get up there and something really broke loose."

"Well, don't borrow trouble," Rob told her. "Nothing's going to break loose with Martin on hand. And I'll bet in the long run even Martin is going to be glad to have that blood storage unit in there." He looked at Chris. "Need a lift home?"

"Nope. I've got the company jeep." She laughed. "There, now. You see how I kill my chances."

"Well, that's for *you* to think about," Rob said. "And touché. I'd better get on home."

Ellie was still up, hand-stitching a blouse she was working on, and he told her about the meeting. "Well, I hope the directors don't just bury it," she said.

"I don't see how they can. They've just *got* to be responsive to a committee of citizens like this."

"I hope so. I'll sure be glad to see the end of these meetings."

Rob looked at her. "You could go to them too, you know."

"No, I think you're wrong. I really couldn't. This is town politics you're getting into now, and there's not a way in the world a new doctor's wife here can fit into that kind of scene. Maybe *you* can get away with it, on a medical question, but *I* can't."

"Well, maybe you're right." He watched her doggedly stitching a seam as though it were all that existed in the universe. It struck him, then, that she had been exceptionally short with him all week. "Ellie —I'm really trying to break things open and get away from this perpetual call. Okay?"

She looked up. "Have you talked to Martin about the OB coverage?"

"Yes, I talked to him."

"And what did he say?"

"He said he'd think about it."

"Great," she said. "And meantime I guess you just stand by and hold your breath."

"Well, I really can't cram it down his throat," Rob said. "Jesus, honey, it's his practice. . . ."

"Oh, *that's* clear enough. You're just here to do piecework, so to speak."

"That's not true," he said. He crossed the room, took the sewing out of her hands. "That's really not true, and you know it."

"I know," she said, defeated.

"I'm here to do a decent job of practicing medicine."

"I know."

"And I'm here for *us*, too."

She looked up at him, then looked away. "I guess."

"So let's stop digging at me. Give me a chance."

"But I need something too."

"Of course you do. I know that."

"I don't mean just a pay check once a month, either," she said. "I need a husband, somebody to *live* with, not just to get dinner for now and then. Somebody to start a family with—"

"Do you really think this is the best time for that?"

"No, of course I don't. The thing that scares me is that maybe there isn't going to *be* any best time."

"But that's silly."

"Is it?" She looked up at him. "You know, at least we used to *talk* about it once in a while—us having a baby someday. But not anymore. Not for a long time."

"I know that. But what's the point of talking about it until we're ready? And *I'm* sure not ready for it right now. Of course we're going to want to have a baby someday. Maybe it ought to be someday pretty soon. Maybe we should really start talking seriously about it in another few months. But *now?* Until I can get some kind of thumb on this practice, I haven't even got time to be a decent husband—as you keep pointing out—much less a decent father."

"I suppose not. But you might give it some thought, just the same." She met his eyes. "I'm sorry. I've got to get to bed. I'm tired."

He watched her go, then found a beer in the refrigerator and walked out to the quiet of the patio for a few minutes. The river below made a cheerful gurgling sound, magnified by the darkness. The air was incredibly sweet, the stars incredibly bright. He sat on the chaise longue, staring at the dark ghost shapes of the cottonwoods across the river, thinking of what Ellie had said, and of Chris's sharp words earlier in the week. *She was right, of course. It's not just the practice, not by a long shot. A whole lot of it is us.* He shook his head. *I should have done what Ellie said—just told Martin we'd be gone this weekend, and then packed up and left. Too late now, but something's sure going sour.* He cast about in his mind for solutions, found none. *Maybe tomorrow I'll just sign out to Martin, for a couple of hours at least, and take Ellie for a drive up into the mountains, explore some of the back roads. She'd like that, and Martin could spare me for half a day.*

He was more weary than he knew; it was almost ten o'clock next morning when he woke, to find Ellie dressed in a trim pants suit instead of her usual dungarees and blouse, putting finishing touches on her makeup. "What are you up to?" he said.

"Maybe you have to stay around all weekend waiting for the boss to call," she said, "but I don't. I'm taking Belle into Missoula shopping for the day. Of course, you can come too, if you want."

"No—I guess I'd better stick around."

"Well, that poor dear hasn't been into the city a single time in the last seven years, so we're going to shop up a storm. She says there's a farmer's market on Saturdays too, just outside of town."

"Sounds great," Rob said without enthusiasm. "Just don't bring home a pig on a string."

A few minutes later Belle turned up at the back door, her powder a little too thick on her nose, the usual blue beret replaced today by a bright red one, but still wearing her old woolen overcoat, with shopping bags in either hand. She gave Rob a sly glance. "You're not going along?" she said.

"No, I don't think so."

"Well, that's *your* loss, I guess. But I brought you a consolation prize." She dug down into a shopping bag and handed him a loaf of bread wrapped in plastic. "See what you think of that."

"It's still warm!" Rob said.

"Of course it's still warm—I just baked it this morning. Princess helped; she always helps me with the baking."

"But you must have gotten up at five A.M."

"Always get up at five." Belle grinned. *"Carpe diem,* I always say." Then, bright-eyed and chipper, she climbed into the car beside Ellie, eager as a child on circus day.

"You're not taking Princess along?" Rob said.

"Not Princess; she's got to take care of the house and the other cats while I'm gone," Belle said. "I left the oven door open, though, so she can lick up the apple pie drippings when it cools down. She loves that, Princess does."

With that, they were on their way, and Rob went back in to cook some breakfast. *So much for a drive in the mountains,* he thought sourly. *Damn. One day I do get off and she takes out of here so fast . . .* He sniffed the fresh bread suspiciously, made a piece of toast and nibbled it, then devoured a second and a third. *Well, hell. I guess I can't*

203

*blame her, but Jesus! Maybe tomorrow . . .*

After breakfast he puttered for a while, wandering around the place like a lost soul, picking up a journal and leafing through it for a few minutes, then tossing it aside, thinking about washing the car but deciding not to. It was hot for mid-September, but the chilly nights were nipping the cottonwood leaves, already turning them orange-yellow. He turned on the radio, got only country music, turned it off again. Presently he went up and swept pine needles out of the roof gutters, then patched a couple of places where the sun had cracked the roofing tar. Some kids came floating down the river on inner tubes, splashing and shouting. Around one o'clock he had a sandwich and a beer, took a long, cool shower, afterward stretching out on the chaise longue on the patio. He tried to nap, but couldn't even doze, increasingly bored, increasingly disgusted with himself. *Damn! Should have gone with them. Better than just sitting around . . .*

Then at two-thirty the phone rang and he fairly leaped for it. An old diabetic he'd been seeing in the office had just collapsed on his living room floor. "It's probably just insulin shock," the man's wife said. "He's done it before, you know. Forgets he already took his insulin and gives himself a second shot on top of the first one and then passes out like a poleaxed mule. I've already started rubbing honey under his tongue, like you told me, but sometimes he has convulsions and he's too big for me to handle. If you could come out . . ."

"Oh, sure, no problem. You live on Camp 18 Road?"

"That's right. Eight miles back from the highway."

"Okay; I'll be right along."

He knew the road, taking off up a canyon a few miles north of town. First it wound for a mile or two through an old logged area, then upward through a beautiful dense forest of old-growth cedar, fir and ponderosa pine. Here and there he saw small homes nestled back in the woods, many of them built and occupied at the time the very first settlers came to Twin Forks. As he rounded a curve in a heavily wooded stretch he saw an old green jeep parked in a turnoff. *Chris? What's she doing out here?* He hesitated a moment, then drove on up to a plateau a few miles farther along. There he saw a modest house set back against the hill, with his patient's name on the roadside mailbox.

As it turned out, he needn't even have come. The old man, out cold from insulin shock when his wife called, had recovered as soon as the honey had been applied. He was still a little disoriented, but his blood pressure was normal and he was able to move around by the time Rob

204

arrived. Rob checked him over and the man confirmed that he must have taken an extra dose of insulin by accident. "Memory's not so sharp anymore, Doc," he said. "Sometimes it's clear as a bell, but sometimes it's a little hazy."

"Well, you need some way to remember," Rob said.

"Eh? How's that?"

"I said you need a system to remember your insulin," Rob shouted. "Your dosage may be off too. Come see me in the office Monday or Tuesday so we can check things out."

"Oh, sure. I've already got an appointment for Monday."

"Fine. You keep it."

The man's wife apologized for the unnecessary house call, but Rob shook his head. "Don't worry about that," he said. "Insulin is tricky stuff for a man that age. You let me know if he starts to get shocky again."

A warm breeze struck his cheek as he started back down the canyon, and he dawdled along the road, enjoying the clusters of gold-and-red-leafed deciduous trees scattered among the evergreens. The heavy pine scent was reminiscent of hot midsummer days in the woods, but the ground was yellow with fallen needles in the golden tamarack groves. He found Chris's jeep still parked in the little roadside turnoff, and on impulse he pulled in to park behind it, peering off into the woods. At first he saw nothing. Then, as he climbed out, he heard a branch snap in the woods off to the right, and saw Chris in blue jeans and a short-sleeved white blouse, some seventy-five yards back in the woods. She was walking very slowly along the open forest floor, peering down intently, stooping from time to time, then walking on, unaware that he was there. Rob watched with growing curiosity. In her left hand she carried a yellow plastic bucket, and in her right hand something glinted from time to time in the patchy sunlight.

Finally he called out. "What are you looking for? Moths?"

Chris straightened up with a start. "Lord, no! Something far more interesting. Come help me hunt."

He pushed through the dense underbrush at the road edge. Once beyond that the undergrowth was thinner and lower, and he found the soft, mossy forest floor surprisingly open except for a scattering of half-rotten windfalls. As he came up to Chris he saw that the glinting object was a kitchen paring knife. "What *are* you doing in here?"

She grinned. "Hunting for these." She handed him a large, damp yellow object.

He looked at it dubiously. "Looks like a toadstool to me."

"There's no such thing, silly. It's a wild mushroom."

He looked more closely. It was a flaring, trumpet-shaped growth, the orange-yellow color of beaten egg yolks, with a thin, curving stem. The outside seemed wrinkled, with a pinkish, powdery tinge to the yellow. The cap was some three inches across. He flicked off a couple of pine needles with his finger, saw the girl's bucket was half full of similar specimens. "I never saw one like this before," he said.

"They're chanterelles, and you can't get them in stores. Millions of them out here, though."

"The only wild mushrooms I ever saw were the little brown spongelike things I used to hunt with my grandfather," Rob said.

"Those are morels, and they're grand, but they only come in the spring. These turn up in the fall. They're early this year; that rain last week and all this warm weather has brought them out by the score. Come on and look. There are a couple over there."

Rob followed her, and saw two of the mushrooms pushing their way up through the moss. "I'll get them. Oh, say, there are four or five more."

Chris laughed. "You'll get hooked yet. Here, take a bag and use the knife. Just cut the stem off at ground level and then scrape off the pine needles." She fished a plastic bag from a hip pocket and handed it to him along with the paring knife. "Unless I miss my guess, that little ravine over there should be full of them." Her eyes were bright, her cheeks flushed as she pounced on another cluster and popped them into the bucket. She was perspiring lightly and had a smudge of dirt under one eye. "You're not in a terrible rush?"

"Not right at the moment."

"Oh, good. Then help me hunt for a while." She started off down the ravine, motioning him to follow. He watched her admiringly for a moment, then came along.

"What do you do with these when you've found them?" he asked. "Are they good to eat?"

"Oh, they're nummy. Just fry them up with butter and a little salt. You never tasted anything like them."

Rob followed her, searching the ground for signs of the yellow mushrooms pushing up through the pine needles. In one place he found a whole cluster of them growing under some low-standing green shrubs; more were growing in the lee of a huge windfall trunk that he climbed over. As they started down into the ravine he saw additional clusters waiting to be picked. "Hold it a minute—here's a different

206

kind." He pointed to a large umbrella-shaped mushroom with a sticky-looking red cap covered with little flecks of white.

"Better let that one be. It's a fly amanita—poisonous. Here, look." Chris stooped down, took the knife and loosened the soil to lift the red mushroom out, stem and all. "See the cup here at the base of the stem? That's one sign of a bad one. Then there's the ring around the middle of the stem, and the 'oatmeal flakes' on the sticky cap. That one mushroom could put you out of circulation for a week." She tossed it aside with a little shudder.

"Where'd you learn all this, anyway?"

"Oh, I've been a mushroom nut for years," she said. "They're fun to identify, and you can find some good ones almost every season except the dead of winter." They went on with the search, Rob leading the way down the ravine, Chris squealing with delight at her finds. For a quarter of an hour they poked along in comfortable silence, intent on their quest. Rob found his eyes accommodating to close examination of the forest floor, spotting a dozen different mosses and ferns, tiny fall-flowering shrubs, berry bushes. The sunlight filtered down through the dense treetops, spreading an odd diffuse greenish-golden light, mottled with spots of yellow, and the mossy ground was soft and deep as a thick carpet. At one point Rob snapped a fallen branch, and halfway down the slope a doe and a fawn leaped from their beds and went crashing noisily off through the woods. He paused, looked back up the slope to Chris. "Lord, but it's beautiful in here."

"It always is. So quiet, yet so full of life. It's like a different world, a magical place. . . ." She caught his hand for support as she climbed over a gnarled root and he was suddenly, fiercely aware of her small, lithe body and her braless breasts pushing at her blouse.

Further down the slope a huge windfall log blocked their path. Chris began working her way around it, away from him; Rob climbed up on it and then dropped to the ground ten feet below, catching himself against a rotting stump. Looking down, he saw a large, leafy fungal growth at the base of the stump. It was the size of a basketball and looked for all the world like a huge head of brownish-white cauliflower. "Hey, here's a really *ugly* one," he called out.

"What? Where?"

"Right down here."

She climbed up on the log above him and peered down. "Oh, Rob, you're *lucky*—you *must* be a magician! There's at least ten pounds of it there."

"Ten pounds of what?"

"It's called Sparassis—a true cauliflower mushroom. It's very rare, and one of the best-tasting mushrooms anywhere. Here, help me down."

He reached up for her extended hand as she edged forward on the log, preparing to jump. Then her foot slipped and she came crashing down on top of him, clutching at him for support. He caught her full to his body and they tumbled down onto the moss as his footing slipped, his arms around her, his face very close to hers, her body remarkably light in his arms. Then suddenly he was kissing her, feeling her shoulders yield to his grip, feeling her whole body pressing to him urgently, her arms tight around his chest. He brought his lips to her cheek, to her neck, then back again to her lips, hungrily, met her tongue as she responded fully. For a brief moment the cloth of her blouse seemed to fight his fingers, clinging stubbornly to her skin, but then it came away and she was helping him, offering her breast to his lips, aiding his fingers until clothes were torn aside, then coming to him swiftly, eagerly. "Oh, yes, love. Oh, God, *yes* . . ." Not until she exploded in climax many minutes later, gasping and sobbing and urging him on, did his own release come, indescribably delightful, and then they lay spent on the mossy bank in the flicker-filtered half-light of the forest.

Long moments later he stirred against her, looked down at her pixie face. "Chris, listen . . ."

"I know, I know. You think I'm made of stone or something?" She pressed her cheek to his chest. "Well, I'm not."

He pulled himself away, suddenly and blindingly appalled at himself. "I mean, I didn't plan . . ."

"Hush."

"But I've got to tell you . . ." He fumbled foolishly for his clothes.

"Hush, love. Don't *talk*. I know." She stretched voluptuously, smiling at him. "It was magical, but now you've got to go."

"Yes, I've got to go."

"And that's all right too, for now."

"Chris, I had no *right*. . . ."

"Oh, piffle." She tossed him his trousers, slipped on her blouse. "There aren't any rights and wrongs, love. Not in a magic forest. Remember that—and don't forget your mushrooms." Quickly she stooped down, cut the Sparassis free at its base. "You only get half," she said. "It's too good not to share." She scooped his half into his plastic bag, put hers in another and set it in her bucket. "Just one more thing," she said. She looked up at him, put her arms around his neck and kissed him once more, lingeringly. "Now go," she said. "I'll come along later."

He walked back out to his car, still shaken, still appalled at himself. He had never before been unfaithful to Ellie, not once, and a wave of guilt swept through him like a fire storm. It was followed swiftly by another thought, unbidden, unintended, almost pleasurably vicious— *Well, maybe it's about time*—and he felt himself cringe at the very meanness of it. As he backed his car away from the jeep, a blue pickup truck came around the curve in the road from the opposite direction. In a guilty move, Rob ducked his head, then watched in his rear-view mirror until the pickup curved on out of sight. Then he drove on down the canyon as fast as the road would allow.

Moments later he was crossing the bridge and turning left into his own driveway, just a little before four, and he sighed with relief that Ellie was not back yet. It was not until he had turned off the motor and started to climb out that he saw the bulging plastic bag on the car seat beside him. He stared at it as if it were blood on his hands, weighing alternatives. Finally he sighed, and shrugged, and carried the mushrooms into the kitchen for cleaning. It was either lie to Ellie or lie to Chris—and Chris would be the one, he felt suddenly certain, who would be sure to spot it.

# 19

On Monday morning Rob tackled Isaacs with renewed determination about the question of OB coverage. "You said you'd think about it," he said. "So what have you decided?"

Isaacs shook his head. "Boy, I just don't know," he said unhappily. "I talked to a couple of patients, just tossed up the idea, and they didn't like it at all."

Rob sighed. "Jesus, Martin, if you're just going to meekly ask their permission, they're going to say no every time."

"Well, what do you want me to do?"

"*Tell* them, for God's sake! Tell them that's the way it's going to be from now on. Period. And then *do* it."

"Yeah, I suppose you're right," Isaacs said. "Maybe I could just start by telling the new ones, instead of dropping a bomb on the ones who are all set to deliver."

"Then all you're doing is putting it off for six months. Why not start right now? And as for the new ones, why not just cut down on the number you take on to begin with?"

Isaacs looked blank. "What do you mean?"

"Send them across the hall to me," Rob said. "Tell them your schedule is full and have Terry start booking them with me instead."

"Rob, you just can't shove people around like that," Isaacs said. "It might work with women brand-new to the practice, but what about the

210

ones I've delivered before? What about the refugees from Florey who don't want anybody but me? Some of these women are damned fussy, and you can't just tell them to go to hell." He sipped unhappily at his coffee. "On the other hand, I suppose I've got to start somewhere or I'll *never* get rid of this load. Just give me time; I'll think of something," and he lumbered on down the hall.

He didn't sound very convincing, and Rob, disgusted, figured that was the last he would hear. Thus he was startled on Tuesday—Isaacs' regular OB day—when the older man buzzed him on the office intercom and summoned him down to his office. He found Isaacs there with Dottie Hazard. The woman was looking more imminent than ever. "Rob, you've met Dottie, haven't you?" Isaacs said.

"Oh, sure." Rob smiled. "She's chairman of the Blood Bank Committee."

"Oh, yeah? Well, I was just telling Dottie that I've got to go to the Western Obstetrical Society meeting in Spokane later this week, so you'll be covering for me. I'll be leaving Thursday morning and won't be back until Sunday night. I think I told you about it."

It was the first Rob had heard about it, but he just nodded. "Now, Dottie isn't due until sometime next month," Isaacs went on, "but she's been having some false labor, and she might just have her dates wrong, so she's going to call you if her membranes rupture, or anything like that. Okay?"

"Fine," Rob said. "I'll be around all weekend."

"Good. I've told her to come in again Thursday, just to have you check her. So far her cervix isn't dilating, and the baby's head is still high as a kite, but you never can tell." He looked at Dottie. "You understand? Give Dr. Tanner a call if anything happens. And of course Agnes will be around too if you do go into labor."

"Oh, nothing's going to happen," Dottie said. "Last time with Janie I had contractions for weeks before I really got going. But I'll call if I have to."

Later, looking somewhat foolish, Isaacs told him, "You probably won't even hear from her, but if you do you won't have any trouble. She's had two babies already and she's pretty relaxed. She'll go smooth as silk if she goes."

"Fine," Rob said, trying to keep a straight face. "I'll stay in touch. What is this meeting, anyway?"

"Meeting? Oh, yeah. It's a clinical conference the Western OB group holds every year. There's going to be a man from Boston there

I'd like to hear. Anyway, it's time I got away from here for a couple of days." Isaacs hesitated. "I'll give you a Thursday to make up for your Friday sometime when you want a long weekend."

"Don't sweat it; just have a good time," Rob said. "Is Jennie going?"

"No, she doesn't like these meetings. Nothing for the wives to do; she'd just go shopping, and that's hard on the wallet."

"Well, maybe we can have her for dinner one night," Rob said. "I'll check with Ellie."

It was clearly ridiculous; it was 100 percent the wrong way to go about turning over OB call, obviously a snap decision on Martin's part, but Rob didn't argue. *He just can't let go, as long as he's around,* Rob reflected, *and he knows that woman's going to pop just as well as I do. But maybe when he's done it once, it'll make it easier. If only he doesn't change his mind . . .*

Isaacs didn't. Thursday morning dawned rainy, with a chill wind coming down from the pass, and Rob was ready to bet gold coins that the older man had altered his plans when he found him at the hospital making early rounds, but Isaacs merely grumbled about the lousy driving weather and the lack of justice in the world and got into his car and left. Back at the office, Rob found that Terry at the front desk had had even less warning of Isaacs' departure than Rob did; there was a panic of schedule-juggling, and both Rob and Jerry were buried under an extra load of patients all that day and Friday too. At least on Friday the weather broke and a cool autumn sun came out, which was fortunate because Ellie had invited Jennie Isaacs for dinner and wanted to try a leg of lamb on the new rotisserie Rob had bought for the outdoor grill. "She sounded delighted to come," Ellie said as Rob arrived home and changed shirts half an hour before the appointed time. "She also sounded almost startled. As if it was something nobody had ever thought of before. Do you suppose they ever go anywhere?"

"Beats me," Rob said. "It sure doesn't seem to matter whether he's on call or not; he's always rooting around the hospital or the office doing *something.* Far as I know, this Spokane meeting is the first time he's been out of Twin Forks since July."

"Not that we're exactly world travelers ourselves," Ellie added. "See if you can rig this roast. I've got it all off balance."

An hour later Jennie Isaacs arrived, looking fresh and autumny in a brown and orange pants suit and bringing as a hostess gift a lovely bottle of a French Bordeaux that had clearly not been purchased in any local liquor store. Ellie glanced at her husband and said, "Too bad Rob

212

is on call; he'll just have to pass up his share," but Jennie, looking inscrutable, shook her head.

"Don't open it tonight," she said. "Keep it until just the two of you are going to have a nice steak sometime. Red wine always gives me a headache."

Then Ellie offered a peppery tomato-juice-and-lime cocktail and hors d'oeuvres and they sat out on the patio while the lamb was finishing, despite a slight chill as the sun set. Jennie seemed somewhat more relaxed than on their first encounter, almost convivial as she listened to them talk about their life together in Philadelphia before coming West —but there was a strained quality to her conviviality, and they both noticed again her odd habit of hesitating before she spoke, as if she were consciously seeking to place her words in just the proper sequence. *Almost as if she were about to stammer,* Rob thought, *or had to have permission to speak.* What was more, although she responded to questions and reacted to comments, she rarely introduced a topic herself; soon both Rob and Ellie were groping to find things their guest was able to talk about. Time and again she would meet a remark, a query or a statement with a two-word response followed by silence. Finally Rob, who was none too facile at small talk under any circumstances, busied himself basting the meat and fiddling with the charcoal. Ellie mentioned her trouble finding a certain wallpaper pattern she had seen in a magazine among Davidson's local selection, and Jennie said, "Oh, it's awful; he doesn't have any variety at all." Then, after an awkward pause, she added, "I even took him in a pattern once for him to try to order it for me."

"That's an idea," Ellie said. "Did you have any luck?"

"No." Silence.

"You'd think he might at least have been able to find something close."

"No. He kept saying an order was coming for three or four weeks, but it never did."

Silence.

Rob asked if she and Martin had vacation plans anytime soon. "Oh, I couldn't say," Jennie replied. "That depends so much on Martin, you know. How much work there is, and all. Of course, you've done a lot to ease the load, Martin keeps saying what a help you've been, but . . ." She made a small, helpless gesture with her hands. "It's so hard to decide where to go." Pause. "Martin's been thinking maybe we should go to Sacramento for Christmas." Pause. "He has family there."

213

Only at one point all evening did Jennie show a flicker of genuine interest. Rob had finally announced the roast was ready, and as they went inside for dinner Jennie's eyes lit on Ellie's little spinet piano in the corner of the living room. "Oh, look," she exclaimed. "Who plays?"

"I play a little," Ellie said. "That was my grandmother's."

"Yes, it's a lovely, lovely old one." Jennie touched it daintily with a finger, then struck a sequence of chords and a fragment of a Chopin nocturne. "And what beautiful tone from such a tiny little thing! It must be two hundred years old."

"Do you play much?" Ellie said.

"I used to, years ago," Jennie said. "I was very good back then; I even played a few concerts. But just when things were opening up, I met Martin, and we were married, and then of course the concerts had to go. . . ."

"Well, anytime you'd like, come out and play," Ellie said. "You're always welcome."

"Yes, that would be so nice. I will," Jennie said. But then, at dinner, the brief flicker of light faded; she seemed almost embarrassed to have mentioned her playing, and sank once again into monosyllabic responses. The lamb tasted fine, but they limped through the meal with straggling and disjointed conversation. In desperation Rob got to telling long shaggy-dog stories about the vagaries of Pacific Northwest weather, stories about his residency in Seattle, stories about Ellie. Occasionally Jennie would smile vaguely at an appropriate moment, but at no point did she laugh. When the phone rang in the midst of dessert and coffee, Rob leaped with ill-disguised relief at the opportunity to go see a sick child at the clinic. An hour later he returned to find Jennie preparing to depart, yet apparently unable to make the final move necessary to take her leave. For a full twenty minutes they stood together by the back door in the midst of constantly lapsing small talk as Jennie examined her car keys for the tenth time, said for the tenth time what a lovely time she'd had, remarked for the tenth time how she really hated to leave but thought she'd better, and at last finally made it out the door to the driveway. For long moments Rob and Ellie stood in suspended animation, almost holding their breath for fear she might have forgotten something. Then they heard the engine start, and a moment later saw her small car drive slowly across the bridge.

Ellie slumped against the kitchen door. "Sorry, kid," Rob said. "It seemed like a good idea."

She shook her head. "Nothing wrong with the idea. It just didn't work."

"It wasn't your fault. The dinner was great. You did everything you could think of."

"I know. But God, that poor woman. Oh, Rob!" She turned to him suddenly, threw her arms around him, buried her face in his chest, weeping.

"Honey, honey, don't," he said softly.

"I can't help it," she said, shaking with sobs. "I just can't help it. I look at her and I see—" She broke off, clinging to him in silence then as he patted her back, stroked her hair. "I'm sorry," she said finally, starting to push away. "I—I've got to do these dishes."

He held her close. "Later," he said gently. "The dishes will keep."

# 20

The night was remarkably quiet, just one minor call after midnight, but Saturday started with a rush and turned into a day Rob was not soon to forget. Isaacs had left half a dozen sick patients in the hospital, so Rob's seven o'clock morning rounds dragged on well past ten. When he finally reached the office, Dora was clucking like an old mother hen. "You're going to have to move right along," she said. "They're stacked up out there like cordwood."

Herman Barney was first in line, in for his weekly weight check and pep talk. With his heart failure really controlled for the first time in ten years, he had actually come in without crutches and was busily showing everybody in the clinic the three inches his wife had taken in on his still-voluminous trousers. "Down another three pounds, Doc," he crowed. "Just like we planned."

"Herman, you're doing great," Rob agreed. "Keep on this way and you'll be down a hundred pounds in no time. And then maybe we can get you off those heart pills for good."

"Don't worry, Doc, I've got it whipped now. I know I can control it."

Rob gave him a sharp look. "If you believe that, you're in trouble, my friend. This next week is going to be the toughest one yet. Never mind having it whipped, just dig in and do it, and I'll see you a week from Monday."

216

In the corridor Dora handed him Dottie Hazard's chart. "She says you told her to come back today," she said.

He had—not because active labor had seemed imminent, but just to play things safe. Now he found Dottie perched disconsolately on the end of his examining table. "Anything going on?" he asked.

"Not much," Dottie said, "except the baby's been kicking hell out of me all night. Does that mean anything?"

"Just means it's in good shape," Rob said. He buzzed for Dora and put on a glove to examine the woman. "Still having contractions?"

"Oh, yes, about once every ten minutes, same as before," she said unhappily. "No change there."

"Well, I can't say they're accomplishing much; the baby's head is still floating. But give me a call if anything changes."

He moved on down his schedule as quickly as he could, putting off one or two time-consuming workups until Monday. By one o'clock the crowd of patients in the waiting room had dwindled and vanished. Dora flipped the office phone onto the answering tape, restocked Rob's black bag with supplies for house calls, and scurried off; but Rob remained for a while in the pleasant, empty silence of the place, charting notes on the patients he had seen that morning, and dictating a couple of insurance letters. Then he leaned back in his chair, enjoying the momentary island of quiet, just sitting, alone and unreachable, for a few moments. Finally he stood up, slipped into his street jacket, locked the office behind him, and drove down to the highway toward home and lunch.

Ellie met him at the door and shattered his wistful visions of a quiet afternoon. "The hospital called twice in the last half hour," she said. "There's been a nasty accident up on the pass, and they want you right away. Here, I've made a sandwich you can eat on the way."

He arrived at the hospital just as the ambulance was pulling in, followed by a highway patrol car with flashing lights. One victim had apparently ridden in the patrol car, a tall man with an injured arm and a huge purple lump on his forehead. Two others were on stretchers in the ambulance: a woman so covered with blood it was impossible to tell much of anything at first glance, and a man lying on his side, doubled up and groaning. The blood-covered woman was insisting that she was "all right" and urging Rob to look at her husband first. "He's the one that's hurt, Doctor—he's hurt bad!" Rob checked her over enough to be sure she had a strong pulse and normal breathing, and signaled the driver to wheel her on into the emergency room.

The man's injuries indeed seemed more urgent. He remained doubled up on his side, moaning, "Oh, it hurts—God, but it hurts," over and over, but could only shake his head when Rob asked what it was, exactly, that hurt so much. With Nellie Webster peering over his shoulder, he tried in vain to pinpoint the site of distress, but one thing was sure: the man's pulse was extremely rapid and shallow and he seemed to be breathing in little painful grunts. "Well, *something's* sure going on," Rob said. "Let's get him right onto the x-ray table and get his clothes off. Get a pressure cuff on him too; I don't like that pulse a bit. Meanwhile maybe Happy can start washing the blood off that woman so we can tell where it all came from."

As Nellie and Raymond wheeled the man in toward x-ray, the patrolman came up to Rob. "What about this guy in my car? He can walk."

"Good. Then walk him inside and plant him somewhere," Rob said. "We'll catch him as soon as the x-ray is free. Looks like he really whacked something with his head."

"He whacked something, all right. Went right through the windshield head first."

"What happened, anyway?"

"This guy blew a front tire and swerved into the opposite lane, going sixty. Took the other car head-on. It's a wonder any of them are moving."

"Well, see that he doesn't fall on his face, okay? I've got trouble enough with this other one right now." Rob walked back into the x-ray room, where Raymond, Nellie and Happy were shifting the first man onto the table. Movement was obviously painful, and the man cried out at one point. "Easy, there," Rob said. "We've got to get a look at you."

"Where am I?"

"You're at a hospital in Twin Forks. I'm a doctor. I need to know where you're hurting."

"Oh, God, Doc, my belly."

"Whereabouts in your belly?"

Gently Rob explored with his hand. The man's abdominal muscles were stiff as boards. "Can you loosen up a little?"

"I don't know. Don't dig around in there. . . ." Momentarily the man relaxed his muscles, then tightened them up again with a groan. "I just can't."

Rob finished undressing him. There was a huge purple bruise low down on his chest on the left; Rob saw it and frowned. "What's his blood pressure?"

218

"A hundred and ten over sixty," Nellie said. "The pulse is one twenty." She lowered her voice. "He doesn't look very good to me."

"He sure doesn't. Let's get a vein open with a plastic needle. A liter of five percent glucose to start with, and have some Dextran ready to go. Better take blood for typing and crossmatch when you enter the vein. He could have a ruptured spleen."

"What about x-rays?" Raymond said.

"Looks like he took the steering wheel in the lower left chest. Get a chest film and a flat plate of the abdomen, and a couple of good rib shots. And make it fast; he's not going to like moving around. Then cath him for a urine specimen too. I've got to be sure he hasn't got a kidney bleeding."

While the others went to work on the man on the x-ray table, Rob walked back to the woman in the emergency room. Happy Cumley was washing blood from her face and neck. "How's Harvey?" the woman demanded as soon as she saw Rob.

"We're checking him out now," Rob said. "He may have some internal injuries, but he's stable for now. How about you?"

"Head aches a little bit," the woman said. "The nurse says I just cut my scalp a little."

"Well, it just takes a nick there to bleed all over. Let's have a look." Carefully Rob inspected the woman, found an inch-long laceration of the scalp that was still trickling blood. Methodically he went on, checking her from head to toe. "Okay, Happy, just shave the scalp around that wound and set up a suture tray for me. I'll be back in a minute." He went over to the third victim, the driver of the blowout car, lying on a stretcher across the room. In addition to a huge welt on his forehead, the man had a contusion of the right elbow and a deep laceration of the forearm. He seemed otherwise stable. When Nellie Webster came up, Rob said, "Let's just clean and dress this arm for the moment. When we get a chance, we'll want skull films and films of the right arm and elbow, but he's going to have to wait. How's the other man doing?"

"Raymond got the films, but the man almost passed out on us, and his blood pressure is slipping—just barely one hundred systolic now."

"Still a lot of pain?"

"It seems worse, if anything."

"How about his urine?"

"Nice and clear."

Rob walked back into the x-ray room just as Raymond opened the darkroom door and hung the wet films up on the view boxes. Normal chest film, no rib fractures. Rob sighed. On the x-ray table the patient was lying on his back, groaning, knees drawn up, still guarding his abdomen. Rob walked over to him. "Harvey, when did you eat last?"

"Eat? A little breakfast about eight this morning. Just coffee and toast."

"Nothing at all since?"

"Nothing. Doc, can I have a drink of water?"

"Not now. You've got some internal injuries and probably some bleeding. We may have to go in to stop it."

The man groaned. "Anything you say, Doc—but can't you get me something for the pain?"

"You bet I can," Rob said. "Then we're going to have to put a tube down in your stomach. All you'll have to do is swallow and let it slide down. Try to help us as much as you can."

He drew Raymond and Nellie Webster aside. "We've got to move," he said. "Raymond, you get that blood in to Missoula for typing and crossmatch—four units, unless I call in for still more by the time you get there. Just stay for the ten-minute crossmatch and get the blood back here as fast as you can. Nellie, you get a sixth grain of morphine into that man's IV tube and then get him shifted onto a stretcher with shock blocks handy if we need them. After that, add a unit of freeze-dried plasma to the IV, and have Happy call Esther Briggs and anesthesia in to stand by. This man isn't stabilizing worth a curse; whatever he's got bleeding in there is still pumping away, and I'm afraid the fat is in the fire. I'm going up to call Harry Sonders."

It had seemed like three hours since he arrived at the hospital, but only a bare thirty minutes had passed. As he headed for the nurses' station he nearly tripped over John Florey and Ted Peterson coming down the hall. "Got a nasty one, eh, Rob?" Florey said.

"Nasty enough." Rob nodded. He picked up the phone and dialed Sonders' home phone. No answer after twelve rings. When he tried Sonders' office he got the answering service.

"I don't have a number for him right now, Doctor," the woman said. "But I'll try a couple places he might be."

"Doesn't he have his Bellboy?"

"Yes, but sometimes he doesn't answer it."

"Great. Look—this is an urgent emergency. If you can't reach him fast you might as well not bother."

"I'll do what I can, Doctor."

Rob gave her the hospital number, then hung up and sat back

angrily. Other times it had just been annoying, but this time it was different. He didn't need just advice this time; he needed Sonders. *Christ! There's just got to be a better way to get hold of this man in an emergency.* He stared at the silent phone, his irritation and frustration mounting. Ten minutes passed, then fifteen. Outside in the parking lot he saw Esther Briggs drive up in her dusty gray Ford coupe. *Well, that's something,* he thought. Of all the nurses, Esther was the really solid, practical, unflappable one, with none of Nellie Webster's insecurity or Happy's twittery effulgence. He pushed the phone aside, walked down to the x-ray room and checked the patient again. The blood pressure was still 105/70, the pulse up to 160; the man was resting easier after the morphine, but there was a gray tinge to his complexion that Rob did not like. Back at the desk, he was about to call Sonders' answering service again and start screaming at them when the phone rang. He picked it up, heard Sonders' nasal voice, abrupt and irritated. "That you, Rob? What's the trouble?"

"We've got a highway case, fifty-three-year-old man in shock with a falling blood pressure. He took the steering wheel hard in the belly, up under the left ribs. No fractures, and his urine is clear."

"Spleen," Sonders said.

"Looks like it. *Something's* sure bleeding in there. His pressure's stable right at the moment, but then I've just thrown a unit of plasma into him. Raymond's on his way to get blood."

"Shit," Sonders said. There was a long silence. Then: "Look—why don't you just pack him into the ambulance and ship him on in here? I can meet him at the hospital."

"Harry, I don't think this man can survive a ninety-minute ambulance ride anywhere. I can get things ready to go here, and probably hang on to him with plasma until you get here—"

"So ride in with him and carry the plasma."

"I can't. I'm on call for the whole practice, and frankly, I don't want to move this guy across the room if I don't have to. I think the ride could kill him."

"Well, God damn it, it just happens I can't drop everything this very instant and trot out there," Sonders exploded. "I'll be three or four hours at least."

"He's not going to last three or four hours."

"You'd better just see that he does," Sonders said. "Or else go in and get it yourself. Take your choice."

Rob started to answer, but Sonders had hung up. Coldly furious,

221

Rob dropped the receiver back on the hook. He found the patient lying on a stretcher outside the OR, with Esther Briggs checking his blood pressure. "Ninety over fifty," she said. "Pulse is a hundred and sixty. Is Dr. Sonders coming?"

"Not in time to help with this. How about anesthesia?"

"Sara's getting things ready."

"Okay, let's get him in there. Add more plasma to that IV and have three or four units on stand-by. He's had all the premedication I dare give him."

Esther looked at Rob over her glasses. "If you're going in after a spleen, you're going to need some help."

"I know it." He picked up the phone again and dialed Jerry DeForrest. There was no answer after ten rings, and Rob hung up, sitting slumped at the desk for a moment. Esther could help—but even if they got Happy in to scrub-nurse the case, it wouldn't be enough. *What if the liver's lacerated? Or the portal vein torn? Or a mesenteric artery?* The spleen itself was buried in the farthest, deepest corner of the upper abdomen, the most inaccessible spot in the entire body. Maybe he could get to it, maybe he could clamp off the artery and get it out of there in time, but he needed hands helping him.

Sara Davis lumbered out of the nurses' dressing room and crossed to the OR, wobbling slightly and reeking of licorice. She helped Esther shift the man onto the operating table, then busied herself with the anesthesia machine. Esther began methodically laying out sterile packs and drapes. Rob watched them with a feeling of numb fatalism. *Like watching a snake swallow a rabbit,* he thought. *It's hideous, but once you start watching you can't tear your eyes away.* He stood up abruptly and walked into the coffee room. Peterson and Florey were sitting there talking. They stopped in midsentence as Rob stood looking down at them. Then Rob said, "I've got a man out here with a ruptured spleen. I've got to go in and get it, and I need another pair of hands."

Florey choked on his coffee. Jaw sagging, he stared at Rob, then at Peterson. The younger man sat frozen for a moment. Then he set his coffee cup down. "I'll change," he said.

In the doctors' dressing room, Rob briefed him. Donning caps and masks, they walked out to the OR anteroom and began scrubbing in awkward silence. Finally Rob said, "Martin may have a stroke when he gets back, but I appreciate this."

"No problem," Peterson said. "Sonders out of touch?"

"Just out of reach, and I can't wait for him."

"I hope you've got some blood coming."

"Raymond's already gone after it. For now we're stuck with plasma. We may get lucky and sneak through and we may not. I don't like it, but there you are."

"If he's bleeding to death, you've got to go after it," Peterson said. "Nobody can fault you there."

In the OR Esther gave both men a startled look, but gowned and gloved them without a word. They waited until Sara indicated the patient was ready. Then Rob stepped forward and took the scalpel.

The procedure began with remarkable smoothness, despite Rob's apprehensions. Surgery had never been his long suit; he had always felt like a misfit in the OR, more onlooker than participant. He had stood at hundreds of operating tables during his training, but only rarely as the operating surgeon, and even more rarely without a skilled and experienced surgeon at his elbow. Yet now, with his back to the wall, this case suddenly seemed little different from dozens of others, and he moved with confidence that surprised him, making the long slanting incision in the left upper quadrant of the abdomen, freeing skin and fatty tissue, gently separating the external abdominal muscles. Ted Peterson worked deftly across the table from him, clamping skin bleeders, nipping the catgut ties as Rob tied them, holding retractors, working calmly, matter-of-factly, responding almost automatically to Rob's needs. As the peritoneum was opened, bloody fluid gushed up from the abdominal cavity between Rob's fingers. He widened the opening, used the suction tube, then scooped out gelatinous masses of clotted blood with his hand. "Something's sure been going on in there," Peterson murmured, and Rob nodded, plunged a gloved hand in, rearranged a retractor.

"Hold that omentum back if you can. I've got to go through over there to get down into that corner." More blood welled up as Rob worked, and Peterson turned retractors over to Esther and himself manipulated the suction tube as Rob explored. "Liver feels all right— yeah, hold it right there—but blood sure does seem to be coming up through the foramen. Damn, that's deep in there. . . ."

Minutes passed, a quarter of an hour. At one point he paused and peered over the shielding drape at Sara Davis, dozing by the anesthesia machine. "What the hell are you doing up there?"

The woman started and began sniffing fiercely as she pumped up the pressure cuff. "Pressure's one hundred over sixty and stable."

"Yes, and the plasma's about to run out too," Rob snapped. "For

223

Christ's sake, Sara, come to, will you? I need some relaxation down here now. I've got to get my hands way down in, and he's tight as a wire."

He went on with his exploration, doggedly, step by step, acutely aware of precious minutes passing. *Stomach intact, no omental vessels damaged, no sign of mesenteric bleeding. It's got to be deep in that left upper quadrant.* "Okay, here goes." With his right hand he went into the upper left corner, groping, going entirely by sense of touch now, with fresh red blood welling up out of the area he was exploring. He searched, feeling his way for what seemed an eternity, trying to find landmarks, trying to identify blind the structures he was feeling. Happy came around and mopped sweat off his forehead before it trickled down into his mask and he turned his head, half closing his eyes in concentration. "Ah!"

"Spleen?"

He nodded, so relieved he was almost trembling. "Split open like a melon. Should have gone right in there first. Now, if I can just get something on that pedicle—have we got a small rubber-shod clamp?"

Esther held it ready. Rob took it in his left hand without withdrawing his right, guided the rubber tip down his right forefinger toward the pedicle of artery and vein that fed the ruined spleen. The position of his hand was wrong, and when he shifted it slightly he lost his tenuous control of the pedicle, felt it slip from his two-fingered hold. He cursed under his breath, groped with the fingers, groped deeper. Nothing. He searched for ten minutes, forcing his fingers to be gentle, controlling them with such rigid discipline against sudden, damaging movement that his entire arm and shoulder began cramping painfully and sweat poured down into his mask. Finally, desperate, he withdrew the hand, let the cramped arm relax a moment as Esther and Peterson waited. Then he went back in again, finding landmarks, and miraculously went straight to the pedicle. Holding it more firmly this time, he guided the clamp down, felt the open jaws on either side of the vessels, then closed it tight just below his fingers. "Okay, now a good strong silk tie, Esther. The biggest rope you've got on the tray."

Still working blind, he brought the length of silk down below the clamp and made a firm tie around the pedicle, pushing as deep with his fingers as he could go. He added a second tie below the first. "Now a blade right along my finger—right. Okay, kids, let's hope that artery isn't torn below my tie. . . ." He worked in silence for a long moment, placing a long-handled clamp on the spleen itself and shifting the handles to Peterson to hold while he slipped his finger guarding the scalpel down beneath the damaged organ.

At this precise moment the operating room door opened and Agnes Miller stuck in her head. "Dr. Tanner, Dottie Hazard has just come in."

"Good Christ." Rob withdrew his hand, straightened up and looked across the operating table toward Agnes. "What's wrong?"

"She ruptured her membranes about an hour ago, and now she's having good hard contractions every three minutes."

"Is the baby's head engaged?"

"I think so. I can't move it with my finger, and the cervix is dilated about two centimeters."

"Well, get her into bed and sit on her. I'm going to be a while yet, like it or not."

Once again Rob reached in toward the spleen pedicle with a scalpel lying along his finger. In a moment he reached the position he wanted. "Now lift it up a little," he told Peterson. "Not too much tension—fine. Hold it right there."

Checking once more to be sure of his position, he used the blade to separate the damaged organ from its stump of tied-off blood vessels. Holding his breath, he signaled Peterson to withdraw the severed organ.

"Got it!" Peterson said.

"Good. Now if we can just suck in here and be sure nothing else is bleeding . . ." He inserted the suction tube, using warm sterile saline to rinse the deep pocket within which the bleeding organ had been lodged. At first deeply stained with blood, the rinsing fluid presently became just pink, then barely discolored. Rob peered down into the pocket, watching, but no new blood appeared. The ruptured spleen, clamp and all, was deposited in a basin and set on an adjacent table as Rob let his held breath out with a sigh.

As he had worked, he was aware that someone else had come into the operating room. Now he saw Harry Sonders with cap and mask loosely tied and a gown thrown over his street clothes, peering into the specimen basin. "Looks like you got it out," he said.

"It's out," Rob said shortly.

The surgeon came around and peered over Rob's shoulder at the opened abdomen. "Be damned sure you have a good double tie on that pedicle before you leave it."

225

"It's double-tied. Now all I'm worried about is getting half a gallon of clotted blood out of his belly."

"Just get it out the best you can." Sonders hesitated. "Want me to scrub in?"

"Suit yourself. You'll be damned little help at this point."

"Well, at least I can take Esther out for a drink when you're through." Sonders stood watching for a moment or two, then walked quietly to the door and out. Rob and Peterson worked for a few moments in heavy silence, scooping out handfuls of clotted blood and dropping them in the basin. Then Peterson said, "Not that it matters, but where's he *been* all afternoon?"

"Out fucking an Indian," Rob snapped, then flushed at Esther's sharp glance. "Sorry. I don't know where he's been, but it sure as hell wasn't here."

They worked on. Someone came in to announce that Raymond had arrived with the blood, and Rob ordered the first unit started. Presently Sara cleared her throat and reported that the patient's pressure was up a little and his pulse was down to 100. "Fine. I think he'll come around all right, if we can just get him sewed up," Rob said. "He's about as clean in there as we're going to get him." Silently, then, he proceeded with the closure and dressed the wound. At last he stepped back, snapped his gloves into the corner of the room and then followed Peterson out of the OR.

"That was a nice job," Peterson said. "We ought to do it more often."

"I know," Rob said. "And thanks for the help. Maybe the two of us can open things up a little, even if Isaacs and Florey can't."

Outside the OR Rob found Sonders sitting on a stool beside a wheeled stretcher, sewing up the arm of the third accident victim—the man with the lump on his head, whom Rob had totally forgotten. Rob dropped his cap and mask into the hamper and walked into the delivery room. Dottie was in the bed in the corner of the room, while Agnes puttered around with sterile packs. Rob looked at the woman. "I thought you were going to wait for Dr. Isaacs," he said.

"So did I. Then all of a sudden I was sitting in a puddle of water, and these pains started up in earnest."

"Well, let's see where you are." Rob checked her and looked at Agnes. "Still pretty high," he said. "Open about two centimeters. Let's get her some Demerol and see what happens." Feeling drained, and suddenly famished, Rob walked back to the coffee room for some cold cuts and coffee. It was just past five o'clock—almost three hours in the operating room—and now, in retrospect, he was appalled at the risk he had taken. He felt none of the euphoria, none of the satisfaction he normally felt after a safe delivery or a neat fracture reduction. Sure, he'd somehow muddled through without a corpse on the operating table, but it was little more than half-skilled muddling, and he was angry and resentful to have been put in such a situation. If he'd even known that Sonders really was coming as soon as he could, it wouldn't have been so bad—but for all he'd known, the surgeon had no intention of coming at all.

He was still fuming when Sonders walked into the coffee room, pausing at the door to toss some teasing remark back at Esther, who was still cleaning up the OR in the wake of the surgery. Sonders poured himself some coffee. "Well, I got that guy's arm put back together again. The skull films are okay, and he's got no neurological problems I can see. You can probably let him go."

"Thanks a bunch," Rob said.

Sonders looked pained. "Look—there's no point getting sore about it. I can't always just come running for any case that comes down the road."

"This wasn't just any case. This one was a bitch, and I needed you here."

"Hell, you did a great job. Couldn't have done any better myself."

"You're missing the point," Rob said, furious. "Sure, I got home free on this one. I could probably do a coronary by-pass too, if I had to, but that doesn't mean I have any business doing one. And I didn't have any business mucking around in that guy's belly, either. If I'd pulled this in Missoula I'd have had my OR privileges yanked so fast I wouldn't know what hit me."

"There are surgeons on call in Missoula," Sonders said.

"There's a surgeon on call here too. He just doesn't respond to calls."

"Oh, shit. I came as fast as I could. Meanwhile you were trapped, and you did the best you could. There wasn't any choice."

"Well, I don't like being trapped," Rob said, "and as far as I'm concerned, it's going to stop. I haven't called you once in the last two months that you haven't given me some kind of crap. If it's not one thing, it's another. Okay; either we've got a surgeon on call for this practice or else we haven't, and I for one would like to know which it is before I get boxed into a *real* corner one day."

227

Pushing his coffee cup aside, Rob went down to the men's ward to check the splenectomy patient. With the blood transfusion going, the man's blood pressure was 120/70, his pulse down to 90, and some color was creeping back into his cheeks as he snored away in his recovery from anesthesia. Sara was nowhere to be seen, but the wife was at the bedside. "Is he going to be all right?" she asked.

"I think so. But you'd better go get some rest. He may just sleep on through the night. We'll get in touch if anything changes."

By then it was almost five forty-five, and Rob checked back with Agnes in the delivery room. "How's Dottie doing?"

"She's in labor, all right, but she's not doing much yet."

"Do I dare go home for dinner?"

"Oh, sure. I'll call you if things pick up."

Driving home, Rob tried to shake off the sense of anger and irritation that still clung to him. At least, he thought, he might have a chance to deliver one of the old fox's patients by default—unless, of course, Isaacs materialized in the delivery room at the very moment of the *coup de grâce.* Not all that impossible, Rob thought, considering the uncanny manner in which the man seemed to sense just exactly when Rob was approaching one of his patients. *Unlikely, though, with the meeting just ending in Spokane about now. Once the ice gets broken, maybe we can move this OB coverage thing off dead center. But our surgery coverage is something else altogether.*

At home Rob peeled off his sweat-soaked underwear, took a quick shower and got into clean clothes while Ellie put the finishing touches on dinner. For a few minutes he prowled the patio, hands in his pockets, staring down at the river and trying to shake off his uneasy mood. He ate in silence, barely listening as Ellie told him about the crowd of foldboaters who had come down the river during the afternoon. Presently she too fell silent. Then: "You're awfully quiet tonight. Busy up there?"

He nodded. "One of Martin's OBs is in the house. I may be up there all evening."

"While the cat's away, huh?"

"You might say." He lapsed into silence again.

"Trouble of some sort?"

"Oh, sort of." Suddenly, inexplicably, he did not want to talk about the afternoon's contretemps. In fact, he didn't want to talk about anything. "There are some problems need straightening out on this coverage business, that's all. It's hard to explain."

228

"Well, you're certainly on the run whenever *you're* covering. Seems as if everybody purposely waits until you're on call."

"I know—but that's not really the trouble. I can handle a whole lot of work if I have to, but Martin's going to have to get some things straightened out pretty soon, and he's not a great one for changing things."

"But surely if it's something pressing . . ."

Rob smiled wearily, wishing she'd be quiet. "I guess we can hope," he said.

The phone interrupted, with Agnes on the line. "Dr. Tanner, you'd better come check this woman. She's having some whopping contractions, and she's really miserable, but nothing much is happening."

"Sure. I'll be right up." He gave Ellie a quick kiss on the cheek, and then drove back up to the hospital. In the parking lot he saw Harry Sonders' little red Porsche still sitting there, but Esther Briggs' old Ford was gone. Neither of the two was to be seen in the hospital. Rob walked into the delivery room, sensing that something had changed since he last checked Dottie. She looked tired and gray now, with wrinkles of distress around her eyes and mouth as a labor pain receded.

"How are you doing?" Rob said.

"Not so good. They're really digging in now. I don't remember anything like this with the others."

Rob checked her, listened for the baby's heart sounds with his stethoscope. When the next contraction came, Dottie turned her head away, biting her lip, clenching her fists and nearly raising her body off the bed as her leg muscles tightened. Then, gradually, she relaxed again and took a quavering breath. There was sweat on her forehead and upper lip. "Anything happening?" she said.

"Dottie, you're doing fine. Just a little slow, that's all. But you're fighting the pains instead of just letting them roll off you. Agnes will get you another shot, and then you try to relax with the contractions. Breathe deep and don't tighten up. You know what I mean?"

She managed a wan smile. "I know what you mean; I just can't seem to do it."

He told Agnes to repeat the Demerol. She nodded. "You'll be sticking around, then?" she asked.

"I think I'd better."

He had already decided to stay until Dottie Hazard delivered, so he slipped into a scrub suit and then made rounds on his other patients. Harvey Temple, the splenectomy patient, was still snoring up a storm;

Rob checked his pulse and blood pressure without waking him. Both were strong and stable. *Incredible, to bounce back like this after the pounding he's taken,* Rob thought. *And at his age too. He must have the constitution of an ox.* The first pint of blood was almost gone; Rob made a note to remind Janice Pryor to hook up the second. He was charting at the nurses' desk when Agnes came out, looking worried. "What's the trouble?" he said.

"I don't know. She's having terrific contractions, and an awful lot of pain, but she's still only dilated about five centimeters. That last Demerol only held her for about fifteen minutes, and she's kind of going to pieces in there. She's never done *that* before, either."

"Jesus, Agnes—I don't dare give her any more Demerol; we'll never get the baby awake. What about a tranquilizer?"

"It might help," Agnes said.

"Okay, get her a good slug of Diazepam, maybe ten milligrams. And relax. She's moving slowly, but she's moving."

Back in the coffee room he wished he felt as confident as he'd tried to sound. The fact was that the woman was moving far too slowly and having far more pain than made any kind of sense, and Rob did not like it. He couldn't see a reason: two previous easy labors, no sign of a breech or other malposition, nothing to suggest an overlarge baby. But what to do? *A caudal would be great right about now, but Martin would go right through the roof. If I tried it and something went wrong, I'd never hear the end of it. This one, of all patients, has got to go right.*

In the end, he waited and did nothing, drinking coffee and staring at the tabletop. Agnes checked from time to time: progress, but slow progress. He waited another hour, then still another, more apprehensive by the minute. It was dark by now, and he thought of giving Ellie a call but decided: *What's to tell her? That I'm tied up? She already knows that.* He wandered out to the nurses' station just as Joe Hazard walked in, obviously just down from the woods, his work clothes filthy. "I just got down to Camp 18 and heard she was here," he said. "Is everything okay?"

"Yes, but very slow. I'm just about to check her now."

As he walked into the delivery room, Agnes looked relieved. "I think you can put in the block," she said.

He checked the woman and nodded. The baby's head was not down as far as he'd have liked, but Agnes had never called the timing wrong before that he knew of, and Dottie was plainly in misery. "Okay. Let's get her up after this pain is over."

230

He moved fast, as eager to get in the saddle block as Dottie and Agnes were. A few moments later Dottie sighed in relief as the labor pain eased. But when Rob checked her, he swore under his breath. He'd jumped the gun; there was still a rim of cervix preventing descent of the baby's head, and the once forceful contractions were diminishing in intensity. "Better get some Pitocin going," he told Agnes. "Three minims by hypo and then ten units in an IV, or we're liable to be here all night." As Agnes headed down the hall for the IV, Rob went back to the coffee room, shaking his head. *What's with this woman?* he thought. *Can't anything go right?* One thing was sure: this was not the sort of smooth, orderly relaxed labor and delivery he had assisted Martin Isaacs with a dozen times before, with everything moving along like well-oiled machinery. This one, of all cases, was different—and if anything went wrong, it would be a long, cold winter before Isaacs let him near another one of his patients.

Quite suddenly he realized how weary he was. The day had been a mess from beginning to end, and fatigue was getting to him now. He was worn out, not thinking well, dreaming up trouble that didn't exist. Some women had long, painful labors, that was all. Hungry for fresh air, he stepped out the back door onto the parking tarmac, then walked across to the grassy area under the trees at the edge of the hill. It was cool, almost chilly now, with a strong smell of autumn in the air—what was it? A musty odor of yellowed leaves falling, moist on the ground in the evening damp, and a strong tinge of wood smoke. Fireplaces, of course. The first fires of fall. He looked down at the town, remembered it in midwinter, cold, white, the snow scooped into piles down the center of the highway through town, cold brilliant stars overhead. It was coming—slowly, after this long, hot summer, but coming. And with it, oddly, a chill of apprehension. *Sonders. DeForrest. Isaacs himself. The elements of a good, solid medical practice, competent men doing competent work under the handicaps of remoteness, making do where necessary, but making do well.* A solid façade, apparently the kind of practice a man could live and grow with—but now, under closer inspection, cracks in the façade. Cracks that went right down to the foundations.

He tried to shake off the sense of pervading gloom that enveloped him. There was nothing here uncorrectable, he told himself, no cracks that could not be repaired. Of course there was conflict—every doctor was an independent, egocentric, irascible and totally different individual. If he wasn't, he would never have made it through training. And

231

when you put a group of independent, egocentric, irascible and totally different individuals together in the same room too long, there is going to be friction. To expect anything else was insane. The notion that such a group could work in perfect harmony, with total and unfailing cooperation, some sort of ideal and selfless dovetailing of skills and capabilities and motivations, was pure childish fantasy. *It could never happen in a million years.*

He walked back into the hospital. Dottie's IV was running and the Pitocin was doing its job, reestablishing powerful, rhythmic uterine contractions. Dottie herself was relaxed, working with the pains now, and Agnes was beaming. "The baby's got black hair, just like Joe," she said. "And I think I know why it's been so slow. Check and see what you think."

Rob slipped on a glove and checked the baby's head. "I'll be damned," he said. "Sunny side up."

"What's that mean?" Dottie asked.

"Nothing bad, except that most babies start down the birth canal facing toward the mother's spine, and this one came face up. That usually means a longer, slower labor."

"I've sure had that," Dottie sighed.

"Well, it's about over. You'll be ready to go by the time I get a gown on." Rob nodded to Agnes, who helped him into sterile gown and gloves, then proceeded to place the sterile drapes on Dottie's abdomen. Then after a final check of the baby's position, Rob placed the forceps, took the stool, and applied gentle downward traction the next time the uterus contracted. . . .

For a long moment nothing seemed to happen. He was suddenly aware of an incredible, almost hallucinatory, extension of time. The sweep-second hand moved around the face of the clock with dogged slowness, and he heard his own pulse pounding sluggishly in his ears. The delivery seemed to proceed in excruciating slow motion, with intermittent traction and relaxation of the forceps, the patch of wet black-haired baby scalp visible at the orifice, enlarging with painstaking slowness; his own motion to make the episiotomy incision proceeding with a cogwheel deliberation, like individual frames of a movie blinking along frame by frame; the welling of blood from the episiotomy wound, promptly stanched as the baby's head stretched and pressed against the severed tissues; and at last—long, long minutes later—the removal of the forceps and the delivery of the baby's head, face up—a blue, sour-looking face and a smeary, bloodied scalp. Rob's fingers slipped a loop

232

of umbilical cord from around its neck, then took the suction bulb to suck mucus from the tiny nostrils and mouth. A moment later the delivery was complete and he held the baby by the ankles, dangling it head down. After a gentle whack on its back, it let out a plaintive howl, first tentative, then wrathfully indignant as the blue face turned abruptly bright pink. . . .

Dottie strained to see over the pile of drapes on her belly as Rob handed the baby to Agnes and clamped and cut the cord. "What have I got, Doctor?"

"A fine pink baby boy."

"Oh, that's nice. That's really nice. Joe'll be so pleased, after our two girls. That's *so* nice. . . ."

Agnes had the baby in the sterile blanket now, brought him up for the mother to see, then placed him in the waiting bassinet, still howling, to await transport down to the nursery. Rob had already ceased hearing the mother or thinking of the baby as he noticed the continuing flow of bloody fluid from the woman's vagina, somehow more excessive and brisk than it should be. "I want to get that placenta out of there, Agnes. Got the basin?" A moment later the afterbirth was delivered, inspected to be sure no fragments had been retained inside. "Now the Ergotrate. And keep that IV running."

The episiotomy incision was bleeding actively, and there was still copious flow from the birth canal. Rob sat on the stool, sponged blood away, then took up the needle-holder with the large, curved needle, sponged more blood away, and began repairing the incision, with one nervous eye on the continuing vaginal flow. Agnes stood by to help, but Rob shook his head. "Why don't you break scrub and check her pressure for me?"

A moment later Agnes said, "It's one hundred over sixty."

"What's it been running?"

"A little higher—maybe one ten over seventy."

"Try massaging her uterus and see if you can't get it to clamp down a bit. There's too much flow down here."

He went on with his work, completing the suturing as quickly as he could, still more concerned with the flow than with the surgical repair as Agnes massaged Dottie's abdomen. "How's it doing now?" he asked.

"Better. But it's still pretty soggy."

Rob slipped off his gloves and stepped up beside Agnes. Dottie's emptied uterus felt like a soft, spongy melon, reaching almost up to her

233

navel, instead of contracting into a hard, grapefruit-sized lump just above the pubis. "That's no good," Rob said. "Dottie, how are you feeling?"

"Kind of light-headed. Hard to get my breath."

"Okay; we're going to tip your head down a bit." Rob cranked the table so that Dottie was tilted slightly head downward. "Agnes, turn that IV up and get her another fifteen milligrams of ephedrine." He stepped to the buzzer by the door, buzzed for the floor nurse to come take the baby to the nursery. "Tell Joe Hazard I'll be out in a minute," he said. Within a few moments Dottie was looking better, and the flow had decreased considerably. "That's more like it," he said to Agnes. "Keep the IV going when you take her down to bed, okay?"

He peeled off his gown and walked out to the lobby to greet Joe Hazard. "Dottie will be down in her room in just a little while," he said. "She had a slow labor, and she lost a little more blood than we usually see, so we'll be watching her especially closely. We may even want to get her some blood for transfusion."

Joe Hazard looked alarmed. "She's not in any danger, is she?"

"Not really, but she had a mean time of it, and then got a little shocky just after the baby came, so we may just want to play it safe."

"Look, Doc, anything she needs, you get it for her. How's the baby?"

"Superfine. A big, fat sassy boy. I'm going down to the nursery to check him out now."

The nursery nurse put the baby up on the small examining table. "Eight pounds nine ounces," she said.

"Jesus. No wonder it was slow coming down." Rob examined the infant carefully. "Good-looking specimen too. No problems here, thank God."

Back at the nurses' station, he saw it was just past midnight. He was feeling rum-dum by now, almost giddy, as if he had a three-martini buzz on. It was fatigue, of course, plus a sense of release that the woman was delivered with no particular disaster to have to report to Isaacs. When he saw Agnes wheeling her down the hall to put her in bed, he heaved a sigh and went back to change into his street clothes. He was down to his undershorts, miles away already, when Agnes banged on the door. "Dr. Tanner? Are you in there?"

He pulled up his pants and peered out. "What's wrong?"

"I'm not sure," Agnes said. "When I got Dottie down to her room, she complained about some pressure down in her groin, so I looked, and she's got a great big lump down there."

"A *what?*"

"A lump in her groin. It's big as an orange."

"Oh, for Christ's sake, Agnes. How could she have a lump in her groin as big as an orange?"

"I don't know, but you'd better come see."

Down in the room, Dottie Hazard looked up apprehensively. "There isn't anything wrong, is there?"

"Let's just see." Rob drew down the covers, peered down at the recent field of battle. Agnes was dead right; one side of the perineum looked massively swollen and bluish, actually pushing the labia off to one side. "Let me have a glove." Checking then, he could feel a hard mass in the tissue below and to one side of the birth canal, as big as an orange or bigger. For a moment he was totally confused, unable to imagine what it might be. Then, abruptly, he knew. "The episiotomy. Something in there is still bleeding. She must have half a pint of blood trapped in there."

Agnes just blinked at him. "I don't understand."

"She had a deep bleeder in there that I saw when I started the repair. I thought I got it with the deep sutures, but it looks like I didn't. Then I closed the skin and the blood couldn't get out. And I was so busy worrying about her damned uterus that I didn't even notice."

"Well—what do we do about it?"

"We take her back and we open it up again, that's what we do."

"We can't use the delivery room. Happy is right in the middle of cleaning it up."

"Then we use the OR. And I suppose her block's gone by now so we'll have to use Novocaine. Well, let's get moving."

Briefly he explained the problem to Dottie, then went back and pulled on a scrub suit again, cursing under his breath. Of all the things that he *didn't* want, something like this was at the top of the list. *Of all the clumsy, stupid, goddamned tricks. No wonder she was shocky, with this piled on top of excessive flow from a worn-out uterus, and all because you just didn't watch what you were doing, for Christ's sake.* He saw the surprise on the night nurse's face as they wheeled Dottie back toward the OR, saw Joe Hazard's startled look as they went past, and there was nothing to do but to stop and explain the problem. " . . . not a common complication, but when it happens you just have to go back and fix it. No, no—no particular threat. It's just one more headache for everybody." He left the man standing there wondering whether to be angry, alarmed or relieved, and went on into the operating room. Then there was the whole process of regowning and regloving, draping the patient, getting the procaine syringe ready. He snipped out the sutures he had just put in, saw the episiotomy incision gape open to reveal a huge reddish-purple mass of semiclotted blood entrapped within. He bent to the laborious task of scooping out the clotted blood, sponging, scooping again, peering into the wound, then suddenly uncovering a small pulsating fountain of bright red blood squirting out at him, spraying his gloves and sleeves and the front of his gown. "There's that bastard—let me have a clamp." He snapped a hemostat on the bleeder, sponged again, then clamped a second bleeding vessel in the depths of the wound. Inadequate anesthesia; Dottie complained of pain at least twice in a certain place, and Rob had to stop, infiltrate more local anesthesia. Sweat dripped down into his eyes and onto his mask; his hands trembled more from sheer anger and self-disgust than from tension as he began a slow, painstaking reclosure after the bleeders had finally been tied. Dottie was incredibly patient despite her exhaustion, but complained as he finished that she still felt sore down there, anesthetic or no anesthetic, and Rob looked at her, thinking: *Sore now? Just wait till tomorrow, babe; you're going to be sore like you never dreamed of. You're going to hate me in the morning, and your plague-taken Dr. Isaacs is not going to be all that pleased, either.* . . .

At last he pushed the stool back and stood up. "Okay, Dottie, back to bed with you. It's all fixed up."

"No more bleeding?"

"No more bleeding, but you've lost more blood than I like, so I'm going to order some up to replace it."

"I'm sorry to be such a bother," she said.

"It's not your fault. You've been a great patient. Dr. Isaacs will be proud of you."

Back at the nurses' desk he added a new operative note to Dottie's chart, then went in to change clothes again. It was now almost two-thirty in the morning, with a chilly breeze striking his cheek as he climbed into his car and headed down the hill. It hadn't just been talk, what he'd said to Dottie. The labor, the delivery and the aftermath had all been pure torment for her, but she had been patient and cooperative through it all. Martin Isaacs would have good reason to be proud of

236

Dottie Hazard. Unfortunately, Rob reflected, he was not so likely to be proud of Dr. Robinson Tanner.

It was not until he reached the bottom of the hill that it struck him that Harry Sonders' red Porsche had still been sitting in the hospital parking lot when he left.

# 21

Martin Isaacs was indeed not pleased when he returned to Twin Forks Sunday evening, but it was not because of Rob's mishandling of Dottie Hazard. On Sunday morning Rob had made rounds and found Nellie Webster starting a second unit of blood for Dottie, as he had ordered. The woman still looked sallow and exhausted, but she seemed at least to be in good spirits. Rob checked her episiotomy again and winced. She looked as if she had been pounded with a sledge hammer —but there was no sign of a recurring hematoma, only a normal amount of flow, and if she was ungodly sore in the area, she didn't dwell on it. He spent a moment talking over the pros and cons of breast-feeding with her—"I'd like to, but Dr. Isaacs isn't so hot on the idea"—and ultimately told her she would have to fight that one out with Isaacs himself.

"At least you'll have a little extra time to get onto it, if you decide to do it," Rob said. "I'm afraid you're going to have to spend a couple more days in the hospital than you'd planned."

Dottie just sighed. "I suppose that figures," she said. "But I guess I can use a little rest, even if it does play hell with the bank account."

Down in the men's ward Harvey Temple was awake and alert, still a very sick man but recovered enough to complain about the food. "For breakfast, yet, they give me lemon jello."

"I know. I ordered it. Anything heavier and you'd plug up like a

238

bloated cow." Rob listened at length and in vain for returning bowel sounds in his abdomen. "As soon as something starts stirring down there, we'll pull out that stomach tube and get you something to eat. Until then, just be glad for the jello."

After rounds, the rest of the day dragged. By noon he was back home, to spend a lazy afternoon reading the Sunday paper, napping, then tinkering with some cabinet plans that Ellie had unearthed to help with the storage problem. They had a patio supper, even though it was too cool. Then about seven o'clock the phone rang, with Isaacs on the line.

"What the hell's been going on around here this weekend?" he roared as soon as Rob picked up the receiver.

"You at the hospital?"

"I sure am, and it looks like the plague has struck."

"Well, just hold on. I'll be up in ten minutes." Rob gulped down his last bite of dinner and headed up the hill. He found Isaacs sitting in the coffee room, looking sour. "If you want to know what happened with that damned woman, I can't tell you," Rob said. "I just plain don't know. She ruptured her membranes yesterday and came up here in labor, and from then on something went wrong every time I looked at her."

"You mean Dottie?" Isaacs said. "Well, don't sweat it; nobody's perfect. Sometimes you get a case where everything you touch turns to shit. At least you stuck with it when you got in trouble, and you got a good baby and a good mother out of it. That's all that matters. But this spleen case is something else."

"You heard about that too, eh?"

"Heard about it? The minute I walked in here, there was John Florey smirking and asking me how I liked my new surgical assistant. The son of a bitch."

"Sorry, but I had no choice."

"No choice but to drag Peterson into a case with you? *Where the hell was Sonders?*"

"He got here in time to mop up the floor."

"But when did you call him?"

"About four hours earlier. As soon as I was fairly sure we were going to have to open the guy up."

Isaacs leaned back, his face dark. "So what happened?"

"First I couldn't get him at all—which seems to be par for the course these days—and then when I did get him, he told me to ship the patient to Missoula or open him up myself."

239

"So why didn't you ship him in?"

"I didn't think he'd make it. The man was busy bleeding to death. I told Harry that, in so many words, and he hung up on me."

"I see," Isaacs said. "So you opened him up yourself."

"I had to. I wasn't sure Harry was ever going to come, and Jerry was off and away somewhere, as usual, and I needed another pair of hands. It was as simple as that. I could have used Esther to assist, with Happy scrub nursing, but Peterson was here, so I chose him."

"Jesus," Isaacs said. "Talk about the blind leading the blind."

"That's about the way I felt—but I was the one that was stuck with the patient. We got home free too—but I didn't like it for sour green apples. We can't go on with this kind of hole in our coverage. I don't want any more weekends like this one."

"Neither do I," Isaacs said heavily. "I can carry Jerry on my back, but I can't carry Sonders. It's a pity too. He can be a damned good surgeon when he wants to get off his ass."

If Isaacs was furious, Jerry DeForrest vacillated when the three of them met in Isaacs' office next morning. "You can't really fault the man for not leaping every time you jingle the phone," he said. "I'm not sure we have all the parts to make a judgment in this case."

"How the hell many parts do you need?" Isaacs said. "He's taking a full partnership share of the money out of this place, and he isn't giving us left hind paw in return."

"I hadn't noticed anything so bad," Jerry said.

"You don't take call, either," Rob said. "Sure, Harry does the scheduled surgery all right, and I guess he makes his office hours, but it's Martin and me that get stuck for a surgeon on nights and weekends."

"He's not even making his office hours worth a curse," Isaacs growled. "He's always got fifty post-op people to see, but he never gets down here before three o'clock on his office days. And it's not because he's still in surgery, either. He's just too damned busy hiking the skirts on that Briggs woman, if you want the plain truth."

"Oh, hell, Martin," Jerry said. "I don't care if he's screwing Esther black and blue as long as he's discreet about it."

"*Discreet!* My God, half the people in this town know he's caterwauling after that bitch—"

"Yes, and the other half are going to know too if you don't lower your voice," Jerry said sharply. "We can ask Harry to take care of our surgical patients, Martin, but we can't legislate his morals."

"In a town like this you've got to worry about morals too," Isaacs

240

snapped. "What's more, I'll be damned if I want him screwing her on my time."

"Okay, but that's not the issue," Jerry said. "The issue is getting him to tighten up his coverage. Well, *I* can't make him do it—I'm just an itinerant pill-peddler to him—but maybe one of you can lean on him somehow."

Isaacs snorted. "I can lean on him, all right."

"Trouble is, a slap on the wrist won't do it," Rob said. "What kind of practice does he have in Missoula?"

"He's limping along," Isaacs said. "We provide at least two thirds of his work."

"Then why not get him out here to live?"

"In Twin Forks? Not a chance. Of course, that's what we really *need* —a surgeon that lives right here. We could find plenty to keep a man busy out here. But not Harry. He'd laugh in our faces."

"Well, I can't take any more deals like that spleen case," Rob said. "We've got to do something."

"There's only one thing to do," Isaacs said, "and that's dump him."

Rob blinked. "You mean just—kick him out?"

"Right on his ass," Isaacs said.

"Well, now, hold it," Rob said. "That wasn't quite what I had in mind."

"Well, I do. He's useless, and I don't want him around anymore."

"So then we'd have no surgeon at all."

"We can always get a surgeon," Isaacs said. "Look, there's something else here I haven't told you guys. I think Sonders is screwing us blind. I think he's taking cases from out here in to Missoula to do and then billing them privately. I think he's been doing it for a long time."

Rob stared at the man. "Martin, for God's sake! What patients?"

Isaacs looked uncomfortable. "Maybe a lot of them," he said.

"Like which ones? I mean, specifically. That's a serious charge you're making."

"Well—I'm not sure, exactly. I've got Bev working on it right now."

"In other words, this is just a vague suspicion you're talking about."

"I can't absolutely *prove* it yet, if that's what you mean," Isaacs said angrily, "but I'd bet you anything you can name that that bastard has been robbing us. . . ."

"Look," Rob said, exasperated. "I don't want the guy kicked out, not on the basis of some wild fairy tale like that. All I want is some coverage. So let's forget about dumping him and see if we just can't get

241

him to straighten himself out. Okay?"

Isaacs spread his hands. "Whatever you want. I still think we should dump him and get it over with. But if you insist, I'll just have a little talk with him first."

It didn't sound too pleasant, and it wasn't. On Tuesday morning Sonders was at the hospital bright and early for three scheduled cases. Rob assisted, and when they finished Sonders checked Harvey Temple and wrote a progress note on his chart. "He's getting some bowel tones now," he told Rob. "If they're still good tonight, pull the Levin tube and start him on a soft diet tomorrow. Be sure he's up and out of bed a couple of times a day too. You can do without a pulmonary embolus." Rob went home for lunch then, returning to the office an hour later for his afternoon schedule.

When he drove up, he saw Sonders' car in back of the clinic. Isaacs' office door was closed, but he heard muffled angry voices inside. Dora was fluttering around nervously. "They've been in there for almost an hour now," she said. "I've never seen Dr. Isaacs so angry."

The fight continued for some time. Finally Isaacs' door flew open and Harry Sonders emerged. He looked as cool and dapper as ever in his crisp white lab coat and perfectly pressed trousers, his curly red hair neat as a fashion plate, but his face was dark with anger. "There's no way you're going to push me around like this," he was saying fiercely, "and let me tell you once again, by God, you keep my wife out of it" —and Isaacs' voice roared back, "Harry, this is just one final friendly warning. If you've got any wits at all, you'd better listen."

"Oh, shit!" The surgeon turned sharply and stalked up the hall. Dora met him with a chart in her hand and he fairly snatched it away. "All right, let's get these people moving. I haven't got all day, now or any other day." He glanced at the chart and charged into the treatment room.

A moment later Isaacs emerged, jacket over his arm. He paused at Rob's office door and threw a malevolent glance down the corridor toward the minor surgery. "I'm going to lunch," he said. "I gave him the word, and he's by God going to straighten out, too. He needs us more than we need him." A moment later he was out the back door and Rob heard tires squeal on pavement as the Buick roared out of the parking lot.

Rob's own schedule was full, and he twice called Sonders in for brief consultations. With the patients Sonders was his usual smiling, affable self, joshing them, pausing to chat a moment. He was decidedly cool toward Rob, but that was all right too. *We don't have to have a love feast, for God's sake,* Rob thought. *All I need from him is competent surgical consultation and coverage, nothing more.* And however angry Sonders might have been, his fight with Isaacs clearly had struck some kind of chord: for the first time since Rob had been in the office the little red-headed surgeon was still busily seeing patients at six-thirty in the evening, when Rob finally finished his schedule and headed for home.

That night Rob finally mentioned the contretemps with Sonders to Ellie. She listened, her face serious, as he told her about the spleen case, his own distress at the situation, and the meeting with Isaacs that followed. When he finished, she shook her head. "I don't know about Martin, Rob," she said. "The more I see of the way he works things, the more I wonder what's going on."

"Well, he can't just throw the man out on his ass," Rob said. "At least, not with Jerry opposed to it. After all, they're supposed to be equal partners in this thing. And as for this silly business about Sonders stealing patients—well, Martin just can't be serious."

Ellie glanced up sharply. "You don't think so? Then I don't think you understand that man very well," she said.

"What do you mean?"

"I think he could be very serious indeed. Oh, not about Sonders stealing his patients; that's obviously phony. But as for getting rid of him —that's something else."

"But *why?* If Harry would just shape up a little bit—"

"Honey, Martin Isaacs doesn't like to be thwarted, and Harry Sonders is busy thwarting him every chance he gets. Well, it's not going to work. Martin is going to dump him. You just watch. In the long run it's not going to matter *what* you or Jerry or anybody else may think. Martin is going to *dump* him, and that's going to be that."

"But what's he going to do for a surgeon?" Rob said.

"I don't know, but I wouldn't be surprised if he already had another surgeon up his sleeve."

Rob laughed. "I suppose it's possible, but Jesus! You really don't trust him very much, do you?"

"Trust him? *Isaacs?* I'd have to be out of my mind."

"Oh, come on," Rob said. "Now you're sounding paranoid."

Ellie picked up a pillowcase she had been crocheting and began poking at it with a needle. "What did Martin have to say about Peterson helping you?"

"Ha! He nearly went through the roof when Ted billed us a hundred dollars for his assistant's fee. It seemed fair enough to me—the guy was tied up in the OR for a whole Sunday afternoon—but Martin nearly had a fit. He's going to pay it, but he sure doesn't like it."

"You didn't really expect him to, did you?"

"I don't know," Rob said. "I guess I was hoping it might warm things up a little bit. The guy sure helped me out of a nasty hole. But I guess Florey's pretty negative about it too. The day after surgery Ted was pleasant as could be, stopped to chew the fat awhile, interested in how the patient was doing. But then yesterday he walked past me like I didn't exist, wouldn't even say good morning. Florey must have got to him, and things seem chillier than ever."

"It sounds like Martin and Florey are going to keep cutting each other's throats no matter what," Ellie said sourly.

Rob looked at her. "You really *are* getting paranoid," he said.

"Well, it's enough to make anybody paranoid, the way things are going around here," Ellie said. "And not just the practice, either. Other things."

"Like what?"

Ellie shrugged. "I ran into Chris Erickson at the Safeway this afternoon. It was very odd."

Rob looked up, instantly wary. "Odd?"

"She was just too sweet for words. Wanted to know how we liked the mushrooms. Then she asked me when I was going to Missoula shopping again, and started to laugh. She seemed to think something was hilariously funny, only I didn't seem to be in on the joke."

"You're seeing spooks," Rob said. "Chris is just another patient."

"Maybe so. But I don't think I like her very much. And Belle says—" She stopped abruptly.

Rob frowned. "Belle says what?"

"Oh, never mind."

"I see. Well, I think it's about time that old hen started minding her own business for a change."

"She's not an old hen," Ellie flared. "She's a very sharp old woman, and she knows more about the people in this town than you're *ever* going to know."

"So what does she know about Chris Erickson?"

"Nothing very flattering," Ellie said. "And I don't want to talk about it very much, either." She poked at her crocheting some more. "What is Martin doing about the OB coverage?"

"Well, at least that should cheer you up," Rob said. "I actually think

244

we're making progress. We're not there yet, but we may make it if we can hang on long enough."

It was true, as well as paradoxical: Rob had discovered that his mishandling of Dottie Hazard's case had not, as he had feared, cooled Isaacs' enthusiasm for trading off calls on his OBs. If anything, it had seemed to quicken his interest in the whole idea. Isaacs did nothing so straightforward as to send his OB patients to Rob to check and get acquainted with, as Rob had suggested—but whereas before he merely grumbled continually about the overwhelming load of OBs he had to carry, he now began calling Rob in for "conferences" with some of his patients who were coming due. These were awkward affairs, with Isaacs explaining to the patients—more correctly, bluntly *instructing* them— that if they should happen to start in labor when he was away, or ill, or otherwise unable to respond, they were to call Rob and he would do whatever was necessary. Isaacs was obviously ill at ease with these presentations, watching the patients nervously, perfectly willing to waffle the issue at the first sign of protest, and it irritated Rob to be presented as a sort of Ugly Duckling on a take-it-or-leave-it basis—but at least it was a step in the right direction. He tried to suggest that a little more finesse might be in order, but Isaacs just brushed his objections aside. "Look, I *know* these women. If I don't hit 'em over the head with it, they're never going to believe me. Now you just let me handle it."

Rob conceded, and over the next couple of weeks he saw a dozen or more of Isaacs' patients this way, some familiar to him, some strangers. There were other ways, too, in which Isaacs seemed to be trying to loosen the reins a little. Since his return from Spokane, he insisted more firmly than ever that Rob assist with every one of his deliveries, call or no call—and on some occasions he even let Rob officiate, himself standing by merely to assist. It was more and more a trial for Rob and Ellie; it made a confusing mess of the call schedule and kept Rob running days and nights on end. It also forced Ellie once again to give up the fall camping weekend Rob had promised her on the next weekend he was free. But at least Isaacs seemed to be moving, at however glacial a rate, inch by inch toward the precipice. The one thing he did *not* do again was to absent himself from the area when a patient was due, and simply let Rob take over. This, it seemed, had to wait for the right occasion, and the right occasion never quite seemed to arise.

In the meantime, slowly but surely, Rob began to acquire an obstetrical clientele of his own. Pregnant patients previously attended by

245

Isaacs were automatically scheduled for Isaacs—the older man would not yield an inch on this—but new patients to the clinic were simply told that Dr. Isaacs' OB schedule was full at the moment, and were sent on to Rob. It seemed clear that if he lived long enough, this in itself would eventually help balance their respective OB loads, and slow as it was, Rob was inclined to be patient. Things at least were moving.

Indeed, for the first time since he had arrived at Twin Forks, Rob began to feel faintly optimistic. Even Sonders seemed to be toeing the line better since the fight with Isaacs. True, there had been no response from the hospital directors on the blood storage unit proposal—the anticipated meeting had been postponed a couple of weeks—but the longer they waited, Rob thought, the more likely they would be to go along with it. And although he found Jerry DeForrest no less frustrating as a medical consultant, Rob devised ways to work around him, and as his own confidence increased, found fewer and fewer patients on whom he needed medical consultation anyway; it was, he found, increasingly easy to live without Jerry. All in all, not too bad a situation, Rob felt— until a sequence of events during a single week in early October shattered his complacency once and for all.

For one thing, Ellie finally and completely ran out of patience. Rob discovered this on the Sunday evening of a call weekend when he had finally returned from the hospital at nine o'clock after taping a man's ribs following an auto accident. The weekend call had been more irritating than anything else, not exactly rushed but never really quiet either; no sooner had he returned home from one call than the telephone was jangling with another from early Sunday morning on. By midafternoon, disgusted with the shuttle trips to and from home, he had just stayed at the hospital dealing with a succession of minor problems, telling Ellie to have dinner without him and bolting down a supper of cold cuts between patients. When he finally got home, exhausted, he found Ellie on her knees in the middle of the living room floor with camping gear, pots, sleeping bags, tents and ponchos spread out in all directions. "What are you doing?" he asked. "Packing that stuff all away?"

She straightened up and looked at him. "No," she said. "I'm getting it ready to use."

"For what?"

"For backpacking." She went on checking items off a list in front of her and setting them aside into a pile. "I got the maps two months ago, and some up-to-date information from the forest service last week.

246

There's a gorgeous wilderness area down in Idaho south of Salmon—a public campground accessible by car, and a dozen trails for overnight backpacking up to some of the high lakes. I figure a half day to get down there, stay overnight at the campground and then pack in for the next night. . . ." She checked another item off her list, then brushed her hair back with her hand and sat on her heels, surveying the scene.

Rob went over to the sofa. "Just when are we planning all this?" he said.

"Tomorrow, if I can get some last-minute shopping done early enough."

"Don't be silly. I've got to work tomorrow."

"Honey, as far as I can see, you've got to work every day, including every day off and every weekend, whether you're on call or not, and I guess that's your choice. As for me, I've got to get *out* of here for a few days, just—just get *away* for forty-eight hours or so—and if you can't go with me, I'm going by myself. You don't have to worry; I've got the laundry all finished for the week and I'll leave a couple of steaks in the refrigerator."

"Ellie, don't be ridiculous. You can't go off backpacking by yourself in a wilderness area you've never seen before in your life."

"Oh, but I can. The trails are good, and I won't be more than seven miles from the highway at any time."

"And if you got snowed in you'd never get out."

"The good weather's supposed to hold for a while yet."

"Ellie, it could start snowing anytime. It's the middle of October, for God's sake!"

"I know that. That's the whole point. This beautiful fall weather is going fast, just going to *waste,* and I've been trying to tear you loose for six weeks now and you just keep putting it off, pushing it aside. If it isn't one excuse it's another, and I've truly had it. I'm going to go while there's still time."

She went back to her checklist, her face flushed, slapping things down onto the pile for packing with an air of finality. Rob watched her unhappily for a while. "Look, maybe this coming weekend we can go," he said at last.

"That's what you said two weeks ago."

"I know; it just didn't work out. I'm doing my best to get this OB coverage thing opened up once and for all so I can *get* some time off once in a while. And Martin's coming around, too, but it's been like watching grass grow; he's just dragging his feet every inch of the way."

247

"Yes, and he'll still be dragging his feet by Christmas time, and the next Christmas too, if you let him," Ellie said bitterly.

"But why blame *me?* I'm pushing as hard as I can."

"Rob, you can't push the man if he won't be pushed. You'll just kill yourself for nothing. Well, that may be okay with you, but it's not okay with *me.* I'm tired of standing around watching."

She clapped the cup on top of the Primus stove and set it aside with the other checked-off items. Rob watched her go on checking things for a minute. "Okay, I *promise* we'll go this next weekend," he said, beginning to feel desperate. "I'll go over Martin's OB list with him tomorrow and see if we can't just get out of here Friday morning."

"That's not good enough," Ellie said. "It'll be just fine until Thursday afternoon and then something will come up and it'll all be called off, and we'll be right back where we started, only a week later. No, thanks."

"Well, what the hell do you want me to do?" Rob exploded.

"Don't check with Martin. Don't ask him, either. *Tell him you're going to go,* period, and let it drop. Then when Friday morning comes, we get in the car and we go."

"All right, I'll *tell* him," Rob said. "God, Ellie, you act like I'm deliberately playing tricks on you or something." He got up and walked into the kitchen, ran a glass of cold water. "You act as if I created this OB situation, just to spite you."

"It isn't just the OB thing," Ellie said. "If that were all it was, I'd say fine, let's just sweat it out—but it's not. It's everything. We've been here almost four months now and already I see *patterns* developing, patterns we're going to be stuck with for years if somebody doesn't blow the whistle pretty soon. This incessant run, run, run and never stop, this week-after-week stuff without a break—days, nights or weekends, never finding a minute for yourself *or* me, pushing and crowding and fighting to get things done and *never quitting for half a day.*"

Rob stared at her. "Ellie, if you're going to practice decent medicine, the practice has got to come first. It always has and it always will. Surely by now you know that. It's true here, no matter what patients I'm seeing. You saw it with your own father; all your life you saw it. It was true all through medical school and hospital training, and you saw it there. You knew it was part of the game when you bought into it, and now all of a sudden you're going through the roof, and I don't get it. What makes it different now?"

"Everything," Ellie said. "When you were in medical school and

248

training there was only one goal: just getting you through. Nothing else mattered, everything else got pushed aside, *everything*—money, a house, clothes, children, even a decent marriage relationship—because you wanted to practice medicine and until you got through that bloody stretch there wasn't going to *be* any practicing medicine. But that's behind us now; you got through that bloody stretch and you've got your chance to practice, nobody can take it away from you—but I see things happening just like before, everything else getting pushed aside, especially *me* getting pushed aside just like I was never there, shoved back on a shelf somewhere so I won't be in the way. Well, I've been sitting on that shelf for seven years now, and I'm not going to stay there any longer. I married a human being, not a medical computer, and I want to see the color of his eyes once in a while, and the time is *now*, not sometime in the dim, distant future. Because there isn't going to be any dim, distant future if things don't change pretty fast."

She was fighting back tears now, turning furiously to her sorting and checking. Rob stared at her, shaking his head. "Well, maybe I've been pushing it a little too hard," he said lamely.

"Too hard! My God."

"There's just so much to *do* in this practice. And it all needs to be done *now*. It should have been started years ago, and it all takes time, and there just isn't that much time, there aren't enough hours. It's like wading through waist-deep mud. Maybe I just don't know when to quit."

"Then somebody's got to tell you when to quit," Ellie said. She leaned her head against his knee for a moment, her face averted. "Honey, I know you've been working like a dog to fit in here somehow, and I know it's different from a training hospital, where everything is set out, one, two, three, and where everything you need is there and everything works and you've got help on all sides, people that can at least help you untie some of the knots. I know you've had to learn an awful lot in a hurry, and put up with an awful lot that isn't the way you think it should be—and I could *understand* that, I knew it would have to be like that for a while. But when it begins to look like forever and nothing seems to be getting any better . . ." She looked up at him, shaking her head. "There have just *got* to be other things too, sooner or later. You know? Whole *days* go by and we hardly even say hello to each other, and that's no good. We've got to have *some* time together when you don't have to jump and run every time a telephone rings."

"But we *do*."

"Not really. And even when we do have a few minutes, you make me feel like I'm on the outside looking in. I know you get stirred up about things that go on at the hospital and the office, but I'm not sure what's happening and I feel so stupid and *useless*. Other people know things, but not me."

"Like what?"

"Oh, I know it's silly, but the whole town seems to know about Harry Sonders' local love life. The girls down at the grocery have been tittering about it for weeks, and they assume that I know too and I don't know *anything from anything.*"

"There's not a whole lot to know about that," Rob said. "Harry has got the hots for the local scrub nurse and they take off together after his surgery is finished. So what's to tell you about? Is this exciting dinner talk?"

"At least it's *something*," Ellie said.

"I suppose."

"And you've got to work with these men, one way or another, and if you're worrying about them, I'm worrying too. You're not in this all by yourself, you know."

"I know." He reached down and touched her hair. "I guess I just figure there's no point to bothering you with all these silly things, that's all. And they really *are* silly, a day or so later. I get pissed off at Martin about some damned thing or another, I really get hot, but then in a couple of days he's still there and I'm still there and it all seems so *trivial*. Or I keep hoping against hope that Jerry DeForrest is going to surprise me and come to life one of these days, and I get irritated when he doesn't—sometimes I could just pound his head against the wall— but then I cool off and realize that he's probably *not* going to come to life the way I think of it, no matter how long I wait, he just isn't made that way, and that particular issue begins to look too foolish to make a fuss over. And I figure why tell you about *this* kind of crap in the little time we have together."

"At least it would be something," Ellie repeated.

"But surely there are things for *you* to do. Get involved in your club meetings, see more of Amy DeForrest—"

"I can't *stand* Amy DeForrest," Ellie said. "Every time I see her I think: God, am I going to be like *that* in another five years? She just hates it here, she acts like this is the creepiest little do-nothing dump south of Circle, Alaska. Of course, there's Jennie too, but Jennie is purely no help. And the other people act like they're walking on egg-

250

shells around me. I try to open up a little, just *respond,* and they act like they've been bitten. You can just see their minds close down, wham! Like that."

"I guess you *do* need to get away," Rob said. "So let's do it, anyplace you want to go. I'll tell Martin tomorrow, and we'll leave just as soon as he picks up call on Friday morning and not come back until Sunday night."

They left it at that, with Ellie returning to her checking and sorting, while Rob looked over the maps and campground guides with more appearance of enthusiasm than he really felt. He turned in early, anticipating a busy Monday, but then lay awake mulling over what Ellie had said long after she had followed him to bed. It was easy, and very tempting, to chalk it up to a blue mood—but on a deeper level he knew it was more than that. Ellie wasn't ordinarily a complainer: throughout his training she had accepted the limited time he had to devote to home life. Of course, in Seattle she had her own work, her own circle of friends—mostly other medical wives—and opportunities to explore her own interests as a buffer against his long hospital hours. They had both known things would be different in a place like Twin Forks, more socially restrictive, more lonely for her—but some of the subtleties of small-town life had caught them both unprepared.

He, of course, faced no barriers in making new acquaintances and finding a welcome here. His position as one of "Isaacs' doctors" was his passport, and he was largely accepted as part of the basic town structure, however different or peculiar he might seem. At the same time, there was the time-honored professional barrier that isolated and insulated him from the people he contacted, a barrier that he could adjust at will, revealing as much or as little of himself as he wished, leaving himself untouchable and invulnerable within. Behind this barrier he could know others but conceal himself, receive the confidence of others, yet never confide. With it he could fine-tune his relationship with patients, office staff, hospital nurses, other doctors—even his own wife.

For Ellie, though, there was no such ready acceptance in the town, and no protective barrier to hide behind. As a doctor's wife she was an unknown quantity, maybe even a threat. She could make acquaintances, but few friends; friendships would ripen only slowly, and she could not force them. And meanwhile, loneliness would be inevitable.

He groped for an answer, but found none. *Maybe I really have to tell her more that's going on, however trivial it may seem. Maybe she needs more support until things open up for her. Maybe just small talk*

251

*would help sometimes.* He thought then of the incident with Chris Erickson, and winced inwardly for the hundredth time. *So sudden, so irresistible—but indefensible just the same. No way could that help Ellie—or anyone else. You just don't get snarled up in that kind of thing in a place like this.*

He finally fell asleep, but was still depressed at hospital rounds next morning. He wished desperately that there was somebody he could talk to about it—but who? Certainly not Chris. Isaacs? He was probably in closer contact with Martin Isaacs than with anybody else in the valley, but hardly in terms of personal problems, and the ever-present specter of Jennie Isaacs pulled him up sharply whenever he thought of confiding in Martin. And as for Jerry—well, not really. Somehow he did not want DeForrest's cool-eyed, dispassionate vagueness brought to bear on his personal life, however much Jerry and his wife might once have weathered a similar storm.

In the end, he consulted no one. When Isaacs arrived at the office that Monday morning, Rob told him about the projected weekend camping trip. Isaacs took it calmly enough. "Sure, you can probably use a rest," he said. "Take off Thursday night, if you want. I can cover all right." Rob said no, Friday morning would be fine. He hesitated, on the razor's edge of broaching the problem of Ellie, but the older man was already halfway down the hall to his office, and the chance was gone.

Then, with his first patient that morning, the whole question was thrust from Rob's mind. "Ed Butler's in for a pre-op exam," Dora said, thrusting a chart into his hand.

Rob blinked. "Pre-op? For what?"

"Oh, didn't you hear? He came in with a strangulated hernia last Friday, while you were off. Dr. Isaacs spent the whole afternoon with him at the hospital getting it reduced."

Rob went into the examining room, frowning at the note Isaacs had scrawled in Ed's chart. The retired millworker sat on the end of the examining table wrapped in a green gown, his bushy eyebrows twitching unhappily. Rob looked up from the chart. "Ed, what the hell is going on here?" he said.

"Damned if I know, Doc," Ed said. "Maybe you were right about me maybe getting a rupture or something. All I know is that Friday morning I was up to the lake fishing and all of a sudden I got this pain down in the crotch here, and I found this big lump the size of a lemon."

Rob sat down on the stool, looking disgusted. "And it all started while you were pulling that damned boat ashore, I'll bet."

"Well, yeah. Matter of fact, I was just trying to get it up a little higher on the beach—"

"Ed, I *told* you to get a winch for that damned boat."

"I know, you sure did tell me. I just didn't get it done. But anyway, this lump started hurting like hell, and all of a sudden I started throwing up, so I got down here as fast as I could. Doc Isaacs looked at it, since you were off, and he hauled me up to the hospital, put me on a stretcher with my ass end tipped up, and give me a shot that made me drunk as hell. Then he poked and fiddled for almost an hour, damned near had the knife to me right then and there, but then all of a sudden the lump went down and quit hurting and I quit puking, so he let me go home. Said I had to go back up there and have Doc Sonders fix it for me on Thursday." Ed shook his head. "I don't like the idea too much, though. Never had a knife put on me in my life before."

"Ed, you get a loop of bowel stuck down in that thing another time and it's just liable to kill you," Rob said. "Once you break one of those things open, you've got to have it fixed. That's all there is to it. Here, let me check it."

There was no question of the change since Rob had examined him last—an unmistakable defect in the groin on the right side. Rob looked grim. "Ed, I'm afraid you're in for it, like it or not."

"Is it real big?"

"No, it's very small. That's why it's so dangerous. If it was nice and big, anything that pushed through could just pop back again. With a little defect like this, about the size of a dime, anything that pushes through is likely to get stuck there. All you've got to do is cough good and hard and you could be in the soup."

"Couldn't I wear one of them belt things they advertise?"

"A truss? Not unless you want to live with one foot in the grave and the other on a banana peel." Rob looked up at him. "Believe me, Ed, you just don't dare fool with it."

Ed sighed. "You're the doctor, not me. So what do we do?"

"First thing, I check you over right now to be sure you're in shape for surgery. If everything's okay, we put you in the hospital Wednesday night and Dr. Sonders will fix you up on Thursday morning."

"You gonna be there?"

"I'll be helping him. Now let's get that gown off so I can go over you."

He wasn't expecting much, since he'd just checked the man thoroughly two months before, so he was listening to Ed's account of

253

late-season fishing up in the lake with half an ear as he proceeded. As a consequence, he nearly missed the moist crackling sounds at the lung bases until he was about to go on to something else. "You got a cold, Ed?" he asked suddenly, cutting the man off in midsentence.

"Cold? Hell, no."

"Well, be still a minute and let me listen here. Deep breath. Now cough. Another deep one." Rob listened, frowning. "You been short of breath lately?"

"Not so's you'd notice."

"What did Dora weigh you in at?"

"Hundred and eighty-five pounds," Ed said. "Seemed like more than it ought to be."

"Yeah, about ten pounds too much," Rob said. He listened again to the man's lung bases, then very carefully to his heart as he sat there, then had him lie down and listened again. He pulled out the extension at the foot of the table and had Butler stretch his legs out flat. The ankles were unmistakably puffy and Rob's thumb left a little dent mark when he squeezed them. "Ed, have you been sick since I saw you last?" he asked finally.

"Nah. Healthy as a horse."

"No chest pain of any kind?"

"Nothing. Why? What's the matter?"

"I'm not just sure, but I'm going to have Dora get another chest film and a repeat cardiogram while you're here. Just sit tight and I'll see you in a bit."

He notified Dora, then went on with other patients as she took Ed to the x-ray room. Half an hour later she flagged him down. The chest film looked normal. When he compared the cardiogram with the one taken two months earlier, he found some minor differences, but nothing he could be sure was significant. He sat gnawing his lip and staring at the cardiogram tracing for long minutes. Nothing on the tracing—but he knew what he'd heard, and he didn't like it.

He put in a call for Harry Sonders at Sacred Heart in Missoula and caught him between cases. "Harry, this Ed Butler guy Martin scheduled for you out here on Thursday . . . Yeah, the hernia case . . . I wonder if we shouldn't hold up on him."

"Why?" Sonders said. "Martin said he was in good shape."

"Two months ago he was clean as a whistle, but I've just checked him now and something's changed."

"Like what?"

254

"I think he's in borderline heart failure," Rob said, "and I don't quite know why. He's carrying around ten extra pounds of water in his tissues, and I think he's also got a heart murmur he didn't have two months ago."

"Oh, come on now," Sonders said. "What kind of a murmur?"

"I don't know. I can only just barely hear it—but I know it wasn't there before."

"Well—hell," Sonders said. "What is he, seventy-two years old? He's probably got a little failure and some heart enlargement that's made one of the heart valves a little floppy. Just give him a dose of Esidrix; he'll dump off that water by Thursday."

"It isn't just the water that bothers me."

"All right, so digitalize him too, if you want to. I'll even do the repair under spinal anesthesia so we don't have that Davis bitch anywhere near his heart or lungs. Hell, all I want to do is fix his hernia. I'm not going to disembowel the man."

"I know it's just a hernia," Rob said, "but I don't quite understand why he's in failure all of a sudden. There's something here that stinks, and I think we'd better scratch the surgery till we find out what it is."

Sonders sighed. "Rob, for Christ sake! Martin had to spend all Friday afternoon talking this guy into the surgery, and now you want to muck it up. You let him off the hook now and the next time he strangulates that hernia up in the woods somewhere he's liable not to get back down in time—or else Florey will end up doing it at two o'clock some morning, and Martin will have a stroke." Sonders paused. "Look, if you'd feel better, get Jerry in there to have a look at him. Then if the two of you agree one hundred percent that he shouldn't be done on Thursday for whatever damned reason, just go ahead and scratch the case. Okay?"

Rob hung up, swearing under his breath, and went to find Jerry. DeForrest looked at the chest x-ray, compared the cardiograms, then went in with Rob and listened to Ed Butler's heart and lungs. When he finished he told Ed to get dressed and took Rob down the hall to the coffee room.

"So what do you think?" Rob demanded.

"Hard to say. His lungs are certainly a little soggy, and he's got some ankle edema and a little distention of his neck veins when he lies down. That all points to some degree of heart failure. There's nothing diagnostic in the cardiogram, and as for the murmur, it's so faint you can hardly hear it. Sonders might be right: Ed's heart might be enlarged just enough from the failure that one of the valves leaks a little." DeForrest paused and sipped coffee. "Maybe he's not the choicest candidate for surgery, but then one has to weigh the risk that he'll strangulate the hernia again. If he got a loop of bowel really jammed down there, he could be out of the picture in four or five hours."

"Okay, so what should we do?" Rob asked.

"About the surgery?" Jerry scratched his lean jaw and shook his head. "Sure is hard to say. You're kind of caught by the short hairs in a case like this. You could be wrong either way."

"Yes, but somebody's got to decide which way we'd be the *most* wrong," Rob said, a little desperately. "I think it's silly to risk elective surgery until we get his heart failure under control and have some idea why he's got it—but all this doesn't seem to bother Harry a bit. So he said to find out what you thought."

"Well, you sure could be right," Jerry said evasively. "No previous history of heart trouble in a man this age, and then this turns up out of the blue; makes one wonder what's going on. But then Harry has a point too. You've got a couple of days grace to get him on digitalis and a diuretic, get him dried out a little bit. Of course, if he still looks sour by Thursday morning, one could always scratch the case then."

"So you think we should plan to go ahead."

"Well, tentatively. If he could dump ten pounds of water between now and then, he might just be fine."

"Okay," Rob said, tight-lipped. "I still disagree, but you're the internist. Just for the record, though, I'd like you to put a consultation note on his chart with your impressions and recommendations."

"Oh, sure. Tell Dora to leave the chart on my desk."

"And what about follow-up? He'll go up to the hospital Wednesday evening. Shall we both check him then before Harry turns up on Thursday?"

"Sure. Or you can. Whichever works out best." DeForrest put down his coffee cup. "Right now, I'd better get back to work."

Back in his office, Rob struggled to conceal his irritation as he outlined the plan to Ed Butler—the digitalis, the diuretic, a low-salt diet, no strenuous physical exercise until after the surgery. Ed took it all in, and then Rob had Dora call Ed's wife, Emma, back to double-check the instructions. "So you come in to the hospital midafternoon on Wednesday," Rob concluded. "I'll be up there before dinner to see you."

Ed nodded, then looked up at Rob. "You look mighty unhappy, Doc."

"Oh, I just don't like this water-retention business, that's all," Rob said. "It's nothing for you to worry about, though. And if I'm still unhappy Wednesday night or Thursday morning, we'll just call off the show, that's all."

"Whatever you say," Ed said, getting up to depart. "I reckon you won't get me in trouble if you can help it. See you Wednesday afternoon."

The man's confidence was touching, but it merely intensified Rob's uneasiness. All that afternoon and all day Tuesday he had Ed Butler stewing on the back burner of his mind, uneasy because he couldn't get a good, clean, straightforward opinion out of Jerry DeForrest, uneasy at Harry Sonders' obvious lack of concern, uneasy with himself for not getting up on his hind legs and screaming, and even more uneasy that there seemed to be no definite, clear-cut and specific threat that he could put his thumb on. *People Ed's age get heart failure,* he told himself. *Who knows why? Old sclerotic arteries get stiff, and the heart overworks pushing the blood around. Water seeps into the ankles and lungs, and the circulation gets sluggish, and the heart works even harder and gets less done, and pretty soon the man's in failure. It's no disaster; it's early, he'll bail out. People can live for years with heart failure, if it's properly treated. So what are you worried about?*

He couldn't say, and that bothered him more than anything. Three or four times on a busy Tuesday he reached for the phone to call Ed, see what his weight had done, see how he felt—and checked himself each time. *You'll just get the old guy all nervous and tense, and that's no good, either. See him Wednesday night, take another cardiogram, and then blow the whistle if you have to and the hell with Sonders. But leave the poor guy alone until then.*

He was still fretting about Ed on Wednesday morning when Dora dropped another patient's chart on his desk, hesitated a moment, and then said, "Something funny is going on here."

"What do you mean?"

"Janice Blanchard is here to see you. She must be six months pregnant now if she's a day, and I'd almost swear she had a long session with Dr. Isaacs last week, but now she wants to see you and nobody else. Wouldn't tell me why."

Rob took the chart, but found no recent note in it. He remembered

Janice Blanchard's leukemic baby all too clearly, and had more recently seen Janice at several of the Blood Bank Committee meetings. He had even noticed her obvious pregnancy at the last meeting, and assumed that Isaacs was taking care of her.

But now, as he walked into the examining room, he wasn't so sure. She was a tall, pale woman with jet black hair and eyes of a startling deep blue. Too thin to be truly attractive, with a ghost-haunted face and a flicker of tragedy about the eyes, she forced a shadow of a smile as Rob came in. No, not attractive, he decided, but handsome, even compelling, as her eyes caught and held his. "Well, Janice, I haven't seen you in here for quite a while."

"No, I know," she said. "Not since the baby died." Her voice was flat and strained, as though she were fighting to control it. "Dr. Bauermann said he'd sent you a report."

"He did. Not much help, but with something like that there just *isn't* much help."

"I know," she said. "It was hard to accept, but Bob and I have made peace with it, I think. Anyway, we already had the real antidote all the time and didn't even know it."

"Oh?" Rob glanced up at her, puzzled.

"I must already have been pregnant again at the time the baby died."

"Ah. When were you sure?"

"Back in July, just after Debbie got sick. My period was more than a month overdue, and I was having some morning sickness, and my breasts were—you know—all funny. . . ."

Her voice trailed off as Rob nodded and leafed through her chart. "Dr. Isaacs delivered that last baby, right?"

"Yes, but I don't want to go back to him."

Rob looked up. "How come? Did you two have a fight or something?"

She flushed. "Not that, exactly. But I've had the three miscarriages now—"

"You mean you've been pregnant three other times since Debbie was born?"

"No, no. I had two miscarriages before I had Debbie and then a third soon after she was born. They all happened in about the third month, and Dr. Isaacs had to do a D&C each time."

"I see." It suddenly struck Rob that there was something decidedly odd about the way this woman was responding, sitting very stiffly on the

258

edge of her chair, watching him closely, yet shifting her glance whenever he tried to catch her eye. "You know," he said, picking his words, "you shouldn't blame Dr. Isaacs for the miscarriages. Nine times out of ten there's nothing any doctor can do to stop one if it's going to happen."

"I know. Dr. Isaacs explained that to me."

"And most doctors today do a D&C afterwards just to make sure there's no tissue retained that might get the woman into trouble later."

"I know that too. I'm not blaming Dr. Isaacs for anything. It's just—" She broke off, flushing, obviously groping for words.

"You think maybe a change of doctor will mean a change of luck?" Rob said.

"Well, maybe." She sat silent a moment, twisting a finger in the palm of the other hand. "Look," she said suddenly, "is there some kind of medical law that says that once you have a Caesarean baby, you absolutely have to have the next baby that way too, no matter what?"

In a flash, then, Rob saw the whole picture. "Debbie was a Caesarean baby, is that it?"

"Yes. I went into labor, but something was wrong, the baby didn't come down the way it should, and then I started bleeding a lot right in the middle of things, so Dr. Isaacs took me into surgery."

"And the next time you got pregnant, he told you you'd have to have another Caesarean."

"Yes. But then I miscarried and lost that one, and then Debbie got sick the way she did, so suddenly. She was always a weak baby, you know, she never nursed the way she should have, and then that horrible leukemia . . ."

*And you figure that somehow the Caesarean was to blame. You wouldn't admit it if I asked you, you've already been told by experts that there couldn't be any connection, but you still think maybe, just possibly . . .* Rob shook his head. "Janice, a Caesarean section isn't just done at the drop of a hat. Ordinarily it's more risky than a normal delivery, and it's only done in the first place if something turns up to threaten the mother or the baby or both. But when it has to be done, it has no bad effect on the baby. No effect whatever."

"I know. That's exactly what Dr. Isaacs said. But Bob and I have decided we just don't want another Caesarean."

"Let me finish," Rob said. "A Caesarean has no effect on the baby, but it does have an effect on the mother. It leaves a scar through the wall of her uterus. A break in the muscle wall, a weak spot. So when she gets pregnant again and the baby starts stretching the uterus, that weak spot gets thinner and thinner. It doesn't usually cause any trouble until labor begins, but if the labor happens to be especially hard or forceful, that weak spot can split wide open, and then both the patient and the doctor are *really* in the soup."

"But does it *always* happen that way? Does it necessarily *have* to happen?"

"No, it doesn't *have* to happen. But who wants to take the risk?"

She looked up defiantly. "Maybe *I* do," she said. "Why can't I? It's my pregnancy, isn't it? Look, I'd do anything you told me to; I'd do all kinds of exercises—"

"Exercises wouldn't cut the risk."

"Well, maybe not, but I'd really work to keep my weight down, I wouldn't get all puffy the way I did with Debbie, and Bob and I would sign papers so you wouldn't be held responsible if anything went wrong. I'd do anything you said, but *I just don't want another Caesarean.*"

Rob watched her, shaking his head, as she dug into her purse, pulled out a hanky and dabbed at her eyes. "You've already been over all this with Dr. Isaacs, haven't you?"

She nodded, tearfully. "He just said no, period. He wouldn't even listen. He said I was crazy, told me if I insisted, I'd have to go to somebody else."

Rob nodded. It sounded like Isaacs. Rob knew the old obstetrical rule perfectly well: *Once a Caesarean, always a Caesarean.* It wasn't just superstition or medical jingoism; there was a very real risk that a Caesarean-scarred uterus would rupture if a normal labor was attempted later. But not all OB men stuck rigidly to the rule. He recalled at least one obstetrician in medical school who had argued that each case had to be approached individually. "A pregnant woman is not a cog in a machine," he had said. "Forget about the rule and look at the patient. If she's young, healthy and vigorous, a cautious trial of labor may be indicated—and you could be saving her an unnecessary surgical insult."

Now, facing Janice Blanchard, Rob saw what his answer had to be. "I could no more promise you not to do a Caesarean at this point than I could sprout wings and fly out the window," he said. "I don't care *what* you and your husband might sign. If I'm to take care of your pregnancy, then I'm responsible for your safety and the baby's, and if this means having to do a Caesarean when the time comes, then that's what I'll do.

260

There's no way I can promise what you're asking. I don't know any doctor who could."

Janice looked up. "Dr. Florey promised," she said.

"He promised you that he wouldn't do a Caesarean, no matter what?"

"That's right."

"Well, with all due respect to Dr. Florey, I don't think he'd keep his word. If he really got down to the wire and then felt a Caesarean was necessary, he'd go right ahead and do one, promise or no promise. If you think otherwise, you're in the wrong office, and you'd better go right back down there."

"Well, I don't really like Dr. Florey that much, I guess," Janice said.

"Okay, then we have to start off without any promises. The best I can tell you is that we won't have any arbitrary rules, either. If everything looked favorable when you got ready to deliver, a trial of labor might be possible. I said *might* be. And in any event, *I'd* be the one to decide, when the time came. Not you or anybody else. Me. Do you understand that?"

"Yes. Oh, yes! But if it's even *possible . . .*"

"I don't know yet if it's possible or not. All I can say now is that we'll keep it in mind—nothing more. Okay?"

"Oh, yes. Yes!"

"And you'll go along with whatever I decide when the time comes? Even if I decide it's got to be a Caesarean?"

"Yes—if you'll at least consider the other way."

It seemed reasonable enough, and the woman seemed sincere. Rob buzzed the front desk and set a time on Thursday afternoon to have her return for her OB physical exam and lab work, and she left his office, positively radiant. He went on with his morning schedule, buoyed up with a sense of accomplishment and satisfaction. *At least something's going right this week,* he thought. *Here's one that Martin fumbled and I recovered, right out of John Florey's lap, the old fraud. And all it takes is a little finesse.*

His self-satisfaction didn't last long. Coming back from lunch, he met Agnes Miller in the hall, and she looked at him over her glasses. "I hear Janice Blanchard is coming to you for her OB care," she said.

"Right," Rob said. "How about that?"

"I don't know. She's kind of spooky, that woman."

"She's just a little nervous. She'll be okay."

Agnes looked dubious. "Maybe so, but she and Dr. Isaacs have gone round and round a couple of times." She plunked instruments down on a tray for the autoclave. "I wouldn't want to butt in, but Dr. Isaacs may not be too happy about it, either. Last I heard, he sent her down to Tintown, and believe me, he doesn't do that too often with an OB case."

Rob didn't have to wait long to find out how the older doctor felt. Before he had a chance to see his first afternoon patient, Isaacs came storming up the hall and into his office. "What the *hell* are you doing with that Blanchard woman?" he demanded.

Rob looked up from his desk. "Seems that I'm taking care of her," he said. "She's obviously pregnant. I guess she went to see everybody else in town first, but it looks like I win the raffle."

"That woman is nuts," Isaacs said. "You can't take her through a normal delivery. She's got to have a Caesarean."

"Well, I know the rule, but she was really pretty adamant. So I guess I just begged the question."

"My God, there isn't any question to beg!" Isaacs exploded. "She's got to have a section, and that's all there is to it. She's a tall, skinny woman with a narrow, cramped-up pelvis, and she's never had a vaginal delivery yet. She couldn't even push a five-pound baby through there the last time; as far as trying a normal delivery is concerned, it'd be just the same as a first baby. So what are you going to do when that scar splits open with the first good cramp? Stand there and wring your hands?"

"Jesus, Martin, it isn't quite all that bad. I really didn't promise her a thing."

"Then what's she doing down at the front desk telling the girls how you thought maybe she could have a normal delivery after all? What the hell *did* you tell her?"

"I merely told her the truth," Rob said. "I told her that Caesareans weren't necessarily a law of God, and that if everything looked good when the time came, a cautious trial of labor might be possible. And that's all I told her. No promises."

"Oh, good Lord." The big man sat down heavily across from Rob, pulled off his glasses and polished them on his lab coat, then looked at Rob with exasperation. "You're out of your fucking mind," he said. *"Nobody* today can take a risk like that, you or anybody else. Do you have any idea how thin that uterus gets when labor starts? Maybe an eighth of an inch, that's how thin. And the scar is even thinner; it's got no strength. It just *tears*. One good hard push and it could split wide open."

"Okay," Rob said. "So it's got to be done under careful control. I'd have to have the operating room all ready to go, so that we could open her up the minute anything went wrong. That's what you do when you think you may have a placenta previa on your hands, isn't it? Before you even try to do an examination?"

"That's right—but God creates that risk, boy, and there's nothing you can do about it. *You're* creating this risk, and you just can't. Sure, with some women you might just poozy them along and get them all prepared to accept a section by the time they're due, but not this one. This woman is off in Neverland somewhere. I've been through the mill with her once too often—three miscarriages and one section—and I'm telling you, she's *nuts.* Right this minute she thinks you've promised her a normal delivery, and if you don't give her a normal delivery, she'll have your ass nailed to the barn door before you know what hit you. She'll slap you with a malpractice suit for a million dollars, and you'll *lose.* I *know* this babe. Why do you think I sent her down to Florey? To hand him a three-hundred-dollar fee?"

"Martin, there's nothing wrong with the woman," Rob said. "Everybody's a little eccentric sometimes."

"*Eccentric!* She's *crazy.* She was in here three or four months ago and wanted me to lend her a speculum so she and some of her women's lib girlfriends could do pelvic exams on each other!"

"So what did you do?"

"Do? I handed her my textbook of gynecology and told her when she and her friends had read all fifteen hundred pages and could pass state boards on it, I'd lend them a speculum. She took off in a snit, the goddam fool. I heard later that they sucked Peterson into giving them a group demonstration so they could all take their own Pap smears. Talk about the blind leading the blind . . ."

"Okay, so maybe she's screwy as a bush full of owls," Rob said. "The fact remains that she's pregnant and she needs somebody to take care of her."

"Well, it isn't going to be me, or you either. The one time she finally got through the first trimester without aborting, she was nothing but grief—never kept her appointments, never did anything I told her, gained weight like a hog in a feed lot, blood pressure up, spotting, cramps, kidney infections. Jesus! You name it and she had it."

"But you're not going to *have* the headaches this time," Rob said. "If there's any grief, *I'll* have the grief. The worst you'll have to do is cover for me when I'm off."

"Or bail you out," Isaacs said heavily. He pushed to his feet. "Well, don't say I didn't warn you. If you want *my* advice, you'll get this Caesarean matter settled without any question-begging, right up front, before you do anything else. Do it before you even examine her. Forget the trial-of-labor crap; wipe it right out of her mind."

"I don't see how I can back off from it now," Rob said.

"Well, God damn it, I'm telling you how. Back off from it, and do it fast, or you'll have grief like you never saw before. And if you're *really* smart, you'll get rid of her. She and Florey deserve each other."

After Isaacs had left, Rob sat staring at the desktop for a long while, tapping the edge of the desk with his pen in a sharp cadence of irritation. The sense of satisfaction and accomplishment was gone, replaced by a vast feeling of frustration. It was unfair; the old bastard's arguments were deliberately loaded. He'd said nothing about the risks of a Caesarean. He'd simply brushed aside the woman's feelings and desires. So maybe she *was* a little nutty. So what? But most jarring of all was the bitterness and vehemence of Isaacs' antipathy to the woman. *Boy, when you get on that man's shit list, you'd better believe it's a shit list. Half of what he said wasn't germane. Hell, half of it wasn't even rational. So she wants to do her own Pap smears.* Rob threw his pen down in disgust.

Presently he stood up and started his afternoon schedule. What Isaacs was deliberately ignoring was that Rob had made some kind of peace with the woman, at least for the moment. There would be time enough to pull her away from her fear of a section, if necessary. Maybe a consultation with somebody would help, some OB man in Missoula. Then at least he'd have an expert opinion to back him up. Or to back her down—one or the other.

Of course, Isaacs might not like that, either—but Rob could worry about that later. One thing was certain: he was not going to yield to irrationality and dump the woman, as Isaacs recommended. Isaacs could go hang first.

# 22

Around four o'clock Wednesday afternoon Miss Pryor at the hospital called to tell him that Ed Butler had checked in for his hernia repair the following morning.

"Fine," Rob said. "I'll be up in a while to write orders."

"Do you want us to notify Dr. Sonders too?"

"Not yet. I'll call him after I've seen the patient."

He buzzed Jerry DeForrest, but Jerry was tied up with some aged relict of his practice and didn't answer. Well, he knew Ed was coming in, and he knew Rob wanted a pre-op consultation. What was more, Rob was going to have one if he had to drag DeForrest out of bed at three in the morning to provide it. Meantime, Sonders could stew if he wanted to—although it seemed somehow unlikely to Rob that Sonders would be stewing very much.

He had hoped to get up to the hospital early, but patients and timing foiled him. It was after seven when he got there and found Janice Pryor more than usually snippy because he'd given her no diet orders for Ed. "He was watching everyone else eat, and threatened to check out and go home if we didn't give him his dinner," she said. "Fortunately, Dr. DeForrest finally came in and wrote diet orders so we could feed him." Rob nodded, listening with half an ear as he leafed through the man's chart.

DeForrest had indeed been there and had indeed ordered Ed's

dinner, not the low-salt diet Rob would have written for any patient with congestive heart failure, just a "Regular Diet" order, which this evening had meant ham. Rob sighed. DeForrest had also examined the patient, it seemed, because there was a brief note on the chart: "Heart failure controlled with digitalis and diuretics. Weight down. Okay for surgery in AM," with Jerry's initials scrawled beneath it. Rob sighed again and pushed the chart aside. *So much for Jerry's consultation.*

Down in the men's ward he found Ed Butler propped up in bed reading a *Reader's Digest.* "About time you got here," he grumbled. "They were going to starve me until that skinny DeForrest guy came in and told them to feed me."

"Did he check you over real well?"

"Well, he listened to my ticker for a minute. Said maybe you'd want another one of them cardiograms; he didn't know for sure."

"I do. How've you been feeling?"

"Well, them pills really gave my kidneys a boost. Been pissin' a regular river for two days now. Must have gone to the can forty-eight times."

"Good. You can do without that water." Rob pushed the covers back, found the ankle swelling almost completely gone.

"DeForrest said my heart's slowed down too."

"That's what we had in mind. Let me listen now." Rob listened, moving the stethoscope back and forth across the man's chest. The heart rate was certainly slower, down to a steady seventy-two beats a minute. The lung bases were also clear of the juicy, crackling sounds he had heard two days before. As for the murmur . . . he listened, closing his eyes. Still there. Fainter now, but unmistakably still there, a barely audible whooshing sound at the end of each *lub-dup* of the heartbeat. Rob set the stethoscope aside, opened the man's chart and studied the copy of the electrocardiogram he had taken two days before, when the heart rate had been much faster. Finally he went to find Raymond and order a new cardiogram. As he waited in the coffee room he stared out the back window at the surrounding woods, wishing he felt more comfortable about Ed Butler, yet still at a loss to know why he was so uneasy. *After all, Jerry isn't a dunce. If he'd been worried, he'd have blown the whistle. You're borrowing trouble, that's all, just because you thought the surgery should be scratched and somebody overrode you. And now you're just sitting and stewing for no reason at all.*

Half an hour later Raymond came in with the new cardiogram tape

266

draped from his fingers. Rob compared it carefully with the earlier one from the office. The heart rate was unquestionably slower, stronger and more regular. Some evidence of digitalis effect, but nothing to suggest recent heart damage. Some cardiac enlargement, which was to be expected, but . . . He cursed under his breath, wishing he were sharper at reading cardiograms, wishing that Jerry would just once take the bull by the horns and order up a repeat cardiogram while he was still there to read it.

He went back down to the men's ward. "Ed, it looks okay. You just do what the nurses tell you. No breakfast, not even any water after midnight. I'll be here in the morning to help Dr. Sonders." He paused, looking down at his fishing friend. "Ed, are you sure you haven't been sick in any way the last couple of months? No way at all?"

"Hell no, Doc. Been feeling fine. Oh, I had a little spell of heartburn a month ago, lasted a couple of days, but it went away."

"I see. Do you have heartburn very often?"

"Maybe once a year. Nothing to worry about."

"No chest pain when you're splitting firewood?"

"Nah, not anymore."

"Why not?"

Ed Butler looked up at him, deadpan. "I let Emma split it now," he said. "She's pretty spry."

*Damn*, Rob thought. *If we could only get a cardiogram with an esophageal lead or something. If we could only somehow get a really good cardiac consultation. But how—and why? There's just nothing to go on, really. How can you explain a vague, unsubstantiated nervous hunch? DeForrest and Sonders would both have fits if you hauled in a cardiologist from Missoula at this stage of the game. Even assuming that you could find one who would come.* Shaking his head, he pushed the idea aside. "Well, Ed, you get some rest. And don't fret. I'll see you in the morning."

He went on to check last-minute orders on other patients, then headed down the hill. Ellie had put a meat loaf in the oven when she saw him drive across the bridge, and they settled down with crackers and cheese and beer while they waited for it to bake, Ellie bubbling over with maps and camping plans for the weekend, Rob morose and preoccupied. "This wilderness area down in Idaho really looks like fun. Only about eighty miles from here, with a couple of nice-looking lakes for camping, and there probably won't be too many others there at this time of year. And one of the places is right at the trail head for a whole collection of high-country trails, if we feel like packing in a few miles on Saturday."

"Sounds fine," Rob said.

"Well, at least it'll be a change." She looked up at him. "And you look like you could use a change. You look absolutely *gray.*"

"So make me a drink. Maybe that'll pick me up. Martin's got call."

"More trouble?"

"Oh, not really. I had another set-to with Martin this afternoon about an OB patient, and let me tell you, when that guy gets an idea in his head there is no getting it out. Talk about stubborn."

"What kind of an idea?"

"Like insisting that you have to do a repeat section on a woman once she's already had a Caesarean baby." Briefly Rob told her about the situation, omitting names and identifying details.

Ellie was silent for a moment. Then: "He could be right, you know. He must know that woman pretty well by now."

"He thinks she's a nut."

"He could be right about that too."

"Yes, except that *his* definition of a nut is anybody who disagrees with him, for whatever reason. That can take in an awful lot of people."

"Well, it may not be fair, but he could still be right. He's been handling OBs for a long time. Maybe he *knows* you can't get away with a trial of labor in a case like this. Maybe he's just trying to spare you having to learn it the hard way."

"Oh, I know it. It's just that he's so damned autocratic he drives me crazy, that's all. He walks in and says, 'Do it this way!' and I'm supposed to do it, period. It doesn't matter what *I* think, or whether it's right, wrong or indifferent, for that matter. He's always got a reason—but the reason may not make any rational sense at all, when you really look at it."

"Seems to me you're talking about politics now, not medicine," Ellie said.

"Maybe so. But I'm always the one that gets his toe nailed to the floor in one of these hassles." Rob stuck a cracker into his mouth. "At least with this woman there's a little time to get her squared away, and I'll be damned if I'm going to tell her one thing one day and something completely different the next. At least I'm not backed up to the wall yet. But this surgical patient is something else. Nobody seems to be worrying about him except me, and he goes on the block tomorrow morning."

268

"Which surgical patient is that?"

"Oh, an old fellow with a hernia." He told her briefly about Ed Butler and his uneasiness about the case. "Harry insists on going ahead, and Jerry is sitting on the fence again, as usual, and I don't know *what's* going on with the old guy's heart. But I hate to take him to surgery this way——"

"So you're going to lie awake all night worrying about it," Ellie said.

"Well, damn it, *somebody* has to!"

"Oh, Rob." She came over and sat beside him on the sofa, leaning her head back against his shoulder. "Doesn't it ever occur to you that maybe you're just barking at shadows?"

He looked at her. "What do you mean?"

"Honey, these other men must have *some* idea what they're doing. They must have been doing a reasonably decent job before you came here, or this valley would be strewn with corpses by now."

"Oh, for Christ's sake!" Rob jumped to his feet. "Ellie, I can tell sloppy medicine when it comes up and kicks me. Obviously they managed, but I'll be damned if I know how. And you don't see the corpses, because they're all buried."

"But don't you think their experience maybe counts for *something?* I don't mean fancy hospital experience, I mean practical experience right here in Twin Forks, Montana. So why do you keep pounding your head on the wall? I know you're a perfectionist, everything has to be just right, all tied up in a neat little bundle—but maybe it's not *like* that here. Maybe it *can't* be like that here."

"Well, maybe you can't have perfection, but you can have a certain minimum standard of good medical practice!"

"Good by whose standard? Yours alone? You can't be the sole arbiter of what's right and wrong here. And you can't go on making yourself the self-appointed scourge of the practice, either. For one thing, you'll tear yourself to pieces, and for another, the other men are going to get fed up, sooner or later, and that's no good. You've got limited resources in a practice like this, and it seems to me you've got to learn to live with them without killing yourself or driving the others up the wall."

"Oh, hell, you don't even understand what I'm talking about." Rob jammed his hands in his pockets and crossed the room to stare out the window into the darkness. "I'm not trying to reform the world. I'm not even asking for very much. But I think it's just plain wrong to tell a pregnant woman who's already scared silly that she has to have her

269

baby according to some blind medical rule of thumb, and if she doesn't agree, just tell her to go to hell. And I think it's wrong to go doing elective surgery *right now* on a man who isn't in shape for it just because you're afraid he might back out if you give him a chance to think about it for a while—"

The telephone jangled suddenly, and Rob snatched it off the hook. "Dr. Tanner," he said. "Yes . . . I see. Any fever?" He listened for a long moment. "Well, it's probably just that ear again, but I'd better have a look at her. Bundle her up and take her to the hospital. I'll meet you there in ten minutes." He dropped the receiver back on the hook. "I'll be up the hill for a while," he told Ellie. "I don't know for how long."

"Rob . . ."

"Oh, forget it. I'll see you later." He banged out the door and a moment later was driving across the bridge. Up at the hospital the mother was waiting with a wailing child. He ordered the usual for an earache: fever control, antibiotics, something for the pain. He was just finishing when Roger Painter came trotting up the ramp and handed him a sealed envelope.

"Glad I caught you," he said. "I was going to mail this to Mrs. Hazard, but maybe you can deliver it."

Rob looked at him and ripped open the envelope. It contained a brief note typed on hospital stationery:

In view of increasing hospital costs and lack of adequate space, the Directors of the Twin Forks Hospital cannot sponsor or support a whole blood storage unit at the Twin Forks Hospital at this time. The vote was 5 to 1 with one director abstaining.

S/Roger Painter
for the Directors

Rob read the memo again. "It was the Judge who abstained?"

"He felt he shouldn't vote," Roger said primly.

"I see." Rob started to crumple the paper in his fist, then straightened it out and put it in his breast pocket. "Okay. So now you figure we'll just let it drop."

Roger Painter smiled. "Of course. What else?"

"I'll tell you what else," Rob said. "If this is how they voted, then we need a new board of directors. In fact, we need to take this whole crappy hospital out of private hands and run it as a community institution, and the sooner the better. You might pass that on to the directors, from me. And if you think I'm kidding, you're very much mistaken."

270

As Rob drove home, the depressing tone of the directors' memo hit with full force. As for his brave words, they sounded fine, but he had no idea how they might be implemented. *Owned by half a dozen private investors, mostly in Twin Forks, a couple in Missoula.* To break a hold like that he'd need help—expert help. Isaacs? Not likely, considering his response to the blood bank idea. Judge Barret? *Maybe. Just maybe.*

He was still mulling this over as he drove down through town. Purely by chance, he glanced up the clinic street as he went past, and thought for a moment that he saw a car in the parking lot by the front door. He slowed down, frowning, then shook his head, deciding against turning back. Just a fleeting impression. The car was probably parked on the street, and he laughed at himself for the sudden flicker of alarm. *Jesus, Ellie's right. You're getting jumpy. And even if it was somebody, they can call you.*

By the time he reached the house by the river he was feeling thoroughly contrite for snapping at Ellie earlier. Maybe she was right, and he just couldn't see the forest for the trees. Maybe a really good weekend rest was all he needed. He didn't like to leave the squabble hanging, but the house lights were down when he arrived and Ellie was already in bed, breathing regularly. *No point in waking her,* he thought, setting his shoes quietly on the floor. *Time enough to straighten it out tomorrow.* Moments later he too was in bed, pushing her over as she snuffled a groggy protest, and falling asleep himself in a matter of moments.

Much later the phone jangled, dragging him up out of a deep sleep. A man's voice, oddly muffled. A voice he did not recognize. "Dr. Tanner?"

"Yeah." He fought sleep away.

"The hospital said I could call you, right?"

"Who's this?" Rob said.

"Swinner. Frank Swinner. We're just passing through—"

"Dr. Isaacs is on call. You'd better call him."

"I did, but he didn't answer. And my wife's having this terrible pain—"

Suddenly alert, Rob sat up on the edge of the bed. "What kind of pain?"

"It's in her back on the right side, Doc. Like she's passing a kidney stone or something. She's had them before, and it's about killing her. I've got to get her something. Can we meet you at your office?"

271

"No. Not my office. Go up to the hospital. I'll meet you there."

"How do I get there?"

"Go to the middle of town, just north of the bridge, and follow the signs up the hill."

"Okay. But hurry, Doc."

The caller rang off. Rob replaced his own receiver, then sat staring into the blackness for a long moment.

He knew the call was phony. He didn't know *how* he knew, but he knew it as sure as he knew his own name. Something about the voice, the pattern of words, the quasi urgency. He *knew*. After a moment he walked out to the kitchen and snapped on a light. He picked up the extension phone, dialed a number, heard it ring twice. . . .

"Twin Forks Police, Vern Bradley speaking."

"Vern, this is Rob Tanner. I've got a junkie call. I'm going to meet them at the hospital. You want to swing around?"

"Sure, Doc. Fifteen minutes?"

"That'd be fine." Rob hung up, pulled on slacks and a sports shirt and went out to his car. It was 5:45 A.M. and the sky was still dark. At the hospital a single car was parked in the patients' parking lot at the front of the building, but the Emergency Room lights were not on. Fine; Jessie Hodges never liked to be alone with anybody down in the Emergency Room at night. He walked up the ramp and found her getting a woman perched on a wheeled stretcher under the bright lights in the delivery room corridor. He was vaguely aware of two men sitting waiting in the darkened lobby near the front door.

Hodges gave him an odd look and turned a sidelong glance at the woman. "Glad you came right away," she said. "This woman says she's got a lot of pain in her back."

Rob nodded and approached the woman. She was maybe forty, dumpy and dough-faced, clutching her back with her right hand and moaning. "I'm the doctor you called. What's going on?"

"I think it's one of those damned stones," the woman said in a gravelly voice. "Caught me all of a sudden, and when I went to the john in the gas station down in town, there was some blood."

"You've had these attacks before?"

"Oh, yes. The pain"—she winced, arching her back, then taking a deep breath—"the pain comes in waves. We're trying to get back to Spokane to my doctor there, but I don't know if I can make it. He usually gives me a shot for it."

"What kind of a shot?"

272

"Dolophine, usually."

"No," Rob said flatly.

"How's that?"

"I said no. I never give narcotics to people passing through. Period."

"Doc, the pain is about to drive me nuts. You could at least check my urine and see for yourself."

"No, I don't want to check your urine," Rob said. "I'll give you some Darvon and have the nurse give you some Thorazine by hypo, if you want, but that's it. You just go on to your doctor in Spokane for your Dolophine, or if you're hurting too much it's just ninety minutes back to Missoula to a big city hospital—"

"My God, I can't make it back to Missoula, you son of a bitch. What kind of a fucking doctor are you to just let a patient sit around in pain like this? I know you hick bastards, you're sadists, every one of you, and I swear to God I'll have your ass in a malpractice suit if you don't do something to help me—"

As she talked Rob saw headlights flash from the uphill road, and now there were footsteps up the ramp. Vern Bradley and another uniformed policeman walked into the corridor. One of them tipped his hat to the night nurse. "Mornin', Miss Hodges. Got some coffee back in the kitchen? Thought we'd just stop for a cup."

The woman stopped her tirade in midsentence the instant she saw the uniform. In the same instant the two men in the waiting room were on their feet, heading for the outside door. The woman slid off the stretcher, almost tripping over Rob to get to her feet. "All right; if you won't help, we won't bother you," she muttered.

"You're sure you don't want me to check your urine?" Rob said.

"Get out of my way, you smart-ass prick." She gave him a shove that nearly toppled him and headed for the waiting room, where one of the men was holding the door for her. An instant later the car roared out of the parking lot—the same car Rob had seen parked at the clinic earlier. It whirled out of the hospital lot on two wheels and careened on down the hill.

"Whew," Hodges said. "I was sure glad to see Vern Bradley turn up here."

"It didn't just happen," Rob said. "I flagged him before I even left home." He pushed through the door into the coffee room, drew some coffee and joined the policemen. "Good show," he said. "The timing was perfect. But what do they do now? Just go on to the next town?"

Bradley shrugged. "All depends," he said. "Our worry is to get them out of *this* town. But we got their license plate and car description and called it to the state patrol. They'll run a fast check, and if there's an alarm on them anywhere they'll pull them in. Sometimes they have something on them, sometimes they don't. In the cities they stay put pretty much, but in the country they travel. They've got regular routes, hitting green new doctors, ripping off small-town drugstores, some-times hitting clinics or hospitals." He cocked his head at Rob. "How'd you pin them on the strength of a phone call?"

"I don't know," Rob said. "Except that you can smell them ten miles off. Of course, I could have read it wrong, too. If that woman hadn't started moving out the minute she saw your uniform, I'd have had no choice but to really investigate her complaint, check out her urine for blood, examine her, maybe get kidney films. But you guys solved my problem for me, so maybe I can go home and get another forty winks before the day's work starts."

He was sitting at the nurses' desk writing a brief outpatient report on the call when Jessie Hodges came rushing up the corridor from the men's ward, white as a sheet and trembling. "Dr. Tanner, Ed Butler is having trouble down here."

Rob followed her down the hall. "What kind of trouble?"

"I don't know. A minute ago the man in the next bed started ringing his buzzer like crazy. He said all of a sudden Ed grabbed his chest and started groaning and couldn't seem to breathe."

"Good Christ. A coronary?"

"I don't know. He said he was hurting on his right side."

"*Right* side? Oh, God. Look, get the EKG machine fast, and have your aide set up a liter of glucose and water in case we want a vein open. I'll see what I can see."

In his bed Ed Butler was rolled over on his side, clutching the right side of his chest with both hands and gasping like a fish out of water with each respiration. Rob pulled the curtains around the bed and snapped on the bedlamp. The man's face was purple-gray, twisted with pain. "Ed, for God's sake, what's going on?"

The man looked up weakly. "It's killing me, Doc. Hit me in the chest like a ton of bricks. . . ."

"On the *right* side?" Ed nodded feebly. "When?"

"Just a minute ago," Ed choked out. "I just went out to the can. Felt fine all night. I was getting back into bed when it hit me, like somebody rammed a poker in there. Jesus, Doc, it's killing me. . . ."

274

"Let me listen." Swiftly Rob pulled off the hospital gown, placed his stethoscope bell over the man's heart. The heart rate was fast and feeble, with an irregular rhythm, runs of fast beats and then pauses. Ed started coughing, a desperate paroxysm, drowning out all other sounds, and his face and neck went gray. The coughing seemed to go on for minutes as the man twisted and writhed, and finally he got some mucus up, streaked with bright red blood. For a moment Ed stopped breathing altogether; then he took an enormous gasp and began once again fighting for breath. "Jesus, Doc, I can't get my breath."

"Okay, easy; I've got to listen again." Now Rob listened to the lungs, first the left and then the right. Meanwhile Jessie Hodges appeared with the EKG machine on its stand. She started shaking out the leads, but Rob took them from her. "I'll do that. You go get the respirator."

"Which one?"

"The Byrd valve. We may have to breathe for this man for a while. And get a sixth of morphine too, right quick." He turned back to the man in the bed. "Ed? We're going to get something for the pain in just a minute. You hold tight. Just get what air you can and try to relax."

"Can't—relax. Hurts too much." He was off in another paroxysm of coughing.

"We're getting you some oxygen too. Just hang in there. I need your arms out now; I want to take a cardiogram." He set up the leads to the man's wrists and ankles, threw the switch for a calibration segment, and found no paper in the machine. With a curse he started down the corridor, met Hodges coming back with the respirator and an aide carrying an IV setup and a hypo. "There's no paper," he said.

"Paper?"

"In the EKG. Where's it kept?"

"Oh, Raymond must have forgotten to reload it. It's in the cupboard under the drug cabinet."

"Okay, get that respirator going, and give him the morphine. I think we'll wait on the IV for the moment." Under the drug counter he found a roll of EKG tape, brought it back and loaded the machine. Hodges had the respirator going now, and Ed Butler was breathing easier, turning aside from the mask for his coughing spells. His face was a colorless gray, and his heartbeat, racing along at 120 per minute, registered as a low-magnitude wriggle on the cardiogram tape.

"What does it show?" Hodges asked.

"No current of injury. Tachycardia and failure, a few ventricular extra-systoles. What's his blood pressure?"

"One hundred over sixty. I just checked it."

"Okay, let me listen again." Rob used the stethoscope once more, shaking his head unhappily. There was good expansion on the left, but air movement into the right lung was sharply impaired. The morphine was taking hold now, and with the pain easing up Ed seemed to relax some, though his breathing was still ragged. At one point he even pushed himself up a bit in bed and said, "Jesus, Doc, we just should have gone fishing."

"You can say *that* again," Rob said. "You just hang on and we'll go yet." He stuffed his stethoscope in his pocket, pushed the curtain aside and walked over to stare through the ward window at the brightening morning sky. Something obviously had happened—but what? A coronary? Unlikely, with this pain pattern, and no sign of it on the cardiogram. Dissecting aneurysm of the aorta? An awful reach, and no sign of obliterated pulses in the groin or wrist. Pulmonary embolus? Yes, of course, by far the most likely. A small, minor coronary which occurred maybe a month ago, maybe in the septum between the ventricles. A rough, fibrin-coated spot inside the heart wall on which a clot could form and cling. Maybe that caused the murmur and the failure too. And then a change in the rate and strength of heartbeat, due to the digitalis, and a chunk of that clot broke off and went out a pulmonary artery into the right lung. Nasty. It could easily have killed him instantly, and another one still could—

"Doctor! Quick!"

Rob whirled. Ed Butler was sitting bolt upright in bed, one hand clawing feebly at the respirator mask, the other clutching at his chest, his face a deathly gray-blue, eyes protruding, mouth opening spasmodically. He sat like that for an endless moment, a muffled gargling sound emerging from his throat. Then, in horrible slow motion, he sagged, slumped to the side of the bed. Hodges dropped the respirator mask, caught the man to keep him from rolling off the bed, struggled under his weight as Rob joined her. They grabbed his shoulders and rolled him onto the mattress on his back. Aside from a spasmodic jerk or two, there was no sign of breathing. "Get the respirator on positive pressure," Rob snapped as Hodges fumbled with the mask. "Then put it over his face and hold it tight, get some aeration going." He went around the bed, pushing the aide out of his way, and snapped on the still-connected EKG machine. The tape showed a feeble twitching of the heart muscle, no real pumping at all. Rob raised his fist and slammed it down on Ed's chest, once, twice, three times. For a moment the tracing showed a brief run of heartbeats, then resumed the deadly pattern of ventricular fibrillation again. Rob pulled a chair to the side of the bed, knelt with one knee on the bed and one foot on the chair, crossed his hands over the lower left side of Ed Butler's chest and began pressing and relaxing, pressing and relaxing, once every second. He looked over his shoulder at Jessie. "Go get the shock box, quick," he said.

"The what?"

"The defibrillator. It's back against the wall in the emergency room. Get it!"

"I can't," Hodges said. "It's not there."

"Oh, come on, for Christ sake—I *know* it's there, right against the wall in the emergency room."

"It's not. It had a short or something and Raymond sent it in to Spokane for repair. It's not back yet."

"Then get the stand-by." Rob looked at her. "Oh, my God. No stand-by machine?"

"No."

Rob rocked forward and back, pausing only long enough to see the same fibrillation pattern on the tape rolling out of the EKG. "Then get the one down in our office. Get DeForrest or Isaacs to bring it up, and tell them we need it *now.*"

Hodges disappeared while Rob continued working over the inert body. He was becoming breathless and his shoulders were aching, but he continued the cardiac compression. *Sometimes it works,* he kept telling himself. *People have been salvaged after an hour or more. Got to keep it up, don't even look at him, just keep it up.* He reached over between strokes to turn off the EKG before the tape ran out, closed his eyes, and continued counting under his breath: *one—and—one—and—one—and—* He heard the rhythmic *whoosh—whoosh—whoosh* of the positive-pressure respiratory valve, one *whoosh* for every four or five compressions, noticed the man's chest rise with each *whoosh.* Minutes passed, more minutes, like hours. He was beginning to tire, someone was going to have to relieve him, but he worked on doggedly. Then, finally, Isaacs was there carrying a small black case, with DeForrest on his heels.

"Better let me relieve you," Isaacs said.

"No, just shock him," Rob panted. "I can hold on. Take a look at the tracing."

Isaacs snapped the EKG switch. "Nothing," Isaacs said. "Not even fibrillation."

"Shock him anyway."

"I will." The white-haired doctor methodically opened the case, drew out the leads, working around Rob's hands to place them. "Okay, pull back."

Rob lifted his hands and Isaacs threw the shock switch, once, then again, eyes fixed on the EKG tracing. "Nothing," Isaacs said.

"There's *got* to be something! Try it again."

"No point to it, Rob," DeForrest said. "There's no conduction at all."

"But there was just ten minutes ago!"

"There's not any now. He's gone."

Rob stared at him, then at Hodges. Sweat was pouring down his forehead into his eyes, and he wiped it away with his sleeve, stared down at the inert body. In a gesture of defeat, he motioned to Hodges to remove the positive-pressure mask. Then, stiffly, he climbed down from the bed. "It had to be a pulmonary embolus," he said. "There was a little one, first, and he survived that. Then I guess there was a massive one. He started fibrillating and there was no shock box. *No shock box!*"

Isaacs looked at Hodges, spread his hands and shrugged. "Better get his wife on the phone," he said. Then to Rob: "Shall I talk to her?"

"To Emma? No, no; I'll—talk to her."

The nurse disappeared up the corridor, followed by Isaacs and DeForrest. Rob stood for a moment, looking down at the dead man's face. *In some places they put pennies over the eyes,* he thought. *In some places*—he pulled the sheet up to cover the man—*in some places they don't die like this, either.*

He walked out and took the phone. Nellie Webster was just coming on duty, and the other day-shift people were huddling around whispering to each other. Rob gave Emma Butler the unhappy message, as gently as he knew how, checked on the funeral home to contact. Finally he put down the receiver. "She says to call Benson's," he said to anybody who was listening.

Back in the coffee room he found Isaacs and DeForrest, both looking glum. Isaacs shook his head. "It was a bad break, but there wasn't much to be done. Pulmonary emboli kill people. Always have and always will."

278

"And no shock box," Rob said. "The fucking thing is in Spokane for repair, and there wasn't any stand-by."

"I don't know," DeForrest said. "I doubt that a shock box would have helped much."

"But we'll never know, will we?" Rob said.

"I guess not." Jerry took a deep breath. "Somebody had better call Harry and tell him. Save him a trip out here this morning."

"Oh, to hell with Harry," Rob exploded. "Let him get out here and find he's got a dead man to operate on. Let him waste some of *his* precious time for a while. If Harry hadn't been in such a Christ-awful rush we might have gotten that poor man some kind of decent cardiac evaluation. We might even have been enough ahead of this to save his life."

"Rob, Jerry checked him out," Isaacs said.

"Oh, my ass. Jerry listened to his heart for a minute and said, 'Very difficult problem,' and wandered off. No diagnosis, no suggestions, no nothing. What kind of consultation is *that?* At least a cardiologist could have read the EKG for us. He might at least have suspected a mural thrombus. He might have had *some* idea what was causing that murmur."

"Rob, I know you're disappointed and frustrated—"

"Yes, but that doesn't really quite describe it," Rob said fiercely. "I'm telling you, Martin, we can't keep on doing this sort of thing. I've really had it, and I'm telling you now that some things have got to change. I can't practice this way. *Nobody* can practice decent medicine with a surgeon who won't listen to common medical sense and an internist who won't give you an honest yes-or-no answer to *any* damned thing. And as for this stupid little one-lung hospital that can't even keep its basic equipment together—" He pushed his coffee cup aside in disgust. "Well, it's senseless. It can't go on like this, and I'm telling you both, loud and clear, that something has got to *change.* And if you can't hear me, you'd better get the wax out of your ears, because right now I'm screaming just as loud as I can scream."

Isaacs started to say something, but Rob didn't listen. He pushed through the door into the corridor and headed down the ramp, almost knocking Esther Briggs flat as she came up. He climbed into his car, gunned the engine and drove out of the parking lot and down the hill. The air was chill and the morning sun was bright, promising a clear autumn day ahead, but Rob hardly noticed. Driving through town, he slowed to let Judge Barret cross the highway from the Bar-None toward his office. The Judge waved, but Rob hardly saw him. All he wanted was to get away—away from the hospital, away from the town, away from the people in it. Beyond the town limits he pushed the gas pedal, took the turn off the highway toward home on a reckless two wheels, finally crossed the bridge, and pulled into the drive behind the house.

Turned off the motor. Sat there. He felt numb, still shaking, as the anger and frustration and helplessness all hit him in a vast body blow, and suddenly tears were streaming down his face, and he laid his arm across the steering wheel and buried his face in it, his shoulders racking uncontrollably. He was still there twenty minutes later when Ellie came out and found him.

# Part III

# 23

The long camping weekend was a heaven-sent change of pace for Rob Tanner, if not precisely the carefree holiday Ellie had had in mind. Still sick from the loss of Ed Butler, and angry beyond words at the other blows of the preceding few days, Rob had stuffed the backpacks into the Vega on Thursday night, and Friday morning at seven, after checking out to Isaacs, he and Ellie piled into the car and fled Twin Forks like pilgrims fleeing the plague. Heading south on Route 93, they crossed the Continental Divide at Lost Trail Pass and dropped down into Idaho just as the sunny autumn day began warming up. The scenery was spectacular, with the dark blue-green of fir and pine in stark contrast to the hillsides of tamarack, flaming gold in its fall colors. At Salmon they stopped to buy cold cuts, cheese and a cold half gallon of California rosé, then turned off the road by a boulder-filled creek that plunged down into the gorge of the Salmon River. Here they climbed on the rocks to munch sandwiches and sip wine, and rest, and forget for a moment the bitterness and frustration of the week just ended.

Somehow Rob had made it through that grim Thursday after Ed's sudden death. Showering and changing at home, he had gone to the office at ten o'clock, hoping to see as little of his colleagues as possible. They obliged: Isaacs, on his day off, did not appear at the office at all, and Jerry DeForrest stuck close to his examining room. Even Dora, somehow aware of the disaster, fairly tiptoed around to keep out of

Rob's way. A little after ten a furious Harry Sonders walked in, tight-jawed, thin-lipped, glaring at Rob as he passed down the hall. He complained loudly to Bev Bessler that nobody had called to tell him his morning case was off, and then demanded that all his afternoon-scheduled patients be called in then and there so he could get on back to Missoula. When Terry protested that some just couldn't come so soon, Sonders brushed her aside angrily. "The hell with them, then. Let Tanner see them this afternoon. I'll be damned if I'm going to sit around here with my thumb up my ass all day." By eleven he was out the back door of the clinic and tooling away in his sports car, leaving Rob double-scheduled for the rest of the day.

Rob hardly noticed. He moved numbly from patient to patient, his mind far distant, wishing only that the interminable day would some-how come to an end. When an almost cheerful Jerri Harlow brought young Bobby in, his rickets receding on a program of vitamins, milk and sunlight, Rob could take no pleasure in the achievement, nor even in the news that Jerri was pregnant again and wanted him to be her doctor this time. And when Herman Barney arrived for his weight check, proud of his loss of over forty pounds in three months, he was totally deflated when Rob merely grunted and ordered him back in another week. It wasn't good, Rob knew that. With a patient like Herman, whole months of progress could be lost in a single visit if the doctor failed to praise and support the effort being made—but Rob could find no heart for praise or support, and Herman waddled back down the corridor, shaking his head and muttering ominously to himself.

After lunch things were even worse, when Janice Blanchard came in for her new OB workup. Since his battle with Isaacs over the case, Rob had decided what he was going to tell the woman: that his main job was to protect her life and that of the baby; that he understood and sympathized with her desire for a normal delivery and might permit a cautious trial of labor if everything seemed favorable when the time came, but that if he or a consultant decided at any point that a Caesar-ean section was necessary, he would need her solemn promise in advance to agree to it, like it or not, if he were to undertake her care at all. It had seemed reasonable, designed to enlist her willing cooperation, so reasonable that even Martin might, on sober reflection, go along. But faced with her that Thursday, it all came out wrong, more blunt pronouncement than reasoned persuasion, sounding like a complete reversal of what he'd told her the first day—and when he tried to soften it in some way, it just got worse and worse. Ultimately she

284

shrugged her reluctant agreement and let the matter drop as he proceeded with her examination—but he could see her disappointment,
her sense of bewilderment and betrayal, in the tight set of her lips, the
paleness of her thin face and the defeated look in her eyes as she
prepared to leave. At the door she hesitated as if framing one final
appeal, then shook her head and went on down to make her follow-up
appointment. Watching her go, Rob knew that something irreplaceable
had been lost; he had somehow failed to forge the vital bond of confidence so utterly necessary from the start if a trial of labor was even to
be considered, thus totally defeating the objective he had set out to
attain. Of course, he might succeed later, but that seemed unlikely now.
The opportunity was gone; to her he had become one more of the
Enemy now, seeking to thwart her, regardless of what he might later
do or say.

By six o'clock he still had half a dozen patients waiting and he called
Ellie to tell her he would be late. At seven Dora packed his bag for call
that night, and he pulled out of the parking lot at seven-fifteen. He did
not, however, turn south on the highway toward home. Instead he
drove a mile or so out the River Road, then turned left and up the hill
through the woods past a number of neatly kept cottages. Presently he
swung into the driveway of a small white bungalow with ED BUTLER
lettered on the roadside mailbox. Emma Butler greeted him at the
door, her white hair held with a black lace kerchief, her eyes reddened
behind rimless glasses, her cheeks as pale as bone china. She introduced
him to two neighbor ladies who were just leaving, and offered him a cup
of tea.

Then, sitting in an ancient wooden rocker with a quilted seat and
balancing a dainty teacup on his knees, Rob explained to Ed's wife as
gently and unhurriedly as possible what he had only blurted out over
the phone that morning: the nature and circumstances of her husband's
unexpected passing, the kind of illness he must have suffered and how
it must have taken his life. "We don't yet know for sure what happened," Rob said. "We may learn more when we get the post-mortem
report early next week. For now, we think something must have happened a month or so ago that we just didn't know about. Probably a
minor coronary attack that night he thought he had indigestion—you
remember that?"

"Yes," Emma said with a sigh. "I remember. I wanted him to call
you right then, but he wouldn't hear of it, two o'clock in the morning
and all. And then by morning it was gone."

285

"Well, it couldn't have been a full-scale heart attack," Rob said, "but it could have been enough to weaken his heart so it started to fail, and it could have caused a blood clot to form inside the heart. And when a piece of a clot like that breaks loose and goes to the lungs, it can all be over in nothing flat. Ed put up a good fight this morning, and I did what I could to help, but it just wasn't enough."

"I know." Emma Butler shook her head helplessly. "At least I'm glad you were there. He never really trusted Dr. Florey, and Dr. Isaacs was just a 'ladies' doctor' as far as Ed was concerned."

She offered him another cup of tea, and Rob sat with her a few moments longer, letting her talk, offering what little comfort he could. There was an odd, otherworldly air to that tiny, quiet living room: the overstuffed sofa with the arms and back protected by antimacassars; the knickknack shelf in the corner; the heavy drapes and half-pulled blinds; the ancient upright piano with a woven tapestry thrown over the top, surmounted by wedding photos—it was a room from another era, nostalgically old-fashioned, dim and musty-smelling. Finally, almost reluctantly, Rob stood up, pulling himself back to the present with an effort. "I'm afraid I have to go," he said.

"Yes, of course. But it was good of you to come."

"I wanted you to know how badly I feel. I'd hoped for many more fishing trips with Ed."

She had smiled then, and taken his hand. "I know," she said, "but we can't always have what we hope for, can we?" And then he was out in the cold, windy dusk, backing his car out, turning it down the hill, feeling once again that a door was closing behind him, never to be reopened. . . .

Now, munching sandwiches and sipping wine by a rocky stream in Idaho, it all seemed far away and unreal—yet he still could not throw off the sense of loss and guilt. He hadn't told Emma everything, of course. *No point to it, it could only have hurt her—but Ed should never have been in that hospital in the first place. He could at least have died in his own bed. You could have told Sonders no, and made it stick. You could have got him to a cardiologist before you started meddling. You could at least have suspected what was going on.*

Could have. But not now. He leaned back against a rock, sick from thinking about it, and dozed while Ellie pored over a Geodetic Survey map she had acquired. Presently she woke him and they drove on south at a leisurely pace for another hour or so, with Ellie at the wheel while Rob watched the splendid mountain scenery, talking from time to time

286

about little, pleasant, unimportant things. The day was bright, but the afternoon sun had an autumn cast to it. "Going to be winter before long," Rob observed.

"I'm afraid so. The mountains are probably beautiful then too, but you can't get to them."

"Wouldn't be surprised if we saw some elk, in where we're going," Rob said. "I thought I heard a bull bugling, back there at lunch."

"Bugling?"

"It's a funny noise they make during the rutting season. Telling the other bulls to get out of their territory."

When they reached Challis, Ellie turned west onto a gravel road, and then suddenly they were plunging into deep forest, following a good-sized stream, then continuing on upward through cool woods and sun-dried meadows. At one high turnout they could see the whole Salmon River valley spread out behind them. A few miles farther along they topped a ridge and saw a lovely blue-green lake surrounded by fir and tamarack a few hundred feet below them. There was a primitive forest camp, deserted except for one other couple well back from the lake, and Rob set up their two-man mountain tent while Ellie scraped up firewood and stuck the rest of the bottle of wine into the lake to cool again.

It was now past four o'clock, with the sun casting long shadows across the smooth surface of the water, and the trout were rising. While Ellie tended the fire and put the dinner stew on to cook, Rob fished from the shore until it was too dark to see. Then, at Ellie's bidding, he fetched the wine bottle from the lake, poured two paper cups full. He found a stump to lean against and settled back, sipping wine and watching his wife prepare a salad and do interesting things with her stew pot. Finally she pronounced it ready, and without a word they devoured a delicious meal.

Later, with coffee poured and the fire dying, Ellie joined Rob by his stump, staring into the yellow flames. "Have enough to eat?"

He nodded. "Too much. I can hardly move."

"I know. It always happens when we camp."

"Is my old pipe still tucked away in the camping box?"

"Could be. Take a look."

Rob rummaged for a moment and came up with an aged and discolored briar pipe and a plastic pouch of very stale tobacco. He threw another log on the fire, poured Ellie the last of the wine, and returned to sit beside her as he packed the pipe and lit it.

287

"Smells good," Ellie said. "I always loved the smell of a pipe."

"Mm. Bad habit, though. Doctors shouldn't smoke anything. Bad image."

"So why worry about image? It's just plain old you underneath."

"Ah, but the patients don't know that." He tamped the pipe and relit it. "Image is everything in a place like Twin Forks. People with problems don't want to see plain old Rob Tanner with all his warts and his sweaty armpits and an old pair of sneakers on. They want to see Dr. Tanner, and he'd better look and act like Dr. Tanner, too. There's always this wall, with the doctor on one side and the patient on the other, and the minute the doctor forgets which side he's on, the image crumbles and he's in trouble."

"But he can have a private life too, can't he?"

"In Twin Forks?" Rob laughed. "Where are you going to hide? Take drinking, for instance. I'd bet you a month's pay that Martin Isaacs has never once had a drink in a public tavern or cocktail lounge in Twin Forks. In Missoula it's okay, he doesn't count there, but in Twin Forks he's a doctor, and doctors don't drink. Bad image, and the image counts." He paused. "Matter of fact, in cases like Ed Butler or my woman with the Caesarean section, image may be all you've got going for you."

Ellie shook her head. "Honey, don't talk about it if you don't want to."

"There's not much to talk about, really. Old Ed could have keeled over on the street just as well as in the hospital, but either way, we didn't offer him much. Maybe a good heart man could have helped, and I'm just sick that I didn't scratch the surgery and get him a good, competent consultation—but I didn't, so that's that."

"It would have served Harry Sonders right if it'd happened right in the middle of his surgery," Ellie said angrily.

"No, that would have been the worst thing possible. Image again. The whole town would have blamed Sonders, then, and me, and by extension the whole clinic, and what good would that do? At least this way his wife can make peace with it—but if he'd been in surgery, she'd spend the rest of her life thinking he needn't have died, no matter what we told her." Rob sighed. "As for Sonders, it wouldn't have changed a thing. He's an arrogant, self-centered son of a bitch, and that kind of guy isn't going to change just because somebody drops dead in his operating room."

"Well, I think it's a miracle you can work with him at all," Ellie said.

288

"What choice do I have? Hell, Ellie, he's *there*. And he's a damned good surgeon too, if we can just get him to turn around a little bit." Rob puffed his pipe a moment. "It's Martin that holds the place together," he said finally. "He drives me up the wall sometimes, but I swear that man knows more medicine than all the rest of us put together. Practical things they don't teach you in medical school; things that *work*. He can do more with his left hind paw than I can do with all four feet at once. Like the woman I had with the rash last week—did I tell you?"

"No."

"One of the town matrons, with this rash that had her scared silly. Covered with big reddish-brown splotches, top to bottom. They just appeared one day, and they itched, and they looked horrid, and she was sure she had psoriasis, and her hair was going to fall out, and so on, and so on, and so on. Well, they looked like secondary syphilis to me, and I was sweating out how I was going to ask this forty-year-old wife of a town councilman, with two strapping boys on the high school football team, just who she'd been playing around with—so finally I asked Martin to look at the rash. So he took one look and laughed and said, 'Oh, yeah, that's pityriasis rosea.' Then he looked at her and said, 'That comes from a mild virus infection, and you'll have it for about six weeks and then it'll go away. Meanwhile, don't waste your money on salves or lotions; they won't help. Just throw some oatmeal in a tubful of cool water twice a day and soak. That'll stop the itching.' So she went home happy as a clam. Martin told me later that the oval-shaped spots were the tip-off, and nobody *knows* that it's a virus, but it makes people feel better to think so, and it usually goes away in three weeks but he always tells them six so that he'll look good when it goes away sooner. So I went back and read up on pityriasis rosea in my dermatology book, but in ten pages of small print it didn't tell me a third of what Martin had told me in one minute flat."

"Well," Ellie said, "it's good there's *somebody* who pulls his own weight."

"Oh, Martin does that."

"If only you could admire other things about him."

"Well, that's a pretty mixed bag. He's crude as hell the way he treats some of his patients; the minute they start to bore him, he just cuts them off at the knees and sends 'em packing. Or this silly blood feud with Florey. Jesus!"

Rob stirred the fire and tossed on another log. For a long time they sat in silence, side by side, leaning against the stump. Then Rob said,

289

"Maybe it's the same with any group practice. Anytime you get a bunch of egocentric individualists trying to work together, there's bound to be friction. You take a surgeon who thinks he's God Almighty, and an internist who won't dirty his hands with cutting and sewing, and a GP who thinks he knows more than everybody else combined, and you put them all together in a place like Twin Forks, and it's a wonder they don't tear each other's throats out. Maybe they need a John Florey around just to siphon off some of the hostility. But a group like that needs somebody to grab the reins and hang on. Somebody big enough to rise above all the ego clashes, and strong enough to keep things going straight. Somebody tough enough to knock heads together when he has to, and smooth enough to get away with it."

"And Martin's the one?" Ellie said dubiously.

"Who else is there? Trouble is, I'm not so sure that even he can do it."

"Well, I hope it gets straightened out."

"Kid, it's *got* to get straightened out—but *I* can't do it. All I can do is kick and scream and hope that somebody's listening." He tossed a twig into the fire. "Hell, right now I don't even want to *think* about it."

"Maybe there are better things to think about," she said.

He leaned over to kiss her, brushed a mosquito out of her hair. "Like washing the dishes?"

"They'll keep until morning."

"Mm. Maybe we should walk around the lake in the moonlight."

"Too many bugs. Anyway, the tent is closer."

He stood up and pulled her to her feet. She came into his arms, clung to him with her cheek against his chest. "I'm glad we came," she said. "Seems like we haven't talked in months."

He stroked her hair. "I know. I just get all strung out and don't want to talk to *anybody.*"

"But I'm not just anybody. And there's no way I can help if I don't know what's wrong."

He pulled her chin up and kissed her, felt her arms tighten around him. "Come on," he said. "Let's get out of the bugs."

They undressed quickly in the firelight and crawled into the tent, zipping the front shut after them. The fire cast an eerie flickering light through the tent wall as they stretched out on their sleeping pads. For a brief instant Ellie looked like a stranger in the dim effulgence, a beautiful stranger half turned to him, waiting for him, eager and yet wary, with something almost like fearfulness in her eyes. Then he

290

moved to her and she met him hungrily, and the strangeness was gone
—her shape, her scent, the rise of thigh and breast pressed to him so
familiarly, warm, totally right. "I trust you've got your gadget in," he
said thickly.

She was suddenly very still. "It probably doesn't matter," she said.

He bent to kiss her again, stopped short and reared up on his elbow.
"Huh?"

"I said it doesn't matter."

"The hell it doesn't. Jesus, kid! That's about all I'd need right now,
having you—"

"Well, I'm sorry," she said, "but I'm afraid that's just what you've
got."

"What do you mean?"

"I mean I'm almost three weeks late right now, and I've *never* been
late before. I've got an appointment to see Martin on Monday."

"But how? We've always . . ."

She turned, avoiding his eyes. "I don't know. I never did trust that
gadget, since I had to go off the pills. Something happened, that's all.
I don't know what."

He stared at her for a long moment, turned to stone. Then, in spite
of himself: "Good Christ."

"Look, it's plenty early, Rob. We can stop it if you want to."

"Oh, come on, Ellie. Really. If you're pregnant, you're pregnant,
and that's that. And as long as it's nobody's fault . . ." He took a deep
breath. "The timing isn't the greatest, but I suppose it doesn't matter
that much. We've always figured on it, sooner or later." He leaned over
awkwardly to kiss her cheek, and saw that she was weeping. "Hey, hey.
It's nothing to *cry* about, for God's sake."

"Then hold me."

He put his arms around her, suddenly clumsy, and her whole body
trembled as she clung to him. "You'd better get some rest now."

"I don't want any rest," she said. "I want *you.*" So he kissed her and
held her close, without excessive ardor, but enough, and then presently
he took her (*gently, gently*) because she wanted and needed to be
taken.

Later, still holding her in his arms, he said, "Maybe we can do
something about what's happening to us."

"Yes. Oh, yes. We *have* to, now, don't we?"

"I don't know what to do, exactly. But we have to try."

"Yes. We surely have to try."

Presently, with the firelight glow almost gone and a chill night wind brushing the tent, she fell asleep beside him, breathing gently against his chest. He lay silent and still for a long while, staring into the darkness and listening to the unfamiliar wind sounds. *So you're going to be a father.* The very thought jarred him. *And nobody's fault? Well. . . .* He heard the faintest rustling noise as a chipmunk nibbled at something near the dying fire, and he found himself thinking seriously, for the very first time, of the meaning and imminence and reality of soon-to-be fatherhood. And then he felt a sudden, irrational surge of joy and pride pushing all else aside as images flooded his mind: A boy on his lap, hearing a drowsy bedtime story. Learning to read. Joining the Cub Scouts. Taking long hiking and fishing trips with him into the mountains. Admitted to medical school. Graduating at last and solemnly repeating those ancient words, "I swear by Apollo . . ."

*And if it's a girl?* He almost laughed at himself. *Every man since Adam has wanted a boy first. But if it's a girl, it's a girl, and you try again. And today lots of girls go to medical school too. . . .*

At long last, the images finally fading, he drifted into troubled sleep, and dreamed of Chris Erickson.

# 24

Monday morning dawned cold and gray, with an icy wind driving the rain down the streets of Twin Forks in ferocious gusts. The men who gathered in Martin Isaacs' office after morning rounds looked equally gray. Isaacs himself sat slumped in his chair, his long white hair already slightly disheveled, leafing through a stack of lab reports. Jerry DeForrest, looking sallow, perched on the corner of the desk, while Harry Sonders, peremptorily summoned from Missoula solely for this meeting, stood across the room in a dark blue business suit, staring bleakly out the window at the rain-swept parking lot. Rob sat across from Isaacs, trying to recapture the sharp spike of anger and indignation he had felt the morning of Ed Butler's death, and failing completely. The cutting edge of bitterness had been dulled by now; there was nothing left but frustration and weariness.

"Okay," Isaacs said abruptly. "We're here because Rob is unhappy with what's going on, and I can't exactly blame him. Ed Butler was a mean case, but maybe we should have done things differently."

Jerry shook his head. "Nothing would have helped the man," he said. "You've seen the autopsy report. He had a minor, unrecognized coronary a month ago, and built up a big clot in his right ventricle, and when a chunk broke off and hit his lung, he went out. I know Rob's upset, but you can't fight God. And the fact that Ed was in the hospital was pure coincidence. He could just as well have been in his own bedroom."

"He could also have been on the operating table," Rob said. "And I don't think Harry would have liked *that* too much."

"Oh, shit," Sonders said. "If somebody throws a pulmonary embolus on the table, that's not my fault. And it's not my fault if you two can't make up your minds whether a patient's in shape for surgery or not."

"I told you what *I* thought," Rob said.

"Yes, and Jerry disagreed," Sonders shot back. "Well, Jerry's the internist around here. If Jerry says a patient's all right, I assume he's all right."

"But Ed never got a really careful, thorough cardiac evaluation," Rob said. "All Jerry had to offer was a lick and a promise, and that wasn't quite enough."

Jerry started to protest, but Isaacs cut him off. "There's no point tearing strips off each other over that one," he said. "I probably would have passed him too. But we've got more trouble than that. Our consultation system isn't working, and that's got to change. There's no point working together if we can't get fast, expert medical or surgical consultation when we need it."

"Oh, crap," Sonders said. "All Rob's got to do is pick up the phone."

"Yes, but when I do, I get your answering service," Rob said. "Then maybe you get back to me a few hours later and maybe you don't. People could be dead by the time you check back. And as for Jerry, I don't know *where* he goes when he leaves the office, but there's sure no point calling him. He's never around."

"Well, you can't expect me to sit by the phone all the time waiting for you to give me a jingle," Jerry said.

"That's not what he means," Isaacs said, "and you know it. Ever since Rob took over your call, Jerry, you've been running and hiding the minute you get out of this office. Rob can't reach you, and neither can I."

"So I go into the city once in a while. So what? There aren't that many medical problems so urgent they can't wait awhile. You're just making a big fuss."

"Damned if I am!" Isaacs said. "When a real emergency turns up, we need your help *then,* not next month. That means we have to know where you can be found when you're not around home. And if that interferes with your precious privacy, that's just too damned bad. You take your full share of the income out of this place, and you can damned

294

well start responding when we need you, beginning now."

Jerry looked sour, then shrugged. "Whatever you say," he said. "But you're still making a big fuss. I work as hard as anybody else during office hours in this place."

"Fine. But you've also got responsibilities outside office hours, just like the rest of us." Isaacs polished his glasses. "As for your consultations *during* office hours, you're just plain getting sloppy. You need to do thorough consultations and file complete consultation reports, just like the internists in town. And charge for them too."

Jerry DeForrest shook his head. "Martin, for Christ's sake! I can't do a formal workup every time Rob stops me in the hall with a question."

"I don't mean minor things," Isaacs said. "But with real diagnostic problems, a half-ass curbstone consultation isn't enough. You do sloppy work, and then all of a sudden we've got an Ed Butler on our hands, and *everybody* is unhappy, but nobody wants to take the blame because nobody's done anything wrong, exactly. They just haven't done anything right, either. Including Rob."

"Me?"

"Yes, you. You're more to blame for Ed Butler than anybody else."

"How do you figure that?"

"I mean you had the responsibility right from the first, and you fumbled it. Harry sent him to you for a pre-op workup, and if you didn't like what you saw, you should have blown the whistle right then and there."

"But I did," Rob protested.

"Like hell you did. You phoned Harry, and then when he balked, you just caved in. You should have told him to take his surgery and shove it until you were happy. If you didn't like Jerry's consultation, you should have called somebody else. There are half a dozen good heart men in Missoula. You could have sent Ed to any one of them."

"Martin, you'd have had a fit on the floor if I'd done that, and you know it."

Isaacs gave him a long look. "So I'd have a fit on the floor," he said. "Does that scare you a great deal? Hell, Rob, you've got a good pair of legs—why don't you stand on them? Worry about your patient, don't worry about me. If I think you're wrong, I may override you, but then at least it'll be *my* responsibility. And if you think *I'm* wrong, or anybody else around here, you'd damned well better override us too."

Rob stared at him glumly. "I suppose," he said finally. "But why should I *have* to override Jerry, or send a patient off for an outside medical consultation, or square off with Harry about scratching a case?"

"You shouldn't," Isaacs said. "We're supposed to be practicing together, not fighting each other. But if somebody's too bullheaded to listen, you may just have to do it your way and fight about it later. Like that spleen case—when you couldn't get Harry, you had to go ahead and do it. You'd have had a dead patient if you hadn't."

Harry Sonders turned sharply away from the window. "For Christ's sake, let's not drag *that* up again," he said.

"Why not?" Isaacs retorted. "Rob was right on that, and you were wrong. Thank God he moved, and it turned out okay—but it was no thanks to you."

"Well, that's ancient history now," the little surgeon said.

"Not to me, it's not," Isaacs said heavily. "It's just one more of the crappy jobs you've been handing us lately—as if we need any more. Your job is to handle our surgery, follow up your patients in the clinic, and stand by for call on the days and evenings you're not out here, and you're screwing us black and blue in all three areas. You're taking three grand a month out of this practice, a full partner's share of the income, and we're not even getting shit in return."

"Oh, crap," Sonders said. "You're getting better surgical coverage than nine tenths of the rural practices in this country today, and you don't even know it."

"Well, that's not enough," Isaacs said, his face darkening. "Every week out here you're cutting your office hours short, running people through here like cattle, with no instructions for follow-up when you're gone. And worst of all, you don't come when you're called. A few years ago you'd be out here at the drop of a hat when we had surgery on nights or weekends. Now we can't even get you on the phone."

"All right, so I don't sit around waiting for calls any more than Jerry does," Sonders said heatedly, "and what's more, I'm not going to start. I could run my ass off coming out here every time Rob Tanner hollers."

Isaacs turned to face him. "You're missing the point," he said. "Rob has his faults, but he's been picking up *surgery* with all these full-scale workups he's been doing. And it's all legitimate work too; he hasn't slipped you a funny one yet. Well, surgery means *money* in my book —but while he's digging it up, you're cutting us short at the office and giving us left hind tit on call, and by God, Harry, that's going to *change.*"

Sonders jammed his hands into his pockets and glared up at Isaacs. "Okay, Martin, now let me tell *you* something. You may be able to boss

296

these other clowns around as if you owned them, but you can't boss *me*. I'm giving you and your little tinhorn practice all the time I can, and as far as I'm concerned, you're getting a gold-plated bargain. I've got better things to do than drive out here every time one of you guys gets a little bit nervous. You can get along on what I give you, or you can go suck wind. And as for right now, I've taken about all the crap from you that I'm going to. I've got a case in town now and I'm going in to do it, and if you've got anything more to say, you can send me a postcard." Sonders glared at the others for a moment, then turned on his heel and walked out of the office.

Martin Isaacs, his face turning purple, had come halfway up out of his chair as the surgeon talked. Now he sank back again. "That son of a bitch," he said softly.

Jerry spread his hands. "So much for Harry Sonders' contribution," he said.

"That son of a bitch. I brought him out here when he was *starving* for work. He was chasing ambulances and giving Christmas booze to every GP in town just to rustle up a few cases. I brought him out here and *fed* him for two years before he even paid for himself."

Jerry shrugged. "That was then," he said. "This is now."

"Yeah? Well, nobody in my practice is going to talk to me like that."

"You did kind of land on him with all four feet," Jerry said mildly.

"So what do you want me to do? Pat him on the ass? Beg him to please come around a little more often?"

"No, but maybe I can talk him into cooperating more."

Isaacs just grunted.

"It's worth a try," Jerry said.

"What we *really* need is a surgeon who lives right here, and forget this commuting-from-Missoula crap," Isaacs said.

"Harry is never going to move out here."

"I know." Isaacs stood up suddenly, as though shaking a weight off his shoulders. "Well, try it your way, Jerry. See if you can talk sense to the bastard. I've got work to do."

The meeting broke up and Rob went back to his office. He was cheered, in a way, that Isaacs had gone to bat for him, but the whole meeting just depressed him. Jerry wasn't going to change, and Isaacs had deliberately forced a showdown with Sonders, and that wasn't good. *Of all the blunt, stupid ways to try to approach the guy!* he thought. *Lord Jesus! Surely there's got to be some way to get through to Sonders, but you can't hit a man like that over the head with a piece*

297

*of firewood and expect to get anywhere. Of course, Jerry won't be able to reach him, either. Talk about sending a lamb in after a lion. Harry won't listen to Jerry any more than he'll listen to Isaacs.*

Because of the meeting, Rob got started late and fell still farther behind as the day passed. Isaacs was buried too, but he flagged Rob down as he returned from lunch. "Say, I saw your wife this morning, and she's doing fine. She's coming back Friday for her lab work and OB physical, but I think she's a good two months pregnant."

"*Two* months!"

"At least. She had a little spotting last month, but it wasn't really a period, and she's just too big for one month. So if you were planning on a baby in late June, you'd better figure on late May instead."

"I wasn't exactly planning at all," Rob said.

Isaacs gave Rob a sharp look. "Yeah, that's what I figured," he said. "I thought she was hedging a little. How come she wasn't on the pill?"

"She was, until she started running a little high blood pressure a couple of years ago. She's been using a diaphragm since."

"I see. Well, that's pretty reliable too. Except when you leave it in the dresser drawer."

"She's always been pretty careful," Rob said.

"Maybe so, but she's also been pretty lonely these last few months. Maybe she just decided it was time to have some company around."

"You think that's what happened?"

Isaacs laughed. "Who knows? I can't read minds. But at least she's not going to be packing up and going South on you this winter. She's pregnant as hell, and that tends to keep 'em at home."

Agnes interrupted at that point with a hospital call for Isaacs. When he returned close to five o'clock, he looked in on Rob again. "I made rounds while I was up there, so you won't need to," he said. "Look, I'm about to head home. Why don't you stop by for a quick one when you're finished here?"

"Fine," Rob said. "I should be through by six. Some problem?"

"No, no," Isaacs said. "Just mulling things over. Come on over when you're free."

It seemed an oddly offhand invitation. In fact, it was the first time Rob had actually been invited to Isaacs' house. *Probably just an impulse,* he thought. But right on the heels of a disruptive confrontation? Odd. Decidedly odd . . .

By six-fifteen his last patient was gone, and Rob walked the block and a half to Isaacs' house. The rain had stopped during the afternoon

298

and the clouds had cleared from the mountains, transforming the threatening day into a clear, crisp autumn evening. He filled his lungs with the cold air and watched the wind tug at red and yellow leaves on the trees. *A beautiful time of year,* he thought. *But not for long. There'll be snow soon, and then we'll see what winter can be like.* He made a mental note to order winter cordwood and check on tire chains and batteries. *Can't have Ellie out pushing that station wagon if she's pregnant.*

Isaacs' house was a small yellow-and-brown clapboard place set well back from the street and concealed by head-high privet hedges. The sun, just setting below the mountain rim, reflected blinding red-gold from the front windows as he walked up on the porch. It was not until the older man opened the door that Rob realized all the drapes were pulled. "Damned sun comes right into my eyes this time of year," Isaacs said, opening the curtains a crack to let in the evening light. A TV newscast was tuned in, with the volume low; Isaacs had been sitting in a reclining chair across the room from it. Now he snapped the set off and picked up a glass from the stand beside his chair. "What can I get you? Bourbon?"

"Fine," Rob said. "Just a short one." He sat on an overstuffed sofa across from the recliner, peering around as Isaacs went to the kitchen for the drinks. The darkened room was tastefully furnished, and totally spotless—as though no one really lived there. A handsome fireplace occupied one wall, but with no evidence that a fire had ever burned in the grate. In another room Rob could see a baby grand piano through the glass interior doors. "That must be nice for Jennie," he said when Isaacs returned.

"What, the piano? Yeah, she plinks around on it once in a while. She's not much good, though." Isaacs handed Rob a huge drink, then sank back in the recliner with a sigh.

Quite suddenly, Jennie Isaacs appeared from the dining room, looking wraithlike in bathrobe and slippers. She stopped abruptly, startled to see Rob. "Martin? I didn't know you had company. Is there something I can . . . get you?"

"No. We're just going to talk."

"I see." She hesitated. "You know, if Rob wanted to stay for dinner—"

"I said we're just going to talk," Isaacs cut in. "Do you mind?"

"No . . . of course not." Jennie looked helplessly from one to the other for a moment, then turned and left as silently as she had come.

When Rob stirred uneasily, the big man made a disgusted gesture.

"Don't mind her," he said. "She's just getting over the flu or something. I'm trying to keep her in bed." He paused. "You know, I never did thank you two for having her over while I was in Spokane. She had a real nice time."

"No great trouble," Rob said lamely. "Ellie likes to entertain once in a while."

"Well, it was nice. We don't go much for the social life, you know. Jen is kind of shy, and I've never had much time for it. Don't even like to go to meetings anymore—same old faces, same old shop talk. Matter of fact, I'm going to send you in to a meeting in Missoula next week. Staff meeting at Sacred Heart on Wednesday night. Dinner in the cafeteria at six, then a short business meeting, and later a pretty good clinical conference with the OB staff. Wouldn't hurt you to meet some of the guys in town, and I've got a school board meeting here I ought to go to. What do you think?"

"Sounds fine to me," Rob said. "I'll tell Terry to clear my schedule after four."

"Good. This month's topic is obstetrical emergencies. You might pick up some pearls."

Isaacs lapsed into silence then, sipping his drink and leaning back with his eyes closed in the failing light. Presently he pulled off his glasses and polished them with his handkerchief. "How long have you been here now?" he said suddenly. "Six months?"

"Just over four," Rob said.

"I'll be damned. Seems like a lot longer." Isaacs put the glasses back on. "So how's it been going? I don't mean the problems; I mean the overall picture."

"I don't know," Rob said cautiously. "There's sure a lot to learn. Dumb little things. Like what do you do about venereal warts? Or ingrown toenails? Or pinworms? I swear every kid in this valley must have pinworms."

Isaacs laughed. "So you're all thumbs for a while. But pretty soon those little things'll get to be old hat, and then you'll wonder why you were so worried."

"Maybe so, but I sure feel like a damned fool sitting there with the patient looking at me, and no idea what to tell him about his sore hemorrhoids."

"So you just fake it until you can check it out. Or get him thinking about something else. Just remember that nine times out of ten the

300

patient's going to get better, no matter what. All you need to do is sit there and nod and pretend you understand, and it all goes away. Nature does the healing and you take the credit."

"I still feel like I'm picking their pockets sometimes."

"Don't ever worry about that," Isaacs said. "You're spending your time. You're listening. You're honestly trying to help. So right there you're doing more than ninety percent of all practicing doctors ever do. That alone is worth your fee—and if it happens to be the one case in a hundred that requires real medical skill, and you happen to do the right thing, that patient is so far ahead of the game that his head should be swimming. Never sell yourself short. The patient doesn't, and your fee is going to be peanuts compared to the peace of mind he takes home with him, if you're any good at all."

"I guess," Rob said. "It sure is a kick to hit one right on target once in a while." He sipped his drink. "On the other hand, it's hard to see beyond the really bad problems we have. Like this miserable hospital situation. You heard about the blood bank proposal?"

Isaacs nodded. "Don't say I didn't warn you," he said.

"Yes, you warned me. But God, Martin! They just *can't* turn it down when fifteen or twenty responsible citizens in this town want it."

"They don't want to spend the money," Isaacs said.

"Then we've got to find some way to make them," Rob said. "That place up there is a death trap. The lack of blood facilities is just one of the rotten apples. What about everything else? Their emergency power system is great on paper—but it doesn't work. That drunken anesthetist is a walking disaster; she's going to kill somebody one of these days. They can't even be bothered to keep stand-by equipment on hand when something vital goes out for repairs, and they lean on Raymond for *everything*. If that man ever broke a leg, the whole place would fall apart."

Isaacs sighed. "Look, it's no worse than it's ever been, and we've managed."

"But the risk! Do you really mean we're stuck forever with what we've got up there?"

"Could be. Things need improving, but there's no money for it."

"The hell there's not," Rob said hotly. "I've seen the room rates up there, and by God, *somebody* is taking *money* home from that place, and you can't tell me they're not."

Isaacs shrugged. "You can't blame the stockholders for wanting a return on their investment, can you?"

"While they let Ed Butler die for want of a shock box? Good God! There's no place in the *world* for a private, profit-making hospital anymore, Martin. The people of Twin Forks should own that hospital, and every nickel of profit should be going back into improvements."

Isaacs laughed. "Okay, okay! Beat your head on the wall, if you want to. Just don't holler to me when it starts to hurt." He took Rob's glass to the kitchen for a refill. When he came back he settled into the recliner with a sigh. "I didn't want to get started on the hospital anyway," he said. "We've got trouble enough right in our own office." He looked up at Rob over his drink. "What did *you* think about Harry's performance this morning?"

"Not much," Rob said. "I just hope Jerry can get through to him."

"*Jerry?* Forget it," Isaacs said. "There's only one solution. Sonders has got to go."

The liquor was buzzing in Rob's ears, but he suddenly snapped alert. "How's that?"

"I said Sonders has got to go. We've got a surgical practice that's going great guns, and we're getting nothing but shit from our surgeon. Well, I've had it up to here."

Rob stared at the older man. "So what do you plan to do?"

"Dump him," Isaacs said.

"But—I thought you three were *partners* in this practice."

"Yeah. Well, I made him a partner, and I can damned well dump him," Isaacs said.

Rob shook his head. "Seems to me a lot more people are involved than just you," he said. "Just this very morning you were telling Jerry to go ahead and talk to the man."

"Rob, Sonders is not going to listen to Jerry. He's not going to listen to *anybody*. He's got to *go*, and that's all there is to it."

Rob took a deep breath. "Then what do we do for a surgeon?"

"Hell, a lot of new young guys would give their upper plates for a spot like this," Isaacs said. "Plenty of work, guaranteed income from Day One, nothing to buy, everything there is in the world to keep a good surgeon busy and happy living right here in Twin Forks." He took a long sip from his drink. "Matter of fact, I talked to a guy over at that meeting in Spokane. Young fellow named Stone. Well-trained surgeon, sharp as they come." Isaacs paused, grinning at Rob. "He could do a great job, and set John Florey on his ass at the same time."

"What do you mean by *that?*"

"Make him cut out all the major surgery he's doing," Isaacs said.

302

"Make it too risky for him. Long as we had nothing but GPs out here, Florey could do anything he chose—gall bladders, gastrectomies, any damned thing in the world. But bring a board-qualified surgeon out here and Florey'll have to back off. If he tries to do a case he's not qualified for, and fumbles it, he's screwed. Of course, Sonders has been putting *some* heat on Florey, but we could never really claim he was practicing here full time. This Stone guy living out here would fix John Florey good. He'd have to think twice about doing a simple appendectomy."

Isaacs took another sip of his drink and leaned back in his chair, stretching like a contented cat. For a long moment Rob just stared at him. Then he said, "Martin, what in the hell are you *talking* about?"

"What's wrong? All I'm talking about is improving the standards of practice out here, making really top-rate surgical care available twenty-four hours a day."

"No, that's not what you're talking about at all," Rob said. "You're talking about some new scheme to gig John Florey."

"Oh, hell, that's just a fringe benefit."

"And you want to shake up the whole practice and dump a perfectly good surgeon, one of your own *partners,* yet, without even *trying* to work things out first."

"I've tried everything there is to try," Isaacs said.

"No, that's not quite true. Harry's a prima donna like every other surgeon I ever heard of, and he's *never* going to bow down to threats and sanctions. But he may respond to other pressures. If nothing else, there's the money he stands to lose. He's obviously benefiting three thousand dollars a month's worth from this practice out here, and to people like him, money *talks*—as long as you don't butcher his pride too much in order for him to get it. But you've got to *work* with the man to get through to him, reason it out with him. You can't just walk up and kick him in the balls."

Isaacs was shaking his head. "Rob, I must have given you the wrong idea or something. I guess I didn't put it very well. I'm not articulate like some of your guys—"

"Well, you sound pretty damned articulate to me," Rob said. "And you also sound like you're forgetting about the practice and turning this thing with Sonders into some kind of personal grudge fight, and I'm telling you I don't want any part of it. Persuading Sonders to go along is one thing. So is leaning on him a little to make him do his job. But just arbitrarily dumping him on his ass is something else, and I don't like it. And as for John Florey, that's another one of your grudge fights, not mine, and I'm not going to get dragged into it."

Isaacs was laughing, holding up his hands in protest. *"Jesus,* Rob, cool off. Relax. I'm not going to dump Sonders tomorrow morning. I wouldn't do that unless you and Jerry agreed, would I?"

"I don't know," Rob said. "Sounds to me like you've already hired this bird in Spokane."

"Oh, for Christ's sake! We just talked a little, that's all. Absolutely no commitments." Isaacs shrugged. "Maybe you're right; maybe I did land on Sonders too hard this morning. Maybe we can persuade him to swing around. We just need to be planning in case he won't, that's all. And I never should have mentioned John Florey. I hate his guts, sure, but I don't really *care* what he does as long as he stays off my corns. So let's drop it, okay? Pretend I never said it."

"Okay," Rob said, slightly mollified. "But since we're hashing over problems, let's hash over another one. What's happened to all our great plans for OB coverage? For a while there I thought it was all settled, that I'd be covering your deliveries by now, anytime I was on call—but nothing's happening."

"I know." Isaacs leaned back with a sigh. "It just isn't all that easy. I've tried putting it to these gals of mine, and they just keep backing away. I hit one gal with it on her second visit, and she never came back. Agnes says she went down to Tintown."

"Well, we figured we might lose one or two that way," Rob said, "but certainly not very many. A couple on my list didn't like it, either, until I pointed out that *nobody* could promise for sure to be on hand twenty-four hours a day seven days a week for nine solid months. They went along when they saw it was for their own protection as much as my convenience."

"Boy, you just don't know these women like I do," Isaacs said. "They get a thing in their minds about their OB doctor, and it gets to be very exclusive, especially when they get along toward delivery time and don't really want their husbands fooling around too much. They lean on the doctor more and more until that baby's delivered, and they don't want anybody interfering at the last minute."

"In other words," Rob said slowly, "you're saying you've got to keep carrying the OB load, like it or not, even with me here to take it off your back."

"Well, not exactly. Maybe we're just going at it ass-backward. What we *really* need is to get more of them into your hands to begin with."

304

"Like how?" Rob asked.

"Well, I've got an idea that might work. I know these women, and if there's one thing that bothers them just as much as who's going to deliver them—maybe even more—it's how much they're going to have to pay."

Rob frowned. "I don't follow you."

"The OB fee. It's a big pile of money to a lot of these people and they really worry about it. I lost quite a few patients when I pushed my fee up to three fifty a couple of years ago. I even lost some of the old faithfuls, women I'd delivered three or four times, when I did that. They went right down to Florey—he only raised his fee to three hundred—and a lot of them stayed down there. Never did come back."

"I—still don't quite follow you," Rob said cautiously.

"It's simple," Isaacs said. "We want to get a lot of these gals onto your list, right? Okay, why not set my fee higher than yours? I'm not board-qualified or anything like that, but I did have two years of OB-GYN residency, and fifteen years of clinical experience—"

"Wait a minute," Rob said.

"No, let me finish. If we bump my fee up to four fifty, say, and leave yours at three fifty, there'll be a whole flock of women who'll go right over to you. Of course, the ones that want to pay for it can stay with me; we'll just put that much more money on the books. And then if you want help with one of your gals, some kind of problem turns up, I'll charge an extra consulting fee, maybe twenty-five dollars or so. Huh? What's that?"

"I said *just hold it a minute.*" Rob was sitting bolt upright, staring at the older man in disbelief. "Martin, I don't know if this is just one of your awful bad days, or what, but I wonder if you know just what the hell you're *saying.*"

"Jesus, what's wrong? We wouldn't lose a single patient, and you'd have most of them over on your side, and my list would be ninety percent lighter, and we'd end up with more money too. Now, what's wrong with that?"

"Just about everything I can think of," Rob said tightly. "And if I have to spell it out to you, then there's something wrong with your head."

"Well, hell, Rob. Other groups do it. Explain to me what's so bloody wrong."

Rob took a long pull on his drink. "Okay," he said. "Number one, your basic premise is very problematical if not dead wrong. You don't drive patients away by raising your fees; any doctor with half a wit knows that by this time. If anything, you drag more patients *in.* They think you must have something extra special, to charge so much, and there must be something wrong with the slob they've been seeing or he'd be charging more too, and the next thing you know, they're crowding you out of your office. That's number one. For number two, a scheme like that will automatically split our OB practice into two classes: the ones that won't go to anybody but the great specialist, regardless of his fee, and the ones that'll go over to the slob in the corner office because he's cheaper. And since you're casting me as the slob in the corner office, you'd better think what it's going to make me look like. Well, it's going to make me look like a heap of shit, and I'm sorry, but I don't like the image." Rob lurched to his feet, pacing the room, suddenly feeling the impact of the drinks on top of his anger.

Isaacs stood up too. "Look, calm down, for Christ's sake. You *have* got a short fuse, haven't you? I'm not trying to put you down. Nothing was farther from my mind—"

"The hell you're not," Rob said. "Sure, maybe in a big city—or even a middle-sized town with lots of doctors—you can do this, even in a group practice, and get away with it. But in a little tiny country town like Twin Forks, if you start doing this, you're telling the whole town, loud and clear: 'One doctor is good, and the other is cheap: take your choice.' And if you think I'm going to be Dr. Cheap around here, you're wrong. I don't care what other groups do. I'll leave first. And if you don't like that, you can shove it."

"Rob, good Christ!"

"Well, there's an even better solution. You're the great OB specialist around here, you set your fee just as high as you want, and you take the OBs. *All* of them. I've got no special training in obstetrics, you're the one with the training, so you do it. *All* of it."

"Oh, good Lord. Rob, go home and cool off. It was just an idea. Maybe it's a bad idea. So forget it, okay?"

"That's the first good thing you've said all night. Right. Forget it." Fuzzily, Rob made for the door.

"But it might *work.* It might get a lot of these women over into your corner."

"Yeah, Dr. Cheap's corner. Well, forget it."

"Okay; go get some dinner. I'm sorry. I guess it all came out wrong." Isaacs opened the door. "You okay to drive?"

"You think I get sloshed on two bourbons?"

306

"Okay, okay, just take it easy. I'm sorry; it was just an idea."

Rob pushed the screen open, misstepped on the porch steps and almost went sprawling. Catching his balance, he turned back and said, "Thanks for the drinks."

"Sure, anytime. We'll—square it all away later," Isaacs said.

Back at his car, Rob realized he was feeling the whiskey far more than he had thought. He was also so furious he was shaking. He was still muttering imprecations under his breath when he pulled in at home behind Ellie's car.

Ellie met him at the back door. "What happened?" she said. "I was about to call the police."

"Martin asked me to stop by for a drink on the way home. I figured it would only be a few minutes, but it turned into two hours. Sorry."

"Doesn't matter." She gave him a sharp look and wrinkled her nose. "I guess that was nice of Martin."

"Oh, sure, it was real nice," Rob said. "I had two stiff drinks, and I think I'm going to have another one right now, if dinner can wait."

"It's just lamb chops, and I haven't started them yet." Ellie followed him to the liquor cupboard in the living room, watched him pour a stiff bourbon for himself and a Scotch and soda for her. "You're really going to reek if you have to see anybody tonight," she said dubiously.

"It's Martin that's going to reek. He's got the call."

"I see. Did he have something special on his mind?"

Rob looked at her and burst out laughing. "Did he ever! Jesus! Martin was all full of neat little schemes tonight."

"I see."

"Oh, but you haven't *heard,*" Rob said, collapsing on the sofa and pulling her down beside him. "First of all, just for openers, he thinks we should fire Harry Sonders and bring in some young guy just out of training to live out here and do our surgery full time."

"Sounds great to me," Ellie said.

He looked at her. "I hope you're kidding."

"Well, Rob, honestly! You've been complaining about Sonders for the last three months, always trying to reach him when he won't be reached, getting backed into corners at two in the morning. Seems to me a surgeon living out here would solve a lot of problems."

"But good God, Ellie! The man's supposed to be a partner in the practice. Martin can't just throw him out in a fit of pique. Don't you see anything wrong with just dumping him?"

"Not a whole lot. What do *you* think's so wrong about it?"

Rob walked across to the windows. "Honey, the thing that's wrong is that nobody's ever once really gotten Sonders' ear about straightening himself out. That's what's wrong. Martin's tried shouting at him a few times, but that's not what I mean. The fact is, Harry Sonders is a very good surgeon. For a small-town practice like this, he'd be a really *great* surgeon, if we could only get him to respond. And I think it'd be a real tragedy for the practice and the town to lose him if there's any conceivable way we can persuade him to take his job out here seriously. *That's* what's wrong."

"But the fact remains that he doesn't," Ellie said, "and you can't live with that much longer. And maybe *nothing* will make him respond. Maybe you've *got* to dump him."

"Oh, for Christ's sake." Rob threw himself down on the sofa again, slopping his drink on his pants. "I suppose you'll think Martin's other little scheme is just fine too," he said thickly.

"Like what?"

"Like pushing his OB fee up a hundred dollars higher than mine, so that all his old OBs who can't stand the extra bite will come rushing over to me."

"Well, I don't know," Ellie said cautiously. "All *I* want is for you to have some kind of predictable on or off OB call, so that you're really *off call* sometimes. Maybe this way makes some sense."

"Sense! So he can play the great specialist over on his side of the hall and let me play Dr. Slob over on my side? What do you mean, it makes sense?"

"Honey, you've been trying for months to get his OB patients onto your list. Maybe this'll work."

"Over my dead body it'll work." Rob was on his feet again, weaving as he tried to pour another drink, spilling half of it on the counter. "My God, Ellie! How can you sit there and *buy* it? We can't have a fee setup like that. There'd be no end to it. I'd not only be the second-class OB doctor around here; pretty soon I'd be the second-class doctor for everything else too. Dr. Slobsky, our cut-rate corner quack . . ."

"Well, if you ask me, I think you're too drunk to think about it," Ellie said angrily, standing up and pushing past him to the kitchen.

"Goddam right I'm drunk, and high time too. Somebody's got to get up on his pegs to that bastard."

"And there's nothing like a little Dutch courage to help."

"Oh, shit." Rob sent the glass crashing into the fireplace. "Go ahead and support the bastard, if you want to. But I'm not going to buy his little schemes, drunk *or* sober."

"I also think you're acting like a spoiled baby. Spank your hands and you have a tantrum." She put the chops into the pan, turning her back to him.

"So now I'm a baby. Whose side are you on, for God's sake?"

She turned sharply. "Rob, I'm on your side, I always have been, but now you're really being unfair. You're unhappy with the practice, and you're fighting Martin, and you can't make *him* budge, so you take it out on me. You act as if *I'm* the problem around here somehow, but I'm *not* the problem. Martin Isaacs is the problem, and I'm not going to be your whipping boy on his account anymore."

"Jesus! Now you're talking gibberish."

"No, just plain straight thinking. I think we made a terrible mistake coming to this place. I've thought so from the first day we came here and got a look at Martin in action. Well, it's done now. Somehow we've got to live with him, and we can't do it by fighting. The man is a power-crazy tyrant, and he's going to stomp down anybody that gets in his way, and that includes *you* if you can't find some way to make peace with him. So I think maybe you'd better make peace with him, even on his terms."

"You mean crawl on my belly like Jerry DeForrest? No. Not me. And you've got Martin wrong. He isn't big enough to be a tyrant. He's just a small-time bullheaded bastard with delusions of grandeur, and he needs somebody to jar him awake."

"And you're going to do it?"

"You just watch. He may think he can cram these things down my throat, but he's got hold of the wrong man. I'm not going to *let* him fire Harry Sonders, because I think it's wrong. And there's no way I'm going to swallow this fee crap, either. He can just go screw himself."

"Well, I know one thing," Ellie said hotly. "You can't keep fighting everybody and everything all the time, the way you're doing, because it's going to tear you apart. And you can't keep beating me into the ground, either. You're just going to have to give a little, somewhere along the line."

"Not on this, I'm not going to give. And as for beating *you* into the ground, maybe you're not all that helpless after all. You might find it charming to hear what your fine Dr. Isaacs had to say about you and your pregnancy when we talked tonight."

She stiffened and turned to him, suddenly wary. "What did Dr. Isaacs say?"

"He thinks maybe you've been leaving your diaphragm in the dresser drawer."

"He said that?"

"More or less. And maybe he's right. A diaphragm's pretty reliable, except when you leave it in the drawer."

"Do *you* think I did?"

"Beats me, kid. Maybe you did and maybe you didn't. You're the only one that knows."

"Yes, that's right." She took a deep breath, like a sigh. "Well, now there's got to be two of us that know, I guess. Martin is right. I did leave the damned thing in the drawer. For several weeks, as a matter of fact." Her voice trembled, defiant. "I couldn't think of anything else to do. I wanted to keep my husband and my marriage, and the only way I could think of to keep my husband and my marriage was to have a baby, so I decided I was going to have a baby, and that was the way it was."

"I see." He looked at her for a moment as if she were a stranger. Something in her eyes told him that this was not the time to react, not the time to lose control, and drunk as he was, he forced his hands to stop trembling. "Well, what's done is done," he said finally. "I guess I think we need a baby right now like we need a pig on roller skates, but if we're going to have one, then it looks like we're going to have one. And as long as it's only got one head and you come out of it all right, I don't suppose it matters too much just *how* it happened."

"No, I don't think that's good enough," Ellie said angrily. "I didn't want you to know, I never planned on telling you. But since I had to, I sure don't want you hating me and the baby too."

"Honey, that's the risk you take when you play this game. And it's a little late now, worrying about how *I* feel."

"No, it's not too late. There's plenty of time. If you don't want this baby, if you've really got serious reservations, I can go right back to Martin tomorrow morning and have him stop it."

Suddenly he couldn't hide his outrage any longer. "No, you can't," he snapped. "I won't let you. You've done enough already. No wife of mine is going to have an abortion in *this* snoopy little town. Or anywhere else, either. So forget it." He lurched to his feet and poured himself more whiskey.

"Rob—"

"I said *forget* it."

310

She stood silent for a moment. "You sound just like Martin," she said finally.

"So I sound just like Martin. Just don't whine to me anymore about beating you into the ground—"

The telephone jangled, cutting him off. He lurched across the room to take it, but Ellie grabbed it first. "No, I'm sorry, Dr. Tanner's not here—"

"My ass I'm not. Give me that phone."

"I mean he can't come right now. He'll—he'll call you back."

She slammed the receiver down before he could tear it away from her. He held her wrist clamped, glaring at her. "Just what the hell do you think you're doing?"

"Let go of me." Her voice was very quiet. "You're in no shape to talk to a patient. You're liable to kill somebody."

"Who was on that phone?"

"Some woman, she didn't say who. She'll call back if it's desperate. Now let me get dinner."

"Oh, shove your dinner." Rob grabbed his coat off the hook and banged out the kitchen door. Moments later he was weaving across the bridge in the Vega. More drunk than he realized, he barely missed colliding with a semi as he roared out onto the highway, but somehow he made it to the clinic in one piece. Letting himself in the back door, he staggered into the supply room and emptied his stomach into the sink. *Beating her into the ground, for Christ's sake! While she's busy pulling this. Here's your baby, father, like it or not. And then dumping it all into my lap, whether to have it stopped.* He leaned over the sink and retched, retched again, waiting and waiting for the liquor-induced nausea to subside.

A long while later he walked into his darkened office and sank down at the desk with his head in his hand. Outside, he heard a car whisper by on the street, and from time to time the telephone made clicking noises as the tape picked up a call. There in the darkness the images of fatherhood came back to his mind, just as they had that night in the tent—the pride, the joy, the great future things fatherhood would bring, the fatherhood he knew in his heart of hearts that he really wanted someday—but now the images seemed tainted. *Well, you've got your baby inside you, and I've got Martin to fight, and he's no insuperable tyrant, either; he just needs to have his head rapped, is all—*

Quite suddenly, then, another image appeared: of a magic forest, and mushrooms in the moss, and a girl with green eyes and skin the

311

color of honey. *You've got your baby, and I've got Martin and maybe something else too.*

He sat there, hardly moving, for over two hours. Then, at last, he got up, walked out to the car and drove back home again. Ellie was in bed. On the dining table was a china plate with two cold lamb chops on it. He picked them up with a curse and hurled them into the sink. Then he collapsed on the sofa in the living room and a moment later he was snoring.

# 25

Ellie sat in bed with a cup of coffee in her lap, feeling gray and wrung out despite the cheery morning sunlight streaming through the curtained windows. It was a bad night, all the way around, she reflected. She'd been so bloody stupid—stupid to consider it in the first place, stupid to imagine it could ever pass, stupid in every possible dimension. Just irretrievably stupid, and Lord, how she regretted it now. Not that it cooled in the least her bone-deep anger at Rob. *He can really be ugly when he wants to,* she thought bitterly. *The bastard. But then, at least he didn't knock me across the room, the way some men would have done.*

Somewhere outside the window she heard a loud *thump!* clear and distinct, as if a bird had struck the window. A moment later there was another thump, and then another. She pushed the curtains aside, looked out, but saw nothing. She threw the window open to hear better. Nothing but silence. Then, once again, *thump!* and she saw something large and brown hit the roof of the old Chevy and bounce off onto the ground.

A large pine cone. High up in the tree over the car she saw the squirrel, a tiny gray creature, scurrying madly from branch to branch, cutting off pine cones and letting them drop *thump* onto the car roof, working as if furies were after him. Ellie smiled, watching him. *My God, in another twenty minutes he's going to have that tree stripped.* She rapped the window sharply, laughed aloud as he scurried up the trunk at the sound, turned around and stared down at her, then almost shrugged and went on to the next pine cone.

She turned away from the window finally, and some of the grayness was gone. *Life goes on,* she thought, *no matter what you do. That squirrel is getting ready for a long, cold winter. What's more, he's going to make it. And so are we.* She went out to the kitchen for more coffee, suddenly feeling halfway hopeful. *The first move has got to be his, after last night,* she thought, defiant. *But one way or another, we're going to make it.* And for a while, at least, she almost had herself convinced.

Rob found Jerry DeForrest sitting in the coffee room at the hospital that morning, unbelievably early for Jerry and looking unbelievably gray despite the cheery morning sunlight streaming through the curtained windows. Rob got some coffee and sat down across the table. "You look about as wrung out as I feel," he told Jerry wryly. "What's the trouble?"

Jerry shrugged. "I came up to talk to Harry when he finishes with his case in there," he said. "But I don't think I'm going to be able to do it. I'm not going to get a single word through to him, and he's going to laugh in my face, and Martin's going to say he told me so, and that's going to be that." He looked up at Rob, his eyes old and tired. "I don't know," he said. "I don't seem to be good for much of anything around here anymore. Not even for talking. Maybe Amy's right. She keeps telling me I should get out of this business and take up gardening. Maybe I could do a decent job of that."

Rob looked at the man, took a sip of his coffee and put the cup down. "Come on, Jerry, for God's sake," he said finally. "In your own funny way you're doing a whole lot of good things for a whole lot of people in this valley, whether you know it or not. *I* know it, and so do a lot of others." He paused. "Sure, maybe I wouldn't do things exactly the way you do them, but then I'm not you. Don't sell yourself short. And don't listen to Amy when she talks like that, either. Ignore it. She doesn't know what she's saying." He took another sip of coffee. "You know, we all start out aiming for perfection right from the beginning, just dead certain that we're going to achieve it. We figure it's only a matter of time. And then one day, somewhere along the line, it begins to seep through that we're never going to get there. You know? But life goes on, no matter what you do. Even I'm beginning to find that out, and I'm a lot younger than you are."

314

"I suppose," DeForrest said.

"Look, you don't have to talk to Sonders if you don't want to," Rob said suddenly. "You two live in completely different worlds. Of course you're going to have trouble getting through to him, and of course he's going to laugh in your face. And he can really be ugly when he wants to, the bastard."

"But *somebody's* got to talk to him," Jerry said.

"So maybe I can try," Rob said. "I'm a whole lot closer to his world than you are. Maybe I can make it where you can't. At least he won't knock me across the room."

Jerry looked up, and some of the grayness was gone. "God, Rob, I'd appreciate that," he said. "I'd really appreciate it if you would."

"Don't sweat it," Rob said. "Forget it. Go on down to the office and read some of those piled-up x-rays. Spend your time doing something you really *are* good at." Rob heard a loud *thump*, clear and distinct, from the OR corridor as a nurse banged through a door somewhere with a tray in her hands. He went out to the kitchen for more coffee, suddenly feeling halfway hopeful. "I may not catch him right this morning," he told Jerry. "It was a bad night, all the way around. But I'll catch him in a day or two, and somehow I'll get through to him. And one way or another, we'll make it, don't worry." And for a while, at least, he almost had himself convinced.

If Rob had expected Martin to be angry that morning when he turned up at the hospital a few minutes later, he saw no sign of it. The older man seemed fresh and bright—far more than Rob himself—and hustled him down to see x-rays of an injured millworker he'd admitted during the night. At the office afterward, as Rob struggled through his morning schedule with a pounding headache and a queasy stomach, Isaacs stopped him for a couple of minor consultations, but didn't even mention their discussion of the evening before. Whatever he'd thought of Rob's outburst, he didn't seem bothered; if anything, he seemed more than usually warm and congenial.

Rob felt anything but, his anger now tempered by hangover and remorse. He'd made his own breakfast, with Ellie in icy silence in the bedroom, and headed for the hospital, wishing desperately that one of them could have said something, anything, to help soothe the abrasion. But the first move had to be hers, and she hadn't made it. Now, later, anger and irritation won out. *Let her sit and sulk, if she wants to. I can manage. And if she wants to fret about me scrapping it up with Isaacs,*

315

*that's fine too. Just let her keep it to herself. I'm the one that has to deal with Isaacs, not her, and I can sure live without a Greek chorus in the background.*

A little before eleven o'clock Terry buzzed Rob's office intercom. "Chris Erickson's on line four, Doctor."

Rob took the call. "Hi, Chris. What's up?"

"Plenty," she said. "You heard about the blood bank thing?"

"They turned us down."

"They sure did," Chris said. "Dottie showed me the letter last night. She's mad enough to take an ax to the place. We tried to call you, but all we got was a frantic female on the line, with growling in the background."

Rob winced. "So that was you. Sorry. It was a bad night."

"Well, we just wanted to check with you." Chris paused. "So what's the next move, Merlin?"

"I'm not sure," Rob said. "Either we tackle the stockholders one by one, or we go around them. See about getting a Hospital Improvement District on the ballot, and move from there. I'm going to see Judge Barret in his office at one-thirty. Want to come along?"

"Sure. I'll take a late lunch hour."

She came roaring up in her green jeep just as Rob crossed the highway to Judge Barret's office. A moment later they were facing the tall, lean lawyer across his desk. "I guess we just don't understand the complete lack of response," Rob said. "If the vote had split a little, we could at least respect it, but this was just a kick in the teeth."

The Judge spread his hands. "I know. But I could have predicted it. The board voted *their* interest, not the public interest."

"But can't they see a *moral* obligation?" Chris protested.

"With money at stake, moral obligations get lost," the Judge replied. "It's sad, but it's also true."

"Then you think there's nothing we can do?" Rob said.

"There may be things you can do, but I'm not sure they'll accomplish much," the Judge said. "If you built a broad enough base here in the valley, got a petition signed by just about everybody, you might make them listen—but I doubt it."

"If they won't listen to twenty, they won't listen to three thousand," Rob said angrily.

"I'm afraid that's true."

"Unless the three thousand are voting to force that place into public hands."

316

The Judge looked over his glasses at Rob. "I'm not too sure you want to get involved in that," he said quietly.

"Why not? If the board won't listen to reason, then maybe it's time to start shaking things up."

"You could find yourself in a very awkward position."

"Like what?" Rob flared.

The Judge raised his hands. "No offense, Rob. You just might find shaking things up more painful than you think, that's all."

"Well, we'd certainly need some good legal advice," Rob said, glancing at Chris. "And there's nobody we'd rather have helping us than you."

The Judge shook his head. "Not a chance," he said. "I can't help you."

"Why not?"

"Conflict of interest, plain and simple. I'm not only attorney for the board, I also represent some of the stockholders. I can't help you threaten these people."

Chris gave Rob a crestfallen look. "But I thought you were on *our* side," she said.

"Privately, I am. Privately, I think they were damned fools to turn down this blood bank thing—and I've told them so. But they're still my clients, and I have to protect their interests whether I like their decisions or not."

Rob stood up slowly. "Well, at least you're honest. But surely you can give us a list of the stockholders, tell us where the incorporation papers are filed—"

"Sorry. All I can do is warn you, and wish you luck. You're going to need it."

Outside on the street, Chris gave Rob a bleak look. "Well, Merlin, where do we go from here?"

"I don't know," Rob said wearily, helping her up into her jeep. "Missoula, I guess. Find a good lawyer. But it's going to be an uphill climb. I'll get back to you and Dottie after I've had a chance to mull it over."

He started to close the door, but Chris caught his eyes. "Hospital business aside, when am I going to see you again?"

He returned her gaze. "You're sure you want to see me?"

"I wouldn't ask, otherwise."

"You know this town has eyes and ears," he said.

"There must be someplace."

317

Something clicked in his mind then, and he answered before the censor could stop him. "Yes. There's a little cabin up on Lake Marian. Belonged to a friend of mine. Nobody ever goes there."

"Then how soon?"

"Next Wednesday night. I'm supposed to go to Missoula to a meeting, but I can shuck it. I'll call you."

"Yes, love. You do that." She smiled briefly and cranked the jeep motor alive. A moment later she was roaring up the highway as he walked back toward the office. He was fighting the censor all the way, but his headache was suddenly gone and a wave of exhilaration replaced the morning's depression. It was wrong, it was absolute idiocy, but somehow he didn't care. Foolish or not, it was done, a new door was open, and all the week's bitterness and frustration suddenly grew dim: the hospital board balking, Ellie sulking, Martin raving like a madman. Well, screw them all. Chris wasn't sulking, and one night wouldn't burn any bridges.

He plunged into his afternoon schedule, ignoring the nattering censor buzzing in his ear, moving swiftly and keeping Dora hopping double time. Then at three-thirty Isaacs was on the intercom, and suddenly even Chris was pushed out of his mind.

"Rob, can you go up to the hospital? They're taking Happy Cumley's daughter Nan up there in the ambulance. She's had some kind of accident on her way home from school, and I'm in the middle of sewing up a guy's leg."

Rob heard the ambulance siren as he walked out to his car. On the highway he saw it come hurtling along the River Road and head up Hospital Hill without even slowing for the turn. He followed up the hill and pulled in beside it at the emergency room door. Bill Peters, the driver, came over just as Janice Pryor emerged from the emergency entrance, followed by Raymond wheeling a gurney. "You'd better take a look before we move her, Doc," Peters said, shaking his head grimly.

"What happened?"

"She was riding her bike down the River Road and swung in front of a logging truck. Must have hit a stone or something. Johnny Yelenich was driving and didn't even have time to hit the brakes. Front wheel caught her and threw her thirty yards across the pavement." He shook his head again. "She's a real mess, Doc."

As Peters talked he had been throwing open the rear doors to the ambulance. His assistant, a younger man, emerged. "She's still breathing," he said tightly. "But I don't see how."

318

Rob looked at Miss Pryor. "Where's Happy?"

"She's on her way up."

"Better just take her inside when she gets here." Bag in hand, Rob climbed up into the ambulance van. "Get me some light in here, Bill."

Bright overhead lights flicked on. Rob knelt beside the small, slender figure on the stretcher, pulled a towel away from the head end, and almost gagged. The girl, about fourteen years old, was on her back, facing away from him, with makeshift bandages, sopping with blood, wrapped loosely around her head. Gently he moved the gauze wrapper and grimaced. Jaw, cheek and forehead were all one huge, oozing abrasion; above that a large flap of scalp had been thrown back and the skull underneath was broken open like a gourd. He could see some yellowish, flocculent material dripping out onto the dressing. *My God,* Rob thought, *she can't still be alive*—but at the same moment he saw the girl's chest rising and falling, heard stertorous, gargling breath sounds. He eased her broken jaw forward gently and the gargle became a snore, grating and ugly in the small ambulance enclosure.

Carefully Rob loosened clothing, examined the rest of the girl's body without moving her head and neck. An arm and a leg were both fractured, but the spine appeared intact. Her heart tones, racing at 120 beats per minute, sounded fluttery but steady. *Still alive—yes, barely. Massive skull fractures. Obvious brain damage and coma. The face— well, a good plastic man can help with that if we can keep her alive long enough. Good enough airway for now; hate to suction back there until I know how much damage to the skull base.* He backed out of the ambulance to face Raymond and Janice Pryor. "There's nothing we can do here," he said. "We've got to get her to a neurosurgeon, fast." He turned to the driver. "Bill, let's go right on into Sacred Heart. I'll ride with her and see if I can keep an airway open. Janice, call Isaacs and tell him where I've gone—and give my wife a ring, if you think of it. Then tell Sacred Heart emergency that we're on our way and need a neurosurgeon." He started to climb back into the ambulance, then stopped midway. "When Happy gets here, see that somebody drives her to Missoula—got that? I don't want her going off the road on the way in."

Bill closed the ambulance doors, then clambered into the cab of the ambulance with his assistant. Through an intercom Rob heard his voice. "She still okay, Doc?"

"She's still breathing. You'd better hit the hammer, Bill—but don't take any unnecessary chances. An extra five minutes isn't going to

319

change anything." He felt the vehicle start moving and found a spare pillow to sit on, clutching a handrail as they lurched out of the parking lot and down the hill. He heard the siren start wailing, as though from a great distance, and moments later they were out on the highway heading north.

The snoring continued, an eerie, discordant sound in the stuffy interior. Rob looked around, checked the suction apparatus on the wall of the ambulance and put it back. The girl's waxen color was unchanged, her pulse still racing and thready. Rob took her uninjured arm, found her blood pressure stable at 120 systolic. *Maybe, just maybe, there's a chance,* he thought. *Maybe there's no basilar skull damage, maybe a good neurosurgeon can plate the fractures, or wire them or something. She's young, healthy—maybe she can pull out of it alive. But the brain damage—oh, Christ.* He thought again of the yellowish stuff he had seen seeping out between the fractured bone edges, the filamentous network of blood vessels torn by the skull-breaking impact. *Alive, maybe, but what else? Five years of snoring coma? A living, breathing turnip? A brain reduced to scrambled eggs?*

He forced the image from his mind, checked the girl's airway again. Nothing to do, really, as long as air was moving freely. He sat there, cramped in the close quarters, feeling helpless, stupid. The rumble of the moving vehicle merged with the snoring breathing of the child and he found himself half mesmerized, his mind wandering, almost dreaming . . . images of Chris Erickson sitting in the jeep, tawny hair, honey-colored skin, elfin tilt to the eyes, the smile, and then suddenly, startlingly, as if rushing for sanctuary, he felt an almost overpowering surge of physical hunger for her, of tension building like a drawn bowstring. He jerked himself awake, rubbed his forehead. Jesus, he *was* dozing— but the dream image lingered, tantalizingly; a sense of fervent anticipation lingered too, and he shifted position, chagrined and almost embarrassed by his own obvious arousal. He checked the girl's blood pressure again, then leaned back against the wall, wondering what he was doing there, wishing he'd brought a book, wishing that this seemingly endless trip would come to an end.

The snoring continued. For all the girl's pallor, her skin was hot and dry, and he was aware of the faint medicinal odor of the dressings. He watched, listened, waited as ten minutes passed, then ten more. Then at last the siren began screaming and he saw the houses and buildings on the outskirts of Missoula passing by. Interminable minutes later the siren died and the ambulance swung into the Sacred Heart emergency bay.

Rob was so cramped he could hardly crawl out when the rear doors were thrown open. Already a white-coated orderly and an intern were moving to take the stretcher. Then a tall, gray-haired man in a gray business suit came up and shook hands with Rob. "Dr. Tanner? I'm Henry Lanovitz. Neurosurgery. Let's get a look at this girl before we move her too much." He leaned over the child, took scissors from the nurse and snipped and parted the head dressing slightly. "Oh, boy. She really got it, didn't she? How did she manage on the trip?"

Rob shrugged. "Not too bad; her vital signs are stable. She's got closed fractures of her right humerus and left tibia and God knows what else. I didn't try rolling her around much."

"That was very wise," the neurosurgeon said. "No response?"

"No. She's been comatose all the way."

"Well, let's get some skull films and see what we're really dealing with. You planning to stick around?"

"I thought I'd wait until the mother gets here."

"Good. The permission forms can wait, of course, but you could explain that we really had to get this girl into the OR as fast as possible."

"The mother's a nurse. She'll understand."

The neurosurgeon helped move the girl from the ambulance stretcher onto the x-ray table adjacent to the emergency room, with people working swiftly and all the life-support apparatus in the world converging around her. A few moments later Lanovitz called Rob to see the films. "Pretty classic major skull trauma," he said, "and a bad scene, I'm afraid. That skull plate is caved in a good inch at this point here. We'll have to free it and elevate it, and those spicules of bone penetrating the brain there will have to come out. Hard to tell how much underlying brain damage there is, but we're already so far behind that the chances are pretty slim."

"You mean for recovery?"

"For survival," Lanovitz said. "She's young, but shock is bound to catch up with us, and with this much crushing of brain tissue . . . ." He sighed and shrugged his shoulders. "We'll try, but don't expect too much. And don't encourage the mother, either. Just tell her we're doing all we can, and let it go at that. Okay?"

"I understand."

"There's nothing you could have done," Lanovitz added, "so don't

321

fret about that. I'm just amazed that you got her here alive." He took another look at the films and shook his head. "You might as well go get some coffee. The office will page you when the mother gets here."

Numbly Rob walked down the corridor to the cafeteria. It was just past six o'clock, and the place was full, a huge glaring room with white-tiled walls. *Like a morgue,* Rob thought, falling into line behind a gaggle of nurses, picking up a cup of black coffee and sitting down at one of the brown slab tables. *Or a prison. Everybody should be pounding on the tables at once.* Two gray-faced doctors in scrub suits sat down across from him, started eating their dinners in methodical silence. He sipped the tasteless coffee, thinking gloomily about the surgery. How could people like Lanovitz live with these cases, day in and day out? Trying to rebuild human wreckage, week after week—hemorrhage, stroke, trauma—and only really winning in one case out of forty. How could they stand it? The OB man, by contrast, saw patients who were strong, healthy, happy, increasingly eager as delivery day approached. He wondered idly how Martin Isaacs would do as a neurosurgeon. Not too well, probably. Isaacs didn't care much for the mess and misery that went with medicine. *Trust him to pack somebody else off on an errand like this one,* Rob thought, half bitterly, *even when the victim is the daughter of one of his most loyal aides. Let the new man handle the dirty work.*

He heard his name on the loudspeaker, and picked up a wall phone to answer. "They want you in the business office, Doctor," the operator said. "Mrs. Cumley just arrived."

"Fine. Where's the business office?"

"First floor, off the lobby."

He found Happy Cumley sitting before a desk, her eyes red-rimmed but dry, her face grief-stricken, with Raymond standing uneasily nearby. Her face brightened a little when she saw Rob. "How is she, Dr. Tanner?"

"I don't know," he said unhappily. "They've taken films, and Dr. Lanovitz has her up in the OR right now."

"Yes, I was just signing the permission forms. Did he—did he think—"

"He didn't say much, but he looks like a careful, competent man. He'll do everything he can."

She nodded and finished signing the papers. "I'm so glad you came in with her. At least I knew somebody was—right there. And Raymond insisted on driving me in."

322

"Well, if they've assigned a room yet, you may be more comfortable waiting there."

The clerk nodded. "A nurse will be down in a minute," she said.

Raymond looked up. "You want a ride back, Doctor?"

"No, but you go ahead. I think I'll stay awhile. I'll work out a ride home later."

A nurse appeared at the door, and led Rob and Happy to an elevator. The third-floor room reserved for the injured girl was bright and airy, with a view west toward the mountains and the setting sun. Happy stood by the window, staring out, insisting that Rob take the single chair. "I don't think I can sit very well anyway," she said. "Will they—tell us as soon as she's out of the operating room?"

"I'm sure they will."

"It's just so sudden, I can't grasp it. So unfair. She had a volleyball game after school, so she took her bike instead of riding the bus. But I can't understand what happened. She must have lost control somehow. We've known Johnny Yelenich for years; he's one of the most careful drivers the timber company has. He *always* watches out for kids on bicycles." She fumbled in her purse for a handkerchief. "It's strange it was Johnny," she said. "Almost weird. Johnny was my husband's partner up in the woods when he was killed eight years ago. The very same man."

Rob cleared his throat. "I didn't know about your husband," he said.

"No, of course not. You wouldn't have. They were working on the yarding cables then, up in the hills, dragging logs down to the loader. Johnny was on the donkey engine they were still using then, and Mike, my husband, was setting chokers."

"Chokers?"

"The big steel clamps on the end of the cables they wrap around the logs. One man sets the choker, and the man on the engine hauls the cable up tight. Then the man on the choker jumps free before the log is dragged down. Mike had already jumped, but the choker broke loose. Ten pounds of steel flailing through the air on the end of a tight cable." Happy spread her hands with a helpless shrug. "It hit him in the head, and that was that. Johnny was so sick about it he swore he'd never run a donkey again. So they had him driving logging trucks. And now this." Her voice broke as she fought back tears. "That girl is all I've got left, Doctor."

"Happy, you've got your own good health, and work you love, work

323

that's helping other people, work that people depend on you for. And you've got a long, full life ahead, and people who love you—"

"But without my baby?"

"We don't know that yet. There's no sense thinking about that yet."

"No, I suppose not, but I just can't help it."

Quite suddenly Martin Isaacs was standing in the door, his face grave, his long white hair ruffled. "Well, Hap, how are you holding up?" he said.

The woman whirled, then rushed to the man and threw herself into his arms, burying her face in his chest. "Oh, Martin, I'm so glad you came. I'm—I'm not holding up too well, I'm afraid."

He stood there, holding her close, trying to gentle her weeping. "I know, girl, I know. And the hardest part is sitting and waiting, and not a damned thing we can do about it." He rubbed her shoulders, stroked her hair as if he were comforting a child. "Hey, hey, ease up there. Chin up now."

"But, Martin, she's my baby."

"I know. I know. But you've got to fight, kiddie. You've just got to keep on fighting, no matter what. You know that."

She nodded, wiped her eyes on Isaacs' handkerchief and allowed him to lead her to the chair. Isaacs sat on the edge of the bed, and Rob now stood by the window, watching the brightening lights of the city evening. Somewhere in the distance a siren wailed, and traffic, stopped on the busy street below, surged forward as a light changed.

"Have you—been upstairs?" Happy asked, hesitating.

Isaacs nodded. "I just came down. They're still working." He lapsed into silence for a moment. "Oh, yes; Dottie Hazard said she'd come on in as soon as her husband got home to stay with the kids. She's probably already on her way. She'll get you a motel room and stay with you tonight."

"Oh, that's sweet of her. Dottie's a peach. I hadn't even thought about where to stay. . . ." Happy's voice trailed off and she glanced at the bedside telephone, then leaned back wearily in the chair and closed her eyes. Isaacs made no move to go, sitting in silence, his head bowed a little. As the sun dropped below the mountains, the light in the room faded. Out in the corridor dinner trays were being distributed, and an aide offered them food, but no one was hungry. Twenty minutes passed, then thirty.

When the telephone rang, Martin took it. Rob could hear the scratch of a man's voice over the wire. "I see," Isaacs said. "I see. Yes, she's here. I'll tell her. And thanks, Henry."

He put the phone down slowly, pulled off his glasses and rubbed his eyes. "I guess that's it," he said. "She never recovered consciousness, and she never felt any pain, but there was just too much brain damage to support life."

"She's dead," Happy said dully.

"Yes. They did what they could, but it wasn't enough."

"I guess I knew it wouldn't be." The woman bowed forward, rested her forehead in her hand, but she was dry-eyed now and her voice was under control. "There isn't any point to you men staying," she said.

"We can stay just as long as you want us to."

"I know. You'd stay forever, if I asked you. But I think I'll be all right, if I can just—rest here a little. Dottie will be here soon."

"Yes, and Dr. Lanovitz will be down to see you, so maybe we'd better be going." Isaacs stood up, touched her hair for a moment. "I'm sorry, Hap. If I can help, just tell me."

She took his hand, held it to her cheek, then released it. A moment later they left her by herself in the darkened room. Down in the lobby Rob called Ellie to tell her that Martin was driving him home. Later, as the lights of the city thinned out and the highway stretched ahead of them to the south, Rob said, "I'm glad you came. It meant a lot to her."

"There wasn't much I could do."

"Maybe more than you think."

"Maybe. Little Nan was one of the first babies I ever delivered when I came to Twin Forks. A footling breech, and I didn't even have Agnes helping me in those days. But Hap and the baby both came out okay, and Hap's been loyal through thick and thin ever since. And it's been pretty thin sometimes, too—a couple of miscarriages after Nan was born, and then her husband killed up in the woods, and now this. I don't know. A lot of people couldn't take it, couldn't keep going, but she will. She'll fight back. There's a lot to that woman you don't see on the surface."

"You must be very fond of her," Rob said.

Isaacs was silent for so long Rob thought he hadn't heard. Then he said, "Fond of her? I guess that's a safe way to put it. Sometimes a patient gets to be far, far more than just a patient. Sometimes something else altogether takes over. But when that happens, you have to be careful." He paused and took a breath like a sigh. "Yes, indeed. You have to be very, very careful."

# 26

In the days that followed, the entire town of Twin Forks went into mourning at the tragic death of Nan Cumley. The funeral was on Thursday morning, and most of the shops closed up. The Twin Forks Community Church was filled to overflowing half an hour before the service. Martin Isaacs, who swore he couldn't stand funerals, *any* funerals, appeared in spite of himself, standing by the wall in the back, looking tired and out of place. Johnny Yelenich and his family arrived, the huge truckdriver awkward in an ill-fitting dark gray suit that reeked of mothballs. Happy Cumley and her aged mother appeared, and she embraced the big driver tearfully in the foyer before entering the church. Johnny's craggy face crumpled as he held her tight for a fleeting instant, and it seemed as though his wife half-supported him as they went down the aisle to a pew near the front. Once the service began, it was mercifully brief, yet Rob, returning to the clinic when it was over, felt drained and exhausted.

Ever since the accident Martin Isaacs had seemed increasingly remote and withdrawn, barely nodding to Rob when they passed in the hall, and spinning through his office schedule with such manifest disinterest that even Agnes was muttering under her breath. Harry Sonders had only one case scheduled Thursday morning, and again he badgered Terry to bring in his afternoon follow-up patients late in the morning so he could get away right after lunch. Isaacs glowered but said

326

nothing as he went about his business, and Sonders himself had little to say to anyone.

As for Rob, the atmosphere remained frigid at home too. Ellie was civil but distant, apparently still rankling from their Monday evening fight, but with his mind busy with Nan Cumley on one hand and Chris Erickson on the other, Rob let her stew, although he'd never seen her quite like this before. He kept telling himself that Friday, when he was off, there'd be a chance to sit down with her and talk things out rationally, but when Friday finally came, Ellie was off to a rummage sale in a town up the valley before he even woke up, leaving him a sharp note to please clean the pine needles out of the roof gutters so the place wouldn't flood the next time it rained, and that was the end of talking things out rationally on Friday. He skulked around the house, debating whether to make rounds or not, then trying to call Chris at the lab and missing her ("She just left for Missoula to pick up a new sterilizer, Doctor"), and feeling furtive telling the secretary that he was calling with a lab report. He was entertaining wild thoughts about driving to Missoula himself, thinking he might meet Chris on the road, when the phone rang and Jerry was calling, wonder of wonders, to ask Rob for a consultation on a patient he'd just hospitalized.

It was an old man with an old hepatitis and borderline liver failure whom Jerry had been nursing along for years. "He just gets better or worse week by week," Jerry said. "You know how *that* can go. But now all of a sudden he's started having funny spells—disoriented, confused, odd behavior, like he's halfway into liver coma while he's still walking around."

"Well, maybe he *is*," Rob said. "What kind of odd behavior?"

"Like getting up at three A.M. this morning and going out to wash his car. Didn't even recognize his own wife when she came out to get him." Jerry paused. "I never saw liver failure act like this before. Maybe you could take a look at him."

Rob did. The man was disoriented, all right—almost totally—and he had a hard, cirrhotic-feeling liver. He also had a blood pressure of 220/170, and eye-ground changes suggestive of a staggeringly elevated intracranial pressure. When Rob finished his exam he went back to the coffee room to find Jerry. "I don't know about that guy," he said. "I sure don't like his high blood pressure."

Jerry frowned. "What high blood pressure?"

"The high blood pressure he's got right now. His eye grounds are a mess too. I can hardly see the retinal vessels."

327

Jerry whistled. "I hadn't checked that, either," he said. "Let me go take a look."

Rob waited in the coffee room. Ten minutes later Jerry was back, shaking his head. "I'll be damned," he said. "I'll just be goddamned."

Rob looked at him. "That guy's either got a brain tumor in there the size of a grapefruit, or else something else is pushing his pressure up till his eyes are popping out. I don't think his liver's got anything to do with it."

"You sure could be right," Jerry said. "What should I do? Get skull films and kidney x-rays tomorrow?"

"Sounds like a good place to start," Rob said.

"Maybe a spinal tap too."

"Jesus, Jerry! With that much pressure inside his skull? You're liable to kill him."

"Yeah, that's right, too," Jerry said, chagrined. "I just wasn't thinking. And I just can't believe that blood pressure. I'd swear it was normal six months ago."

"Maybe so," Rob said. "But *Jesus*, Jerry! An awful lot can happen in six months."

The lean doctor sighed. "I know. I guess I've just been so close to it that I couldn't see the forest for the trees."

Rob wrote a note on the patient's chart as Jerry went on making rounds. Stopping by the office, Rob asked Terry to pull the patient's clinic chart. Then he sat down and studied it from the first note in Jerry's handwriting two years before to the last hasty scrawl, dated that day, saying: "Admitted to hospital for evaluation. Dr. Tanner to consult."

*Dr. Tanner to consult, indeed,* Rob thought. *It's just incredible. He's seen the man twice a week for months, and never once really looked at him.* A succession of cryptic notes: "Feeling better?? . . . " More nausea, thinks losing weight . . . Complains left flank pain, urine okay." A constant juggling of medicines—anti-nauseants, tranquilizers, barbiturates, bile salts. *Jesus, is there any pill he missed?* Blood pressures had been recorded by Dora at each office visit, sometimes up, sometimes down, with no sign DeForrest had even noticed. *Sure, you can get so close you can't see the forest for the trees once in a while, but for weeks on end? What kind of excuse is that? That's what you trained for, that's why people go see you. You've got to see the forest.*

Finally, wearily, Rob tossed the chart aside. Maybe, between the two of them, they could come up with some answers for the poor bastard. *But how many others are there? How many others in this practice are piddling along getting sicker instead of better because Jerry can't see the forest for the trees? Maybe he really* should *get out of this business and go into gardening.* Rob sat for a long while, staring into space, before finally rousing himself and driving on back home again.

# 27

If Martin Isaacs had been smoldering all that week, the fire burst out on Monday, and Rob Tanner was in the middle of it, up to his ears.

His duty weekend had started off the dullest that Rob could remember since first arriving at Twin Forks. Aside from a child who had swallowed a bottle of iron pills and a man who broke his ankle falling down the cellar stairs, Rob had one or two minor calls between Saturday noon and dawn on Monday; no OBs had delivered, and there were only a few patients to see at the hospital. He spent his time leafing through journals and avoiding Ellie, who was busy repairing a lovely old quilt Belle Foreman had given her and didn't solicit any advice from him. The "talking things out" that Rob had planned still had not taken place, and ultimately he had pushed the notion aside. *Let her break the ice if she wants to, God damn it. I've got other things to think about.*

Then at 5:30 A.M. on Monday the hospital called him out to deal with a singularly messy highway accident, and he was up to his neck in frantic work for the rest of the morning. A superannuated Oldsmobile with defective brakes and a drunk at the wheel had skidded on wet pavement and crashed broadside into a pickup truck driven by a man and his wife, hurling the pickup off the highway and down a ninety-foot embankment and killing the man, while the Olds disintegrated going through the guardrail. The woman, hauled from the burning truck by a passing motorist, had extensive burns on her thighs and legs, the rest

330

of her body having been shielded from the heat by the down parka she wore, as well as a fractured forearm and innumerable deep lacerations of the face and neck; the driver of the Olds had one side of his chest crushed, with open fractures of three ribs. He was, however, still stone drunk, and kept climbing off the litter and staggering around, hindered only by violent paroxysms of coughing and spitting of blood, splattering the walls with it, until Rob finally ordered restraints and a nurse's aide to control the man until he could move the woman onto the x-ray table for Raymond to shoot the broken arm, and get an IV running at the same time to control shock.

Rob had taken one good, long look at the mess and sent Hodges off to call Harry Sonders: "I know it's not his regular surgery day, but keep trying till you get him anyway. I need him now." Patrolmen were hovering around like blowflies, trying to get statements from the victims and ending up with cough-punctuated curses from the drunk and hysterical garble from the woman. It was almost two hours' work before he got all the pieces sorted out, respiratory support started for the drunk driver and a treatment priority set up, and he was much relieved when Sonders in the flesh walked in a little after eight o'clock.

The little surgeon took over. Esther Briggs was there to help, along with Happy Cumley. "Better get Sara to set up anesthesia for this woman," Sonders said. "We'll need to debride those burns and see what we're really dealing with. The arm is a single-bone fracture; we can do a closed reduction on that and cast it up at the same time. Plenty of plasma on hand? Good, we'll need it. As for that bird over there, he's got a pressure pneumothorax for sure, with all those splintered ribs, and he's liable to go out on us if we don't get a tube into his chest pretty damned soon. Hap, you get that set up, with a water trap and one of those big trocars, okay? And just a little procaine in a syringe. He's already about as anesthetized as he can get. Rob, for Christ's sake stop wringing your hands and help me get this woman's clothes cut off."

For the next three hours he and Sonders worked side by side, hardly exchanging a word, concentrating on the work at hand. Once again Rob was struck by the surgeon's cool, unruffled smoothness, his economy of action, the quick, sure decisions taken and acted upon, without fanfare. Not a movement was wasted, not a moment squandered, with Esther supplying instruments, dressings, solutions exactly when Sonders wanted them, like a perfectly integrated second pair of hands, her dark eyes watching his masked face, responding to every motion, every fleeting eye signal.

331

At one point Martin Isaacs came in, peered over their shoulders and grunted. "Some kind of mess," he said to Sonders. "But since you're already out here, I've got a woman with an ovarian cyst I want you to see down in the office before you leave. I'll have her in there at one-thirty."

Sonders looked up sourly. "Shit, Martin. You going to keep me out here all day?"

"Better than hauling you out twice," Isaacs said. "One-thirty. Remember that." And he stalked out of the room.

By eleven-fifteen the accident cases were under control except for some of the woman's lacerations, and Rob and Sonders took a coffee break. The surgeon looked comfortably relaxed, and it seemed like a golden opportunity to Rob. "That was a beautiful job," he said, "cleaning up that mess that way."

Sonders shrugged. "Not a hell of a lot to it, really. Just a matter of doing the right things at the right time in the right order."

Rob laughed. "I suppose. But it really is great, having surgical help here on a case like that. And you know, Harry, I think a guy like you is a whole hell of a lot better surgeon for a little country practice like this than a lot of big-name hotshot big-city surgeons I can think of."

Sonders grinned. "I don't know. Surgery's surgery, wherever you do it and whoever you have."

"Maybe so—but we really do need top-rate surgical help like this out here when we need it. We need it bad. It truly isn't just a matter of us getting nervous about little things we ought to be taking care of ourselves. The need for a surgeon we can count on every time is really here."

Sonders sighed. "Hell, Rob, I know that as well as you do. It's just that Martin keeps gigging me till I can't stand it anymore. He's up my ass about something every time I turn around, and I won't take it from the son of a bitch. It gets to the point that I don't give a shit *what* happens out here."

"But others are involved besides Martin," Rob said. "Like me. And a whole bunch of patients who need a good, reliable surgeon on tap."

"I know. Maybe I've been crowding it too far. If he'd just lay off for ten minutes." Sonders pushed his coffee cup aside. "Look, Esther and I can finish sewing up this babe's face," he said. "You'd better get on down to the office before the boss man shits on the floor."

Rob didn't see Martin when he got to the clinic, but his own patients were stacked up six deep waiting for him. Janice Blanchard was first in line. It was only two weeks since he'd done her OB workup, but she had already gained over twelve pounds. "Good Lord," Rob said. "What happened?"

"I don't know," Janice said. "I stayed on the diet, and hardly gained at all, and then just puffed up a few days ago." She hesitated. "I tried calling you Friday but couldn't get you, so I called Dr. Isaacs. I guess he's mad at me, though. He just told me to take one of my water pills and see you today, and then he hung up. When I tried to call back and ask him what water pills he meant, he wouldn't even answer the phone."

Rob frowned. "So what did you do?"

"One of my girlfriends gave me some water pills Dr. Isaacs has her taking. They seemed to help yesterday, but the weight was right up again today."

Rob sighed, shaking his head. "Well, it's bound to be water you're puffing up with. But I sure wish you'd let *me* order the medicines so I know what you're taking, and when, and how much."

"Well, I know. But shouldn't I call Dr. Isaacs when something funny is going on and I can't reach you?"

"Yes, you certainly should. I'll remind him. But meanwhile, I want you here every Monday morning to weigh in, like clockwork, until I'm sure this weight gain is under control."

With all the patients waiting, Rob skipped lunch, merely pausing for a cup of coffee about one-thirty. At a little after two Martin Isaacs came charging along the corridor. "What the hell was Harry doing up there when you left him?"

"Sewing up some lacerations," Rob said.

"Well, Jesus. He ought to be done by now. I've got this woman here to see him, and she's been waiting for over an hour. Maybe I'd better call the hospital."

"Uh—Martin. Why not let him be?"

Isaacs just gave him a black look and stumped back down the hall as Rob went on with his schedule. At three-fifteen the hospital called him to come check the man with the crushed chest: they thought the chest tube was plugged, they said, and Dr. Sonders was gone. Rob started for the door, bag in hand, when Isaacs stopped him, fairly sputtering. "You going up to the hospital?"

"Right. Just for a minute, I hope."

"Well, if you see that goddamned Sonders, tell him I said to get his ass down here in a rush, and I mean *now*. Pryor says they've been out of surgery since one-thirty."

"Maybe he stopped for lunch."

"He stopped for something, that's for damned sure, and my woman with the cyst is about mad enough to chew nails."

"Well, I'll tell him if I see him." Preoccupied with his own late schedule, and concerned with the accident patient, Rob pushed Sonders out of his mind as he drove up to the hospital, and the sight of the red Porsche in the parking lot hardly registered. Mostly Rob was hoping it was just a plugged tube to get unjammed, so he could get back to the office fast; he was already hurrying up the ramp when he heard a muffled sound from down below in the basement isolation room.

He stopped, peered back toward the closed door. A patient? The room had been empty that morning when they brought the accidents in. He listened, then shrugged, about to start on, when he heard it again: a thumping sound and a stifled groan.

He turned back down the ramp, pushed the door open, and then gaped at the tableau: two people mother naked on the high hospital bed, startled faces turned to the door, then a flurry of movement as one of them grabbed at a sheet to pull up over them. Rob said, "Good Christ!" and slammed the door, stared at it a moment, then said, "Good bloody God!" and almost ran up the ramp to the hospital corridor.

The man's chest tube was plugged; just a moment's work to clear it. As Rob walked back to the nurses' station, a chastened-looking Esther Briggs came up the ramp, uniform askew, eyes averted, and started folding surgical packs for the autoclave as though her life depended on it. By the time Rob finished writing his note on the chest case, the Porsche was gone from the parking lot—but it was not parked at the clinic when he arrived there.

Isaacs was waiting, furious by now. "Did you tell him?" he snapped.

"Well, not exactly."

"What do you mean, not exactly? Did you see him?"

"Yes, I saw him, but—oh, hell, he was just resting. He should be along any minute."

Rob tried to duck past the big man into his office, but Isaacs didn't budge. *"Resting!"* he said. "And me with a patient waiting for the last three hours." He looked at Rob, and his eyes suddenly narrowed. "Wait a minute. Just who the hell was he resting *with?*"

"It's none of my concern. I've got work to do."

334

"That goddam Esther Briggs, wasn't it?"

"Martin, it's none of my business. Nor yours, either."

"Yeah, that's what I thought. What did you do—walk right in on them?"

"In a word, yes."

"That son of a bitch." Isaacs turned and started down the corridor. Then he turned back. "God damn it, we can't afford this nonsense anymore. That bastard is supposed to be doing our surgery, not screwing the nurses."

"Oh, Martin, come off it."

"*Damned* if I'll come off it. I'm telling you, we can't risk it anymore."

"Risk what?"

Isaacs threw up his hands. "Use your head for once. This is a little town, a *very* little town, and all we need is one big fat scandal to make us all look like horses' asses. Well, this does it. This is too much."

"Martin, there's no law that says Harry can't climb into bed with his scrub nurse if he wants to."

"Maybe not, but small-town doctors just can't do it. Somebody else catch him and the people would run the two of them out of town in a dump truck. That Briggs woman's reputation is bad enough— she'd gang-bang the whole Loyal Order of Moose if they'd have her— but I'm not going to stand around and have one of *my doctors* nailed to the wall—"

The back door opened and Harry Sonders walked in, smiling, dapper and cool. "Somebody mention my name?" he said.

"Oh, you son of a bitch." Isaacs turned away abruptly. "There's a woman down in Room 3 who's been in there with her legs spread for three hours. But you're just supposed to examine her, not screw her."

"Sure," Sonders said mildly. "That the cyst you were telling me about?"

"Right. And when you get through, you might just drop down to my office. We're going to have a little talk."

Rob returned to his patients, brushing a bewildered Dora aside. A few minutes later he found Dora and Agnes huddled with Terry in the coffee room, whispering to each other. They stopped abruptly as he poured some coffee. Rob forced a laugh. "What are we having back here —some kind of a wake?" he said.

Agnes flushed and turned away, while Dora busied herself with the autoclave. But Terry said, "Dr. Tanner, what's going on? Dr. Sonders and Dr. Isaacs are in that office and I swear they're throwing things at each other."

"Don't sweat it," Rob said lightly.

"But the patients are all upset. They could hear Dr. Isaacs shouting clear down in the waiting room."

"He's just a little stirred up. He'll cool off. Now let's break this up, okay? We've all got work to do."

In half an hour, Sonders emerged from Isaacs' office and walked out the back door, curiously subdued. Then about four-thirty Isaacs himself took off without a word or a glance at Rob. Two hours later he called from the hospital to tell Rob that he'd already made rounds so Rob wouldn't have to bother. Even over the phone there was an odd, cool distance to the man's voice. Rob hung up and drove on home, his mind filled with a sense of impending disaster he could not shrug away.

Next morning he started for the hospital early, since it was Sonders' regular Tuesday operating day and Rob was scheduled to assist with a long and tedious varicose vein stripping. As he started up Hospital Hill he was amazed to see Sonders' car come careening down, swerving to miss him, barely pausing at the highway and then turning north to roar off toward Missoula. Rob nearly stalled his Vega, staring back over his shoulder. He had caught just a glimpse of the surgeon, a snarl on his face as he skidded by. Moments later Rob met Martin Isaacs coming down the ramp from the hospital. "Where's Harry going?" he said.

"Back to Missoula," Isaacs snapped.

"But he's got that vein case at eight."

"That's been canceled." Isaacs started to push by, then paused. "I've got a new baby in there for you to check, and then you'd better hop down to the office. I'm calling a meeting for eight-thirty."

Rob walked into the hospital, now thoroughly puzzled. *Something* had obviously happened during the night. Esther was busy mopping down the OR floor, Happy was tied up in the newborn nursery, and Sara Davis was hovering over a woman—apparently, a new mother—recovering from general anesthesia. Sure enough, the vein case had been canceled, with Isaacs' initials on the order. As Rob checked out the newborn he looked up at Happy. "What's going on here, anyway?"

"I don't know, Doctor. I just walked in at seven and they handed me this baby."

"Caesarean?"

336

"I guess. It's Francine Stein's baby. Agnes brought it out of the operating room."

Down at the clinic, Rob found Terry fluttering timidly outside his office door, talking in whispers to a grim-faced Dora. "What's wrong now?" he said.

"I've got to squeeze some patients into your schedule today," Terry said.

"How come?"

"Dr. Isaacs told me to. He said Dr. Sonders won't be in, and I don't know *what's* going on. . . ." The girl's voice wavered; she was close to tears.

"Well, I'll find out." Rob walked down to Isaacs' office. The big man was sitting at his desk, polishing his glasses. His face looked blanched and somber, almost chalky. "About time," he growled when he saw Rob. "Get Jerry in here too."

Rob summoned Jerry, and they went back to Isaacs' office together, closing the door behind them. The older doctor blinked up at them owlishly. "Okay," Rob said. "What's going on with Sonders?"

"He's gone," Isaacs said.

"Gone?"

"Washed up. Finished. I fired him this morning. He won't be back. Our new man will be here in two weeks, and that's that. We can backlog our routine surgery until then."

Rob and Jerry looked at one another. Then Rob said, "You just fired him—like that?"

"That's right."

"But last week we all agreed to ride things out for a while."

"I changed my mind," Isaacs said.

"Why? Because I caught him with the nurse?"

Isaacs flushed. "It's not just that. Other things too."

"Well, you didn't talk to *me* about any other things," Rob said, "and I haven't changed *my* mind. I was even making a little headway—"

Isaacs' hands clenched into fists. "Look, I don't give a shit whether you've changed your mind or not. I got crowded into an emergency Caesarean on a woman last night, and I called that bastard to come help me and he said to call you. When I told him I didn't want you, I wanted *him,* he told me to go fuck myself. Well, that was the last straw."

"Why didn't you want me, all of a sudden?"

"Because I happened to need a surgeon, that's why. That woman had fat on her two feet thick. I needed some real expertise, not just more hands, so I spent a whole damned hour up there on the phone trying to reach the bastard, and by the time I got his load of lip, there wasn't any time to call you."

"And you've already hired this new man?" Rob said.

"You bet your ass I have. No point messing around. He's been ready to come for the last three months, so I told him to come ahead."

"And we don't even get a look at him first?"

Isaacs looked startled. "What do you think, he's got three heads?"

"Who knows?" Rob said.

"Now, what in the hell do you mean by that?"

"I mean you seem to have this all tied up in a neat little bundle before anybody else has a chance to say anything."

Isaacs' face turned angry red. "What's there to say? We had to get rid of Sonders, but we also need a surgeon. And we haven't got time to screw around, either."

"Well, Rob's got a point," DeForrest said mildly. "We're all going to have to work with this new man. We should at least have a chance to sit down and talk to him before we're all committed."

"Oh, Christ!" Isaacs said. "All you ever want to do is sit down and talk. Well, that's not good enough. We've got to *act,* and if you guys can't trust me to act for our own best interests, then I've got the wrong set of partners."

"Martin, trust is a two-way street," Rob said. "I don't know about Jerry, but this looks like a power play to me, and I don't like it. I'm not so sure we have to fire Sonders, and if you want to keep pretending that we're some sort of a partnership here, then let's back up and see what Sonders has to say."

"*No.*" Isaacs slammed his fist down on the desk and lurched to his feet. "We're not backing up, and we're not going to sit and talk about it, either. I don't want Sonders in this office again. I fired him, and I hired his replacement, and if you two don't like it, you can go suck rocks, because that's the way it's going to be."

Isaacs glared at them, first Rob, then Jerry. Then he hunched his shoulders forward and walked out the door and up the corridor. Moments later they heard his car leaving the parking lot. For a long moment Rob and Jerry stared at each other. Then Jerry shrugged and pulled himself to his feet. "Well, so much for Harry Sonders," he said. "And up the organization." He opened the door and shuffled down toward his office. Rob Tanner sat in silence for a long while before he, too, came to life and went back for a tasteless cup of coffee.

One thing was sure, he thought. The ambiguities were over. Now the battle was joined.

# 28

For Ellie it had been the longest and coldest week of her life. Her anger and resentment had faded into remorse as she watched her husband move from day to day like a stranger she didn't know. She should never have let it go on this long, she told herself over and over. She should never have let a ridiculous, nasty fight freeze into day after day of wordless hostility—but she could not find the words to break the deadlock, and Rob didn't seem to care, and that made it even more impossible. She knew, of course, that there was far more here than some trifling minor conflict. They'd had their fights before—he could be arrogant, and she could be stubborn, and friction caused heat—but never anything like this. And now, to top it off, the word about Sonders, and the overwhelming sense of disaster closing in on her, as Rob drifted further away, and absolutely nothing she could think of to do about it.

She finished the Tuesday morning breakfast dishes, made the bed, then wandered about restlessly. Rob had told her about Sonders the night before at dinner, bluntly, angrily, the outrage unmistakable in his voice. "He's out. Martin fired him last night. Martin had a Caesarean, and Sonders wouldn't come, so Martin fired him. Just like he said he would."

Ellie had shaken her head. "If the man just refuses to come when he's needed, how can you argue?"

"You can't," Rob said tightly. "That's what's so goddamned frustrating."

"So what do you do for a surgeon?"

"By strange coincidence, there's a new man waiting in the wings. Name of Tom Stone. He'll be here in two weeks. And if he happens to be a lemon, we're stuck."

*And even if he doesn't, we're still stuck,* Ellie thought now, helplessly. *With Martin Isaacs. And who knows whom he's going to stomp on next? Or what will happen to Rob if he keeps on fighting?* Staring out at the river in the pale morning sun, she wished desperately for someone she could talk to. *But who? Belle? She's a dear, but I can't torment her with this sort of thing. She needs help more than I do.* Her hand touched her abdomen, and she almost thought she felt life there, even though it was far too early. *And the baby, too. Of all wretched wrong times—*

The telephone jarred her alert. For a moment she couldn't place the woman's voice on the line. Then: "Jennie! Is that you?"

"Yes, it's me." There was a long pause. Then Jennie said, "Did you hear about Dr. Sonders?"

"Yes, I heard."

"I wondered . . ." Jennie paused again. "I was thinking, if it was possible . . . maybe you could . . . come have lunch with me?"

"Today? Of course."

"I thought maybe . . . about one?" The voice was distant, almost ethereal. "Unless you have other plans . . ."

"No, Jennie. I'd love to come. At one."

A moment later she was staring at a dead receiver. Slowly she set it back on the hook, turned back to morning housekeeping chores. About eleven she showered, found herself wondering, inanely, what she ought to wear and settling for a sweater and skirt. With an hour still to wait, she debated having a glass of sherry, then vetoed the notion and cringed inwardly as the thought came: *What if she's drunk when I get there? Then what do I do?*

Jennie wasn't drunk, or at least showed no sign of it when she admitted Ellie into the darkened living room. Nor had she dressed up for the occasion, either; she was wearing a shapeless pink and gray garment that could have been a robe or a morning coat or almost anything else. The kitchen was brighter, with windows looking out toward the mountains, and Jennie led Ellie back there while she put finishing touches on the shrimp Louis she'd prepared for lunch. She offered a cocktail, which Ellie reluctantly accepted, poured herself some tomato juice, sipped it, and then said, "Maybe I'll have a small drink too," and poured a glass heavy with bourbon and ice. For a while the smallest of small talk limped and staggered and lurched along, haltingly. Then finally, with lunch before them in the dining nook, Jennie took a deep breath and said, "I understand you're pregnant."

Ellie nodded. "I suppose Martin told you."

"Oh, my, no. Martin never tells me anything about . . . patients. He's very strict about that. No, I think it was Ernie at the gas station."

"Ernie's a regular fountain of information," Ellie said wryly.

"Yes, he is." Jennie hesitated. "I suppose Rob's . . . pleased."

"Not exactly," Ellie said.

"Oh, dear."

"But he's adjusting. I guess."

Jennie poked at the shrimp, hardly eating. "We had a baby once, you know."

"No, I didn't know."

"Oh, yes. It was years ago. A little boy, but he was defective. Badly retarded. I wanted to keep him, but Martin wouldn't hear of it. They took him to the state hospital, and then of course he died. We've never had another. Martin . . . wouldn't hear of it."

Ellie stared at the woman, at a loss. "I'm sorry," she said.

"I hardly think of it anymore," Jennie said. "Hardly ever." She turned back to her lunch, and silence reigned for a moment. Then: "I suppose Rob told you about Dr. Sonders."

"He told me last night," Ellie said. "He was very angry."

"Oh, he mustn't be. Martin just gets carried away . . ."

"He must have hated Harry Sonders, to do a thing like that."

"Oh, yes, he hated him." Jennie glanced out the window, almost furtively, then leaned forward as if passing a secret. "Harry wouldn't do what Martin wanted, you see, and Martin won't tolerate that. Martin has . . . to have everything—" She turned away suddenly, her voice breaking, fists clenched at her side. "Oh, I don't know what to do," she said, barely audible. "I don't know how I can stand it any longer."

"Jennie, don't," Ellie said.

"No, no, I've got to tell you," Jennie said. "That's why I asked you here, to tell you, to warn you. Rob mustn't be angry, he mustn't try to fight him, because Martin will *never let him win.*"

"Jennie, that's crazy. You make him sound like some kind of a monster."

*"Monster!"* She stared at Ellie. "You just don't know that man."

"But I can't make Rob stop fighting him."

"You've *got* to. Listen." Jennie leaned forward, her voice almost choked. "You've got to listen. You've still got a chance, the two of you. I'm trapped here; there's nothing left for me to do in this hell hole but wish I were dead. But you're not trapped yet. You're young, you can still go somewhere else, get away before he crushes you both, or turns Rob into a carbon copy—"

Ellie stood up abruptly. "I'm sorry, but I've got to go," she said.

"You don't believe me."

"I don't know. I—I don't know what I believe anymore."

"You've got to believe me. You've got to get away." Jennie trailed behind her, wraithlike, tugging feebly at Ellie's sweater as she headed for the front door. "Please believe me. Get away while you can—"

Ellie whirled on her. *"Stop* that. Don't *say* that anymore." She took Jennie's shoulders, shook her hard. "Now I've got to go. I'm sorry, but I've got to think."

She started down the porch steps, then heard a sound like a sob from Jennie. "Ellie? Will you help me?"

Ellie stopped. "I don't know how to help you."

"I . . . need help."

"Yes, of course I'll help. I'll do whatever I can. But you'll have to tell me what." She found her way to the car then, and drove off, refusing to look back. Numbly she headed for home, back toward the river, to the little house. Once in the driveway, she sat clutching the wheel for a long moment before going in.

Belle Foreman was sitting at the kitchen table having a cup of tea. "Hope you don't mind, dearie. These old legs of mine wouldn't take me another step, with those bags to carry."

"No, no; of course I don't mind."

Belle peered up at her. "What's the trouble, dear? You don't look too good."

"I don't feel too good." Ellie slumped into a chair, then suddenly put her face into her hands and started weeping.

Belle watched her keenly for a moment, then reached out and stroked her hair with a gnarled hand, touched her cheek. "Now, now, now. It can't be that bad."

"I don't know," Ellie sobbed. "I just had lunch with Jennie Isaacs."

"That must have been dreamy," Belle said.

"Oh, Belle, you just don't know. It was absolutely awful." Ellie looked up at the old woman. "I don't think I've ever seen a woman so frightened in my life. She was just terrified. And she kept babbling things about how Martin was going to destroy Rob, and how we had to get away while we could, and how she wished she was dead . . ."

"Well, that's nothing new," Belle said dryly. "She's pretty near made it a couple of times, too."

Ellie stared. "What do you mean?"

Belle looked uncomfortable. "Silly things, mostly. Like last spring when she ate a whole bottle of tranquilizers, and they spent all night pumping her stomach out, and then Martin took her to some private funny farm in Spokane to get her head straightened out. Not that it helped much. Couple of years ago she tried slashing her wrists, but she made sure Martin found her in time. And then another try a year or two before that. It's an old story."

"Not to me, it isn't," Ellie said, "and I think it's appalling. How do you know all this?"

"Never mind how I know," Belle said. "I've got eyes and ears. And I've known about Jennie and Martin for years." She sighed. "It wasn't always as bad as this. Martin's not an *evil* man, exactly. He's just got his values all scrambled up. He's probably helped more people in this valley than he's buried, and that's saying something, for a doctor." Belle paused, ruminating. "And it wasn't all Martin's fault, either. Never has been all his fault, I suppose. Jennie was weak, and passive, and dependent, clinging to him like a rock on his back. She'd never stand up to him, even when she should have. She'd never get up gumption to say, 'No, it's going to be like *this,*' and sometimes a woman just *has* to, with a difficult man on her hands, if she wants to keep on living like a human being. And even at that, things didn't really get bad until Mike Cumley got killed in the woods, and Happy turned to Martin, and Jennie found out."

"Oh, dear," Ellie said.

"Well, I'll give the devil his due," Belle said. "Martin was good to Happy. He got her back on her feet, and he loved her and made her whole again. And he was discreet—but of course Jennie soon got wind of it. She really tried to fight him then, but it was far too late; he was too strong, and didn't care anymore, and he just beat her down to a raw stump. And it hasn't gotten any better with time, either. Jennie's a

344

game woman, in her way; she just gets to where she can't take it anymore, is all."

"But why should she come to me with all these horrible things?"

Belle shook her head helplessly. "Maybe she's honestly trying to warn you," she said, "and maybe you need to be warned. Maybe she sees history repeating itself—and maybe you ring a bell in her mind somehow."

"But *I* can't make Rob give in to Martin. And we can't just pack up and leave, either. That's ridiculous. Rob would never stand for it."

"No, I suppose he wouldn't. And what Rob won't stand for isn't going to happen, I suppose." Belle pulled at her lower lip and gave Ellie a sharp look. "You know what I think, dearie? I think Rob sounds more like Martin Isaacs every day. Kind of scary, in a way." She struggled to her feet with a sigh and began groping for her bags. "Yes, it's downright scary. The resemblance is just uncanny."

"But what can I do?" Ellie said as she followed Belle to the door.

The old woman shook her head. "I wish I knew, dear. Maybe you should listen to Jennie."

After she had gone, Ellie walked to the windows, leaned her forehead on the glass and stared sightlessly out across the river. A long while later she took a deep breath, walked briskly into the kitchen and pulled the evening's roast out of the refrigerator, her jaw tight. *Maybe Belle is right,* she thought grimly. *Maybe I just haven't seen it quite that way. And scary it is. But the last one I'm going to listen to is Jennie Isaacs. . . .*

# 29

While Ellie was talking to Belle that afternoon, Rob was on the phone from his office.

"I thought you were never going to call," Chris said over the line.

"It's been a bitch of a week," Rob said. "I'm not sure who's on first anymore."

"But the date's still on?"

"God, yes. If I don't get out of here soon I'm going to blow apart in ten pieces."

"Well, we certainly can't have that. So where and when?"

"I can get out of here by four tomorrow," Rob said. "Take your jeep up the Lake Marian road. A mile beyond where it runs into gravel there's a turnaround and the road becomes a jeep trail. I'll meet you there at four-thirty." Rob glanced up at Dora, fluttering at his office door. "Got to cut it now. I'll see you."

At dinner that night he told Ellie about the medical meeting in Missoula. "Martin usually goes," he said, "but he thinks I should go for a change, and meet some of the other docs in person."

"Good," Ellie said firmly. "I can go along and do some shopping."

Rob set his fork carefully down on his plate. "This may not be the best time for that," he said.

"Don't be silly. I need a change."

"Hell, you can go any day of the week."

346

"Oh, I don't like to drive to Missoula alone, and I can't stand Amy DeForrest. Anyway, she never decides to go till the last minute, and by then I've always got something else planned."

"Well, look, this really isn't a very good time," Rob said. "I have to leave the office before four, and it's strictly a business affair anyway. I don't think wives are invited."

Ellie laughed. "I don't want to go to your old staff meeting. I'll just go shopping. I really need a new winter coat. And the wallpaper trim I want for the kitchen. I can't find *anything* decent out here."

Rob picked at his roast beef. "We wouldn't even get there until six," he said. "The stores would all be closed."

"Not on Wednesdays. They're all open till nine. Look, if it's like the Graystone staff meetings, they'll serve up last week's salmon croquettes, and you won't eat anyway. We can go out somewhere after the meeting and have a nice steak dinner, maybe have a chance to talk a little. We haven't had a night on the town for years, it seems like."

Rob took a deep breath. "I know, and we probably need to do that, too, before long. But this time I've really been hoping to go by myself. Just get in the car alone and drive away from this crappy little town, just shake the whole thing off for a few hours, all by myself. Okay?"

"Well, sure, I suppose so." She looked at him. "It just seemed—but it doesn't really matter." She took up her plate and went quickly into the kitchen.

Rob followed her. "Look, Ellie, this whole damned scene keeps crowding me until I've got to have a breather. And this firing of Sonders —I don't know what Martin's going to do next, and somehow I'm right in the middle."

"Oh, I *know* you're fretting, but I don't have any *answers* to those problems," Ellie burst out. "All I know is you never tell me what you're thinking, and we hardly ever see each other anymore, and we practically never talk to each other, and whenever we do we end up fighting—"

"Honey, we just had a nice camping trip."

"One camping trip isn't enough."

"Well, all I'm talking about is one foolish meeting."

"I know. It doesn't matter."

"You want to go shopping, fine. We'll take my next day off and go shopping all day long, do it up brown, anything you'd like."

"Sure. That'd be—great."

"So come on back and drink your coffee, huh?"

347

She came back to the table with coffee cups. "You want me to heat up your roast?"

"No, it's fine." Rob ate without enthusiasm, then put too much sugar in his coffee, went to the sink to dump it out and poured another cup. Back at the table his hand was shaking as he stared at the coffee cup.

Finally Ellie broke the silence. "I had lunch with Jennie today."

"Oh? How did things go?"

"She was very upset."

"Far as I can see, she's always upset," Rob said.

"Maybe so." Ellie paused. "Belle says she's attempted suicide. Took too many pills or something."

"That's not hard to believe, either. But that's got to be Martin's headache, not mine."

"It could be why he goes off on these tangents all the time," she said.

"Well, if that's true, then we're *really* in trouble. Because somehow I don't think Jennie Isaacs is going to get well real quick." He pushed away from the table, sensing that he had to get out of there while he was still ahead. "Look, I'm going up to make rounds. I'll see you later."

Turning out onto the highway, his heart pounding like a kid almost caught stealing, he felt a wave of self-loathing at the lies he'd just told. *Very smooth, a regular three-star performance, really tugged at the old heartstrings. A little more practice and you may get good at it. But then, what else? You knew there'd be lying sooner or later.* At least, he thought, she didn't sound suspicious. And if he hadn't moved fast, cooled it right then and there, she'd sure as hell be trotting off to town with him, and that would be that with Chris. And what would he tell *her?* That the little wife decided to go to Missoula with him, so the date was off? Make him look like a goddamned ass. *Well, maybe so. Maybe that's just what you are, Bright Eyes. What do you think you're planning with that woman? Just a nice social evening at Ed's cabin? Somebody new and exciting to talk over your troubles with? Sure, like pigs have wings.*

He pulled into Ernie's gas station, sat waiting for the tank to be filled, tapping the steering wheel angrily. Christ, it wasn't *his* fault things were sour with Ellie. What the hell *was* happening, anyway? Every time she came near him lately he tightened up, pulled back, wanted to get *away*. It wasn't just the baby; things were going sour before that turned up, the old emotional contact was fading—or had

348

they ever really touched at all? Why did he feel trapped whenever she came close, feel this fierce need to keep her off, to defend himself? Sometimes it seemed she was always in the way, every way he turned, until recently always agreeable, sweet, submissive, but always *there*. . . .

He paid for the gas, started up toward the hospital, but then changed his mind and drove around to park behind the clinic instead. Letting himself in, he sat down in the darkened office, rubbing his forehead with his hand. He needed to think, needed to work things out without interruption for a minute. Seemed that every time he really started to get to the bottom of things there was a phone call, or some new hassle with Martin, or some squabble with Ellie, and now the thing with the baby to top things off . . .

Ellie. There was the trouble. An Ellie he couldn't talk to anymore. An Ellie who wouldn't let him alone. An Ellie who made him cringe every time he thought about her. *What had happened with Ellie?* It hadn't always been like that. There was a time, once, when they'd talked, laughed, had a good time, really *enjoyed* each other—

*Or had they, really? Or merely thought they did?*

Oh, God. The illusions. The will to believe. So many things they took for granted, and never talked about at all. Christ knew they'd both been busy beyond endurance back then, he with his endless succession of clinics and lectures and conferences and rounds, running his ass off just to keep on top of things—and she with her nursing work on the special pediatrics floor, taking care of the toughest of all problems, all the Christ-awful, tragic kids' cases that wouldn't respond to routine nursing, where they watched the *child*, not the shift, and sometimes worked twenty-four to forty-eight hours straight through. Sure they'd seemed close in those days, the few minutes a day they saw each other at all. Sure things were smooth when connecting at home by chance was like an unexpected date. The sex was always good, when they had a chance; she had a good healthy appetite, a "reaction to her Puritan upbringing," as she told him, only half laughing, and he was not exactly indifferent, either. But *talk?* Well, hell. There wasn't any time to talk in those days.

*And now?*

He shook his head, angry at himself, angry at his sense of helplessness and frustration. *There's got to be a way somehow.* But now there was also Chris Erickson, and that was something else. So he should forget her? No way. Why should he? *So she doesn't fit in with the rules.*

349

*So the hell with the rules. What actually happened, anyway? An unexpected thing, a brief instant of contact, a minute of vulnerability. But nothing that mattered. . . .*

*Sure. So lie to yourself too. That'll help.*

He shook his head helplessly. He knew it sounded phony—but was it, really? It wasn't just some girl to be laid. More than anything, he had to *talk* to somebody, talk his heart out. Why not to Chris? He could control it, keep it above the waist. Two civilized people pausing in the middle of a hurricane . . . *Candles blowing on the table, the wind ruffling her hair, her eyes catching his in a simple honest moment of human contact, her breasts*—well, never mind her breasts. She might have thoughts, ideas, suggestions. A warm, open discussion, but stopping it right there—telling her reasonably, dispassionately, that it was really a foolish risk; if somebody found out, nobody would understand —and she agreeing, regretfully but dispassionately, yes, it *was* foolish, another time, another place and things might have been different, but under the circumstances . . .

*You ass. You puking, pusillanimous, pluperfect ass. As if there's anything dispassionate about her. And you're going to control things!* He pushed himself to his feet, suddenly fiercely angry at himself. Well, why not stop it right now? One quick phone call, that's all it would take. He reached for the phone, started to dial, and heard the curiously tape-distorted sound of Terry's voice saying, "I'm sorry, the clinic is closed for the night. Dr. Tanner is on call. You may reach him by dialing WEstwood 2–4577, or call the hospital, WEstwood 2–3335. I will repeat the numbers. . . ."

He dropped the receiver back on the hook. After a while he locked the clinic door behind him and drove on up to the hospital. It was quiet, the patients were all asleep, and there were no calls for him. After a solitary cup of coffee or two he went home.

He had to talk to Ellie; that was obvious. Hell, why not tomorrow night? Go ahead and *take* her to Missoula and let Chris cool her heels at the turnaround, and that would be that. Maybe he should even say something to Ellie tonight, make some kind of a start, get something going. . . .

But the night light was on over the back door, and Ellie was already in bed, asleep, and she moved away as he undressed and slipped into bed, and the moment passed. And after a restless, ragged night of sleep, Wednesday started at 4:30 A.M. with a phone call from the hospital. There'd been a fight at the Wagon Wheel and Matt Harlow had been

350

sliced up pretty bad with a broken beer bottle, and maybe he'd better come sew him up, and when he finally surfaced from that it was pushing noon and Martin was storming like a madman and he was overdue in the office, and talking with Ellie was far from his mind, and the notion of scratching his date with Chris was the last thing in the *world* he was going to buy, and that was the way it was. . . .

# 30

When he saw daylight that Wednesday morning, it was raining—not the half-hearted on-and-off drizzle so common during the past autumn months, but a pounding, drenching downpour of a winter rain, sweeping in sheets across the highway, driven against rooftops and windows by an icy wind coming down from the pass. By ten o'clock there were travelers' warnings out for all the mountain passes, and trucks lumbered down the highway, piled high with wet snow and dropping huge, splashy chunks behind them as they ground on through. When Rob headed to the office after sewing up Matt Harlow, the storm sewers in town were overflowing and the gutters carried muddy rivers, while outlying roads lay under six inches of undrained water.

At the clinic he found Jerry DeForrest back having coffee. "Say, what happened to your nutty patient?" he asked. "The one that was washing his car at three A.M."

"Him?" Jerry shrugged. "I shipped him into town. Lanovitz thought we'd better move. He wants his own x-rays, maybe a cerebral arteriogram, maybe a CAT scan, and then he's going to open up his skull. So I packed him off by ambulance."

"What does Lanovitz think?"

Jerry grinned. "He's too smart to try to guess without having all the parts. Maybe a tumor, maybe a brain abscess—he wouldn't be pinned

352

down. But it's something above the ears. He'll be calling me in a day or so."

"Well, keep me posted." Rob turned to go, then paused, listening. "What's Martin hollering about down there? Sounds like he's giving Bev Bessler hell."

"Production figures," Jerry said with a sigh. "We're not putting enough money on the books, and he's telling Bev to get after us to charge more for night calls."

"Money's bound to go down without any surgery," Rob observed.

"Yeah; well, you can point that out to him if you feel like it. I'm not going to." And with that, Jerry disappeared down the hall.

Moments later Isaacs himself came roaring up to Rob's office, waving a big sheaf of papers. "Look at these figures," he fumed. "They're absolutely awful."

"So I've heard," Rob said.

"Well, we've got to do something about it," Isaacs said. "We've got more patients coming in here than ever before, but our total charges are going *down*. At this rate we're barely going to be able to pay the new surgeon when he comes. *My* charges are up, all right, but you're hardly breaking even."

Rob sighed. "Martin, I haven't exactly been sitting on my hands lately."

"Then you're not charging for your work," Isaacs said. "You're giving your time away free. You can't spend two hours doing a physical exam and charge just twenty dollars and expect to pay the overhead. And all these no-charges! A mother with a kid for a well-baby checkup brings three other kids along too, and you check all four of them and then only charge for the baby—"

"The others only take a minute or two."

"Okay, but then you see some kid with a mile-long problem and spend forever with him and only charge an office call fee. Or people like old Maggie Muldoon. You had her in your office the other day for *three solid hours,* just talking to her."

"It was only one hour. And old Maggie's got nobody else to talk to these days, since Harry died."

"Then *charge* her for one hour!"

"Hell, Martin, she can't even pay for an office call."

"Then let her go on Medicare. That's what it's for."

"Yes, and Maggie must be one of the last of the Hoover Republicans, too. She wouldn't go on Medicare if the President himself knelt down and begged her."

"Oh, shit," Isaacs said. "So shoot down everything I say. But I'm telling you, if we don't get our production up pretty soon, we're *all* going to be on welfare. What's more, we can't go on without some major improvements around here. We already need another wing on this building, but the practice can barely pay me the rent on what we've got. Ginny in the lab has been begging for new equipment for the last three years, but that's three thousand bucks we haven't got. And as for that old x-ray machine back there—well, Jesus. We're irradiating the whole damned valley every time we take a chest film, it's a wonder Dora's fingers aren't dropping off, but a new machine with proper shielding would cost us fifty grand at least. So go tell *that* to your Maggie Muldoon."

Isaacs started off down the hall again, still clutching the tally sheets in hand. "By the way," he said. "I just sent a woman up to the hospital with an atrial flutter. Take a look at her when you make rounds."

"I can't," Rob said. "I'm going to that meeting in Missoula tonight, remember? I'll be leaving at four o'clock."

"Yeah, that's right. Well, say hello to the guys for me." Isaacs turned back down the corridor.

Rob began seeing the few of his patients who had braved the foul weather outside. Around two o'clock Ellie called. "Honey, you don't really want to drive to Missoula in a storm like this. Why not just bag it?"

"It'll probably stop before I leave," Rob said.

"The forecast says all afternoon and night. The wind's so bad I'd swear our roof is coming off, and there's a great big puddle in the fireplace."

"It'll be all right," Rob said. "Quit worrying."

"Well, be careful. How late will you be?"

Rob hesitated. "Maybe pretty late, if those guys go out for drinks after the meeting."

"Honey, don't drink too much. You don't know that road very well."

He gripped the phone tightly. *Patience, boy. Don't blow it now.* "I know, kid," he said finally. "I'll be careful. But don't wait up."

By two-thirty the waiting room was empty, with dozens of cancellations because of the storm. A few minutes later Martin Isaacs emerged, muttering that the place looked like a goddamned morgue, and took off,

354

leaving word that he'd be back by four. A little later even Jerry left, in haste, with some comment about water in his basement.

And still it rained. Rob leafed through some journals impatiently. Then Dora appeared, with an odd look, and pointed to his examining room. "You've got a patient," she said.

Belle Foreman sat perched on the end of his examining table, her long woolen coat drenched with rain and draining puddles onto the floor. Rob looked at her, startled. "Good Lord! What are *you* doing out on a day like this?"

"Oh, these old legs of mine have been aching a bit," Belle said, with a vague gesture toward her extremities. "And I figured you wouldn't be too busy today."

"Well, let's take a look." Rob checked her joints and reflexes, listened to her heart and lungs. "Belle, there's not a thing in the world wrong with you."

"Of course there's not," she said, looking indignant. "Leastwise, nothing serious. I never said there was."

"Then what are you doing in my office?"

"It's the only way I could figure to see you," Belle said. "You don't seem to be home much anymore."

Rob took a deep breath. "So what's on your mind?" he said.

"I came here to talk about Ellie."

Rob flushed. "Look, with all due respect, Ellie's problems and mine are none of your business."

"Maybe *your* problems aren't," Belle flared, "but Ellie's are, and I just can't sit still and watch it any longer. I've seen what's happening to that girl, and I'm telling you straight out, you'd better start listening to her while you've still got a chance."

Rob's lips tightened. "Belle, you're a fine lady in your way, and I have a lot of respect for you, except for one thing: your nose is too long."

"Maybe so, but I don't care. I'm going to say my piece anyway." She leaned forward intensely. "That woman of yours is too precious to be treated this way, and if you can't see that, you need to be *told.*" She looked up belligerently. "Now let me tell you something, Dr. Tanner. This is the first time in twenty long years that I've left my house to go plead with somebody for something. That wife of yours has done incredible things for me, and she doesn't even know it. Before Ellie came to Twin Forks, I sat back there hiding in my nest in the woods with my cats and my memories and twenty years of bitterness, but in a few short months Ellie has changed all that. She's brought me back to life. She's made me care, actually *care*, about somebody else—and believe me, that is no small thing. She's warm and she's loving and she's sensitive, and she deserves far better than she's getting from you, and I see bad trouble coming. I think you'd better start sniffing the wind while you still have time. Now, that's all you're going to hear from me. I've said it, and I'll be going." She eased herself down off the table.

Rob stared at her. "And now what are you going to do? Walk back home in the rain?"

"Little rain never hurt anybody," Belle said, adjusting her blue beret.

"Well, don't be silly." Rob threw open the corridor door. "Dora! Get on your coat and drive Belle home, will you?" *Goddamned old fool.* He swung on Belle. "And *don't argue* with me."

They went on out to Dora's car and Rob went back to his journals, drinking coffee, half angry and half bemused at the old woman's visit. It was three-fifteen now, and he began glancing at his watch every five minutes, growing steadily more restive, almost expecting a call from Chris at any minute canceling their plans—but no call came. Finally, at three forty-five he packed his bag, told Dora he was on his way, and headed out the door. He made one brief stop at a small grocery at the edge of town to buy steaks, potatoes, a jug of wine, a bag of ice and some bourbon. *Might as well do it up brown,* he thought. Then he headed south on the highway with the rain pelting his windshield.

He almost missed the Lake Marian turnoff, then drove through water up to his hub caps before the road started to climb. Soon he reached the gravel, and drove slowly, avoiding soft spots and puddles as best he could as the road wound upward through the forest. It was almost pitch black now and his headlights cast only a feeble glow. *Christ,* he thought. *I hope she hasn't chickened out. And I hope Ed's roof is sound up there, or we're going to be cold and wet.*

Finally, with his wheels spinning in mud for the last fifty yards, he reached the turnaround, nosed the car into the brush and turned off his motor and lights. There was no sign of Chris's jeep. He looked at his watch. *Four-thirty. Well, she's bound to be here soon.* He cranked down the window, felt the rain on his face. Then he saw an arc of light down the road and the old green jeep pulled in behind him. He could see Chris's gamin face peering out at him from under the hood of a red plaid rain slicker.

He waded through ankle-deep mud to the jeep, motioned her over to the passenger seat, and climbed in behind the wheel. She leaned over to kiss him soundly. "Whee!" she said. "That's some road."

"It gets worse before we get there," he said. Water was pouring through cracks in the jeep shroud. "God, you must be soaked."

"Oh, I am, I *am*—isn't it wonderful? First decent rain in six months; I could just get out and *wallow* in it if it weren't so bloody cold. *There.*" She finally got her head free from the rain hood and shook a damp curl back from her forehead. "I hope you brought some food. I'm ravenous."

Rob grinned and threw the jeep into gear. "Just pray that the firewood's dry or you'll eat raw steak."

"Raw, cooked—what's the difference? Drive on, Merlin."

Slowly Rob drove up the muddy trail, sploshing through foot-deep puddles, slithering off the higher shoulders into the ruts and then ramming the jeep sideways to get back out of them. For all the hard driving, he found himself relaxing more completely than at any time since the morning Sonders had been fired. Suddenly it seemed as if the practice problems were sliding away behind him, the nagging depression, the medical worries, the irritating infighting, even the scraps with Ellie, and he felt completely at ease. *Well, wasn't that what Chris was all about, really? An escape from the practice, and Isaacs, and Ellie, and everything else intolerable?* Glancing at the girl beside him, he felt a sudden wave of exhilaration more keen than he could remember for years. A whole long evening without problems, without worries, without arguments or hassles . . . "It's just a little way now," he said. "Up over this notch and down to the lake."

Chris leaned forward like an eager child, peering through the windshield at the blackness. Suddenly the car started downward, slithering through the mud. At one point they glimpsed black water covered with whitecaps in the car light. Then the road turned suddenly, and the little cabin was directly ahead. "Oh, Rob, it's *beautiful*. Like a magic cabin in the forest. And I do so love storms."

He helped her out and they ran for the cabin door, leaning into the wind and rain. Rob found the key, undid the padlock on the door, and they pushed inside. He groped for the kerosene lamp he remembered on the table, got its flickery light going. Then he turned and caught the girl in his arms, felt her press to him as he kissed her. "Hey, let's get a fire going," she said, laughing. "Time enough for this later."

There was dry wood and paper on the hearth, just as Ed Butler had left it, and the roof was sound. Rob sniffed the air, slightly musty with odd overtones of pine scent. As he got the fire started, Chris seized the lamp and went about the cabin peeking and poking and prying with squeals of delight, like an excited puppy, totally entranced with the simple rustic charm of the place—the hand-hewn beams and split-cedar roof, the massive granite fireplace. Once the fire was roaring there, the tiny cabin was snug and dry and warm, the interior reflecting the simple tastes of the man who had built it: a cedar-slab table; chairs and bed built from tamarack poles; the majestic antlers of a royal elk rising above the mantelpiece log, with a sweat-stained red hunting cap and a sheath knife hanging from its spikes; a huge elkskin rug, fully four inches thick, on the floor before the fire; heavy homemade quilts on the bed; and a pantry packed with cans of cocoa and pork and beans. "Rob, it's like out of a fairy story."

"I know." He threw a log onto the fire. "Now, then. Maybe a drink to finish warming up."

"What do you have?"

"I brought some bourbon, but I see a bottle of Irish over there on the shelf. Old Ed wouldn't mind."

"Oh, good, make it Irish—and put some out for the leprechauns."

He made drinks and they sprawled in the rustic chairs before the fire. Chris's cheeks were already glowing from the heat. "So how are the moths?" he said.

"Okay, I guess." She sighed. "Sometimes I think I'm spending lots of time getting nowhere at all, and other times I think I'm really on the right trail. Pheromones are very spooky things."

Rob nodded. "Thomas had a lovely description of them in *The Lives of a Cell*," he said.

"Yes, and he was so right—nobody knows exactly how they work. They may have special odors, or maybe even colors or some other wave characteristics we can't pick up, but when an insect or an animal releases them, there's a powerful response. A sex response, or a feeding response, or a migrating response—hard to pin down or isolate. It's like the falling tree that only makes a noise if somebody's near enough to hear it. You can only tell the pheromone is there by the way some creature responds to it. Primitive, but subtle."

"And you're working it all out?"

"I don't know. It's all very slow. If I were really lucky, maybe in two or three years I might end up with a pure strain of moths with males that can't detect or respond to the female sex pheromones, and then maybe—just maybe—I could try some controlled testing in the field. But you can fiddle for *weeks* getting something ready to go, thinking out all the pitfalls in advance, and then something you've completely

358

overlooked screws it all up and you're back where you started." She sighed. "Sometimes I think you doctors have it made. You wave your wands and lo and behold, in two days you've got *results*. You start to treat somebody's ache, and three days later it's gone, and you're the magician."

"Well, not always," Rob said. "Sometimes we fiddle around for months or years and they've still got the same problems and all we've been doing is plugging leaks."

"Even that must help, if the people keep coming back."

"I guess so. You try to show that you care, that you're doing all you can, and sometimes that's enough. But other times you feel like some kind of snake oil peddler, pretending something will help when you *know* it won't, and taking their money week after week."

She sipped her drink and looked up at him. "But can't you just tell them there's really nothing you can do?"

"Sure—but you can't make them believe it. If you tell them not to come back, they'll just go somewhere else—and you never know who might get them then. Maybe somebody even more unprincipled than you are, somebody who'll just take their money and won't even *try* to help. So you hang on."

"Then I guess you have to do the best you can and not worry about it," Chris said. "You just have to follow your heart and your conscience."

Rob smiled. "That sounds very old-fashioned," he said.

"I know. But it still has meaning." She laughed. "Now with moths, you don't worry about hearts and consciences. The problem never arises. You work like a machine and jot down the results. But medicine is humane, at the bottom of it all, or it isn't any good. That's why computers will never put you out of work. Computers don't care. You can make them *act* like they care, but it's all a fraud, down at the bottom. There's no heart, no conscience there. Nothing but wires and electronic responses."

He watched her as she talked. Even in the dim light her eyes were startlingly green, slanted slightly at the corners, her face, framed with honey-colored hair, mysteriously piquant in the light and shadows—the small, slightly tilted nose, the full lips and firm chin. Her ears, hidden by curls, were not pointed, he thought, but they should have been, and the odd elfin quality of her face almost startled him. "You're very lovely tonight," he said.

She smiled. "We try harder."

"It doesn't show. What's your secret?"

"Steaks cooked on an open fire. So take a hint, Merlin."

She refilled their drinks while Rob got the potatoes roasting and later put the meat on. Presently they sat together, cross-legged before the fire, devouring the steaks and sipping the wine and listening to the roof creak and sigh as the rain and wind strafed the cabin from outside. Later they threw the last two logs on the fire, watched as they blazed up. Then they lay back on the elkskin and he kissed her, touched her cheek with his hand. "I'd better get some more wood in first," he said.

"Yes, do."

The wind nearly blew him off his feet as he went outside to the woodshed and loaded his arms with tamarack logs. When he returned he found her standing shimmering naked before the great fireplace, baking herself, her tawny hair glowing with the ruddy aura from the flaming logs, her elfin face suddenly, enchantingly beautiful. She came to him with a little cry, clung to him as he kissed her lips, her neck, her breasts. Then slowly, in delicious ritual, they made love on the soft elkskin, oblivious of the wind, oblivious of anything but their bodies and their urgent hunger. At one point she became the aggressor, taking him with her mouth until he could stand it no longer, then coming to him again feverishly as he entered her. . . .

For a long time later they lay close to each other, naked and wordless, watching the fire subside to glowing coals, sipping the remains of the wine. Presently, at his urging, she talked about herself: her childhood on a central Iowa farm, the lean years after her father's death, with barely enough to meet her undergraduate tuition at Drake, her decision for graduate work in Montana after her marriage fell apart. And then he was telling her about his early training days in medical school, his fledgling ambition to go into a medical specialty, cut off by the realities of marriage and financing. "I finally saw it just didn't add up," he said. "It would have meant another four or five years of residency, with nothing much but Ellie's salary to live on, which wasn't much in those days—nurses hadn't started striking yet—and then there was all the debt piled up from college and medical school too. Finally I saw that the only plausible route was a two-year general practice residency that paid enough to limp along on and start paying interest. And then when I was wrapping that up, I met Isaacs at an Academy of Family Practice meeting out in Seattle." Rob smiled wryly. "His offer looked like manna from heaven, just what I was looking for, and too good to pass up."

360

"So you came to Twin Forks," Chris said, "and found it wasn't quite as heavenly as it sounded."

"Not quite. Oh, the salary was good enough, there's no problem there—"

"But there's more to it than the salary."

He nodded. "Yes," he said. He sat up, hunching his shoulders forward. "But you don't want to hear about it."

"Don't I?" She looked at him soberly, then touched his hand, his shoulder, his clenched jaw, and shook her head. "All that muscle, love, tied up in knots," she said. "Do you know how tense you are? Like a tiger in a cage, ready to spring and tear and claw if only you could wrench the cage open. Maybe you need to talk more than you know."

"Maybe. Things are going wrong, I *know* they're going wrong, but I don't know why and I don't know how. I feel I've got to do something, fast, before everything blows to pieces, but I'm right in the middle of it, and I don't know what to do. . . ." And then, in a desperate burst, he was telling her the whole thing, forced out by his anger and frustration, even finally, painfully, the trouble with Ellie: his irritation at her failure, as the "doctor's wife," to fall neatly into her allotted position in the pattern of small-town life; her increasing demands on his time and his increasing compulsion to draw back, to hide behind the shield of practice demands, to shut her further and further out of his mind and emotions.

Through it all, Chris listened intently, stroking his bare shoulder, pressing the tense muscles in his back and neck, interrupting once or twice to clarify a point. As he talked she found a cigarette in her purse, leaned forward to light it from a coal, smoked it silently. She glanced up sharply when Rob touched on his troubles with Ellie, and when he stopped talking she was silent for a long moment as if waiting for something more. Then she took a long breath and tossed the cigarette stub into the fire. "You really don't get along with people very well, do you?" she said.

"Huh? Well, of course I do. I mean, I see patients day after day—"

"Well, sure. You tell the patients what to do, and as long as they do exactly what you tell them, you get along fine." She smiled. "As for other people, you're pretty obsessive. Either they do things your way, or you start climbing the wall. They've got to be perfect or better just for openers. . . ."

He looked at her for a moment, startled, and then shrugged. "Okay, maybe you're right. In medicine, you either do things right or you get out. There isn't anyplace for compromise or being pleasant or diplomatic or just overlooking fuck-ups. It isn't a cocktail party where everybody's got to be politely civil, no matter what." He laughed. "Jesus. I run into Jerry DeForrest, down in the dumps over his many inadequacies, and I try to cheer him up, you know? Tell him it's okay, it doesn't matter, nobody's perfect and all that. And then I run into one of his more spectacular blunders, some confused old guy he's almost killed with his neglect and laziness and stupidity, and I realize that it's *not* okay, it *does* matter. When you're dealing with people's lives you've got to be *right.*"

"And of course you're always right."

"You bet your life I am." He caught her eye, and flushed. "Well, hell, of course not. I make mistakes. I can be wrong like anybody else. But I can't just sit there and accept it. If I'm wrong I've got to find out why, if I can, and straighten it out. That's my job. But God, Chris, it's not my job to straighten everybody else out too."

"No. But you can't stand by and ignore what you know is wrong, either." She gave him a wistful smile. "And on top of all that, there's the baby coming."

He blinked. "How did you know about that?"

"Oh, come on, love. Everybody in Twin Forks knows about that. Specifically, Ernie at the gas station told me, at least ten days ago. That was after Connie Treadleman at the bank told me that she'd heard it from Dottie Hazard, who was getting together with Happy Cumley to plan a surprise baby shower. That was aside from getting the news from Al Davidson at the lumberyard when I went in to get some silicone sealer for my moth cages." She looked up at him quietly. "Not that it matters that everybody knows it, because four months ago I would have bet a month's pay it was going to happen pretty damned soon. And now it has, and you're not too happy."

"Well, you couldn't say it was planned."

"Maybe not by you," she said.

"But the baby's not the problem, anyway. The problem is everything else plus the baby."

"And especially Isaacs."

"Right. I don't like what I see, but I'm right in the middle of it, and nothing I do seems to help. The more I fight, the tighter it gets on all sides. I just feel—"

"Trapped," she said.

362

"I guess."

"Boxed in, with the walls getting closer all the time." She sighed. "Well, I know what you mean. You're trapped by the town on one side, and the hospital on another, and Isaacs on another, and Ellie and the baby on still another, and you're right in the middle, and the chains are getting tighter every day. Already you can barely breathe, and it's getting worse, and there's no way out that you can see, no way out at all. So you kick and fight and scream, but nothing happens, it just keeps getting worse, with no end in sight. I know."

He stared at the firelight for a long moment. "You make it sound horrible," he said.

"Not me. You drew the picture. All I did was put it in words. Am I right?"

"Oh, you're right. Lord, are you ever right!" He stared at her. "But what can I do?"

"You can always hope things will get better."

"But you don't think they will."

"Not really." Chris shook her head. "Is the new man going to help?"

"Who knows?" Rob said. "Not if he plays Isaacs' game."

"And being hand-picked, I suppose that's in the cards." Chris sighed. "Well, there's no easy answer. There's no painless way to break out of a trap, and you don't have many choices. Just three that I can see."

"Three?"

She looked up at him somberly. "Well, you can always lie down and let Isaacs win. But somehow I don't think that's your answer."

"Let's forget that one," Rob said tightly. "What else?"

"You can plant your heels in the ground and bend your neck and just slug it out to the end. Fight Isaacs to a standstill. But that could mean fighting the hospital and DeForrest and the new man and Ellie and everything else as well. It could be murder, and there might not be much left of you when you're through."

"I know," Rob said. "But I don't see any choice."

"Oh, there's a third way. Painful, but final." Her green eyes caught his and held them. "Trapped foxes have been known to do it. You could gnaw your leg off and get away."

Rob blinked. "What do you mean?"

"You could leave behind whatever you have to, and go."

"You mean just walk away?"

"That's right. Just pack your suitcase, and get into your car, and start driving—and never look back. Leave everything right where it is and go." She looked up into his face, her eyes bright. "You could do it, you know. God, Rob, you're young, you've got so much skill, so much talent—why piddle it away in Twin Forks, Montana? You could go anywhere in the world that needs a doctor." She turned her eyes away. "You wouldn't have to go alone, you know."

Something in the fireplace snapped, and the roof creaked in a sudden gust of wind. Rob took a deep breath. "Chris, I—don't know how I could do that."

"It might be easier than you think," she said. "How else are you going to break free? Think about it. I'll tell you one thing: you're a person too, and somehow, in the long run, you have to consider *you*. Not Isaacs, not Ellie, not anybody but *you*. And if the walls close in so you truly cannot stand it, you always have that third choice."

"And Ellie?"

"Well, Ellie!" Chris made a vulgar gesture. "That would be for *her* to think about, wouldn't it?"

"I don't know," Rob said.

"Then maybe the time isn't ripe," Chris said. "When it comes, you'll know, all right. And meantime, you'll just have to slug it out."

"I guess." He looked down at her, tousled her hair. "It's getting late. Maybe we'd better go."

"I suppose. If we have to."

"Unless there's something else that needs doing first." He leaned down to kiss her.

"Yes." It was a sound almost like a sob as she moved to him, met his lips fiercely, pulled him close. "Oh, yes. Indeed there is. . . ."

# 31

It was past 3 A.M. when Rob drove across the bridge and rolled into the driveway, flicking out his headlights as he turned. The light over the kitchen door was dark, and he stole silently into the house. He banged against a kitchen chair, cursed under his breath, and found his way to the sofa to remove his shoes and socks. Standing to undress, he tiptoed into the bedroom. He tossed his clothes over a chair, slipped on his pajamas, and set the clock on the headboard by the illuminated dial. It was not until he actually crept into bed that he realized the other side was empty.

"Ellie?"

No answer. He sat bolt upright. "Ellie? What the hell!" He snapped on the bedlamp, peered around the empty room. Her nightgown lay crumpled on the floor, slippers nearby. Her purse was gone from its usual place on the dresser. *"Ellie!"*

Out in the living room he flicked on lights, searched the house. Two or three kitchen pans sat in scattered places on the living room floor, each containing brownish water, and he saw wet stains on the ceiling board above them. He even checked the patio, found nothing.

The place was empty.

Really alarmed now, he snatched up the phone, hesitated a moment, then dialed Martin's number. After four or five rings he heard Isaacs' sleepy voice.

"Martin, do you know where Ellie is?"

"Where the hell are *you?*" Isaacs said. "What time is it?"

"It's three o'clock, and I just got home. Damned car broke down and I had to get help. It took forever. But Ellie's not here."

"I know. She's up at the hospital."

"Oh, good Lord. What happened? The baby?"

"Nothing too serious," Isaacs said. "She got home from the grocery and found water dripping from the ceiling, so she went up on the roof with a shovel and broom to clean out the rain gutters. When she got back down she was spotting, and it kept on all evening. So I came and took her up to the hospital and slugged her out with Nembutal. It's probably all right; she wasn't having cramps or anything. I just wanted to be safe. But Jesus, Rob, you've got to find some way to keep her off that roof."

"Yeah, I know. Look, can I see her?"

"*Now?* Hell, no. I want her resting. See her in the morning. They'll call me if there's any problem in the meantime. But Jesus, Rob, three o'clock? What was wrong with the car?"

"I don't know," Rob fumbled. "Distributor full of water or some damned thing; it doesn't matter. It's all right now. You're sure I can't—"

"No, you can't, so go to bed." Isaacs hung up, leaving Rob holding a dead phone. He set it back on the hook and stared at it for long moments before he finally turned out the lights.

By morning the storm had subsided to a persistent gloomy drizzle, matching Rob's mood to perfection. His head, already aching when he had finally got to sleep, now throbbed relentlessly as he hauled himself out of bed, his mouth bone dry, his stomach queasy. Tomato juice and toast were no help, and his morning coffee left him more jittery than before. Since there was no point in appearing at the hospital before Isaacs had been there, he dawdled through a shower and shave, dressed reluctantly and stood staring out the window at the gray sky and the swollen, muddy river. His mind turned to the evening before, and he winced. The hours with Chris, the jarring shock of finding Ellie gone, the lying to Isaacs, and now, irrationally, the wave of sullen anger he felt at himself, at Ellie, at Isaacs, at everything. *Of all the goddamned miserable, sloppy messes,* he thought. *And then he's got to throw her in the hospital, for God's sake. And what is Chris going to say when she hears about it?* He shook his head, still jarred by the contradictions of

366

the evening before. No telling *what* Chris might say. Such a strange woman, so cool and sensible as they talked, so curiously able to put her finger on the aching nerve, ruthless as she prescribed her alien cure— and then later, the ruthlessness falling away like a veil to reveal the passion, the hunger, the almost incredible abandon as she met him. He felt himself stirring again, felt perspiration starting out. *A passionate woman—but dangerous. And her solution so God-awful tempting . . . just to turn his back and walk away.*

He met Isaacs leaving the hospital as he arrived. "Ellie's going to be all right, I think," the older man said. "Maybe I jumped the gun a little, hauling her up here, but with you not back . . ." He shrugged. "You know how it is with doctors' wives; if anything can go wrong, it will. I just decided not to take any chances."

"She can come home, then?"

Isaacs frowned. "Better leave her here for the day, and then take her home tonight, okay? Just to be safe."

"But can I see her now?"

"Yeah, but make it short. Just let her rest."

Rob walked into the hospital, glanced at Ellie's chart, and went down to her room. She was still groggy from the sedative, looking shockingly gray and wan, and she didn't brighten perceptibly when she saw him. He touched her forehead with his finger, tried to smile and suddenly found he couldn't. "So how are you doing?" he said.

"Okay, I guess."

"You look awful."

"I suppose so. I'm sorry."

He groped for words, something gentle to say, but nothing came. "You could at least have left me a note," he said finally. "You damned near scared me silly."

"It just happened so fast, that's all, and you were so late, and I got scared." She turned her eyes away. "At first it was just a little spotting, and I thought it could wait till you got home, but then there was more and I got panicky." She extended her hands helplessly.

"You and your goddamned roof," he said. He turned away, fumbling through her chart. It was coming out all wrong. He knew he should be saying something sensitive and supportive, reaching out to her, trying to comfort her, but a surge of guilty anger welled up and blocked him off. "Martin wants you to stay here today," he said finally. "I'll come get you tonight sometime."

"Rob?"

He looked at her.

"I said I was sorry—but I was *scared*. Can't you understand that?"

"Sure."

"And you were so late I *had* to call Martin." She looked up at him. "What made you so late?"

"It doesn't matter. You get some rest now. We'll talk about it later."

She called his name again as he started up the hall, but he didn't turn back. At the nurses' desk he checked charts, made a pretense of making rounds, and then fled down toward the office.

Dora met him in the hall, full of motherly solicitude, merely intensifying the guilt and anger and chagrin churning in his mind. "Nellie Webster just told me," Dora said. "I do hope everything will be all right."

"I think it will."

"These things just happen so fast—"

"Come on, Dora! She had a little spotting, that's all. She's going to be fine. Now let me have about ten minutes by myself before we start the parade, okay?"

He retired to his office, grappling for control. For an eerie moment he could see his own mind working, in grisly slow motion, as a distant observer might see some nauseating entity creeping by under a dissecting microscope: the bitter sense of guilt and self-loathing that gnawed at him; the frustrated anger welling up in defense of the indefensible; the horrid flare of hope he'd felt, when he saw her this morning, that maybe the baby would be lost—and the instant, almost simultaneous, blocking; and his absolute inability to face Ellie with any of all this but the anger showing. *Christ! You couldn't even pretend for a minute, couldn't find a decent word to say. You had to play the bully—just like Martin Isaacs.*

He froze for a moment, then pushed the thought away. Patients were piling up now. There wasn't time to think about that. There wasn't time to think about Ellie, either. Later, when Isaacs came by with some new announcement, Rob hardly heard him the first time. "Eh? What's that?"

"I said the new man's coming early. He'll be here Monday morning. So start lining up the surgery."

"Sure, I'll rush right out and create some." Rob looked up. "How come he's coming so soon?"

"Because we need him, that's why. We've been shipping too much to town to wait any longer. So I called him up and told him to get his ass out here." Isaacs looked enormously pleased with himself.

"Well, there's nothing like having a tame surgeon on the line," Rob said, and walked away, shaking his head. *And that's just for openers,* he thought. *Oh, brother!*

Later, pleading an intolerable headache (which he certainly had), he took off early, dumping the rest of his patients in Jerry's lap and driving home to empty the catch basins and mop up the leaked-on floor and make the bed with clean linen and start some chicken baking for dinner before bringing Ellie home. It was therapeutic, in its way, but not quite therapeutic enough. More than once, before he was through, he found his mind drifting back to the thought fragment that had jarred him before and thoroughly chilled him now, ridiculous as it was: *just like Martin Isaacs. . . .*

# 32

Something had changed, Ellie knew, but she couldn't tell what and she wasn't sure why. He'd come up to get her before five that evening, after her interminable hospital day. He'd written the discharge order himself and packed her off home and deposited her in bed with a gruffness she couldn't quite read and then spent the evening watching her, covertly, as if he expected her to burst into flame at any minute. He'd clearly made some kind of effort: the place was clean and dry, if musty-smelling, the bed was fresh, and the chicken was only partly burned, so she choked down a little, even though her rebellious stomach warned her not to. He didn't seem as cold and angry as he'd been when he saw her that morning; he even seemed solicitous, in a way, which probably should have pleased her, except that it seemed so strange from Rob these days that it made her nervous instead. He wasn't off and away to the hospital after dinner, as he usually was, and seemed content to do the dishes and leaf through a journal or two and suggest four times that she probably ought to get back to bed again. But the words she hoped for didn't come, and presently she was annoyed with herself even for hoping. *It wasn't his fault, after all. And there's bound to be tension, with this new man coming and nobody knowing what to expect, and when Rob gets tense he clams up, you know that.* She retired finally, sensing that he was waiting impatiently for her to have time enough to be properly asleep before he came to bed; and she didn't sleep, but he did, the bastard, like a poleaxed mule; he hardly rolled over the whole night long.

By morning, when she awoke, he was coming down from thumping on the roof ("Got to stop the damned leaks somehow") and taking off for the hospital to make rounds. "And then I've got to stop at the office and catch up on some charting," he said as he went out the door. "I'm way behind."

*Day off or no day off,* she thought sourly. *And maybe he'll be home for lunch and maybe he won't.* She showered and dressed, had some coffee and toast. Somehow, she sensed, she needed something to act on, some positive plan of approach—but the imminent arrival of the new surgeon seemed to suspend everything in limbo. *You can't fight shadows; there's no way to get hold of them, no way to pin them down. They shift and twist, whatever you do.*

She debated walking down to see Belle, but it was Belle's baking day and she wouldn't welcome company. Finally she decided to repot some of the heart ivy she'd got from Belle some time before, a task she'd been putting off for weeks. She was into the potting mulch up to her elbows when the phone rang.

Jennie's voice sounded blurred and muddy over the line. " . . . just heard this morning about your trouble. I do hope you're going to be all right."

"Oh, yes. It was just a false alarm," Ellie said. "I'm fine."

"I'm glad to hear that. I was afraid . . ." There was such a long pause that Ellie thought she must have hung up. "But I'm glad . . ."

"Jennie, are you all right?"

"Me?" Another long pause. Then: "I guess so."

"You sound very odd."

"It's just my throat," Jennie said thickly. "You know, I've been thinking I ought to get away somewhere."

"Get away?"

"You know, just for a few days, down to California maybe, somewhere I could be by myself for a while."

"Maybe that's a good idea," Ellie said cautiously.

"I thought so too," Jennie said. "I even talked to Martin about it. But he said no. He said he wanted me around, with the new man coming." Another prolonged pause. Then: "I—I don't know what I'm going to do."

A chill prickled Ellie's neck. "Jennie, there's bound to be something." She looked around helplessly. "Look, right now I'm covered with mud, but I'll be through in a while. I'll run over later and we'll figure something out."

"Yes, that would be nice." Jennie's voice sounded flat, almost detached. "Maybe . . . you can come over later."

Ellie put the phone down slowly and went back to her pots. *Drunk? Maybe, but not just that. The flatness in her voice, the emptiness . . .* She went on working another half hour, with Jennie's voice still nagging at her mind. Finally, half disgusted, she pushed the work aside unfinished, washed the mud off her hands and dialed Jennie's number on the phone. *Maybe she just needs contact, somebody to talk to.* She waited as the phone rang six, eight times.

No answer. She dialed again. Still nothing. Frowning, she slipped on a jacket and went out to the car. A bitter wind had come up, sweeping the valley, and the old Chevy wagon swayed as she turned out onto the highway. She saw Judge Barret crossing from his office to the Bar-None, holding his hat clamped to his head as his coattails fluttered. A left turn and another left turn brought her to the Isaacs house.

There was no sign of life as she walked up onto the porch. She pushed the bell, heard it chime in the back of the house, but nothing happened. Then, in a gust of wind, the front door blew open with a bang and she peered into the darkened living room. "Jennie?"

No answer.

She stepped inside, closing the door behind her. All the curtains were drawn. She looked around the empty room, walked into the dining room, sniffed. The place reeked of whiskey, cold and raw in her nostrils. In the corridor to the bedroom she saw the bathroom door ajar, the light inside blazing, a whiskey bottle smashed on the tile with a great brown puddle soaking into the corridor rug. *"Jennie?"* She walked to the bathroom door, pushed it open.

She was hanging from the ceiling light fixture, suspended by a silken bathrobe cord, her neck swollen, head wrenched grotesquely to the side, her face purple and bloated, eyes unblinking. Even as Ellie watched, the body swung slightly.

She didn't scream. She caught the doorjamb as her knees buckled, then sank to the floor, clutching her throat as she started to retch. When the wave passed, she inched her way back down the corridor, away from the thing in the bathroom. Long moments later she reached the living room telephone, controlled her hands until she could dial. An instant later she heard Rob's voice on the line. "What's the matter? Where are you?"

"Where's Martin?"

"He's up at the hospital, delivering a baby." She heard him take a sudden breath. "Ellie? What's wrong?"

"You'd better come over to Martin's house. I think Jennie's dead."

She waited in the dark room, alone, then, shivering, shaking her head and pressing a clenched fist to her lips, her mind echoing a threnody, over and over and over: *No more. No more. No more of this. . . .* Dimly she saw Rob come in, walk back to the bathroom, return a moment later to phone Vern Bradley.

He put the phone down and stared at her. "The bastard," he said. "The bloody, brutal bastard."

"Yes."

"Well, he's going to pay for this. I don't know how, but somehow—"

"Shut up, Rob." Ellie looked up at him then, a frozen look, tired and bitter and old. "Shut your mouth for once, and just get me home."

# Part IV

# 33

The arrival of the new surgeon came with far less friction and furor than Rob Tanner would ever have believed possible. A brief news account in the weekly *Twin Forks Examiner* a week before he appeared had simply stated that Dr. Harry Sonders had resigned from the Twin Forks Medical Clinic to pursue his full-time surgical practice in Missoula; a week later the same paper carried a discreet professional announcement of the arrival of Dr. Thomas Stone, surgeon, with office hours at the clinic commencing at once, and that was the extent of the formal introduction.

In part, of course, Stone's arrival was eclipsed by the hubbub over Jennie Isaacs' suicide. A perfunctory coroner's inquest laid to rest any doubt that the death was self-inflicted, but tongues wagged just the same. Last rites, by fixed intent, were kept as low-profile as possible: the briefest of memorial services in the funeral home, followed by a sad trek through drizzling rain to the cemetery at the foot of the mountain west of town. There were no notices, and only a few accompanied Isaacs to the graveside: the DeForrests, Judge Barret, a couple of the nurses, Rob and Ellie and, surprisingly, Belle Foreman. No one said much until it was over, when Martin turned to Rob. "You know, I'm pretty shaken up about this," he said. "I'm going to need a little help for a while till I get back on my feet, with the new man coming."

"Well, sure," Rob said. "Like what?"

"Oh, you know." Martin waved a hand. "Like smoothing over the trouble a little. Getting all the rumors settled down. Getting things off on the right foot. . . ."

*Yeah,* Rob thought, *which means getting things going your way again,* but he said nothing and went along to drive Belle and Ellie home.

Rumors were a problem, but from the first Tom Stone proved unpromising grist for the Twin Forks rumor mill. The very antithesis of Harry Sonders, Stone was tall and angular and gawky, a shambling figure, slightly hunched forward, like a vulture regarding its prey. His face was all jaw and forehead and hawk nose and disturbingly cool gray eyes; his hands all long spidery fingers, thin and delicate and translucent as fine porcelain. His shock of black hair apparently defied all assaults of the comb. Though he was young, his clothing spoke of another era —long, musty, mournful tweeds with baggy knees and black leather patches at the elbows, white shirts starched stiff, and narrow dark ties that might have been fashioned from widows' weeds. He came to town with his small, quiet wife and two small, quiet children in a weather-beaten Volkswagen of uncertain vintage, painted bright green and incongruously bedecked with a flower-child daisy on the hood, and the spectacle of the man unfolding his seemingly endless limbs from the tiny driver's seat had to be seen to be believed. His voice, when he spoke, was quiet, with a dispassionate calm that suggested he might well have neither shouted nor cursed in the entire span of his thirty-four years; his pace, when he worked, was deliberate and precise, not swift or slow, but above all meticulously thorough. He rarely seemed to smile, nor frown either, but how much this was his normal façade and how much a cautious approach to a new environment, no one could say. He had none of Harry Sonders' easygoing charm with patients; rather, he listened intently when they spoke, fixing them with those pale gray eyes, and when he spoke in return it was with a quiet authority Sonders had never achieved. Where Sonders had wheedled and cajoled, Tom Stone *explained,* with simple reasonableness, the nature of the problem and the decision the patient had to make for a surgical cure.

"You've got to hand it to Martin," Jerry DeForrest said to Rob the second or third day Dr. Stone had been with them. "The man has good training. A fellow I know in Seattle says he's a brilliant operator. Fussy as hell, meticulous is his middle name, but brilliant."

"That's great for Seattle," Rob said, "but there's no fancy medical center out here, just a little town with precious little to work with. I hope he can make the switch."

"Well, at any rate, I'll bet he answers calls," Jerry said. "And maybe the practice can use a little meticulous surgery for a change. As for other things, we'll just have to see."

In point of fact, Rob saw very little of Tom Stone the first few days, and thought about him even less. In addition to the regular press of patients, suddenly intensified by a wave of flu in the valley, Rob was heavily preoccupied both with Ellie and with Chris Erickson. Ellie had changed since the day of Jennie's death. There was a wan, withdrawn coldness about her, a bone-deep chill, and her usual quiet good cheer was conspicuously absent. She remained silent and reflective, with little to say even to Rob's direct comments, indifferent to his practice problems and totally uninterested in the new surgeon. Rob found himself watching her with a mixture of concern and irritation as she went about the house as if she were walking on eggshells.

Finally, exasperated, he said, "Come on, Ellie. What the hell is wrong?"

"I just don't feel good, that's all."

"If you don't feel good, go see Martin."

"I don't *want* to see Martin. I just want to catch my breath." She turned away. "Mostly, I'm scared," she said.

"You mean because of Jennie? Well, sure, a suicide right next door is a kind of a scary thing, but God, Ellie—"

"I don't mean about Jennie. I mean about you and Martin. And me."

He looked at her. "And the spooks under the bed too, I suppose. Maybe you'd better take some Valium."

"I don't want Valium, either. Why don't you just quit badgering me?"

"It just seems kind of ridiculous to go around here acting like you've had a subtotal disembowelment or something," Rob said.

"Well, I could go up and finish fixing the rain gutters, I suppose."

"Okay, so I forgot the rain gutters," Rob said. "I admit it. So call Al Davidson and tell him to come fix them. Or let them overflow. I don't care which; I just wish you'd quit moping around." But Ellie turned away and pulled her robe tighter around her and went on about her business, doing the dishes slowly, carefully and silently.

Rob's temper was not improved when his several efforts to tele-

379

phone Chris came to nothing. More and more he found himself fiercely anxious to hear her voice, to reconfirm the warm words she'd left him with when they'd come back from the cabin, especially to be reassured that their stolen evening had not been some kind of fluke, some freakish confluence of wine, weather and circumstances, unlikely ever to recur —or worse yet, a matter of cool indifference to her now that the moment had passed. By Monday morning in the office, after three more weekend attempts to reach her, he was wondering if maybe *she* had packed up and fled, when Dora trotted in with a chart in her hand. "Chris Erickson, Doctor. She's back in to check those last lab tests."

She was dressed in work shirt and dungarees, looking wryly amused when Rob appeared. "Temperature, pulse and blood pressure," she said. "Your Dora can't be put off."

Rob closed the door behind him, and she came to his arms, hugged him briefly before turning her face away and gently disengaging him. "Hey, Merlin, all we need is to have that nurse walk in."

"I know, but God, I've missed you. I've been trying to get you for four days."

"I've been buried in moths." She reached up to kiss his cheek, then stepped back. "And I didn't dare call you. This was the only thing I could think of."

"Well, we'll have to do better," he said. "I was beginning to think I'd scared you off."

Chris broke into a happy laugh. "You're very sweet, love. You just don't know this little girl, is all." She looked at him soberly. "You listen now: I wanted you the other night and I want you right now, and it's been murder not seeing you or talking to you these last few days, okay? And as for what comes next, it's merely a question of when and where, as far as I'm concerned. There's just one practical problem: you can't really go to too many meetings in Missoula."

"No; I guess that excuse is queered for a while."

Chris chewed her lip thoughtfully. "I hear by the grapevine that Ellie walked right in on Jennie Isaacs."

"Yeah." Rob looked at her. "And she's jumpy as a cat these days, too."

"Then we're going to have to be *very* careful."

"I'll think of something, don't worry," Rob said. "Maybe we can just get in the car and drive somewhere. Let's plan on later this week. I'll get in touch."

"Fine. But take care."

It was the first tentative step toward a long series of clandestine meetings, sometimes for a whole evening, sometimes only for an hour, that sustained Rob on a wave of euphoria as he thrust his anger with Martin Isaacs and his growing impatience with Ellie to the back of his mind. Preoccupied with such things, Rob barely noticed the new surgeon during those first days. But his mind snapped back with a jolt toward the end of Tom Stone's second week in Twin Forks when the man suddenly revealed himself as a force to be reckoned with and not ignored.

The occasion was a small welcoming cocktail and dinner party that Amy and Jerry DeForrest threw for Stone and his wife, inviting all the town's doctors—including John Florey and Ted Peterson—and their wives. Not until Florey had declined did Martin Isaacs agree to come at all, and then he came late. Ted and Betty Peterson appeared for the briefest acceptable time, congenial enough in greeting the new man, but leaving before dinner, with Ted begging a difficult case he was dogging at the hospital. ("Probably because the old bastard made him," Isaacs grumbled.)

All in all, it proved less than a gala occasion. Stone and his wife both refused cocktails in favor of tomato juice, and the woman seemed so shy —or else so reserved—that the others could not draw her into conversation at all. In fact, both Stones were exquisitely polite but distant, as though warily confronting a group of alien beings of uncertain temper. Even with Jerry leaping into the breach with his rambling monologues, the conversation faltered repeatedly and Rob found himself wishing everyone would go home. Finally dinner helped save the evening—a mouth-watering *risotto alla Milanaise* followed by an incomparable scaloppine of veal served with red Italian wine (again politely declined by the Stones)—but a sense of warmth and earnest exchange never quite surfaced. Regarding literature, the arts or current world events, Tom Stone seemed totally disinterested, even somewhat baffled; it was only when the conversation turned to the surgical problems of the practice that he came to life a little, listening intently, fixing his gray eyes on Isaacs' face and raising his eyebrows ever so slightly as various points were made.

"Call has been the biggest headache," Isaacs was saying. "Missoula is ninety minutes away, and Harry didn't like having to hop out here every time somebody had a problem. So after a while, it got hard to get him to come at all, and we began having some tight surgical squeezes."

Dr. Stone shrugged. "Itinerant surgery never did work very well," he said. "And it's especially hard to justify in this day and age."

"Well, it wasn't exactly itinerant surgery," Isaacs said cautiously. "He had regular operating days out here, you understand, and regular office hours."

"Oh, I understand all that," Dr. Stone said, "but it rather amounts to the same thing, wouldn't you say? He still had to have others follow his cases—and a surgeon can't really do that. Too many—ah—difficult things might happen, eh?"

"Well, maybe, up to a point."

"I mean, a surgeon can't very well half cover a practice. He either covers his work or he doesn't, wouldn't you say? But then, that shouldn't be any trouble for me, living right here."

"That could solve nine tenths of the problem," Rob said. "I don't know about the others, but I plan to call you anytime I need a surgical opinion."

"Well, I should certainly hope you would," Stone said, looking bemused. "That's why I'm here, wouldn't you say?" He studied his long white fingers for a moment, then looked up at Isaacs. "For me, I suspect the problem will be with the hospital. Some of the facilities seem—ah —terribly limited."

"They're a little limited," Isaacs conceded. "We just work around the limits, that's all."

"Ah, so. But perhaps the management might consider—ah— smoothing off some of the rougher edges."

"Well, you met Roger the other day. What do *you* think?"

"That frosty chap with the toupee?" Stone pursed his lips. "Frankly, he seemed a bit more hostile than I'd hoped for."

"Not so much hostile as defensive," Isaacs said.

"Ah—perhaps. But then, he may have been having a bad day." The new man cleared his throat. "The problem is, with certain surgical procedures the hospital simply *must* provide certain standards of supportive care, or you just can't do the procedures there, wouldn't you say?"

"Like what procedures?" Isaacs said.

"Well, thyroidectomies, for instance. Did you say that Dr. Sonders did them out here?"

"Of course he did."

"But *how?*"

Now Isaacs looked bemused. "He just went ahead and did them," he said.

"I see." Dr. Stone looked faintly distressed. "I only asked because, as you know, thyroidectomies can present some extremely tricky post-op nursing problems. And I'm not convinced, for instance, that any of the nurses up here would know how to handle a thyroid storm. The ones I asked thought I was talking about the weather. But with that kind of a crisis, you've got to have skilled nursing care or you may suddenly have a dead patient on your hands."

Isaacs laughed, shaking his head. "Tom, I just don't think we've ever had that problem. Jerry's taken care of the pre-op medical workup, and made sure the patient's thyroid activity was normal before the surgery, and that's been that."

Stone grimaced. "Perhaps you've been luckier than you realize."

"Maybe it's just the difference between big-city medicine and small-town medicine," Isaacs said. "Out here in the sticks we have to make do with what we've got. You'll get on to it."

"One must hope. But of course I'll need surgical privileges at one of the city hospitals too, for cases I just can't do out here."

"There won't be too much of that," Isaacs said. "We're going to keep you so busy out here that we can afford to refer those few. We already know commuting to Missoula doesn't work, unless you like driving awfully well, and with winter coming on—well—" He shrugged. "We'll see how it works."

The party limped on a bit longer until the Stones finally excused themselves, with Tom begging early rounds in the morning and some time scheduled with Roger Painter to familiarize himself with the hospital's operating room supplies and procedures. "Go easy on him," Isaacs admonished. "He knows the shortcomings, all right, and he's a little touchy. He's just afraid you're going to make a lot of costly trouble for him, but he can help you if he wants to. So go slow at this point, okay?"

"Don't worry, I won't make a bore of myself," Tom Stone said. "Not this week."

After the Stones had left, a subdued Martin Isaacs took off his glasses and polished them. Jerry cleared his throat. "I don't know, Martin," he said. "Stone doesn't strike me as the most pliable man imaginable. In fact, he sounds like he has some pretty rigid ideas."

"Oh, he'll be okay," Isaacs said. "He's just full of big-city hotshot medicine, that's all. Those guys live on a different planet; they want to snap their fingers and it's all right there waiting for them. Well, he's sharp, and he'll learn. Right now he's worrying about what we can't do

383

out here. Drop a couple of three-car accidents in his lap and he'll begin to see what we *can* do. Even if we have to train Rob to give anesthesia."

"No way I'm going to give anesthesia," Rob said. "But maybe he can goose Roger into finding a decent anesthesiologist to cover us."

"I wouldn't hold my breath," Isaacs said.

"Well, he's dead right, you know. If he's any kind of a surgeon, he won't buy this 'small-town medicine' business. He'll figure there's only one way to do surgery, and that's the right way. And I'm going to be right there with him."

Isaacs laughed. "Rob, maybe you'd better just keep out of it. For the moment, let's just watch and see how he works out, eh? He may surprise us all."

Surprise or no surprise, Tom Stone soon made his presence felt in the clinic and at the hospital. He moved in quickly to pick up on the active surgical patients, whether preoperative or postoperative, that Harry Sonders had left behind. More than once he came away shaking his head, and turned to Rob with his comments. A case in point was a burn patient, twelve-year-old Terry Hyatt, whose dressings Rob had been changing since Sonders was fired. Three months before, the Hyatt boy had been rescued from a house fire, with serious burns of his trunk and arms. Sonders and Rob had treated the boy together from the start, through the first critical days of staving off shock, fluid loss and kidney failure, then later fighting infection and pain as the burned areas were gradually prepared for skin grafts. Tom Stone had examined the boy carefully the day he arrived in Twin Forks, clucking his tongue and shaking his head. "I assume he was treated in the city initially," he said.

"No, Harry chose to treat him right here. I didn't think it was smart, and we were working pretty much around the clock at first, but Roger got the freeze-dried plasma we needed, and the nurses were awfully good with him."

"Amazing," Stone said. "He must have had thirty or thirty-five percent second-and third-degree burns."

"We figured about thirty percent," Rob said.

"But what did you do for lab work—electrolytes, all that?"

"Raymond took blood samples into the city every day, and we got telephone reports back every afternoon. Not as handy as a lab downstairs, but we managed. We did the routine blood counts and urine checks and bacteriology down in our own lab."

"Amazing," Stone repeated, half to himself. "But you haven't run electrolytes for a week now, and he's still losing fluids from those burns."

"Order them up, if you think we need them. Of course, he's taking food and fluid by mouth now."

"True, but imbalances can still sneak up on you." Stone wrote the lab order on the chart in a spidery, precise handwriting. "Sonders seemed to think he'd be ready for grafting next week. Let's schedule a dressing change Monday, and plan to go ahead with the graft if it looks okay."

"Make it Tuesday and I can help you," Rob said. "That's the anesthetist's regular day too."

Stone looked distressed. "Do we really need this anesthetist? If we can give the lad a really good soak in the Hubbard tank first, maybe we can spare him the risk of anesthesia."

"There isn't any Hubbard tank, unfortunately, and when the nurses tried soaking the dressings off a couple of weeks ago with warm saline and peroxide, it didn't work too well. Took two of them three hours, and there was still so much pain I had to use anesthesia."

"Well, maybe we can keep it light. You've been just fantastically lucky so far. Damned shame to knock the kid into left field with an aspiration pneumonia at this point."

With another of Rob's patients, however, the new surgeon was not nearly so malleable. Hattie Carmichael had already been scheduled for a hysterectomy on Thursday of the week Sonders left; Rob had re-scheduled her so that her case could be reviewed by the new surgeon. Hattie was a small red-faced woman of forty-five, married to a construction worker who was off building highways much of the time. She was also an all-too-familiar daily habitué of the Wagon Wheel Tavern. More than once Rob had been called out by her distraught husband to revive Hattie when she passed out on her living room floor; and more than once Rob had patiently tried to explain to her that her drinking habits were surely going to shorten her life. But Hattie's Monday morning resolutions were forgotten by Monday evening; and soon she would have gone down in Rob's book as just another refractory alcoholic if she hadn't come up with a more treatable complaint: excessive bleeding during her periods.

At first Rob thought this was just Hattie's normal exaggeration and embellishment. But after he was called to the hospital twice when Hattie was allegedly hemorrhaging—with bloodstained bath towels to prove her point—Rob did a diagnostic dilatation and curettage to rule out any possibility of cancer, and then appealed to Isaacs for advice. "Hell," Martin said, "take her uterus out. It's not going to solve her problem, but at least it'll stop the bleeding." Sonders had agreed to the surgery on the spot, checked the woman over in a brief ten-minute office visit, and scheduled a hysterectomy—still undone when he left.

Dr. Stone saw her the Tuesday afternoon of his second week, and spent over an hour with her. Rob's own schedule was full, and he didn't catch up to the surgeon until late in the afternoon. "Well, did you get Hattie Carmichael rescheduled?" he asked.

"Actually, no," the surgeon said.

"Oh, really? Why not?"

"Matter of fact, I canceled her."

"*Canceled*—you mean you just scratched the case completely?"

Stone nodded. "What else could I do?" he said. "She hasn't any real bleeding problem. She's just playing you and her husband for sympathy."

"For God's sake, Tom—I've *seen* her bleeding."

"Oh, I'm sure she puts on a very convincing production, tears and hysteria and all that, but it's phony. You can quit worrying about it."

"Just how the hell do you figure that?"

"Well, for one thing, these episodes always happen just after you or her husband—or both of you—have been leaning on her about her drinking. That's one point. Then when you ask her how much she actually bleeds, she can't really tell you. Three drops, and off she goes, clutching for the bath towel. But the clincher is her hemoglobin level. If she'd been bleeding all she says, she'd be white as a sheet by now, but she's pink as an English schoolgirl, and her hemoglobin is slightly *above* normal for a woman her age." Stone pulled on his ear. "So she's not bleeding much; certainly no more than normal. If we took her uterus out, we'd just be playing *her* game—and complicating her problem by letting her get away with it. Christ knows what she'd do next for sympathy. We'd just be letting childish behavior win, that's all."

Rob shook his head angrily. "Look, I'm no psychiatrist, but I know one thing: three of us here have been telling Hattie Carmichael she needs a hysterectomy, including me. You're going to make us all look like asses if we back out now."

"I realize that," Stone said quietly. "And of course, I regret it. But really, that's *your* problem, not Hattie Carmichael's. Wouldn't you say?"

386

"Well, it's easy for *you* to say, but you're not the one she gets out of bed during these bleeding episodes."

"Oh, I wouldn't mind," Stone said. "I'll be happy to pick up her care if you want."

"So what do *you* plan to do?" Rob said, exasperated as much at Stone's quietly rigid reasonableness as at his decision. "Wave a magic wand over her head?"

"No magic; no. I'd just ignore these childish displays and concentrate on the real problem. Try to get her to stand on her own pegs like any other mature adult. As soon as she sees that the 'bleeding' doesn't work anymore, she'll forget about it."

"Well, I wish you luck," Rob said bitterly, "and many happy night calls."

"Oh, the night calls are also childish behavior," Stone said confidently. "I'll take care of them, too, in time."

"And you say you're a surgeon?" Rob said, exasperated by the man's cheerful self-certainty. Stone looked at him and almost smiled.

"That's on Monday, Wednesday and Friday," he said. "The rest of the time I practice voodoo."

Other irritations with Tom Stone turned up as the days passed, some minor, some major—but bit by bit Rob became accustomed to the young surgeon's curiously fixed ideas and awkward behavior. It was clear from the first that he would not be intimidated by anyone, from Martin Isaacs on down. It was also clear that, slowly and painstakingly as his opinions were formed, he was exceedingly difficult to shake once he'd decided something.

For Jerry, who could change opinions three times in the course of one conversation, this was a totally baffling quality, and the two men spent the first few weeks eying each other nervously and edging away from each other. When Stone wanted a patient worked up, he referred to DeForrest at first—but he also repeated the workup himself, and more often than not found Jerry's work lacking. Presently, quietly but firmly, he began sending the patients to Rob instead, a pattern that was not lost on DeForrest and did nothing to endear the new surgeon to him.

Rob, on the other hand, soon recognized a solid ally in the practice. Stone was not a mover and shaker, but he wouldn't be budged when he'd made up his mind, and he supported Rob consistently in his continuing conflict with Isaacs. This was not entirely painless for Rob, since Tom could be an extremely trying man to have around. Rob soon

387

realized, for example, that Stone was a person who could not, and would not, let well enough alone. No matter how carefully Rob examined a pre-op patient, Stone in his quiet, insistent manner invariably had some fault to find. Perhaps another lab study would be helpful, he would say. Maybe a certain x-ray would help clarify a fuzzy point. In this patient there were lymph nodes Rob had neglected to check for, in that one a slight liver enlargement Rob had written off as insignificant. This sort of "nit-picking" (as Isaacs called it) just infuriated the older man when it came his way, though he fought valiantly to control his irritation. Rob came to accept it, first with impatience, then with chagrin and finally with a mixture of amusement and admiration. Oddly enough, he discovered, the man was almost always right. The overlooked lab study proved illuminating, the x-ray useful, the physical finding of more importance than it seemed. And one day, when Stone discovered a small ovarian cyst that Isaacs had missed in a patient, even Isaacs came away shaking his head. "By *Christ*, but he's sharp," he said to Rob that evening. "Irritating as hell, but *sharp*. I should never have missed that."

Stone had a counterquality, however, which seemed to Rob to compensate for all the irritation. For all his infuriating self-assurance and his wide clinical acumen, Tom Stone recognized his own limitations. This was brought home in the third week, when Rob suddenly faced the first real emergency to turn up in his obstetrical practice.

Ellen Trotwell had been a difficult patient at best—a large, florid woman of thirty-three, mother of four, who had neglected to see a doctor at all until the sixth month of her pregnancy, and then studiously ignored everything Rob had to advise regarding prenatal care. She had missed her seventh-month appointment altogether and then appeared three weeks later, smiling and complacent and thirty pounds heavier than six weeks before. Rob had fumed, but she just laughed. "That weight gain, I always done that," she said. "You doctors just like to make a big fuss, that's all."

She was not laughing, however, when she called Rob on the phone in the middle of her ninth month—the third week Dr. Stone was with the clinic. "Dr. Tanner, I think I broke my bag of waters."

"Okay," Rob said, "then you'll probably be starting into labor. Come on down and let me check you."

"Well, I don't know," the woman said. "My pains have already started, but something seems to be sticking out."

Rob froze. "What do you mean, *sticking out?*"

388

"Looks like a loop of chicken gut or something, big around as my finger."

Rob cursed under his breath. "Ellen, if that's cord sticking out, your baby's in bad trouble. Can you get somebody to drive you to the hospital?"

"My husband's still at work."

"Then I'm sending the ambulance to get you. While you're waiting, get down on your knees and lay your shoulder and cheek on the floor and *stay there*—do you understand? That way gravity will help keep the baby from pushing on that cord. Don't fool with the cord itself, don't even *touch* it. Have you got that?"

"I—I think so. Doctor, am I going to die?"

"Not if I can help it, but the baby's in terrible danger. You go with the ambulance as soon as it gets there, and I'll meet you at the hospital."

He heard the siren howling through town as he and Agnes pulled into the hospital parking lot. A moment later the frightened woman was in the labor room. She was certainly in labor, and a loop of umbilical cord had dropped down to protrude below the baby's head, so it was compressed with each labor pain. With a stethoscope Rob could hear the rapid *tic-tac* rhythm of the baby's heartbeat, normal in tone between pains but speeding up frantically at the height of each contraction as vital blood flow to the baby was literally pinched off.

"Any way to push the cord back up?" Agnes asked.

"Not a chance in the world." Rob stood. "You keep her in a knee-chest position and try to push the baby's head up so a little blood gets through that cord during contractions. I'll call Esther to set up the OR for a section, fast, and then try to get Dr. Stone up here. The sooner we get that baby out, the better chance it has."

Faced with a crash emergency, Esther Briggs moved swiftly, delegating the floor nurse to call in the anesthetist and commandeering an aide to help her get the operating room ready. Tom Stone arrived ten minutes later with Martin Isaacs on his heels; in another ten minutes Sara Davis was in the OR, gowned and masked, checking the valves on the anesthesia machine. Although Esther's hostility to Stone was plain on her face, she pushed it aside to consult him about special instruments. But Stone shook his head and turned to Isaacs. "Martin, you're the expert here. You'd better take over and have Rob and me assist."

"Why don't we both assist Rob? He can use the experience."

389

"No, this baby's in trouble. You'd better do it and let Rob wait for a section that's planned."

Rob stood by to meet Agnes just moments later with a wailing infant in her arms. "A lovely pink baby," she said proudly. "Just four minutes from opening to delivery. Want to check her over now?"

Rob examined the infant quickly. "No problems I can see," he said, "but put her in the Rockette just the same. She's had a rough go of it for the last hour."

In the operating room he found Stone and Isaacs engaged in the tedious process of repairing the uterine incision. "That baby sure recovered from the anesthesia fast," he said as he joined them at the table.

"It hardly got to the baby at all," Stone said admiringly. "Never saw such a fast Caesarean in all my life. Very neat job. Uh—Martin, don't you think you should double-tie that bleeder?"

Later, in the coffee room, Isaacs said, "Thanks, Tom. That was a good case."

Stone shrugged. "When it comes to sections, it's your ball game. They scare me silly, all that blood all over the place."

Isaacs laughed. "I thought there wasn't any surgery you wouldn't tackle," he said.

"Oh, I'd tackle one in a pinch. But not with two guys around handling OBs. Even with me, there are certain limits."

# 34

Within a month the new surgeon was well enough entrenched that no one even thought of Harry Sonders anymore. Not that Stone became any more comfortable to work with. More than once Martin Isaacs emerged from a round of argument almost speechless with fury, tearing his hair and swearing under his breath that he didn't know why he'd ever hired the man. DeForrest drew steadily further into his shell, consulting Stone only when he had to, and rarely exchanging more than superficial morning greetings otherwise.

At the hospital, a huge battle with Roger Painter finally exploded, with Tom Stone insisting quietly but firmly that there were certain things, including reliable anesthesia and really skillful post-op nursing care, that the hospital simply *had* to provide if he was going to practice surgery there, and Roger, red-faced and shouting, insisting that he had no money to finance major personnel or equipment changes, and complaining bitterly that Harry Sonders and John Florey had both been doing surgery there for years without requiring special considerations. Isaacs got trapped into moderating this exchange, trying to calm Roger down while also attempting to get Tom Stone to relent a little, without noticeable success in either direction. It ended in a Mexican standoff, with Roger muttering about young wise guys from the city trying to run his shop, and Stone growling ominously about charnel houses and medieval pest holes.

Others reacted to Stone in varying ways. Esther Briggs, still smarting from Sonders' peremptory dismissal, slowly came around to admire the new man's surgical skill, much as she disliked his critical personality, and the two worked together in a sort of armed truce. John Florey quickly dispensed with politeness and dealt with Stone in open hostility, siding with Roger on the issue of hospital surgical facilities, while Ted Peterson, formally neutral, privately applauded Stone's viewpoint. "High time somebody else stood up and screamed about the way this place is being run," he said to Rob over coffee one morning. "If Roger would just try a little bit, he could get the things we need. But he won't even try until somebody pinches him where it really hurts, right in the OR schedule."

For all these problems, there were compensations. Tom Stone answered call any day and any hour that anybody wanted him. He seemed to thrive on lack of sleep, and tended his surgical patients closely, the first to arrive at the hospital for morning rounds, the last to leave the office at night. What was more, the new man's medical counsel almost always proved remarkably good. For a surgeon, Stone seemed to command an amazingly deep knowledge of other fields of medicine as well —and had no hesitation applying what he knew. More than once he caught Rob short on points of general medicine or pediatrics, and despite his insistence that he "knew practically nothing" about obstetrical care or gynecology, he had raised more than one awkward question with Isaacs, to the older man's chagrin. "I swear he spends every free minute reading the journals," Isaacs grumbled. "If he isn't on me to do more amniocentesis, then he's objecting to my weight-control program. Claims these women shouldn't have *any* type of thiazide diuretic, even if they puff up like poisoned pups. Next thing you know, he'll be telling me which forceps to use." Isaacs managed to put up with this sort of adventitious advice, perhaps because Stone seemed so naïvely unaware that it might be offensive, but DeForrest turned surly when the new surgeon challenged him on medical procedures.

"My God, Jerry," Stone would say in front of doctors, nurses, patients and all, *"nobody* uses the string test for ulcer diagnosis anymore. That went out with therapeutic bleeding. It makes your patient miserable, and it doesn't *tell* you anything. You stick *any* foreign body down a patient's gullet and his gastric lining is going to bleed a little. Show me the ulcer on an x-ray and I'll believe it, but don't bother me with string tests!"

"What if the x-ray doesn't show the ulcer?" Jerry returned angrily.

392

"You think that means it isn't there?"

"Of course not. If he's got the history and symptoms, you go ahead and treat him anyway, and maybe pick up the scar on later films. But as for making him swallow a ball of string—yech! That's witchcraft, man, that's not medicine." And DeForrest would go off muttering to himself and pull even further into his shell.

The hospital problem showed no sign of resolution. Roger insisted he'd contacted every M.D. anesthesiologist west of Great Falls to come out to cover scheduled surgery and emergencies, and failed to find a single one who would take on the job. Rob doubted that he'd gone to any such effort, but what could be done? The problem became especially acute when Stone's application for staff membership and surgical privileges at Sacred Heart Hospital in Missoula met with unexpected—and mysterious—resistance. First the application went to the Staff Credentials Committee, where it seemed to get buried. When Stone repeated his request for a prompt decision, he was told he needed letters of recommendation from all the hospitals where he had trained, regardless of his formal specialty credentials from the American Board of Surgery. He would also have to be formally presented to the rest of the Sacred Heart staff by a sponsor. Finally he and Isaacs drove in to a staff meeting in Missoula, where Isaacs gave him an introduction that, to Stone, seemed considerably less than impassioned. He was told his application would be considered "soon"—but a week passed, and then another, and nothing happened. Finally, angry and frustrated, Stone faced Rob and Isaacs with the question. "Somebody's blocking it," he declared. "There's no other reason for this delay."

"Nah, you're just impatient," Isaacs said easily. "They'll come around pretty soon."

"It couldn't be Sonders, could it?" Rob asked.

"Sonders couldn't care less," Isaacs said. "And who else would want to block it?"

"I don't know," Stone said, eying the older man soberly. "Who would?"

Isaacs laughed. "Well, certainly not me."

"Maybe not, but without surgical privileges somewhere in Missoula, I'm stuck with doing my cases out here, whether I like it or not," Stone said bluntly, "and it didn't seem to me you exactly knocked yourself dead getting our problem across to that Credentials Committee."

Isaacs laughed again. "Well, I'm not much of an orator, I guess.

393

Truth is, you're just up against a bunch of little tin gods in there. They want to make you sweat a little, that's all."

"Mm. And in the meantime, what do I do when I have a case that requires tricky anesthesia or really good nursing care?"

"Not much you can do but handle it here," Isaacs replied with a little smile. "Or hand it over to somebody in town. Wouldn't you say?"

If Isaacs seemed to find the issue somehow amusing, Rob Tanner didn't. More and more it seemed to him that Stone and the hospital were on a collision course, and he could not see how Isaacs could remain so unperturbed. For a while he clung to the hope that one side or the other would presently yield, at least enough to show good faith and open the way to compromise—but as days went by, neither side budged an inch. In private Rob urged Isaacs to use his good offices to break the deadlock somehow—either to press Roger into making a token improvement of some kind, or else really to exert himself to get to the bottom of the roadblock at Sacred Heart. "I'm telling you, Martin, this is a bad scene," he said. "We've got the whole hospital staff taking sides, and I think we're heading for trouble."

"Oh, hell, Rob, relax. Young Tom here is just bonehead stubborn, that's the real trouble. He'll get over it after a bit."

"I'm not so sure," Rob said. "If he's stubborn, he's smart stubborn. He's right, and he knows it. Roger is stubborn too, but he's also stupid, and that's bad. He's not bright enough to see that he's going to lose this fight, sooner or later, and maybe jeopardize the hospital to boot. Right now, he's just begging for a disaster to happen."

Isaacs laughed. "Rob, for Christ's sake! If a fraud like John Florey can take out gall bladders in the OR for the last fifteen years without a disaster, a man like Tom can stay out of trouble."

It made sense, Rob had to admit—but it also begged the question. Maybe Stone could stay out of trouble, but maybe others couldn't. It was an unsettling thought—and in fact, when disaster did strike, it was none of Stone's doing at all.

It came without warning, when everyone was least prepared. The patient was one of the first Rob had seen when he came to Twin Forks: a thin, gray-looking fifty-year-old spinster named Elsie Cobbell. A teacher in the local grade school, Elsie had come to Rob with a multitude of complaints including chronic bronchial asthma and frequent stubborn bouts of depression. Thrown over by a lover in her mid twenties, Elsie had drawn back from real human contact; with no family, few friends and little to vary the dull routine of crowded classrooms and

394

evenings by herself in her tiny room in the Twin Forks Hotel, she was a desperately lonely woman, too old to make major changes in her life, too shy to reach out for companionship.

Something in this sad woman's plight had struck a chord of empathy in Rob, and he had devoted extraordinary amounts of time to her care, urging her to open herself to more contacts with people, to become active in her church's Altar Guild and to join the local Business and Professional Women's group. Gradually her depressions had improved, but her asthma grew worse until the slightest hint of a cold or sore throat would leave her wheezing and gasping for breath. She lived in dread of chills or drafts, and even at her best she could often be seen visibly struggling for air, her squeaky breath sounds audible clear across the room.

Considering Rob's past efforts on her behalf, it was hardly surprising that Elsie called him at two o'clock one Monday morning when she began suffering sudden and severe abdominal pain, even though she knew that Dr. Isaacs was on call. Rob met her at the hospital, expecting a case of indigestion, but he soon changed his mind. Whatever was causing the pain, it was not indigestion. Elsie Cobbell had an acute surgical abdomen.

Tom Stone came up a short while later, at Rob's bidding, and checked the lab work and screening x-ray Rob had obtained. "Urine's clear, so it's nothing there," he murmured. "You say her appendix and gall bladder are both out, so it can't be those things. White count's up, though, eighteen thousand with a lot of young cells. Any fever?"

"Yes; 100.6 degrees," Rob said.

"And this has been coming on since eight o'clock last evening?"

"That's right."

"And some blood in one bowel movement around midnight?"

"That's what she said."

"Well, let's have a look at her." At the bedside the surgeon repeated Rob's examination, except that he spent long moments with his stethoscope listening to the woman's abdomen. Finally, with a sigh, he straightened up.

"You're certain you heard bowel tones before?"

"Positive."

"I don't hear a sound now."

"Obstruction?"

"Has to be that. And I don't like that bleeding episode one damned bit. I'm afraid we're committed to go in and look."

395

"Oh, dear," Elsie said. "Can't we wait just a little and see if it gets better?"

"I'm afraid that's too dangerous."

She looked up at the surgeon. "You think it's cancer," she said.

"Not necessarily. But even if it is, the sooner we get at it, the better, wouldn't you say?"

At the nurses' station Jessie Hodges was on the phone alerting Esther Briggs and Sara Davis of the emergency surgery. Esther was there in ten minutes, and presently Sara drifted in, reeking of licorice. Tom and Rob retreated to the doctors' dressing room to change into scrub suits. "What do you think it is?" Rob asked.

"I'd lay odds on a lower bowel obstruction with a gangrenous segment."

"From a cancer?"

"Most likely. Could be in the cecum or lower down." Stone paused. "You say she has trouble with asthma?"

"I'm afraid so."

"Damn." Stone scratched his chin. "I just dread the thought of Sara giving her an inhalation anesthesia."

"How about a spinal?"

"I'd give my left leg if I could sneak by with a spinal." He scratched his jaw again. "But I can't. I'll need all the relaxation I can get down there. *Damn.*" He pulled on the baggy green scrub pants. "We'll just have to see that she gets good respiratory support, that's all. And you watch the Davis woman like a hawk and yank her off if she starts dozing on the job."

Twenty minutes later the OR was ready and Tom Stone got started, with Rob assisting. In contrast to Harry Sonders' swift, almost casual operating technique, Stone was painfully slow and methodical, completing each step to his entire satisfaction before progressing to the next. Where Sonders would have left a poor tie on a skin bleeder, Stone would shake his head, snip it off and replace it himself. The overhead lights were hot and Rob started sweating under his gown, shifting from one foot to the other, taking the retractors from Stone when the peritoneum had been breached and hanging on for dear life. He moved over as the surgeon crossed to his side of the table to insert his left hand into the abdomen, waited patiently as Stone silently explored the cavity. Then, after endless minutes, Stone said, "Jesus."

"What is it?"

The surgeon shook his head. "Can't tell if it's a big tumor mass or

396

what. Adhesions all over the place." He withdrew his hand. "We've got to extend this incision. How's she doing, Sara?"

The anesthetist nodded. "Fine, fine. No problems."

"Is she getting plenty of oxygen?"

"She's pink as a baby."

"Okay; I'm going to need lots of relaxation in a minute. I'll tell you when."

He extended the incision lower and placed self-retaining retractors so that Rob was free to help hold internal organs aside. Stone worked intensely, peering into the incision and muttering to himself. At one point he stopped, straightening up and shaking his head. "Talk about a mess."

"What are you finding?"

"There's a big lump of something down in there, all tied up in adhesions. Last guy in here must have left her half full of blood."

"Is it something in the bowel?"

"Seems to be. Or in the mesentery. Or somewhere. Esther, I need you to retract for me too, and let's see if we can't kick that overhead light for a little better angle, hm? Little more. Okay, that may help."

Five minutes passed in silence, then ten as the surgeon slowly worked the mass from the depths of the patient's abdomen up closer to the incision. Finally Rob could see it in the angled light—a large, blackened lump of tissue the size of a softball.

At the same moment Stone said, "Well, I'll be damned."

"What?"

"That's no tumor, that's a volvulus. A loop of small bowel caught up and twisted in all those adhesions. Obstructed and gangrenous, all right, but it may not be cancer at all."

Once they could actually see the mass, Stone worked more swiftly, preparing to resect the damaged segment of intestine and then rejoin the healthy, pink ends of bowel from above and below the twisted loop. From time to time he checked the patient's vital signs and respiratory condition with the anesthetist, found no evidence of respiratory distress or shock. Finally the crucial part of the task was finished; Stone then changed gloves and explored the rest of the patient's abdomen, nodded his satisfaction, and finally began closing the long abdominal incision. "You say she's had no abdominal symptoms recently?"

"Nothing she's told *me* about," Rob said.

"Well, there *may* be a tumor in that loop of gut we took out—but small-intestine cancers are rare as hen's teeth. More likely she's had that loop all bound up in adhesions for months or even years, and then something happened to pinch it a little too tight, and she got some gangrene developing. Could have been anything that did it."

"Maybe she swallowed a peach pit," Rob said, so relieved at the outcome that he was feeling a little silly.

"Ah, yes. The Peach Pit Kid. Well, the pathologist should be able to identify peachpititis, if that's what it is. We'll see." Dr. Stone stepped back from the table, the closure completed, and stripped off his gloves. "Lord, it's almost dawn. So much for *that* night's sleep. Maybe I can get home for breakfast, though, if I get moving. I'll dictate the operative note if you'll write an admission note on her chart—okay?" He turned to Sara Davis. "Be sure that tube stays down in her stomach while she's recovering," he said. "That bowel of hers is going to lie there like a dead dog for a good forty-eight hours before there's any activity, and we need to keep her stomach empty. We don't dare have her vomiting. And keep the respirator right by the bedside, just in case she has any respiratory distress at all."

They helped Sara move the still-sleeping patient from the operating table onto the wheeled gurney. As Stone disappeared into the doctors' dressing room to dictate his operative note, Rob sat down at the nurses' desk to write an admission note on the patient's chart. He was aware of Sara Davis wheeling the patient down to a room, then bringing in the oxygen tank and respirator as Dr. Stone had ordered. Esther and an aide were busy cleaning up the OR. Presently Stone appeared, glanced into Elsie's room, nodded to Jessie Hodges as she helped the anesthetist, and finally went out quietly, leaving a page of postoperative orders for Rob to insert in Elsie Cobbell's chart. By a quarter to six Rob too was driving down the hill, reflecting sourly that one quick hour of sleep before rounds would at least be better than none.

Ellie was waiting in bathrobe and slippers at the back door as he turned in the driveway. "They want you back at the hospital right away," she said. "Your post-op patient is in trouble."

Rob stopped dead. "What kind of trouble?"

"She threw up a tube or something and she can't breathe. Jessie Hodges called and she sounded frantic."

"Oh, good Lord. Call her back and tell her to get that respirator going. I'll be there in five minutes." Rob gunned the engine back to life and backed out onto the road. A moment later he was whizzing across the bridge, turning onto the highway on two wheels and flooring the accelerator. He ran the red light in the center of town and skidded to

398

avoid a dog on the road up to the hospital. Moments later he was running up the ramp, bag in hand.

The corridor and nurses' station were deserted. In the patient's room he found Jessie Hodges hovering tearfully over Elsie Cobbell's inert form, emesis basin in one hand, ineffectually dabbing at the patient's mouth with a towel.

"What happened?" he demanded.

Hodges leaped as if she had been stung. "Doctor, I don't know. She's trying to breathe but she's not getting any air."

Rob pushed the nurse aside, bent over the patient. Elsie's face was gray, her eyes closed, body flaccid, with only an occasional convulsive movement of her throat and mouth to suggest she was even alive. The nasogastric tube lay on the pillow beside her head, and a trickle of thick, yellowish, sour-smelling stuff oozed from the corner of her mouth. With a swift movement Rob reached out and pulled her jaw forward with one hand, inserted a finger in her mouth to scoop out more of the sticky emesis. He snapped on the bedside suction and inserted the metal tube into the patient's mouth. "Get me an endotracheal tube," he said.

"There's one right there on the shelf."

"That's great; get it open for me." He snatched the pack from Hodges' hand, ripping it open and unwrapping the curved tube. "What in the hell happened?"

"I don't know. She was recovering just fine, and then I had to go answer the phone, and when I came back she'd thrown up tube and all and her mouth was full of that stuff and she wasn't breathing."

"Where was Sara Davis?"

"She had to go take her husband to work."

"With a patient still under anesthesia? Good Christ. And Esther?"

"She left when she finished the cleanup."

More stuff was coming up through the suction tube, and finally Rob got the tracheal tube inserted. By then Elsie Cobbell was totally flaccid; even the occasional breathing movements had stopped. "Have you got that respirator ready? There's still a lot of junk down there, but we've got to get some air in fast—" He broke off, staring at Hodges. "My God, woman, what now?"

Hodges was in tears. "The valve's stuck and I can't get it going," she sobbed, looking fearfully at the respirator. "Half the time I can't make it work at all."

"Well, then give her mouth-to-mouth while I fiddle with it." Rob stepped aside and virtually pushed the nurse toward the patient, then turned his attention to the respirator tank and mask. In a moment he had the tank on and the respirator mask and valve functioning. "Now hold this in place over her mouth. You don't have to do anything, just hold it snug." He placed the mask properly, heard the machine administer a wheezy puff of forced oxygen every five seconds like the ponderous swing of a low, heavy pendulum. While Hodges held the mask in place, Rob stripped away Elsie's gown, watched to see if her chest was rising and falling with the respirator. He shook his head, listened momentarily with the stethoscope and shook his head again. "She must have gotten a quart of vomit down her windpipe," he said. "Let me try that suction again."

A second time, frantically now, he worked the suction tube, pulling Elsie's jaw and tongue forward, again sucking a quantity of sticky yellow stuff up from her chest, some of it tinged with blood. Once more he tried the respirator, found some movement of air now but not enough. The woman's pulse was so rapid and thready he could hardly detect it. He shook his head again, turned to the aide, who was standing transfixed at the foot of the bed. "Get me a tracheostomy set," he said. "Open it up, and bring a pair of gloves too. Hodges, you keep that respirator going for dear life. I'll be right back."

Stepping out into the corridor, he grabbed the phone on the nurses' desk and dialed Dr. Stone. "Tom, you'd better get up here. That Cobbell woman is going out on us. Aspiration. She's got a chest full of gunk, and I can't even push air in with the respirator."

"Have you got a tube down?"

"Yes, but it's plugged tight."

"Then get her trachea open. I'll be right there."

Back in the room Rob had Hodges hold the respirator mask in place from the far side of the bed while he pulled on sterile gloves, then made a small incision through the midline of the patient's throat and into her windpipe. Fixing the small metal air tube in place, he again used the suction tube to clear out the trachea. Finally he adapted the respirator tube directly to the new, open airway, and for the first time saw Elsie Cobbell's chest fill with oxygen-rich air, then fall with expiration, in a regular, even rhythm set by the respirator. "Check her blood pressure, will you?"

The elderly nurse bent over the blood pressure cuff, listened with the stethoscope. "I can't get it."

"Let me try." Rob took the cuff, pumped it up around the woman's arm, listened to catch the first sound of pulse—but no sound came. He

shifted the stethoscope to the left side of the patient's chest, but found
no heart sounds. He thumped the patient's chest twice, three times,
with his fist, furiously, and was listening again, in vain, as Tom Stone
walked in.

Rob handed the tall man the stethoscope grimly. "I think she's in
cardiac arrest," he said.

Stone listened intently for a moment. Then he tossed the stethoscope aside and leaped onto the bed over Elsie's inert body, pressing
her chest down and releasing it at one-second intervals in a rhythmic
attempt at external cardiac resuscitation. The man seemed so intent, so
determined, that for a few moments Rob actually thought it might
work, and busied himself adjusting the respirator pressure—but the
patient remained inert, unmoving except for the effect of the artificial
breathing and circulation aid. The room was hot, the air stinking of
emesis; sweat formed on Stone's forehead, and he swiped it away angrily with his sleeve between compressions. "All right," he said breathlessly, "now tell me what happened."

Rob told him what Hodges had said, what he had found when he
arrived back at the hospital, what he had done since.

"And where was Sara Davis all this time?"

Rob told him. Stone turned to look at Hodges. "She just walked out
and left you in charge?"

Hodges nodded. "The aide was here, but she was busy with Mrs.
Cone down in Room 5."

"And this patient wasn't even fully recovered when she left?"

"She was just muttering and moving her head. Sara left her on her
side, but she must have rolled over on her back when I went to get the
telephone."

"And drowned in her own vomit." Stone looked at Rob in cold
anger. "Rob, you get ready to relieve me here. I'm going to get Roger
Painter over here to see this, and Isaacs too."

"You think it's helping?"

"Hell, no. She's gone. But we've got to try for a decent interval, and
get encephalogram leads on her for documentation too. Those bastards
just wouldn't listen when I told them they were going to start having
bodies on their hands if they didn't shape this place up. Well, they're
going to listen now, or else."

Rob moved in to take over the cardiac compression as Stone moved
aside. There was no sign of response from Elsie Cobbell, no indication
of life now, and it seemed to Rob that he actually could feel a slight

401

coolness of her body, a sense of waxy plasticity of her flesh that had not been present before. *It's no good,* he thought. *She's gone and this is just a pointless exercise. You were just too late, too slow, too trusting. You should never have gone down that hill. If you'd been here when she first vomited, you might have helped her, but you weren't.* In the steamy room he was pouring sweat, feeling the muscles of his wrists and forearms cramp as he pressed, released, pressed, released. Five endless minutes passed, then ten, before Stone returned with the electroencephalograph machine, placed the basic leads at the patient's temples, forehead, scalp, snapped the switch for recording, let the tape run and run and run. Finally, with a sigh, the surgeon snapped off the machine. "You might as well give up on that. There's nothing coming through."

Rob had expected it, yet the stark words jarred him. He leaned back and straightened up, staring at the waxy pallor of the woman's face, her head turned away from him, eyes closed. He walked around the bed, removed the respirator mask, noticed the purplish marks it had made around her nose and mouth. He snapped off the respirator, and in the sudden silence in the room, moved the dead woman's hands up across her chest, and drew the sheet and blanket up.

"What the hell is going on here?" Martin Isaacs demanded from the doorway. He was bleary-eyed and unshaven, his white hair rumpled from sleep.

Rob looked up at him. "You'd better ask Tom Stone," he said coldly.

"But this looks like Elsie Cobbell. I was just talking to her in the dime store last night." Isaacs walked in, staring at the dead woman. He reached down and picked up the encephalogram tape, ran it through his fingers and let it flutter to the floor again. "My God, it *is* Elsie Cobbell. *What happened?*"

"She died, that's what happened. The anesthetist took off, and the nurse couldn't get the respirator valve working, and Elsie choked to death. That's what happened."

"Anesthetist? Respirator? I—I don't get it."

"Oh, hell; check it out with Stone," Rob snapped, pushing his way past the big man. "Me, I'm sick of talking to you."

Isaacs flushed. "Well, now, hold it! I'm not going to have some lightweight surgeon preaching to me about what's wrong with this place—"

"Oh, Martin, climb off it. I told you long since that we were going to have one like this sooner or later. I told you loud and clear, and all you did was laugh. Well, now maybe you'll stop laughing. Maybe you'll

402

shut your mouth for once and try to listen. Maybe Stone can knock some sense into you. I can't. I'm tired of trying."

He started for the door. Isaacs turned slowly. "Rob," he said.

"What is it?"

"Maybe you're right," Isaacs said tightly. "Maybe I should have listened. Maybe I can even get Roger to listen. But where are you going now?"

"Me? I'm going home. I've been up here since two o'clock this morning, and I've had it up to my ears. I'm going home to bed for a while. But don't worry, I'll be down at the office by nine." Rob turned and walked out past the nurses' desk, past a grim-faced Nellie Webster just coming on duty, and down the ramp to his car. As the wet morning breeze struck his face, he thought of Chris and what she had said that night at the cabin. *You can plant your heels in the ground and bend your neck and just slug it out. . . . Or you could leave . . . get into your car, and start driving—and never look back.* Suddenly there was nothing he wanted to do more, nothing in the world, than to get in his car and start driving and never look back. Instead he drove down through the town, stopped for a morning paper, and then headed back toward the river through the wintry rain.

Later, at the clinic, Tom Stone walked into Rob's office, carefully closed the door and sat down facing him across the desk. "Got just a minute?"

"Certainly."

Stone sat silent for a moment, as though selecting his words. Then he said, "We should never in the world have lost that woman."

"I know," Rob said.

"I can't put up with something like that again," Stone said. "I won't hang around for it."

"I know." Rob looked at him. "But maybe you'd like to stay and fight."

"Sounds interesting," Stone said. "Like how?"

"I'll tell you how. I've been fighting for six months, and gotten nowhere—but I haven't had the right weapons. They don't really *need* me, you see. But they need you badly. Without surgery that place will fold. And with both of us fighting, and both of us hanging tough, we can break that place right open."

"I'm beginning to see," Stone said. He looked at his fingers. "It might get a little bloody, what you're proposing. I'd need you right behind me, all the way."

"Don't worry about that."

"Martin won't like it very much."

"Then that's for *him* to think about."

"Yes, of course. I see." Stone stroked his chin thoughtfully. "It's a nice little town here. I'd like to stay. So you know what I think?" He looked at Rob with those cool gray eyes. "I think you've got a deal."

# 35

For Ellie, the shock of Jennie Isaacs' death slowly faded, but the resolve she had taken did not fade. Instead it intensified day by day. The awful message was too agonizing by far for her to put it aside any longer. If it meant confrontation, it meant confrontation, but much as she might dread that, she dreaded the alternative more.

The new surgeon's arrival was no aid to her resolution. Rob was preoccupied—Lord, everyone in *town* seemed preoccupied—with how the new man would work out, and the waiting backlog of surgery piled up since Sonders' firing had buried the doctors in work. The times that she saw her husband at all were more and more fleeting every day, his temper more and more uncertain when he was home. And now, increasingly, there were more and more evening intervals when he was —inexplicably—*gone. He can't just be running and hiding,* she told herself, *and hospital rounds on his off-duty evenings just can't take four or five hours, night after night after night.*

She caught him at low ebb, the morning Elsie Cobbell had died. She'd known there was trouble from Hodges' frantic call, and she'd read it in his eyes when he returned home two hours later. He'd sat drinking coffee, a thousand miles away, while she cooked breakfast. "What happened?" she said finally.

"We lost a patient."

"Oh, dear."

"No damned reason we should have lost her; we just *lost* her, that's all," he said bitterly.

"We?"

"Tom and I. Look—I've got to eat and go."

She brought more coffee to the table, sensed his suppressed fury, and then rejected it fiercely. *Not again. Not one more time.* "Martin has call tonight," she said. "Isn't that right?"

"On Monday night Martin always has call."

"That's good. Because tonight we've got to talk."

He looked up from his coffee. "I may be held up," he said.

"Perhaps you'd best not be, tonight." She turned back to the stove, her hands trembling, fighting to control herself, forcing herself to concentrate on the bare mechanics of breakfast-making—turning the bacon again, pouring the grease into the can by the stove, cracking the eggs into the pan and salting them. "We've got to talk, with no interruptions. No calls to take, no rounds to make, no nothing—just talk."

"About what?"

"About us. You and me. Nobody else but us. Now eat and go. I'm taking my shower."

He was gone when she was finished, and she went about the house doing busy work—cleaning up the breakfast dishes, making the bed, dusting. About noon she drove to town and shopped for pork chops and mushrooms for an easy casserole dinner. On the way back she stopped to pick up Belle, who was hobbling along the highway, both bags laden. "Feel like some tea?" she asked the old woman as they drove across the bridge.

"Not today, dearie. Princess has been irritated with me, being gone so much. I've got potting to do this afternoon, and baking bread this evening that I didn't get done last week." Belle tucked a string of white hair under her beret. "Maybe I'll bring you a loaf or two when I'm through."

"Maybe not tonight," Ellie said. "Rob and I have got some talking to do."

"I see," Belle said, tugging at her lip. "Biting the bullet, eh, dearie?"

"You might say."

"Well, we'll let you be, then, Princess and me. Bite hard while you're at it."

As Belle went on up the road, Ellie set down her groceries and then descended to the riverbank and sat for a long time, staring at the dark water swirling past the rocks, listening to the wind rattling the few remaining leaves on the cottonwoods on the farther shore. *Almost December, and a long cold winter coming up. A gray time of year, a bad time—but there isn't any good time, is there? Not for some things.*

It was almost dark when she went back in and started dinner. An hour later Rob appeared, seeming remarkably cheerful, snooping in the casserole, actually whistling a bit as he showered before dinner.

She waited until they were through eating and Rob had a fire going. "You must be bushed after last night," she said.

"Sure am. Think I'll turn in early, for once."

"Something good must have happened today."

"Could be. Tom and I had a talk. Between the two of us, we may get some changes made."

"That sounds good," Ellie said. "That's what we have to talk about. Some changes being made."

"I mean up at the hospital," Rob said.

Ellie took a deep breath. "Well, I mean right here."

"What kind of changes?" Rob said. "What's there to talk about?"

"Just about everything. You and me, and what's happening to us. All the things you've been ducking and dodging and shying away from all these months."

"Is this going to be a lecture about all my shortcomings as a husband and father-to-be?"

"Rob, we can't run and hide any longer. We just can't. I've waited and I've waited, but it hasn't done any good. And now I just won't wait any longer. If we can't talk now—oh, *damn!*"

Someone was thumping on the kitchen door. Ellie went to answer it, pulling her robe tight as she went.

Outside in the darkness she saw Belle Foreman standing, beret askew, the old woolen coat only half buttoned, tears streaming down her face. Her hands were coated with flour and she seemed hardly able to stand. "Belle! What on earth—"

"Oh, Ellie." The old woman staggered through the door, then buried her face in her floury hands. "My Princess," she croaked. "I've killed my Princess. I've murdered my darling."

Rob came up with a chair for the old woman, who sank down into it, sobbing. "That old yellow cat?" Rob whispered, and Ellie nodded fiercely.

"Belle, what happened?"

"I was making my bread, just like always. I didn't get it done last week, so I had to tonight, and Princess was helping me, just like always. And then when I'd put the first two loaves in to rise and bake, I couldn't find her." Belle looked up helplessly. "I hunted and I hunted. I thought I heard her crying, a long way off, but I looked high and low, and then the crying stopped but I still couldn't find her. And then I went to get the bread—"

"Oh, Belle. Oh, *God*, Rob."

"She'd jumped inside the oven to get the apple pie drippings from last week, and I didn't see her when I put the bread in—" Belle choked and buried her face, weeping inconsolably. "I murdered my sweet Princess."

Rob started to get his jacket, but Ellie shook her head. "I'll take her back," she said, helping the old woman to her feet. "I'll do what I can." She looked up at Rob, tears of defeat in her eyes now. "I'm sorry, but there's nothing else to do. Maybe tomorrow night we can talk. Maybe —tomorrow."

# 36

Rob was late to the office next morning, delayed by a heart patient in massive failure up at the hospital. When he finally reached the clinic, it was almost noon and Isaacs was buzzing his intercom fiercely. "Rob? Come on down here a minute before you get started," he growled.

Rob found the older man sitting at his desk, polishing his glasses furiously. Isaacs was clearly distraught; when Rob came in he leaped to his feet and peered out the window toward the parking lot, then opened the door to his examining room to be sure no one was there. Rob stood awkwardly, watching him as he finally went back to his desk. Presently Isaacs looked up as if just seeing Rob, and said, "Say, I just checked your wife this morning, and she's looking okay. The baby's fine, and she's fine, so you can quit worrying." He put his glasses back on. "I —uh—thought you might like to know that," he finished lamely.

"Great," Rob said. "Is that all?"

"Oh, hell, sit down a minute," Isaacs said. "What do you want me to say, for God's sake? I know that was an awful thing with Elsie Cobbell up there yesterday morning, and I feel lousy about it. Elsie was one of my oldest patients. But Jesus, Rob, there wasn't a thing either one of you could have done about it."

"Yes, there was," Rob said. "If we'd sat right there by her bed, it never would have happened."

"Well, that's ridiculous. You've got to count on your help some-

409

times. You've *always* got to count on your help to some degree, you *can't* do it all yourself, and if your help lets you down . . ." He spread his hands. "At least we can be glad the woman doesn't have any family to come back at us."

"What do you mean, come back at us?"

"You know what I mean. We've never had a malpractice suit yet out here, and I'm not eager to start now."

"Malpractice!" Rob stared at the man in disgust. "Well, I guess every cloud has a silver lining, if you want to look at it that way."

"Yeah, a silver lining; that's about it," Isaacs said. "But listen, Rob, you've got to help me rope this Stone guy in a little bit. I swear to Christ he's gone right off the edge. He just hasn't got any *right* to talk to Roger Painter like that."

"What do you mean?"

"Up at the hospital, this morning. I never heard anything like it. Stone just laid into Roger like he was some kind of public menace. Told him he could take his crappy little hospital and shove it up his ass sideways, and man, I'm quoting verbatim. Told him his nurses wouldn't make good hog-callers, and as for Sara Davis, the next time he saw her anywhere near one of his patients he was going to break her neck over his knee."

"Sounds good," Rob said. "I'll be right there to help."

Isaacs blinked at him. "Oh, come on, now."

"I mean it. We need that woman like we need gangrene. The same goes for that stupid Hodges. How long has that respirator been in the place? Five years? And she still can't get it to work right half the time."

"Oh, for God's sake, Rob. You can't expect Roger to throw out his whole damned staff just to please some smart-ass surgeon who's only been around for six weeks. Why, you should have *heard* him this morning. I tell you, this guy Stone is nuts."

"Then two of us are nuts."

"Rob, you don't know what Stone was *saying* up there. My God! He's going to wipe out our surgical practice." Isaacs lurched to his feet and leaned across the desk. "You know what he said? He said he wouldn't do another surgical case in that place any worse than stitching up a cut lip until Roger had an M.D. anesthesiologist hired on a regular basis for both scheduled work and call. He said he wouldn't do another case up there until Roger had a competent surgical nurse on full-time call for post-op nursing, and *he* was going to be the one to decide whether she was competent or not. He said he wouldn't do another case

410

until every nurse and aide on the staff had learned to run all the emergency equipment, with *him* deciding when they'd learned well enough. He said a lot of other things too, including calling the hospital a goddamned pest hole, and until everything is up to snuff according to *his* way of thinking, he's going to take all his surgery to Missoula, and if the hospital there won't give him surgical privileges, he's going to *refer* it all."

"Sounds good to me," Rob said. "Wouldn't you say?"

"But that's *half our practice* he's talking about giving away."

Rob raised his eyebrows. "If he can't do surgery up there, he can't do surgery. And if we have many more dead bodies up there, we aren't going to have any practice to worry about. Or any hospital, either."

"Oh, hell," Isaacs said. "He's making a mountain out of a molehill. It just isn't that *bad* up there. I mean, open heart surgery might be one thing, but for just ordinary cutting and sewing—"

"You mean 'just ordinary' like Elsie Cobbell?"

"Well, of course not. Hell, you know what I mean."

"I'm not sure I do," Rob said. "But I know damned well what Stone means. He's through taking chances up there, and I'm with him one hundred and forty percent."

"But you *can't* be with him! He's going to send our surgical practice right down the tube." Isaacs, whose voice had been rising, glanced at the office door and went on in a lower tone. "Look, Rob, I guess I'd like Roger to straighten things out a little up there just as much as Stone would. Okay, fine. Maybe I can nudge him into action now. But it's going to take a bit of time."

"God, Martin, you've had fifteen years now. How much time do you want?"

"All right, maybe I haven't really worked at it before this, just sort of let things ride when I shouldn't have, but I need time *now*. And believe me, having Stone going in there kicking and screaming and threatening isn't going to help a damned bit."

"So what do you propose?" Rob said slowly.

"First we get Tom Stone to cool off a little bit. You get along with him better than I do; he seems to listen to you. Maybe you can get him to pull back a little—"

"No dice," Rob said. "For one thing, I don't think Tom is going to cool off for anybody. I think he's going to do just what he says he's going to do. If Roger wants to get moving fast, that's fine. If he doesn't, then the surgery goes to town. As for me, forget it. There is no way I'm going to intercede for you. Not after Elsie Cobbell."

Isaacs stood staring at him for a long moment. Finally he sat down behind his desk again, fighting to control his anger. "Rob, you're making a bad mistake. This is no piddly little squabble. This could wreck the practice. If you and I can't stick together on this, we're in real trouble —and John Florey is just going to clean up on our surgical cases."

"Not if Tom can take cases to town, he won't. And between you and me, Martin, it might be a real good move if those people at Sacred Heart suddenly changed their minds and okayed Tom's surgical privileges— like, say, tomorrow."

Isaacs flushed. "I can't do a thing there."

"Oh, come on. It's no accident they're stalling him. With his credentials, there shouldn't have been any question at all. Somebody is purposely blocking him."

"And you think it's *me?*"

"Who else? If the shoe fits, wear it."

"Oh, for God's sake! You're as paranoid as Stone." Isaacs sat back, his face florid. "Well, let me tell you something, buddy. Stone is going to have to bend a little on this issue, or he isn't going to have any surgery around here to practice. And that goes for you too. You guys seem to think that you can just walk in here and run things any way you want, but you're going to find out different. I didn't spend the last fifteen years building up this practice just to have a couple of young punks come in here and tear it apart for me. As far as I'm concerned, I've been crowded as far as I'm going to be crowded. Now you'd better go back to your little office and do a little thinking before you come shooting off your trap to me again."

It was hardly more than he might have expected, Rob reflected later. He hadn't planned to accuse Isaacs of blocking Stone's staff appointment at Sacred Heart; the words had popped out without thought —yet they made a certain amount of twisted sense. Isaacs wanted Stone doing surgery in Twin Forks, whatever the hospital's shortcomings— and without Sacred Heart to resort to, the surgeon would seem to have precious little choice. If Isaacs had sensed that Stone might really rebel against the local hospital, he might very well have exerted some quiet pressure to block Stone's city appointment. But if so, he had clearly not considered the risk of a disaster case such as Elsie Cobbell's—and he had seriously misjudged Tom Stone's reaction to a squeeze, and Rob's frustration as well.

Whatever Isaacs had done, it soon became clear that Tom Stone was not backing down. Turning up at the office just as Rob's meeting with Isaacs ended, the surgeon picked up a phone and quietly canceled two elective surgical cases scheduled for later that week, explaining to the patients quite matter-of-factly that he was dissatisfied with particular aspects of the care at the hospital, and since the scheduled cases were not urgent, he preferred to wait until certain improvements had been made. Another patient—a woman Rob had found with a lump in her breast—Stone handled differently. After reviewing the woman's history and examining her carefully, he referred her to a Missoula surgeon for an immediate breast biopsy to rule out cancer. "Too bad," he told Isaacs, "but there's no excuse for delay, and I'm not about to get trapped into a radical mastectomy up in this monkey house. Jack Finley's a good man. I've talked to him at meetings a couple of times, and he's invited me to assist on the case, privileges or no privileges."

Throughout the next few days Stone followed the same course, to the obvious distress of both Isaacs and Roger Painter. Minor cases requiring local anesthesia that Stone himself could administer were scheduled at the Twin Forks Hospital. So also were a few cases Stone could do under spinal anesthesia that he or Rob could administer personally. Any other cases were simply not scheduled at all. If the surgery was elective, Stone offered the patients a choice: they could wait until he was satisfied that "problems at the hospital" had been corrected, or they could go to Dr. Finley in Missoula. But patients requiring immediate major surgery were referred without the blinking of an eye. And as these cases mounted up, first one or two, then a dozen, Martin Isaacs grew more angry—and more frantic—by the day.

"He's getting the whole town up in arms," Isaacs raged to Rob one morning a week after the disaster. "Everybody's asking me what's wrong with the hospital, what's happened, why do they have to go to some stranger in Missoula? So what am I supposed to tell them? It's an outrage! And the fees we're losing—my *God!* He's given away *ten thousand dollars' worth of work!*" But despite Isaacs' fury, Stone did not waver, and neither did Rob. While Isaacs fumed, Stone quietly refused to schedule, and nothing Isaacs said would budge him.

One major confrontation involved a patient of Isaacs', a middle-aged woman with a huge ovarian mass. Isaacs asked Stone to see the patient and confirm the need to remove the mass and determine its nature. "No question in the world," Stone said. "It's either a cyst or a tumor, and at her age it could well be cancer. It's got to come out."

"Fine. Then schedule her," Isaacs said.

413

"Up here? You're crazy. I wouldn't touch it up here."

"Look, I'll be the surgeon of record and you can assist. This is as much my field as it is yours."

"I meant what I said, Martin. I wouldn't touch it up here. If it's cancer, we could end up doing a whole pelvic cleanout, and for that you need top-rate anesthesia, to say nothing of a pathologist to do frozen sections. There's no way in the world I could justify doing a case like that up here."

"Then by Christ, I'll do it without you," Isaacs exploded. "I'm not going to ship a case like this off to somebody else."

"Well, that's your decision, of course," Stone said mildly. "But you might have trouble defending yourself if something went wrong, especially if your own surgeon testified against you."

"Nothing is going to go wrong. You're paranoid, that's all, just plain paranoid. You're looking for spooks under the bed."

"Perhaps."

"Oh, hell, just forget it." He glared at Stone and then at Rob, who had sat silent through this exchange. "I'll schedule her myself, and I'll do her myself if I have to get Jerry to scrub with me." Isaacs turned and stalked out, returning to his office, where the patient was dressing. He remained sequestered with her there for over half an hour—but ultimately he did *not* schedule her case, referring her instead to a man in Missoula. "It's absolutely insane," he told Rob later, still fuming. "There's no reason in the world I couldn't take care of that case up here —but what can I do? With him opposed, if something went wrong I wouldn't have a leg to stand on. *My own surgeon,* and he makes me give away good surgery. God! Why the hell did you guys ever let me bring him in here in the first place?"

"*Let* you! Much choice *we* had."

"Yeah; well, I must have been out of my mind. He's just going to have to give a little, that's all. This is impossible!" And Isaacs stormed down the hall to his office again, muttering to himself.

But Stone did not give, and Rob did not give, and in the next few days the clinic took on the aspect of an armed camp. More and more, Isaacs began pointedly ignoring both Rob and Stone, passing them in the hall in icy silence, responding to direct questions with monosyllabic grunts, and brushing aside greetings and other remarks with no response at all. When he needed information or consultation with one or the other, he would summon them to his office like an emperor to his court, make his query as abruptly as possible, and then dismiss them

414

with a wave of his hand. His hospital rounds and office hours both became erratic; he would appear suddenly, an hour or two late, and then be gone again with equal abruptness, sometimes simply vanishing and leaving scheduled patients waiting for hours before he reappeared, if he reappeared at all that day. More often than not the nurses, thoroughly confused by the signs of open warfare, shuttled the patients in for Rob or Jerry to see as they could, and then suffered in silence when Isaacs later berated them for "messing up" his schedule. When he *was* in the office, he began tormenting the nurses mercilessly, complaining bitterly over minor sins of omission and commission, leaving Dora nervous as a cat and more than once reducing Agnes to tears in front of his OB patients. Sometimes he spent hours on end in closed-door conferences with Bev Bessler in her little cubbyhole office, while at other times *nobody* knew where he might be, and Terry took to tiptoeing warily down the hall and talking in whispers whenever she had to consult with Rob or Stone or DeForrest on some scheduling problem.

Jerry DeForrest remained carefully aloof from it all, avoiding Stone like the plague, drawing back even from Rob, and spending his time diligently minding his own business with his own patients in his own office and emerging only to go to the men's room. As for Rob, he set his jaw and plowed along through his daily schedule, feeling the tension mounting day by day as the great gaping hole in the practice that Isaacs had predicted—the sudden sag in surgical cases—became increasingly acute. Ellie watched him warily, aware that something was very wrong, but uncertain precisely what; and when she asked Rob point-blank, he brushed her aside. "Tom and I are in a big fight with the hospital, that's all," he told her. "And we'd better tighten our belts, too, because it may go on all winter."

Of them all, Stone alone seemed totally unperturbed, moving about the clinic with the same bland, noncommittal expression as always, speaking quietly, always politely, seeing such surgical patients as there were to see and doing whatever surgical work he could do in the office and hospital according to the terms and limits he himself had set down, seemingly unmindful of, or unconcerned about, the atmosphere of tension and siege that was settling down about the clinic. "It's just fantastic," Rob said to Chris during one of his brief stolen evening visits to her apartment. "He acts like nothing is happening while the roof falls in on all sides."

"He's a stubborn man," Chris said reflectively. "And he knows he's

415

right. That's a tough combination to beat."

As day followed day it became increasingly clear that something had to break. But even Rob hadn't realized the true desperation of the other side until one evening when Roger Painter flagged him into his office as Rob was finishing rounds. The man looked hollow-eyed, his fingers nervous, one eyelid twitching erratically. "This is terrible," he said. "This is just terrible."

"Whatever do you mean?" Rob said innocently.

"You know damned well what I mean," Roger flared, then caught himself, forced his hands to sit still on the desk. "I don't know quite how to put this," he said finally, with an almost pathetic tremor in his frosty voice. "I know you and I have had our differences before, but now I need your help. I can't keep this place open without surgical revenues, and Florey and Peterson just don't bring enough in. I can't pay a surgical crew to sit on their thumbs all day, and I can't stay open without them. I've got to have Stone's work, or we're going down the tube. That's the long and short of it."

"So what can I do?" Rob said.

"You can talk to him," Roger said. "He seems to like you. Maybe he'll listen. Maybe you can press him a little, make him see—"

"Sorry," Rob said, standing up. "I've got no magic wand, and I wouldn't use it if I did. Matter of fact, I *agree* with Stone—and as far as this place is concerned, I'm just plain talked out."

Roger cleared his throat. "I—I know you've been upset," he said slowly. "But I'm not entirely asking for favors. Some time back the board turned down a request for certain things you thought desirable. A blood storage unit, an incubator for typing and crossmatching. I—um —personally thought their action was a little hasty, thought perhaps they hadn't fully appreciated the need." Roger looked up coldly. "In fact, I'm quite certain I could get them to reverse that decision, if I felt I had your support in this current conflict. Your positive support, I mean."

Rob looked at the man and scratched his ear. "You know, Roger, there's one basic difference between you and me," he said finally. "The difference is that you're all prick."

Roger flushed. "Doctor, there was a committee of twenty solid citizens in this town who wanted that blood storage unit—"

"That's right," Rob snapped. "And they're going to get it too, and a whole lot more as well. But I'm not going to sit here and be blackmailed by some little shit of a hospital manager. You're far too late for bargaining, Roger. We're going after bigger stakes now, and we're going to win. We're going to clean up this pest hole, or we're going to close it. Now you can go tell your board of directors I said that."

"You stupid ass!" Roger was on his feet, shaking. "You don't even know what you're saying! You bloody idiot! What do you mean, tell the board of directors? What do you think *they're* going to do? Who do you think pays them? Who do you think owns the stock they vote?"

"Well, who?"

"Maybe you'd better find out who, before you sit here and tell me you're going to close this place down!"

"Oh, Christ, what am I doing here?" Rob stared at the man for a moment, then walked out, slamming the office door behind him. He drove on down the hill, feeling physically ill at Roger's shabby little offer, furious at him for talking riddles. *What does it matter who does what, anyway? The place has got to change or it's got to close, and that's what really matters.*

Five days passed, with Isaacs growing increasingly ugly and Stone more coldly obdurate. And then, on a Tuesday morning, quite without fanfare or warning, Tom Stone received a certified letter from the administrator of Sacred Heart Hospital: a cold, formal one-paragraph letter informing him that he had been admitted to the courtesy staff of the hospital with full surgical privileges. In short, he could now admit and treat his own surgical patients without the need to refer them to another surgeon. When Rob saw the letter he whooped and congratulated the tall surgeon, who seemed to take the decision with absolute calm, almost indifference. Isaacs glanced at the letter and brushed it aside, handing it back to Stone and saying, "Yeah; well, I told them they'd better get off their asses," and walked off down the hall.

Two days later Rob and Stone were interrupted at morning coffee at the Twin Forks Hospital by a perspiring and red-eyed Roger Painter, looking as totally miserable as any one man could look at eight o'clock in the morning, with news that his search for personnel had borne fruit. "There's a man in Missoula just retired from full-time practice, an M.D. anesthesiologist named Sternig, very highly recommended by all the surgeons there. He's sixty-five, wants to ease up a bit but still keep his hand in. He's willing to come out here for scheduled cases on Tuesday and Thursday mornings, at least for a trial period, providing there's enough scheduled work to make it worth his trouble." Roger paused, looking pointedly at Stone. "That means it'll only work if you schedule all the surgery here you possibly can. If you keep boycotting us, it'll fall through."

Stone pursed his lips. "You checked his credentials?"

"He checks out fine; board certified and everything. I checked, but you can check too, if you want to."

"Has he been out here and looked at your anesthesia equipment? I mean right here on the spot?"

Roger looked uncomfortable. "He's been out. There are quite a number of things I'd have to get for him, but I'll get them as soon as you agree."

"What about night and emergency call?"

"He's not too eager for much of that, but he'll back up Sara Davis on any cases you think may be especially tricky." The harried man spread his hands. "Look, I know you're down on Sara, but there are some things she can do, and she *will* respond to call, even with me taking most of the scheduled cases away from her. But I've got to give her *something* or she's just going to tell me to stuff it. Look, for God's sake, there's got to be a *little* give and take here. Florey and Peterson are perfectly happy with Sara, they *like* Sara, but they're willing to go along with the new man for scheduled cases just to help me out. I mean, they're willing to compromise. I should think you could compromise at least a little on Sara."

"And who decides if the emergency case is too tricky for Sara?"

"Well, you do, except if you just keep boycotting her on that basis it's not going to work."

"Well, maybe some cases might work out," Stone said reflectively. "What about the post-op nursing care?"

"That's something else. You can't just create a good surgical nurse out of the air, but Janice Pryor, our head nurse three to eleven o'clock now, has had five years surgical ward experience in San Francisco. She's willing to take over post-op care on all the surgicals if I can get somebody else to take evenings. In fact, she'll do double duty for a while to give me time to find somebody."

"Yes, I think Pryor might do very well," Stone said. "She's the one nurse around here who seems to know which end the patient's mouth is at. So that leaves the question of teaching the girls to run the special equipment."

Roger sighed. "Okay, it's going to cost me money, I'm going to have

418

to pay them for the time, but if you want to do the instructing, I'll work it out somehow."

"Sounds fine," Stone said cheerily. "I felt sure you'd find some way around these problems. So let's give this setup a try and see how it works."

"You mean you'll go along with it and start scheduling again?"

"Of course; why not? I told you right from the first that I'd start doing patients up here again just as soon as I thought it was safe, didn't I? So this sounds like it's worth a try. Of course, there are still some limits. Without a pathologist out here I can't do patients who require frozen sections and a preliminary path report while the patient is still on the table, so I'll have to take those cases to town, right?"

"I—suppose so."

"But then, there aren't all that many of those, anyway, and for the routine things—well, we'll give it a try. Let me know when Dr. Sternig can be here."

"He can be here next Tuesday morning at seven-thirty," Roger said.

"Fine. I've got two or three cases hanging fire right now. I'll get them scheduled this morning."

When Roger had left, Rob looked at Stone with a mixture of wonder and admiration. "By God, you got him to move," he said.

"Well, of course," Stone said. "He had to move, sooner or later. What did you expect?"

"I didn't think he'd move that far," Rob said.

"He had no choice; that was obvious from the first. There was no way he could keep this place running without operating room revenues and surgical beds filled. It was just a matter of how long it would take to convince him, that was all."

"Well, we've got what we wanted," Rob said. "Maybe things will settle down now."

"One must hope, as Jerry would say." Stone looked at Rob with the faintest hint of a smile. "Of course, there are a few other minor items. This lab setup is ridiculous, trotting samples to Missoula by hand and then waiting three days for a written report. And this whole Mickey Mouse x-ray setup he's got here—God! Raymond Potter doesn't know x-ray technique from finger painting. And your blood storage unit, and a few other things. But there's no rush on them. We can let them wait until next week—wouldn't you say?"

419

# 37

Winter came to Twin Forks the first week in December with a suddenness and ferocity that surpassed anything in the memory of the oldest residents. Throughout October and November there had been alternating rain and sunshine, dismal days interspersed with balmy Indian summer, days of shimmering golden tamarack groves on the mountainsides, with the alders, cottonwood and aspen in the valley clinging to their yellow leaves with fierce determination. Even the occasional snowfalls in the mountains had washed off the pass highways with the ensuing rains as though they had been premature accidents of nature, and the brushings of white appearing on the mountaintops on nippy mornings had vanished before evening. Thanksgiving, early that year, had come on a day more fitting for September, with gentle sunshine and balmy wind carrying clouds of yellow leaves scurrying down the main street and cluttering lawns all over town. Rob had drawn call for the entire four-day Thanksgiving weekend and had found that what he suspected was true: when it came to calling doctors, the people of Twin Forks were no more reluctant to seek out medical care on a home-and-family holiday weekend than any other time of the year. From the summons at 4:30 A.M. Thanksgiving morning from a mother whose child had tippled from the Clorox bottle to an all-night wait on a reluctant delivery on Sunday night, he was kept running almost constantly for four days, and ate his Thanksgiving dinner at the DeForrests'

420

in four or five broken installments scattered through the day as he hustled off to clinic or hospital to answer calls.

Then, on the first day of December, the snow had come, beginning late the evening before as a gentle sifting of white velvet in the windless night, piling up to eight inches of fluff by morning and continuing steadily and heavily throughout the day, landing in great piles and billows, filling streets and alleyways and driveways with the soft, dry powder and reducing transportation in the town to a standstill by evening. The river, already swollen by the fall rains, became filled with great clots of sodden snow falling in from the banks and carried downstream; the trees around the river house bent down under their load of white, breaking the power line and necessitating an emergency call to the electric company. By afternoon the air was filled with the groan and roar of the snowplows fighting to keep the highway clear as the feeder roads became so drifted that travel was impossible.

Rob responded to Ellie's call and came home early from the office —no problem, since patients had been canceling all day and the waiting room was empty by 3 P.M.—to shovel the driveway. By then there was almost a fifteen-inch accumulation, and after finishing the drive he looked nervously at the house, remembering what he could of the roof construction, and scratched his head, and then went up and shoveled the roof as well. Later, going to the hospital for evening rounds, he nearly buried the car on the road to the highway before finally getting out and putting on chains. In town, Ernie from the gas station was doing a land-office business plowing parking lots with his old chained-up jeep with the plow blade on a hydraulic lift on the front, and helping the town snowplow make a great heap of the white stuff down the center of the main street. Hospital Hill had been plowed and replowed (first on the snowplow's agenda, he'd heard) and Raymond was busy on a diminutive tractor-plow scraping newly collected snow from the parking lots.

The change in weather was uplifting—mostly because it was a change. The fragile truce between Tom Stone and the hospital had held up through the first week, despite Roger Painter's inability to work out a time that all the nursing and operating room staff could meet for instructions on the use of emergency equipment. Tom chose to assume that at least Roger was trying, and perhaps he was. Stone had scheduled three cases on the first Tuesday with the new anesthesiologist—a T&A and two hernia repairs that he had merely postponed through the period of the boycott—and on the following Thursday he undertook the

421

removal of a Baker's cyst from the back of a logger's knee, a procedure which Harry Sonders would have whipped through in twenty minutes but which took Stone an hour and a half of puttering. Dr. Sternig, graying and patient, proved the soul of competence at the anesthesia end of the table, and for the first time in months Rob had the feeling of working in a real, bona-fide operating room again.

In addition, Stone had accepted Sara Davis's services for an emergency appendectomy which had turned up on Thanksgiving night. Janice Pryor had been on hand for the postoperative nursing care, her normal, quiet, competent self; and Stone had also stood by, extra-wary; but no problems had arisen. By the end of that week it seemed to Rob that the surgeon was easing his vigilance at least a trifle, and the entire staff was also beginning to relax visibly. There was a sense of a watershed behind them, a milepost finally passed, and it was not until then that Rob fully realized to what extent the entire hospital had been enveloped in a sense of crisis since Elsie Cobbell's death two weeks before.

The truce did not, however, carry over to the clinic—at least not in any way that mattered. Martin Isaacs did not like Roger's resolution of problems at the hospital; to his mind, they were problems Stone had created in the first place. He clearly resented the fact that Stone had won, not only at the hospital but in the clinic office as well. Isaacs remained withdrawn, frosty and sullen; and if he resented Tom Stone's triumph, he was flatly furious at Rob's stand in the battle. To his mind, a breach of faith had occurred, a breach of loyalty, and he was not inclined to forgive or forget.

Isaacs' ire presented Rob with a difficult problem. From the first, informal "curbstone consultations" had always simplified daily practice to an enormous degree. Hardly a day had passed that Rob had not called on Isaacs' knowledge and experience to resolve some problem—and Isaacs had called just as freely on him for problems of child care he encountered. This exchange of information was never precisely even: Rob really needed help, while Isaacs was never so helpless in dealing with infants and children as he professed. But now, with Isaacs licking his wounds—and actively at war with Rob—such hallway consultations became difficult or impossible. Isaacs' hours became increasingly erratic. Whenever there was a lull in his schedule, he would simply walk out, leaving Agnes with instructions to call him at home when he had more patients to see. When he *was* on hand, he seldom came out of his office, and when he emerged for a cup of coffee he was invariably

422

preoccupied and distant. More often than not, when Rob brought up a question, he would say, "Oh, hell, Rob, *I* don't know, why not check the book?"—or equally often, he would simply turn and walk back down the hall before Rob had time to finish his question. Nor did Isaacs call Rob in for informal consults anymore. He would simply mark a child's chart *Dr. Tanner to assume care* and send the mother down to the front desk to make an appointment with Rob.

It was irritating, but there was little Rob could do. He hoped, at first, that Isaacs would presently cool off—but days and weeks passed without a sign of change. Of course, Stone was there as a permanent thorn in Isaacs' side, but like it or not, Isaacs had to deal peaceably with Stone. Stone was the surgeon Isaacs had hired. There was a stream of surgery to be done, and that meant money; where Stone was involved, Isaacs was trapped. He could not relegate Stone to a status of nonexistence, much as he might have liked to; the man, unfortunately, was indispensable. But Rob was different. . . .

For Rob it was especially trying because a sort of negative feedback began working. With Isaacs inaccessible, Rob turned more and more to Stone for consultation, as well as for coffee-break bantering and give-and-take. Increasingly, when Isaacs did emerge, he found their heads together, and read conspiracy in the air. He glared at Rob, and shunned him further, as if his blackest suspicions were being confirmed day by day.

Rob soon learned to manage without the curbstone consultations, but occasionally a patient needed a careful, thoroughgoing gynecological or obstetrical workup. Barred from informal access to Isaacs, Rob followed the more formal route: making special appointments for his patients to see Isaacs. Even this ran into problems. One such patient was a middle-aged woman with bleeding and spotting after her menopause. Rob knew she needed a diagnostic D&C to rule out cancer; he merely wanted Isaacs' confirming opinion. But next thing he knew, Isaacs had admitted the woman to the hospital and was scrubbing to do the D&C. When Rob complained, Isaacs just shrugged. "You sent her to me, so I assumed you wanted me to do it." And that was the last he saw of *that* patient.

Another case was even more distressing: a twenty-two-year-old woman two months pregnant, thin and sallow, with a terrible case of acne and glasses so thick they looked like the bottoms of soda bottles. The problem was classic, and insoluble. The girl had been severely diabetic since age eleven, with total loss of insulin control during her

423

adolescent years. Since then she had had two previous pregnancies, both mercifully ending in early miscarriage, but her diabetes had worsened. Now she was almost blind from the disease, using huge doses of insulin to keep her condition under some semblance of control. She had come to Rob for the care of her pregnancy only after John Florey and Ted Peterson had both turned her down, recommending she seek out an OB specialist in Missoula. "But I can't," she told Rob plaintively. "My husband's been out of work since they closed down the plywood plant this summer, and the car don't run well enough to get to Missoula."

Rob examined her and reached the only conclusion possible: the pregnancy was a threat to her life. "You just won't survive it," he said as gently as he knew how. "It's a dirty trick, but when it happens, there's only one thing to do, and that's get rid of the pregnancy."

"You mean have an abortion?" the girl said.

"I'm afraid so."

"But I don't want to," she said. "I want my baby."

"I know," Rob said. "But it doesn't make sense."

The girl's eyes filmed with tears. "Anyway, I can't," she said. "I'm Catholic, and Dr. Peterson already talked to Father Stowe, and he said no."

"Then we've got to get you the most expert care we can," Rob said. "Come see Dr. Isaacs this afternoon and see what he says."

She saw Isaacs at three o'clock. At four the big man came back to Rob's office with her chart in his hand. "This diabetic woman," he said. "She's got to get rid of that pregnancy."

"That's what I told her," Rob said, "but she can't."

"Then get rid of her. Pack her off to town." He dropped the chart on Rob's desk and turned to go.

"Martin, it's not that easy. She's got no way to get to town."

"Let her ride the bus or something. If she hangs on to that baby, she's going to die. If you want to play the big hero and take care of her, go right ahead; just don't call on me. I wouldn't go near her myself."

"But I'm referring her," Rob said.

"Not to me, you're not."

"Look, Martin, *somebody* has to help this girl, and you've got a whole lot more experience than I do."

"That's right. I've got enough experience to know when I'm whipped. Do anything you want with her, but count me out."

It was obviously no solution, and the next day he talked again to the

424

girl. "There's a bus each way every day," he said. "It wouldn't be hard to see a doctor in town."

"But *why?*" she insisted. "I haven't had trouble since I got pregnant this time. I'll do anything you tell me to do."

"That may not be good enough. You could be in trouble no matter what I tell you to do."

"But maybe I won't."

"Three months from now we might just have to pack you off to the city in an ambulance."

"If you have to, you have to. But can't we at least see how it goes?"

Finally he gave in, much as he hated to. "What else could I do?" he asked Tom Stone later. "Martin says I'll have a mess on my hands —but at least I'll know what's going on with her. If I send her off and she won't go, she'll have no care at all for six months—and then when the fat's really in the fire she'll be right here on my doorstep again anyway, and then I won't know *what's* going on."

Stone shrugged his shoulders eloquently. "Martin's right. She's going to be a mess. But you're right too. If you're going to have her on your hands anyway, you might just as well be in the driver's seat from the start. And there's always a chance you might pull her and the baby through clean as a whistle. All you need is just fantastic good luck."

Other consultations were equally frustrating. Sometimes Isaacs merely wrote a terse note in a chart; other times he would stop Rob in the hall with a scathing remark and then stalk off. What was more, quite suddenly he began to set steep consultation fees. Marlene Daly, the diabetic woman, came to Rob in tears the week after her visit with Dr. Isaacs; an additional fifty dollars had been added to her obstetrical bill. "I only saw him for a few minutes," she said, "and he didn't tell me nothing at all, and we just haven't got the money." Rob reduced his obstetrical fee by an equivalent amount, determined to jump Isaacs about it at the first opportunity—but the opportunity never came. Soon other consultation fees began appearing, to the point that Rob began to think twice about consulting Isaacs at all.

It was during this period that Janice Blanchard came in for her regular OB check near the end of her seventh month, and Rob decided that like it or not, Isaacs should see her once more as her term drew near. Janice was still adamantly opposed to a Caesarean. Contrary to Isaacs' early predictions, she had followed Rob's instructions to the letter, keeping her weight under control and behaving like a model OB patient in every way. The baby, moving for three months now, seemed vigorously healthy, with good heart tones and a pattern of intermittent rest and activity that suggested no threat to the pregnancy. Indeed, everything seemed favorable for a trial of labor—but Rob was determined to leave no stone unturned. If something were to happen to tie him up at delivery time, Isaacs would have to step in, and he wanted both patient and doctor prepared. He even held some faint hope that Isaacs might finally agree to the trial-of-labor idea.

Janice objected. "Why bother?" she said. "All he's going to do is lecture me about Caesarean sections. And anyway, I think he's mad at me. I said hello to him twice on the street this past week, and he just turned around and walked off."

"I still think you should see him," Rob insisted. "You're only two months away now, and we have to be prepared."

"But you're going to be here, aren't you?"

"I'm sure going to try. But who knows? I might be delivering somebody else at the critical moment—or be dying of pneumonia, for that matter. I can't promise to be right by your side for the next two months."

"I suppose not."

"And this is for *your* protection, just in case he has to step in."

"Don't worry," Janice said tightly. "It's you I'll be calling, not him."

"Fine—but if you can't get me for some reason, then call him and don't fool around. Do you understand?"

"I suppose so."

"Okay. Now take this slip down to Terry and she'll set up a time with Dr. Isaacs."

However reluctantly, Janice Blanchard kept the appointment on Isaacs' next regular OB day. Rob saw her come down the hall to the older man's office. How long she stayed he didn't know, but the meeting was clearly stormy. Within a few minutes Agnes was back in the coffee room, shaking her head and muttering to herself. "I swear I don't know what's gotten into that man," she said. "The way he lit into Janice was just disgraceful."

"What do you mean?" Rob said.

"Oh, telling her she had to have a Caesarean whether she liked it or not, and how she should have been seeing him right from the first, and how disloyal she was after all he'd done for her, and a whole lot of other rubbish. She didn't say a word, poor thing. Just sat there and listened. Seemed kind of strange, in a way. She's got a sharp tongue, she

426

used to tell him off right back, but not this time. She just sat there."

"Well, I hope he checked her over."

"Oh, he checked her, but he was sure in a bad mood—"

At that point Isaacs himself appeared and Agnes went on about her chores. Isaacs glowered at Rob and thrust out Janice's chart. "What the hell are you sending this woman to *me* for?" he demanded.

"Just routine," Rob said. "In case she goes into labor when I'm tied up and you have to cover."

"Well, you've sure got her straightened out fine," Isaacs said bitterly. "I tell you, that woman's got a head full of mush. You can talk and talk and talk, and she just won't listen. She's still babbling about a trial of labor."

"I know. The way she's been doing, it might just work."

"Well, if you're still planning that, you've got big, round holes in your head," Isaacs said.

"I don't see why. She knows we may have to do a section after all, and she agrees that it'll be up to us to decide on the spot. I don't know what else you could ask."

"Well, as far as I'm concerned, you should never have taken her on in the first place. You're playing with fire, and you don't even seem to know it. And if you keep insisting on this trial-of-labor crap, you're on your own. Don't holler for me when the fat's in the fire."

"Oh, hell, Martin," Rob said wearily. "If I have to holler for somebody, I imagine it'll be you. And if something happens that you have to handle things, I suppose you'll do what you think best. So let's let it lay for now."

"Well, it's your grief, not mine," Isaacs said, setting his coffee cup down with a *thunk* and starting up the hall. "Just so you know where I stand."

The crowning insult fell that same week, on Isaacs' day off, when Agnes dropped a chart on Rob's desk and said, "Looks like another new OB for you."

"Really? Who?"

"Mollie Hart. You worked on Tommy's broken arm, remember? Well, she's pregnant again, and she says if this one isn't a girl she's going to throw herself off the West Fork bridge."

In the examining room Rob found Mollie waiting, with the usual faint aroma of stove oil about her, a little chubby, a little grubby, but cheerfully complacent. He remembered how she rode herd on her flock of irrepressible boys when Tommy was coming in with his arm, and he

427

had seen her other places too—in the supermarket, the drugstore or the gift shop, always surrounded by children and friends, always joking and laughing, the sort of person to whom everyone else in town was a pleasure and joy. She'd always been treated by Dr. Isaacs, and had had her share of trouble, to judge from her chart: a couple of miscarriages as well as six deliveries; an almost fatal case of viral pneumonia several years before; the loss of an early child to spinal meningitis; and a leg fractured in an auto accident only a year before. Now here she was, accepting the fact of another pregnancy even though she'd been on the pill, or thought she was. Rob examined her, and sighed. "You're pregnant, all right. Three months or more. But why do I get the nod this time? You have a fight with Dr. Isaacs?"

"Fight?" Mollie threw back her head and laughed. "Mercy, no, I'd never fight with him. He's the only doctor I've ever seen in this valley, until you came along." She paused, turning suddenly sober, looking down at her hands. "No, it's really just the money."

"The money?"

"Right. Of course, everything's going up these days, but George doesn't earn much at the mill, and I can't work, with the kids to take care of. And with all these mouths to feed, that extra hundred dollars is just more than we can manage."

"The extra hundred dollars," Rob repeated.

"Yes. Dr. Isaacs said if I'd been a month earlier, I'd have gotten under the wire, but once he made the change he had to make it for everybody."

"I see," Rob said slowly. "Well, I suppose that's right. But we're still trying to hold the line on this side of the hall, so you don't have to worry. Okay, Mollie, I'll want to see you again next week. We'll have the lab work finished by then, and we can get you going. Got to watch your weight like a hawk this time, and get you some flu shots, keep you out of *that* trouble this winter."

When she was gone, Rob walked down to Bev Bessler's office. Bev was busy with the day's postings, but pushed her work aside when he came in. "Yes, Doctor?"

"Bev, tell me about Dr. Isaacs' new OB fee."

"Oh, he put that into effect last Monday. He's charging four fifty now."

"Since last Monday, you say."

"Yes." She looked up at him. "You knew that, didn't you? He said you'd both talked it over."

428

"Point of order. *He* talked it over. I told him no way was he going to charge more than I did for OB care in this office. If he's done it, he's just gone ahead and done it on his own."

"Oh, my." Bev looked distressed. "Well, Dr. Tanner, I'm sure there's some kind of misunderstanding. He didn't say a word about you objecting."

"There's no misunderstanding," Rob said. "He knows *exactly* where I stand. He just decided to slide it under the door whether I liked it or not."

"Oh, dear," Bev said. "I can't imagine—I mean—" She glanced at the phone. "Do you want me to call him?"

"Not really. If he wants to charge four hundred and fifty dollars for OB care, I certainly can't stop him."

Relief showed in Bev's eyes. "Well, I'm glad you look at it that way. Things have been so tense around here, Dr. Isaacs just hasn't been himself. So if you don't object . . ."

"I couldn't possibly object. But of course, if he can raise his fee anytime he chooses, so can I, and I just did. Better mark it down so the girls get it straight. If he charges four fifty, I charge four fifty, beginning today."

"Oh, my." Bev's face was white. "But, Doctor, the whole idea—"

"I don't like the whole idea."

"But that's higher than anyone else charges around here. If you *both* raise your fees, a lot of these women . . ." Her voice trailed off.

"Yes. Well, if you can figure that out, so can he. And if enough of these women trot down to Tintown fast enough, maybe he'll wake up before he's torn the whole OB practice apart."

"But what about Mollie Hart?"

"She's home free—but nobody else. Whatever he charges I charge. And if he doesn't like it, he can come check with me."

He started for the door, but Bev stopped him. "Doctor—are you going to tell him about this?"

"I don't see why I should," Rob said. "He didn't tell me. And this really is a two-way street, you know. If he can't see that, it's high time he got new glasses."

Furious, Rob walked to his office, pulling charts from his box on the door as he went. *That* was where he'd seen Mollie Hart so recently, coming out of Isaacs' office last Tuesday—but not a word to *him*. He pushed the charts aside in disgust. Well, Martin had made the move, now Martin could back off from it. A $450 fee didn't make *sense* in a little town like this, full of loggers and millworkers. It was more than city specialists were charging, for God's sake. There was no excuse for it here. But that was for Isaacs to think about. If the women went to Florey in droves, all the better. If enough of them left that it really began to hurt, maybe that white-haired bastard would think twice before he kicked Rob Tanner in the crotch again.

He got through the rest of the day somehow, drove to the hospital for rounds, still seething, then headed home. Over a silent dinner he turned aside Ellie's queries with brief answers. Ellie fought his silence valiantly. "There's a pre-Christmas sale at Jorgen's," she said. "Some really nice things."

"Nice prices too, I'll bet."

"That's true. They had a lovely winter sweater there, but eighty-nine dollars was a little too much."

"God, I should hope so."

"But you do need some shirts."

"There's always the Sears catalogue."

"True." She lapsed into silence as she served a pudding for dessert. "I hear it's going to be a long, cold winter," she said.

"Where'd you get *that* good news?"

"Ernie at the gas station."

"What does Ernie know about the weather?"

"He heard it from the Indians. They say it's going to be a long, cold winter."

"The Indians are in touch with God somehow?"

"I don't know, but old Chief Hanging Dog reads buffalo chips or something, and he hasn't been wrong in forty-five years."

"Well, I wish somebody could get Ernie to shut his mouth once in a while and plow our road a little wider," Rob said. "Ernie has got diarrhea of the brain, if you want my clinical opinion."

"Oh, Rob, he was just making pleasant conversation."

"Well, I don't find his conversation so pleasant. Ernie's a fucking snoop."

"Okay," Ellie said. She cleared the table in silence and loaded the dishwasher while Rob moved to the living room, stirred and refueled the fire in the fireplace and collapsed to the couch with a couple of journals. He was angry at Martin, yes, but also angry at himself for his outburst. He just couldn't seem to respond to Ellie at all anymore without a snarl or a put-down. It wasn't what he wanted, he told himself. What he wanted was to be left alone—but even that wasn't true.

430

He was more depressed now than at any time since he had come to Twin Forks. He wanted desperately to tell somebody about the day's indignation, the tension at the clinic, the bitterness he felt at Isaacs' unilateral fee-fiddling. He could barely tolerate the growing sense of frustration, of humiliation, his sense of being helplessly trapped in a sequence of events that he could neither control nor alter. But faced with Ellie, he felt an unscalable barrier appeared. Even when he tried, he could not enunciate the words to his wife; and with each failure he found himself pulling back further, pushing her away. With Chris, at least he could talk—yet the very fact that Chris came to mind in this context made him block Ellie still further. He could talk to Chris, but it was Ellie he was faced with, and with every passing day there was a growing conviction, deep in his mind, that an end point was approaching, that something was going to break. . . .

Presently she joined him in the living room, dressed in the dowdy green bathrobe she'd worn for as long as they'd been married. She had some sewing, a needlepoint pattern held in a ring. He sat leafing through a journal, his mind turning back to the afternoon's disclosure and his own explosion of bitterness.

"Rob?"

"Uh?"

Ellie looked up for a moment. "Have you had another big fight with Martin?"

"Not yet. That comes tomorrow. Why?"

"I just wondered. I saw him on Tuesday, my regular appointment. He seemed very odd."

"Odd?" Rob put the magazine down and looked across the room at her.

"Like I was a total stranger he didn't quite know how to deal with. Nervous. Almost clumsy. And then after he'd checked me and said everything was okay, he muttered that maybe you'd be happier if he had somebody in the city take over my care—just to be on the safe side, or some such thing."

"Well, that's ridiculous," Rob said.

"I thought so too. I told him if I needed help for some reason I sure didn't want to have to drive seventy miles to get it, and he just sort of shrugged and said, well, he thought he'd mention it, and then he hustled me out of there like he was embarrassed or something. But what do you suppose he meant?"

"Christ only knows," Rob said. "He's been shitting square bricks

431

ever since Tom Stone turned up and started making waves about the crappy hospital setup, and he's been climbing all over me for the last two weeks."

"Why you?"

"Who else? He can't tackle Stone directly, and Jerry only peeks out of his hole once a week, so that leaves me. What that's got to do with your OB care, I just don't know. But when he gets pissed about something, he churns around like an angry bull until he gets it straightened out, and he's sure been pissed lately."

"Well, I just thought I'd tell you," Ellie said.

"Yeah." Rob lapsed into silence, staring at the journal in his lap. Ellie picked at her needlework. The silence lengthened and thickened. Rob got up, walked to the kitchen, looked half-heartedly in the refrigerator. He wished fiercely that the telephone would ring, wished he could go up to the hospital again, but he went back to the sofa instead. Something was wrong in the room. He saw Ellie look at him, then glance quickly away. Finally he slapped the journal down. "Okay, what's bugging you?" he demanded.

She shook her head, peering intently at her needlework.

"Come on, something's wrong. You've been watching me like a hawk ever since I walked in tonight. What is it?"

"We never got to finish our talk," Ellie said. "Poor Belle—"

"Yes, Belle and her goddamned cats."

"They're all she's got. She's quieted down a little by now. I finally got her to go to town today."

Rob studied her across the room. "You wanted to talk to me about Belle?"

"No, no. Belle's going to be all right. But seeing Martin got me to thinking again. About the night I started bleeding." She poked at her needlework. "Martin was very upset that night. He thought I was going to lose the baby right then and there. That was why he tried so hard to reach you."

"Reach me?"

She nodded. "In Missoula. All evening long." She looked up soberly and steadily. "Where were you that evening, Rob?"

"Oh, for Christ's sake. I've been through that a dozen times."

"No. Just once, I think. Something about being at Sacred Heart until ten and then having engine trouble in the rain. But Martin tried to get you at Sacred Heart just after nine. He had you paged, and finally

432

called his friend Ted Bonney out of the meeting to look you up. But nobody'd seen you at that meeting. Not a soul."

"Okay, fine," Rob said angrily. "So I went for a secret tryst with my paramour."

"Who is your paramour, Rob?"

He sat up, knocking the journal to the floor. "For God's sake, Ellie, what's got into you? Can't you tell sarcasm when you hear it?"

"Maybe not," Ellie said. "I don't know. I'm not sure of lots of things I thought I knew. But I know one thing for sure: something's gone very wrong with us in the last few months, and I don't know what it is, and you aren't telling. I don't know where you were that night and I don't want to know. But you're a very bad liar, and wherever you were, you're lying about it. And ever since then, you've been cutting me dead. You've been practically living up at that damned hospital, and the few times you happen to be here, the minute I try to say something you slam the hatch down so hard it's a wonder you don't get your fingers caught. You haven't so much as laid a hand on me for two solid months—"

"You're forgetting your delicate condition," Rob cut in.

"Oh, *balls*, my delicate condition. Even I know better than that and I'm no doctor. And I don't think you've suddenly turned into a monk, either—"

The telephone rang as they stared at each other. Rob grabbed it before the second ring. He muttered something into the speaker, listened, then muttered again and hung up. "It's the hospital," he said lamely. "I'm on call."

"Great," she said. "I wish that place would burn to the ground."

"The pass is a mess with all this snow and ice. I may be up there all night. I can't help that, but you can call and check anytime you want."

"I'm not going to check. I don't care if you're at the local whorehouse."

"There isn't any local whorehouse. All the loggers go down to—"

"Oh, God, *shut up.*" She whirled on him bitterly. "Go on, get out, go up to your crummy hospital. But let me tell you one thing, Rob Tanner. This little girl isn't going to be another Jennie Isaacs. The practice is important, but it's not holy, and there's something very wrong when a man's work tears people's lives into shreds. There's something wrong in this house, and I'm not going to sit around and take it anymore. I'm not going to be whipped and stomped and frozen into

433

some sad little shadow by you or anybody else. I'm still young and I've got a life that matters to *me,* and the life we've had this last few months is not the life I'm talking about. And if there's a whole lot more of it, you may just find yourself living it alone."

# 38

The invitation arrived that Monday morning: a personal note from the chief of surgery at Graystone Memorial Hospital in Seattle, inviting Rob to attend the annual Graystone Clinic Day conference the second weekend in December—now just two weeks away—and participate in Graystone's special Alumni Program of clinics, lectures and social events planned the following day for all departed interns and residents of the hospital's training program. A printed announcement had crossed Rob's desk weeks before, but he'd thrown it out, preoccupied with his problems. This letter, however, caught his attention. "As one of our most recent Family Practice residents at Graystone, we especially hope you can attend and perhaps chair a panel discussion on the problems facing family practitioners in a semi-rural practice setting," the letter said. "Please let us know if you can be with us." Rob read it, lifted his eyebrows and read it again more thoughtfully. Then he took it down to Isaacs' office before the first patients of the day arrived.

"Semi-rural practice setting, eh?" the big man said sourly. "Why doesn't the condescending bastard just say out among the cows and pigs? They'll probably expect you to come in a horse and buggy. So what's your problem? You want to go to this thing?"

"It might be worthwhile," Rob said. "It sure would be some kind of a change, and I haven't got an OB due for a couple of months yet."

"So go ahead; I can't stop you. Better leave Ellie home, though. I

435

don't want her jouncing around in an airplane right now. Could be that having you gone for a few days wouldn't hurt there, either."

Rob opened his mouth to say something and then closed it again. That evening, though, he hadn't even mentioned Isaacs' cautionary edict when Ellie ruled herself out. "There's a Sacred Heart bake sale that Saturday," she said, "and I've promised to be on hand. Anyway, I don't feel like taking a trip right now, or wandering around Seattle shopping, either. You'll just have to go by yourself."

"Okay," Rob said. "I'll see about a plane ticket." Since her outburst the week before, Ellie had had little to say to Rob, or he to her. A half-dozen times over the weekend he had tried to say something to break the ominous mood she had set, but what could he tell her? That he'd fallen in love with Chris Erickson, and that that was the way it was? Whether it was true or not, he wasn't ready for *that* yet. And as for Ellie, having shouted in his ear, she had little else to say. Angrier, perhaps, than even she realized, she was of no mind to try to patch things up. The next move was Rob's, and now that she'd taken a stand, she clung to it.

Rob phoned Chris the next evening after his last patient had gone. "Bad night to try to see you, I've got the call, but I wanted to let you know."

"Seattle, hm? I've always liked Seattle."

"Liable to be pretty sloppy this time of year. But all the stores will be open dawn to dark on the Saturday, and there are only a few things I absolutely have to appear for. We could make it a long weekend, fly out there Friday night and be back sometime Monday, if you could get away."

"No problem; I'm pretty much my own boss. And I've got to be in Missoula that Friday anyway—a seminar at the U."

"Then let's plan it. I'll order the tickets and meet you at the airport." Rob paused. "God, we can actually have some time to talk for once, without peeking out windows and wondering what kind of egg old Ernie is going to lay the next day."

"True." Her voice was thoughtful. "We haven't done much talking lately, have we?"

"Too busy with other things."

"Yes. One might say." She paused. Then: "How are things on the home front?"

"Christ! Between Isaacs and Ellie and Roger Painter, if I don't get

436

out of here pretty soon, things are going to blow right out of my left ear."

"Well, be discreet, baby. Why things haven't blown out long since I'll never know, but be discreet. Is Wednesday night still on?"

"Right. Call me about eight-thirty. If I'm not there, you'll know something's queered it. Otherwise, the same as usual. See you then."

When he had rung off he sat back for a moment, closing his eyes, consciously willing his tense shoulder and neck muscles to relax. It was risky, these desperate meetings with Chris, fleeting and ephemeral as they were, sometimes at her apartment, with his car left parked at a discreet distance, sometimes a swift trip to Darby or south over the pass to Gibbonsville, or more often up at Ed Butler's cabin. He knew exactly how risky it was, yet increasingly and perversely he found himself caring less and less about the risk. Taking Chris along to Seattle would be even riskier; although plausible excuses could conceivably be made if they were seen together in the vicinity of Twin Forks, being found together in Seattle could hardly be excused. Yet he threw caution to the winds. In part this devil-take-the-hindmost attitude came from a growing weariness of dissembling, and the knowledge that it would hurt Ellie if she ever found out, but in larger part it was something else: an intensifying, almost fatalistic conviction that something was going to break soon, that the fragile, enchanted world with Chris could not last as it was, that the world of Isaacs and Stone and Ellie and the practice was approaching a crisis that could not now be averted or altered and that the shape of things that would ultimately emerge simply could not be foreseen.

Certainly he did nothing to break the impasse with Ellie, and the approaching holiday season brought their discordance into ever sharper relief. Ellie busied herself with Christmas cards, but not the hand-drawn products lovingly made in previous years, nor did she spend the hours she had once devoted to lengthy once-a-year messages, the "keeping-in-touch" notes she had always insisted on before. Instead she finally brought a list to Rob and said, "I've sent cards to all the people I want to. If you want to send any more, do them yourself."

Especially trying were the series of pre-Christmas parties which started in the town almost immediately after Thanksgiving, beginning with the big annual party thrown by the mill manager and his wife. All the upper crust of Twin Forks were invited, and attendance, according to Isaacs, was obligatory. "You go, that's all," Isaacs told Rob. "When

437

John Stanley asks you to his Christmas party, you don't insult him by not turning up. He sends John Florey enough work from that mill as it is. Don't make it worse." The party was early, the second week in December, and a grisly affair at best, with multitudes of people whom Rob and Ellie barely knew greeting them like long-lost friends, too many drinks and a too-long-delayed buffet that must have cost more than a mill-worker's annual wages, catered by uniformed waiters from Missoula. Among other delights, there was the grotesque spectacle of Martin Isaacs and John Florey attempting (in vain) to be civil to each other, while Ted Peterson slunk around pretending (in vain) that he was somewhere else; for Rob there was the even more distressing spectacle of Chris Erickson, in an almost obscenely stunning dress, paying far too avid attention to a handsome, unmarried and pathetically eager young mill foreman who had just arrived in town—allowing him to help her with her spilled drink, accepting a buffet plate from him, and later dancing exceedingly close to him after the band arrived, with Rob raging and burning inwardly, until they passed on the dance floor and Chris favored him with a long wink and a wicked grin over Ellie's shoulder; and through it all, Rob and Ellie trying desperately to project an image of solidarity and holiday cheer until Rob couldn't stand it any longer and said, "Christ, let's get out of here," and they drove home in uncheerful silence.

Other gatherings were less dreadful, but not much less: a small cocktail and dinner party the DeForrests gave; a hospital staff gathering, also obligatory, featuring very sweet cookies and very weak punch, with Roger Painter nauseating everyone with his air of forced conviviality; the local tree-raising and street-decorating, with the center block in town closed off to traffic for the raising of a huge Noble Fir, and with Ernie from the gas station falling off the ladder while trying to place the star on the top and nearly breaking his neck. ("Damned shame he didn't hit harder," Rob muttered, and Ellie responded with, "Good Lord, Rob, he's just a harmless old man—what's *wrong* with you?" and Rob bit his tongue to keep from replying.)

Plans also were laid for the forthcoming clinic Christmas party. Rob objected bitterly that he was so sick of Christmas parties the thought of another one made him want to vomit, but Isaacs was adamant. "We've got to do something for the girls or they'll all be sore, and it's a whole lot cheaper than Christmas bonuses. You can sweat it out for one evening." In the end he did (Ellie's presence was not required), and spent an hour or so with tree-trimming in the waiting room and punch and cookies and phony good cheer until he was at last mercifully delivered by a call from the hospital.

Quite aside from the general distastefulness of these pre-Christmas festivities, the two weeks before the Seattle meeting were flawed by certain more serious developments. For reasons best known to himself, Martin Isaacs chose this interval to mount a fiercely accelerating campaign of nit-picking and fault-finding, with Rob as his major target. Hardly a day passed that Isaacs was not viciously harassing Rob with complaints or accusations, some close to the mark, some irrelevant, some completely ridiculous, but all pursued with a surly peevishness that crowded Rob's self-control to the limit.

One morning, for example, he walked into Rob's office complaining bitterly that Rob had discontinued a sleeping pill order on an OB patient of his the night before. "When I order a sleeper for a woman, by God, I want her to get a sleeper! What are you doing, mucking around with my orders?"

"Hell, Martin, she was already so slugged out on Valium she was barely breathing," Rob said. "I figured she could make the night without a sleeper piled on top."

"Well, that may be *your* opinion, but it's not *my* opinion. When I order medicine for these women, I want them to get it. I've had enough of your high-handed crapping around with my order sheets!" And he stumped on down the corridor, muttering to himself.

Another day it was the clinic charts Isaacs homed in on. "We've just got to have more detail," he complained. "If your charts ever got pulled into court, you'd look like an ass, a perfect ass."

"But I spend half my life charting already," Rob protested.

"Then maybe you'd better put in longer hours. These charts are a disgrace, and I'm not going to have that in *my* practice, by God!"

Yet another morning, out of the blue, Isaacs said, "Whether you like it or not, we're just going to have to drop our OB fees down again."

"How come?" Rob said innocently.

"Too damned many complaints is how come. Women I've treated for years are going down to Tintown en masse." He shook his head indignantly. "Why, we haven't had but one new OB in three weeks now."

"Well, you wanted a lighter load," Rob said.

"I didn't want them all to go to Florey," Isaacs snapped.

"And that's *my* fault?"

"Damned right it is," Isaacs said peevishly. "Everything would

439

have been fine if you'd left your fee alone."

"You set the figure, not me."

"Oh, shit. Well, we've got to bring it back down again, that's all there is to it. We can't stay in business the way it is."

"Well, fine, Martin. You drop yours down, and then I'll drop mine. It's just that simple. Now I've got work to do." And Rob brushed past leaving him fuming.

And so it went, day after day, progressively more vicious. Rob began bracing himself every time he saw the older man, fighting to control his tongue and growing coldly furious as things went from bad to worse. Whether Isaacs was purposely seeking to anger and humiliate him, or was merely trying to reassert his control of things, Rob could not tell. But much as Isaacs seemed determined to goad him into reaction, Rob was equally determined to deny the man the satisfaction of an angry response as he waited doggedly for the time for the Seattle trip to arrive. Unfortunately, his growing tension exploded in other areas. He became increasingly short with Dora and Agnes, jumping them for trivial oversights and errors. He exploded at Terry over a scheduling snarl-up, leaving the bewildered girl close to tears. He precipitated a minor crisis at the hospital when he refused to come up at three in the morning to catheterize an aged gentleman who refused to use a bedpan, telling Hodges to call Raymond to do it if she couldn't manage herself; and he became so irritable at home that Ellie gave up speaking to him at all. Even his two meetings with Chris during this interval were marked by unaccustomed tension, especially the night they got so mired in snow returning from Ed Butler's cabin that they had had to chain up all four wheels of the jeep and spend two hours digging to get ahead of the falling snow and extricate themselves, returning home exhausted and chilled through at 2 A.M. Worst of all, he became so short with his patients that the nurses began apologizing for him, and the patients themselves left his office shaking their heads in bewilderment.

The climax came on the Friday he was to leave for Missoula to catch the Seattle plane. Flight time was six twenty-five in the evening, with arrival at SeaTac Airport scheduled for eight-thirty; the tickets were paid for and waiting at the Johnson-Bell Airport at Missoula, and Chris was to meet him there no later than five. He had a rental car reserved at SeaTac, and prepaid reservations at the Edgewater Inn. He had also instructed Terry to close his schedule that Friday no later than two o'clock to give him time to finish packing and get on his way.

Inevitably, it turned out to be the busiest day in the past month, with patients double-booked all morning, and at least five to be seen between one and two. Equally inevitably, a couple of thorny diagnostic problems turned up, patients who required time, attention and patience that he simply couldn't muster that day. He managed to postpone the workups to the following week, but even so was running straight through his lunch hour, looking for a ten-minute break to go get a sandwich at the Bar-None, when Dora came into his office with a chart in her hand. "Dr. Tanner, could you see Francine Stein for a minute before you go? She had that Caesarean six weeks ago, and her baby's got the colic."

Francine Stein was short and fat and cheerful, chattering a blue streak as Rob checked the baby. She was also pregnant again, she thought. "Have to see Dr. Isaacs pretty soon," she said. "Seems like every Christmas I have to see Dr. Isaacs for the same old thing."

"Well, at least your Caesarean won't be a surprise this time."

"Never was," the woman said. "Not since the first one four years ago."

"You mean this last Caesarean didn't catch you off guard? I thought it was a crash emergency."

Francine Stein laughed. "Heavens, no. Dr. Isaacs planned it weeks in advance. Always does, with me so fat and all."

She went on her way, with colic drops for the baby, and Rob ducked out the back door for the short walk to the Bar-None for a sandwich—but something was picking at his mind. Nothing important, exactly. Just—odd. Back at the clinic, he found Agnes Miller eating her lunchtime cup of yogurt. "That fat woman who had the section," he said. "Did you help Martin with that?"

"You mean Francine Stein? Sure. But then, I always help Martin with sections. Saves calling one of you fellows out."

"I see." Rob sipped coffee. "But that was a pretty frantic case, all of a sudden at three in the morning, and Martin trying for hours to get Harry Sonders out—"

"Oh, piffle," Agnes said. "There was nothing frantic that *I* knew about. He'd been bumping her with Pit in the office for the last two days. He'd even ordered up blood in advance to have on hand. So when she came in with contractions he whisked her into the OR and took the baby, like always with her. He never called Dr. Sonders on cases like that. Why should he?"

It was a little thing, of course, a very little thing. Ordinarily he might have shrugged it off as just one more of Isaacs' little foibles. But things were far from ordinary these days, and a surge of anger came welling up. *A repeat section,* he thought, *planned well ahead and perfectly routine. But he told us—*

Momentarily he pulled back. *Maybe Agnes just didn't know. Maybe she didn't realize everything going on. You'd better be certain before you go off half-cocked.* With sudden grim resolve, he buzzed Terry and told her to cancel the few patients he still had remaining. Then he headed up to the hospital.

The clerk in the business office was puzzled at his request. "Telephone log? You mean the long-distance list from the phone company?"

"That's right." Rob gave her the dates he wanted. She rooted in a file and came out with a folder. Rob took a seat and went down the list item by item.

There were no calls listed to Missoula that day.

He sat staring at the list for a long time. *So Agnes did know, after all,* he thought. Martin's frantic effort to reach Sonders that morning hadn't happened. It was a fraud, a setup, and like idiots, they hadn't even questioned it. The "reason" Sonders had been fired that morning wasn't a reason at all. It was nothing but a lie.

# 39

The flight for Seattle was an hour late coming in to Missoula from Bismarck because of high winds and blizzard conditions farther east, and lost another hour taking off due to ice and drifting snow on the runways. Finally airborne again, the plane had headed south to climb above the storm, amid rumors that Spokane International was closed with heavy snow, and that Portland and SeaTac were both fogged in so the flight might have to be routed to Vancouver. Once they were finally aloft, Rob Tanner refused to worry, leaning back to the soothing roar of the engines, with Chris beside him, snoozing, her head nestled against his shoulder. For a while he leafed through a magazine, then snapped out the seat light and tried to sleep, but nothing came of it. Finally, alone with his thoughts, he stared into the darkness outside the plane's tiny window, wishing the flight might go on forever.

The past eight hours had been harrowing, and never before had he been so totally happy to leave time, place and people behind. For him, right then, the roar of the engines meant total, idyllic escape and the girl beside him was a part of it. Some natural instinct of self-repair was at work here; slowly he could sense the anger and bitterness leaching out of his mind as he thought once again of the shabby little falsehood he had just uncovered a few hours before.

It made perfect sense, of course: so obvious, so predictable, so very much the sort of thing Martin Isaacs would do. *When in doubt, lie. Lace*

443

*it up with a little bombast and then cut off argument by stomping
angrily out of the room. Nobody's going to check it out.*

Except that by chance somebody did. For a long while Rob had sat
staring at the telephone list, angry beyond words or caring. It was
disgusting, yet in a way it fit. Part of a pattern of things, things that had
almost caught his attention but not quite. One other thing in particular,
a matter involving a fight with Roger Painter, a fight that had ended in
riddles. He looked back in the administrator's office, but Roger was
gone. Then, with sudden resolve, he sat down at the desk and dialed
Judge Barret's office.

"Yes, Rob? What can I do for you?"

"You can tell me something," Rob said. "It's important, and urgent.
I don't mean to ask you to break professional confidence, but I want to
make a statement and have you tell me if it's true or not."

"Might depend on the statement," the Judge said cautiously. He
listened then, and there was a long pause. Finally, reluctantly: "Yes, I'd
say that's true."

"He owns all the stock?"

"Substantially."

"And what does he pay the others?"

"A thousand apiece a year, plus a case of good Scotch whisky,"
Judge Barret said. "Except for Al Davidson. He prefers gin."

Rob set the phone down and went out to his car. *When it comes to
confrontations,* he thought bitterly, *there's no time like the present.* It
wasn't even the lying so much as the manipulation, cold and contemptuous, and he suddenly couldn't wait to nail Martin Isaacs to the wall
with it. But Martin was not in his office. Agnes shook her head helplessly. "I don't know where he went. He took out of here like a shot half
an hour ago and I haven't heard from him since. Maybe a house call or
something." Rob rang his home, but there was no answer. A quick
canvass of the bank, the Bar-None Café and the hardware store turned
up no sign of him. By this time it was well past two o'clock and Rob gave
up, heading home to finish packing for his trip.

When he walked in the door Ellie took one look and said, "Something's wrong."

"Nothing's wrong," Rob snapped.

"Rob, come off it. What's the trouble?"

"It's nothing you can help with. Forget it."

"Rob, *please.*"

"Look, are you deaf? I said nothing's wrong. I don't want to talk

444

about it. All I want is to get my bag packed and get out of this fucking place before I kill somebody. Now, are you going to help? Or are you going to stand there and wring your hands?"

She followed him into the bedroom, watched him stuff clothing into his bag and finally gently shouldered him out of the way and began refolding shirts. "If you want your good shoes, get a plastic garbage bag to wrap them in," she said. "I can do this."

He stood by, pulling things from the closet for her to pack. "Honey, it's only for two days," she said. "Do you really need three suits?"

"I suppose not."

"Then put this flannel one back and just take the tweed. It's not going to be that cold. You'll be at the Olympic?"

"The Edgewater. I like those rooms on the Bay."

"And you'll get back to Missoula about noon on Monday?"

"Unless the flight's delayed, or I end up in Boise because of the weather."

"I could drive you in, and then come meet your plane."

"Don't be silly. There's heavy snow forecast, and I don't want you hassling with chains."

"I could always get somebody to stop and help."

"Look, I don't *want* you to drive me in, okay? Now forget it."

She finished the packing in silence while he devoured a sandwich, checked his briefcase for reference data, and finally just paced. Outside, the sky had turned heavy gray and a filtering of snow had begun to fall. "Look, I've got to get out of here before this turns into a blizzard," he said.

"Everything's ready."

He lugged the suitcase out and stowed it in the trunk as Ellie watched him apprehensively. As he climbed into the car she said, "Rob?"

He paused and looked at her.

"I—I'm sorry."

"For what?"

"For whatever hasn't been right the last couple of months. For whatever I've done."

He shook his head impatiently. "Forget it."

"Maybe a couple of days away will be a good thing," she said. "For both of us."

It was after three when he finally turned onto the highway and headed north for Missoula. The drive was a nightmare, with glare ice

445

on much of the road and new snow falling heavily all the way. Missoula itself was one huge snow-clogged traffic jam, and it was almost five-thirty by the time he reached the airport. There was no sign of Chris in the lobby. He dropped his bag on the floor, looked at his watch again, then peered around at the small clots of people moving here and there. He checked the newsstand, glanced into Dorothy's Airport Café, and went over to pick up the tickets at the ticket counter. Flight 723 was still scheduled for six o'clock, although its arrival from the east had not yet been listed. Back in the lobby he waited, more frantic by the minute. What to do now? Have her paged? Call the university and see if she'd left? Check with the state patrol to see if she'd gone off the road on the way to the airport? The clock moved on to 5:46, 5:47, 5:48—and then he saw her, clutching a huge suitcase, ducking her way through the crowds, a snow-laden scarf over her hair. When she saw him she waved, and a moment later she was in his arms, laughing breathlessly. "Bet you thought I was never going to make it."

"I ought to break your neck. Where on earth were you?"

"Jammed up in traffic. A truck jackknifed out on the highway."

Rob took a deep breath. "I was beginning to think you'd changed your mind, decided to hell with it."

"Oh, love, you know better than that." She shook her hair free of the scarf, then looked up at him sharply. "You really *were* worried."

"Yes."

"Well, we'd better get checked in now. We've only got ten minutes."

At the baggage check they learned that the rush was unnecessary. "Flight hasn't left Billings yet," the clerk told them blandly. "It'll be at least two hours late leaving here."

The cocktail lounge was busy, but they found a table for two in a corner at the rear. When their drinks arrived Rob stirred his once or twice, fiddled with the swizzle stick until it snapped in his fingers, then took half the drink at a gulp. Chris watched him in bemusement. "You're in great shape tonight," she said finally. "What's happened now?"

"Nothing, really. I just found out today that Isaacs was lying about his reason for firing Sonders, is all. The bastard."

"Lying?"

"Just a few embellishments."

"And finding this out *surprised* you?"

"In a way."

446

Chris sipped her drink. "Somehow I don't think I'd be surprised at *anything* that man might do. So what are you going to do about it?"

"Confront him with it, I suppose. Get the others together, and confront him, and . . ."

"And what?" She looked up at him sharply.

Rob shifted in his seat. "I—don't know."

"So you confront him and he says, 'Forget it, kid, you're bothering me.' Then what?"

"I'm not sure."

"Of course, he won't do that; it'd be too honest. He'll probably just put on a Contrite Sinner act and say he *knew* it was wrong, he felt just *terrible* about it, but he couldn't control himself. So then what?"

"I—I just don't know."

Chris stared at him. "Rob, can't you see what the man's done? He's got you whipped any way you turn. It's obvious you can't bring Sonders back; he wouldn't come back now if you begged him."

"No, we can't bring Sonders back."

"And he *needs* Stone. He doesn't dare dump him yet, much as he'd like to."

"You think he wants to dump Stone?"

"Oh, doesn't he, though! Stone must be a *real* thorn in his side—but he's stuck with him. He can't turn against *Stone* yet. So that leaves you. You're the ugly duckling. You're the one in Isaacs' way now, and he isn't going to quit until he has you snuffed out or under control, one or the other."

"I know." Rob looked at her leaning across the table at him angrily, her green eyes burning, her fist clenched under his nose. "I've been living with it for the last month, every day worse than the last, and I've had about all I can take."

"Then don't you think it's time you *did something?*" Chris looked up, startled, at the cocktail waitress. "Yes, you'd better bring me another before I start smashing glasses on the floor." She reached out and took one of Rob's hands in both her own. "Ah, sweet, I suppose I sound like an awful shrew, but it makes me so *mad.* I sit and watch you getting deeper and deeper into this mire, beating yourself to pieces trying to do something about it and just sinking deeper all the time, and it just makes me *boil.* It's tearing you apart, and I just about can't stand it."

"Well, I'm getting there too," Rob said wearily. "Your fox is about ready to gnaw his leg off."

"And leave?"

447

"It sounds better all the time."

"Oh, Rob! I've been waiting to hear that. You don't *know* how I've been waiting." Chris touched her tongue to her lip. "But what else can you do? There's no point confronting Isaacs if there's nothing you can do about it anyway. And you'd still be working with a man you could never trust."

"I just have to think it out, that's all."

"Then *think it out*. The best I can do is point the way. I can go with you too, help with the rough spots—but you're the one that has to decide. Nobody can do that for you."

"All the same, a swift kick can be a big help."

"Then consider yourself kicked." She smiled. "But *decide.*"

The flight came in at long last, and began boarding Missoula passengers. Arm in arm, Rob and Chris went aboard and found seats near the rear of the plane. Once they were airborne Chris leaned her head against his shoulder and soon was asleep. Rob leafed through a magazine, then leaned back himself, peering through the window into darkness. Staring decision in the eyes, really *facing* it for the first time, he found the prospect profoundly disturbing. There was so much truth in what Chris had said. Certainly there was no going back to the way things were before. A bridge had been burned, a wall of confidence breached. No conceivable confrontation could ever restore that breach, nor was there any point in confrontation unless something could be gained.

*And what could that be? An apology? Well, words are cheap, no sweat to Martin Isaacs. A pledge that things would change? Sure, great —until he chooses to break it.*

The engines thrummed, half mesmerizing him. Of course, confronting Isaacs would accomplish one thing: it would let Jerry DeForrest and Tom Stone know the whole story. But really—what good would *that* do? Would it tell them anything they didn't already know? They could hardly threaten the man—he was the backbone of the practice. True, Jerry had a few patients who were loyal to him, and even Rob had his Maggie Muldoons, but to Isaacs, Rob and Stone were "his doctors," mere hirelings and nothing more. *And no one knew that better than Isaacs.*

There was no way out that he could see. Except what Chris had said. *Trapped foxes in Iowa used to do it. You gnaw your leg off and get away. . . . Just pack your suitcase, and get into your car, and start*

448

*driving—and never look back. You cut off whatever you have to cut off and leave.*

But to *go?* Actually turn his back and walk away? He stared out the black window, felt the airplane engines rumble. It would mean escape, all right—and with her, too. Escape from Isaacs, and Ellie, and all the other headaches. Just walk away, right now, and never come back.

But God, was this really *him?* To come to a place like Twin Forks to practice good medicine, and fail, and turn his back and leave? To marry a woman, and hang on until things got tough, and then turn his back and leave? *And where would that leave the others you committed yourself to? The Ed Butlers and the Elsie Cobbells and the Tom Stones and the Janice Blanchards? Where will that leave them, when you turn your back and leave?*

Well, Ed Butler's dead. Elsie Cobbell's dead too. No bringing *them* back. Stone'll manage all right. He'll move out too, and end up in some big surgical center where they can really *use* the talent he's got. Janice —well, she's kind of nutty anyway. A no-win situation. What are you really offering her?

*And Ellie? What was really there once? And what's there now?* His wife of seven years—did that mean anything? The mother of his child-to-be—did that mean anything? Suddenly, as he sat there, leaning back, engines thrumming in his ears, the images came back, fiercely, in living color. *A boy, tousle-headed, sitting on a man's lap, drowsing to a bed-time story. An older boy, so proud, being invested in the Cub Scouts. Still later, the same boy, hiking hard and steadily, with a man behind him, up a trail to a high mountain lake you almost couldn't get to for a week of fishing—trout as long as your arm. . . .*

*Ellie's boy. Or girl, as the case might be. And the man?*

He knew then, without any question, that Chris's answer was no answer at all. He wasn't going to leave Twin Forks. He wasn't going to walk away—he was going back. He looked down at Chris, stirring in her sleep, suddenly aware of the odd fragrance she wore, aware of the warmth of her head on his shoulder. *I'll have to tell her,* he thought. *She won't like it, but I'll have to tell her, and she'll understand.* He felt her hand on his arm, took it gently in his own and closed his eyes, succumbing to a great wave of weariness, and soon was sleeping himself until the landing signal sounded and they stirred, ruffled and yawning, to disembark at SeaTac airport.

# 40

The Saturday medical conference at the Graystone Clinic proved everything that Rob had hoped it would be: a galvanizing change of pace for him, a stimulating intellectual and professional challenge, a chance to meet and mingle with physicians in a dozen different fields from communities large and small, and—perhaps more important—to reassure himself that the horizons of medicine really did extend farther than the confines of his own office and examining room in Twin Forks, Montana.

The meeting started early, with registration at 8 A.M., and Rob was not at his freshest. It had been almost midnight by the time he and Chris finally arrived at the Seattle hotel. Even then they had stayed awake for hours in the comfortable darkness of the waterfront room, watching the fireboats patrolling Elliott Bay as they talked about Chris and her work, drawing rapidly to a close at the Twin Forks mill, his own anticipation of the forthcoming conference, his experiences in training, anything and everything except the practice problems he had left behind him, until finally Chris was yawning and dozing and finally asleep in spite of herself. He didn't tell her his decision. He wasn't ready for that yet, wrong time and place, and he had lain awake yet another hour before he too drifted into sleep.

He had snapped awake in the morning moments before the alarm rang and dressed himself silently, leaving Chris a note and the keys to their rented car, and taking a cab to the clinic building, feeling seedy but alert as the first morning presentations were read. Most of the early program was devoted to the problems of selecting patients who might benefit from coronary artery by-pass surgery to restore good circulation to hearts threatened by hardened and plugged coronary arteries—a couple of sharp young heart surgeons presenting a really dynamic review of the "state of the art" in a field which had always excited Rob. Luncheon was served in the clinic cafeteria, with conference attendees breaking up into small groups for lunchtime workshop seminars in various medical fields. Rob had signed for the OB-GYN group, an hour-and-a-half interchange on ways and means of meeting women's growing demands for more participation and less male chauvinism in handling gynecological examinations, a discussion that got hot and heavy at times but was, on the whole, perceptive and intelligent, all served up along with the chicken croquettes—a juxtaposition that no one present seemed to find even remotely odd. After lunch attention turned to new advances in the medical and radiological treatment of breast cancer, as opposed to more widely favored forms of surgical treatment, with the chief of medicine from a large Southern cancer center as a very stimulating guest speaker. Between papers, Rob chatted with the men from Graystone who had been his mentors and supervisors during his residency training, and reaffirmed that he would be present the following day at the conference and the cocktail party and dinner for the hospital's house staff and "alumni." By the time the meeting broke up, Rob decided to duck the reception scheduled to follow at the Rainier Club, and with an odd mixture of weariness and keyed-up exhilaration from the day's proceedings, he walked down to the rainy street and hailed a cab to take him back to the hotel.

It was just after five o'clock, and Chris was not yet back from her shopping. Rob took a quick shower and shave, changed his underwear, and then sprawled on the bed, falling asleep instantly. Two hours later he woke at the sound of a key in the lock and Chris came in, piled high with boxes. "Oh, good, you're back," she said. "That reception sounded like it might go on all night."

"I skipped it," Rob said. "Enough was enough. You can just pack in so much at a stretch and then you need a breather."

"Got a nap, hm?"

"Right. And you?"

451

"No nap, but did I ever shop! I went into every store there was, from the Bon to I. Magnin, and I bought myself into a stupor. Here, let me show you."

He sat back and watched as she unpacked boxes and bags—dresses, shoes, two robes, a new purse, a dozen other things pulled out with the excitement of a little girl in a candy store. "Now I see why you brought that huge suitcase," Rob said finally.

"Sure, I'm not so dumb." She sat down on the edge of the bed and took his hands. "And how was your day?"

"Absolutely tops. I'll tell you later. Right now I can't think of anything but dinner. Tonight we're on the town. Where do you want to go?"

"Anyplace. You choose."

"Then it's El Gaucho. Best food in town, and I was always too broke to go there before. I'll call and be sure there's a table."

"Good. And then build us a drink while I get myself gathered together."

As Chris vanished into the bathroom, Rob called to make the dinner reservation, ordered up ice and mixer, and prepared drinks. He handed one in to Chris, then propped himself up on the bed to savor his own. Getting herself gathered together took longer than he had expected, and he was well into his third drink and basking in a warm, spreading glow when Chris finally emerged, radiant, to slip into the dressiest of the dresses she had purchased, modeling it for him, then begging his help with the zipper. "There," she said, turning a pirouette. "How do you like it?"

He pulled her down beside him and kissed her. "It's beautiful," he said. "Fantastic. It's really unbelievable what the right new dress can do."

She looked at him. "That's not quite the right answer," she said.

"But I mean it. It's just plain miraculous how a new dress can turn a drab, colorless, unattractive mouse of a woman into—"

"Oh, phooey." She jabbed him in the ribs and leaped to her feet. "For that I'll order lobster tail and crêpes suzette and the costliest wine in the house."

He pulled her back, pinned her shoulders to the bed. "The gentleman orders the wine. And for a drab, colorless, unattractive mouse of a woman like you I think I'll probably order"—he kissed her, ducking a wildly flailing arm—"the costliest wine in the house."

He kissed her again, felt her respond, then stir, turn her head. "Oh,

452

Rob, if we're going to eat we'd better go eat, I warn you."

"Okay, Drabkins, if you put food before other things . . ."

"You'd better watch it or I'll fix you so you don't have any energy left for dinner, new dress or no new dress."

"No, not that." He sat up, pulled her close and smoothed her rumpled hair. "Oh, it's been a good day. I'm glad we're here."

"That's good, love. So am I."

"Maybe tomorrow we can just have breakfast in bed and loaf and go up the Space Needle or something. I don't have to appear at Graystone until one o'clock and it should all be over, reception and all, by six or so. Ladies not invited, I'm afraid."

"What do you all do—sit around and tell dirty stories?"

"Dirty *medical* stories. They're more revolting than most. Like the definition of scrutch—"

"Oh, God. Let's go eat."

The restaurant was busy yet uncrowded, with a quiet table in a secluded alcove waiting for them. They dawdled over a cocktail, decided on their order and scanned the wine list together; the meal, when it came, was as superb as Rob had promised, served with quiet and unhurried competence; the surroundings were warm and congenial, the atmosphere reflecting a private intimacy, as though they were isolated on another world, unobserved yet able to observe others. They talked sporadically about a dozen things as they ate, carefully skirting the unhappy topics of the evening before. It was not until the cheese and fruit platter arrived and coffee and brandy were served that Chris broke the ice. "So tell me about the conference."

"It was just great," Rob said. "Like a breath of fresh air. You have no idea what it was like to sit there and realize that exciting things are still happening out here in the real world."

"Like what?"

"Like these coronary by-passes for people who are dying of heart disease. Fifteen years ago nitroglycerin for angina and lots of rest after a coronary was the end of the line for these people. You waited for them to die—which they did, in most rewarding fashion. Today, though, that's all different. Take old Ed Butler, for instance. If we'd been alert, we might have spotted his trouble in time. But we weren't and we didn't. I'd have given my right arm to save Ed Butler, but I just wasn't sharp enough."

"And you really think you could have done something?"

"I don't know—but I'll bet these crackerjacks out here could have."

"But only with a top-rate hospital to work in, and really good consultants, and modern facilities, and a lot of other things they'll never have in Twin Forks, Montana." She looked up at him. "Did you check on any open positions?"

"Well—not really."

"But, love, aren't you missing a golden opportunity to let some important people out here know that you're available?"

"Yes. Except that I'm not," Rob said.

Chris set her coffee cup down and looked at him, her smile turning tight around the edges. "What do you mean?"

"I mean I've thought this all out very carefully, and I'm not going to leave Twin Forks."

"That's not what you said last night in the airport."

"I've changed my mind. I was confused last night."

"Confused! My God. I guess you *are* confused! With your talent and potential you could go anyplace in this country and go right to the top, do the best medical work there is. And you're going back there and waste your time fighting pukey little fights with phonies and liars?"

"I'm afraid so."

"Well, I think you're an idiot. An absolute, blabbering idiot!" Her voice had risen, and other diners were suddenly watching. Chris flushed, ducked her head down and went on in a fierce whisper. "If you don't leave now, you'll never get away, never! You go back to that place for one day now and you'll be sandbagged for life, and if you're too stupid to see that, you need to be *told.*"

"Maybe so. There's just one trouble with leaving. Somebody's got to grab the ball and run with it in Twin Forks, Montana. There are people there who matter, and they need help."

"And you're going to be Sir Galahad!"

"I have to. I'm the one that's committed, and there's nobody else to do it." Rob shook his head. "Hell, Chris, there's more to it than just standing up to Martin Isaacs or trying to get a blood storage unit for the hospital. There's the whole matter of decent, honest medical care to fight for. Back in training it was easy. The hours were awful and the pay was lousy, but that didn't matter. The hospital had everything, and the men around me were experts and I was the perfect medical machine. I thought good medicine was merely a matter of asking the right questions and ordering the right lab tests and getting the right consults, and the patient was just a living cipher, a warm body to be worked on. I actually thought that was what medicine *was*. And then I came to Twin Forks and found out I'd been living in a dream world. For the first time in my life I began meeting the Isaacses and the Sonderses and the Roger Painters and the Sara Davises of medicine, and I couldn't believe what I was seeing until they came up and kicked me in the teeth. And I also met the Ed Butlers and the Elsie Cobbells and the Dottie Hazards and the Janice Blanchards, and I found out they weren't ciphers, they were real people who were depending on us for their health care and their very lives. When push came to shove, *we were all they had to turn to,* and they deserved far, far better than they were getting."

"But you can't remake the world," Chris said wearily.

"Maybe not, but I can change one small part of it. If I walk away from Twin Forks, I'm throwing those patients to the wolves, and I can't do that. And I can't walk away from Ellie and the baby, either."

"So you're going back and fight."

"I'm going back and win, somehow."

"Well, I don't think you've got the guts," Chris said. "Isaacs is not going to *let* you win. He'll do anything he can do to crush you. It's going to be you or him, and frankly, right now, I wouldn't give you sucker's odds."

"If nothing else, maybe I can turn him a little."

She laughed bitterly. "You think you're going to turn *that* man? You're out of your mind. He's run that practice his way for fifteen years, and he's not going to change for you or anybody. But then, that's your headache, not mine. Go on back to your Twin Forks, if that's what you want. Go on back to your creepy little practice and your crappy little fights and your mousy little wife and *suffocate,* for all I care. But count me out. If you think I'm going to—"

Her voice broke off abruptly as she saw Rob stiffen and look up at the man who had suddenly appeared at their table, sleek and dapper in his well-tailored suit and trim red hair, deeply tanned and smiling. "Well, Rob!" Harry Sonders said easily. "So it *was* you we saw over here." The little surgeon's eyes slid to Chris for a moment, then back to Rob, and his smile broadened. "Karen said, 'Isn't that Rob Tanner over there?' and I said, 'Nah, you're crazy, that sure isn't *Ellie,*' but by God, she was right! So how are things in Twin Forks?"

Rob had leaped to his feet so suddenly he jarred the table and sent his coffee cup spinning. "Twin Forks? Uh—fine. You come over for the Graystone Clinic Conference?"

"No, we just came over for a weekend on the town. A little shopping, a little fun, get away from the old grind." He looked again at Chris. "Haven't we met somewhere?"

"Uh—yes," Rob said. "That party at Jerry's last summer. Chris Erickson—Harry Sonders. Harry was—I mean he used to—"

"Yeah, that's right; the girl with the moths," Harry cut in. "Well, I see your waiter here has your check ready, so I won't hold you up. Glad to see you're taking some time off for fun and games, Rob. Little change of pace never hurt anybody." Sonders' smile broadened again for a moment, and then he was walking away to rejoin a group at a table just beyond the alcove.

"Damn," Rob said as he eased himself back down. "Damn, damn, damn."

"Small world, isn't it?" Chris said with a tight little smile.

"Of all damned times for *him* to turn up."

"So why worry?" she said. "He's seen two people having dinner, that's all."

"Yes. The wrong two people."

"Well, he probably won't go back to Twin Forks and spread the word," she said, smiling. "He's too nice a guy for that. And it won't bother me anyway, one way or the other." She stood up, her face suddenly cold. "Let's get out of here."

Rob left money for the waiter and they walked out, with Rob nodding grimly to Harry and Karen Sonders as he passed their table. Outside it was raining as they walked to the car. "You want to go somewhere else?"

"Let's just bag it. I don't feel like romping around." She sat away from him as they drove in silence to the hotel, and followed him without a word as he led the way to their room.

Once inside, Rob turned to her. "Look, I'm sorry you're upset."

"Don't sweat it," Chris said shortly.

"Maybe tomorrow we can talk."

"Sure, there's always tomorrow." She turned away, unsnapped her dress collar, tore the zipper and cursed. "Right now I'm dead tired and I'm going to sleep." She took the unused twin at the far side of the room, turning her back to him and beginning to snore in a matter of minutes. Rob poured some bourbon, undid his collar and stared out at the black harbor water. A long while later he lay down on the other bed without even undressing.

456

# 41

It was late when they awoke, well past ten, with gray December light coming in the window and a sad drizzle of rain ruffling the water of Elliott Bay outside. Rob was up first, ordering room-service breakfast with extra coffee and the Sunday paper thrown in; Chris roused herself when it arrived and sipped coffee, silently and somberly. She seemed cold and withdrawn to Rob, almost dissociated, her green eyes distant. She glanced at the paper a moment, then tossed it aside impatiently and went in to shower. Presently she came out, dressed in bra and panties, and fiddled with her hair for a seemingly endless period. Finally she threw the comb down in annoyance and began applying eye makeup with incredible care and concentration. Rob watched for a while, then crossed the room and bent to kiss her cheek, but she shook her head, leaning closer to the mirror with the makeup brush in hand.

"Gilding the lily?" he said.

"You're in the light."

"You seem very gray today."

"I feel very gray."

"Maybe some fresh air will help. My meeting doesn't start until one. We've got time to go up the Space Needle, walk around the old fair grounds."

She merely looked at him obliquely in the mirror and went back to her eyes. He slipped into fresh underclothes and slacks, found a

457

sports shirt in his bag, then retrieved a bow tie from the dresser and stuck it in his jacket pocket. Her eyes finally finished, Chris donned the slacks and blouse she had worn shopping the day before, picked up her purse. "If you don't mind, I think I'll take a walk by myself," she said.

"Look, there's no sense sulking," Rob said. "We're here; we might as well make the most of it."

"Sorry, but the fun and games, as Harry Sonders would put it, are over. I've got some planning to do, and you'd better think about the mess you're going back to."

"It's going to work out somehow."

"Famous last words."

"It's *got* to work out. I've got to confront Martin, and take it from there." He paused. "And then there's Ellie to confront as well."

"Yes. Well, I hope you enjoy yourself. And I dearly hope there's something left of you when you get through." She fished in her purse and drew out a small oblong box tied with a plain ribbon. "I guess I'm not so dumb after all," she said bitterly. "I bought you something yesterday."

He stripped the ribbon from the box, opened it and blinked at the object inside: a silver tie clasp in the form of a caduceus with small star sapphires for eyes. "It's beautiful," he said. "But—"

"Just a memento," she said. "It's probably too corny to wear."

"A memento?"

"A going-away present," she said. "I'm not going back to Twin Forks, Rob. I never intended to."

"What about your work?"

"It's done, for all intents and purposes. There's a lab assistant who can wrap things up. There's nothing for me to go back for, that I can see."

"But what are you going to do?"

"Loaf around Seattle for a while. Take a new post when I get good and ready. I've had three nice offers in the last six months."

He stared at her for a long moment. "So *you're* going to walk away," he said at last.

"You'd better believe it."

"Well, think it over awhile," he said angrily. "Go get some air and think it out. We can talk about it tonight."

"Sure. We'll do that."

After she had gone, Rob paced the room restlessly, read the morning paper, sketched out some notes for his seminar, then went down for

458

a sandwich in the coffee shop. Finally he drove on up to Graystone Hospital. The seminar was a ghastly charade of the conference the day before, an endlessly dull discussion of the problems facing the family practitioner in the world of modern medicine, badly moderated, badly presented, missing all the real, pertinent points in so many ways that Rob had trouble even following the arguments. The pleasure he might have taken in rejoining the men he had trained with and exchanging ideas with them, many of them men in practices much like his, had completely drained away; the things they did not seem to comprehend about the realities of rural practice seemed boundless, and the very things he could have told them were precisely the things he couldn't imaginably talk about here, didn't for a fleeting moment want to share with anyone else in the room. By midafternoon he was feeling almost physically ill, and again and again the thought kept coming back: *What am I doing here? Why am I wasting my time here, with all the things that need doing at home? How can I sit here and listen to this blabber?*

Free at last, he walked back to his car in the driving rain, thinking bitterly of the rain that first night with Chris at Ed Butler's cabin. *And you couldn't see it, you blind ass! You walked right into it, like a fatuous idiot without enough wit to see through a cellophane bag.* Back at the hotel, he let himself in with his latchkey.

She was gone, of course, just as he had known she would be. The room was dark; her bag was gone from the closet, with empty shopping bags and boxes carefully jammed into the wastebasket. His own bag was neatly packed on the bed, the folder with the two return airline tickets lying on top of it, together with the box containing the tie clasp. For a moment he sat down in the darkened room, staring out at the harbor lights, dim in the fog and rain, aware of the lingering fragrance of her perfume—and of an overwhelming sense of relief. *At least that's over,* he thought. *And now there are some other things long overdue. Things that can't wait any longer.*

He turned on a light and took up the ticket folder, found the airport number on it and rang the reservations desk. Yes, there was a Minneapolis flight leaving SeaTac at nine-thirty, putting down at Missoula at 11:10 P.M. Yes, a seat was available. He asked them to hold it, canceling the two reservations he had for Monday, and then rang off.

The journey back was a nightmare in aggravated slow motion. The plane was an hour late arriving at SeaTac, circled Spokane's Geiger Field for over an hour before coming in to land, and finally disembarked him at 1:30 A.M. at Missoula, where he found his car in the parking lot

459

buried in twelve inches of fresh snow.

The drive to Twin Forks was a madman's dream; he should never even have started in darkness, with the half-plowed road covered with three-foot drifts in some areas. After thirty miles he stopped and chained up. Later, at a gas station, he was told that the pass might be closed. Somewhere the heater conked out, and he began shivering in his light tweed jacket. He made the long crossing of the grazing flats, hitting drifts across the road hard in order to plow through them, seeing no oncoming traffic whatever, and then took the long zigzag curves down into the river valley. Presently he slowed, searching for his turn-off, found it at last and plowed through another hundred yards of drifts before finally crossing the bridge at twenty minutes to five—and pulled up, blinking in confusion, because every light in his house was blazing, and Ellie was sitting, coffee cup in her hand, waiting, at twenty minutes to five in the morning.

He struggled through the back door with his suitcase, dumped it on the kitchen floor, found Ellie in his arms, kissing him. Carefully he disengaged her. "What are you doing up at this hour?"

"Oh, Rob, I tried to get you. I called the Edgewater and they said you'd checked out, so I knew you were on your way."

"I came back early. But what's wrong?"

"I don't know. Something up at the hospital."

He froze. "What do you mean?"

"A woman called at one o'clock and had to talk to you, insisted on talking to you. She sounded just awful, and I said you were in Seattle and wouldn't be back until tomorrow and that she should call Martin. She hung up like I'd kicked her, and I sat and thought about it awhile, and then I called Martin myself, and he just laughed and said to forget it, the woman was hysterical, it was nothing, so I went back to bed." Ellie looked up at him, her face sheet-white, her eyes pleading. "But I guess it wasn't just nothing, because at three o'clock Tom Stone called and asked if I knew where you were, could I possibly reach you, and I said I'd try, and I called the Edgewater, and they said you'd checked out hours before. So I called Tom back—he was at the hospital by then—and I told him that, and he just swore and hung up. And then ten minutes later *Dr. Florey* was calling, of all people. I'm sure it was from the hospital—it was Miss Hodges' voice making the connection—and Florey wanted to know when you'd be home. I said you'd left the hotel in Seattle, but I just didn't know, and then—it was very odd, he sounded so *formal*—he said, 'Mrs. Tanner, tell your husband that I called. Mark

460

down the time, right now, and tell him that I called,' and then he rang off."

Rob stared at her. "It doesn't add up. Who was the woman?"

"The woman? I don't really remember, it all happened so fast. Is there—is there a Janice Blanchard?"

"Oh, Christ. What time is it? Five? I've got to get up there." He threw the thin tweed jacket on the dining table, pulled on a heavy wool coat and started for the door. "You stay by the phone," he said. "If anybody calls, I'm at the hospital."

In the hospital lot he saw Tom's car parked, and Esther's. There was also the moth-eaten green Olds that John Florey drove. At the top of the ramp he ran almost full tilt into Jessie Hodges, who said, "Oh, Dr. Tanner, thank God you're here. There's never been anything like this," and then rushed full speed down the corridor toward the newborn nursery.

There was no one else in the corridor, but the operating room lights were ablaze. He turned right, into the scrub room, and pushed open the operating room door.

Tom Stone was hovering over the figure on the table, with the pudgy form of John Florey in mask and gown across from him. Sara Davis was at the head of the table. As he walked into the room, Stone raised his head and looked around. "Well, what do you know!" he said. "So you got back after all."

"What's going on here?" Rob demanded.

"Your Janice Blanchard," Stone said. "A couple of months early, and a placenta previa. We had to move."

"Two months early . . ."

"She started to bleed, and she wouldn't stop. The baby's in the Rockette, might be okay. I don't know yet about Janice."

"Good God, Tom. Where's Martin?"

"Go on back and sit for a spell. I'll be with you in a little."

"Tom, *where's Martin?*"

"I said I'd talk to you later. You might check that baby out, if you've got a chance."

Out in the corridor Rob found Hodges and followed her down to the nursery. "I never saw such a thing," she muttered ominously. "I'm getting too old for this. . . ."

"For what, a new baby?"

"For the fighting that's going on."

"Well, let's see the baby." He found it in the Rockette, a four-

461

pound-two-ounce boy, with the odd plastic appearance of the premature, but pink and strong, responding to his interruption with a lusty wail. "Thank God," Rob muttered. "Thank bloody God."

"What's that, Doctor?"

"I was thanking God. You might try it too. And better get the child in the incubator. He's a good baby, but he's early. No more than five percent oxygen. Got that?"

"That's what he's getting, Doctor."

He found his way back to the coffee room. The clock on the wall said 5:25. Half an hour later he was still waiting, clutching himself as if unnaturally cold, when Tom Stone came in and threw his cap and mask onto the table. "Sorry, Rob," he said, "but I had no choice."

"Where was Martin?"

"Good question. She called you when she first started spotting, but you weren't there. So she called him. He said she was hysterical and told her to get lost—in so many words, I guess. Finally she called me, when she was already in shock, bleeding down her leg and cramping every three minutes or so. Of course, I had to set up the OR to examine her, assuming it was a previa, and it was. Placenta pushing right out the cervix and bleeding like you wouldn't believe. So I had to move."

*"And she'd called Martin?"*

"Oh, yes. Just like you'd told her to, and he wouldn't see her. Said she was your patient. Told her it was your headache, not his, and hung up on her."

"You mean she was bleeding and in labor *then?*"

"Oh, was she ever."

"And he wouldn't come."

"No. So I hauled her up here myself, and sent Raymond in for whole blood, and got plasma started and the surgery set up, and meanwhile looked for help. Jerry wasn't back from Missoula yet, and Ted Peterson was sick, so that left John Florey, and he came through. He's not all that bad a surgeon, as a matter of fact. He was mostly worried that you'd take offense."

"Offense! I'll shine his shoes for him any day. And the woman?"

"It was touch and go right from the first. We got the baby out, but I had to clamp the uterine arteries to stop the bleeding, and that old scar was ready to split open anyway, so I had no choice but to do a hysterectomy. We've got her riding on plasma right now, and if Raymond gets back here with that blood sometime this week, she may

462

make it. She's down in Room 1 coming out of the gas right now, if you want to go see her."

In Room 1 Sara Davis was watching Janice Blanchard like a mother fox watching a cub, keeping her positioned for recovery and adjusting the IV running into her arm. When Rob touched her shoulder, Janice looked up at him as if he were slightly out of focus, shook her head, looked up again and half smiled. "Dr. Tanner. I'm glad you finally got here. Looks like I had a section after all."

"I know, Janice. That was the way it broke. There wasn't any choice."

"And the baby?"

"Fine and healthy, a boy. Just over four pounds. He'll have to be in the incubator for a while, but probably not for long."

"Thank God for that." She closed her eyes for a moment, then opened them again. "I was so scared, I didn't know what to do. Two months early and you gone off to a meeting, and all of a sudden I was bleeding and cramping, all at once. And I called Dr. Isaacs and he wouldn't listen to me."

Rob fought to keep the cold fury from his voice. "You told him what was happening?"

"Yes. I could hardly hold the phone, I was so scared, and I couldn't *believe* him when he just said it was my problem and hung up on me. And Bob was on the crane at the mill and they couldn't seem to reach him, and then I finally got Dr. Stone and he came right to the house and said he thought the placenta was in the baby's way, and brought me to the hospital himself."

"Well, it's all right now."

"I know."

"You've got a good baby."

"I know. And Bob?"

"He's waiting in the lobby. I'll go talk to him, and then he can come in when Sara here says it's all right."

He gave the woman's hand a squeeze and walked out into the lobby, threw himself down into a chair beside the tall, frightened-looking man waiting there. "She'll be all right," Rob said, "and the baby too. It had to be a section, there was no other way to get the baby out, and the uterus had to come out too."

"But she's all right?"

"Yes." Rob hesitated. "There won't be any more babies, Bob."

463

"I know. Dr. Stone told me. But if she's all right . . ." The man looked up at Rob, a cigarette trembling in his fingers. "Just one thing I don't understand. I know you were gone; it was way early and you weren't expecting this. But where was Dr. Isaacs?"

"I don't know, Bob. But I tell you for true, I plan to find out."

He found Tom Stone dictating his operative note in the doctors' dressing room. Rob poured coffee, his hands trembling. He didn't sit down. He just stared at the lanky surgeon. "She really *did* call him," he said finally.

"Oh, yes; she called him, all right."

"And he turned his back on her."

"Yes."

Rob set the coffee down. "I'm going to break him for this."

Stone looked up and nodded once, slowly. "Somebody has to," he said.

"I'll need you to back me up."

Stone nodded once more. "Any way you want it, Rob. It's your show."

Rob walked out past the nurses' desk and down the ramp to his car. It was almost seven o'clock and a gray half-light was filtering through the snow-filled sky. He backed the car out, drove down the hill, turned off at the Bar-None corner and rolled to a stop in front of Isaacs' house. The gray Buick was gone from the driveway, an hour's worth of new snow drifted in the tracks. Rob walked up on the porch anyway, rang the front doorbell, pounded on the door. He waited in the cold, snowy silence, waited like Pinocchio waiting for the snail, looking at the snow piled heavy on the ground, on the porch, overhanging the eaves. Finally he got back in his car, drove to the clinic and let himself in with his key. His watch said 7:35. Isaacs' office was empty. Rob took the phone, dialed the hospital and asked for Stone. "Tom? Has Martin shown up there?"

"No sign of him yet."

"Then you'd better get down here. We're going to sweat him out."

"I've got a tonsil case at eight-thirty."

"Postpone it. This can't wait. I'm calling Jerry." He hung up, dialed the DeForrests, got a sleepy Jerry on the line. "Better come down to the office," he said.

"Trouble?"

"There's trouble."

Stone came in and began dictating some notes on industrial insur-

464

ance cases. Jerry arrived a few minutes later and briefly Rob told him what had happened, saw the flesh sag into weary folds around Jerry's eyes. "I guess it figures," he said finally. "It was going to happen sooner or later."

Rob went back to the coffee room, saw the clinic staff appear one by one: Terry, wrapped in a great woolen muffler, peering at him with frightened eyes and fleeing for the front desk; Agnes Miller coming in, grim-faced and silent; Dora, looking worst of all. "I just heard from Nellie," Dora said, "and I want you to know where I stand. I'm with you, no matter what."

Rob looked at her and gave her a quick hug. "Then go tell Terry to hold the patients up. Later on I'll see anyone we have to see, but not now."

Thirty minutes later Martin Isaacs walked in, tall and stooped, snowflakes flying from his unruly white hair. "Welcome home," he said to Rob as he walked down the corridor. "How were things in Seattle?"

Rob didn't answer. He followed the big man into his office. Tom Stone was sitting there facing the desk. DeForrest stood by the window, looking sick and gray. Isaacs looked around. "Well, what are we having down here?" he said. "A coffee hour?"

"You son of a bitch," Rob said. "We're going to talk about Janice Blanchard."

Isaacs looked around again, and the bravado peeled away like an extra skin. He pulled off his glasses and began polishing them as he sank down behind his desk. "I'm not really at my best right now," he said slowly. "Maybe we can talk later."

"Sorry, but it's going to be now."

"All this snow. We just have to get Ernie's plow over here. Patients can't even get into the parking lot."

"Martin."

"You want to talk to me?"

"Yes. Now. I want to know why you hung up on Janice Blanchard last night."

Martin Isaacs looked up at him and said nothing.

"You knew what was going on with her. You sat through her pregnancies and miscarriages before. You knew I was away, and you knew what seventh-month bleeding could mean. Why didn't you see her when she called?"

For a moment Isaacs lifted his head, opened his lips as if to speak, then closed them again.

465

"Martin, you've got to talk; we aren't just going to let it pass. *Why didn't you see her?*"

Eyes fixed on his desk, Isaacs said nothing.

"You knew she could have died, but you didn't care. We were supposed to be practicing together in this group, covering for each other, helping each other, and you hung up on a woman in mortal danger just because she'd been seeing me and you didn't like that."

Silence.

"But there's more," Rob said. "No life-and-death matter, just a minor matter of lying. You told Jerry and me you'd called Harry Sonders the night of Francine Stein's Caesarean, and that he wouldn't come. You said that's why you fired him. But the truth is you didn't call him at all. It was a fraud. Agnes told me all about it."

Isaacs stared at the desktop, silent.

"Martin, do you hear what I'm saying? I want *answers* now. I want to hear *why*. Now is the time to speak up if you want to salvage anything from this mess."

Silence.

Rob took a deep breath then, glancing at the others. "All right; if you won't talk, then I will, because somebody's got to. You dumped Sonders because he got in your way. He wouldn't behave. He wouldn't do what you told him to anymore, and you couldn't stand that. *Your own surgeon,* sassing you back, telling you where you could go and what you could do! You made him and you could break him. You decided to break him, way back last summer before you even met Tom Stone. You didn't go to Spokane to attend a meeting; you went to find a new surgeon, so you'd have one all lined up when you got ready to move. You had Stone all ready to come—and then at the last minute, Jerry and I balked at your firing Sonders. We got in your way. We acted as if we thought we could actually *stop* you, so you cooked up your little lie and put on your fine indignant act and dumped Sonders anyway, and that was that."

Isaacs continued staring at the desktop. From across the room Stone was watching Rob intently, suddenly very alert. "Trouble was, it didn't work out quite the way you planned," Rob went on. "You got a good surgeon, but you also got a very stubborn man. Stone took one look around, and he wouldn't play your game. He wouldn't put up with the hospital crap that you and Sonders had been satisfied with. He wouldn't go for half-assed follow-up, and he wouldn't go for unnecessary surgery, and when you tried leaning on him, he wouldn't bend. Worse yet, I lined up with Stone one hundred percent, and when you tried leaning

466

on me, I wouldn't bend, either, and that you *really* couldn't stand. I'd been a thorn in your side ever since I came here, with all my smart-ass ideas, but this was too much. You had to live with Stone, at least for a while, because surgery was half your practice—but you could live without me. It must have seemed very simple to you. Either you'd break me, or you'd drive me off—and the fastest way to drive me off was to hit me where it hurt the most. So I went to Seattle, and Janice Blanchard fell into your lap, and you figured that was your chance: the one final outrage you knew I couldn't tolerate."

Isaacs had been sitting motionless, his eyes downcast. Now, slowly, he lifted his head and looked from one to the other. DeForrest stood motionless at the window, staring out at the gloom. Stone said nothing. "Well, you were right about one thing," Rob went on. "Janice was an outrage I cannot tolerate. But you were wrong about everything else. You're not going to break me, Martin, and I'm not going to be driven out. Neither is Stone, even though he was next on your list if he didn't shape up. I'm not leaving Twin Forks, and neither is he. You're the one who's leaving."

For the first time Isaacs seemed to come to life. He lifted his glasses, sitting up straight and staring up at Rob. For an instant he seemed about to laugh, but no sound came. Then he said, "Just what in hell do you think you're talking about?"

"I'm telling you how it's going to be, Martin. You're leaving. Today. I don't mean permanently; don't misunderstand. You're far too capable a doc for us to just pack you off for good, unless you really absolutely won't adjust yourself to realities. You'll just be gone for a while—a couple of months, maybe three; we'll see. You can take off for California, or Miami, or you can just go sulk in your living room, for all I care. Where you go and what you want to call it is up to you. Call it a nervous breakdown, or a long-overdue vacation, or getting over the shock about Jennie—hell, call it anything. We'll go along. You'll just be gone long enough for us to get this practice settled down again into some sort of a sane routine. Long enough for us to get the staff here over the jitters and get this clinic operating like a medical office instead of a madhouse. Long enough to get the hospital straightened out so we can use it to practice decent medicine in. Long enough for us to get Janice Blanchard back on her feet and home with her baby and maybe, if we have just fantastic good luck, tiptoe by without having her and her husband suing everybody in sight for everything we'll ever own, which they may very well do anyway—and the nervous breakdown story might just be

467

worth considering, Martin, because you're the one who's *really* going to be crucified if they sue. And then, when all that's behind us and Tom and I have things running here the way they're going to be run from now on, then we'll see about letting you come back, as long as you very carefully do things our way."

"Well, I thought I'd heard everything," Isaacs burst out, red-faced, "but I guess I was wrong." He glared up at Rob. "You can't just pack me off, you simple-minded ass. This is *my practice* you're talking about stealing—"

"Not your practice," Rob cut in. *"Our* practice. You've run things here like a medieval fiefdom for fifteen long years, but that's all over now. We aren't stealing anything because you don't own anything but a couple of buildings and a parking lot and a few medical tools. You don't own the town and you don't own the people in it. As far as medicine is concerned, Tom Stone has done more to raise the quality of medical practice in this town in the last two months than you did in the last ten years. Well, Tom and I took a vote this morning, and your days of playing God are over. While you're gone, we're going to set up some standards for this practice. Some guidelines, things we're going to do and things we're not. Professional standards, and ethical standards. They're going to be high, and we're going to make them stick. Among other things, there's going to be an end of conflicts of interest. We'll all buy shares in your clinic building and equipment here; that's easy. Then all this rent money we pay out to you every month will start building us some equity. And before you come back, you'll divest yourself of that hospital, so we can get busy turning it into a community-owned medical center like it should have been all along—"

Stone blinked. *"His* hospital?"

"Of course it's his," Rob snapped. "I even got Judge Barret to confirm it. He owns it lock, stock and barrel, with a few paid flunkies to front for him on the board, and a nice, tame whipping boy like Roger to keep the money rolling *his* way all these years. Right, Martin?"

Isaacs said nothing, his face slowly draining of color.

"Well, we don't have to talk about that right now. You'll have plenty of time to take care of the details, and if Judge Barret won't help us work it all out, we'll get some sharp young lawyer who will. No problem there. The only real problem is going to be *you.* When you come back, you're going to have to toe a new line. And there won't be any grace period. You've worn out your grace period already. One misstep, one stupid move, and you're out, just like that."

468

The older man sat silent for a long moment, staring first at Rob, then at Stone. "And you two really think I'll go along with this fairy tale?" he said finally.

"Oh, yes, I think you will," Stone said. "It's far more than you have coming, wouldn't you say?"

"And if I won't?"

"I was hoping you'd ask," Rob said. "In a way, that would be easiest of all. If you won't go along, then it's really very simple. We'll move across the road from you and we'll open our own office, maybe share lab and x-ray facilities with Florey until we can buy our own, and we'll pound you into the ground, inch by bloody inch. We'll take your staff with us, because Agnes and Dora and Terry aren't going to want to keep on working for a monster anymore. We'll leave you here with an empty building and a big, fat tax bill to pay. And then we'll start working on the town. There's a built-in gossip factory in Twin Forks, and we'll feed it. We'll see that the whole town knows what happened to Janice Blanchard, and why. We'll see that the whole town knows why that hospital has been so bad for so long, and why so many people have died up there, and who's *really* been responsible. We'll close the place down if we have to burn it, and help this town build its own community hospital instead. We'll end this ridiculous feud with Florey and Peterson and get them to work with us, and we'll turn your name into a rotten word in this town. And in the meantime, we'll be working on your credentials. The Medical Society is pretty flabby, but the boys are very nervous these days about bad apples in the profession, and when really serious charges get pressed—charges like criminal negligence while covering other doctors' patients and things like that—they sometimes even pull licenses. One final thing you'd better understand: once we start on this, we won't quit. We're young and we don't need a lot to live on, and we'll fight just as dirty as we can. Am I right, Tom?"

"Oh, yes." Tom looked up coldly. "I should certainly say so."

"So you see, Martin, it's all up to you. Our way or no way. Take your choice."

For a long moment Isaacs said nothing. Then: "I don't think you've got the guts."

"Seems to me I've heard that once before this week," Rob said. "But you can always try us and see."

"Agnes would never go with you. She's been my nurse for years."

"Shall we call Agnes in here now and ask her?"

The older man took a deep breath and put his hand to his forehead.

469

"I'm—really not at my best right now." He sat silent for a moment. "Jerry? You aren't in on this, are you? You and me, we've worked together too long. . . ."

DeForrest turned from the window with a nervous gesture, avoiding Isaacs' eyes. "Martin, one would have to make a very tough decision. Put all the parts together and see how they add up."

"I see." After another long moment of silence, Isaacs slowly pulled himself to his feet. "The snow's still falling," he said in an odd, choked voice. "Bad snow. Worst I've seen for years." He peered about the room as if trying to focus. "Glasses are going bad on me too. I'll have to get them checked." He started for the door, paused once more. "Rob? For what it's worth—I'm sorry."

"So am I. But that's not good enough now."

"I've *tried* to be a good doctor, do a decent kind of job, the best I could. I just haven't been myself since Jennie died—"

"I'm sorry, Martin. But that's not good enough, either."

"I see." Isaacs took another deep breath then, glanced around once more, and walked out the door and down the hall. A moment later they heard his car stir to life, muffled in the snow.

Jerry sighed. "He'll go along," he said. "He'll kick and he'll scream and he'll fight and he'll raise bloody hell, but he'll go along."

"I don't know," Rob said.

"Nor I," said Stone. "But I daresay we'll find out soon enough."

"I put you way out on a limb, Tom."

Stone shrugged. "It was that, or leave—wouldn't you say? And I really don't want to leave." He looked at Rob. "So now?"

"If you can hold the fort for a few minutes, I've got some unfinished business at home. Something that can't wait any longer. I'll check back this afternoon."

Outside, the cold hit him like a physical blow as he bent into the wind to reach his car. Suddenly he was bone weary, drained, hardly able to fit the key into the slot, but he managed finally, and drove to Ernie's gas station. He sat inert, barely listening as Ernie filled the tank and bombarded him with the morning's gossip. The highway was reasonably open, and the plow had been down the road and across the river once, an hour before, down the spur road not at all. Rob turned beyond the bridge and spun wheels to inch into his own driveway. He waded through snow to the kitchen door and walked in. He found Ellie dressed in her work blouse and slacks, hair pulled severely back behind her ears, sitting at the dining table writing notes on a pad of informals he had

470

given her a year ago. She didn't look up.

There was coffee made. Rob poured a cup, came in and sat down across from her. "It was Janice Blanchard," he said. "She had a placenta previa, started bleeding and cramping two months early, and Martin wouldn't go when she called him."

Ellie looked up at him briefly, a flat, venomous look, and went back to her writing.

"The woman could have died. The baby too. Thanks to Tom Stone and John Florey, they both made it."

Ellie looked up again and set the pen carefully down on the table. "You bastard," she said. "You stinking, rotten bastard."

Rob blinked, confused. "What do you mean?"

"You know damned well what I mean."

Something cold caught him, and he shook his head. "Ellie, if Karen Sonders has gotten to you already, I can only tell you—"

"*Karen Sonders!* My God, does the whole damned state of Montana know what I don't know? What does Karen Sonders have to do with *this* thing I found in your jacket pocket?"

Rob saw it then, lying on the table: the airline folder with Chris Erickson's return ticket inside. "I see," he said.

"Yes; well, so do I, finally."

"The thing is, that it—doesn't matter."

"Ah, that's really fine," she said furiously. "That covers everything, doesn't it? Well, it may not matter to you, Buster, but it matters quite a good deal to me. I've absolutely had it with you this last three months, and I'm not living with it one day longer. As soon as they get these miserable roads plowed, I'm getting *out* of here. You can have your ever-loving girlfriend; I just don't care anymore. All I want is *out*, and I'm getting out, fast."

"Ellie, she doesn't matter. She's gone. She isn't coming back."

"Well, I guess that's your headache. It sure isn't mine." She took up the note pad and started past him for the bedroom.

He caught her arm. "Ellie, this is crazy."

"Don't you touch me."

"What about Belle? You're just going to leave her too?"

"Belle's going to do all right. You don't need to worry about Belle."

Rob turned to her, suddenly desperate. "Ellie, listen. Things are going to be different. Please don't go."

"Sorry, my friend, but that's not good enough now. I've begged and pleaded and beaten my head against the wall for just one civil word

471

from you; I've done everything I could think of and I'm through fighting now. You can take yourself and go *screw.*"

He looked at her and felt suddenly unsteady, as if the floor were shifting slightly under his feet. "Look, I know you're right," he said. "I've been acting like a shit for months now, and I'm sorry." His eyes caught the airline folder, and he pointed. "I—I know how that hurts—"

"*Hurts!*" Her laugh was short and harsh. "You're standing there telling *me* you have some serious idea how that hurts?"

"Okay, maybe I don't. Maybe I thought you'd never know. But I *do* know a doctor's life can be hell on a wife, and I know I've been hell on you. I've been fighting something with Martin that I didn't know how to handle, and the more I fought the worse it got, and I couldn't see why—and then somehow *she* was tangled up in it, and I didn't mean her to be but she was, and it all came out wrong, just plain *wrong.* But it's all over now. She's gone, and last night snapped the last strand with Martin."

Ellie stared at him, uncomprehending. "You mean you're leaving the practice?"

"Not me. Martin is leaving. Tom and I are pitching him out until he gets his head on straight, if he ever does; at least long enough for us to clean up the mess he's made in this town. Then if he wants to come back and do things our way, we'll give him a chance. If he won't go along, we throw him to the wolves."

"I don't believe it. He'll twist you around—"

"No more, he won't. He's betrayed me for the last time. For a long time he had me fooled. Sometimes he seemed almost like a father. I admired him, looked up to him. If he'd ever let me, I could have come to love the bastard, but he didn't want love. He wanted power, power to run things *his* way, and that meant he had to tear me down, fight me at every turn, cut my legs off at the knees. But it didn't work because I finally wouldn't let him. He could dump Sonders like a sack of rocks, and beat Jerry into submission, and plan on cutting Stone's throat if he didn't finally submit, but he couldn't get me out of the way. He could drive his own wife to suicide—"

"Yes, and butcher everyone else in sight."

"Well, it took me time to figure out what was happening, but I finally saw it, and Janice Blanchard was the final blow. It was a foul thing, but it made it easier when we met with Martin this morning."

472

Ellie shrugged. "So you had another meeting."

"Not just a meeting. A showdown." Rob took a deep breath. "It could have been so simple, a few months back, to make the changes and salvage things and put the pieces back together. The practice had so much that was good about it: good minds, good training, years of hard experience you can't get any other way, faithful patients. There was a point, back there, where everything could have been altered. If only he could have said, 'Maybe I've been wrong.' If only he could have said, 'I've made a bloody mess of things, let's try again.' "

"But he didn't."

"No, he didn't. And then it was too late and there wasn't any way back; not like it was. It had to be smashed from top to bottom."

"And you and Tom are going to put it back together again?"

"Somehow, yes. Jerry'll stay; he's not a man for hard decisions. The nurses will stay. Isaacs may come back and toe the line—maybe. But any way you cut it, it's going to be hard. I'm going to need your help."

Ellie stood up with a wan smile, touched his hand briefly and then walked to the window. "Not really," she said. "Not in any way that matters."

"You mean you're still going?"

"Yes."

"The girl is completely out of it, Ellie."

"It isn't the girl I'm leaving."

"But where are you going?"

"Anywhere. It doesn't matter. Somewhere to have the baby, first."

He stared at her. "But that means I won't—"

"No, you won't be there, but that shouldn't tear you up too much. And then after the baby I'll go back to nursing, I suppose. I'll keep in touch with Belle." She stared out at the snow-shrouded patio and the water below, carrying great clots of blue-green snow downstream in its current. "I'm going to miss that river," she said. "But not much else."

"Ellie, please change your mind."

She shook her head. Silence hung cold in the room, a wordless vacuum. He came to stand beside her as the silence lengthened.

"Martin couldn't say it," he said, finally, "but I can. I was wrong, Ellie. I've made a bloody mess of things. Let's try again."

She turned, buried her face in his chest, clung to him for a moment. "Do you love me, Rob?"

"I—don't know. I'm not too sure of anything right now. But I know

I did once, and I want to try again."

She looked up at him then, solemnly, and brushed his cheek with her lips. "Then maybe someday later," she said. "When we both know. Maybe then we can try again."